AN
ODOR
OF
SANCTITY

AN ODOR OF SANCTITY

A Novel of Medieval Moorish Spain

by

FRANK YERBY

The Dial Press

NEW YORK

PROLOGUE

The land—said the ancient African desert dwellers who saw it first, looking down upon it from that bare hump of rock that would have to wait some thousands of years more before one of their own descendants would give it his name, calling it "Gibel al Taurig," The Mountain of Taureg, insuring himself thus a corrupted immortality in the name Gibraltar—is a land of rivers. So they called it that, "Iberia," Land of Rivers, because to them, newly come from their own blistering sand-whipped wastes, its creeks and rivulets and half-dried stream beds were mighty floods. The land, said the Celts who followed them, is a bull's hide staked in the sun to dry; but what they called it, no man can say. Galicia probably, Land of the Gauls, because that much has survived as the name of a province. The Carthaginians called it "Ispahnia," Land of the Rabbits, with much justice, for the skip and scamper and skitter of the small furry beasts then, as now, were loud upon the crisp, dry air. The Greeks, sweet singers, poets, named it "Hesperia," Land of the Setting Sun. But the Romans, being matter of fact, having scant patience with poets—even their own—took their Semitic foemen's name for it—or rather had that name hammered into their thick skulls by Hamilcar Barca's mighty fist—called it Hispania, ending the matter.

That being settled—a name having been found and given to that tortured landscape resembling, if anything, the dark side of the moon; that sweep of climates from the mist and rain and fog of Galicia, from Soria's near-Siberian cold to Andalucía's desert heat—only one thing remained: to complete the weird and wonderful alchemy, the witches' broth, hellbrew, that compost of arrogance, towering pride, intolerance, mysticism, sanctity, faith, genius, individualism, stubbornness, greatness of the race itself. So now the Alani and the Suevans came and went, leaving scarcely a trace of their passage. After them, the Vandals, who would give their name to a whole region—"al Andalus," the Arabs called it, Land of the Vandals, so Andalucía, sweet land of oranges, olives, figs, and wine, would be forever branded with the name of one of the cruelest tribes of barbarians who ever lived—scourged and ravaged and destroyed their way across the entire peninsula within a single generation, to drown themselves at the end of it in a sea of blood, washing in the last sunset of their brief, awful history, against the sandy shores of North Africa. And, last of all, some four hundred years before this story begins, creaking over the Pyrenees in their wagons, bearing with them their women, children, chattels, slaves, practicing their strange Arian form of Christianity, designed to impose their towering stature, fair hair, and blue eyes upon whole segments of the population, the Goths.

They dwelt in the land. Semicivilized even before they came, they softened easily, forgot their rude Teutonic tongue, spoke, by the time the sons of the original invaders had come to manhood and begot sons of their own, only "Romance," that musical vulgar Latin that had not yet been Arabicized into Spanish, made themselves feudal lords over the smaller, darker mixtures of all the valiant breeds who had come before them; and were there when the Crescent unsheathed its sword; when Berber, Arab, Yemenite, Syrian, Bedu—all that fierce complex of desert peoples whom they and their Hispano-Roman vassals and allies compressed into the single, and all but meaningless, expression "Moor"—swept up from the south to pour their blood, their speech, their habits of thought into the caldron, and more, to build for a time, for an all too brief time, one of the most brilliant civilizations the world has ever seen.

It is of one [truncated] instant snatched from the context of that last great meeting, one spark struck white hot from that anvil of opposing wills, bloods, creeds, upon which the Spanish race was forged, [one half heartbeat's compendium of the nothing a man is—fleeting joy, boredom, anguish, futile grope for meaning, love, hope, dreams, death, all—] one puny, gesticulating figure outlined for a meteor's flash against the dust clouds of history, endlessly piping his shrill, impotent "I! I! I!" above the hideous cacophony of battle, [through the intervals of quiet, standing apart for one immeasurably brief identity granting hiatus from that] the long, slow duel grinding men to carrion dust under that Iberian sun, where so many things were won, and so many, many more lost, that we will attempt to treat here.

And now, Reader, if you will, or can, or must—turn the page.

Book One

ALARIC TEUDISSON

I

It was cold and the sun was a pale blaze hurting his eyes and all the morning was loud with birds. Alaric lay there on his bed in his bare room in the tower; but though he was awake, his dream would not let go of him. He had had that dream often, and it was always the same: he stood on a high place above a landscape gloriously, unimaginably bright, while below him lay all the splendors of the world: castles and walled cities, with legions of horsemen, armed cap-a-pie, drawn up before them in brave array, and fair maids watching from the battlements and piled-up riches gleaming in the sun. And it seemed to him that fawning liegemen of the lords of those castles, the ruling princes of those mighty cities, came out of the gates and knelt before him in homage, offering him kingly gifts: pearls and rubies and gold and slaves. Then out from the ranks of these courtly vassals always there stepped a fair youth dressed as a page who offered him a velvet cushion upon which lay the golden keys to the gates of those castles and those cities; but, as Alaric extended his long and nimble fingers to take those keys from the youth kneeling before him, out of nowhere hands unseen, ghostly, awful, yet matchlessly tender, reached out and drew him back. The curious part about it was that the brooding, tender clasp of those great hands was not exterior to him, coming from without to grip his slender waist, his arms, but was quietly, secretly interior, a force that had always lived within him, and tugged now at his heart. He struggled with that force, those hands, fiercely shouting: "Let me go! Let me go! I am not ready yet! I am not fit—"

And, at that precise point, always, he woke up to find his cities, riches, and fair maids gone; himself once more upon his narrow bed, sick at heart, and quaking a bit with fear. He never told his dream to anyone; not to Ataulf, his brother, whom he loved beyond all measure, for Ataulf would only laugh at him; nor to his sister Gelesvinta, whom likewise he loved, though with that careless, mocking, half-exasperated fondness that boys of eighteen generally reserve for their sisters, for she would surely repeat it to his father and his mother—which was to be avoided at all costs! For his father would frown like Olympian Jove and boom out in his drum-deep bass: "You're right, Godsuinta, this puling milksop you've given me hath God's mark upon him. Commit him to Father Martin. Let him be a priest!"

But Alaric did not want to be a priest. There was nothing on earth he wanted less. He wanted to be such a warrior as his father and his brother were. He wanted to do brave deeds, rescue damsels in distress, have men bow before him, pile up wealth and fame. Only he was lath-slender, and lacked his father's and his brother's thews; and, worst of all, he had the face of an angel or a girl.

He held all his long thin body achingly still until the shivering went out of his limbs; and now, somewhere far below, he could hear his father, Count Teudis, Lord of Tarabella the Greater, roaring like a bull.

"Ha!" Count Teudis' voice boomed, the spiral staircase leading to the tower distorting it, and the stone walls of the castle adding a whole contrapuntal orchestration of echoes so that it seemed as though a hundred men were shouting at once: "You should have seen him, Godsuinta! Those nigh onto thirty years you've thrown his gentility and his grace into my teeth! Count Leovigild of Tierraseca, and his son Eigebert, who, but for your folly in choosing me, might have been your very own! Ha!"

The Lady Godsuinta, Alaric's good and gentle mother, said something in her good and gentle voice; but, since she lacked her husband's mighty lungs, Alaric could not hear what that something was.

"Ha!" Count Teudis said; and now Alaric knew that curious note in his father's bull bellow was laughter. "Dressed in a turban, oh my soul! With his beard clipped to a little point. Wrapped in a burnous. Rings on all his fingers, including his thumbs. Fairly reeking of aromatic scents. And Eigebert—"

Again the Countess said something that Alaric couldn't hear.

"But I forget!" Count Teudis laughed: "He's Leovigild no more. Nor Eigebert. Now they're the banu Djilliki, loyal subjects of the Emir, may Allah the Compassionate grant them long life! The filthy renegades! Why—"

His father's point being made, Alaric didn't listen anymore. Apostasy of that sort was common enough in the year of Our Lord 822, among both the Gothic and Hispano-Roman nobles whose lands lay to the south within the territory conquered by the Moors. Alaric puzzled the matter over for a minute or two, then gave it up. Why any man should leave the True Faith for the abominations said to be practiced by the Moors was beyond him. He'd ask his brother Ataulf. Ataulf would know. Ataulf knew all there was to know about mundane things.

He lay there, reluctant to get up. And now his young face twisted into a quick grimace of pain. He brought his left hand up and let his fingers—long, slim, and almost as delicate as a girl's despite all his efforts to toughen them—stray over the barely healed sword cut on his arm. The expression of hurt in his blue eyes deepened. But its cause wasn't physical anymore. His arm scarcely bothered him at all now. What troubled him was another thing.

The day they had borne him, half fainting at the sight of his own blood, into the courtroom of the castle, his mother Godsuinta and his sister Gelesvinta began to scream at the top of their lungs; but his brother Ataulf had laughed at him.

"Better keep your nose glued to your books," Ataulf said, "and leave the fighting to me, Alaric. Here, let me have a look at that. . . ."

The two *bucelarios*, Sisberto and Julio, brought him over to the fire. They were both free men, holding their lands in fief from Count Teudis, which was more or less what the word "bucelario" meant in the vulgar Latin the Goths spoke, having forgot completely their own rude German tongue in the some four hundred years they had been in Spain.

"Hmn," Ataulf said. "It's none too good. What think you, Father?"

"That the boy's a milksop," Count Teudis said. "We'd better make a priest of him. Who hit him? You, Sisberto?"

"Yes, my lord," Sisberto said. "I've tried and tried to teach him to keep his guard up, so I thought a little scratch might lend him caution."

Ataulf's voice was harsh suddenly. Ataulf dearly loved his younger brother.

" 'Tis more than a scratch, you fool!" he said. "Look at it bleed! We're going to have to put iron to it, or risk a mortification which could cost him his sword arm!"

"Oh, no!" Gelesvinta said.

"Oh, yes!" Ataulf said. "Gele, go fetch a flagon of the best. Better that he has a skinful of wine, because, God knows, the kiss of the iron is far from loving. Canst bear it, little brother?"

Alaric nodded. He didn't dare open his mouth. Or else, he knew well, his breakfast was going to gush out of it. Which wouldn't do. Which wouldn't do at all. Not before his old lion of a father.

"Your kerchief, Gele!" Ataulf said.

Gelesvinta untied her *couvrechef*, a sort of wimple or head covering of clean white cloth, and handed it to Ataulf. Ataulf pressed it to Alaric's arm, stanching the flow of blood.

"Now go get the wine, as I told you, sister," he said.

Watching Gelesvinta's graceful skip and scamper as she ran from the room, all at once Alaric felt better. The reason he did was simple. He could no longer see his own blood. The wound was bad enough; but he had inherited enough of his father's taurine strength, along with his mother's slender grace, to have borne that. What had sickened him really was his own overactive imagination, which saw death in every red drop that flowed from the cut. That sight removed, his strength came back.

"My lady Mother," Ataulf said, "had you not better retire? This will not be a pleasant sight, you know. And fond as you are of the little Alaric—"

The Countess' head came up. Her fine nostrils flared.

"And leave him in the hands of Turtura or another of those careless Spanish wenches?" she said. "You'll find my nerves are up to anything, son Ataulf. I have not endured your father these thirty years for nothing!"

Alaric smiled, suddenly. His lips were white and bloodless; they trembled a little; but it was an authentic smile for all that.

"And we, Mother?" he whispered. "We are not?"

"God bless the boy!" the Countess said. "He is bleeding to death; and yet he must poke questions at a body! We're not what, son?"

"Spanish?" Alaric said.

"God's blood!" Count Teudis roared. "We're Gothic nobles; and never forget you that, little clerk! Spanish! By the incorruptible arm of Saint Fredegunda! We—"

"Father," Alaric said, "say something in Gothic."

Teudis stared at his youngest.

"God's blood!" he said again, but less fiercely now. "Why look you, boy—" He stopped dead, his face baffled. He turned to his wife. "By all the saints, Godsuinta, the boy has a point! We speak Romance. I was born here, and so were you, and so were our fathers and our grandsires, as far back as—"

"Four hundred years ago, Father," Alaric said. "When a tribe of blond, blue-eyed barbarians came over the Pyrenees in oxcarts—"

"Barbarians!" Countess Godsuinta said.

"Barbarians," Alaric said. "Dressed in bearskins. With their beards reaching to their knees. The women, my lady Mother, having bone pins in their hair, whose chief use was to scratch the lice with which they all were infested. Speaking a language they'd learned, mayhap, from the bears themselves, from the sound of it—"

"God's death!" Count Teudis said. "I think we'd better clap the iron to his mouth!"

"Thus have we always dealt with truth!" Alaric said. "I am a Spaniard, Father! This is my land. I know no other. I have as much right to it as Julio here, or Turtura, whose black hair and eyes mean nothing! Their grandsires were invaders and barbarians, too! Why—"

He stopped short, because Ataulf had taken away the cloth from the wound and again he saw the red tide of his blood. The green, vile sickness rose up from his middle and with double force, choking off his breath.

"This, too, is truth, little brother," Ataulf said. "Mother—since stay you will, suppose you prepare some clean cloths for the bandages, and heat some water to cleanse the wound. Or shall I call Turtura to do it?"

"No!" the Countess said. "I can attend to my son's hurts, God willing! Besides, as you know well, I cannot bear the sight of that lascivious wench! Always eyeing you and Alaric both as if—"

"Mother!" Alaric said.

The Countess put out her hand and stroked his bright blond hair.

"My poor baby!" she cooed. Her baby was eighteen years old now, but that made little difference to Countess Godsuinta.

Gelesvinta came in with the wine. Alaric tried to get it down; but he couldn't. It kept meeting his breakfast on the way back. The Countess busied herself with the hot water and the cloths. The two bucelarios, Sisberto the Goth, and Julio who by the Countess' definition was Spanish, knelt before the fire, heating the irons. They were dressed in chain mail, as was Alaric himself. But that hadn't turned aside Sisberto's blade. All it had done was to make the wound uglier, because some of the broken links of the chains had gone into his arm along with the sword's edge.

Alaric turned his face away from those irons, already beginning to glow. Sweat beaded upon his forehead. His lips went whiter still.

"Steady, boy," Count Teudis said, not unkindly. "This will be all over in less time than it takes a hare to jump."

Alaric didn't say anything. He couldn't.

"Ready, my lord," Julio said.

"All right," Count Teudis said, and gripped Alaric's wrists so hard that the boy was sure his bones were crushed. "Sit on my knees, boy."

Alaric sank down on his father's lap. Count Teudis smelled of wine and sweat, and the rich odor of horseflesh. Like most Gothic nobles, the Count wasn't given to overfrequent bathing. The smell of him made Alaric sicker than ever.

Julio picked up the iron. Alaric found his voice.

"No! Let Ataulf do it!" he said.

7

"All right," Ataulf said, and took the iron from Julio. The end of it glowed cherry red. "Hold him, Father!"

Count Teudis' grip tightened.

Alaric turned away his head. Then all the fiends out of hell bit into his arm. He heard his own flesh sizzle, smelled that charred meat stench. The castle began to revolve about his head, slowly at first, but gaining speed every second. Then it wasn't there anymore. Neither the castle nor the bucelarios, nor his mother, nor his sister, nor his brother, nor his father.

From black oceans away he heard his mother scream: "Oh, my poor baby! My poor, poor baby!"

Then he saw he was lying on the floor. And he had lost his breakfast after all.

" 'Fore God," Count Teudis said, "I've half a mind to geld him and sell him to the Moors. They've a taste for pretty, girlish boys, I'm told!"

Just remembering it, now, was enough to propel Alaric from his pallet like a stone from a catapult. Like all the Goths, he slept completely naked. He had inherited his mother's delicate slenderness rather than his father's mighty bulk, and his body was very fine and fair. But he was stronger than he looked because his muscles were deceptively long and smooth, giving him the look of an Apollo of the classic age, rather than having the knotted, seam-bursting Herculean bulge of thews his father and his brother displayed each time they moved. His face was his mother's but little hardened, if at all, by masculinity. Which meant that he was astonishingly beautiful. More so, the spiteful were quick to point out, than his sister Gelesvinta.

Shivering a little in the sudden cold, he went to the window of his tower room and leaned out of it into the pale, watery, morning sunlight. Though it was April now in that high table land which had no name —having forgot its old one, Bardulia, and having not learned or accepted what the Arabic-speaking invaders called it, "Bilad al Qila" or "Qashtalla," Land of the Castles—the wind that swept down from the mountains still had the bite of winter in it; but Alaric disregarded that. He hung there, unflinching, listening to the shrilling of the myriad birds. Then, with deliberate cruelty, he lifted the stone pitcher which stood on the little table beside the window and dashed the icy water all over himself. His milk-white skin reddened and roughened with the cold. He picked up a rough cloth and dried himself. Then he slipped his *chainse*, or undertunic, over his head. His sister Gelesvinta, had woven it for him from the finest, softest lamb's wool. It was very warm. He tied it at his throat and wrists with the tassels sewn there for that purpose. Bending over, he pulled on his stockings which were actually a kind of tights covering not only his legs, but his hips and belly to the waist; he belted them tightly about his slim middle, sat down, cross-gartered them from knee to ankle; finally, he drew his pointed, soft red leather shoes over feet that were smaller than even his sister's. Standing up once more, he pulled over his head his *bliaud* or blouse, a long-sleeved smock that fell to his knees, ran a comb through his silken, pale blond hair, and was dressed. In his mirror—of polished silver, because the Arabs had not yet taught the Europeans how to make glass —he examined his jaw. The all but invisible fuzz on it was still, at his newly passed eighteenth birthday, as soft as swans-down, and maddeningly sparse. On his chin was one lone pimple. Outraged by this lingering reminder of adolescence, he squeezed it fiercely, wiping away the little smear of blood and pus, and leaving his chin fiery red. He clapped the cap on his head, adjusting it so that its cock pheasant's feather stood rakishly askew. Then he started toward the door; but before he reached it he heard his brother's heavy footsteps on the stair, so he stopped where he was and waited.

Ataulf came into the room and brought down a huge and horny hand on Alaric's shoulder.

"God's death!" he said, laughing. "You're dressed for a wedding, I'll vow! Who's the lucky maid?"

Alaric's mouth turned down at the corners. The expression gave him a sulky look.

"I've no maid, as you know right well, Ataulf," he said. "And equally as well know you why!"

Ataulf stared at his younger brother.

"Now you wrong me, Alaric," he said. "I thought your chastity was a matter of conviction—a preparation for a monastic life. Father always says—"

"—that I've the makings of a priest! God's blood and eyes, Ataulf! I am as much man as he and you! Only—"

"Only what, little brother?" Ataulf said.

"The maids laugh at me. They say I am too pretty to be a boy! Even —even your Clothilde says our mother dresses me thus to deceive our father because he wanted another son. And Turtura's worse! She says—"

"What says that little piece of goods?" Ataulf grinned. "Something right rank and foul, I'd vow!"

"She says I should unsheath my weapon and impale them upon it, thus removing from the matter all doubt—"

"Ho!" Ataulf roared. "She would! And starting, of course, with her. Ha, brother mine! Don't you know an invitation when you hear it? Don't

9

tell me you haven't lifted Turtura's skirt? Now there's a juicy piece, all hot and panting for it! And you've not mounted that wild mare? God's blood, boy!"

"I don't like her," Alaric said. "She's dirty. She stinks."

"She is a slatternly slut for a fact," Ataulf said. "I'll have to look around and see what I can find you. You spend too much time in the monastic cell. Books! God's eyes, boy! You'll blind yourself with reading. You mean you've read all this?"

"And more," Alaric said proudly. "For instance, these—can you read them, brother?"

"God's teeth! What manner of hen-scratching is this?"

"It's Greek. When our great-grandfather drove out the perfidious Jews, he found a whole library of these in the house of one of their rabbis. Half in Latin. But what no one until I came along realized was that the Latin works were translations of the Greek. So I was able to puzzle them out. Then you captured that lot of slaves come overland from Marsella—"

"So that was why you insisted upon keeping that ancient Byzantine!"

"Yes. Poor Paulus! He lived but two scant years; but in those two years he taught me to both read and speak his ancient tongue. That was an ugly thing you did with the rest, though, Ataulf. . . ."

"Ho! I only beat the Moors to it. Though if I had known I was lowering their price by deflowering all the maids I'd have had less sins on my conscience. That Mozarab brigand ibn Ha'ad swears he could have got double for them in Córdoba if I'd left them virgin—"

"And yet," Alaric said "you scarce dare touch Clothilde's hand—" Ataulf frowned.

"That's different. She's highborn and—I say, little brother! Have you made me another poem for her? You know I've no head for such fripperies—"

"Yes," Alaric said. "Here it is."

Something in his tone came over to his brother. Ataulf stood there holding the scroll in one hand. Then he put out his other, and let it rest on Alaric's shoulder.

" 'Tis a hard thing I ask you, little brother," he said, "and had you more years I'd give her up to you. But she's your elder by three winters —and, truth being told, not nearly so great a lady as you think. Now it amuses her to be courted thus—with verses, and flowers, and gifts. But, deep down, she's as earthy as I am. She'd only make you unhappy. By all the Saints! I think we'd better ride forth, you and I—Let me think! The Count of Avila now—they say he has naught but daughters. Surely among them—"

"Don't let it trouble you, Ataulf. Now come, I must be about my practice at arms—"

Ataulf looked at his younger brother more keenly now.

"Why do you bother?" he said. "You're the finest archer in all the land."

Alaric's face flushed.

"I mean not archery," he said. " 'Tis a baseborn weapon. Only a coward would kill a man from afar off, courting no risk himself—"

"Only a fool," Ataulf said, laughing, "will court risk when he doesn't have to! Could I shoot the way you do, I'd never pick up a sword. God's death! When you bend a bow, a foeman needs must commend his soul to Our Lady, for he's already dead! As for the rest, you've skill enough, God wot. What you lack in strength you make up in quickness. If I were you, I'd never mount a great horse or bear armor. I'd stick to that barb of yours, ride rings around those great clumsy chargers, and—Oh, all right! You must fight by the rules. Even at that you'd do well. Sisberto and Julio both admit you beat them fairly now. So why not forget all these exercises of war? There is scant need. After all, we're at peace with the Moors—"

"Thanks to you," Alaric said.

"No—only because I know how to toss a pretty bird. How was I to know that young beggar was a Moorish prince? Blond as you or I, his eyes as blue—"

"They brought no women with them when they came," Alaric said, his voice gone stiff and dry. "They've been here an hundred years. And Gallegas and Vascas bring the highest prices on the slave market, precisely because they're blond. So no wonder Prince Abd al Rahman looks like us."

"It wasn't the Prince," Ataulf said, "at least not the heir to the throne. A brother of his, al Mugira ibn Hakam. Younger brother, I'd guess. Anyhow, from his looks I thought he was a renegade like the ibn Djilliki, so I was rather stiff with him. But he was so fascinated with Babu, my gyrfalcon, and so sincere in his praise of my hawking that I ended up by promising to visit him in Córdoba and teach him the art. God's eyes! What a time I had convincing Father to let me go!"

"Father was right. You came back in a bad way. More than half a renegade yourself," Alaric said. "Truth to tell, brother, I doubt that any place short of heaven could be like the Córdoba of your tales."

"Just wait till you go there, and you'll see!" Ataulf laughed. "The Moors know how to live, little brother. Women, music, wine—"

"I'll wager," Alaric said. "But truly, Ataulf, I must be off. There's a trick of a backhand stroke that—"

11

"Nonsense! Come with me to see the procession. All the maids of the mark will be there, praying to Saint Fredegunda's never-rotting arm to snatch them up husbands. Mayhap among them you'll find a 'sheath for your weapon,' in Turtura's gentle words. To divide one's life between a monkish cell and swordplay—ugh! These are civilized times, brother! Even though my thick fingers make horrid sounds upon the lute, I like it better."

"The result being you're getting soft and fat," Alaric said sternly; but then his fondness for his brother overcame him. "Very well, Ataulf," said he, "I'll come."

From where he stood with Julio on the corner of the rutted cobblestone street that dated back to Roman times, Alaric could see the villagers waiting for the procession. They were very few. Most of the houses on that street were roofless. The church had its roof, though. The church was untouched. It was the only building in Tarabella that was.

"God's death!" the bucelario said. "What sins have we done, my young lord, grave enough that we should suffer so?"

Alaric turned away his face to escape the miasmic cloud of wine and garlic on which Julio's words were borne. He was fond of Julio, but he resented the bucelario's presence here, armed cap-a-pie on such day. The Countess had sent Julio along to guard and protect him. To take care of her baby boy! Alaric thought bitterly. As if I were not capable of defending myself! So it was that when he spoke, anger lent sharpness to his tone.

"Drunkenness, for one, Julio!" he said.

Julio grinned.

"A fair hit, my young and noble lord!" he said. "But, then, since today is fiesta—why not?"

"As an excuse for swilling a skinful, all days are fiestas to you, are they not, Julio?" Alaric said.

"I don't mislike a cup or two," Julio said. "That I'll avow. But, then, Lord Alaric, the life of the poor is hard. Would you deny us our simple pleasures?"

"Since you'd only indulge them behind my back, I'll save my breath," Alaric said. "By'r Lady, this procession takes its saintly time!"

"I can wait," Julio said. "I've seen plumper arms than Saint Fredegunda's—even had more than one pair wrapped around this neck, I'll make bold to say. . . ." He looked up at the belfry tower. "Strange the Moors spared us our church, infidels that they be," he said.

"No, it's not," Alaric said. "Look you, Julio; the fiends of Mahound would teach us a lesson in chivalry. We, according to them, are not entirely lost from the standpoint of the teachings of their camel-driver Prophet. Our Lord Jesus, they are kind enough to grant, was also a prophet—a minor and unimportant prophet who preceded and made way for their great Muhammad, but still a prophet. Generous of them, is it not?"

"God's death!" Julio said. "What a blasphemy!"

"Wait, my good Julio, there is more. They do not touch our churches, nor the temples of the rascally Jews because both faiths, they condescend to admit, have much of truth. We have one God, as do they, though we have not got His name right; and we, too, have our holy book, the sacred Bible—vastly inferior to the Qur'ân; of course; but a holy book for all that. Thus we—and the Jews—being 'People of the Book' are, in their lordly view, not entirely pagans, so our churches are sacrosanct, and we, poor devils, under their kindly guidance must be led to find the true way. God's death! I prefer open persecution! I'd rather be treated as a man and an enemy than an idiot, backward child!"

"Hmnn—" Julio said. "Look you, my lord Alaric, that would be scanned. A slit gullet has no remedy; but an overlord, even one too ready with the knout—"

"—like my father," Alaric said.

"—like the Count, God cool his blood—" Julio said, being drunk enough to be bold "—can be outmaneuvered, as it were. Besides, the Count's a kindly soul, once you've let him bellow for a while. The Moors now—apart from their religion—Look you, my lord, my cousin Urbano has a Moorish master, and he says—"

"—that he has never been so well treated before. I've heard that song from more than one filthy Mozarab. The knaves! Why—"

"My young lord," Julio said, "look you now, this business of religion is beyond a simple man. Mayhap 'tis beyond so young a lordling as yourself, begging your pardon right humbly—"

"Go on," Alaric said grimly.

"Didn't you yourself, my lord Alaric, tell me that when your own people, the Goths, came to Hispania they were not of the True Faith? Or did my poor ears deceive me?"

"You heard aright. We were heretics—Arians," Alaric said.

"And who was it, Lord Alaric, who whacked off Saint Fredegunda's breasts and arms?" Julio said triumphantly.

"We did," Alaric said grimly, "but that was before King Recared—"

"—made True Believers of you. Which of course gave poor Frede back her tits 'n hookers?"

"I'll vow!" Alaric laughed. "You're a sly churl, Julio! Yet you're right. A man who's got himself killed has no hope. But apart from the matter of religion, the Moors are cruel enough. Look what they've done here in Tarabella. Like your roofless houses, Julio? Or your maids snatched away to warm their lascivious beds? See how few people there are left! Why—"

"None of which would have happened if my lord Count Teudis, your noble father, had paid the Emir his tribute!" Julio said.

"God's eyes, Julio. My father has his pride!"

"For which pride we poor 'uns paid with our poor hides," Julio said. "But then, we always have, for the follies of the rich and great. God wot the times your father and Marquis Julian, the Frank, have gone to war over this very town. And now, look! Your brother Ataulf, bless him—there's a brave lad for you—pledged to wed the Lady Cloth-ilde, the Marquis's fair daughter. Both noble houses at peace, and united, which not only does not bring us poor folk back our dead, but now you both war on the Moors—or would were it not for Lord Ataulf's having a mite of sense!"

"I like not that kind of sense," Alaric said.

"Methinks you like not sense at all, young Alaric," Julio said. "By all the saints, what harm was there in your brother's spending a month or two with the Emir's second son to teach him the art of falconry?"

"None," Alaric said. "But this business of sending the Prince a cast of peregrine eyases, every year since, or gyrfalcons when he can't take peregrines, in their stead, along with a half-dozen common hawks, ac-companied by his own austringer to train them, that smacks overmuch of tribute to my taste!"

"A light one, in any case," Julio said, "which demeans your brother not at all. What a brave lad is he! All the maids are fair daft over him. 'Tis said the reason that the Lady Goissuintha took the veil is that he preferred her sister the Lady Clothilde to her. . . ."

"If so, 'tis a pity," Alaric said, "as few highborn maids as there be hereabouts—"

"The pity's greater than you think, Lord Alaric. The Lady Gois-suintha is fairer than her sister by far. Just wait till you see her in the procession. Not even the habit of a nun can hide her beauty!"

"Fat lot of good that will do me now," Alaric said. "But if she's so pretty, why did Ataulf—"

"—choose the other? Methinks he found the Lady Goissuintha over gentle. Too refined, as it were. That Clothilde's a spicy bit—at least to judge by her tongue which has no bridle on it—"

"That I know, right well," Alaric said. "Strange that the Lady Goissuintha has a name so like my mother's. Almost the same, isn't it?"

14

"That, my young lord Alaric, is still another tale!" Julio laughed. "My lord Julian, Marquis of Tarabella the Lesser, was mightily smitten by your lady mother when they both were young. As what man was not hereabouts? Beautiful as she was, and is—'tis from her you get your looks, you know—"

"God curse them!" Alaric said.

"Now, lad—when you're older and filled out, and with, mayhap, a scar or two to take away the girlish air, you'll find it is no disadvantage to be fair favored. Anyhow your lady mother chose your father the Count—God alone knows why—and years later Count Julian, the Frank, gave his second daughter her name, spelt Frankish fashion, of course, to hide his design, which proves how long that hurt had lingered. Methinks that 'twas your mother and not this worthless town who was the cause of all their battles. Tarabella was but an excuse, God wot! But, now with age cooling their blood, and their children to be wed—"

"Don't speak of that," Alaric said. "Tell me, Julio—what's the Holy Relic like?"

"You mean you've never seen it? God's eyes, boy! But of course not! How could you? You were not big enough to mount a nag when Count Teudis installed the chapel in the castle and brought in Friar John to say mass, hear confessions, and shrive your sins—for fear the Moors would take you en route to church—"

"For fear of my lady mother, you mean," Alaric said, "who has always seen danger where none exists as far as I'm concerned. Come on, Julio, tell me what it's like—"

"Why?" Julio said. "You're going to see it yourself within the hour. God's thirst, but I'm parched! Look you, my lord Alaric—"

"Oh, get you to your tavern! But you'd better be back before Mother appears, or she'll have your hide in strips for leaving her poor helpless baby boy unprotected—"

"Scant need you have of any man's protection now. My pate aches yet from that blow you fetched me last week with your mace! Good thing 'tis solid bone, or you'd have cracked it for fair! Have I your permission truly, my lord?"

"On the condition that you walk back from the tavern, instead of being carried, Julio," Alaric said.

"My lord, my lord, to reduce me to such a state there is not wine enough in all the world!" Julio said, and clanked away in his armor as fast as he could, plainly fearing that Alaric might change his mind.

Alaric stood there alone, wondering what impression the Holy Relic would make on him. One of his own forebears, tradition held, had hacked off the Saint's arms and breasts with his sword, because she would not renounce her Catholic faith. Dying, the lovely maid—for Saint Fredegunda had been most fair—had both forgiven and blessed her murderer, thanking him for the privilege of martyrdom. Whereupon, struck to his soul by her courage, her beauty, and her faith, the rude Goth publicly renounced his heretical beliefs, and proudly suffered martyrdom in his turn.

Fortunately leaving a son to carry on his line, or there'd be no Counts of Tarabella the Greater, Alaric thought. But then he saw Ataulf coming around the corner with Clothilde on his arm. All Alaric's breath froze inside his chest, splintering to ice-slivers of pure pain. How lovely Clothilde was! How achingly, tormentingly lovely. So flowerlike, so slim—

And my brother's betrothed, Alaric reminded himself; soon to be his bride! I'll not bear it! I cannot! The day Ataulf brings her home, I'll ride forth to—to seek my death! By Saint Fredegunda's arms, I swear it!

The young lovers were not alone. A step or two behind them came the Lady Ingunda, Clothilde's mother, walking arm in arm with the Lady Godsuinta and Gelesvinta. Sor Fidela, Sister Faith, formerly the demoiselle Goissuintha, was, of course, not with them. But later, Alaric knew, he would see her as well, walking barefoot in the procession behind the image of the Saint—for all the good that would do him.

"Dear Holy Mother," he prayed under his breath, "send me a maid of my own!" Then fiercely: "No! I pledge myself to Clothilde while I live! I shall die in battle wearing her gage—or—or become a monk!"

He stood there watching his great lout of a brother—such was the power of jealousy to alter a beloved image!—and the lovely Clothilde coming closer. By the customs of the times, they were never allowed to see each other alone. But all the chaperonage seemed not to trouble Ataulf one jot. He was his own bluff, gay, hardy self. Now he said something that made Clothilde blush all the way down to where her slender neck disappeared into her gown. She slapped him with her glove, right smartly.

"For that I claim a forfeit!" Ataulf roared, and kissed her, before the eyes of all the world.

Alaric turned away from that, his two fists knotting helplessly at his side. He heard his mother's crisp voice say: "Ataulf, I vow you have no manners at all!"

"Oh, leave the boy be, Godsuinta!" the Lady Ingunda said laughing. "Have you forgot quite what it was like to be young?"

"What it is like is death and hell," Alaric muttered between set teeth; but, then, they had reached the place where he stood.

"Why, 'tis your Alaric!" the Marquise said. "How tall he has grown! Come, lad, turn your face so that I may have a look at you. . . ."

Sullenly Alaric turned, bowed, said the Romance equivalent of: "My homage, ladies—"

"Now, by my troth," the Marquise Ingunda said, "here is a living marvel! Godsuinta, dear, how came you to bear such a paragon? By'r Lady, he is too pretty by far to be a boy!"

Alaric stood there trembling, a fact that Clothilde saw at once.

"Now, Mother," she said, "you've hurt his feelings! Alaric, dear brother, you must tire of people remarking your beauty in such terms. . . ."

"I do," Alaric said.

"Yet 'tis true," Clothilde teased. "Until last summer, I was of those who held your lady mother dressed her second daughter thus, because Count Teudis needs must have another son. . . ."

"But now you're not?" Ataulf said sharply. "How account you for your change of heart, my dove?"

Clothilde blushed; but her smile was mocking.

"That's a secret 'twixt Alaric and me," she trilled. "Isn't it, brother dear?"

" 'Fore God, Clo, you'll get him killed!" Ataulf roared in not entirely mock wrath. "I like this kind of secrets not at all."

"Nor I," the Lady Ingunda snapped. "You'd better explain yourself, daughter!"

"Well—" Clothilde said, " 'tis a secret that does the pretty Alaric no dishonor, though it shames me the tiniest bit, I'll vow. Have I permission to tell them, Alaric, dear brother?"

"Oh, stop plaguing him, Clo!" Gelesvinta said. "You know right well there is no secret 'twixt you and Alaric, nor could there ever be—"

"Ah, so?" Clothilde said. "Be not oversure of that, my sister yet to be! Tell me, Alaric, if you will, who was that dark-skinned maid playing Lady Eve to your Lord Adam, when I surprised you both in the river splashing so merrily that fair and flowering day of—let me see—'twas August last, wasn't it?"

"God's death!" Ataulf got out. "You're a bolder baggage than I thought, Clothilde!"

By then, hidden though they were by his pointed leather shoes, even the soles of Alaric's feet were red.

"So it—it was you!" he stammered. "That gray palfrey! Of course! By'r Lady, Clo—I—"

"Ill-bred of you, dear brother, not to invite me in to share your sport.

17

'Twas such a day that made one pity the lost souls in hell. But then, two maids are one too many, are they not, Alaric—particularly under such delicate circumstances?"

"Clo—til—de!" her mother said.

"Yes, my lady Mother?" Clothilde said. "But you may all rest assured, upon my oath—there is at least one dark-haired wench—who knows past any doubt that our Alaric is no maid!"

The Lady Godsuinta and the maid Gelesvinta were staring at him with horrified fascination. Then they both said it, upon one great, explosive rush of breath: "Turtura!"

"Mother, you're wrong!" Alaric almost wept. "Gele—you must not think—"

"Think?" the Countess rasped. "About that slatternly slut, what need is there for thought? What else, son of mine, could persuade her to expose her filthy hide to water? I vow me she has not bathed above that once these nineteen years!"

"Mother, we did not! I—I didn't even know she was there. I heard her splashing and Clo's mount's hoofbeats at the same time! I chased her away, and—"

"God's death, little brother!" Ataulf laughed. "Never admit before a mortal soul that you refused the favors of a maid—highborn or base; or else the world will think—"

"—what they have no right to," Clothilde mocked. "Our Alaric is well weaponed, that I trow!"

"Daughter mine," the Lady Ingunda snapped, "I doubt not that a sound thrashing, followed by a week's confinement in the tower upon bread and water, would do wonders for the delicacy of your speech, and the purity of your mind!"

"Oh, nonsense, Mother!" Clothilde said. "Am I not to wed this gross lout come Eastertide? What good will delicacy do me upon that night? You tell me, Ataulf, dear, what good?"

"No good at all, my dove!" Ataulf laughed. "I fear me 'twill get ripped away along with—"

"Ataulf!" the Lady Godsuinta said.

"Your pardon, my lady Mother," Ataulf said.

"As for you, you mannish boy," the Countess said, turning upon Alaric, "I mean to have a word with your father about your behavior as soon as we're home again!"

"Who, doubt it not, Mother, will be delighted at the news that he need no longer fear our Alaric's turning into a whey-faced canting priest," Ataulf said.

"There you have much right," the Countess said with a sigh. "But at least I can have of him the boon of putting that filthy trull off the place before night!"

"Mother—" Alaric began, but the Countess cut him off.

"No more!" said she. "I must have time. To compose my spirit—return my mind and heart to the piety proper for such a day. By'r Lady, they tarry with their Holy Processsion do they not, Ingunda?"

"There is reason for the delay, Godsuinta," the Lady Ingunda said. "The new image of the Saint—you've heard of it, no doubt? No? Well, it seems that among the Emir's Christian slaves there is a wood carver of wondrous skill. 'Tis he who, says my daughter Goissuintha—can you explain how two sisters can be as unalike as Clo and she?"

"No. Any more than I can explain the differences between Ataulf and Alaric," the Lady Godsuinta said. "Get on with it, Ingunda—what about your wood carver?"

"Oh, 'tis quite a tale! He carved some statues of animals and birds for the Emir—for all that their superstition forbids the representation of living things—so marvelously lifelike that the Emir offered him what reward he would—short of his freedom, of course. And being a pious man, instead of gold, he begged the Emir to send him under guard to make a holy image for the nearest Christian church, which is, of course, our own—"

"Begging my lady's pardon," Alaric protested, "there are churches in Cordoba itself! The Moors permit them. So why should the Emir have to send him here?"

"The wood carver insisted upon it, young Alaric," the Marquise said. "He claimed as part of his reward that he should have the right to choose the church his holy image would grace—"

"And he chose ours?" Alaric said. "By all the saints, my lady, why should he do that?"

"Because it is the nearest one," Lady Ingunda said. "He is old and unfit for much travel."

"By that token he should have chosen one of the Mozarab churches in Córdoba itself, just as Alaric says," Gelesvinta declared in her reasonable voice.

"He would have, says my poor daughter lost to God," the Marquise said, "but for the fact that the Moors often enter the churches there, and then go home and spread scandalous lies about the proceedings. Although he didn't dare say as much to the Emir, the image that he planned to make is much too holy for heathens' eyes—so our wood carver needs must find a church that only godly folk can enter—"

"Considering who enters this one," the Countess snapped, "he missed his mark by far, I'll vow!"

"At least we profess belief, Mother," Alaric said, "and have a chance at repentance and ultimate redemption; while they—"

"Spoken like a true clerk!" Ataulf laughed. "By all the fires of hell, boy, I think I'd better get Turtura to redeem you, after all!"

"Ataulf, one more flippancy from you, and I'll have your father put you in irons for a fortnight!" the Countess said.

"Ah, Mother—" Ataulf began; but then they heard the music of fifes and tambors, and the clank of marching men.

Count Teudis and the Marquis Julian, lords of Tarabella the Greater and the Lesser, came around the corner first, bareheaded, their helmets in the crooks of their left arms, to show their submission to a higher power. They were followed by part of their men at arms bearing not the standards of their noble houses now, but the banners of the church. Behind them came Father Martin, soon, rumor had it, to be elevated to bishop's rank. As he passed, the people fell on their knees, awaiting his blessing, which right regally he gave.

Behind him, borne on the shoulders of more of Marquis Julian's bucelarios, was the image of the Holy Mother—Our Lady of the Sorrows, her radiant and quite visible heart pierced by a multitude of swords. After her came a file of penitents, their faces exposed to public view, for not yet had the Mother Church granted repentant sinners the merciful anonymity of the tall, conical hoods. Chains clanked about their feet. Not a few of them staggered under the weight of huge, heavy crosses in imitation of Our Blessed Lord. One or two, stripped to the waist, laid unmercifully about their own shoulders with the knout, until the blood ran down their backs.

Alaric turned away, shuddering at the sight.

"Look you! Look you!" his mother shrilled. "See what's in store for lewd and sinful men!"

Alaric dutifully turned back his gaze, just in time for Saint Fredegunda's incorruptible arm, miraculously preserved in token of her piety, to catch his eye. He had eaten little, but that little hit the back of his throat in an explosive rush. Manfully, he swallowed it again. He tried to tear away his gaze, but he could not. There, on a velvet-lined silver casket, borne on the shoulders of four men at arms, lay a long bone, or rather several long bones, over which a shriveled, brownish-black length of hide had shrunk, cracking badly about the joints, especially the knuckles of the fingers, so that the dingy yellow of the bones showed through.

He gazed at it, and the cold sweat popped out of him all along his considerable length. His eyelids seemed glued open. He could not so much as close them, any more than he could turn his rigid head.

But more was yet to come. Around the corner now, the wood carver's masterpiece swayed on its velvet-covered stand, borne on the shoulders of twenty stalwart bucelarios, half of them bearing the Count's coat of arms upon the tunics which covered their armor; and the other ten the Marquis's. And masterpiece it was, of stark, uncompromising, merciless realism. Having reached but a month or two ago his eighteenth summer, the question of what it had cost the sculptor, or what it said about him, never entered Alaric's head. He hung there sweating, staring at it, mouth and eyes opened wide, so that he seemed to be screaming without making a noise. On the inside of him something was; and what it cried unvoiced, unheard, tearing out of him below, above, beyond all sound, as true anguish always is, was: "No! oh, no! Oh, no, no, no!"

Saint Fredegunda's image had its one remaining arm spread wide—in defiance of the tradition that his ancient grandsire had lopped off them both, or perhaps in deference to the fact that only one uncorrupted arm had been found, the wood carver being unwilling or constitutionally unable to accept the villagers' common-sense explanation that the other, along with the rest of poor Fredegunda, had been devoured by dogs in the ravine where her saintly body had been thrown. In the palm of her outstretched hand lay as saucy and delectable a pair of rosy-tipped breasts as ever had sinful eyes of man feasted upon. Like all the rest of gentle Fredegunda's marvelously lifelike body, they had been richly polychromed.

"God's death!" Ataulf said flatly. "No grandsire of mine ever whacked off such a pair! Fondled them right lovingly, I'll vow; planted a hungry kiss on both those cherry buds: but cut them, never!"

"Ataulf!" his mother gasped.

Alaric did not hear his brother's uttered apology. He hung there lost, staring at the painted gore dripping between the image's fingers, at the flood of it that dyed her stomach and flanks from those gaping wounds which could only have been carved by a man who had actually seen a woman's breasts cut away. Everything about the image was lifelike, except, of course, the draperies which in miraculous defiance of the laws of gravity, rose in a cunning little peak to hide the Saint's pudenda, while leaving her milk and ivory derriere entirely exposed.

Ataulf leaned close to his brother's ear. His voice came over to Alaric thick, and heavily spiced with wine.

"Nothing wrong with that wood carver that a night with Turtura couldn't cure!" he said.

But Alaric had whirled by then, already running. Through the dreamlike silence in which he was enwrapped his own footfalls came over but faintly, and fainter still his mother's voice, calling his name.

Two streets away, he stopped, doubled over, clutching his middle, and was most thoroughly sick upon the ground. He straightened up, leaning back against the wall of a house, white of face, panting, tears glazing his eyes. But what was in his mind, his heart, he couldn't put words to. Not yet.

Then he began to move, slowly at first, but ever quicker, until he was running hard by the time he came to the square in which he had left his horse. He untied the beast, mounted, clapped spurs to its flanks.

Some time later, reeling from the tavern, Julio was frightened into near sobriety to find him gone.

II

He could not sleep. The moon was at the full, flooding his tower room with light, leaving it awash with mist, silver and subtle, so that he could not be sure whether it floated through the open window or whether his eyes were themselves forming it along with that scald, that salty sting.

His head, pressing against his down-filled pillow, had transformed itself into a caldron in which a legion of witches stirred up brimstone and nightbane, and mandrake root, the tongues of adders, the eyes of newts, the jewel from the frogking's brow. There was no order of discipline to what went on there. Blue flames cackled through his mind, shaped words: "He let them nail his own Son to a tree, between two thieves, so, to Him, a woman's arms or her—ugh! Ataulf—he has not come home and methinks I heard a cock crow. Surely those are larks singing now, not nightingales! Ay, Clo—Clo—you must not think that! I did not touch that trollop! By Saint Fredegunda's arm—Ay-ya! Such a dried and shriveled bone as carrion birds would scorn! Dragged off by dogs too surfeited to devour it and left—God, forgive me! Our Father who art—What is that blasphemy Julio says? Ah, yes—if a man collected all the splinters of the True Cross he would have more useless wood than exists in all the forests of the world—Forgive me! Ay, forgive me! But do You truly love death and anchorite saints who sit in their own excretion, devoured by vermin to the greater glory of Your Name? Is the odor of sanctity anything more than a foul smell? Or is it You we worship or filth and pain? Forgive me! 'Tis a punishment for the sinful mind that You caused Clo to love Ataulf not me. . . ."

Ataulf did not come home. He rode away after the procession with Clo—and by accident or design they—Father said that. He was roaring about it till he fell asleep. God's death! Could they not wait, not wait, not wait? Why wait! What matters the mumbling of a priest? Does all the Latin nonsense in this world cure death or heartbreak—or make us any less food for worms? Father, forgive me! I rave. I believe! I believe —what? Mayhap that You delight in cruelty, in pain. In crucifixion and women's breasts lopped off. In fire. In the lash. In—Holy Mother, save me, for I—

All the castle crawled with night noises. There were creaks, as it settled under its own weight into the hill atop which it was built. Hollow groans came from the wind caught in pockets between the battlements. And other noises without explanation, unless they were the faint moans of doomed souls in hell, or the echoes of what was going on in his mind. But that sound—that sound was real! That dry whisper of footsteps on the stair. Feet unshod and bare from the sound of them.

Ataulf! He has taken off his shoes and comes up here to sleep because he does not dare pass by Father's door—left open, surely, to catch him upon his return. The lout! The oaf! The knave! If he has—if he has—

But that image would not come, nor even the words for it. His mind refused to picture Ataulf and Clo coupled in lewd embrace. His boy's mind could not visualize Clo doing such a thing any more than it could so picture his own mother, despite three living proofs that she sometimes had.

He lay there listening. And knew with cold certainty it was not Ataulf. These were the footsteps of someone who weighed half or less than half what his brother did. He remembered his dagger now, tossed carelessly on the table across the room, three yards—three leagues—three lives away. Before he could get to it, his ghostly assailant would be upon him.

"Holy Mother," he whispered. "Now and at the hour of my—"

Then all the room was flooded with scent. An odd, strange, exotic scent—a perfume brought surely from the Orient. Not the simple scents his mother and his sister wore. Nor the lavender and roses Clothilde had left in his nostrils to torment him out of sleep. No, this was a headier scent, high spiced, right rare, that penetrated to his very blood.

He sat up in bed, staring toward the door. The figure in it was still in shadow, but her voice came over to him.

"Lie down again, my handsome lord—"

"Turtura!" he said.

"Ssssh! Would you wake your father?"

"What do you want?" Alaric said suddenly.

"You," Turtura said.

Her voice sounded odd. Then she stepped out into the moonlight, and he saw the tears upon her face. It was an uncommonly pretty face, now that it was clean. Her hair had been combed, too, and its night-black plaits coiled high upon her head in exactly the same coiffure that Clothilde wore. In her life, Alaric was sure, she had never worn it in any other fashion but hanging loose, and always with wisps of straw from her bed tangled in it to prove no comb had violated its depths. But now it was combed; and that perfume came from Turtura as well. The white shift she wore—and plainly nothing else—was snowy.

"Look you now, Turtura—" Alaric began.

"I bathed," she said, her voice humid with tears, "and put on scent —a scent bought from a wandering Jew. I stole three ounces of silver from the Countess to buy it, and I'll be beaten bloody; but I don't care! 'Cause I heard what you said to my lord Ataulf! You said I—I was dirty! I died hearing that. But now I smell nice, don't I, my lord? And I'm going to be clean as anybody! I've taken my oath to bathe all over every fortnight, at the least—"

"Turtura, by all the saints—"

"Can I help it if I have feelings, my lord Alaric? Even a poor serving wench has a heart, y'know. And blood in her veins! 'Tis not my fault you are so gentle and so fair! So wondrous fair! Your brother now—I like him well; but you—"

"But me, what?" Alaric said.

"But you, I love! My bones turn water at the sight of you. Let you but say, 'Turtura, my kerchief!' or suchlike, and I'm afire! Ayee, Lord Alaric, is there no pity in your heart?"

"Pity?" Alaric said; then: "What would you of me, wench?"

"This!" Turtura gasped; and with one swift movement, jerked her shift over her head.

Alaric sat there. In all his life he had but once before beheld a naked maid—and that maid this same one, on that fair and flowering day Clo had described. But that had been different somehow. For one thing, Turtura had come wading toward him in midstream where the water was deep, veiled in its greenish muddy swirl up to her shoulders. For another, all that limpid wash of light had lent innocence, blended with playfulness to the occasion. Even his wrath, God wot, had been false. But now—now the moonlight was kind to Turtura; it slimmed down the broad span of her hips, the bulge of her little round belly well stuffed with all the rough food the Countess gave her, and all the dainties she could steal. The night shadows hid the cracked redness of her hands, her splayed and calloused feet, blurred the places where she was dark-furred with her own healthy she-animal's youth. Besides, at nineteen, Turtura was not yet truly gross; her curves were generous; but they were firm still, unsagging. Alaric's breath tangled in his lungs; he felt his flesh stir, rise up.

She took a step toward him, and the moonlight fell upon her breasts. What happened then was a curious thing. Out of nowhere, Saint Fredegunda's disembodied hand floated between them on the dark, holding up her own pink-white, delectable, severed globes; and when

Alaric looked at Turtura again he saw, instead of her warm, sun-ripened golden melons, two gaping holes, that crimson flood.

"Get out of here!" he screamed, his voice gone high and shrill. "You hear me, Turtura, go!"

She hung there, staring at him. Then, from somewhere far below, the Countess' voice floated up to them.

"Alaric! Alaric! What ails you, son!"

Turtura bent, picked up her shift from the floor, and fled.

"Alaric!" the Lady Godsuinta cried.

"Nothing, Mother!" Alaric called back. "I—I was dreaming. A—a nightmare, that's all. . . ."

He could not hear what his mother said to that, but he knew what she would do. So he lay back down, covered himself. Then, exactly as he had expected, he heard his mother's footsteps on the stair.

She came into the room, holding a taper in her hands. Her long blond hair, but faintly streaked with gray, hung loose. She was clad in a loose wrap; and, despite her forty-seven years, she was fairer by far than Turtura would ever be.

Alaric stole a puzzled, guilty look at his mother's form.

Yes, his mind mocked, she would attract a man that way! Think you your gross beast of a father was enthralled by the music of her dulcet voice?

The Countess sat down on the edge of the bed.

"What ails my baby boy?" she cooed.

"Oh, Mother, nothing! I was dreaming," Alaric said.

"Tell me your dream, son," the Countess said.

Alaric seized the first thing that came to his mind.

" 'Twas the image. You know, Mother, Saint Fredegunda's. It seemed to me that she entered by that door holding out her—her—"

"Her breasts. Be not overshy with your mother, at whose own you suckled, my son. A woman's breasts are not shameful things, but givers of life. 'Twas my good milk that made you so fine and fair. Go on with the wondrous dream, Alaric—"

" 'Twas strange," Alaric said, fighting for time, "but 'twas no image, but she—the Saint herself, I mean. The blood—the blood—agh—"

"You must conquer your squeamishness at the sight of blood, Alaric," the Countess said. "You know, of course, that we women, each moon—"

"Do not speak of that, Mother!" Alaric said. "Anyhow, the blood flowed from her wounds; but she was smiling. And not as the image smiles, Mother! As—as Clo does! With mischief. And she—she wore—"

"—little, if you could see her wounds." The Countess laughed. "I'll have Turtura bring you up a cup of hot milk, well laced, so that you may sleep. Good thing you convinced me of your innocence, or she'd be gone from here now! What was it that your dream image wore?"

"A scent," Alaric said, without knowing why, except that that odor tugged at the edges of his consciousness still. "A strange Eastern scent, unknown in these parts, I'd vow. . . ."

The Countess' head came up. She sniffed the air. In the light of the candle, Alaric could see her face go pale.

"Holy Mother of God!" she whispered.

"What ails you, Mother?" Alaric said.

" 'Twas—'twas no dream!" She stared at her son in awe. Then she sank down on her knees beside his bed, her hands folded in the attitude of prayer; but her blue eyes were wide open, fixed upon his face. "Bless me, my lord Alaric," she said.

"Bless you? I? Mother, what nonsense is this? And why do you call me 'lord' ?"

"Because," the Lady Godsuinta said, her gentle voice filled with pride, "it is as I thought: God has granted unto me to bear a saint. Such a one as is worthy of holy visitations! Note you not, my blessed son, how the odor of sanctity still perfumes the air?"

"Mother, please!" Alaric almost wept. "This is a blasphemy you utter, though you know it not! Don't say these things of me! I dreamed, I tell you! I—"

"No, my saintly son, you did not dream. Cannot your nostrils catch the perfume with which the room is filled? Even with the window opened, it lingers still! Upon the morrow I must send riders to fetch Father Martin! Friar Juan would only hem and haw, and misdoubt himself much! And this case must be laid before the highest ecclesiastical authorities in the land. Perhaps 'twould be wiser for you to enter a holy order, after all. But about that, Father Martin will advise. Now I must go fetch your father that he may witness it! I'll close the shutters so that the scent cannot escape. . . ."

"Oh, Mother, please!" Alaric said again. But the Lady Godsuinta banged the shutters shut, dropped the bar across them, lit Alaric's rushlight from her candle, and was gone, carefully closing the door behind her.

"God's death!" Alaric groaned. "What a monstrous piece of folly is this! Far better had I sheathed my flesh in Turtura's than—Oh, Holy Mother, grant that the wench comes no closer than five yards of Mother for a fortnight!"

Then he heard his father's heavy tread, and his mother's lighter one on the stairs.

The first thing the Count did when he came into the tower room was to inhale as loudly as a bull does when he is preparing to charge. Then he let his breath out upon a great bull bellow of laughter.

"Scent it is, my good Godsuinta!" he guffawed. "But whore's scent, not saint's, by my troth! What a daft creature you are, over the boy! Some village maid he picked up after he ran away from the procession. I doubt not the whole thing was planned. Look, I'll prove it to you. Get out of that bed, boy!"

"But, Father!" Alaric said. "I have on no clothes! And Mother—"

"—has seen me naked nightly these thirty years," the Count said, "and has bathed your own besmeared arse often enough when you were a tot. Get out of there!"

"Mother—" Alaric wailed.

"I'll turn my back," the Countess said. "Get up, son."

Alaric got out of bed and stood there shivering in his nakedness.

The Count picked up the taper, bent down, and examined the sheets for semen stains. There were none. The bed smelled faintly of Alaric's own clean male youth; but there was no odor of perfume there at all.

The Count lifted his great head with a baffled jerk. He sniffed the air again. The cheap, bad perfume Turtura had bought from the Jew hung on the night long after a finer scent would have blown away.

"Where is she?" he roared.

"Where is who, Father?" Alaric said.

"God's death, boy! You take me for as big a fool as your mother?" the Count said. He dropped to his knees, bending the taper down so that the wax dripped and sizzled on the floor, and peered under Alaric's bed. Then he got up and looked around the bare room, peering behind Alaric's arms and armor where they hung upon a clothes tree. Crossing to the great chest, he opened it. It was filled with clothes, but right diligently did Count Teudis poke and prod among them. He turned now, what showed in his little blue eyes was another thing. A thing Alaric had never in all his life seen in his father's eyes before: fear.

"Son Alaric," the Count said, a curious little quaver shaking his bull bass, "are you willing to take your sacred oath no maid's been in this room?"

"How could she have gone, Father?" Alaric said quickly. "Not by the stairs, or Mother would have met her on the way—" His mind shot a startled question at him. Why did she not? Turtura had no time, no time at all to— "and from the window she needs must have an angel's wings!"

"Or a rope!" the Count said with grim satisfaction, and crossed to the window. He looked down toward where the keep dropped dizzily away into the dark. Clearly there were neither rope nor lovelorn maiden dangling there. He turned back toward his son.

"God's eyes, boy!" he rasped. "We'll have this out! You dreamed, you say?"

"Yes, Father," Alaric said, reflecting that much was true; a man did not have to be asleep to dream. And Saint Fredegunda's arm had got 'twixt Turtura and him; it had!

"And you'll take your oath that no maid's been in this room?"

Alaric hesitated; but a highly sophisticated bit of subtlety popped into his head; born, no doubt, of his having trained himself upon the complicated dialectics of the Church Fathers.

"Yes, Father, that will I swear!" he said, and his voice rang out boldly; for all sure things upon the earth, the surest was that Turtura was no maid! Save alone Alaric himself, every man on the place, from the kitchen scullions up to Ataulf, had enjoyed her gamy favors. As long as his father used the word "Maid," Alaric knew he could swear upon the True Cross itself, and still not lie.

The Count hung there, his heavy face slack with wonder. Quickly he crossed himself.

"Get back to bed, lad," he rumbled. "Your mother's right. We'd best consult Father Martin about this thing. . . ."

After they had gone, Alaric lay there shivering, not from cold, but from nerves. The way that accursed scent clung, his mother would be sure to smell it upon Turtura in the morning. And the wench's unwonted cleanness, the artful way her hair was combed, would beyond all doubt catch his mother's or his sister's eye.

"God's death!" he swore. "I wish I had let Mother throw her off the place! Father will have my hide! There's no way out—no way at all—"

But though he knew it not, he was wrong.

The way out blasted him from his bed at daybreak in a blare of trumpets. He rushed to the window and saw all the Marquis Julian's bucelarios drawn up before the castle in battle array. The morning sun blazed gold upon their armor; their standards whipped from lance shafts, their swords were blinding, lifted in the air. 'Twas a brave sight, calculated to stir any man's blood. But now the trumpets blared again; and a great fanfare rolled out from the drums.

Hanging there, Alaric saw a herald ride out from the Marquis's hosts, a scroll of parchment in his hands. The man unrolled it. His great voice rang out:

"Hark ye! Hark ye! Unless within the hour, the fair and honorable maid, our lady Clothilde, basely abducted by Lord Ataulf, Count Teudis' son is to us returned unharmed, my lord Julian will to this castle lay siege with all his forces!"

Alaric whirled away from the window. In seconds, he was pulling on his tights; but over them he put only his chainse. From the corner where it hung upon its crossbarred perch, he yanked up his heavy shirt of chain mail, dragged it over his head. Over that he pulled his war bliaud which bore his father's coat of arms. Sitting down, he busied himself with his greaves and his armored boots, with their cruel spurs.

He was drawing on his hood of chain mail, which fell about his shoulders, leaving only his face exposed, above which his tall, conical helmet would be perched, when the herald roared out once more: "One hour ye have! After that, we attack!"

Alaric clapped on his helmet, picked up his broadsword, sheath and all, buckled it about his waist, ran his left arm through the loop of his shield, and was off, clattering down the stairs.

When he reached the portcullis, his father was already there. But the Count was dressed in ordinary clothes, and bore no arms beyond a jeweled dagger.

He eyed Alaric's battle dress.

"Go take that armor off!" he growled. "Besides the fact that if you get a scratch you'll faint, there is no cause for war. . . ."

"But, Father—" Alaric protested.

"You heard me, you puling milksop! Go take that arm—" The Count stopped, staring at his son. When he spoke again, the anger had drained out of his voice.

"Let's see whether 'tis true, as your mother claims, that you enjoy heaven's favor," he muttered. "Sisberto, give him the white banner!"

"Yes, my lord," Sisberto said, and handed Alaric the flag of truce.

"Now," the Count said, "you ride over there, boy, and tell that ass Julian I want to talk to him. Outside the walls, both of us unarmed—so that I'll penetrate even that thick skull of his that I mean no trickery. And if the hotheaded old fool balks, tell him I'm as worried as he is, because Ataulf hasn't come back, either!"

"Mayhap they eloped, my lord," Julio said.

"God's death!" the Count roared. "Today I am surrounded with magi, soothsayers, and sages! Why should they, you impudent clodhopper? Tell me that! They have both lord Julian's consent and mine. And the wedding was to be a brave affair which pulls much weight in the mind of a maid. And, albeit that little Clo's a saucy minx, yet I much doubt that Ataulf could persuade her to this folly—"

30

"And I, that he even wanted to, Father," Alaric said. "Ataulf set much store by Clo's chastity. I don't think he'd spoil his own wedding this way. No later than yesterday he admitted to me he'd scarcely touched her hand."

"So?" the Count said. "Then what do you make of it, my little clerk in warrior's dress?"

"I—I don't like it, Father! It—it has an ugly cast! My dream, Father! What was it that Saint Fredegunda wished to tell me? I saw her arm floating upon mid-air with her fair breasts in her hands; and there was blood—"

The Count's little blue eyes opened wide, staring at his son.

"God's death!" he said again; then: "Julio, you fool, bring him a mount. And now!"

Lord Julian's face was white and grim.

"I tell you, boy, that if you lie I'll—"

"I never lie, my lord," Alaric said. "Father's as troubled as you are. Ataulf didn't come home at all last night, nor has he come even yet. And an elopement makes no sense. Just the feast, and the brave, bright show with which you and my father together had planned to celebrate the union of our houses, would make them think a second thought. Besides, my lord, whoever heard of a couple eloping when they already enjoyed the consent of both their sires?"

That stroke was a telling one, and silently Alaric blessed his father for it.

"That's true," the Marquis muttered. "Still—"

"Still," Alaric said, "there is another thing, my lord of Tarabella the Lesser. Last night—the Holy Image of Saint Fredegunda came to me in a dream—bedewing all my room with blood! I fear me there is more amiss than a pair of foolish lovers fleeing what they have no need to fear. My lord, we waste time! Meet my father! Hear him out! Then let us both join forces and ride—"

"Where, Alaric?" the Marquis said. "Tell me that, boy! By all your saintly looks, and the gleam of prophecy in your eyes, tell me: Where should we ride?"

Alaric closed his eyes. He held them closed a long time. What went on inside his head was something like this: "No. They haven't run away. So? No enemies now that Father and this old fool have made peace. And Ataulf's shrewdness about that business of falconry has stopped the Moors from—the Moors! True the Emir's son has kept his word. But what if a wandering band were to happen upon such a maid as Clo? God's eyes! Maddened as they are by blue eyes and fair hair! Did not the old Emir, this one's father, specify that the women sent him as tribute be Gallegas? And—and one thing more! Those renegades—enemies of my father. Turned Moor now, what might *they* not do if—"

"Where, Alaric?" the Marquis said again. A shake had got into his voice by now.

Still Alaric did not answer. What he had thought was very swift and simple and logical; but like all overly bright lads, he was something of a mountebank and a charlatan, especially when he held the center of the stage as now. All his life Ataulf had overshadowed him; but at this rarely intoxicating moment, with the eyes of a half a hundred burly, battle-scarred warriors upon him, he had to play his newfound role to its furthest limits, exult in his newly discovered powers of prophet-saint. So he kept his eyes closed, dwelt upon the horror in his own mind—a swarm of swart, beturbaned fiends holding Clo down, tearing at her clothes—until his own face was a most convincing white.

"Where?" the Marquis all but screamed.

Alaric opened his mouth, let the words come through slow and deadly.

"South!" he whispered. "South, my lord: Where a band of Moorish slavers ride, with thy daughter gagged and bound!"

"And Ataulf?" the Marquis said.

Now truly Alaric paid for his boyish sins of fakery and pride. Because if his shrewd guesswork were correct, if the Moors or a band of renegades had taken Clo, they could only have accomplished that feat one way, if Ataulf were there. "Ataulf!" he wept inside his heart. "Ataulf! Ataulf! Ataulf!"

Lord Julian had him by the arm now, and his mailed fingers bit even through the boy's shirt of chain.

"Your brother!" he said. "What about him, lad?"

"I don't know!" Alaric moaned. "I don't know! I don't see him in my mind at all!"

They rode hard. Lord Julian had not waited for Count Teudis and his bucelarios to arm themselves. Instead he had headed south with his men at arms, telling the Count to follow as soon as he could. But Alaric rode with the Marquis, his face white and drawn. What stabbed into his brain like arrows was as near to prophecy as mortal men are capable of: a thing both less and more than thought.

South. But beyond the town, of course. And not by the main highway that led to Cordoba when it was ours. No. By this one. This goat track of road. Why? No whys. This one.

"Alaric!" Lord Julian boomed. "Why do you turn?"

"This way, my lord!" Alaric cried. "This way!"

By now the Marquis was convinced the boy had the gift of prophecy. He signaled his men, and they all thundered down the goat track single file.

There were no tracks. The path was too rutted, stony, for hoofprints to show. Yet Alaric galloped on, drawing ahead of them now.

This one. Where a man would take his maid to be out of sight of prying eyes and wagging tongues. In all innocence, God knows—a kiss or two, a fond and foolish vow exchanged; and for that, for that—Lord God of Hosts! If he's—if he's—

But his young brain would not shape the terrible word. Not then; not until he saw that broken clump of thorn bush, trampled surely by furious hoofs; that one branch not broken off but cut razor clean by—a sword stroke, certainly; the slant of white wood too long, to smooth, too angled for any ax to have—

"If he's dead, I'll curse Thee and die!" Alaric got out his awful oath, and yanked his foaming charger to a halt, so cruelly that even that great-boned war horse, bred to bear the weight of his rider's armor and his own all day long in battle, danced, rolling his bloodshot eyes red and wild at the sudden bite of the bit.

In his turn, Lord Julian pulled up his own great gray, and sat there in the saddle, staring at the boy. Alaric's face had gone white again, his blue eyes sick.

"What ails you lad?" the Marquis said.

"I do not know," Alaric whispered. "But here, or not far from here, something has occurred. Some great and terrible thing!"

He stared at the ground. Then, very slowly, he climbed down from his mount, knelt upon the ground. His dagger flashed in the sun. Carefully he dug loose that clod of earth, took it in his hand, and, rising to his feet, held it up to the Marquis.

"Tell me, my lord," he said, his voice gone almost out of sound, "is this not—blood?"

Lord Julian looked at the black-stained earth, crumbled a bit between his powerful fingers. Smelled them.

"Aye, so it is, young Alaric," he said, "but whether of man or beast, I cannot say."

But Alaric was gone from him, clanking in his weight of mail toward the thorn thicket, scarcely two clothier's yards away. And now the Marquis too saw how the bush was broken, trampled as though great beasts had thrashed about there, saw that sword-severed bough; but before he had time to sort out the meaning of all that, he heard Alaric's cry: "Ataulf! Ataulf! Oh great and vengeful God!"

Then it rose to a scream keener than a woman's, so dreadful, shrill that the heart went out of the day with the sound of it. When Marquis Julian burst through the brush, he found Alaric kneeling there, his brother's head cradled in both his arms, and his young eyes blue-glazed, scalded, blind.

"They've killed him!" he wept. "My lord, they've killed my brother!"

Then from that bloody, terrible head a slow bass rumble came.

"Not yet, boy! Though I am done, I fear. So leave me and ride— ride—"

Ataulf's voice trailed off.

The Marquis knelt beside them. "Wamba! Luvildo! Theodulfo!" he called.

The bucelarios came through the brush.

"Take him up," the Marquis said. "Bear him to yonder tree, that we may dress his hurts. Ye've a flagon, have ye not, Wamba? We must try to get some sense into him that he may tell us where they've borne the lass—"

At that, Ataulf's eyes fluttered open. The words came out between teeth set against his pain.

"Córdoba!" he said. "Leave me! Ride! Or else—"

"My lord"—Alaric's voice was the scrape of steel on flint—"You'd leave him? You'd let him die?"

Lord Julian sighed. The choice was hard.

"Look you, boy, there is no time," he said. "I'll leave three men with you to do what they can. He is your brother, but he was my son-to-be. I loved him much. But she is my daughter and my flesh. You understand that, don't you?"

Cothilde's small, heart-shaped face came out of nowhere then, filled up Alaric's mind.

"Yes!" he said. "You're right, my lord! Mount you now, and ride!"

The sword cuts across the face were slight. The lance thrust in the shoulder was an ugly thing; but a man as strong as Ataulf should have been able to walk home with worse wounds. Then they turned him over and saw the broken shaft of the arrow that disappeared into his back low on his left side, about where his kidney was.

The bucelario Ludvildo looked at Alaric.

"Shall I draw it out, my lord?" he said.

Alaric nodded. He knew well that unless they got that arrowhead out of Ataulf's back the wound would mortify, and no power on earth could save him.

Ludvildo put his powerful hand on the broken shaft, and pulled.

Ataulf's scream split the sky apart. The bucelario let go, turned to Alaric, his dark eyes sorrowing.

"My lord, I cannot; 'tis barbed," he said.

They made a kind of litter by binding two long, oval shields between the shafts of two lances. On that they laid their own tunics to make what cushioning they could. Placing Ataulf facedown on it, they started out, taking turns two and two, bearing Ataulf's great weight. Half an hour from that place, they met Count Teudis at the head of his men at arms, coming on.

Never before had Alaric seen his father weep, but the Count wept now, unmanned by his grief. He raised his gauntlet-clad fist toward the sky.

"What right," he roared, "What right have you, Oh God, to take away my son? To end my line thus?"

"Father—" Alaric said.

"And leave me only this milksop? This whey-faced, canting little priest? What sin have I done that You—"

"Father"—Alaric's voice edged itself— "say what you will of me; but Ataulf lives. And you waste both your time and his chances, defying heaven thus. Best that we get him home."

The Count brought down his mailed fists from their threatening gestures toward the sky. His voice dropped from its taurine roar, into a bleak, froglike croak.

"He lives?" he said.

"Aye, Father. Come, men, bear him up!"

"Wait," Count Teudis said. "Sisberto, I place you in command, with Julio as your second. Ride to the Marquis' aid. And bear you bravely, now!"

"Yes, my lord," Sisberto said, "and I thank you for the honor—"

"All right. Alaric, if you have aught of God's grace in you, as your mother claims, send up your prayers! I am a sinful man, and—"

"Father, we'd better march now, and pray later," Alaric said. "Theodulfo! Wamba! Bear him up!"

That selfsame night, after their arrival at the castle, Count Teudis sent a rider to the convent to beg of the Lady Abbess a sister skilled in nursing, offering his pledged word as a Christian and a nobleman as guarantee for the safety of her person and her honor during whatever time she needs must bide within his walls. And upon the morrow, the rider returned, escorting a mule cart, in which rode a young and strikingly beautiful nun, accompanied by two others, both ancient, wizened crones, who, as evidenced by their wrinkles, warts, toothlessness, and the witchlike tufts of gray hair on their chins, had been selected by the Abbess for no other reason than to chaperone their young and lovely sister.

Alaric was in his wounded brother's room when she came into it. So it was that he saw her for the first time in his life. He recognized her at once, because her face was very like Clothilde's. But at one and the same time, it was most unlike, because it was almost translucent in its purity. And not even her monastic garb could hide her beauty. It seemed to Alaric that the dark room glowed with a soft light that surrounded her; that music accompanied her as she came, lauds and flutes and even the voices of angels, somewhere behind, beneath, beyond all sound. Step by step she crossed to where Ataulf lay. She stood there looking down at him. Then she sank down on her knees, folded her hands together, raised her eyes toward heaven. Alaric saw the candlelight catch in the tears on that angelic face, and blaze. He was conscious of a strangling in his throat, which increased intolerably until the very walls and ceiling reeled. Even so, long moments passed before it came to him what that sensation was.

Very simply, he had ceased to breathe.

He was aware at last that she had risen once more to her feet, had, in fact, turned toward him, that her gentle eyes were fixed upon his face; and they were grave and sorrowing.

"God bless you, Sor Fidela!" he blurted, for lack of something more to say.

"And you, my lord Alaric, for you, too, have loved him much," Sor Fidela, the former maid Goissuintha said.

The combined forces of the Marquis and the Count returned to the castle after three more days. They were dust-covered, spent, nearly all of them nursing wounds. But they came in triumph, for behind her father, with her two hands wrapped around his armored bulk, the lady Clothilde rode.

Seeing her face, what was in it now, was more than Alaric could bear.

"My lord Count," she whispered, "Ataulf—is he—?"

"No, daughter," Count Teudis said. "He lives; but his suffering is great. Come, get you down, lass, and let the women attend you—"

"No!" Clothilde said. "Ataulf! I must—"

"Better that you rest a while first, Clo," Alaric said. "There's time enough—"

Her small, heart-shaped face was absolutely venomous.

"Yes! In this world where brave men die and pretty, girlish cowards live, there is always time, is there not, dear brother?" she said. Then she swept past him into the great hall.

Alaric stood there. He did not think. What he did was to feel. And what he felt was the precise, unacceptable enormity of his own death; the dagger iron hard between his ribs aquiver still from the force of the blow, needing only to be yanked free again for his life to follow it on one great foaming rush. And it was youth's tragedy and its glory that he had not yet lived beyond the capacity for joy or pain. Or even wonder. But that was no consolation for young Alaric, Count Teudis' son, then. For him, considering his hurt and its source, consolation was not possible; did not, in fact, exist.

"Don't mind her, son; she's upset," the Marquis Julian said. "Teudis, I thank you for the loan of your men. But for them we'd have been doomed. Even so, those infidel beggars outnumbered us. Bold as brass, lingering in the mark to pick up another pretty maid or two, no doubt. Which is the only reason we caught up with them. God's death, how those Berber horsemen can ride!"

"Berbers?" the Count said. "You're sure of that, Julian?"

"Quite. Some of them wore turbans. Their fakirs, likely. Have you ever known a Moor to wear a turban?"

"No, I haven't. But I thought the Berbers kept to the mountains."

"They do," Lord Julian said. "But these were led by renegades. A great blond man with a spike beard. I could see it gleam in the sun. Another, slightly smaller, whose beard was forked, but red-gold, too—that I'll vow. What I don't see is—"

"God's eyes and death!" Count Teudis roared. "Julian, you fool, you never see! What man on earth is there who hates us both? To whose emissary did you refuse Clo's hand before my boy won your grudging consent to pay her court? I ask you, you thick-skulled idiot, who?"

The Marquis stared at Count Teudis.

"Teudis," he said, "are you sure?"

"Sure? As I am of death and hell! The banu Djilliki, oh, oh, my soul! That swine Leovigild of Tierraseca! Eigebert, his son! Apostates! Renegades! Filth! So now they're stealing Christian maids! Especially *your* daughter and *my* son's betrothed! And mark you, Julian, they'll be back! This time with all the Emir's hosts behind them. And you and I, my friend, will be smashed like worms on the field, or we'll die of hunger within our castles' walls, after having cut our women's throats to save them from some swarthy bastards' beds! I tell you—"

And now the idea was big within Alaric's breast: here at hand, the means of his liberation. Since his life was over in any event, his spirit drawn and quartered between Clothilde's contempt and Goissuintha's indifference, what better than this chance to throw it away gloriously? To earn a tear or two from eyes that while he lived wept only for his brother.

"Father," he said, "give me a horse and your leave to ride to Córdoba—"

"Are you daft, boy?" the Count said.

"No, Father. Don't you remember that the Emir's second son loved Ataulf well? That he pledged eternal peace between his house and ours? I'll go to him. I'll tell him of this. He'll make justice, of that I'm sure!"

"Justice on his own? On the men his own father sent out?" the Count said.

But the Marquis was staring at Alaric with new hope in his eyes.

" 'Tis possible the boy's right, Teudis," he said. "I've heard the Emir's a man of his word. He and his son are mostly of our blood, anyhow. That's one thing. Another is that there's no love lost between Berber and Moor. 'Tis like as the Gallegos or the Asturians. If we could make peace among ourselves, we could drive the Mussulmen into the sea! As we will, one day. But surely the banu Djilliki acted on their own. We've been at peace with the Moors these three years. Thanks to Ataulf's diplomacy. Methinks the Emir prefers it that way. He's got troubles enough without having the frontier marks break out in war. So it seems to me the boy's judgment's sound—"

"For the first time in his life, then!" Count Teudis said. "So you think it's worth a try?"

"Yes. And there's one thing more to be added in its favor. A thing that wood carver told my daughter Goissuintha—"

"Sor Fidela," the Count corrected sardonically. "What a waste! By the way, Julian, you know she's here?"

"No," the Marquis said. "Why the devil should she be, Teudis? 'Tis highly irregular and—"

"I know. But she came at her own request. Seems the Abbess heeded her plea that her prayers and ministrations might help. Two other nuns came with her, so her precious honor's safe, Julian; not to mention the fact 'twas never in danger, what with my lady Countess to watch me like a hawk, Ataulf wounded unto death, and this milksop wanting even the inclination! Now on with it, my friend: What did that wood carver say?"

"Well," the Marquis said. "With two others, eh? Then I suppose it's all right. The wood carver? Oh, yes—He said the Emir has a favorite Jew—one Solomon ben Ezra—so skilled at medicine that rumor has it he revives the dead. Mayhap because of this friendship between Ataulf and the Prince—"

"God's eyes!" Count Teudis roared; then his big hands came together in a clap like thunder. "Khinsvilda!" he shouted. "Witza! Theodorico! A horse! A horse for this wilting flower of mine! But a glib tongue he has; and he can ride. God's blood and death, a horse!"

III

Afterward, Alaric could never quite remember the country he passed through, except that it was nearly all mountainous. He rode very slowly away from his father's stronghold, the fire of impatience checked by the ice of fear, alternately burning and freezing his heart. From where Count Teudis' castle—a small rectangular box of stone with four square towers projecting up at the corners—sat, on a little hilltop sticking up like a pustule out of the vast flat high table land of Castilla, to Córdoba was a very long way. The journey involved his having to ride over the Sierra de Guadarrama until he reached the central plains on which stood a tiny village so small that as yet it had no name; and from there, moving southwest until he had crossed the River Tajo, carefully avoiding fortified Moorish city of Toledo, because its largely Mozarab and Muladi population was always revolting against the Emir, and hence probably wouldn't let him leave if he entered it. From there his route led still southwest over more mountains, called in those days the Sierra of Toledo, across the Guardiana River, then through a linked chain of valleys until he came to the mighty capital of the Emirate, which was on the near bank of the River Guadalquivir.

He had to keep a tight rein on his fear, his impatience, and especially on his horse. If he killed the poor beast by riding it to death, the chances of his being able to buy, or even steal, another one in the frontier marks through which he rode were so slight as to be unworthy of consideration. His preparations for the journey had caused many a roar from Count Teudis, but in the end he had made his father see how sensible they were. First of all, he flatly refused to wear armor, on the score that it weighed too much, or to ride a war horse, on the equally sensible grounds that the huge horses, bred to bear the weight of their riders' armor and their own, were too slow.

"If I meet foemen, Father," he said, "I'll be outnumbered from the outset—and my only chance will be to run—"

"At which, God knows, you're right handy," the Count snorted.

Alaric looked at his father then.

"Mine own worthless life means nothing to you, good my lord," he said quietly. "That you've made abundantly clear these several years. But

40

since my brother's now depends upon my reaching Córdoba alive and bringing back the heathen skills we need, best that I postpone my glorious heroic death until another day, don't you think? In this, it seems to me that a live coward on a fast horse outweighs a legion of doughty warriors—for even a battle bravely won would cost us time we do not have. Have I your permission to go now, my lord Father?"

"God's death!" the Count muttered. "Your tongue has a well-honed edge, in truth, boy! Still—" He put out his big hand suddenly and let it rest on Alaric's shoulder. "Still," his drum-deep bass came out, steady and slow, "you're right. I have been less than fair to you, Alaric. You're not the sort of lad I'd have chosen as a son, and Ataulf is. Yet—who knows? —mayhap 'twill be you who will carry our name to greater glory. All men remember Saint Isidore while many a warrior princeling of his time is quite forgot. And this you do is a brave thing, right enough. Yes—get you gone, my son. No, wait!"

"Yes, Father?" Alaric said.

Then, astonishingly, Count Teudis had gathered his younger son into his great arms, and planted two sound bewhiskered, wine-scented kisses on both Alaric's cheeks.

"Now, go with my blessing," he said gruffly.

Alaric had whirled then and run out of the hall, lest his father see the sudden tears that unmanned him. But even so, he was not to escape further leave-takings.

His mother had already wept and prayed over him, had, in fact, taken to her bed in a fine excess of grief and fear for his safety. All he had been dreading was his parting from his father, which now had turned out well enough. But when he crossed the courtyard to where Julio waited with that superb descendant of the desert barbs which could equal its ancestors' feats of a hundred miles a day if pushed, Clothilde was standing there; and, at her side, her sister in blood, and in faith, Sor Fidela, the former demoiselle Goissuintha of Tarabella the Lesser.

"Alaric—" Clothilde said.

"Ladies," Alaric said, taking off his skullcap, made them both a bow.

"Oh, have done with your nonsensical courtesies!" Clothilde said. "I want to know—"

"Clothilde, please!" Sor Fidela said.

"Oh, shut up, Goissuintha!" Clothilde said. "I want to know, brother Alaric, how soon you can return with your Jew? 'Tis only Ataulf's great strength that is keeping him alive, now; and his even greater heart, which, methinks, you lack! So tell me—"

"Clothilde," Sor Fidela said, two spots of pink showing in her cheeks, "have you given no thought to what the marks are like 'twixt here and Córdoba? You who were dragged through them as a captive?"

"They're hell's own image; that I know, sister! But what matters that? Ataulf is dying, you silly fool of God! Him for whom you took that veil, out of your jealousy of me! And he'll not last a week, once the heat of summer comes! So don't plague me with things that don't matter! I only want to know—"

"And I," Sor Fidela said. "But I should ask it in a gentler way, without questioning the valor of the man who rides the marks but lightly armed, and alone. So, permit me, sister! Alaric, brother of my spirit and my heart, how long do you think it will take you to return—if, by God's grace and my prayers, you survive to return at all?"

"Ten days—a fortnight," Alaric said, naming an impossibly short span to give them hope. "But return I shall, having your prayers, sister. And I'll bring back the Jewish magus, if I have to drag him by his beard—"

"See that you do!" Clothilde said. "And don't destroy your palfrey's lungs by spurring him bloody each time you fancy you hear a noise. Now off with you, you pretty knave! You heard me, brother, ride!"

Alaric stood there, looking at her. What was going on in his head was no such ordered thing as thought. A little vein stood out on his temple, and beat with his blood. His breath was a hot tangle inside his chest through which his heart did not so much beat as labor. All his life he had been a timid lad, the more so since reaching the age when blood and nerves and even flesh can be stirred beyond the will's control by the mere sight of a maid. But each man has his limits, and Alaric's had been reached and passed by now. His shyness, his timidity drowned in a mounting tide of anger.

I ride out, mayhap to die, and she—she treats me in this scurvy fashion! She'd question my courage at the moment I display it! By heaven and hell, I—

But when he spoke, his voice came out light, dry, a little mocking. It needed an ear more attentive than Clothilde's to catch the tremor in it. Such an ear as, doubt it not, Sor Fidela in that moment had.

"No, dear Clo," he said, "you've offered me insult—wounded me by questioning my valor. For that I claim a forfeit—"

"That I should kiss you, you mean?" Clothilde said. "God's death, Alaric! Go kiss that fat, greasy serving wench of yours. Your lips are not clean, methinks! So now—"

"You think Ataulf's are?" Alaric said; and at once regretted his words. They were petty, less than a man's part, and he knew it.

"Ataulf is a man," Clothilde said slowly, "and men—"

"You think I'm not?" Alaric said, and took her in his arms.

She looked at him a moment, her blue eyes wide. Then she shrugged.

"Oh, well," she said, " 'tis but a little thing—" And touched her lips to his as lightly as a breath. Then, having delivered her small, deadly insult, more offensive than a slap, because to have struck him would have been to grant him proud possession of such virility as a maid needs must defend herself against, while this cool, sisterly kiss reduced him— precisely as she intended—out of his own uncertain pretensions to manhood into lackeydom or worse, she stepped back against the circle of his arms, and looked up at him with a mocking smile.

Anger burst in him, leaped, cackled, stood tall. He tightened his arms about her with all his considerable strength, seeing, with a kind of bitter joy, that smile fade, her face go pale. Her fair brows came together above his nose; she opened her mouth to cry out to say—what would never in life, after that moment, be said, because he ground his mouth into her half-opened lips, cruelly, hurtfully, while time itself stopped and the very air was still.

That interval, that taut-stretched hiatus clawed out of the spans allotted their separate existences—and ending for the nonce, even that separation—was long. He became aware of that when she tore her mouth from his and allowed the universe to move again. But he was aware of something more, with a paean of triumph that soared above the sudden guilt that flooded him, the pain: that her mouth on his had gone soft, gone yielding; had at the last slackened, parted, then clung to his, adhesive and molten as Greek fire.

Yet, the first thing he saw, as she arched her head away from his, was not her face, but Sor Fidela's. It was very white.

"Your pardon, Sister!" he stammered. "I—"

Sor Fidela smiled.

"Now certain 'tis you are a man, Alaric," she said, "and a sinful one, I think! Now get you gone before more mischief crosses your path. And you, sister mine, come. I doubt not you have need of prayer—"

"I?" Clothilde said, her voice curiously aquaver. "I did nothing! He—"

"Did you not?" Sor Fidela said, her voice both crisp and dry. "That kiss was far from sisterly, Clo! Now, come. . . ."

But not even yet was he free. For life does not leave a man his triumphs for long—not even so small a triumph as Clothilde's kiss. He sat there on his barb, looking at his father's castle. And, mayhap because he was leaving it, was like not to see it again, he saw the castle with clear eyes. It was, he realized, small, rudely built, and totally unimpressive. Yet, if he would accept his father's word, the Count had taken it away from the old Duke Atanagild—known throughout the mark as the "Black Duke" for his crimes—after a bloody battle. Only in this, as in so many things, he couldn't quite depend upon his father's word.

For as that irreverent miscreant Julio put it: "My lord Count's tongue is nobody's prayer book. The truth now, lord Alaric—the truth is such a scurvy thing. Can a body blame him if he feels the need to embroider it a mite? Look you now, my boy—what happened truly was this: The Black Duke was old—nigh onto three score years by some reckonings. And those fiends from hell of sons of his had got themselves all killed by then. And without issue—oh, they had bastards enough! Half the mark wears their evil faces. Some say that even I—but no; I would not claim *that* blood, noble though it be, God wot! But without legitimate issue, largely because they tormented the poor maids foolish enough to wed them into their graves before the first year was out. So the old Duke sold this cold, vermin-infested, stinking pile. Oh, yes; 'tis better now. The good Count, your father, chinked the bigger holes with clay, and furnished it right royally, I'll vow—

"What's that? Of course your father bought it! The Black Duke was down to three retainers by then—all of them as old as he, so how could he fight? Besides, the suggestion came from him, not from your father, lad. The Duke wanted to move to Tarragona, and live out his days in peace and comfort; so when he heard your father'd lost his own place—

"How's that? The Moors? God's eyes, my young and noble lord: If the Count had fought half the battles he claims, he'd have been dead long since! Oh, he and the Marquis Julian knocked each other about a bit, but that's all. What happened to the castle your great, great grandsire built—way back in King Wamba's times—was this: Every time it passed down to a new Count of Tarabella, he had to add something to it. Such a collection of towers, battlements and the like as ever eye did see. In a word, my lord Alaric, it got too heavy, like a fat old dowager stuffed with sweetmeats—especially if due regard be given to the fact 'twas built upon a hill of clay. And that winter, it started in to rain. God's death, how it rained! Forty days and forty nights, as in good Lord Noah's time. I was but a snot-nose of eight winters then, but my bones ache yet, remembering it. The clay softened and began to slide out from under us. Fortunately the north keep, the farthest from the town, went first, and gave your father warning. So he started roaring like a bull, and got us out of there. I remember how your lady mother wept—standing there in the rain with my lord Ataulf in her ams—for neither your fair sister nor you were more than lusty twinkles in the good Count's eyes then—

44

as she watched the castle slide down the hill, turning into a broken heap o' stones as it went. The Count saved his jewels, and his gold— that was all. And with them, he bought—

"How's that again? God's holy tongue, boy! Of course I speak the truth! Why else would your castle be above six leagues from the town 'tis supposed to guard? God's eyes!"

It has truth's unpleasant ring about it, Alaric thought, and tugged his barb's head about; but then he heard that voice.

"My lord! My lord!" it wept. "Wait—wait for me, please!"

He pulled up the barb, and waited. Turtura came flying out of the brush, her long black hair streaming in the wind. She caught at his stirrup, clung to his leg, panting and sobbing like an idiot child.

"Don't go! My lord, don't go!" she wept. "The Moors are cruel men! They'll kill you or—"

"Or what, Turtura?" he said.

"Or alter you, and use you like a maid! They do that, you know. They have right rare tastes, and pretty as you are . . ."

"God's death, wench!" he swore. "Turn me loose! I have leagues to ride, and you—"

"Then take me with you!" she sobbed. "I'll serve you well, my lord! I'll make the fires, and cook for you, and—" a flash of mischief lighted her streaming eyes— "keep you snug and warm o' nights! Oh, please, Lord Alaric, I—"

"Oh, get you hence, Turtura," Alaric said wearily. "I can't be burdened with the likes of you—"

But she clung to him, still crying.

Alaric lifted his whip and brought it down smartly across her arms. She howled and turned him loose. He clapped spurs to his mount and galloped off; but before he had gone twenty yards he reined his mount in again.

A thought had hit him with sudden force. When he had ridden out of the courtyard, Julio and Sisberto had lowered the portcullis behind him. And he was sure he had seen Turtura's face peering at him sorrowfully from one of the low, barred windows of the scullery. Yet, here she was. He knew full well that Julio and Sisberto hadn't gone to the trouble of cranking up the portucllis to let her out. For one thing, it was too much work; for another, the Countess would have had their hides for allowing Turtura to get into more mischief. And once the portcullis was down—since the chief reason for a castle's existence was immunity from attack—to get out of Count Teudis' stronghold, one needs must have wings. He knew that well, because he had tried it more than once himself for the—to him—good and sufficient reason that he wanted to wander alone through the moonlit night and dream of Clo. So he knew it couldn't be done. Yet, Turtura had done it. This plump little serving wench had scaled those frowning walls, or learned to fly. He stared at her, then rode his barb back to within five yards of where she stood.

"Turtura," he said sternly.

"Yes, my lord Alaric?" she said, her round face becoming a full moon of pure joy. She started toward him.

"Stay where you are!" he said. He didn't want to have to untangle her fat arms from about his leg again. "Tell me—"

"What, my lord?"

"How the devil did you get out here?"

She grinned at him impishly, through the traces of her tears.

"Are you going to take me with you?" she said.

"God's eyes!" he swore. "How did you, Tura?"

"Does not my lord recall the night I came to his room in the south keep, and my lady Countess came up the stairs before I had time to hide?" Turtura said. "And yet, she found me not, my sweet lord. How do you account for that?"

"I don't account for it," Alaric said, "nor even see what it has to do with this—"

Turtura laughed. The sound of it was chilling somehow, even on that warm May day.

"I am—a witch, my lord!" she said, then dropping her voice into a hoarse whisper: "I can walk through walls. There is no castle that can hold me, no keep, nor any dungeon either. So now—"

"So now?" Alaric said.

"My lord had better take me with him, before I cast a spell on him, and turn him into a monkey or a goat!"

Alaric sat there looking at her. Inside of him, something crawled —a cold and slimy thing he couldn't put a name to; but that was very like to fear. Feeling it, half knowing what it was, caused anger to rise in him. So he did an ugly thing: he kicked his palfrey into a gallop and headed toward her as if to ride her down. At the last possible instant he pulled the beast up, sawing at the bit so cruelly that the palfrey reared. Turtura threw herself down and to one side to escape those terrible hooves. Alaric fought the barb back down again, and jerked its head about. Then he pounded off at a gallop, riding hard. Southwestward. Toward Córdoba.

With such confused and troubling memories mounted upon his heart, roweling his brain, small wonder that young Lord Alaric, Count Teudis' son, was unaware of the glorious landscape through which he rode. He failed to even question the highly unusual circumstances that he did not so much as sight a patrol of Moorish or Berber horsemen, beating through the mark, attributing his all but miraculous good fortune to Sor Fidela's prayers. Perhaps with some justice; though the absence of the Emir Abu'l Asi al Hakam's marauders from the mark had another, simpler cause, as he would learn. But, at the moment, he was content that the only living souls he met were all Christians—woodcutters, a hunter or two, peasants seeking a strayed cow—who touched their forelocks to him right respectfully and bade him Godspeed.

And now, late upon the afternoon of the eighth day of his ride, he saw it at long last: a thousand, thousand golden towers glittering in the limpid air. Minarets and mosques and churches, too; and the frowning keeps that stood above the gates in the mighty walls. He sat there on his barb, staring at Córdoba, then, in that year of Our Lord 822, the greatest city in Spain, if not in all the world. Magic, it seemed to him, and fey and fairylike; a magician's ghostly image conjured up with rare spells. Its sweep and grandeur reduced him in his own mind to what, in goodly part, he was: a country-bred lordling come from a rude heap of poorly hewn stone to this princely city. And his heart sank within him.

Never, he thought, never will we vanquish men who can build a splendor such as this!

Then he clapped spurs to his barb and rode down toward where the Guadalquivir lay supine and dull golden, lazy in the sinking sun.

Even before he came up to the New Gate, that sound came over to him. It was a strange noise, as though a hundred thousand voices were shrieking one shrill, semibestial note, either of rage or of joy. But, when he reached the gate itself, he forgot that sound. It went on, just as before, as shrill, as bestial; but his ears refused to hear it. He sat there on his palfrey, his jaw dropping like a country oaf as he stared at the two men guarding the New Gate. They were both giants, taller, it seemed to him, than even his brother Ataulf; and Ataulf was said to be the biggest man in all Castilla. But it was not their size that held him there, but rather the contrast between them. The one to the right was normal enough except for his bulk. He was blond and ruddy and clean shaven save for a pair of mustachios that stuck out from his broad Germanic face like the horns of a bull. But for the fact that he wore a Berber turban wrapped around his conical steel helmet, one could have taken him for an outsized Christian. The other—God's eyes!—the other—had skin like black velvet, a nose plastered across his face, and lips like great bluish sausages. Alaric knew from his reading that there were

black men in the world; but formerly he had considered the idea on
the level with that of those men who have their heads beneath their
shoulders, or those with one eye in the center of their foreheads, or
those called pygmies who are so small as to scarcely reach a Christian's
knee; all of whom his studies had told him existed, as well. He hadn't
rejected these strange ideas; the world, God wot, was full of wonders; but
from his father he had inherited a somewhat skeptical turn of mind,
so he hadn't fully accepted them either. But to see with his own eyes
such a marvel as a man with crow-black skin was enough to send his
head reeling and make him doubt his own reason. Yet here the marvel
was! The Negro was dressed in exactly the same fashion as his white
companion; very likely he was no bigger; but his stygian blackness aug-
mented him in Alaric's mind. It was to the black that he addressed himself, in the belief that this inky giant needs must be a ruler over men.

"My lord Blackman—" he began.

The Negro opened his little bloodshot eyes a trifle, and nodded toward his white companion.

"Address yourself to me, young lord," the white giant said, speaking
Romance with a Frankish accent much more marked than the one that
lingered still in the speech of the Marquis Julian. "Bishr is one of the
mutes."

"You mean he has no tongue?" Alaric said.

"Nay, my lord. Bishr can talk, but only his own heathen language.
The city mob call the Emir's foreign guard that, because most of us
are either blacks or white Easterners—Slavs, that is—and therefore can
speak neither Romance, *aljamia*, nor Arab, hence, to all intents and purposes, the majority of our corps might as well be the mutes the people
call us—"

"You speak Romance might handily," Alaric said.

"Because I was born to it, or the Frankish variety of it, anyhow.
'Tis much the same. Though God wot, I'm an exception. There're
very few like me. The Emir prefers that we be unable to communicate
with the populace. Now tell me, what would my young and noble lord?"

"Permission to enter the city. I must find one ibn Ha'ad, who will
guide me to the house of a Jew called Solomon ben Ezra, who is skilled
in the art of healing. My brother, good Captain, lies at death's very
door, and—"

The big Frank frowned. "You are a Christian, are you not, my lord?"
he said.

"Yes," Alaric said. "And you, good Captain?"

The Frank shrugged. "Your Lord Jesus and His Holy Mother did not
prevent my being taken by the slavers near Narbonne, and brought here

to be castrated by the very dog of a Jew you name," he said. "But seeing my size, Count Rabi saved me from being unsexed, and made me a member of the Emir's guards. Scant wonder I pray now to Allah the Compassionate. Look you, my lord; my advice is that you do not enter the city upon such a day. Wait you till next week and—"

"God's death!" Alaric swore. "There is no time, good Captain! My brother is dying of his wounds and—"

"And you are like to die at the hands of that howling mob should you enter Córdoba now," the big Frank said.

"Why?" Alaric said. "Why should they want to kill me?"

"Because you're a Christian, and look it, young lord! You see, the master whom I served is—No. Let me put it another way. The fact is, young lord, that the old Emir, al Hakam, died these four nights agone; and the new one, Abd al Rahman, his eldest son, has chosen to seek the favor of the plebes. Hence, today, he has turned over Count Rabi to them. I do not like to think what they have done to my former master by now. . . ."

"Why?" Alaric said again, seeing the Frank was willing enough to talk, finding it, doubtless, a relief from the daylong silence he had to maintain.

"Because as captain of the Emir's guard he has had to put down many an uprising and afterward to cut the mutineers' throats at the Emir's orders. Al Hakam was not tenderhearted. The plebes claim that Count Rabi had no orders from anyone which permitted him and his soldiery to ravish their wives and daughters; but, look you, my lord, a soldier's life is hard; and a little sport has to be permitted him from time to time. . . . But the worst of it all was that some years ago, the old Emir made my master head tax collector as well. Now a broken maidenhead costs a man nothing, and only makes his labor easier on his wedding night; but lighten his purse and you earn his undying hatred. So I'd advise you not to enter Córdoba this day. . . ."

Alaric looked at him.

"Do you forbid it, good Captain?" he said.

The big Frank scowled. "Aye, that I do!" he said. "For I would not have the blood of a comely lad, of the faith I was born to, on my conscience. Now get you hence, young lord; and return another, safer day!"

"And if I were to tell you my brother is the Lord Ataulf, Count Teudis' elder son—"

"Never heard of him. Get you hence, boy!"

"—who is a friend of Prince al Mugira ibn Hakam, the late Emir's second son? Who has visited the Prince here, and taught him the art of falconry?"

"God's eyes!" the Frank swore. "I thought I'd seen the like of that pretty face of yours before! Of course! The Gothic lord, as big as I who —God's eyes! Wait you here, my lord, while I see what can be done—"

Alaric waited. Within a scant half hour the Frankish guard came back with a man who actually bore the rank that Alaric had naïvely awarded the simple guard. In fact, this official had a much higher rank than even captain, being the chief of the lower of the two groups of the city police. Alaric looked at him in some surprise; except for his dress, this Moorish officer could have been the brother of Julio or Umberto or any of the Romance-speaking Spaniards of Celto-Iberian race; that is, though his hair and eyes were dark, his skin was white, fairer in fact, than most of the Hispano-Romans ever were. His dress was the richest stuffs, but he wore his tunic over a shirt of mail, and his high Persian bonnet, which city dwellers wore instead of the Berber headcloth, did not entirely hide a close-fitting skullcap of Toledo steel. He had a poniard at his belt, a sword that was the most beautiful weapon Alaric had ever seen. In his right hand he had a little silver horn, while from a strap about his waist dangled a mace which, from the blood and hair on it, had already been used to crack a skull or two that morning. He was sweating, and his fine clothes were in some disarray.

He threw questions at the big Frank in Arabic. To Alaric his speech sounded like the growls and barking of dogs. The guard answered him more slowly, and with evident difficulty. Arabic, Alaric decided, was no easy tongue to master. Then the officer turned upon Alaric. His Romance, learned doubtless from his own Spanish mother, was flawless.

"You know His Highness, the Prince al Mugira, you say?" he said impatiently.

"No, my lord Sherif," Alaric said, having caught that word from the big Frank's speech. "But my brother is a friend of his. I have come to seek a favor of the Prince—"

"What favor?" the Sherif snapped.

"That he send the physician Solomon ben Ezra to save my brother's life," Alaric said.

"How do I know you do not lie?" the Sherif said.

Alaric stopped and thought.

"There must be many among the Prince's servants who know my brother well," he said, "especially his master falconer, if he has one."

The Sherif al Surta Sugra stood there, staring at Alaric.

"Very well," he said at last, "come with me. No, wait!" He lifted his silver horn to his lips and blew a blast. Within seconds, it seemed to Alaric, a swarm of armed guards came flaying toward the gate, knocking over whatever passersby got in their way. The Sherif barked commands in Arabic. They opened ranks, forming a square.

"Be good enough to dismount, young Goth," the Sherif said, "and give your weapons to Yusuf, here."

"Am I under arrest, then?" Alaric said.

"Only protectively. And temporarily until the master falconer confirms your statement. You see, my lord Goth, there is unrest in the city today. 'Twould not be wise for an armed Christian to be found in the streets. The plebes are in a rage and not a little drunken. . . ."

"Is that not against your faith?" Alaric said.

"It is," the Sherif said, "and this morning the young Emir gave orders that the wine sellers' stalls outside the Old Gate be destroyed. The Alfaquires led the mobs to them, but could not prevent them from drinking all they could in the heat of the work. Now desist from your questions and come."

They moved afoot through the streets swarming with people. One of the guards led Alaric's horse. Alaric found everything a wonder: the goldsmiths' shops; the workers in tooled leather, in ivory, in perfumes. The sweetmeat stalls; the curious and beautiful designs of the houses; but what caused him to stop dead and stare into one of them was the sight of an inky black girl of some fifteen years, who stood before some ten or twelve other maids—all of them white, all of them veiled—and read aloud from a book in a piping childish treble, while the others diligently copied down every word she said. Alaric asked the Sherif what was the meaning of this trange thing.

" 'Tis a copy house," the Sherif said, looking at him as though he were a dolt. "Thus do we multiply a single book into hundreds. Do not you infidels have the like?"

"No," Alaric said, sadly. "You have many things that we have not, my lord."

"If you do not lie," the Sherif said, "and your brother is indeed the Prince's friend, mayhap His Highness will invite you to bide with him, and accept Islam. He has a certain weakness for beauty in either sex, and you, my lord, are wondrous fair. . . ."

Alaric wondered what he meant; but he did not ask. He didn't like the way the Sherif's voice sounded then.

The crowds were thicker now. The policemen had to beat them out of the way with their staffs and the flats of their swords. Then, as they were crossing a square, Alaric was conscious that he had arrived at the source of the sound he had been hearing ever since he entered Córdoba, and he realized at last what that sound was: the voice of the mob, raised as one man in fiendish shrieks of pure, bestial joy. He turned wondering eyes toward the Sherif. The Sherif pointed with his mace. Alaric followed the gesture with his eyes—and stopped dead.

From nowhere, a very long way off, he heard the Sherif say in Romance to one of the guards, a Mozarab by his looks: "Catch him! The pretty mancebo's going to swoon!"

Alaric straightened up. He was deathly pale; but since Clothilde's verbal attacks upon him, he had sworn to show weakness no longer. Still, it was one thing to see a holy image in a church, and quite another to gaze upon a living man hanging in absolutely insupportable agony upon a cross. It was evidence of the mob's hatred for Count Rabi, Thodulf's son, and their rage at having a Christian set over them as prefect of the city and tax collector, that they had not merely bound his arms to the cross, and left him to dangle till he died, which usually took days; but had nailed him to the cross, after the fashion copied from the images of Our Crucified Lord they had seen in the Christian churches. By so doing, they had done him an accidental kindness; for, in a way, this rarely used form of crucifixion was the more merciful of the two: because, while it made his early sufferings much greater, it shortened them considerably. A strong man might linger on for four or five days while his vital organs slowly sagged down into his abdominal cavity; and the shutting off of the circulation of his blood finally killed him in unbelievable agony if he were merely bound to the cross by his arms and ankles with ropes in the classic fashion, whereupon the more patient of his tormentors might have the exquisite pleasure of watching his belly swell like a balloon, his feet and hands turn blue, his tongue protrude and choke off his own moans, his head twist from side to side to shake off the flies invading his nostrils, his mouth, and finally his eyes, watching him befoul himself with his own urine and excreta, prodding him awake with poles when mercifully he fainted, inventing what other torments they could to prolong his incredible sufferings. Yet, on the other hand, the strongest man on earth could not survive being nailed to a cross more than eight to twelve hours, for the very simple reason that the flies attracted to his bloody wounds blew them at once, and the gangrene thereby produced racing through his helpless body ended his sufferings in that much shorter space of time. But any way it was done, Alaric saw now, one thing was beyond all doubt: no means of execution ever devised by man at his fiendish worst—not even burning at the stake— came even close to crucifixion in cruelty.

Yet now Alaric forced himself to watch Count Rabi's agony, and neither vomit nor faint, as he would have surely done less than a week ago. He was gaining domination over his delicate nerves. Which was just as well. He was going to need it.

"Come," the Sherif said gruffly: " 'Tis yet far to the Alcázar—"

They came up to the Emir's palace of Alcázar. Here the Sherif prudently stopped and stated his mission to the Chief of the Royal Guards.

The Chief cried out: "Al Sahib al Bayazira!"

Immediately another voice within the Alcázar repeated: "Al Sahib al Bayazira!"

Then another and another, each farther away until the sound died away altogether.

The Sherif saw Alaric's puzzled face.

"They call him whom you asked for—my lord of the Falcons," he said.

Then from within a faint voice called out again. And all the other voices took it up.

"He comes," the Sherif said.

The interview between the Sherif and the head falconer was brief. The falconer freely confirmed every word that Alaric had said. More, he sent Alaric's barb around to the royal stables by one of his own grooms, and bowing respectfully before the "brother of my lord Ataulf ibn al Qutiyya, offered to personally visit the Prince's chamber to announce him.

Five minutes later the Sherif was congratulating himself upon his own astuteness at not having followed his first impulses—or, more justly, his natural instincts—which had prompted him to throw the fair young stranger into a dungeon, or simpler still, cut his throat, an act that afterward could have been attributed, easily enough to the 'amma, or mob. Because the head of all the Emir's servants, the eunuch Abu l'Fath Nasr, came himself to conduct Alaric to the Prince al Mugira's quarters in the Alcázar. This was a signal honor, the more so because of a shrewd action the old Emir had taken some days before he died. Reflecting, perhaps, that his own harsh rule had sown all the land of al Andalus with the dragon teeth of hatred ready to spring up as warriors to rebel against his line, al Hakam had designated not only his own successor, as the custom was, but the successor to his successor if death by assassination or accident should remove the new Emir, Abd al Rahman II, before any of that lusty prince's swarm of male children should come of age. So, therefore, al Mugira was heir apparent to the throne, and surrounded with but little less protocal than the new Emir himself.

"Sahib," the head eunuch said, bowing low, "you honor our house with your presence. His Highness bids you come."

Alaric followed the fat little man. They went down what seemed to him leagues of corridors, all richly decorated with the intricate leaf and flower and star motifs of Arabesque bas relief. Then Nasr pushed open a door, and stood aside.

"Have the goodness to enter, Sahib," he said.

Alaric lifted his head, got a grip on his nerves. He was conscious suddenly of the dust that covered every inch of him from his ride, of his own rank, sweaty smell. God's death! he thought: the Prince will understand that I haven't come from across the street and—

Then he entered that room. To his vast surprise, it was empty. He stood there perplexed, staring at the tapestries that adorned the walls, the divan piled high with cushions of yellow silk; the teak and ivory stools; the bronze urns that glowed like gold; the screens worked with mottoes in the flowing Arabic script, all of them from the Qu'ran, though he knew that not; at, in fact, more wealth, more luxury, more taste than he had known existed in the world.

He turned back toward the head eunuch, his mouth already opened to say: "But the Prince—"

Then he closed it again. Like one snatched away from jinn and demons, the *al fata al kabir* Abu l'Fath Nasr was gone.

Alaric crossed to the door, tired the latch. It was not locked. He stepped out into the corridor, looked down it in both directions; but the head eunuch was nowhere to be seen. Alaric hung there. Then he crossed himself, muttered a prayer. That corridor ran arrow-straight for two dozen yards in either direction; so far as he could tell there were no other doors in it except the two at each end of it and the one out of which he, himself, had come. And in the time it had taken him to cross to the door, even the fastest runner in the world could not have reached the end of that corridor. Yet the fat, perfumed little eunuch apparently had—or had vanished into the insubstantial air. Alaric crossed himself again.

"Our Lord and His Holy Mother aid me," he muttered, "for either I have fallen into the hands of wonder-workers and magicians—or I am mad!"

Slowly he turned and went back into the room. He sank down on the divan, cradling his head on his two hands. The moment he did so, something—the rustle of breathing, perhaps—told him he was no longer alone. He sprang to his feet, clapping his hand to where his dagger should have been. But his fist closed on empty air. The Sherif al Shurta had forgotten or had deliberately refrained from returning him his weapons. And he, fool that he was, had been so obsessed with all the wonders crowding in upon his senses from every side, that he had not so much remembered as to ask for them.

"God's death!" he swore. "I—"

Then the two youths came out from behind the screens. They wore turbans of snowy silk, damasked trousers, bracelets of gold and silver upon their slender arms, necklaces of beaten gold around their necks; but their bodies from the waist up were bare, their skin seemed to have been oiled, they reeked of scent. They were both as fair as young male angels.

They salaamed deeply.

"Sahib," one of them said in a curious kind of Romance that despite its odd sound was perfectly comprehensible, "if our lord will deign to follow us, we will lead him to his bath. . . ."

"Thank you," Alaric said, and got up. "But I have no time! I must—"

The youths smiled.

"There is always time, Sahib," they said. "His Highness will receive you presently. . . ."

Alaric sighed and gave up. In this world of magicians, a simple Gothic lordling was beyond his depth. Better to keep his eyes open and his mouth shut. He inclined his head a little, and followed them.

They moved down the corridor ahead of him, opening doors, going on.

There seemed to be no end to that labyrinth of corridors, salons, halls. Then they opened a richly carved double door of Lebanese cedar, and stood aside, bowing, so that he had to pass between them. He went through that doorway, and stood there, lost. The room was vast. Its floors were of marble; its walls alabaster; urns of jade and porphyry stood around them; there were green plants growing in stone jars, a profusion of columns with flowered crests, made of veined marble; and in the middle of the room a pool big enough for a party of ten to swim in, out of whose center a sizable fountain played.

Alaric saw the steps leading down into the water, smelled the perfume that rose from it. Then he stood there, remembering the big wooden tub whose staves were bound together with iron hoops, into which he crowded his long, slender body every Saturday night, a custom which his mother insisted upon, and which he, alone of the males of his household, followed—this, too, being one of the things that earned him the reputation of being too effete for his own good. That his mother and sister indulged in a bath every week was commented upon as a curiosity among the ladies of the mark, the most refined of whom considered once a fortnight often enough to court chills and lung fever—in theory. In practice, he doubted not, most highborn ladies washed all over once a month—and some, more modest, and more pious than the rest, once every three. As for the men, aside from swimming in the river when the heat was on the day in summer, Alaric was sure that bathing was a thing they indulged in every half year, or every year, or not at all. And now it came to him why the perfume of the head eunuch and the two *fityan*—male servants—who stood beside him now had a different, more pleasant scent from those his neighbors used—even, his dismayed mind told him—Clo's. The Goths bought their perfume from peddlers who brought them from the Moorish towns, so their aroma should have been exactly the same. But it wasn't. And now he knew why. For the first time in all his life, Lord Alaric had smelled perfume unmixed with the stench of unwashed humanity.

He stood there in the splendid bathing hall, and what weighed upon his heart he could not put words to; but it was a crushing thing. The essence of a man is pride. All his life, Alaric Teudisson had been proud of his race, his lineage, his nobility—and now, without a word, with the most exquisite courtesy, these Moorish devils had reduced him in his own eyes to a stable boy, rude of dress, awkward of speech, clumsy of motion, and filthy of person.

"God's blood!" he murmured to himself, "I must take care. For 'tis by such subtle traps as these that Satan ensnares—"

Then he felt something touch his arm.

"My lord," one of the fityan said, "allow us to divest you of your garments, that you may refresh yourself in the bath. . . ."

The water was warm. It seemed to have been artificially heated elsewhere, and then allowed to flow into the pool through hidden pipes. Looking closely, Alaric could see the small leaden tubes protruding from beneath the artificial seashells that formed the fountain. It wasn't the first time he had seen running water. The city of Segovia had an aqueduct built by the Romans, and one or two public fountains—likewise built by the Romans. But his own ancestors had destroyed the *thermae* or Roman baths in the belief that bathing made a man soft and effeminate. Yet these Moors, who bathed daily and sometimes twice daily, beat us right handily whenever we meet, he thought; and certes it is that we live in a poorer, shabbier world than the men who went before us—at least in part. My people have risen—we Goths are more civil than ever we were before; but do we—does any man—live as men did in the days of Cicero, or Caesar? Yes, he answered himself, these Moors do—or better.

God's eyes! he thought. Were we to dam the river a little above the castle and then lay tubes like these—bigger, of course—in the stream bed, we—

Then he frowned, and the happiness went out of his eyes. "Pipe water into the house?" he could hear his father roar. "God's blood! For what, boy? Don't we have villains enough to fetch it in in buckets?

Now, if, my dreamer sage, you can figure out a method to pipe in wine! That would be a boon, right enough! But water? God's eyes! What use have I for water?"

The water was perfumed. It was wonderfully relaxing. He could feel the tiredness ooze out of him. When he came out of it at last, the fityan dried him with great towels that were very soft and warm. After that they conducted him to an alcove off the bath, pushed him gently down upon a low table, and proceeded to rub perfumed oil into his skin from head to heel. Only after that was done did they aid him to put on the loose-fitting Persian trousers of heavy silk, the linen shirt, the long brocaded cloth-of-gold coat, and were bending down to slip the jeweled slippers on when they saw how jagged, cracked and broken his toenails were. Instantly one fata caught his hands and looked at them, too. Then he said something to his companion in Arabic. This one went away through the cedar doors. After a time he came back again. And he had with him—God's eyes!—

Two maids. Two maids clearly designed by Lord Satan's hand to turn a man's heart away from pious paths. Two enchantresses. One of them had black hair and eyes. The other was blond with bluish-green eyes. They both wore half veils, extending from just below their eyes to a little beyond their chins; but those veils were as transparent as spring water, making subtle mockery of the Prophet's command to female modesty. The mouths that showed through their veils were enough to induce delirium in themselves; and when he saw what the two slave girls wore —short brocaded jackets opening over a breast-binding woven, he was sure, of spider web, above bare midriffs, and below that harem trousers made of mist, and smoke, and air—he staggered where he stood.

But now the door opened again, and a monster came through it. He stood there just inside of it, three hundred pounds of black flesh, holding in his hands a naked sword big enough to lop the head off a bull at a single stroke. That the black was an eunuch was abundantly clear. For though his arms and legs were still mighty, the rest of him had gone to fat; and the utter indifference in his eyes when he gazed at the two all but naked slave girls would have betrayed him, even if his shapelessness had not.

"God's death!" Alaric said, looking at him.

Green-eyes laughed. Her laughter was the tittering of birds, the ring of silver, the gurgle of wine in a crystal goblet.

"He is ugly, is he not, this sexless dog?" she said in that curious Romance they all seemed to speak. "Now if you, my lord and master, will deign to sit—"

Alaric sat down on a teak and ivory stool. At once the dark-haired slave girl knelt at his feet and began to pare his nails with a wonderfully sharp little knife with a curving blade. Green-eyes went to work on his hands. She clipped his jagged nails, began to smooth the edges of them with a bit of rottenstone. Alaric looked at them both with real pleasure, and some puzzlement.

"What are you called?" he said.

"Yumn," Black-eyes supplied at once.

"Racha," Green-eyes said in her turn.

"And he?" Alaric said, nodding toward the black.

"Yaqut," Racha said. They both seemed to think the name was a huge joke. So did the fityan; because all four burst into great gales of laughter.

Alaric could not know that the two maids' names meant "Happiness" and "Hope" respectively; and that Yaqut meant "Hyacinth," and thus the joke escaped him. He imagined instead that it meant "Monster," but he did not inquire. What he wanted to ask he dared not, because it was too curious and too delicate a thing. The clothes the two slave girls wore concealed absolutely nothing. And yet—God's eyes!—they were clearly in their late teens, mayhap even in their twenties. They were beautifully, perfectly formed; and yet—Twice now he had seen Turtura bereft of clothes, so that now he knew that the body of a maid, like the body of a man, was not entirely bare. Barer than a man's, but still—Yet these were. When they stood up, having finished their tasks, he could see, through the filmy gauzelike silks they wore, their bodies like two naiads, statue-like in their lissome, perfect nakedness.

By heaven! Alaric thought; these Moors can torment a man past madness unto death, and leave not a mark upon his hide. The fruits of Tantalus, with that black monster standing there to see that I pluck them not. God's eyes!

But now again, with that mysterious way they had of coming and going before a man became aware of their presence or absence, the head eunuch was bowing before him.

"My lord," Nasr said in his dry, dead whisper of a voice, "His Highness awaits you. I pray you, come."

Alaric sat at the Prince's right hand. Around them, al Mugira's other guests sat, or sprawled on cushions. The Prince was as Ataulf had described him: white and ruddy, with the look of a Galician or a Basque. So—because they were of the highest aristocracy, and therefore the product of selective breeding—were several other of al Mugira's guests.

58

But for their dress, who'd say they were Moors? Alaric thought. Their raiders must not have left a fairhaired maid in all the provinces to the north. That one, now—ugh!—how rare he is! I wonder—

What Alaric wondered then, he had no words to express; because among the Goths such a man as this would have been speedily—and secretly, lest the very knowledge that such vices were possible among them be noised about—put to death. But here this man, the Sahib Ahmad al Hussein, enjoyed the Prince's friendship and his favor. Looking at Ahmad now, Alaric had to admit that he was fair. In fact, fair was not the word for this highborn Moorish lordling. Ahmad al Hussein ibn Maliki was beautiful—in precisely the way a woman is beautiful. He was—Alaric could see, despite the kohl used to darken his lashes and thus brighten and enlarge his great blue eyes, despite the rouge on his cheeks and lips, the elaborate way his beard was divided in the middle and fluffed out until it looked like fine-spun gold—late in his forties; but even so, his beauty had not yet gone to ruin. And yet his gestures and his speech were not unmanly. He had with him two pretty, rather plump boys whom he was forever fondling and caressing, putting sweetmeats into their mouths with his own long, slim, richly bejeweled fingers. And all the time—a fact that Alaric found disturbing—his eyes never left the young Goth's face.

God's eyes! Alaric thought; he looks at me—as—as Turtura does! I like it not, that look! Why—

But the slave girls, Yumn and Racha among them, were clearing away the great silver bowls in which the banquet had been served, and bringing others, with the dessert, consisting of sliced oranges swimming in rose water with the rose petals floating among them, mingled with the shredded meat of coconuts, grapes, and crystalline sugar. Alaric recognized all these ingredients except the coconut meat and the sugar, neither of which he had ever before seen, not to mention tasted, in all his life.

It was delicious, just as all the other courses had been—the chickens boiled in grape juice with nuts and whole grapes; the roast whole lamb, garnished with leeks, oil, and spices, the glorious peacock served in its feathers, which, opened, contained a fair-sized goose, which in turn contained a duck, which contained a pullet, which contained a dove, which contained a wren. Again Alaric had been forced to contrast his own way of life with theirs to his own's disfavor. He felt a pang of shame at his own ready disloyalty to customs instilled in him since birth, of which his parents were so proudly sure; but he couldn't help it. This—this was his world! This was the kind of life by nerves, by temperament, by inclination he was suited for.

Now the Sahib Ahmad al Hussein said something to the Prince. Al Mugira listened, then laughed gaily. Alaric turned a puzzled face from one of them to the other.

"My lord Ahmad says," al Mugira translated, "that he would give all his fortune for one night with you, my lord Alaric. I have told him that you have no such custom among your people. It is true that you confine yourselves to women, is it not?"

"Confine ourselves, my lord?" Alaric said. "What else is there?"

Al Mugira put that in Arabic for the benefit of those of his guests who could not speak Romance. The whole salon rocked with their laughter. Alaric's face turned fiery red.

"Forgive me, my lord," the Prince said pleasantly. "We mean no offense by laughing. I suppose you must find many of *our* customs strange and amusing. . . ."

"And most pleasant"—Alaric smiled at the memory—"such as having one's nails pared and buffed by pretty slave girls. . . ."

"Ah, so?" the Prince said. "I was wondering what present I might make you that would please you most. I shall give you Yumn and Racha, then, who are trained to that art. Though, be it said, they can make themselves useful in other ways. I shall send them to your castle along with the Jew."

"Your Highness, no! I thank you, but—" Alaric said.

"But what, my lord Alaric?"

"My mother, good Your Highness! She would have my hide in strips! Why—"

This time the laughter began before the Prince could translate, thus proving that many, if not most of his guests understood Romance, whether they spoke it or not. The dainty Ahmad said something to the Prince. The Prince smiled.

"My lord Ahmad says that he will give you a fully furnished house upon a pleasant street, and stock it with all the slave girls you can use, so long as you save a night or two for him each fortnight," the Prince said. "Provided, it goes without saying, that you remain with us, my lord Alaric. I call that offer fair enough, don't you?"

"My lord, I—I cannot," Alaric stammered. "I must go home tomorrow. To lead the Jew, you understand. For, if not—"

"Oh, he can find his way," the Prince said. "Besides, I'm sending along a strong escort for him. What say you, my lord Alaric? Methinks you like our customs well!"

"I do—some of them at least," Alaric said, looking at Yumn as he spoke. "But good my lord, you don't understand. I am a Christian—"

"We have nothing against your faith. Your Jesus was one of our prophets—"

Alaric swallowed even that. He was rapidly learning that self-control was essential to survival in this glittering, luxurious, subtly dangerous world.

"Your highness, I cannot. Among us, highborn women have a most respected place—and my lady mother loves me much. Were I to leave her, she would surely die. . . .'"

"Touching." The Prince yawned. "Very well. But you will vist us again, will you not, my lord?"

Alaric looked at green-eyed Racha—though sad truth it is that 'twas not her eyes he gazed upon.

"Of course, Your Highness!" he said, and his voice rang loud and true.

After the banquet was done, and the other guests—including, much to Alaric's relief, that right rare Lord Ahmad—had taken their leave, the Prince conducted him to a small sitting room, as lovely and as richly furnished as the rest of his quarters.

He peered at Alaric closely. Then he said: "You look tired. But if you can endure a while longer, 'twould be well. I have already sent for our wonder-working Jew, that you may describe your brother's case to him. . . ."

"I could do that on the way," Alaric said, for in truth he was faint with weariness, though, strangely enough, despite all the food and wine he had consumed, he was not sleepy at all. His fatigue had gone beyond the need of sleep now; and it was his tingling nerves he lived upon.

"You could indeed," al Mugira said. "But don't you see, fair Aizun that is the equivalent of your name in our speech—'twould do no good? The good leech must prepare what medicines and what implements he thinks needful for my lord Ataulf's hurts. And that, my pretty friend, he cannot do on the way."

"I'll wait," Alaric said; then: "Tell me, Your Highness, this Sahib Ahmad—are there many such as he?"

"Too many," al Mugira said ruefully. "I think it grew up from the conditions of our desert life, and the strict setting apart of women by our religion. Then the question of wealth enters in: since a rich man may have four wives and many concubines, too few maids are left for the poor, which, 'tis said, caused men to turn to men for love. Yet, truth to tell, this explanation, it seemeth me, explains nothing; because it is precisely among the rich and idle, like Ahmad, that the vice is most often found. Personally, I like it not. But since there is no prohibition against it, we—"

He broke off, because a slave stood bowing in the archway.

"What is it, Zuhayr?" al Mugira said.

"Sahib, the Curer of Illnesses begs to be excused," Zuhayr said. "He is boring holes in the head of a sinner to let out the demon and cannot come, or the man might die. He begs that he be sent a description in writing of the Sahib al Qutiyya's hurts, so that he may prepare his herbs and implements for the journey. . . ."

"Jinn and demons!" al Mugira said. "Where will I find a scribe at this hour? All who have not left the palace can only be taking dictation from my brother, who'd have my head!"

He looked at Alaric suddenly.

"My lord Alaric, would it be overmuch were I to send you to the house of the Jew? You can rest on the way, because I'll bespeak a chair borne on the shoulders of slaves—"

"I shall be glad to go," Alaric said at once. "I have some curiosity about this learned Jew—"

"Good!" al Mugira said. "Zuhayr, go call the Sahib a chair!"

While they waited, al Mugira smiled a bit, and said: "Since you, my pure young lord, will not accept slave girls as a gift, might I be informed what boon you crave? I cannot let you return empty-handed to your house. 'Tis against all our customs of hospitality—"

"Nothing at all, Your Highness," Alaric began; but then he stopped. "One thing, my lord Prince, I do ask of you," he said.

"And that is?" al Mugira said.

"That my weapons be returned to me. The lord Sherif of the City Police took them away. And even though you send me with an escort, I like not the thought of riding the frontier marks unarmed—"

"I do not blame you," the Prince said. "It shall be done. But surely you wish something else?"

"No," Alaric began, but al Mugira halted him with a lifted hand.

"Come in, Zuhayr!" he said.

But it was not Zuhayr who came through the curtained archway. It was the head eunuch, Nasr. He bowed almost to the floor.

"My lord Prince," said he, "the Sword of Allah, the Conquering Lion of Islam, the Terror of Infidels, the—"

"In short, my brother the Emir," al Mugira said dryly.

"Even so," Nasr said with a little smile. "The ruler over all our lives and destinies bids Your Highness come to the royal chambers and bring the Goth. Reports have reached his noble ears of the youth's great beauty, and he—"

"—would see for himself. All right. But why, Nasr? Tell me that, you beardless lump of worthless fat? My brother is not of that persuasion which prefers pretty boys to maids. Rather too much the opposite, methinks! You're forever having to fetch him more concubines, because he keeps all his women big of belly at the same time. So what interest has he—"

The head eunuch shrugged.

"Your Highness, I do not know," he said, "for though I possess many skills, they do not include the art of reading noble minds. But I should suggest that you obey the Emir. His temper at the moment is not at its best—"

Al Mugira stood, extending his hand to Alaric, who had sat there staring from one face to another, trying to divine the meaning of the flood of crackling Arabic that had beat about his defenseless ears.

"The chair has come then, my lord?" he said.

"Not yet," al Mugira said. "My august brother, the Emir, wishes to see you. The dainty Ahmad, or this sexless fool, has told him of your beauty, so he is curious. Come. 'Twill be not amiss to gain the attention of the Leader of the Faithful. Who knows but that his favor may not serve you in good stead?"

"But how will I talk to him, my lord?" Alaric said. "I have no Arabic and—"

"Oh, don't worry! He speaks Romance better than I do. His mother was a Celtic slave girl, descendant of a great Romanized family. While mine, as you can see from my hair and eyes, was a Goth. Which accounts, I think, for my fondness for your race—since I am of it, too, at least by half. Now, come. . . ."

When they came into the Emir's chambers, the Lord of all the Moors was storming at his secretary. Alaric could not understand his words; but from the fury that shook them, he was sure that the secretary's head and shoulders would part company ere long. He looked at the Emir with wonder, and some fear.

Abd al Rahman the Second was utterly unlike his brother. He was, Alaric thought, the very picture of a Moorish prince. In the first place, he was very dark; his skin had the hue of burnt copper; his nose was as thin and hooked as the beak of a falcon; and though his hair was red, a second glance showed Alaric that it was dyed, because his long beard was as black as night. So were his eyes, which seemed now to flash lightning in their wrath. Curiously, they never seemed to wink. He was standing, the better to berate the unfortunate secretary—who cringed before him, his head prostrate against the floor—so Alaric could see the Emir was very tall.

Seeing them enter, he broke off from shouting, and said to al Mugira: "Ah, brother! You bring me your pretty Goth, when what I need is a Greek!"

"At your command, my lord!" al Mugira said with a slight ironic bow. "You should have made your meaning clearer—though Greeks are hard to come by, with those Byzantine dogs as strongly armed as they are. But tell me, Sword of Allah, what need have you of a Greek?"

"To read me this!" the Emir said, flourishing a scroll. " 'Tis a treatise on the arts of love that my trader ibn Ha'ad brought me back from Constantinople from whence he arrived but a se'en night agone. And think you that there is one among my scribes, sages, and learned men who can read Greek? Not one, brother, not one!"

Then, apparently something about Alaric's face caught his attention—the baffled expression, doubtless, with which the young Goth listened to the harsh gutturals of Arabic—so he said, in a more kindly tone and in easy Romance: "Come closer, my boy, for you are fairer than any Greek, even than the statues of Praxiteles, by the Prophet's very beard! And though you speak not that ancient tongue, yet are you welcome for you refresh these eyes. . . ."

Alaric bowed low. Then he straightened up and said boldly: "But I do speak it, my lord Emir."

The Emir's black brows knitted into a frown. But his eyes continued to blink disturbingly beneath it.

"Do not make mock of me, boy!" he said. "Right well do I know there is no man west of the Byzantine Empire—save a Jew trader or two; and they at best mouth a sort of lingua franca of commercial terms —who knows Greek! I am in no mood for jests, for this scroll—"

"If my lord Emir wishes, I shall read it to him," Alaric said.

"Fair Aizun—" al Mugira said warningly.

"Have no fear, Your Highness," Alaric said. "I had in my youth a Byzantine slave called Paulus who instructed me in his tongue. Right well I can speak it, and read it readily enough, I vow. If my lord Emir will permit me—"

He put out his slim hand. Wonderingly the Emir passed over the scroll of parchment. Alaric unrolled it, scanned it with his eyes, began to read.

" 'Now this of fleshly love is no simple thing, but an art, comparable to that of holy dancers, or even, in some ways, of skilled equestrians—' "

"Wait!" the Emir said. "Al Mi'tar, you fool, get up from there! Go get your papers and your pens!"

The secretary leaped to his feet, fled from the salon. The Emir clapped his hands. From a dozen hidden doors a swarm of slaves appeared.

"A chair!" the Emir said. "A chair for the young sage! And tapers! He needs must have light!

The slaves brought chairs, cushions, a candelabrum of silver, placing it so that the light from the candles fell over Alaric's left shoulder, making no shadow. The Prince sat down beside him, and held the top of the scroll for him so that it would not roll back upon itself as parchment was wont to do, performing this service as humbly as though he were himself a servant.

By then al Mi'tar, the secretary, was back with his folding tables, pens, pots of ink, papers, sanding box, all those brought, of course, not by al Mi'tar, but by his two slaves, who set up the equipment, and stood behind their master, busily cutting quills, handing him papers, making ready to sand the finished ones, and to perform such other services as their learned master should require. Alaric saw all this with wonder, realizing at last how important an official among the Moors the Sahib al Catib, Abu Kitab al Mi'tar was. He looked, too, with great curiosity at the substance the secretary prepared to write upon. It was very smooth and white and much thinner than parchment. The secretary seemed to have an immense quantity of it, not rolled up, but cut into handy sheets.

Al Mi'tar dipped a quill into the ink, looked at Alaric; said in Romance: "When you will, my lord Sage!"

Alaric began to read. He saw with astonishment that al Mi'tar was retranslating his translation of the Greek into Romance, directly into Arabic once again, his hand moving from right to left, while the long, beautiful, serpentine, decorative script flowed out from under his pen. Alaric was so fascinated by the secretary's skill that at first he paid no attention to what he was reading.

The Emir lifted a hand. Alaric looked at him, seeing his eyes were still blinking furiously.

"Wait," he said. "Al Mi'tar, read back what you have set down, that I may be sure you've got it right—"

Al Miltar read it back in Romance, not Arabic, having actually written it in *aljamía*, using the Arabic letters to form the Latin sounds, probably because he was ignorant of the Roman alphabet. And now, for the first time, Alaric became conscious of what he was reading, and his young face turned fiery red.

"Good!" the Emir said. "Pray continue, young sage!"

Alaric went on reading. The work was a piece of erotica, of a type not uncommon in the East; but to the Western mind, the hand of the Evil One was clear upon it, setting up this devilish web of seductive words to entrap the immortal soul of the unwary. Yet Alaric did not dare halt or protest—and truth, sad truth being told—he could not have stopped, even had he gained the Emir's unlikely permission to do so, because he was utterly fascinated by what he read. Thus ever hath Satan ensnared the minds of men, he thought, by making evil so much more attractive than God's eternal dullness! Moreover, this particular *ars amoris* was a masterpiece; the language scintillated, shone, sparkled; the humor was endless and rich; and even though it described in precise detail some twenty-odd positions that lovers might use to vary the tedium of the act of love, the descriptions were so matter of fact, so playful even, that it was hard for Alaric to remember Father Juan's warnings against such abominations. Only once did it succeed in shocking him, and that was in the section devoted to the restoral of jaded appetites. There the practices recommended made his hair stand on end, particularly when he remembered how infrequently his people bathed.

But he finished it at last, though his voice was a hoarse whisper by the time he was done.

"Wine!" the Emir said gaily. "He is a dog of a Nazarene, is he not? So his faith does not forbid it. Bring him wine to restore his voice. And prepare him a chamber wherein to rest. What think you, Mugira, brother mine, will ten thousand dirhems monthly be enough for my new Greek secretary? Or shall I offer him more? For, by the Prophet's beard, he is a treasure!"

"My lord," the Prince said, "I much doubt that money would tempt him. He is come upon a sad errand. And as the Prophet himself has instructed us to show mercy to those in need of it . . ."

Abd al Rahman frowned. Clearly he found al Mugira's words not to his liking.

"Tell me about it, brother," he said.

The Prince told the story of Ataulf's wound. The Emire remembered the huge Goth and his visit well.

At last he sighed and said: " 'Tis *gismah*, Allah's will. But—" He switched sharply into Romance: "Look you, young Gothic magus, my brother has explained why you cannot bide with us. Yet I am loath to part with a skill so necessary to me as this. Would you consider dwelling among us several moons each year? I should make you head secretary in charge of Byzantine matters—and enrich you beyond the dreams of avarice. What say you, my lord Goth?"

Alaric considered this. He reckoned up the dangers to his soul from this strange way of life. He called up Father Juan's sternest diatribes against luxury. "What profiteth a man to gain the whole world," he began to tell himself, "an he lose his immor—" But then he saw the slave girl Racha bending over to pick up a silver tray. Her little round buttocks gleamed through the thin stuff of her harem trousers like twin moons at the full.

"I—I am your servant, my lord Emir," he said.

IV

The Moors, Alaric saw, paid scant attention to the clock. It was hard upon midnight—by which time, at his father's castle, he would have been these four hours abed—when the Prince's slaves bore him in a covered litter, cushioned with silk, perfumed with the scent of jasmine, and suspended on long, springy poles which rested on their stalwart shoulders, to the house of the Jew.

Solomon ben Ezra received him at once, and again Alaric's world turned upside down. For the physician simply would not fit inside his preconceived conception of a Jew—likely because the prejudices with which men armor their hearts to hide their own weaknesses and their fears are too ironclad to be capable of the expansion necessary to hold a living man. And that, precisely, was what Solomon ben Ezra was; a man. A knightly man; even, God wot, a lordly one.

He was in his early fifties, though the enormous beard that covered his chest was already well streaked with white. His eyes were a cool and steady gray. They studied Alaric's face with a well-controlled look of hostility that took the boy aback.

"Sit you down, good my lord," he said; then he raised his deep, soft voice. "Zoë!" he called.

"Coming, master!" a girl's voice floated back, ghostly and disembodied from somewhere within the house. Alaric heard the whisper of footsteps. A moment later, the girl herself appeared.

"Yes, master?" she said. The voice was sullen.

"Bring wine. And fruits—no, wait. Have you dined, my lord?" the doctor said.

"Yes," Alaric said, looking at the girl. After all the beauty he had been subjected to this day, she was rather unimpressive. She was small, and very thin, though not uncomely—which meant little; for, by now, he was convinced there were no ugly maids among the Moors. There was something odd about her—a certain air of malaise, of profound disquietude. He decided at once that he didn't like her. She has, he thought, a shrewish air— Then she raised her eyes to his, and abruptly he changed his mind.

Shrewish was not the word. Shrewish wouldn't do. Hurt, mayhap.

Yes, surely, hurt. Wounded unto death. A small, pitiful doe-thing, lying trapped in the dark thicket of her fears, with no voice left to cry out, to say—

What? What were the words? What name, good fathers, learned sages, might be set to this—this unspeakable thing? Call it madness. Say the wench is daft, bereft of her wits. Say that some foul crone, with nightbane and hemlock and mandrake root and cunning spells hath—robbed her of certitude and peace and joy. But need one postulate witches to this effect, good fathers? Is not life itself enough? Is not the hand that strikes down the good, the noble, and the just, like a buzzing fly, and leaves the wicked grown great upon their crimes to stride the broad world in mastery, sufficient cause for the troubled and troublesome thing?

I rave, he thought; this face unsettles me! These eyes—

He studied her eyes. They were brown and almond-shaped and enormous. They looked at him now from under heavy black brows which grew together over her ruler-straight, classic, unbridged Grecian nose, so that but for a slight thinning of the hair in the middle, she seemed to have but one single brow. Yet, gazing upon him, unwavering, they departed from him; their amber glow dimmed, turned inward, became opaque; flared suddenly with what was almost surely a kind of anguished tenderness, girt about with pain.

He felt a curious stab of jealousy. God's blood! he thought; she sees me not; she makes of me an effigy, a thing of straw to mind her of—*him*, his mind supplied with achingly acute perception, whom she has loved, and doubtless, lost—in some cruel fashion, upon some evil day. Look you, fair Zoë . . .

And, having thought the words, he saw now that she was most wondrous fair in a hauntingly subtle way. It was a blessing of his imagination, his dreaming poet's mind, that he could see it; that he was not so bound about by the narrow limits of his world that the strange, the exotic, could not get through to him. Goissuintha and Clothilde, those fair and rosy beauties of the transplanted Nordic tribe he belonged to, might uplift his heart and quicken his pulse; but he was capable of letting this rare new intoxication invade his blood, of kneeling rapt, bemused, lost, before a half-stagnant pool upon which this lotus blossom floated, of standing amid rank jungle vegetation to cup this brown and golden orchid in his hands.

But now her eyes came back again, grew wide and most wondrous soft, delineating his face. Neither comparing nor contrasting it with another's but shaping it as it was, with savor, in her mind. She turned to her master.

"Bring wine and fruit, Zoë," Solomon ben Ezra said.

The girl said something in Arabic, her hands spread wide, as though she was begging for her life.

Solomon ben Ezra laughed. His laughter had a pleasant sound. He answered her, out of deference to his guest, not in Arabic but in Romance. "Oh, get you gone, Zoë," he said.

She ran from the room, came back again with fruit and wine. Ben Ezra dismissed her with a curt nod.

"Eat, and drink, my lord Goth," he said, "while I read this missive from the Prince, brought me by one of the guards who escorted you."

Alaric sipped the wine, nibbled at an apple. He was painfully, tinglingly awake—in that extreme state of near exhaustion when sleep will not come. Which was just as well. Jews, he had been taught all his life, were tricky scoundrels. And, if you didn't watch them every minute—

"So," the doctor said, looking up, "you know Greek! That is a valuable accomplishment. I have some Galen manuscripts that ibn Ha'ad procured me in Constantinople. Were there time—"

But without warning the door burst open. The girl Zoë stood in it. She began to speak in a strange tongue, so rapidly that she'd got more than twenty words out before Alaric began to catch their meaning. And now, hearing what she said, understanding her, Alaric knew what that language was—an old, almost classic Greek, spoken with a lilting music that old Paulus' tongue had never been able to match.

"Fly!" she said. "Fly, oh young and handsome lord! Your beauty moves me—much. For you are like unto him I loved. Do not remain in this house of evil—or he, this monster whom I serve, will unsex you, as he did my Alexis! He will leave you beardless, dropsidical, fat, and useless to me—or any other woman! I tell you, fly!"

"Zoë!" ben Ezra said. "Will you leave our guest in peace? He is in no danger from the knife. He has the Emir's protection. . . ."

Alaric looked at him. There was a thing in all this that—

"If," he said, "you have no Greek, sir Jew; how do you know what she said to me?"

"Because," ben Ezra said wearily, "I have heard her say it too many times before, in Arabic, or in Romance. She is slightly mad, my lord. And, I freely admit, she has some right to be. . . ."

"Too mad to Latinize your Greek scrolls?" Alaric said.

"She has no Latin, save only this bastard aljamía Romance. But I have tried putting them into Arabic with her help. The effort was a failure. Oh, she reads and writes her ancient tongue like a scholar; but her attention wanders. And she interpolates whole passages out of her splendid imagination that I much doubt are in the original at all. For in-

70

stance, when she had gone on for five pages about the art of castration being forbidden by the gods, I gave it up. You see, my lord, she is obsessed by that subject. . . ."

"Do you," Alaric said, "actually geld men, as though they were horses?"

"Yes," ben Ezra said. "At least I have—at the old Emir's orders, and over my own protest. One did not say no to al Hakam, young Goth—not if one had any desire to keep one's head upon one's shoulders. What would you? I am a surgeon; the best in all Córdoba. And the Moors have this fiendish custom of making use of eunuchs to guard their harems. They trust no man, nor their own women, either. In this, they're right; neither are to be trusted, from what I've seen. Still this operation is an ugly thing. Most do not survive it. But now, with young al Rahman on the throne—he is a kindly soul; I know him well—I think I shall be able to refuse with impunity to perform this crime any longer, the more so because that factory at Verdun supplies them now with castrates cut and well healed. . . ."

"Do not believe him!" Zoë shrilled. "He'll—"

"Zoë," ben Ezra said kindly, "leave us now."

She stood there, and her great brown eyes were awash.

"Oh, handsome lord, take care!" she said, and ran through the doorway.

"What ails her, sir Jew?" Alaric said.

"An excess of suffering, I think." Ben Ezra sighed. "She claims—and I believe her, for her speech and ways are most gentle—to be of high birth in the East. She says her mother was one of the ladies in waiting at the court of the Empress at Constantinople, which, too, is possible, even probable. Only on her honeymoon voyage among the Greek isles, poor Zoë and her husband—he was a pretty lad, strongly resembling you, but darker of skin and hair, though his eyes were blue, I recall—were taken by Moorish pirates. And because they were a striking pair—Zoë had more flesh then than she has now—those sea brigands decided not to sell them in Alexandria, as usual, but to bring them here to al Andalus, for, by then, word had spread throughout the whole Mediterranean of the fabulous prices old al Hakam paid for unusual slaves. I suppose, however, that even slavery would have been endurable had they been able to remain together—for much she liked what she had use of, it seemed to me. But, as I told you, Zoë's husband was almost too pretty to be a lad. So al Hakam decided—the old scoundrel was given to odd whims—that the boy would make a handsome page for his favorite of the moment, one Fatima her name was, I think, so he ordered me to cut the pretty Greek. . . ."

71

"And you did?" Alaric whispered, trying to keep the shudder out of his voice.

Solomon ben Ezra smiled sadly.

"You will note that my head is still upon my shoulders, young Goth," he said.

"What happened to him?" Alaric said.

"He died. Eight out of ten do. And she, poor thing, went mad. Old Hakam had put her among his female slaves; but neither he, nor anyone else, had touched her, methinks. By then she was far too skinny to suit a Moor. And when she lost her reason, the Emir freed her. For, according to them, 'whom the Finger of Allah hath touched' is a sacred person. I found her dying of starvation in the streets, filthy, half naked, covered with sores. Brought her here, cured her, restored, even, I think, most of her senses—treated her more as a daughter than as a slave. But she has this obsession still—"

Alaric looked at the Jew. He said roughly, crudely, what was on his mind. "And you do not make use of her?"

"Of course not," ben Ezra said. "I am happily wed. I have daughters above her age. And we Jews, young sir, do not practice these Moorish abominations. We are, within the limits of human frailty, faithful to our wives. Now, if you will, my lord Alaric, tell me of your brother's case. . . ."

Before they had finished that, another hour went by, then two. For ben Ezra plied him with questions, even drew diagrams of a male body upon which he asked Alaric to indicate the exact location of the wound, the angle of entry of the arrow, the degree of penetration. He asked the young Goth shocking things; such as the odor of the sick man's stools, whether blood or corruption had been detected in his urine, whether the wound itself stank, the color of the flesh about it.

All of which Alaric answered as best he could. But despite his best efforts his fatigue overmatched him, causing his tongue to stumble.

"Much do I fear we shall arrive too late," ben Ezra said, "but we'll do our best. I'll have Zoë prepare a bed for you. 'Tis nonsense for you to return to the palace at this hour. . . ."

"But," Alaric said, "will not the Emir or the Prince take affront?"

"The Prince," ben Ezra said, "is too indolent and pleasure-loving to bother. The Emir will not be angered, but for another reason. Ever since the old Emir, his father, forced him to witness the *al jurs* cutting the rebels to bloody bits in Toledo, a sight that shocked him so that ever since his eyes hath not ceased to wink—trying, methinks, to shut even the memory of it out—he has sworn to rule as far as that be possible by kindness and by love. Look you now, youth Goth; 'twas well within his power to keep you in Córdoba by force in order to make use of your knowledge of the Byzantine tongue—of which, as the Muslimn grow in power, the Emir will have ever greater need, because only Constantinople stands athwart their path in the East. Yet, he did not, because, as he told me, he is resolved never to use force until the last hope of persuasion fails. I'll send him word by a runner that you're remaining here; and that we both will appear to take our leave of him before our departure on the morrow. With that he will be content, I assure you."

"And," Alaric said, "the slaves?"

"They'll sleep in the street. Prince al Mugira's slaves often do, when he is about one of his pranks, such as visiting some poor Christian's wife. They're quite used to it. Well?"

"I'll stay," Alaric said, "because, by my troth, I'm sick of weariness. Yet much do I fear I shall not sleep. I've witnessed too many wonders this day, so that my mind hies about from one thing to another, and fidgets with fatigue, like an overridden horse. . . ."

"I'll prepare you a draught," the physician said. "Zoë!"

She came at once. Tired as he was, Alaric saw that something was different about her. He sought details: she had changed her way of arranging her hair; wore a flower above one ear; but it was more than that. Ben Ezra spoke to her briefly in Arabic. Alaric saw how the light in her brown eyes flared. She bowed to him, almost reverently.

"Come, my handsome lord," she said.

Alaric said, more respectfully than he'd ever dreamed of speaking to a Jew, good night to his host, and followed her. Once in the dark passage, another oddity reached out and smote him. Now she wore a scent. He was quite sure she had not worn perfume before, but now—

Alaric was most observant; and that day, among other things, the Moors had commenced to educate both his palate and his nose. The perfume Zoë wore now was no simple fragrance, such as his mother or his sister used; nor even that cheap, violent sort of scent Turtura had bought of the peddler with her stolen ounces. Nay, the faint, subtly insistent aroma that floated back from Zoë, enveloping his head in a warm cloud, was a deadly weapon. It was musky, intoxicating, languid, endlessly and effortlessly aphrodisiac. He drew it in, and his veins stood up and beat with his blood.

She opened the door of the simple chamber, put the candle on a low table by the bed.

"Now I go to bring you your sleeping potion," she said. "So lay you down, good my lord."

As soon as she had gone, he left the gorgeous robe in a heap upon the floor and dived into the bed. He scarcely had time to pull the cover up over his nakedness, before she came back again, bearing a silver bowl in her hands.

"Here, drink this, my lord," she said. " 'Twill do you good. . . ."

He took the bowl from her hands. As he did so, accidentally their fingers touched. She shivered, noticeably, and sparks and slivers of ice ran through his veins.

Zoë pointed to a cord dangling above his bed.

"If you have need of aught, my lord," she said, "pull that cord—and I will come to see to your wishes."

"But how?" Alaric said.

"It rings a little bell in my quarters," Zoë said. "So small a bell that no one else can hear it, so do not hesitate, if you have need of me. . . ."

The need I have of you, Alaric thought, would damn your soul and mine to hell, Zoë. Best that I drink this potion and quiet my blood with sleep. . . .

"Rest well, my lord," Zoë said.

He drank the contents of the cup. It was cool and pleasant, without taste at all. It might as well have been water.

An hour later he decided that it was. He lay there awake, trying to control the direction of his thoughts; but that perfume of Zoë's lingered in the little room. He remembered Yumn and Racha, contemplated in his mind their startling nakedness, made more provocative by partial concealment. He stretched out his long legs, in acute misery, while whole phrases from that damnable parchment of the Emir's moved, insidious and slow and fevered, through his mind. The words made pictures, made coiling naked figures, entwined and twisting before his eyes. God's blood! he thought; and began to pray: "Our Father take from me the temptation of the flesh! Remove from me this carnal lust I feel—"

For Zoë. For a maid he hadn't known existed two hours ago. Why? She was small and dark of hair and thin and—God's eyes! Those coupling naked figures on the wall! Each of them had his head on their shoulders now, and hers! I am mad, he thought; mad and damned! Lord Satan, I pray thee let me go! She is a sweet maid, and innocent by my troth; and he who'd dishonor her deserves—

Only that scent of hers lingered on, too strong, too strong—sending quick shocks and trills and bursts of excitement through his aroused blood until his male flesh awoke and grew and throbbed beneath the coverlet, erect now, anguished. He leaped from the bed, to see if she'd left a pitcher of cold water by the window. If she had, he'd dash it all over himself. That was his favorite remedy for such a state; for he loathed and despised and rarely surrendered to the act of solitary sin. But

now, at once, his nostrils told him that her perfume was endlessly re-
newing itself. He stole to the door, opened it a crack. Looked down.

There on a pallet on the floor she lay, clad in but a shift, a curved
Moorish dagger clasped in her hands.

He stole back to the bed, get into it, covered himself.

"Zoë . . ." he called out, quietly.

He heard her get to her feet. The door opened. She was between
him and the light, so that her body was outlined through her thin
shift. God's eyes!

"Yes, my lord?" she whispered. "What would my lord?"

"Come here," he said.

She crept closer to his bed.

"What was in that potion, Zoë?" he said sternly. "A philter to arouse
the blood?"

"Oh!" she replied. "Oh, no, my lord: I—I poured the potion out.
'Twas naught but water from the fountain. You see, I feared—"

"What, Zoë?"

"That—that he would make you sleep and—and cut you, after all!
I—I have such a horror of that, my lord! They—they suffer so. And like
as not they die. The—the bleeding's too hard to stop; and the mortification usually sets in—"

"Is that why you slept before my door with a naked blade in your
hand?"

She bowed her head.

"Yes, my lord," she said.

"And if your master had come?"

Her voice was lower still.

"I should have killed him," she said.

He looked at her. She had left the door open, and though the light
was dim, he could perceive her face.

"You do this each time your master has a young male guest?" he
said.

He heard the sharp intake of her breath.

"No, my lord," she said.

"Only upon rare occasions, then?" he mocked.

She shook her head.

"I have never—guarded this door—before now, my lord," she said.

He stared at her.

"Come here, Zoë!" he said.

She came toward him, timidly. When she was close enough, he
put out his arms and dragged her down; ground his mouth into hers,
savagely; brought up one big hand and caught at the neck of her shift,

75

ripped it from her body with one great pull; straightened up a little so that he could see her. She had not been depilated like the Moorish slave girls; but her body was nubile and slender, fine and fair. Slowly he brought his eyes up to her face; then he saw her bruised mouth's quiver; saw her tears.

And had, in that moment, his icy bath.

"God's death, Zoë!" he said. "What would you of me?"

"That—that you do not abuse me, good my lord," she whispered.

He lay there, propped up on one elbow, staring at her—at the bitter, hopeless way she cried. It was too much. He was not his brother Ataulf; he was himself: soft-hearted, tender as a maid. Fool! he howled within his mind; milksop, weakling, fool! Canting priest! No man! No man at all—

"Oh, get you gone, Zoë!" he said; and turned his back.

He heard her leap from the bed, heard her skip and scamper toward that door. But then there was silence. No creak of hinges, nothing. Except—God's blood—the soft rustle of her breathing.

Slowly he turned. She was standing there facing him, like Niobe, bathed in tears. He did not move or speak, holding his breath while she took that first step, that second, the third—

Now she was there beside him, inches away, but crying still. Very quietly she bent and found his mouth. Her lips were a warm salt tremble, wonderfully tender, quivering upon his like a breath, a prayer, a sigh. He did not raise his arms to her until she had sunk down once more at his side.

"I pray thee—be very gentle with me, good my lord," she said.

Riding along beside the Jew, Alaric closed his eyes. He felt hollow. There was nothing in him. Except peace. Except the slow and drowsy murmuring of his blood. He tried to shape the words to beg God's forgiveness for his sin; but they would not come. Instead what came to him were the first slow, groping seeds of future rebellion. All his life he had been taught to despise the flesh; the eschatological age he lived in had, or tried to have, no use for corporeal things. But now remembering Father Juan's favorite phrase, "Who embraces a woman, embraces a sack of excrement!" anger stirred in him dimly—he was too soothed, too quit of tension, anxiety, pain to give it vent—at the way it seemed to him now he had been lied to, cheated, deceived.

What I would have done, what I set out to do, he thought, that verily, Fathers, would have been ugliness itself, and a sin as black and foul as ye canting unwashed croakers could want! Because that word sin would be scanned, would it not, good my fathers, sages, and clerkly lords? If I had hurt my Zoë, ripped her, brutalized her flesh, that, I grant you all, is sin's very essence. To violate another. To force one's will, one's greeds, one's angers, one's lust—and, good fathers, one's dogmas and one's cant!— upon another is the stuff of sin.

But this—this mutuality? This wanting, this seeking, this acceptance, this delight? God's eyes, but ye are fools! Ye who turn from this to a monastic cell. Ye who deny the flesh that God gave you to delight each other in his Name, and bring forth children to his service, and his glory.

He frowned in sudden puzzlement. How came this about? What madness had crept through the world to make men hate their own flesh, despise loveliness, warmth, ease, comfort, joy? Who could despise his Zoë? His now! Forever his!

There'll be no other! Upon Saint Fredegunda's arm, I swear it! Lifelong my honored lady and the mother of my sons! The Greeks are a wise and noble race. The fathers, said old Paulus, of civilization. My sons, mayhap, will be nobler than I, wiser, kinder, better—as she is wiser, kinder than—than any of us! Yes—even than—than Clo—

But that way of thinking brought back unease; brought back trouble, questioning, doubt. So he put it from him. Opening his eyes he looked at his clothes. Though they were cut Gothic fashion, they were not his own. Instead they were of far richer stuffs than any he had worn in all his life. And these weapons—how splendid they were! The sword was lighter than a wand; yet, as the slave who had brought it to him had demonstrated, it could cut through a length of heavy chain and keep its edge. The hilt was of massive gold, encrusted with jewels. The blade was inlaid with flowing Arabic script in gold, worked into that Toledo steel. His dagger matched it. He wore a shirt of mail, made of thin scallops of steel sewn to a fine leather tunic so that they overlapped like scales of a serpent. It was far lighter and more flexible than either chain mail or plate. The lance puzzled him at first, because it was too short and light to charge with against an armored man. But then he remembered that the Berbers were said to throw such a lance as this so cunningly as to take a man in the throat between the joints of his armor every time. He'd have to practice that. He hefted the little round leather target that had replaced his huge and heavy shield. It could not cover a man's body like a shield; but, since it weighed practically nothing, it was possible to move it so rapidly as to catch missiles and ward off blows far more effectively than with a shield, and it had the added advantage of tiring its bearer far less on the march.

But best of all was that bow. He took it out of its saddle sheath again, and examined it curiously. It was not, like the puny weapon that Christians left to the baseborn knaves who formed their foot soldiery, made of a single stave of any available wood whether sufficiently elastic or no. Instead, it was built up, layered with various woods; yew, and blackthorn, and hickory and oak, each with a thin strip of horn between it and its neighbor, the whole gracefully double-curving sweep glued together under vast weight, then scraped and oiled and waxed and polished till it shone. He strung it, tried drawing it, and was surprised at the effort it cost him. God's death! It had at least four times the pull of the bows he was accustomed to. It would, he was sure, throw an arrow completely out of sight. If this be a coward's weapon, he exulted, long live cowardice!

He longed to try it, but he did not want to waste one of the long, beautifully made steel-tipped arrows. He was, curiously enough, wholly reconciled to the bow as a weapon now. Life was good; and any method that could be used to preserve it, worthy. If God had not granted him his father's thews or his brother's strength, in compensation the Creator had made him fair, appealing to maids, and master of this skill that enabled him to transfix gross louts come to ride him down from five hundred yards away. Question of honor and bravery be damned! What counted was to live! To live! To return to Córdoba, win the Emir's favor, gain wealth enough to purchase Zoë. And Yumn, his mind added impiously; and Racha! God's eyes! he thought; already I am become a Moor!

He hefted the purse the Emir had sent him in recompense for translating that Byzantine "Art of Love." Heavy as it was, perhaps he had enough to buy Zoë already. But first he'd better feel out the Jew; the world knew their cunning and their avarice; still if he played this right—

"Sir Jew," he said, "what is the cost of a common female slave?"

Solomon ben Ezra looked at him, trying not to smile.

"That, my lord, depends upon many things: her age, her looks—even her color. Black girls come right high, because they are rare in Spain; and every great lady of fashion must have one among her slaves to show how modish she is. . . ."

"And—white ones?" Alaric said.

"Again that depends upon the purchaser. Among the Moors, your fair-haired maidens with blue eyes bring the highest price; because blondes do not exist among them, and every rarity attracts—"

"Then," Alaric said, too eagerly, "dark-haired maids are cheap?"

Ben Ezra smiled. "Such as Zoë?" he said.

"Such as Zoë!" Alaric snapped. "What will you take for her, sir Jew?"

The physician pointed with his whip.

"The contents of that purse," he said.

Alaric untied it from his belt with trembling fingers. He tossed it to the physician with a gesture of contempt.

Deftly ben Ezra caught it, tucked it into his belt.

"Aren't you going to count it?" Alaric snarled.

The physician smiled.

"No," he said, "since I do not mean to keep it, there is no need."

Alaric stared at him.

"You don't mean to keep it?" he said.

"No," ben Ezra said. "The girl cost me nothing except less food than we ordinarily throw to dogs in my household, and little care; so 'twould be unseemly for me to keep this silver. I shall give it to the chief rabbi at our synagogue to distribute among the poor. Oh, don't worry, the purchase stands. When we camp for the night I shall give you a receipted bill of sale in writing. Will you come after her, or shall I send her to you?"

"I—I—" Alaric said. "Oh, keep her yet a while! I'll send you a letter, telling you what to do. . . ." He went on eyeing the doctor. "You're a strange man," he said.

"For a Jew," ben Ezra supplied.

"No," Alaric said. "I wasn't going to say that. Methinks you'd be as strange were you a Christian. Don't you?"

"If I were a Christian," ben Ezra said evenly, "I should be stranger still, for then I needs must be mad!"

Alaric frowned. But too many of his notions had been roughly handled here of late; and who knew to which world his heart belonged now?

"Why do you say that?" he said, and his voice was calm, with no trace of anger in it.

Now it was ben Ezra's turn to stare.

"You truly want to know?" he said.

"I do, truly," Alaric said.

The physician sighed. "No," he said. "We live forever on your sufferance or the Moors'. So 'twould be a folly to—"

"No folly, good physician!" Alaric said, and put out his hand. "And here's my hand on it."

Solomon ben Ezra hesitated, eyeing that fair young hand.

"Why?" he asked.

"A long tale, learned leech!" Alaric said. "Say that truth is a treasure of many parts—of diverse jewels, coins, ingots, bars—of which no man possesses the whole. Say, because upon a day not long ago, I lost my dinner at the sight of a saint's incorruptible arm. Or that—" his young face went serious now—"my brother, who is nobility's very self, is at death's door; while his assassins walk the world, and likely eat and drink and enjoy fair maids. Oh, I know not how to put it! It is that—"

"You've lost your certitude of being right?" the physician said.

"Yes," Alaric said soberly.

"Then I take your hand, young lord," ben Ezra said. "For by these tokens you have joined humanity. . . . Strange . . ."

" What's strange?" Alaric said.

"How oft wisdom—or at least humility—enters a man from betwixt a woman's thighs. Poor Zoë—you must have used her right royally, because she looked like death's twin sister this morning. . . ."

It was late upon the third day that one of the Moors of their escort sighted that dust cloud behind them. He called out sharply in Arabic: " 'Ware, Oh wise and noble lords!"

Alaric turned in the saddle, looking back; then his eyes sought ben Ezra's face.

"Better to make a stand my lord," the physician said. "To outrun them we needs must ruin these mounts we cannot replace. And from that cloud they seem very few. Besides, who knows, mayhap they come in peace—"

"At that speed?" Alaric said. "Tell the Moors to form ranks, Doctor!"

The physician barked out commands in the Prophet's tongue. The Moors drew their mounts off the road. Within moments they had taken positions amid a broken jumble of rocks. Now the whole escort troop was out of sight. Only he and the physician remained upon the road. Solomon ben Ezra nodded toward the right side, then drew his own gray desert Arab off to the left. Alaric bent his barb into a clump of bush.

He waited, while time crawled along his nerves like a host of migrating ants—until at last he saw that it was not a troop of marauding cavalry that pursued them, but a single rider upon a single horse. The horseman drove into a little hollow in the road—and vanished. As far as Alaric could tell, neither the horse nor rider came out again. The dust cloud settled. Above the trail stood only the blue and limpid air.

"Good Doctor!" Alaric called.

"He has fallen, surely!" ben Ezra called back.

Alaric crossed over to where ben Ezra stood.

"You think he's hurt?" he said.

"Or dead," the physician said.

"What should we do?" Alaric said.

"I leave that up to you, my lord. To go back means a delay; and your brother's life hangs in the balance. 'Tis you who must decide—"

Alaric looked at that bare and pitiless desert sweep. Each day was hotter than the last, now.

"We'll go back," he said.

When they entered that little hollow, afoot because the Moors had dismounted in order to use their bows, which were, among them, an infantry weapon, too long to be used from the saddle, each man already had an arrow fitted, and his bow drawn; but when they saw what lay there, they slackened their draw, and slipped the arrows back into the quivers. For a pitiful little bundle lay in the road beside the fallen horse. Alaric could see the animal's sides heave, saw how foam-flecked it was, saw the blood that flooded from its nostrils and its mouth. He moved toward the fallen rider, but nodded to one of the Moors and pointed to the horse. The Moor whipped out a knife and deftly cut the dying animal's throat.

Alaric turned that tiny, dust-covered bundle of cloth over. He saw the veins beating behind those lids above the half-veil, saw that straight brow that swept across her forehead without a break, whitened with dust now; opened his mouth to cry out to say—then closed it again, holding her to him, rocking back and forth, in the excess of his fear, his grief, murmuring brokenly, like a child: "Zoë—oh, Zoë, Zoë!"

Her eyes fluttered open. They were unfocused, blind; then they cleared. She put up one dust-covered, trembling hand, and touched his cheek, holding her fingers there while his tears spilled over them, turning the dust to muddy streams; then with her other hand she tore away her veil, and pressed those tear-wet fingers to her swollen, dried, cracked mouth.

"God grant me nectar such as this in Paradise, my lord!" she said, and fainted.

Alaric raised streaming eyes to the doctor's face.

"Bear her over there, where there is a bit of shade," ben Ezra said. "Now lay her down—and straighten out her limbs—"

Alaric stood there while the doctor ran his big hands all over Zoë's body.

"There are no broken bones," ben Ezra said at last. "We think she suffers from nothing more than heat, fatigue, and thirst. Not even sunstroke, for she has no fever. Here, give me your flagon, good my lord—"

Alaric passed over his leather water flask. The physician poured a little on a cloth and bathed Zoë's face and throat. Then he dripped a drop or two on her cracked and blackened lips.

Instantly she revived, and clawed at the flask.

"No, child," ben Ezra said in Romance, "too much would kill you now. A sip, no more. Promise me!"

Zoë nodded faintly. The doctor put the flagon to her mouth, drew it hastily away.

She opened those enormous doe's eyes then. She smiled.

"My lord Alaric—" she said.

"—is here," ben Ezra mocked: "The master of black, eastern, carnal magic is here—and I would have his secrets! I'd know, fair Zoë, what arts he practiced upon you that after one scant night in his arms, you ride a horse to death to come to his side!"

Her eyes widened. She struggled to sit up.

"No, child," ben Ezra said. "Later. Now you must rest—"

"No!" she got out. "No—time. The perverted one has paid those Muladi brigands who lead the Berbers to—"

"Hush, child," Solomon ben Ezra said.

An hour later, when the sun was down and the heat gone from the day, she told them. Ben Ezra had got enough water into her by then to restore her fully. She had gone to the market, which as a Christian slave and the servant of a Jew she was allowed to. And there, as was the custom, she had met with other servants, other slaves— usually, when they belonged to Moors, old and ugly women, whom their masters were sure could tempt nobody. But among them she had encountered a special friend, Afaf, a young and strikingly beautiful girl belonging to the Sahib Ahmad al Hussein.

"Which is why she can come to market," Zoë said angrily. "What other master in all Córdoba would let a girl as lovely as Afaf come and go as she wills? Often I have seen her with her face bared to the lecherous eyes of commoners and slaves, wearing not even a half-veil! Yet she is true to her name. For, my lord Alaric, Afaf means chastity in thy tongue. I think this is, master and my lord Alaric, because Afaf is in love with her lord Ahmad. But he—as all the world knows—despises women and the normal uses of the flesh. And, as there are no secrets safe from slaves, she heard from one of those fat and pretty baby boys he uses to gratify his lusts the news that he was cloistered in his chambers with the terrible bandit and murderer, the Sherif ibn al Djilliki."

"Not the banu Djilliki?" Alaric said.

"The same," ben Ezra said. "Go on, daughter. What did the dainty Ahmed want of that Goth renegade?"

"That he—capture my lord Alaric," Zoë whispered. "That he bring him not into Córdoba himself, but sell him to ibn Ha'ad who is known as a slaver. Whereupon ibn Ha'ad is to arrange a private sale, to which— such is the Sahib Ahmad's cleverness—two or three buyers are to be invited, these innocently to provide more verisimilitude to the trickery, but none of such wealth that al Hussein cannot outbid them easily. Then, if by chance the matter should come to the Emir's ears, the pederast can plead convincing innocence of wrongdoing—having at least enjoyed my lord the while—"

"To which you have some small objections, eh, Zoë?" ben Ezra said.

"I'll kill him!" she flared. "Or turn him over to you, master—that you may remove the repositories of the seed he wastes and the weapon he dishonors!"

"A lioness!" Ben Ezra laughed. "But if you do not wish Lord Alaric converted into 'ism al-mafu'ul, the victim of a pederast's lust, you must find another solution than offering me the task for which you've so oft berated me in the past. Besides, you have no claims upon me any longer. I am not your master; I have sold you. . . ."

Zoë's face went white. "Oh, no!" she wailed.

"But I thought you hated me," ben Ezra said gruffly.

"No, no, master!" Zoë wept. "For you have always been kind—'twas not your fault that the old Emir forced you to do what you did to Alexis. He would have killed you had you not obeyed—and you did not even know me then. Why have you sold me? And to whom? Not to ibn Ha'ad? Oh, no master, no!"

Solomon ben Ezra put one big hand under her chin. Very slowly he turned her tear-streaked face toward Alaric.

"Behold your new master, child," he said.

Zoë stood there. Her eyes were very wide. Seeing how she looked at him, Alaric felt humbled to his very soul. "Oh, no!" he cried inside his heart. "You must not Zoë! I am not worth, not worth—"

But he could not turn away his gaze. He stood there watching, rapt and lost, as step by slow step she came toward him with what was, despite her small size, the stateliness of the legendary queens of her own race: of Iphigenia going to the sacrificial altar at Aulis; of Medea welcoming Jason; of Clytemnestra watching the beacon fires that announced the return of her loved and hated lord. When she was close enough, she went down on both her knees, and bent forward until her face rested in the dust at his feet. Then blindly, for she did not raise her head, her two hands came out, closed about his ankle and lifted his right foot with surprising strength, bringing it to rest upon her slender neck in that age-old rite of absolute submission—which now to him was absolutely and finally not to be borne. The sound that burst from young Lord Alaric's throat was not even a word, but had the feel of tearing. He lifted his foot from her neck, and bending down, raised her to her feet; he stood there holding her and staring into her small, perfect Grecian face, or into what he could see of it through the shifting curtain of his tears.

Then, with that sudden inspiration, or that monumental folly, which comes only to the very young, he cried out: "Know all men by these presents that this maid is free! I manumit her from this very hour, and take her unto me—as my wife!" Then he bent and kissed her mouth.

Solomon ben Ezra smiled, but even his gray eyes were a little misty.

"A noble gesture, by my troth!" he said. "But, my rash young lordling, just how do you propose to implement it?"

Alaric took his mouth away from Zoë's long enough to stare at the Jew.

"I bought her from you," he said, "so I have the right—"

"—to free her, which no one questions," ben Ezra said. "That is simple, even easy, requiring only two documents which I shall prepare this very night. The first, a receipted bill of sale from me to you; the other, a declaration of manumission signed by you. And since our good leader ka'id, Abdul here, can both read and write, he will affix his signature to them both as witness, and certify, moreover, the mark of one of the common soldiers as another witness. I can, of course, witness the manumission myself, since I am no longer an interested party—"

"Than I don't see—" Alaric began.

"The young never see," ben Ezra said with a sigh. "Look you, good my lord. I have full oft wandered through the kingdom of the Goths; and have been called upon, more than once, to treat the ills of noble Visigothic families like your own. For though you label us Christ-killers, forgetting that your Christ, if he lived at all, was himself a Jew, and subjected to our laws, you, when the fear of death is on you, call us to your cold, evil-smelling halls. So I know your customs, know, in fact how little submissive your women are—"

"Go on," Alaric said grimly, having already caught the doctor's drift.

"How do you, Lord Alaric, propose to silence your lady mother's shrieks of rage and anguish when you appear at your castle with this skinny dark-haired serving wench on your arm, proposing to wed her forthright?"

"You yourself said she was highborn," Alaric said sullenly; then he burst out: "Besides, she's not skinny! Slender, rather, and—"

"You should know," ben Ezra said imperturbably, "just as I know that pretty lads like you are always the apple of their mother's eye. I doubt not that were the Kings of the Franks, of Asturias, Aragon, Navarre, or what have you, to appear at your father's castle with all their fair princess daughters in tow, my lady your mother would find some grave fault in one and all. Am I not right?"

Alaric could feel the chill rising around his heart.

"You are," he muttered, "but—"

"No buts about it! Our Zoë is a gentle creature, and likely, as she claims, highborn. But who can prove it? Is my lady of Tarabella the Greater, or, for that matter, my lord the Count himself, like to take her word for it? Or, for that matter yours—or mine? And you, young lord, I doubt it not, are scarce of sufficient years to question their authority. That's one thing—"

"God's death!" Alaric swore. "You mean there's more?"

"Of course. There is the matter of the fact that while a Christian, our Zoë is of the Eastern rite, of a church that hath fought bloody wars with your own, does not recognize your Pope, claiming authority for their own long-bearded Patriarch. Though that's a lesser obstacle, I doubt not that to remain at your side, Zoë would embrace the worship of Lord Satan himself, would you not, child?"

"Yes," Zoë whispered, "although it damn my soul!"

"And," ben Ezra went on, "there remains the other delightful circumstance, that if I know those renegade Gothic swine, the banu Djilliki, they are by now lurking on the trail with their Berber cutthroats, waiting to return you to the joys of sodomy. As for you, Zoë, 'tis a pity you have not more flesh on your bones, for now—"

"For now, what?" Alaric said.

"They'll cut her throat, since she'd bring too poor a price on the market. After—of course—having made use of her themselves in order of rank," ben Ezra said.

"God's death!" Alaric said. "Not while I live!"

"Which won't be long," ben Ezra said, "unless we begin to consider the future with less feeling and more sense—"

"Listen to him, my lord Alaric," Zoë whispered, "for he is very wise."

"I doubt it not," Alaric said. "What do you propose, good physician?"

"That Abdul's soldiers ring the camp about, their weapons in their hands. That when they sleep, two and two watch by turns, making a circuit of the camp. That way we may all stay alive until tomorrow, and you, my lord Alaric, may escape playing a woman's role in bed. Then we draw up your documents which I will present to the head judge when I return to Córdoba, if I live long enough to return anywhere—"

"You seem to be enjoying all this!" Alaric said tartly.

"I am. Life's sardonic, satanic humor appeals to me. Now tell me one more thing, young Goth. "Do you not know another route by which we may reach your father's stronghold?"

"Aye!" Alaric said eagerly. "Twelve leagues from here, we turn off to the right onto a goat trail that climbs over the mountains. 'Tis much shorter that way, but difficult for the horses. Still, with some care . . ."

"And could you find that goat trail in the dark?"

"Yes—I think so. Yes! I'm sure I could."

"Then let us break camp now and march!"

"But—but," Alaric said, "the documents!"

"Dead men and a pervert's slave have no need of documents," ben Ezra said, "while living freemen can make them tomorrow. Come!"

When day broke, they were high upon that mountain trial, following Alaric where he walked and led his horse, lest the barb go over the edge in the dark. And, when the sun had stood above them for an hour or two, long enough to clear away the mists, they could see the main road, winding far below. Alaric stopped suddenly and doubled in half with laughter.

"What ails you, Lord Alaric?" ben Ezra said.

For answer, Alaric pointed. Like white mushrooms growing amid the rocks below, clear in the sunlight they could see the turbans of the banu Djilliki's Berbers, hiding on both sides of the road.

"May Allah grant them patience!" ben Ezra said.

That danger passed, they rode until nightfall, and then made camp. Under Zoë's guidance, Alaric learned to form in Arabic his name, Aizun ibn al Qutiyya, which was as close as one could get to Alaric, son of the Goth, they having decided to use that form instead of son of Teudis, since there existed no close Arabic equivalent of his father's name. With a right brave flourish, Alaric signed it in the flowing Moorish script to those documents, and watched while the others affixed their signatures in turn.

"Now you are free," he said to Zoë."

"Bless you, my lord and master," she said, "but it does not lie in your power to free me from you. Only God can do that—by granting me my death. That it may be long in coming, tranquil, and at your side!"

"Amen," Alaric said, and crossed himself. He looked a little uneasily at ben Ezra.

"Oh, take her apart to a private bower!" The doctor laughed. "In one way or another she's yours, to do with her what sport you will. And you'd better enjoy this night, and tomorrow and the next; for after that, according to your reckoning we arrive, do we not?"

"Yes," Alaric said; "Good physician, what then? You are wise. What shall I say to my lady mother?"

"Nothing," ben Ezra said.

"Nothing!" Alaric echoed.

"Exactly. Upon our arrival at your fortress, Zoë shall be once more my slave girl, whom I brought along because of her skill at the art of nursing. You will treat her with indifference, indeed with contempt—"

"God's eyes—" Alaric said.

"—see all," ben Ezra said, "but your lady mother's won't, if you are cunning. Then, when my task is done, I shall take Zoë back to Córdoba—"

"God's death!" Alaric said.

"Which He endured until the Resurrection, according to your faith. So must you endure this parting. For shortly you will receive a summons from the Emir couched in such terms that even the Count, your father, will see the advantage of letting you go. By then, we'll have made a Trinitarian Nazarene of your Zoë, and you can wed her in the Church, with my lord the Bishop himself performing the ceremony. Then if you have aught in that fair head of yours, you will remain in Córdoba in a civilized land, and grow great and rich upon the Emir's favors. When you come, I'll have her dressed in bridal white, a lovely gown worked all over with seed pearls, that is, if you have not pumped up her belly too big to get into it, by then. . . ."

"God's—" Alaric began.

"—beard—or the Prophet's—" ben Ezra yawned "—or any other nonsense you want to swear by. Now get you hence, and let her draw the temper from your weapon, till it grow prostrate like a Moor at prayer!"

Solomon ben Ezra's advice as to how he should deal with the Lady Godsuinta, his loved—and, he admitted to himself, feared—mother, was perfectly sound, Alaric knew. The only trouble with it was the achingly simple fact that he never got a chance to put it into practice. For he had forgot one thing—or more truly, had never even taken into consideration such a contingency—that on this very good track of a trail there was a little chapel shrine to Our Lady, much venerated in all Tarabella the Greater, and the Lesser, too, for that matter, in direct proportion to the really great difficulty it took to reach it. Inside the chapel there was an ugly and commonplace image, called by the Celto-Iberian Romanized Spaniards who had placed it there long before Alaric's ancestors crossed the Pyrenees into Spain, Our Lady of the Forsaken, which had the reputation of having worked many miracles, particularly in the cases where all other recourses had failed.

From the shrine, on a clear day, one could see Count Teudis' castle, tiny and insignificant upon its pimple of a hill, rising out of the plain far below. So, when Alaric reached that place, he pulled up his barb, and helped Zoë down from where she rode behind him. He pointed it out to her.

"My father's stronghold," he said. " 'Tis, God wot, a paltry thing, yet—"

Zoë took one of his hands and raised it to her lips. Then she rubbed it against her cheek. Zoë was like that, full of small, unexpected tendernesses. She had suffered much, so now she lived both by and for her love.

"I knew not that my master was so great a lord!" she said. "Too great, I fear, to—"

"To what, Zoë?" Alaric said.

"To grant this poor slave of his body and his heart—a kiss?" she teased.

Alaric complied—with enthusiasm; with—be it said—considerable art, as well. Zoë was of the East, and possessed all an oriental's finesse in the ways of love. On that long ride she had taught him much. So occupied was he with his newfound joy that he did not hear the sudden gasp from the doorway of the shrine.

Clothilde reeled back into the dark interior of the chapel.

"What ails you, sister?" Sor Fidela said—or tried to say, for before she had it out Clothilde had clapped a hand over her mouth and held it there, hard.

"Would God it were dark!" Zoë said. "Oh, good my lord, when I think that this night, and for many nights to come, I must sleep apart from thee, truly I could die!"

"And I," Alaric groaned. "But there's no help for it, my Zoë. Come, let us ride back a bit and meet the others, for we've drawn so far ahead that I fear me they might miss the trail. . . ."

When the sound of his palfrey's hoofbeats had grown faint in the distance, Clothilde took her small hand away from her sister's mouth. Sor Fidela looked at her sister sorrowfully. Clo was white as death. Her whole body shook.

"The villain!" she hissed. "The knave, the lout, the churl!"

"Methinks our Alaric is none of these," Sor Fidela said, "but only a man, given to a man's venial sins. . . ."

"Venial!" Clo spat. "Why came we here, Goissuintha? Have you forgot that Ataulf has not moved or spoke these three days gone? Venial! While he dallies with his trull, his slut, his whore—"

"You are in God's House, sister!"

"I know it well! And do but speak the truth, you whey-faced fool of Christ! His lechery, his clipping and coupling with that foreign strumpet are, God wot, his own affair, and mayhap no more than venial sins. But if my Ataulf dies because of the delay, because of the nights entire he has wasted in his sport; what then, Sister Faithful, Bride of God? Tell me that!"

"Clo," Sor Fidela said, reasonably enough, though, oddly, a tear stood glittering in her eye, "one cannot ride day and night over a distance so great as Córdoba is from here. To do so would be to kill one's mount, as you well know. So if Alaric chose to forego sleep—"

"You'd excuse him!" Clothilde whispered. "You who are sworn to chastity defend his lewdness!"

"I don't defend it. I shall pray to Our Lady to incline his heart toward purer ways. I say only that Alaric's sins, such as they are, have not occasioned much loss of time, if any. He loves Ataulf too well to have forgot him quite, even in the heat of that sort of play. . . ."

"Methinks you know a bit too much of what you speak, sister," Clothilde snapped, "for all your veil!"

"And I," Sor Fidela said gently, "think there is something unseemly in your anger, Clo. Now, come, let us mount and be gone, before they come back again. . . ."

But Clothilde stood there, eyeing her sister.

"Not until you say the thought I see behind your eyes," she said, "or explain what you think unseemly about my wrath. . . ."

Sor Fidel's head came up. She was all woman still; her prayers, her faith, had not yet quenched her pride.

"I think that upon the day of his departure, Alaric put a thought into your head, Clo," she said. "All unwittingly—by kissing you like a man, instead of after the fashion of a boy. And as poor Ataulf has sunk day by day, until by now there exists no hope at all beyond a miracle of God, so has that idea grown. . . ."

"Go on," Clothilde said, her voice dangerously soft. "What idea is this, my sister, of which you speak?"

Sor Fidela smiled.

"That three winters are not too great a space to be bridged, Clo—no matter on which side they lie. . . ."

Clothilde's arm made a white blur in the gloom of the little chapel. The sound of her hand was loud, as it smashed open-palmed across her sister's face.

Sor Fidela bowed her head; when she looked up again her face was very pale, so that the marks of Clothilde's fingers stood out startlingly across it.

"I pray God to forgive thee, Clo," she said, "for I already have. Now, come. . . ."

Alaric rode toward the portcullis. He was well ahead of Solomon ben Ezra and Zoë, who, as prudence dictated, rode behind her former master now. Alaric had forgot she existed. His eyes hurt, so hard did he stare at those blank and silent walls. For long moments he forgot to breathe. His lips moved in silent prayer. To God, to the Holy Mother. To all the saints.

He even invoked Saint Fredegunda's arm. His fear, his anguish vanquished all his doubts; drove them completely from his mind. He rode on until something caught his eye: his father's banner, displaying the arms of his noble house, whipping brave and bright on its shaft above the north keep, under a cloudless sky.

And his heart expanded in his chest, until it was like to burst from joy.

"He lives!" he exulted. "My brother lives—Oh, thank Go—"

He stopped short, the words sliding down a long, atonal scale into what was less than silence. For there were figures on the north tower now. They were—God's death!—They—

He saw the flagstaff quiver, bend, slant downward, fall into the hands of those pygmy figures. It lay there a while; then slowly, slowly it slanted up again, stood erect. But his father's banner of green and gold flew from it no more. There in its place—in its place—

He sat looking at that inky banner. It seemed to him it grew and grew until it filled up all the sky. Until there was no blue left. Until there was nothing left, except that fearsome, screaming sound that ripped and tore, gurgled and slobbered, beastlike, demented, wild—

Unaccountably, he lay on the earth, beneath his horse's hooves. He was pounding the earth with his fists, while that mad animal howl burst endlessly from his throat with a taste of brine and blood, soaring up in a series of ululant pulsations to affront deaf heaven, to assault the very ears of God.

He felt soft hands tugging at his arms; through his blurred field of vision he saw figures running from the portcullis, which was somehow lifted now. A moment later, Julio and Sisberto had dragged him to his feet, where hurrying him toward the courtyard, while Zoë clung to his arm. She was crying too. For him. And for his grief.

They stood there in the courtyard. His father. His mother. His sister. Clo. Sor Fidela. Then, as he stumbled toward them, they turned their backs to him. One by one silently. His mother lingered longer than the rest, her face a fair field wherein love for her son and duty toward her lord warred visibly. Then she, too, turned. Only Sor Fidela was left, facing him still, her angelic countenance awash with tears.

There was no sound at all. The bucelarios, the servants, and the serfs, weeping to a man in bitter grief for their lord Ataulf, for that big, fine, lusty, strapping lad, so brave, so kind, so gay, cut off like this in the heyday of his youth, the very flower of his manhood, followed their gentlefolks' example, turning their shoulders to Alaric as they had seen their masters do.

He hung there. His eyes, all uncomprehending, moved like those of a trapped beast from the back of one rigid head to the next—

Until Zoë found her voice.

"Who are you?" she cried. "Who are you that you dare treat thus my lord? He who is as brave and noble as he is fair! He, whose very thumb-nail outweighs you all upon the scales of God! I ask you, who?"

The motion Clothilde made, turning, was curiously graceful. Her face was lovely, too; set, purposeful, and cold. She said not a word. Instead, step by step she walked over to where Zoë stood. She stopped there, staring into Zoë's brown eyes from a hand's-span away. Then coolly, carefully, and with perfect aim, she spat into her face.

V

It was dark now, so Zoë knew she had been in that little chamber a long time. Ever since that gentle nun had led her there after publicly calling for water and washing the spittle off her face before them all. That had shamed them, Zoë knew—except the blond one who had spat upon her. Nothing would shame that one; nothing in this world.

She sat there listening to the night noises, and feeling her nerves crawling just beneath the surface of her skin. It had not been so bad at first, because her former master had been with her then. But some two hours agone that great grizzled lion of a man whom Alaric had called Father had come into the room without a knock or a by-your-leave, and stood there eyeing her up and down as though she were some rare and distinctly unpleasant beast.

Then, without a word to her, he had turned to Solomon ben Ezra, and said: "Look you, Jew—mayhap your skill can be of use after all, though you come too late to save my son—"

"I came, my lord," ben Ezra said evenly, "as fast as a good horse could bear me, and remain alive to cover the whole distance."

"Oh," Count said, "I do not lay this tarrying upon *your* head, Jew; well do I know the cause of it! Now come with me—for if your alchemy and black arts avail me not to ease the grief I suffer, yet might they restore some semblance of his former beauty to my son; so that when we bear him forth the the sacred ground, those who watch by the roadside will find him as fair in death as he was in life. 'Twill be of some comfort to his mother. Come!"

But two hours had rolled by since then, grinding her heart between the upper and the nether millstones of their passage. No more, she thought, no more! I'll not endure it! I can't!

She got up, walked to the door, tried the latch. The door was not locked. She pushed it open, feeling the rusty whine of protest its hinges made like a dull blade sawing across her halted breath. But no one came. She stood there in the corridor, shivering. Here and there in niches in the walls, rushlights burned, but they only served to drift the darkness deeper in the shadows. It was dank and cold in the castle, despite the spring warmth that flowered through Castilla; 'twould be some weeks yet before the sun could thaw away the last of the chill in that grim old pile. But the quivering of her meager flesh had a deeper cause than the cold she was scarce conscious of, hardly felt; what made her quake to the very marrow of her bones was fear.

She thought: I must find him! I must! He's all unsettled by his grief. He—he might harm himself. Oh, Holy Mother, no! Oh, Most Sacred Mother, before thy icon I pray—

Then she saw the bobbing candlelight on those stairs. A serving wench came down them, a scullery maid, by the looks of her. Now that she was closer, Zoë could see the tears on her face. It was an uncommonly pretty face, round and plump, though, as Zoë saw from the white furrows the tears had plowed through the dirt on it, it had not been washed in many a day. Nor, Zoë's nostrils told her now, had the rest of the wench.

"One moment, child," Zoë said. "Can you tell me where to find my lord Alaric?"

The wench jerked her head toward the top of the stair.

"Up there," she said; then—"Why you're—No, no, you can't be!"

"I can't be what?" Zoë said. She thought: In this grim heap of stones even the servants are mad.

"That Moorish maid my lord Alaric brought back with him. You—you talk like a Christian! And—your skin is fair, not dark! And—and—Oh, but you're—pretty! No, you're beautiful!"

"Thank you, child," Zoë said. "Yet I am she. Tell me, what are you called?"

"Turtura," the girl sniffed.

"Good Turtura, go before me with your light, and lead me to your lord."

Turtura's face changed. It grew more sullen still.

"That you may take him away from us?" she sobbed. "No! I can't! I won't! You keep away from him, you Moorish witch! You've put a spell on him now and—"

Coolly Zoë put out her hand and took the candle from Turtura. "Now stand aside, child," she said in the same calm, dry voice she'd used before.

Wonderingly, Turtura did so. Zoë went past her, and up those stairs.

As she neared the top of them the first thing she heard was the sound of the knout. She stopped dead, listening to the sick, ugly, sodden sound it made as it bit flesh. Again. And again. And yet again. And then she heard him groan.

They dared! she raged; they dared! Because he tarried on the way a little—so little. And that little not his fault, but mine!

"Animals!" she shrieked. "Beasts! Have done! Or I—"

She took the rest of the stairs two at a time and burst into that tower room, her fingers already curving into talons to rake from their sockets the eyes of whoever it was that dared to touch—

—That fair young body, that was her body now, so that she felt in her own outraged flesh those sickeningly cruel stripes from which his warm red blood—equally her own blood since that hour of unquieting—fleshly magic, of disturbing carnal alchemy when they had ceased to be two entities, separate and apart—ran down. He knelt before a rudely carved crucifix on the wall. There were no chains on his ankles or his wrists; no whipping post to hold him bound; nor even any masked, ugly, sweaty giant of a torturer to lay on the lash. He was alone. More alone than any man in life has any right, or can bear to be. And the hand that wielded the knout was his own.

"Zoë leaned against the doorframe waiting for the mailed fist clutching her heart to turn it loose; for the ice that filled her lungs to thaw. She let out her breath—measured it out—upon the dead-stopped air.

"Oh, no!" she breathed. "Oh, Alaric, no!"

Then, as he brought that ugly whip whistling around to lay another laceration across the ones already there, Zoë came alive. She put down the candle carefully, crossed with dreamlike slowness to where he knelt. She bent and put her full, warm, opened mouth upon his shoulders, let it trail downward slowly, slowly across those ugly, brutal stripes, as if to draw from him his anguish and his pain.

"No!" he shuddered. "Don't! I am not fit! Not fit!"

"Alaric—" she whispered. "Look at me. . . ."

"No! Get you gone, Zoë! Leave me! 'Tis for the sin we did together that God took away my brother's life! You hear me, Zoë! Get you gone!"

"I am yours, my lord," she said gently, "and I will obey you—in all else but this. For I cannot make a murderer of you in God's sight. . . ."

"A murderer?" he muttered. "How—"

"My blood would be upon your hands," she said, "since without you I would die."

"Then die!" he howled, whirling upon her. "Die, strumpet! Die, whore! I care not! Get you hence and die!"

She stood there before him and her face was very white. She did not move or speak. She simply stood still and let the great luminous tears brim on her lashes in the candle glow, flash diamond-bright, then fall. That sight was beyond his bearing. And because it was, because he knew that in another instant it would unman him, he summoned up his rage.

"Get you gone, Zoë!" he cried, his voice gone high and woman-shrill, and swung that ugly, heavy whip with all his strength. It caught her across the face, slanting upward from the corner of her mouth to her cheekbone. Under its impact her fair young flesh broke open like a plum.

Still she did not move. She stood there uncaring while her tears rained down, joined now and mingled with that crimson flow. Head up, erect, she faced him, crying what seemed to his sickened eyes great tears of blood.

He opened his nerveless, gray, and trembling hand, let the knout fall to the floor; took a stumbling, shambling step toward her, another, put out his fingers and touched her whip-torn cheek, staring at the thick red flow that covered them at once. Then he dropped to his knees and wrapped his arms about her waist, burying his sick, hurt, baffled boy's face into the heavy yellow silk of the Moorish woman's trousers that she wore, clinging to her like that, shuddering, soaking her with his tears.

She put down a slim hand, tenderly, and let her fingers stray through his hair. Then she brought both hands under his armpits, tugging at him until he got to his feet. She smiled at him, and going up on tiptoe clung her mouth to his, so that he felt its wonderful warm tremble, tasted the hot wet salt of mingled blood and tears.

She led him to his bed, forced him to lie facedown while she dipped cloths in the cool water he kept in the stone jar by his window, and bathed the whip stripes on his back.

"But, Zoë," he groaned. "Your face! How it bleeds! You must—"

"Presently," she said. "Is it not yours, like all the rest of me? And have you not a perfect right to break the thing you own?"

Later she lay at his side, cradling his bright head against her breasts, and talked to him gravely, tenderly, as a mother does a child.

"Tell me, my lord and master, how many days did it take you to reach Córdoba?" she said.

"Eight days," Alaric said.

"And how many to return—with me, with the good physician, and the Moors?"

Alaric frowned, reckoning in his mind.

"Seven!" he said. "By all the saints, Zoë!"

"So then—" she smiled "—despite my lord's sinful dalliance with his strumpet and his whore—"

"Zoë! I—"

"—he actually made faster time. Now do I crave that you explain this thing, good my master and my lord! In what way, then, did your favoring me in the night cause your brother's death?"

"The sin," Alaric burst out. "To punish me for my lewdness, He—"

"—took your brother's life. Odd. Methinks I like not this God you serve. To punish one man's sins, he takes another's life. You are not Christian then, Alaric? You worship some Gothic pagan god?"

Alaric raised up then, staring at her, seeing the thick crust of blood that had clotted hideously into the lint and threads she had torn from a cloth and packed into that cut to stop the flow. Her brown eyes were filled with cool, amused tenderness.

"My God," she said, "pardons sins, and slays no man. He healed the ear of the high priest's servant come to take him; said from the Cross itself, 'Forgive them, Father, for they know not what they do.' I cannot imagine Him killing my lord Ataulf because you lay with me. I cannot even imagine Him killing us, for such a joyous, pleasant little sin. At the most, He'd say—"

"What, Zoë?" Alaric said.

"'Go you, My children, to My house, and consecrate your bodies to each other before My altar in lifelong faithfulness; and the living fruits of your love, to My service.' Does this not seem reasonable to you, my lord?"

"It does. God's eyes, it does! I've been a fool! Oh, Zoë, how wise you are! If only my father and mother could see things as you do—"

"They will," Zoë said, "after I am gone. . . ."

"Gone!" Alaric said. "Gone where, Zoë? You'll not leave my side! I'll not let—"

"Listen to me, Alaric, listen, my pretty baby boy of a lord! For what I'm going to say *is* wisdom—of the kind it cost me many a tear to learn. I want us to be happy together. I want no shadows 'twixt my love and me. If I stay here, knowing my own sex as I do, you will never earn your parents' forgiveness; nor, by my troth, their consent to take me unto you as your wife. Your mother will find me hateful, your sister more so—and that jealous and vengeful Clothilde, whom greatly do I fear, will plow up hell itself to win you for her own. I shall fear her even more being gone from you; but as for that, I can only trust in you, in God, and in my prayers. So upon tomorrow, I shall return to Córdoba with my former master; I shall dwell in his house until you come—bearing with you your father's forgiveness and his consent to our union—"

"Zoë, you ask too much!" Alaric groaned. "You do not know my father!"

"Well enough, I think, to know how to overreach his pride. I will ask of my former master a sum of money—and *you*, my dearest lord, must pay him back!—which I will offer unto ibn Ha'ad, who will procure hell-fire from Lord Saithan if the price is right, as payment for his bringing me from Constantinople proof of my lineage—before which even my lord your father needs must bow! Because I am humble only to love, my lord Alaric; your sons, if got of me, will have the blood of kings in their veins. This I can prove. Now kiss me, and sleep; for tomorrow I must undertake a journey and you—"

Alaric grinned at her suddenly, impishly.

"If I kiss you, I *won't* sleep," he said.

"Then don't kiss me," Zoë said gently. "For though all my body longs for yours until I faint of desire, still your brother Ataulf lies below. That *would* be sin, Alaric; such a sin as even the merciful God I serve could scarce forgive. Now close your eyes, my young and lusty lord—and sleep!"

Though he knew it not, as he lay there in his mistress's arms, young Lord Alaric, Count Teudis' son and heir, had another more potent *advocatus diaboli* arguing his case.

"Look you now, Teudis," his gentle mother said, "they came back from Córdoba in just seven days! I had that of the Jew. . . ."

"Hummmph!" Count Teudis snorted. "After having tarried in that den of iniquity sufficient time to find himself a wench to warm his bed!"

"Which didn't take him long," the Countess snapped. "Is he not, after all, *your* son, Teudis?"

The Count's frown lessened; there was a thing in this strangely to his liking. *God's eyes,* he chuckled inside his heart, *and me calling him a little priest!*

"Reckon it up," Lady Godsuinta said. "He left here—let me see—he left here—Look you, Teudis! The boy left here a fortnight and a day agone! Eight days there, seven days back—that left him but a night in Córdoba! Scarce time enough to *find* the Jew, not to mention—"

"—this dark-haired skinny little wench." The Count chuckled aloud now.

"Oh—for her, he didn't have to look! That strumpet found *him,* you may rest assured, my lord! After all, my Alaric is wondrous fair; and, mayhap, she saw him pass, and feigned some excuse to speak to him and—"

"No," the Count said. "She is a servant in the house of the Jew."

"A servant! And a Christ-killer, herself, from the looks of her! I thank the saints that she leaves here at dawn! God's eyes, Teudis! The boy is fair daft over her! Over this ugly little Jewish wench who—"

"One," Count Teudis said, "she is not a Jewess, but a Greek. And a Christian, after the Eastern fashion. Two, apart from needing to be force-fed like a Christmas goose, she is *not* ill-favored. Three, that she is a servant counts for little, since the Jew swears on the Holy Bible, the

Old Testament, which is sacred unto them as well as to us, that he bought her of Moorish pirates who'd stolen her away from Constantinople itself, where her lady mother is dame in waiting to the Empress. 'My lord,' said he with that sly look of his, 'when I procure you her proof of lineage from the East, 'tis you and your lady who must bow to her, for verily she is nigh onto a queen!"

"And you believe *that*?" the Countess snorted. "God wot but you men have no sense at all! Don't you see—'tis all Jew lies and trickery? He'd worm her into our bosom to his own advantage! I doubt not she's his own daughter! Why—"

"Godsuinta, by God's Holy Breath, you try my patience!" the Count said. "Now close both your eyes and your mouth if such a miracle is possible. We have a hard day before us tomorrow—and a sad one, by my troth. In your daft folly over the boy, have you forgot who lies below?"

"No," Lady Godsuinta whispered, and began at once to weep. "Still, Teudis—Ataulf loved his little brother much—he'd have you forgive him, of that I'm sure. . . ."

"I have forgiven the lad," the Count said, "already, Godsuinta. Much do I prefer this sin to certain others. I'd feared he'd turn into a boy-lover like the Moors, to say it out. Or cheat me of grandsons by turning priest. I'll tell him so in the morning. God's blood, woman! Where are you going?"

"To tell him now!" the Countess exulted. "Or else the poor boy will not sleep! He'll lie there weeping nightlong, and—"

The Count grinned at her wickedly.

"I should not do that, Godsuinta, were I you," he said. "At least not without passing by that little bedchamber down the hall to see whether the wench is still in it. Or if she's alone, if there. By so doing, you, my dove, may save yourself both embarrassment and grief. . . ."

The Countess tossed her head.

"What an evil mind you have, Teudis!" she said. "Think you my poor gentle Alaric would dream of such a thing with his brother lying dead below?"

Then she flounced from the bedchamber, headed for the stairs. Five minutes later, the only ears in the castle that had not heard her shrieks of grief and rage were Ataulf's. And, mayhap, not even his escaped; for my lady Countess's voice rising scream-shrill at the sight of her baby's lying there in that Jew-Greek-Moor strumpet's arms, rose through purgatory to heaven's very gate; and drilled down and through sand and earth and rock to drown out the cries of the damned in hell.

Need it be said that young Lord Alaric gained not his mother's pardon on that day?

He rose in the gray of dawn and dressed himself. What was in his mind now was hot rebellion's sting.

"I'll wait for Zoë and the Jew along the trail," he raged, "for I have neither sister, father, nor even mother, more! I'll not be treated like a scurvy knave! Nor have my Zoë insulted thus! I—I'll embrace the Eastern rite; become myself a Greek! They'll never see my face again in this filthy heap of stone! And the Counts of Tarabella will end with you, Father! For you have no longer any son—"

Dressed now, and armed, he crossed to his window and looked out, for from that vantage point high in the tower he could see with one long sweep of his eye all of what had been, almost to that hour, his world. He saw how the light slanted along the land of Castilla, luminous, limpid clear, about its daily business of giving birth to form, sculpturing plains, walls, the other towers or keeps out of the dark. He saw the portcullis go creaking up, saw a cart drawn by two mules rattle out it. The cart was driven by the Count's oldest retainer, one Jacobo, a graybeard of more than three score and ten winters, a little daft, garrulous, and half blind. In the cart were the two aged nuns the Abbess had sent along with Sor Fidela, not so much to guard a chastity in absolutely no danger at all, as to protect the young sister's reputation—and the convent's—from tongues too prone to wag without just cause.

"Get you gone, foul hags!" Alaric stormed. "For not even the habit you disgrace can hide the fact that witchcraft's your true avocation, and Old Cleftfoot, inky Satan, the Lord you serve! Aye, get you gone!"

He clattered down the stairs in his fine new Moorish armor, bearing his target, lance, and bow. About his waist was belted both his new poniard and his sword; his quiver full of arrows was strapped across his chest, and hung down his back. Upon that morning with his blue eyes blazing wrath, he appeared a young Mars, girt about for war.

But early as he went, he found his father up and dressed before him. Above his somber funeral black, the Count's face was grave and sorrowing.

"Thus do you dress for your brother's burial, my boy?" he said, his voice curiously gentle.

Alaric stopped short. In his rage, he'd forgot quite what must be done that day.

"I—I'll go take them off, Father," he said.

"No, don't!" the Count said. "Moorish raiders have been seen in the mark, my lord Julian sends me word. Best you go armed, and mounted too. I'll put the bucelarios at your command, since, God wot, I'll bear no arms today. . . ."

"But, Father," Alaric said, "those two old nuns! I saw them sally forth—"

"I sent them away, much to their sorrow. They'd dearly have loved to sniff and slobber above your brother's bier. But since today Goissuintha returns to her convent and Clothilde to her father's protection, there's no further need of them; and by my troth they offend my eyes!"

"But if there are Moors in the mark?" Alaric said.

"Ha!" the Count said. "The Moors have no more use than any other man for what rots unwashed betwixt their withered thighs. They're safe enough, God wot. And now—"

Alaric sank down on one knee, took his father's hand.

"Do you forgive me, good my lord?" he said.

"Of course," the Count said gruffly. "A bit of wenching becomes a man, though you chose your moment plagued ill, my son. I was upset yesterday because I believed you'd put playing the beast with two backs above your brother's life—"

"Oh, Father, no!" Alaric said.

"I know you didn't now. The Jew told me what speed you made, and says he, the lass is gently born, though sadly reduced in station. Has she proof of that?"

"No," Alaric said, "but she can procure it within a twelvemonth! Father, you don't mean—"

"I don't mean anything, son," Count Teudis said. "Get you that proof and then we'll see. I wed your mother for love's pure sake, not for castles, dowries, or to link together our domains. And, the truth is, I don't mislike your lass. If she be what the Jew claims, I'll not oppose this match. God's eyes! These are modern times; and tyrannical fathers should belong to a ruder age. I—I've been happy with your mother, boy. I would not less for you. Now, come—we'd best be about the preparations—"

Reverently, Alaric kissed his father's hand.

"My lord," he wept, "you have my obedience and my love. My life, too, should you require it! For to God himself, now do I vow that I have the best father in all the world!"

"Oh, stuff and nonsense, boy!" the Count said gruffly. "Now get you up; there's overmuch to do. . . ."

Among those things was to prepare Ataulf's body for the long march to the sacred ground. For one of the unexpected consequences attendant upon Count Teudis' having won—or bought, depending upon which version of those long ago events one cared to accept—the Black Duke's castle, was that the departed young lord's ancestors lay in the churchyard of Tarabella, some six good leagues away. When my lords of Tarabella the Greater had lived in their own castle just outside the town itself, it had been logical enough to bury their dead there; but now, as the Countess pointed out, it made no sense at all. But in this world of sin and sorrow, seldom is it that sense wins out over sentiment. Count Teudis was not to be budged from his stand. His son, too, must lie beside the mighty of his father's line.

So it was, that young Lord Alaric had time to kiss his brother's cold mouth and say a humble prayer for his soul's repose—which, be it said, required some excess courage on his part. For, despite the Jew's best efforts, poor Ataulf looked like the corpse he was now.

Shuddering a little despite himself, Alaric kissed his dead brother once more, crossed himself, and came out into the courtyard—to find his father talking amiably enough with Zoë and the Jew.

Hearing his footsteps, Count Teudis turned, and Alaric saw his father's face go red with sudden anger.

"Did you do that?" the Count roared, and pointed to the ugly, bloodcrusted stripe across Zoë's face.

"Yes, Father. I—" Alaric began; but that was as far as he got, for the Count fetched him such a blow as to send him sprawling in the dirt.

At once poor gentle Zoë came flying to his side, knelt beside him; wrapped her slim arms about his neck.

"Oh, no, my lord!" she said to the Count reproachfully.

"Knave!" the Count said. "Oaf! Lout! Churl!"

"My lord," Zoë said, "he was right. I—I—provoked him! I—"

"Nonsense!" Count Teudis said. "You don't have it in you to provoke anybody, child! You're much too gentle for your own good. Besides, a wellborn man doesn't hit maids, no matter if they be of high degree or not. I'll not stand for such behavior from a whelp of mine. We owe women either our protection or our respect or both—never our brutality. Now, fair Zoë, turn that lout loose and get up from there! And you, you changeling knave, get down on your churlish knees before her and beg her pardon right humbly, or by heaven, I'll—"

"Gladly, Father!" Alaric said, and knelt before Zoë, taking her hand in both of his. "Have I your pardon, my lady and my queen?" he said.

"Oh, Alaric, I—" Zoë said.

"Or do you want Father to throw me in the dungeon for half a year?" Alaric said with mock solemnity. "On bread and water, at that!"

"You've been cruel to me," Zoë said, mischief lighting her eyes. "Still I'll forgive you; but on one condition—"

"And that condition?" Alaric said.

"That you get up from there and kiss me!" Zoë said.

Alaric looked at his father, fearfully.

"You heard the maid!" Count Teudis roared.

Alaric got up, took her in his arms, stood there looking down into that little face.

"Zoë," he began.

"Kiss me, my lord!" she said. "Then let me go, while I still can. Before my strength and my will both desert me. . . ."

Alaric kissed her. A long time. A very long time.

"Hmmmph!" the Count said. "She said kiss, boy, not devour! Besides, I have a word or two to say to her myself."

Alaric turned her loose.

"As my lord wills," Zoë said.

"Look, daughter," the Count said, and pointed. Alaric turned and saw Julio coming from the direction of the stable, leading a dainty snow-white palfrey. " 'Tis my gift to you," the Count said. "Some small recompense for all you've suffered at our hands. For—God's eyes!—I like you well, lass! This whelp of mine shows more sense than I ever gave him credit for. Besides, the distance from here to Córdoba is overlong for you to ride double behind the Jew—"

"Oh!" Zoë whispered. "You mustn't, my lord: 'Tis far too much! What a pretty beast! I'm sure I don't deserve—"

"That and more," the Count said. "Our good physician, this wonder-working Jew, told me how you rode your nag to death to save the one worthless son I have left. For that alone, my blessings on you, lass. Now come here!"

Wonderingly, Zoë came to him. When she was close enough, the Count stretched out his great arms and clasped her to his bosom. Then he planted a fatherly kiss on her forehead; and, dropping his voice to a bass rumble intended only for her ears, but which none the less carried halfway to Tarabella, he whispered: "Get you proof of your lineage, and then we'll see. I'll tame the Countess down ere that day comes. And, daughter—"

"Yes, my lord?" Zoë whispered, her eyes bright with tears.

"Eat you some solid food, four times the day, or five! A man needs a bit o' flesh beneath him to cushion his weight! And, God wot, no son of mine will be overpleased to hear his wife's bones rattle in bed!"

"I'll come back fat as a Moorish sultana, good my lord!" Zoë laughed; then, upon sudden impulse, she kissed the Count full on his bearded mouth.

102

"Zoë!" Alaric roared in perfect imitation of the Count's best bellow. "You'll make bad blood 'twixt my father and me! Kissing him like that—"

"He's handsomer far than you are, my lord Alaric," Zoë teased, "and bigger and stronger, too, I'll vow. Good thing your lady mother lives or—"

"You were of another opinion last night," Alaric said, and took her in his arms. "Zoë—" he said.

"Alaric—" she whispered. Then wildly, blindly, she went up on tiptoe and clung her mouth to his for a small eon, a little age. She tore free of him at last, her face not streaked but flooded; and stood there bent over a little, her two hands doubled into helpless fists, her mouth not quite closed, nor yet fully opened, trembling like an idiot child's with the wild, wordless sobs that ripped through it; until the sight of her grief was not to be borne, becoming a kind of nakedness. Alaric took a step toward her, but she whirled away from him, and hiding her face against her palfrey's rich caparison, wept silently, terribly, while her whole body shook.

"Zoë, please!" Alaric croaked.

"Oh, leave her be, boy!" the Count said gruffly. "For, by God's eyes, if your mother had wept for me just once like that in all these years, I should have burst with pride!"

Then he, himself, put his big hands under her armpits.

"Up with you, daughter!" he said. "And don't spoil your pretty eyes over this worthless knave. For, if he means so much to you, have him you shall, if I have to write you out your patents of nobility myself!"

Then my lord of Tarabella the Greater did another, stranger thing —a thing that made Alaric afterward wonder whether or not some premonition had not prompted him to greatheartedness and generosity for the ultimate benefit of his soul. He strode toward where Solomon ben Ezra sat, already mounted on his gray, and put out his hand to him. Wonderingly the doctor took it.

"I bid you Godspeed, good physician!" Count Teudis growled. "For Jew or not, by my lights you are a man!"

The funeral procession moved out of the gates of Count Teudis' castle. At the head of it, bareheaded and clad in somber black, the Count himself marched. Behind him came the bier, on which all that was mortal of greathearted Ataulf lay. It was borne on the shoulders of eight stout men at arms, who were followed by sixteen more; for six leagues under that now blazing sun were not to be taken lightly, the Count knew, so he had arranged for three full changes of pallbearers on the way. Ataulf's body lay covered with a great standard bearing his father's coat of arms. Only in the churchyard itself would it be placed in one of the immense granite coffins, which the Count had ordered long ago for himself and each member of his household.

After the men at arms, the ladies came, riding in a cart, above which an awning of white cotton cloth had been spread to guard their fair and delicate skin from the sun. The cart was drawn by four night-black mules, caparisoned in black velvet, with black plumes nodding from their ugly stubborn heads.

And last of all, young Lord Alaric rode, armed cap-a-pie, at the head of the bucelarios of the guard. Which was a signal honor, of which he would have been proud had he been capable of pride on that day. But nothing was further from his heart. He rode bent under a double grief: the brother of his heart whom he had loved, and been loved by in his turn, was gone from him, forever gone; and his Zoë had ridden off in the company of the Jew to that strange, glittering, magic world, so beautiful, so unquieting, so subtly perilous, which lay to the south. He wondered bleakly if he would ever see her again, for, even with his father's good will, the odds were against them, and he knew it.

Then he became aware of something—a thing so passing strange that at first he thought that he imagined it. In the cart, scant yards ahead of him, his mother and his sister rode, heavily veiled, bowed down in tears, their fingers moving ceaselessly upon their rosaries. At their side, Sor Fidela sat, head up, gently weeping, her pale lips murmuring her prayers. But Clothilde sat behind them on one of the two seats that ran, unlike the one on which Countess Godsuinta, Gelesvinta, and Sor Fidela sat, not crosswise but lengthwise the cart. She, too, was veiled, and dressed in black; but now, Alaric saw, with amazement, she had thrown back her veil and was looking out at the countryside through which they passed. She seemed utterly calm; of a certainty she was not crying!

Alaric studied her with some care, knowing as he did that the Marquis Julian and the Lady Ingunda, together with their men at arms, servitors, and serfs, would join the funeral procession at the church; that afterward they would bear both their fair daughters off; and God alone knew when he would see them again. He was not conscious of any disloyalty to his betrothed as he stared at Clothilde. It was only that— God's eyes—she was so wondrous fair! How a body and a face so lovely could house so mean and spiteful a temper was truly beyond his ken. . . .

He was thinking that, when it happened for the first time. Slowly Clo turned, and stared full into his eyes. A long time—a very long time, until 'twas he who dropped his gaze, not she. And, at the very last moment, before his renascent timidity overcame him, he saw—or thought he saw, of that he could not be sure—her pale pink lips curl in a small, slight smile.

He rode on behind her, confusion in his heart, at that snail's pace at which the funeral procession needs must go. He had no way of knowing that from her casement window she had witnessed his tender parting from Zoë, and had he known, still would he have been incapable of divining its effect upon her.

She had watched that parting with a slow, calculating smile. She had displayed none of the anger or the jealousy her sister had accused her of. She had made no effort to sort out her own feelings in the matter. She didn't need to. All she thought, and even murmured to herself, was: "Good! He'll do, after all!"

For Clothilde, Julian's daughter, was of those—by no means rare among her sex—whose minds instruct their hearts. Ataulf, whom truly she had loved, was dead. Too bad. She'd weep for him awhile—for the exact short season the world considered due. But she'd enter no convent nor surrender her life to grief. That grief she felt in the same small measure that she was capable of feeling any sensation not purely physical. She'd not spoil her looks with overweeping; the roses in her cheeks must bloom for another eye. What eye? That eye was here at hand. Since the Moors had come, the frontier marks had been swept increasingly bare of the people of her race; to which must be added the bitter fact that she needs must wed a noble, if she wed at all. Which meant, if she were to have any choice she'd have to leave the mark—very nearly an unthinkable thing. She did not know that five hundred years before her time, men sped from one end of the known world to the other over paved, well-guarded roads, or sailed the seas in biremes, safe from piracy. The Romans, whose tongue she spoke—sadly debased and corrupted like all else in her world—thought nothing of ranging from Britain to Palestine. But in Clothilde's day, save for an infinitesimal fraction, men lived all their lives within two hours' walk from the house where they were born; with order, law, discipline, control gone from the world—save as such burly brigands as her father and Count Teudis might impose a limited local version thereof with their great two-handed broadswords —to leave one's valley was to court slavery, or death—and to a maid, certain ravishment. Now in that tiny fragment of Bardulia, Qashtalla, Castilla—call it what you will—there had never been more than three noble houses; and of those three but two survived, now that Duke Atanagild's line was extinct before him, and the old fiend himself howling in hell for his sins. Such arithmetic as this scarce required the use of her dainty fingers to count upon. Two noble houses in all the mark, one of which was hers. The thought needed no extension: Ataulf dead, the only man left within the few leagues that encompassed her world whom she could marry without stooping considerably below her rank, was the youth who rode behind her now, Lord Alaric, his much-too-pretty, somewhat effeminate younger brother. Of course, her father could scout about—travel beyond the mark to the upper end of Castilla—as bare, God wot, as this part in which they lived. Nay, her lord father, the Marquis Julian, needs must range farther afield: to Asturias, or Navarre, to Galicia, to Cataluña, and make some shrewdly bargained contract for the son of some noble house—a man she'd never seen. Too much of a bother! As a risk, far too great! How many noble maids had lived to weep their lives out as they lay beside some battle-scarred, gouty, smelly old warrior twenty years their senior to whom, for reasons of interest, their fathers had seen fit to wed them.

None of that for her! Alaric was most wondrous fair. Not even his three winters less than hers counted now. And he was rich enough, though Clo was not one to put wealth too far ahead of beauty. She was quite capable of being satisfied with Alaric's moderate fortune, when it was combined with the looks he had. Did she love him? That would be scanned. Probably not. He was a sight too much of a milksop for her taste—though, if this morning were any evidence, she might be quite happily wrong about that. It troubled her not at all that he had lain with that dark foreign strumpet—now that the strumpet was gone, that is!—to her the intriguing thing about that affair was that pale, pretty Alaric had acquitted himself so well in his first passage at arms that the Moorish wench was like to die of her grief at losing him.

Clo remembered that day she had surprised him naked in the river. God's eyes, but his body was fair, and fair to look upon! And—for be it said that the coldness of Clothilde's heart didn't extend to her loins—nobody's gelding! A young stallion, rather. . . .

She smiled to herself as she recalled her behavior in the courtyard when she'd spat into the Moor's face. How much of that occasion had been honest emotion, and how much calculation, she couldn't really say. But it was the feeling she feared, not the calculation. And she had been uncommonly stirred upon that occasion, she had to admit. Better watch that, my girl! The die was cast; the battle joined; and clear eyes and a cool head were the best weapons in this world.

So thinking, she lifted her eyes and saw that Alaric was staring at her again. This time she didn't even hesitate: locking her gaze in his, slowly, warmly, invitingly, provocatively, she smiled at him—after, of course, having taken the precaution to bite her lips hard, so they would glow a deeper rose, designed to put the notion of kissing them into a man's head to the total confusion of all sense.

The confusion was greater than she'd planned, because it extended beyond sense to delicate questions of loyalty. He had pledged his troth to Zoë—whom he loved. God's blood and death! Of a certainty he did— yet—

Yet he had loved Clothilde all his life, from the hour he'd seen her first—his ninth birthday. She'd been twelve then. Strange, he'd always been attracted by maids older than he. Or had he? What maid his age or younger did he know? The answer to that was simple: none.

To ease his confusion, he took refuge in righteous anger—or tried to. In my brother's very funeral train she—she dares to smile at me! Why, the highborn trull! They're all alike! There's no decency in them! They—

Then his anger died. He'd been too recently happy; he no longer had in him that soured bile of disappointment that makes a man a critic or a reformer—if he had ever had, which was debatable. In a strange way, Alaric Teudisson was not of his own age, but of another yet to come or mayhap of some golden age long gone. His senses, his young and healthy blood, taught him that life is indifferent to morality, for- ever deaf to the carping of those who wear their lusts not in strong- thewed loins but in their benighted heads. He was on the threshold of a discovery: that words like trollop, strumpet, trull, slut, slattern, whore, had no meanings of their own, and only reflect the state of mind of those who utter them; that there was an endless maze of sub- tleties between the words *good* and *bad*. Given time, he'd go on to some useful, if inexact simplicities: that the only bad men were those who were tight-fisted, unsmiling, ungenerous, hard; and the only bad women those who were cold!

Only, he was not to be given time. He had lifted up his head to gaze at Clothilde once more; made up his mind that if she smiled at him he'd smile back, when he heard the confused shouting at the head of the column. Then he saw them: a double file of beturbaned Berber horsemen, riding down upon them, and screaming like all the fiends in hell.

The air in his lungs went solid; turned ice. His stomach contracted like a knotted fist. In his middle a thousand loathsome furry things with wings fluttered about and beat and beat. I don't want to die! he wailed in- side his fear-sick, quivering mind; I want to live! I want my Zoë!

He yanked hard on the bridle to turn the barb out of line, to get out of there, to fly; but then suddenly, appallingly, he saw Clothilde's eyes. Her face was white with the fear that as a maid she had some right to feel; but the expression that played about her mouth, causing it to curl, the look in her eyes gazing at him, were pure, abysmal contempt. Seeing her, he could picture how he looked, discern as if in a mirror the panic written large across his face; and the shame in him was a mace blow to the guts, shattering the ice, blasting the loathsome things, leaving him empty until his blood raged back. He lifted up his head, opened his mouth. What came out of it was a female quaver that carried not even to where Clo sat.

He tried it again, his eyes bright with bitter tears. This time he hit the proper note; the bull bellow that burst from his throat might have been his father's own.

"Ho, bucelarios!" he roared, the fear gone from him now, to be replaced by a great and terribly joy. "For God and Saint Fredegunda! Charge!"

Then he was gone, leaning forward on his barb's neck, that light wandlike Berber lance extended in his hand, slanting out and away from the line in a long diagonal toward the Berbers, his swift descendant of desert-bred nomad horses drawing away from his bucelarios' great war changers at every stride. So it was that when he hit the head of the Berber column he was utterly and terribly alone; sufficiently far head of the others to give Count Teudis an exhibition that caused that doughty old warrior's heart nearly to burst with pride. He took the leading white-turbaned rider with his lance, lifting him dead or dying from the saddle with a single thrust; sweeping over and past him, he dragged the point free; caught the second in the throat so hard that the lance point parted the vertebrae and protruded through the Berber's neck behind, so that Alaric could not free it and the Berber's dead weight, falling, snapped the shaft, leaving a yard of useless wood in his hands.

He hurled it into a swarthy, bearded face, drew his sword. Screaming "For God and Saint Fredegunda!" he laid about him, emptying saddles on every side; surrounded now, he hacked his way free, roaring like a young lion, bleeding from a dozen cuts he did not even know he had, the Teutonic berserker in him in full control, smashing into them until now the bucelarios came up to him and lent their immense weight and power to the fray.

Which should have ended it, but for the fact that they were fighting Berbers, not ordinary Moors. For, against the swift desert horsemen, the only effective tactics were their own; precisely the ones that Alaric had used: speed, maneuver, dash—all of which called for light armor and a fast horse, instead of the Goth's great clumsy power. The Berbers whirled around them in rings, cutting them to pieces. The turbaned marauders did not wait to receive a charge; mockingly they evaded it; fencers against broadswordsmen, they let the Goths spend their ponderous fury upon the naked air. Only one man, it was pitifully, terribly clear, was any danger to them: young Lord Alaric, Count Teudis, sole surviving son, like now to carry the line of the Counts of Tarabella the Greater down into the dust with him, when those Berber horsemen did the only thing they had to do to win the day, which was to cut him down.

Yet this, by a whole heart-stopping series of miracles, they failed to do, until Count Teudis, standing unarmed and helpless by Ataulf's fallen bier, began to allow himself to hope, to believe even that Alaric fought under a special blessing—which, be it said, he did; but it was Mammon's, not God's. What stayed the hands of those desert tribesmen was the specific orders they had been given to take Alaric Teudisson alive at any cost. What insured their obedience even in the heat of battle was the added warning that the man who caused his death, even by an accidental stroke, could be certain of perishing himself, inch by awful inch at the hands of the torturer. Dead, Alaric would be but a lump of useless carrion; alive, their master, the Sherif ibn Djilliki, could for all this lithe male beauty to al Sahib Ahmad al Hussein ib Maliki name his price!

So it was that a brigand's greed, a pervert's lust, and a maid's gesture of contempt combined themselves into accidental glory. Under those peculiarly sardonic circumstances, Alaric's feats of arms seemed to his horrified, weeping watchers—struck dumb with astonishment at his unexpected valor, with fear for his tender life—far more brilliant than they really were. Be it said in sober justice, that the fight he waged was very fine; be it remembered that he, too, believed it was his very life he sold for this high and bloody price; but be it at the last admitted in sad, inglorious truth that he would not have lasted thirty seconds if those Berber swordsmen had dared disobey their orders and cut him down. But they did not dare. So it was that time and time again they ringed him about with gleaming steel; time and time again he won free.

For what his gentle mother had to endure, there are no words. She was standing up in the cart now, screaming: "Fly! Don't be a fool, Alaric! Fly! You are the last! Save yourself, child! Oh, God, my son! My son!"

Beside her, Gelesvinta knelt, shaking all over with a great gale-storm of weeping, while Sor Fidela, crying just as hard, albeit she knew it not, tried vainly to comfort her. But there was one among them who showed her mettle: dry-eyed and mocking, the light of battle hard and clear in her blue eyes, Clothilde climbed upon the seat beside the driver, stood fully erect there, tore off her black mourning veil and waved it, her voice fluting above the battle din, triumphant, soaring, like a Brunhild's, like a Valkyrie's.

"For God! For Saint Fredegunda! And, my brave and gallant lord —for me!"

Below them, Count Teudis was roaring like a bull, tears in his small eyes.

"A horse! A sword! For God and Saint Fredegunda! A sword!" And then, but little lower, his great and terrible prayer: "Don't let them kill my boy! You hear me, God? Don't let them kill this lion cub I've bred! Whelp of my own loins, full fit to preserve my line! If he dies—if he dies—I'll curse You and burn in hell!"

Then Julio broke from the press, and rode up to the Count. Leaping from his charger, he passed over the reins to his lord; extended him his sword, hilt first; gave him his shield.

"Take them, my lord of Tarabella!" he said, grinning through the blood and sweat on his face, "for there are pressing matters that require my presence elsewhere!"

"What matters are these, you knave?" the Count growled as he armed himself.

"Swilling a skinful, my lord Count! Lifting full many a dainty skirt! Singing a merry ditty in the tavern in the town! In short, my lordly noble fool—staying alive!"

With that he took to his heels right briskly.

Try as he would, Count Teudis could not reach his son to aid him. In fact, within seconds he had sore need of succor himself. In truth, he was harder pressed than Alaric was, for no one had been ordered to spare his grizzled head. But Count Teudis was a warrior born; with his great height and reach and strength, he held his own, watching Alaric out of the corner of one despairing eye.

But Alaric was not to die that day, nor under such warlike circumstances. He fought on grimly, tiring now, bathed all over with his own blood from two dozen light cuts designed to bring him down alive. He was aware at last there was no hope; that all he could do now was to sell his life as dearly as possible. Slowly he gave ground before a gleaming forest of swords; in another five minutes or ten, they would have taken him.

But Eigebert ibn al Djilliki, the renegade lord of Tierraseca's renegade son, that Goth turned Moor for greed and gain, chose that moment to make his mistake, that fatal error upon which fate hinged in multiple, hideous irony, in senseless, extravagant cruelty, as is her way. At the head of a flying column of horsemen he had so far held in reserve, Eigebert roared in and surrounded the cart bearing the women.

Both the Count and Alaric saw it all, from where they fought on, separately and hopelessly engaged, each fifty yards or more from each other, and double that from the cart, each ringed about with six or eight swordsmen to hold off with his single blade; they saw Eigebert's lance thrust take the cart driver in the belly, lifting him, spitted and clawing at the death that held him, from his seat, to dump him in a spreading pool of his own blood on the ground; the black-bearded horsemen swarming from their saddles into the cart; one of them taking the reins, and whipping up the mules; the others, manhandling the women, snatching off veils and peering into their faces to decide their value as merchandise, whether or not they were worth being carefully preserved intact in hope of their bringing a rich price upon the slave markets in Córdoba, or whether they were such inferior goods as a man might despoil at once, and afterward rid himself of by a knife slash across the throat. Gelesvinta passed the test, but barely; there was some grumbling among her captors, by now from long experience connoisseurs. They bore her down, binding her hands and feet, stuffing a gag into her mouth. Clothilde, fighting like a tigress, followed her, thereby raising her asking price by her spirit; dearly did the sahibs and sherifs of Córdoba love a fierce wench, offering them much sport in her taming; and a beauty like this one, with sunset hair and Allah's skies for eyes! By the Prophet's beard, they'd struck it rich! The Countess' turn was next; they ripped off the heavy black veil she wore in mourning for her son, then seeing her fair face, tired, lined, the white of forty-seven winters in her hair, their poniards flashed in the limpid air; and Alaric heard his mother's screams.

The Berbers had Sor Fidela by the chin, twisting her face this way and that, debating her life in their harsh gutturals, not because she was not fair, but because their own faith bade them respect a nun. Sell her they could not without bringing down upon their own heads a terrible punishment; free her they dared not, lest by some chance she be brought to testify against them before the head judge, the terrible Kadi l'djama'a. So again their poniards flashed; but this time Eigebert cried out to them.

"Have done, ye desert dogs! Long have I desired to enjoy a nun!"

So they bound Sor Fidela in her turn; and started off, dumping the Countess' poor lifeless body unceremoniously into the dust. But now their greed proved their undoing; because there is in a man reserves of strength he does not know he has until some great and terrible emotion release them. So it was with the Lord of Tarabella the Greater now, and so, in equal measure, with his son. Not all the Prophet's desert hosts could have held them then, though aided by all Lord Saithan's fiends from hell. Count Teudis cleft a foeman from pate to naval, crashed his war horse through the gap, won free; but to no further than the spot where the mortal remains of his good and gentle lady lay; there hurled he himself down, to gather her in his arms, cover her still warm dust-caked face with great slobbering kisses, lift up his head and split deaf heaven with his awful, wounded beast's howls of demented grief.

So the rest was left to Alaric. He cut down all three Berbers who barred his way, roweled his poor heaving, foam-flecked barb into its last gallop, gained on them apace; then Eigebert of Tierraseca, Eigebert ibn al Djilliki now, turned his own dappled gray Arab and blocked Alaric's path—which was like trying to block the path of an avalanche. Sitting there with his wife's head cradled in his arms, Count Teudis saw Alaric's barb crash at full gallop into the gray; there was a momentary thresh and broil; a dying mount's unbelievable scream; and both horses went down into a man-made tornado, a whirlwind of dust that blotted sight.

Out of the dust cloud, the Count saw two warriors rise; two blades were silver in the light, making lightnings, clanging, showering sparks, two targets banged against each other, two poniards flashed in double-handed play; then one man went down; boneless and supine, clearly never more to rise. Count Teudis lifted his free hand doubled into Mars's fists, threatening the sky; then he saw it was his own lion cub who stood above his fallen foe, so the Count brought his fist down, muttered: "For this, at least, I thank thee, God!"

Afoot, breath gone, his mount down and dead, Alaric was not even aware that the fight was won. Their leader slain, the Berbers had lost both heart and head. At once they swung out on a long tearing line, plunging southward, fleeing now, riding, going on. But Alaric noted that fact with eyes alone, not with his mind; all he could see with clarity were the mules, whipped on by a screaming Berber, curving across his path in a wild gallop, dragging the careening, bouncing cart behind them. The despair in his heart was a naked blade, until he saw his own shadow slanting out across the barren mesa land toward the flying mules; saw the light-sculptured image of the feathered shafts he bore over his shoulder. Instantly he turned to his fallen mount. His bow was in its sheath, and miraculously unbroken. He strung it in half a heartbeat, whirled, fitted the arrow's notch to the bowstring, drew, let fly, all in one unbroken chain of motion.

The shaft leaped out, raced skyward in a long, long singing curve; whistled downward. The lead mule screamed, high and clear, like a woman in pain; lunged, reared, bucked, went down. The ones behind him piled into him in a thrashing, braying, screaming heap; the cart went over on its side, the bottom wheel splintering into kindling, the top one spinning free.

At once a swarm of Berbers were upon it; three of them lifted the three maids out, tossed them like so many bundles across their saddles, galloped off. Alaric drew his bow again, eased off without letting fly; because at that distance he was as like to kill a maid as her abductor; then turning he saw a clutch of Berber horsemen hurtling by; and drawing, sped an arrow from five scant yards with such force that it transfixed the nearest rider completely. Alaric was at the snorting, dancing, maddened horse's head before its dead master had time to fall; he clouted him from the saddle with a mailed fist, swung up himself, and flew after the three, who, doubly burdened, had already fallen behind.

Sitting there with the slow tears dripping into his beard, Count Teudis saw him go.

When the rider appeared over the brow of the hill, at first Count Teudis thought it was Alaric come back again. Then, when the rider came laboring into their shattered, broken troup, the Count saw his beard was gray, and saw too the Moorish arrow in his shoulder.

The man reeled down.

"My lord," he gasped, "my noble lord—" Then he saw what Count Teudis held, and swept off his helmet with his good hand.

"I see—I come too late," he said.

"Aye," the Count said, "that you do. But speak your piece, then let my good Sisberto attend you—"

"My lord, the Marquis Julian begs your aid," the rider whispered. "He is besieged within the town where he waited to pay his final respects to—"

"I know! I know!" Count Teudis growled. "Get on with it, man!"

"He is besieged within the town, my lord! My lady Ingunda's with him. And the Moors have both a mighty host—and siege engines!"

"Siege engines?" the Count muttered. "A mighty host? Whenever have slave raiders—"

"I know not, my lord!" the rider wept. "But unless you come at once, my lord and likely his lady, too—will die—"

"Aye, that she will," Count Teudis said, "for God knows she has not my poor Godsuinta's beauty. They'll cut her throat, too, right enough. . . ."

"My lord!" the rider cried.

"Very well," the Count said slowly. "Look you, my men, ride you to aid—"

The men stood there, staring at him in pure disbelief. They could scarcely stand; not one of them was unbloodied by a dozen wounds, and yet this gray-beared madman of a lord was ordering them once more to ride.

Then Julio pushed his way to the front. He was clad in a dazzling Moorish scallop armor, at his side was a Toledo blade; all his fingers were heavy with rings. While his fellows fought and bled; fine Julio ran; but not so far as not to be able to creep back and rob the dead.

"Look you, now, my lord Count," he roared. "We had enough! There's not one sound man among us! If you persist in this folly, we'll—"

"You'll what, Julio?" the Count said.

"Do your bidding, noble lord," Julio retreated smoothly, "but in great sorrow, knowing that our deaths will be on your head!"

"Aye, you're right, Julio," the Count said. "Look you, my man—in simple sense, would it change things if we come? If the Moors are as strong as you say, what could the twenty-odd I have still on their feet do?"

"Nothing," the rider sighed. "That's true enough. I—I'd hoped for miracles; but now—"

"Sisberto, attend him!" the Count said.

Sisberto came up and looked at the broken arrow shaft protruding from the rider's shoulder. "I'll have to dig it out," he said. "The Jew told me never to leave an arrow in the wound. . . ."

An hour later, young Lord Alaric was back again, reeling in his saddle, drunk with fatigue, with weakness from his really considerable loss of blood, with pain. But with no such simple pain as his wounds caused him. That he noted little if at all. The pain that tore him was interior. And it would go on lifelong, this Promethean vulture's beak in his flesh, this Orestean fury in his mind. Because, behind him, the maid Clothilde rode, while his own sister—and hers—were gone.

He reined in his captured mount before the Count, started to dismount, would have fallen had not eager hands eased him down. He looked his father in the face, but his own blue eyes were bloodshot, rolling, wild.

"I bring—Ataulf's bride—back—once again, my lord!" he grated. "And once again—at great cost. I wonder—if—she's worth the—price. Father—"

"Yes, my son?" Count Teudis said.

"I had—a choice. I—I must not lie. I could have—saved—Gele. Or Goissuintha. I had time to save one. Just one, Father! So, I—saved Clo. Let—my sister go—to warm—some swinish Moorish—lecher's bed—let Goissuintha—let Sor Fidela—go to—to be—"

"Now, son," the Count said kindly, "don't blame—"

"—to be dishonored—in her person—and her faith. I could have put an arrow through them—both. Only I—I couldn't, Father! I hadn't heart enough! I—I—Father, I beg you, decree my death! I am not fit to live!"

"Son," the Count said gruffly, "you talk rot! This day you've played the man, and to spare! And I have need of you. Now sit you down and rest, for we—"

"Yes, Alaric, dear," Clothilde said. "You're tired and hurt, Come, let me—"

"Don't talk to me, wench!" Alaric howled. "Or by heaven and hell, I'll—"

Then he saw what lay at his father's feet; saw that bloody, pallid image of slaughtered virtue on the ground.

"Moth—" he began. "My lady Mother—" Slowly he sank to his knees; but he could not maintain that posture; his whole body inclined, sank, gave, until he stretched out full-length, his dust-caked head pillowed on those breasts where so often while yet life beat in them he had lain. He lay there a long time, crying very quietly, but his tears availed him not, nor even his prayers—for, as he knew now, beyond the tender mercy of a doubt, to this one hurt there was no cure at all.

VI

And one thing more: As they shouldered Ataulf's bier once again, and the improvised one they'd made for the dead Countess by lashing two long shields between the shafts of two lances, and started back toward the castle, leaving their baseborn dead, and their foes where they lay in crumpled, dust-covered, butchered heaps, a wounded Berber cried out to them in Romance—for among the Berbers, too, there was many a man now who had his captive mother's look and her native tongue, learned at her knee long before, and with greater mastery than his father's harsh desert gutturals—"My lords, mercy! Do not leave me here to die!"

The Count nodded to Julio.

"Cut his throat," he said.

"With pleasure, my lord!" Julio grinned.

"Father, in God's name!" Alaric said.

Count Teudis frowned. Then he said; "No, don't. Let the whoreson live. And bring him along. We might have useful information of him."

Julio looked up. Alaric followed his gaze. High up, three black specks scribed arcs against the blue. And farther out, against the mesa land's rim where the mountains sawed the sky with white and jagged teeth, a line of others arrowed in, swift, purposeful, sure.

"He'll take a Christian's place, my lord," Julio said. "The cart's smashed, y'know. So we have only the mules. Certain is that some might walk, and lead their horses with the wounded laid across 'em. But—"

"But nothing, knave!" the Count said. "At the moment, this Mahound's fiend outweighs a Christian. Or what's in his head does. You heard me, pick him up! Put him on one of the mules!"

Julio shrugged, and turned to the wounded Berber. There was no accounting for his lord's ways, and well he knew it.

"My lord," Sisberto said, pulling his own gaze down from that circling in the sky, "there are many of ours that I fear we cannot save. . . ."

The Count looked at his chief bucelario. His mouth made a poor imitation of its usual sardonic smile.

"Not even after having spent every minute you could, cloistered with the Jew?" he said.

"Not even after that," Sisberto said; and his voice was grave and sorrowing. "My lord knows too well my skill at curing wounds is but a paltry thing; but who else among us hath any skill at all? The good Jew gave me many a pointer; more, my lord, than this poor head could hold. Well would I like to spend a six-month in his house, then truly might I render services of value to my lord; but now—"

"But now what, Sisberto?" Alaric said.

Sisberto pointed skyward.

"Those birds of evil omen don't care whether a man's a Christian or a Moor, my young and noble lord. Or even whether he's truly dead or not, so long as he cannot lift a hand to fend them off. I shouldn't like their scaly beaks and claws atearing at my eyes and tongue while yet I lived—"

"Ohhh!" Clothilde said, and tightened her grip on Alaric's arm. She had not loosed her clasp upon him from the moment that he rose from the spot where his mother's body lay.

Alaric passed his tongue tip over his cracked, blood-crusted lips. "Father—" he said.

Count Teudis stood there, his head thrown back, staring at the sky. He lowered his gaze, looked at Sisberto. When he spoke, his voice was very bleak.

"I pray thee—do what must be done, good Sisberto," he said.

"Father!" Alaric said.

"We have not transport enough, son," the Count said, "nor time, nor skill. And if we tarry, we'll have not even life. Get to it, Sisberto! Julio, you and the others aid him!"

Alaric stood there, watching them move out among those dusty bundles of bloody rags and broken chain-linked iron sprawling bonelessly upon that dry and pitiless ground. They'd bend above a man, Christian or Berber alike, and hold a hand a scant inch from his mouth. If breath stirred against the flesh, a poniard would rise glittering in the light, flash down. There'd be no sound at all, for the most part; only a sudden stiffening of the limbs and afterward a new, slow spreading stain that the dry earth drank in thirstily. But now and again a moan, a gurgling cough, a fearsome scream would come over to his ears, likely, he guessed, when the wounded man was a special friend, and the hand that drove the poniard home trembled, despite itself. And, as they went on, it seemed to him their clumsiness increased. The screams were far more frequent now.

"Stop it!" he cried. "Father—couldn't we come back? With carts, I mean? Mayhap that way—"

Count Teudis looked at his son.

"Think you the carrion birds would wait for your carts, boy? Or the Moors who besiege Julian and his lady in the town? Carts! Why they'd thank their Lord Allah for so easy a slaughter! Besides—"

"Besides, what, Father?" Alaric said, hearing the curious note that had got into Teudis' voice; the uncertain way it trailed off into silence.

"I know not what credence can be lent to the word of Julian's man," the Count said, "though, methinks, that Moor's shaft in his shoulder is certificate enough of verity. Look you, son Alaric, I've traded blows with the Moors before; but up till this very day I've never seen them count more than an hundred men. Yet, today, Eigebert alone had twice that many at his command. And Leovigild—"

"—commands a host," Alaric said, "and that host with gyns! Father, that would be scanned. Wound fever plays strange tricks with the mind. What need have Berber slavers of such great and heavy tools of war, suitable only for taking fortified towns? Or of such numbers? Methinks his hurt, his fear, the heat—"

"And not that the Emir's taken it into his head to raise another Holy War against Alfonso the Chaste?" the Count said.

Alaric stood there, reeling a little from loss of blood, and fatigue. But bleeding, according to the learned doctors, clears the mind.

"Why should the Emir's hosts detain themselves before Tarabella, Father? Before that ruined and roofless town, offering them neither glory, booty, nor even worthwhile slaves—since their raiders have carried off every comely maid long since? If it's the Asturians they're after, why entertain themselves with us—naked, poor, without populace and with scant defense? All they need to do is smash King Alfonso and we'll fall into their hands like an overripe plum, having not even a refuge to fly to anymore. They've left this mark alone—save for the raids because it suited them—and the Asturians—to have a buffer zone between both kingdoms. Why should they change now? Or use a mace to kill a flea?"

"God's blood!" the Count muttered. "You talk sense, boy. Still, there's our messenger who—"

"—whose fear for my lord Julian and his lady caused him to count each single Moor as ten! I tell you, Father—"

He heard, then, Clothilde's choked-off sobs.

"Your pardon, Clo," he said wearily, "but truth must be faced. To go to your father's aid now, with this battered handful that we have, would mean—"

"—that both your house, daughter, and mine would end," the Count finished for him, "while this way—"

"While this way," Clothilde said, "my mother and my father die—

if not of cowardice, then of lack of faith. My lord, I bid you look upon your son! Look upon my lord Alaric and witness—"

"What, daughter?" Count Teudis said.

"A man with God's special grace upon him! Know you how my father found poor Ataulf and me? Did my father not tell you that, my lord?"

"No—" the Count said. "I reckoned they'd followed your tracks—"

"No tracks, my lord of Tarabella! A goat path, too stony to admit of them. But he—your son Alaric, rode straight as the crow flies to where his brother lay, at a gallop, not even looking down! Stopped his horse at the exact spot Ataulf took that fatal shaft, cried, 'Here, my lord Julian, has occurred some great and terrible thing!' "

Count Teudis was looking at his son with something like unto awe.

"Is this true, son?" he said, "or is the lass daft?"

"It's true—in a way," Alaric said. "I—I didn't look down. I seemed to—to know—where Ataulf had gone, which way he'd turned and—"

"And today," Clothilde said, "how do you explain that, my lord? I saw his face when the Berbers struck, saw it go white with fear. Why, even his lips were white! He turned his barb aside to fly. Then it seemed to me the heaven's opened, and a light—"

"God's eyes, Clo!" Alaric said. "You're mad!"

"No, my brave and gallant lord! The heavens opened and a light came down and shone about your head! I saw it, I tell you! Then your lips moved, as if in prayer—and your voice! Your voice was a whole pride of lions roaring at one time! It shook the very ground. And after that—my lord Count, would you tell me that even all his valor, which no man on earth can gainsay now, is explanation enough for the fact he lives? Can you deny that not one but twenty miracles occurred this day? A host of angels fought at my lord Alaric's side! Again and again those beturbaned fiends aimed a fatal stroke, only to have a shield no mortal eye could see ward it off! Again and again I could not see his face for the forest of blades ringing him round about—half a score of swordsmen at a time; battle-scarred champions of many a fray, who cut down your best men to get to him. And then, my lord Count? And then?"

"God's blood, daughter," the Count muttered, "you've a point. Still—"

"And this holy visitation of which your poor lady Countess was so proud?" Clo said. "You'd deny that, too, my lord? You'd say to me that if Alaric took three men or even rode alone, he could not save my parents' lives?"

"I say it, Clo," Alaric said. "There've been lies enough—and half truths—and even some mysteries I cannot myself explain. But they have explanations. All things do. God doth not violate the laws he himself made to govern the workings of his own creation, nor shed his grace upon so miserable a sinner as I am. For whatever powers I may have had, have gone from me, now. They dropped from me in that hour I had not the heart to—to slay—chastity—before letting it—" He stopped, his hands knotting into fists, his tears plowing furrows through the blood-caked dust upon his face. "Oh Son of Purity Incarnate in Womanflesh, why dids't thou not let me die!"

"Alaric—" Clothilde said.

"He whirled upon her, his eyes bloodshot, rolling, wild.

"Aye, Clo!" he howled. "I'll ride to my lord Julian's and his lady's defense! Julio, my horse! My horse, you knavish churl!"

"Son, I'll have you put in irons, first," the Count said, mildly enough. "Look you, daughter—your mother and your father are well along in years. One day or another, they must die. So must we all, but our line, our race, must live on after us. That, child, is your sacred duty—and his. I sometimes think 'tis the only immortality we have—to live on in the blood and thews of sons begotten by our sons. But ye go against life when you send youth out to die for age's gray hairs. I'll not permit it. I should not were it I and my poor slaughtered Godsuinta who were be-sieged. I hope you'll not hold this decision against me, or my son; but though you do, I make it still. And in your filial piety, think on this: would you a father—or a husband, lass? Mark me well—and mind what you say!"

Clothilde stood there looking at him. Then she bowed her head.

"I would—both," she said, "but since that cannot be—"

"It cannot, daughter," the Count said, and turned his gaze toward were Sisberto and the others waited. "Look you, son—" he said. "Say Julian's man is wrong. Say Leovigild has five hundred men; nay, two—what difference does it make? We could not best fifty on the field now. And that means—"

"—we'll be bottled up in our little heap of stone—with scarce food enough to feed those who can draw a bow. That's it, isn't it, Father?" Alaric said. The rage had gone out of him now, leaving only the tired-ness, the slow ache of his stiffening wounds.

"Aye. And what we do here and now would needs only be done a week or two hence within our walls. Moreover, we'd have to throw their bodies like offal from the keep, having no place to bury them. . . ."

"We leave them to bait crows now!" Alaric said.

"And do ourselves the kindness of not having to watch their poor carcasses being beaked and torn," the Count said softly. "Whereas out-side our walls that sight would assail our eyes all day. And the dogs at

120

'em, too. And their smell. Nay, son, the dead I leave to God. 'Tis life and the future I would serve. Clothilde, daughter—"

"Yes, my lord?" Clothilde said.

"What think you of this whelp of mine now, child—aside from his reputed saintliness, I mean?"

Clothilde stared at the Count. Then she turned her eyes on Alaric's face.

"That he is worthy of any maid's admiration—and her love," she whispered. "Is that the response you'd have of me, my lord?"

"It is," Count Teudis said. "Sisberto! Finish your work! And you others, bear up my lady and my son!"

They moved out in a long, weary line, crawling under that pitiless sun, that brazen sky. The heat was on the day now. On that long march back to the castle, they suffered the tortures reserved for damned souls in hell. Alaric's shirt of antelope to which the steel scallops were sewn to make his light and flexible coat of mail, stuck to the self-inflicted stripes on his back, to the multiple small wounds on his shoulders, chest, and arms. And now Clothilde, who rode behind him, laid her head against his broad back and tightened her arms about his waist. What this tender gesture was meant to convey, he didn't know; and cared less than that, for what it did in truth was to almost intolerably increase his pain.

He bore that pain in silence. He endured the raging thirst that parched his throat. He had himself given the order that the water in the leathern flagons be reserved for those who bore his mother's bier and Ataulf's; but it was not for honor's sake that he accepted heat, thirst, pain. Nor yet for Clo's. His reasons were subtle things, lying in that shadowy zone between mind, spirit, flesh. He opposed one hurt with another; accepted—nay, welcomed—these simple comprehensible torments because they kept him from thinking too precisely on far deeper hurts, festering where no balm could reach, beyond in fact, any physician's skill.

So gained they the castle on the very edge of night. But not even then could they rest.

"Find me Father Juan!" the Count called out. "Rouse me up the scullions and the grooms! That they bring crowbars, picks, and spades!"

The bearers laid the biers down. The worst wounded sank to the paving stones and lay there.

"Let me down, my lord," Clothilde said. "There's work for my hands, too, now—"

Alaric helped her down. She went into the hall. After a time she came back with Turtura, Florinda, María, and one or two other serving wenches, all of them bearing water from the well. They moved among the tired, broken men, while highborn Clothilde gave to drink to each in his turn with her own gentle hands.

She came to him now, with a silver chalice in her hands. But instead of merely extending it to him as she had to the others, she knelt before him with such a show of reverence, of respect, that somehow it angered him.

"God's death, Clo!" he croaked. "Get up from there! What mean you by this folly?"

"I—" she whispered. "Nothing, good my lord. 'Tis your august father who hath made his meaning clear."

"My father?" Alaric said; but then he saw what the scullions and the grooms were doing now. Under the flickering light of the torches, they were prying up the stones in the center of the courtyard with iron bars. He looked at them uncomprehendingly and at Father Juan's pudgy form. The priest was kneeling beside two covered bundles on the ground. Alaric could see his hands flying, now making the sign of the cross, now peaking in the attitude of prayer. But for the life of him Alaric couldn't understand what the little priest was doing; his unfocused mind, retreating along an oblique tangent away from horror, away from pain, drove his eyes upward toward the torches. He saw how they flared, saw the great clouds of sooty smoke they sent up.

"Pitch!" he muttered. "There were some tuns of it below, methinks. And pitch hath its uses in defense. It seems to me San Isidore in his *Etymologies*—the 'Book of War and Games'—Pitch! To be sure! You heat it and—or dip the heads of arrows—And gyns! There's some smaller ones that our smith could at my directions make—Khinsvilda!" His voice roared out suddenly, "Get me Khinsvilda! The smith! For I—"

"My lord," Clothilde's voice came over to him, "take this and drink. And don't roar so! 'Tis unseemly. You disturb your father and the *cura* at their prayers—"

He looked down and saw her again now. In the light of the torches, her young face was ghastly, her eyes blue-ringed, deep sunken with fatigue. He took the cup from her and drank, or tried to. Most of the water spilled down over his chin and neck. It was cool. The feel of it was pleasant.

"Come, my lord," Clothilde said, "come with me and rest. 'Twill be some time yet, before the graves are ready. . . ."

"Graves?" he said, peering at her owlishly. "Graves, Clo?"

"Your mother's—and my poor lord Ataulf's. Now, come—your mind wanders, methinks. You've suffered much, and borne you bravely, so—"

"No!" he got out. "No! I'll not leave them till they're safe abed. I'll not—" He reeled drunkenly toward the place where Count Teudis and Father Juan knelt; sank down beside them and folded his hands in prayer. But no prayer came, nothing came to his mind at all. No higher, pious thoughts, no supplications, nor any vows. The sound of the picks biting the earth. The scrape of the spades. The flare of the torches sending up their dense inky clouds. He tried to gather his mind inward, to concentrate his thoughts. And now he saw his mother's face. It was much younger and fairer than now, and was smiling at him.

"Look you, my son—how he dances!" she said.

And he, the nine-year-old boy, shrank against her as the great clumsy bear pirouetted on its keeper's chain. Jugglers tossed balls in the air, earthen plates, knives. Acrobats walked on their hands, their heels in the air. He could hear his father roar with laughter.

"God's death, Godsuinta, you've put to great expense to make the fiesta for your puling baby boy! But 'tis worth it, I think! God's eyes, look at that smirking knave!"

And the maids: the elder, Clo—already flower-like and slim at twelve; and Goissuintha, ten, round and rosy and utterly delectable. Gele, standing there with them. So plain, poor thing! Smiling in her matter-of-fact way. But Ataulf, of course, great and tall and already sure of himself at fourteen, laughed and teased his fair guests, and whispered in their ears, while the Lady Ingunda and the Marquis Julian—

Besieged within ruined roofless Tarabella now! And brave Ataulf is that long shape under my father's banner. That yellow, shrunken parchment, bound tight o'er gristly bones. She smiled at me—my lady mother smiled. Lifelong she smiled, whose smile is no more. For those Berber fiends hath—say it, say it—cut her throat. And she lies there now beside my brave and noble—long bones rotting hulk—my brother. While Gele— Gele. Gele. Goissuintha. How they scream! Those swart hands rip off their clothing now. Their fair limbs—are bare. See how those turbaned Mahound fiends drag their legs apart. See—

God! I pray to you, who visit the sins of the father's upon the children's heads, who let me inherit my father's lewdness and his lust. And to punish me—But you do not, Zoë said. Zoë! Gone from me! And I—

The bucelarios were lifting those wrapped figures now. Bearing them toward that mound of damp, clotted earth, that gaping hole.

"No!" he screamed. "Not yet! Not yet! Oh, Mother! Oh, Lady Mother mine!—"

His clumsy, feverish hands tore at the cloak that swathed her head. And now she stared up at him with terrible eyes. He bent and kissed

123

her mouth, his lips rolling away from coldness, the dry leathern feel, until the earth and sky upended themselves, and the torches flared high above his head. He lay upon the stones, his chin resting on his mailed forearm and stared—at moving feet and legs, and bending backs. He heard Clo's muffled sobs, his father's deep-throated groans. Father Juan was saying things: "In nomine patris, filii, spiritus sanctis—requiescat in pace—" and making the sign of the cross. The spades scraped again. Clods of earth thudded down upon—

Her face. His mother's face. And Ataulf's. Dust unto dust. All that love and tenderness and gentle pride. That bull-roaring lust for life; that gusty laughter. Dust. Clod of muddy earth thudding down. In a little while putrefaction, rot, the pallid, blind crawling things—

To deny which we postulate heaven. Invent God.

Hands were tugging at his arms. He looked up into Clo's face. She was crying. There were tears in her eyes.

"Alaric," she said. "Oh, my love! My poor, poor lost and broken—"

He lurched to his feet, shook her off. He reeled toward the doorway of the great hall. Behind him now the grooms and the scullions were fitting the stones back in place. To hide those graves. So that if the castle fell, no heathen hands might profane—

Inside the hall, the wenches had laid the table. There were great flagons of wine, and cold meats, and loaves and—

He seized a flagon between two hands, lifted it high. The wine ran red and hot and sweet down his throat in long, long pulsating gulps. It pooled in his belly, making a warmth. He clawed a joint of mutton from a trencher, bit into it, chewed wolfishly. But it wouldn't go down. He spit the half-masticated mess out on the floor, and lurched toward the stairs.

Up them now, reeling from wall to wall, his mailed shirt making a clanging. His room. His monastic, tower room where he'd lain nightlong and sinlessly with Zoë. How his mother had screamed—"Jew witch! Moor strumpet! Whore!"—who'd scream no more now for any sin of his. Nor weep. Nor mourn. Nor pray.

The tower was high. Some faint residue of light spilled into it still. He could see the rudely carved crucifix on his wall. Slowly he sank to his knees before it, folded his cut, bruised, dirt-caked hands, began to pray. Or tried to. But what rose to his lips was not prayer. It was closer to blasphemy.

"I cannot blame you, can I, O Savior, Redeemer, Lord? Savior of what? Who could not even save Yourself! Who cried out from the tree—'Why hast thou forsaken me?' Thirty pieces of silver and a traitor's kiss. Is life ever more than this, O Son of God? Ever more than death and

124

pain? Zoë said that Your Father doth not punish the innocent for another's sins. And I—I called her wise! But what sin, what sin at all hath
my lady mother done? The fond folly of loving me too much? You count
that sin? Does Your—Your Father's awful jealousy extend to so small a
thing? 'For I the Lord thy God am a jealous God visiting the sins—' Upon
my sister's head. Upon Gele—as virgin as thy Holy Mother! Upon Goissuintha, as faithful and as pure! What had they done? I ask you, what? I
—I've sinned right enough! And my father, too, God wot! Yet we live,
while they, the innocent, the chaste, scream now in lecherous hands. O
Great and Vengeful God! You bade me worship You, to pray, believe—
and I've kept my vow! But when are You going to keep yours? To succor
the hurt, the defenseless, the good, in their hour of need? To show Your
face in comfort to them, in wrath toward their enemies, to—"

But the tower room was drifted deep in night now, and he couldn't
see the crucifix anymore. He knelt there before it while the hurts in his
bruised, cut, striped, abused young body deepened, moved inward toward his heart. He peered toward that rude wooden carving on his wall
but he couldn't see it. Then, for the first time, he posed that question:
"Are You—there?"

It would not be the last.

In the silence, thick, unbreathing, he got clumsily to his feet. Taking
flint and steel, he struck sparks to tinder, blew them into flame enough
to light a candle. The crucifix reappeared upon the wall. He stood there
staring at it. His cracked, blood-crusted mouth twisted into a grin.

"Count Rabi of Córdoba, Head Tax Collector, I salute you!" he said.
"Or any other madman, criminal, thief! Or murderer. Who lets the
guiltless die is himself a—"

He put down his hands and caught at the bottom of his shirt of mail,
began to draw it over his head. But he couldn't. It was stuck to all his
wounds.

"Turtura!" he howled. "Where are you, you worthless slut? I have
need of you! Come—"

He heard the whisper of footsteps on the stair. Waited until they
were close.

"Fetch water, slattern!" he said over his shoulder. "This accursed
shirt is stuck to all my wounds, of which I have God's plenty, it would
seem. And heat it, mind you! Or else—"

"As my lord and master bids me," that voice said.

"Clo!" he said, and whirled.

She leaned against the doorframe smiling at him.

He stared at her. Weary as he was, the sight was pleasing. God's
eyes, but she was fair!"

"Get you hence, Clo," he muttered. " 'Tis not meet that a highborn maid come to a man's bedchamber. Go call me Turtura, for I—"

She shook her head, still smiling.

"No, Alaric, I'll not call that trull. She has too fond an eye for you now, methinks. I'll attend your hurts myself—and gladly. What boots it now what men call meet or ill? Now lie you down till I come back with water, cloths, and balms. I have some skill at this. Mine own good mother taught me. Besides—"

"Besides what, Clo?" he said.

"There is no highborn woman to company me. in your house, Alaric. Your lady mother's dead, your sister, and mine, taken. Those two ancient fools of God have gone back to their convent. Is not all this so, my lord?"

"Yes," he got out, "but I don't see—"

"Then," Clo said, "permit me the immodesty of pointing it out to you: When these troubled days have passed—and my poor father—if he lives—comes for me, I needs must have taken you—or your father—unto me as husband, before God, and at the hands of his Holy Representative, Father Juan, or else be branded strumpet in the eyes of all the world. . . ."

She looked at him then, seeing his face drawn beneath the dirt and blood upon it, his eyes appalled.

"Which shall it be, good my lord Alaric?" she mocked. "Shall I become your lady mother—or your wife?"

"Clo—in God's name: I—"

"Which, Alaric?"

"I am pledged to—to Zoë. I—I cannot—"

"That Moorish wench? That swarthy little bag of bones? Small obstacle, Alaric! Forget her. For I, God wot, prefer youth to age. Your father's a handsome figure of a man, but he has his fifty years and more, while you—"

She came toward him now. Stood there, her mouth inches from his own.

"While you, methinks I could learn to love. 'Twould cost me some effort, that I will avow—strange as you are; troublesome and strange. But certain is I could. I've known that from the day I surprised you in the river with your trull. I wept bitter tears that night—the more bitter because I knew not why I wept. I was already pledged to your brother, and yet—and yet, my vagrant heart kept shaping your image in my mind. I called myself fool, reminded me that you were more than half a priest, given to study, prayer, and meditation. I invented new epithets to hurl at you; milksop, puling babe, maid in boy's clothing, coward, knave—none of which you were, methinks my heart knew, even then. So now—"

She went up on tiptoe, and kissed his mouth. The touch of her lips on his drove pain into him like a knife. Screaming, crippling pain.

"Now lie you down, my husband soon to be!" she whispered. "For I shall not be long!"

She whirled and left him there. He stumbled toward his bed, fell sprawling across it, burying his face in his hands.

"Zoë!" he wept. "Oh, Zoë, Zoë, Zoë!"

Then, quite abruptly, his body vanquished him, conquered pain, terror, sorrow, grief. He swooned. Or slept. Or both.

He came awake to the great red ball of the sun blazing full into his eyes from just above the Sierra's rim. 'Tis dawn, then? he thought; then horror rode in upon him. His tower window faced due west, so that the dawn light stole into it as a gentle glow. This great and bloody blaze was a setting sun! He'd slept not only the night, but the day through as well! He tried to leap from the bed; but he could not. A weight lay on his right arm. A soft, warm weight. His arm had gone to sleep. It tingled and ached and itched, all at the same time. He looked down, half knowing what he must see.

"Clo!" he said. "God's death!"

She opened her eyes. They went a little startled, staring at his face. She swept the chamber with her gaze. A tiny frown knitted her fair brows. Then she shrugged.

"What boots it now?" she said.

"God's blood and death, Clo!" he said. "My father—"

"—has forgotten I exist," she said. "All that occupies his mind now is keeping his belly filled. And mayhap ours as well. Get you to your window, good my lord, and you'll see how a herd of goats drops their excrement upon your lady mother's grave. Victuals for the siege. A needful thing, right enough, still—"

He lay there, staring at her.

"Don't look at me that way!" she flared. "Think you I planned this bootless folly? Why, good my lord! You do yourself too much honor, for all that beauty of yours that so ill becomes a man! And though, God wot, I often find my maidenhood a burden, I'd trick no man into relieving me of it—least of all, you! . . ."

He went on looking at her.

"Yet, last night you said—" he began.

"—that I could learn to love you. I could, and can, and now methinks I must—though the lesson's scarce begun and taught plagued ill. If you want explanations, here they are—though, by my troth, you insult me by asking them. I came, my lord Alaric, with the water, and those cloths—look you! see them there—to remove your shirt of mail and treat your wounds. I tried to wake you; but, by then, not even the final trump of judgment could have accomplished that. I am but a maid—and though I took no blows, I endured heat and thirst and terror and fatigue, and those black swine's manhandling my poor flesh. I know, I know you saved me from them at great cost, for which you reproach me, and yourself, now. Which hurts. No matter. The point is, Lord Alaric, I am not made of iron. I was sick of weariness when I came to minister unto you. And since sweet sleep's contagious, I laid me down for forty winks, and here I am—compromised, dishonored, and with no joy of it!"

"Clo, in God's Holy Name, you—"

"I am a vixen, my father says. Poor Father! That your foes have not come means he still holds his own." Her eyes were blue ice suddenly. "I'll have my vengeance upon you and upon your father—doubt it not—for failing to succor him. Oh, I know! Your reasons are most sound! But I am a woman, and all women know that reasons count for nothing in this world. Nothing, my sleepy lover, my poor bedeviled husband yet to be, has been accomplished by reasonable men since the dawn of time. The world belongs to madmen, poets, prophets, Saints—and most of all to warriors, like my father who holds the breach against a host awaiting the succor that will ne'er come, holds it without reason, Alaric, with his good broadsword, and his pride! Now wait you here while I bring newly heated water for your hurts. For that I brought last night is too cold now. . . ."

He waited, puzzling over her words; but the tiredness was in him still, and once again he slept. He came awake to the feel of her hands. They were wondrous soft and warm. She had rolled up his mailed shirt an inch or two, reaching the place it had stuck to the first of those self-inflicted stripes. Now she applied a hot wet cloth to it, and tugged gently at the shirt. It clung to the wound. She ceased to pull it, and applied the cloth once more. Still it stuck.

"God's blood, Clo, have done!" he cried. Then, with one great lurch, he got to his feet, clawed at the tail of the shirt, and yanked it over his head. It tore the crusts from all his stripes, his wounds. He stood there swaying a little, all his upper trunk bathed in blood.

"Oh, Alaric!" she whispered. Then she dipped the cloth in the basin, and proceeded to bathe his hurts. She clotted them with lint rubbed in balm. With gentle insistence she pushed him down upon the bed, bathed his face, his mouth. She was, as she had said, quite skilled at such ministrations. He lay there, looking at her.

"I know not, Clo," he said, "whether you are a devil or a saint. There is much of both in you, I think—"

"And more of woman," she said. "Alaric—"

"Yes, Clo?"

"You—don't want me, do you?"

"Clo—" he groaned.

"No matter. I'll go far away, where no one knows me. Or I'll enter the cloister in my turn. Or—"

"Clo, for God's love!"

"Cease to torment you, you mean? Nay, Alaric; this torment will go on lifelong. I'll have my vengeance of life, what it hath done to me—for robbing me of father, sister, mother, lover at a stroke—"

"Clo, you can't say; you don't know—"

"Oh, yes, I do, my lord Alaric! By now my father and my mother both are dead. I am orphan and alone. Having only you whom I love—and hate—"

"Hate?" Alaric said.

"Hate. For being nothing like my dreams. For being so much less, and so much more. For being too tender, where I would have strength. Too brave, where I'd save myself from you by calling up contempt. For being the roaring lion of a man I could adore; and the indrawn mystical saintly fool I must, being me, despise. For being nothing simple, whole-some, lusty, sound. For lying there now, looking at me with those great sorrowing eyes, instead of dragging me down beside thee and soaking thy sheets with the blood of the virtue I'd preserved—against many a temptation, doubt it not—for a man less complex than thou art, more my own, in a way you'll never be. Yes, Alaric Teudisson, hate! I hate you, you hear! I hate, hate, hate—"

Her small head, arching downward, was like a serpent's striking. It crashed into his face, teeth bared. She seized his lower lip between them, and sank them in until his blood spurted, hot and salt into her mouth. Her hands made claws digging into his back that scarce had a single inch left whole to tear; and she rolling against him now, grinding her body into his until he could feel the whole of her against him through the cloth, panting, sobbing, wild.

Then, terribly, they heard that scream.

It echoed through the whole castle. The walls multiplied it, threw it back. It died. The silence rode in upon them. Then it came again. Louder now. More anguished.

Alaric hurled her from him, so hard that she fell to the floor. She lay

129

there, sobbing, hearing his feet thundering down the stair. Then she got up and followed him.

She found him in the dungeon, unused up until now, at least since the Black Duke and his sons had departed this life, to receive heaven's vengeance for their crimes. He was facing his father and their mingled roars shook the very walls. On the rack, the wounded Berber moaned, and Julio stood there grinning, the knout, the pincers, the irons glowing red in their brazier of coals, the thumbscrew, the spike-lined boot, and a host of other implements upon which the race of man throughout the long chronicle of history has expended more care, more science, and more art than upon any other, lay ready to his overwilling hand.

"God curse thy bloody soul to hell!" Alaric roared. "I'll have this not! You doom us from the outset, Father, when you stoop to this! Julio, release him! You hear me, churl!"

"Good my lord Alaric—" Julio grinned, but Alaric whirled upon him and brought the back of his right hand across his mouth in such a blow that measured that whoreson knave's length upon the dungeon's floor. Then he turned to his father.

"God wither the hand I raise against thee, Father," he grated, "but raise it I will, unless—"

The Count stood there, staring at his son. Then very slowly he inclined his grizzled head.

"I would but know what plans they have," he muttered. "Besides, it's no good. This Berber swine will die before he'll speak. Julio, get you up from there, and turn him loose! You hear me, knave! Do as my son says."

The Berber's eyes were on Alaric now. They glittered like a wounded beast's. Julio came up to him and began to release the manacles that held his wrists.

"May Allah the Compassionate shower blessings on your head, my young and noble lord," the Berber whispered. "Now ask me what you will, and I will speak. For the Prophet bids me recompense mercy shown us. Though not to yield to—"

Alaric stood there staring at that poor broken body. Fortunately Julio had not been at him very long.

"I'd not have you betray your Emir," he said, "who dealt well and kindly with me, sending even his own physician to try to save my brother's life. Which is what I do not comprehend—why should he order this attack? The banu Djilliki had to have his consent to command so many men, and yet—"

"Nay, Sahib, not the Emir—" the Berber got out. Then his voice died.

"Water," Alaric said, and turning, saw Clothilde standing there. "God's blood, Clo, fetch water!"

She whirled, already running. When she came back again, she was bearing a flagon.

Greedily the Berber drank. When he spoke, his voice was stronger now. "We rode not at the young Emir's command," he said, "but in rebellion against him. His uncle, Abd Allah al Balansi, who holds all the Valencian lands in fief from the departed—Allah grant him rest—al Hakam, would make himself Emir in place of his nephew. 'Tis folly all men know. Al Balansi is very old, and cannot prevail against al Rahman. But those Muladi Demons, the banu Djilliki, obtained of his senile idiocy money, arms, and men, upon their promise to take the frontier marks for the old fool. They'll take them right enough; but they'll keep them for themselves, make themselves lords over territories of more extent than those that wild ass Alfonso holds—"

"God's death!" Count Teudis swore.

"They—they had some—scores to settle hereabouts—'tis said. Against two petty lords—"

"Petty!" the Count Teudis roared.

"Father, be quiet!" Alaric said.

"And commands to take one young lordling—you, my lord, surely you—for you're as fair as they said—as slave for—"

"I know about that," Alaric said. "Get on with it, Berber!"

"And what maids they could steal to sell in Córdoba—"

"How could they, if they've risen in revolt?" Alaric said.

"They deal with ibn Ha'ad," the Berber said, smiling tiredly, "who'd trade twixt heaven and hell, if he can catch an angel and a demon's ear."

"All right. How many men have they?"

"Two *alam*. That is, two thousand men. . . ."

"God's death!" the Count swore.

"Engines?" Alaric said.

"A ram. And a great machine for throwing stones. They had more, but they left them by the way in their haste—"

"You've more to say?" Alaric said.

"Nay, good Sahib—except my blessing and my thanks—"

"And you have mine, Berber. Julio!"

"Yes, my lord Alaric?"

"Take him to Sisberto. See that his wounds are dressed. And handle him gently now, or I'll double the stripes I'm going to lay on your churlish hide when I have time. Father—"

"Aye, son?"

"Let us take council together. And food, too, if there's any left. God's blood, but I am faint!"

The Count bent a little, staring at Alaric's mouth.

"You should be," he roared, "who fornicate above your mother's grave! Clothilde!"

"Y—yes, my lord?" Clo said. Her voice was very low.

"Was that in self-defense?"

Clo smiled. She looked at Alaric, a long, slow time.

"What would my lord have me say to his august father?" she said.

Alaric glared at her.

"The truth, if you have it in you, you trull!" he said.

She bowed her head. Looked up again, completely mistress of herself.

"No, my lord Count, it was not self-defense," she said.

The Count stood there. His face was gray with weariness. He looked very old.

"Willing or no, the harm's been done," he said. "So now to remedy it. Come!"

"Where, Father?" Alaric said.

"To the chapel, knave! Where else can ye be wed? You heard me, come!"

What to say now? What word at all? Ataulf had said it: "God's eyes, boy! Never admit to a living soul you refused the favors of a maid, highborn or base, or else the world will think—" Refused? That would be scanned. Would I have not in another moment betrayed my Zoë had not the Berber screamed? Oh, traitorous flesh! Oh, quarter ell of dangling gut that only rises to confound me! Clo is—a witch. So fair, so fair. Fairer far than Zoë. And yet—and yet she wept not at my brother's bier! Should I die in this siege, she'll hie her to another before my funeral meats are cold! As dry-eyed as now, as much mistress of herself. What would sons got of those fair loins be? Monsters, surely. Ice cold, and cruel and—No, not cold. Not ever cold. For had not the Berber screamed—God's blood!

"Father," he said, "I have a thing to say."

"Then say it, boy!" the Count said.

"A man who breaks his pledged word is a whoreson knave."

"Meaning?" the Count said.

"I pledged my troth to Zoë" Alaric said. "I'll not break it while she lives."

The Count stared at his torn mouth. Upon his flesh the marks of Clothilde's teeth were clear.

"You'd tell me you've not already broken it, whelp of mine own loins? Ha!"

"I'll tell you that. More, upon my mother's grave, I swear it!"

The Count looked at his son. Then at Clo.

"Lass—" he rumbled.

Clothilde smiled at him, right impishly.

"You chose that moment to put your irons to the Moor, good my lord," she said. "His screams distracted us."

Alaric stared at her. Right wondrous was this art of hers: to tell the exact truth, and yet give it the shape and coloration of a lie. And here she had him: the simplest rule of courtesy forbade his saying out that she had been the aggressor, not he. More, 'twould be to cast affront upon his own manhood. The net was closing around him, his struggles futile. And yet, God wot, they must be made.

"Father," he said, "you said you'd not oppose—"

"—your match to the little Greek? True. I said that, son. But on condition that she obtain proof of her lineage. For which, now, there's no time. I am like to die, son. I'd see you wed, and this lass with child ere I go. Come now—enough of silly scruples. You'd have me believe that you mislike the gentle Clo?"

"No—" Alaric faltered. "Still—"

"Still," Clo's voice rang out crisp now, sharp, "there's another thing, good my lord! I'd force no man to wed me! I am not yet bereft of pride. But, my lord of Tarabella, consider this: there is no highborn female in your house, save alone I, myself. I pointed this out to Alaric, but it would seem that this one thing he prefers to forget. Is the gentility of the Counts of Tarabella such that they permit a maid to depart dishonored from their house?"

"God's eyes, child! I hadn't thought of that," Count Teudis said.

"Then think on't, good my lord. Think very precisely on it. For if your son—or you, my lord, gives me not his name—dishonored I shall be before all the world. It matters not at all that I depart as virgin from your house as I entered it. Should I go to my lady Abbess, submit myself to examination by a midwife before her, obtain a certificate—" she paused now, crying from pure exasperation "—it still would not matter, my lord Count! You know the world. 'Ha!' they'd say, 'with gold enough all things can be bought, even an Abbess' compassion for an erring maid.' "

"God's death!" Count Teudis said. "That settles it! Not another word from you, ungracious churl! Now, come!"

"Father," Alaric said, "you have no wife, yourself, now. . . ."

"God's eyes, boy! I know that all too well! And just as well know I

133

that I have two score and fifteen years! No more of this! You heard me, come!"

They knelt before Father Juan. Alaric stole a glance at Clothilde out of the corner of his eye. God's eyes, but she was fair! Especially weeping the way she wept now: hot, rebellious tears of injured pride and grief. He wept a little too; said a silent prayer: "Zoë, forgive me. Oh, eternally lost love, your pardon, for I—"

It was quickly done. He slipped his dead mother's ring upon her slender finger. But when he tried to give her the nuptial kiss, she turned aside her face.

"Till 'tis given with love, my lord, I want no kiss of thine," she said.

"I'll play Lord Alfonso to your Lady Berta lifelong, if you will," he said. "For God wot this wedding was not of my doing! Father—"

"Oh, get you to your chamber, boy," the Count said wearily, "and enjoy your bride, if you have strength enough left after yesterday. . . ."

"No," Alaric said. "First things first, Father! You and I had take some thought to our house's defense or court the risk of perishing one and all amid its ruins. And first of all are those tuns of pitch we have below. They should be heated nightlong, and then transported to the keep above the gate. Then when Leovigild comes with his ram—"

Clothilde stood there, her small hands making fists.

"Good night, my lords!" she said.

"Good night, daughter," the Count said, and kissed her. "I'll send you up this churlish groom of yours within the hour."

"Don't trouble yourself, my lord!" Clothilde said; and fled.

Count Teudis listened while Alaric explained it to the smith. A great bow of flexible steel, with five times the span that a standing man could draw. Cogwheels like unto those used to raise the gate. Orders to the carpenter to make a wooden winch, this sort of framework; the legs so; the channel thus; the bedding for the great crossbow cunningly wrought.

"And this hook, mark you, Khinsvilda!" Alaric drew rapidly on the parchment with a bit of charred wood from the fireplace. "This hook you make me thus! 'Tis to release, or trigger, ye ken? When 'tis pulled here, it lets the great bow fly and—"

"God's blood, my lord!" the smith said. " 'Tis a cunning marvel, for a fact! How come my lord to know such wondrous things?"

"This wonder, as you call it, Khinsvilda, is a Greek Ballista, these thousand years and more lost to men. And I know these things from the books that you—and my lord father—despise—Saint Isidore, for one. Now get you hence, and work nightlong, mind you! I'd have my engine ready to oppose them when they come. And 'tis hard upon midnight now—and I, God wot, would sleep. . . ."

"Ho!" Count Teudis laughed. "See that you do, boy—at least an hour or two, before the dawn!"

Alaric swayed there, drunk with fatigue, albeit the meats and wine had somewhat restored his strength. Then he bent and kissed his father on both cheeks.

"God guard thee, good my lord," he said; and walked out of there. But not to his tower room where Clothilde waited with the door locked and barred, ready to savor nightlong his cries and entreaties to be admitted; rather he went to the little bedchamber off the hall, reserved for the occasional pilgrim friar who was that age's only source of news. There laid he him down; but he did not sleep. Nightlong he groaned and twisted, tormented by sorrow, loss, grief, folly, love and lust, but held there by his egregious, outrageous, erethismic pride.

So passed he the first night of his honeymoon.

VII

The crash made by Leovigild ibn al Djilliki's battering ram as it slammed its iron head against the portcullis almost threw him from his bed. He leaped to his feet and stood there trembling. Outside in the courtyard he could hear the bleating of the goats, men shouting, the clangor of arms, a woman's shrill, almost demented scream. The crash came again. God's blood, but it was great! It seemed to Alaric the whole castle shook. He turned to take up his arms; but then sickeningly, he remembered where they were—they and all his clothes save alone for his woolen stocking tights.

Which will serve enough for modesty's sweet sake, he thought, while I pay a morning call upon my lady wife. She'll mistake my intent, God wot; but that cannot be helped now. For I must arm myself and take command. Father's worse than useless in this sort of fight, where a man's thews count for naught—and his head for everything!

He dragged his tights up over his legs, belted them about his waist; sat down and cross-gartered them; slipped on his shoes, opened the door, raced half naked through the halls and up those stairs. The crash of that ram punctuated his every step.

"God's death!" he muttered. "That the gate hold till I come!"

Then he stopped short, staring at the door to his tower room. He tried it, finding it—as he knew it would be—barred.

"Clo!" he said. "Open! For God's love, Clo, I—"

Her voice came over to him, thick and sullen with feigned sleep.

"No," she said. "Get you hence, Alaric. Go you back to your fat trull!"

"Clo, in God's name! The place's besieged! I must arm myself! My weapons are—"

"Get you hence, my tender, loving lord!" she mocked. "Think you I am to be taken in by such trickery?"

"Use your ears, wench!" Alaric howled. "The ram! Listen to it, you silly fool! Employ your eyes, if they have other uses than luring a man! Look out the window, Clo! Then talk no more of trickery, or of dalliance! For, by God, there is no time!"

He heard her bare feet thud against the floor, their skip and scamper as she crossed to the window. The ram crashed again, terribly.

And now she came to the door. He heard her hands working at the heavy crossbar. The hinges groaned. The light broadened the dark. Alaric took a backward step. His jaw dropped. His breath caught in his throat; made a strangling. For his bride stood there before him, clad only in the long, light-washed shimmering of her own pale golden hair.

"God's eyes, Clo!" he said.

"Come in, my lord husband," she said. "I bid you good morning. Did you sleep well? I hope so, for well it seems you will need your strength today—"

"Clo—" he groaned.

She looked down at her fair young body, as though his gaze had called her attention to it.

"I always sleep thus," she said. "Don't you? Does my nakedness offend my lord? If so, I'll cover it—though a wife's nakedness is her husband's, I've been told. One moment, then. Ah, now. Is this better, good my lord?"

It wasn't. The shift was of the finest, thinnest linen, molded to her form. It exercised imagination and memory both.

"I know not," he muttered. "Better or worse—'tis all the same to me. . . ."

He bent to pick up his shirt of mail.

"Wait," Clothilde said. " 'Twill only stick to you again. Sit you down, my lord husband."

He sat down on a low stool. She dipped her hands into one of the fragrant balms she'd brought to treat his wounds, and rubbed it all over his shoulders, back, chest, and arms.

"There," she said. "That should do. . . ."

He put his arms around her waist. She stood there looking at him. Her eyes were very wide and soft. Then she laughed.

"Oh, get you gone, Alaric!" she said. "You've more pressing bouts, God wot, this day!"

He could hear Count Teudis roaring like a bull.

"There! There! God's eyes, have I not one archer among ye all? There, you asses, you churls, you whoreson knaves! Can't you hit a butt at this range? God's eyes!"

Alaric came up to that section of the wall above the portcullis, stringing his great Mooris bow as he ran. He reached his father's side, looked down, studying that gyn. It was a fearsome engine: a mighty beam of oak, tipped with an iron head, cast to resemble that of a living ram. It was suspended between a long scaffolding of beams but little lighter than it was itself, upon great hempen ropes. The scaffolding ran on wooden wheels, some twenty of them all told, by which means it had been pushed up to the gate. Its size, weight, and complexity explained more than any presumptive heroism on poor Lord Julian's part, just what had delayed the attack so long. A hundred men were working it now, pulling it back against the tension of the ropes, then slamming it forward with all their strength, aided by its own great weight and the pull those thick ropes gave. Its force was a terrifying thing. A few more smashing blows from it, and even so stout and iron-studded a gate as their portcullis was sure to give.

But gazing on it now, young Lord Alaric laughed aloud. For he had already seen its weakness, upon which he looked with savor, for in a curious way it justified his whole life. Ataulf had laughed indulgently at his bookishness; but his father had despised him for it, holding it unmanly. Yet now it was his scholarly ways rather than his father's brawn that was going to save them. Because he knew the history of such weapons, knew moreover what defense might be employed against them; how, even, they might be undone. Which was a definite possibility with this one, since Leovigild of Tierraseca, whose contempt for human life was the toxin of his evil fame, had failed to provide it with what now it needed most; a simple thing, God wot, but as fatal as simple things often are.

For in the days when Caesar strode the world—nay, further off than that; even in the days when young Alexander ruled in Macedon—this ram would have been built exactly as it was now, but it would have been covered with a tentlike, long, peaked roof, made of bull's hide usually, or even of thin plates of copper, to protect the men who worked it from the slingers, javelin throwers, and archers on the walls; but more to protect the engine itself from one of several ways it could be destroyed. But Leovigild's ram was unroofed. And now Alaric could see the bodies of five or six Berbers that Count Teudis' archers had been able to cut down even with the inferior weapon at their disposal.

"Alaric!" the Count roared. "Now, ye clumsy knaves! Now ye'll have a lesson in archery! Shoot them! Shoot them, boy—for God's love!"

Alaric bent his bow. The shaft leaped out. The Berber nearest to the head of the ram crashed back into the man behind him, the arrow driven into him so hard that only its feathered butt protruded from his chest. Then the man on the opposite side of the ram took an arrow through the throat; and the one behind him reeled out of line transfixed; the next, and the next, and the next; until the Berbers broke away from their vast engine and fled.

The Count brought his mailed hand down on his son's shoulder.

"God's blood, boy!" he boomed. "That's shooting right enough! Look you, ye churls! Not one of them has risen. Dead, every man of 'em! God's death!"

"Father," Alaric's crisp voice cut through Count Teudis' roars; "if you'll delegate me command in this, I'll wreck that engine for you."

"Wreck it?" the Count said. "God's eyes, boy! Are you daft? It can't be wrecked! All we can do is what you've done: make it too costly to operate. But wreck it—how?"

"Wreck it," Alaric said. "Have I your leave to try?"

"Well—" the Count said. "God's death! Why not? There's something in what the lass said—something of the soothsaying sorcerer about you. Or God's favor, mayhap. Look ye, you churls! Do what my son commands!"

"Get me Khinsvilda," Alaric said to Julio, "and Wifredo. I'd have a word with them."

Julio came back with the blacksmith and the carpenter. The two skilled workers stood there before Alaric. Wifredo had wood shavings in his hair and beard. His leathern jerkin was covered with sawdust.

"Look you, my lord Alaric," he groaned, "that engine you commanded is plagued hard to make. 'Tis nearly finished now. But I was delayed—the drawings, my lord—I have no eye for such; and this sweaty animal of a smith only came to explain them to me after he'd forged and tempered that steel bow. So I'll need another day. . . ."

"Leave it for now," Alaric said. "Rig me a pivot beam above the gate. Great enough to support a heavy weight. To be swung out above that gyn. You get my meaning, Wifredo? A pivot beam's a simple thing, for which you need no designs. Can you do it?"

"Yes, my lord!" Wifredo said. "And I can make your engine, too, now that this black-stained churl hath explained it properly—"

"Khinsvilda," Alaric said, "how goes the pitch?"

"Well—" the blacksmith said. "Good my lord, I—"

"You didn't heat it!" Alaric said.

"Aye, that I did; but it got so plagued hot that I thought—The smell, you know, my lord—"

"God's death!" Alaric roared. "So now 'tis stone cold again?"

"Nay, good lord! 'Tis hot enough—so hot that by the time this lout ruins half the wood about the place I'll have it to a boil."

"Get to it, then!" Alaric said.

The morning passed. Wifredo and a dozen men were busy above the gate. First they fitted in place the sawed-off bole of an entire tree. In the exact middle of this stump Wifredo hammered in a mighty spike, leaving it protruding from the center of the sawed-off tree trunk some thirty inches high. Then he and his helpers lifted the beam into place. It had a hole bored through it about one fifth of its length from one end. When the hole was lowered onto the spike, the whole beam could pivot about it, swinging the long end out over the Berbers' battering ram.

"God's eyes, boy!" the Count said. "What good is this? You mean to perch yourself on that pole to get a better aim? They'll kill you sure! This accursed thing makes no sense! Dismount it! Wifredo, take this fool thing down!"

"Father, my respects!" Alaric grated. "But if you don't close your mouth all men will see through it to the emptiness of your head! Now, good carpenter—rig me a block and tackle from the long end; and counterweight the short. Hop to it, man, for here they come!"

The Berbers came on sullenly, being driven by their ka'ids with whips and the flat of their swords. Alaric waited until they were close enough before letting fly. He transfixed the three ka'ids driving them with as many arrows. The Berbers broke and ran.

"'Tis wondrous skilled you are with weapons," that dulcet soprano cooed. "At least those you choose to use, my lord! Is it that you have sheathed the one over which you have no mastery? Or is it poorly tempered, its metal base, so that it doubles at the first blow?"

Alaric turned and glared at her. Then he grinned.

"Good morrow, my lady!" he said. "Now get you down from these walls before you tempt a Moor's barbed shaft. And quickly, before I invoke my husbandly privileges here and now!"

Clothilde's face made a small sunset.

"You—you'd not dare!" she said. "I—"

"Not dare?" Alaric said. "Tell me, Father, what says the law? Is it the size of my thumb or my wrist—the stick I now have the right to beat my lady with?"

"Your thumb." The Count laughed. "And you do well, son of mine, to apply it early! For the minx hath need of it, methinks. And a woman's like a slab o' beef; the more you beat her, the tenderer she becomes. So lay on, boy! And do not stay your hand!"

"Oh!" Clothilde gasped. "Men!" Then she turned and left them then, walking away very slowly, her young back stiff and proud.

They could see the Berbers coming on again. But this time neither Alaric nor any other archer let fly. Sullenly the Berbers took their places at the ram. Swung it back, slammed it home. The portcullis shuddered under the impact.

The Count's grin almost decapitated him.

"Now!" he roared. "Now, good lads, now!"

The beam swung out over the ram; but now from its long end dangled a huge black iron caldron. The Berbers looked up at it wonderingly, a moment too long. Alaric yanked on the rope with all his strength. The caldron tilted, tilted. A thick, ropy sheet of black poured down.

And now they could hear the Berbers' screams.

"Bring it back in!" the Count boomed. "Bring it back, Wifredo! Swing it, good lads! We'll affix another pot. Ho, Moors! Ho, Mahound's fiends! How like ye the kiss o' boiling pitch?"

Alaric was looking at the havoc he had wrought, and even his lips went white. 'Twas one thing to read it in a book, but another to see men twisting in that scalding muck, the flesh dropping from their very bones. He could taste the vile green of nausea in his throat; but manfully he fought it down. Those—men, with blood in them, and dreams and love, and sorrow—those insects twisting in that boiling pitch—those fiends— hath cut my lady mother's throat. Companions of theirs hath ravished— my sister—and—

His father's great hand crashed down upon his shoulder.

"God's death, boy! But you're a living wonder! When this is done, you'll fetch your books and read me out these marvels! For, by my troth, this craft of yours is a thing of value. Who wars thus with his head, hath scant need to draw his sword!"

"Father—" Alaric said; then he straightened his back; what must be done, must be done. 'Twas not enough to kill the men who worked the ram, however cruelly. He'd run out of pitch long before the Galician ran out of men to replace the black, scalded corpses that he made. No, the ram itself must be destroyed. "Father, give them three more caldrons of pitch—well laid on—from one end of the ram to the other. I must go below to prepare another thing. . . ."

When he came back, Khinsvilda was with him, bearng a brazier of live coals. Alaric had a bundle of arrows in his hand. The Count stared at them. Instead of points, their heads were shapeless blobs of rags soaked in pitch. Alaric fitted one to his bow.

"Now!" he said; and the smith took with his tongs a coal from the brazier, touched it to that strange arrow's head. It flared. Alaric drew the bow, let fly. The arrow whistled downward into that pool of pitch, trailing a sooty banner of smoke behind it. In one enormous crackling roar, the whole pool exploded into flame. Those of the fallen Berbers who still lived, began to scream in good earnest now. Alaric sped one fire arrow after another until the ram sat there in a lake of fire, burning all along its length. The ropes upon which it was slung coiled like snakes, as they burned through one by one. The great ram dropped into that man-made hell. The tongues of flame stood skyward like a banner of orange, fringed with clouds of inky smoke. They leaped and crackled, making a noise like demonic laughter. That was the only sound. No one was screaming now.

Count Teudis turned to his son. His big face was gray. His mouth trembled a little under his mustachios. All the triumph had drained out of his eyes.

"An awful way to die," he muttered. "Still—look you, my young and noble lord—are you—truly my son? Or hath some witch with cunning spells introduced—a changeling into my house? For, my Alaric was—a gentle lad. Tender as a maid. And now—"

"—he hath become an assassin," Alaric said, his own voice bleak and dry. "Such a one as delights in cruelty, in death. Nay, Father, 'twas no witch, but life, itself, which has changed me. I but return it the blows it deals! Well, there's your ram. I told you I could wreck it. Now what would my lord father more of me?"

"I know not—" the Count said; then he frowned. "Now look you, daughter—" he began.

Alaric turned. Clothilde stood there, smiling at him. There was something in the way she smiled that—

"Accept my homage, good my lord," she said, "for by my troth, you've borne you well and bravely. And now—"

Alaric stood there, looking at his bride. The slow, deep sickness coiled inside him, still. And her voice, the tone of it, increased that sickness. My sister—and hers, he remembered suddenly—wept at the sight of men being slain. They prayed for my salvation. But she—stood up in the cart, and waved her veil—that veil she wore in mourning for my brother!—and screamed with joy—delighted at—at horror—intrigued by blood and pain—

"And now?" he said. Because he couldn't believe it, yet. He wanted to deny the evidences of his eyes and ears.

Her voice descended a full octave from its usual clear soprano note. It was husky, throaty, warm. There was—God's blood—a hint of pulsation in it. He remembered the Emir's parchment with its receipts for stirring the laggard blood. But this one you did not include, did you, oh ancient sage? That a woman can be awakened to lust by the sight of men twisting in the fire!

"And now," Clothilde purred, "come you to your chamber my husband, and—rest. I have prepared a crust for you, some meats, a sop of wine—"

Count Teudis threw back his head and roared with delighted laughter.

"Well spiced, I doubt me not, eh, daughter?" he guffawed. "Laced with many a cunning potion to—"

Clothilde crinkled her short, straight nose; made an impish pouting with her mouth. But her eyes were utterly serene.

"Now you do insult me, I think, good Father-in-law." she said. "You hold me so little woman that I have need to spice his wine?"

"No!" Count Teudis boomed. "God's blood, daughter, no! Methinks you could make a holy image descend from his cold niche in the church and do a dance! Of womanly charms and devilish ways you have your share, and more!"

Clothilde smiled at him, her eyes alight with mischief.

"Then, good my lord, why did you not take me unto you as wife instead of leaving me to this ninny?" she said.

Alaric felt anger stirring in him. Anger—and another thing. His mind, as a man's mind will when confronted with temptation, arranged not materials for defense, but what terms of capitulation it could call up least bruising to his pride. *I am wed to her—before God, and in the sight of men. Thus I have already betrayed my Zoë. For even should I find her again, I can offer her no honorable estate. Concubinage; whoredom—the black bar across the shields of all our sons. The scruple's useless. I must have legitimate heirs to preserve my father's line. Besides—*

Besides, this morning when she opened up that door! God's eyes! In all good truth—Zoë hath not—such—such globes of milky fullness, with the palest rosebuds thrusting toward my lips. That slenderness which yet doth not reveal a single bone; that golden cloud of hair shimmering about her form—so rosy white except for the tiniest pale wisps here and here and there! God's eyes! I—

He took her arm, moved with her away from his father. He didn't say anything, because he did not trust his voice. A yard away, he slipped an arm about her waist. She leaned her bright head upon his shoulder.

"Alaric," she said, "Dost thou—love me?"

He stared at her. His eyes were very black.

"Yes," he groaned. "Yes. God help me, but I do!"

And then, of course, at that precise moment, so rich in future promise, they heard the crash of Leovigild ibn Djilliki's first stone.

It came soaring from a little rise a good five hundred long clothier's yards away, hurled by an engine that under other circumstances would have delighted Alaric's intellect and even, mayhap, his heart. A great beam made of the entire trunk of a huge tree, some seventy feet and more in length, pivoted about a fulcrum, its short end weighted down with two huge baskets containing tons of stone, its long end dragged

143

down by a team of mules against all that weight, until the two enormous basket counterweights were lifted high. The long and hooked down with a cunning triggering device, a stone of sixty pounds and more was placed in a leathern sling attached to it. When the lanyard was jerked, freeing the trigger-hook, the long beam flew up to describe a perfect half arc until it crashed against a stout, leathern padded crossbeam with sudden force, causing the sling to whip, the stone to fly free.

So occupied had young Lord Alaric been with his love, that he failed to see that missile come. But he saw it strike. It landed among the herd of goats his father had brought into the courtyard to provide them with fresh meat against a siege; and disemboweled three of them.

"God's death!" he heard his father roar. "Get me those beasts to shelter! Or else that sorcerer-fiend will slaughter us more meat than we can eat in a month of Sundays!"

Alaric took his arm from around Clothilde's waist. He raced for the stair. Clothilde stamped one dainty foot.

"Alaric!" she cried.

The goats were milling about in a circle, racing about the courtyard. Their cloven hooves thudded over his mother's grave. Over Ataulf's. Another stone crashed home. It shattered. The pieces of it ricocheting off the paved courtyard broke the legs of two more goats. And now the scullions and the grooms poured out, and began to herd the goats, or tried to.

Alaric felt something tugging at his arm. He turned. Stared into Clothilde's eyes. They seemed to be afire.

"Come!" she said. "Let others attend to goat herding, my noble lord! I tire of being a maid! A wife hath some right to her husband's favor methinks! So come!"

Then he saw his father staring at the sky. He lifted up his gaze. The two balls had lifted very high—higher than any stone. They were tied together, and whirled about their common axis. From the great height they reached, Alaric knew they were very light—and likely hollow. He wondered what evil substance they contained. Pitch, or boiling oil—or, God's death! Who knew but what the Moors had rediscovered the secret of Greek fire. Then they whistled downward, to land not two yards from where Clothilde stood. One of them broke like a melon, and splattered her from head to heel.

She stood there. Then she thrust both hands into her mouth. A shaking got into her body; arose along her limbs until she was quavering like an aspen, jerking like St. Vitus. Slowly, she sank to her knees, still without making a sound, put out her hands, and picked up the nearest of those balls. And now, broken, battered though it was, Alaric could see what it was she held.

Her mother's head. Its eyes were open. Its mouth. It was tied to—what was left of Lord Julian's, by her own long, gray-streaked hair, which was doubly knotted into his beard. The Marquis' skull had been smashed when it struck the courtyard. The thick clotting substance dripping down Clothilde's gown was—his blood and brains.

Alaric opened his mouth, tried to say, "Clo—" But her name drowned in the explosive rush of nausea bursting out of him. He bent in half, spewing out a flood of greenish bile. He felt a tearing in his middle; a sharp stab of pain. He retched again, long and terribly. But what spewed from his throat now was blood.

Still he mastered his spasms after a time. There was a weakness in him so great that he wondered if he could stand. Yet he had to. He must stand, offer her what comfort that he could, say—

"Clo—I—"

"Don't touch me!" she said. "Not now. Not ever in this life. For now, God wot, I shall die a maid before being husbanded by the coward who lifted not a feeble hand to prevent—this!"

"Daughter—" Count Teudis began; then he stopped and stared; dropped to one knee, and drew forth the roll of parchment that was thrust into Marquis Julian's poor shattered mouth. He unrolled it, stared at it. His grizzled brows knit together.

" 'Tis written plagued ill—" he muttered. "God's eyes, what a crabbed hand. It says, it says: 'My Lord of Tarabella, greetings! I send you by these presents—' God's Holy Death!—I cannot make heads nor tails—"

Alaric took the scroll from his father's hand. Leovigild's Latin was more than vulgar, it was villainous. But he could read it right enough. "I send you by these presents my terms for an honorable surrender. You need but give into my hands the whoreson churl who cut down my son Eigebert on the field, and I'll withdraw my hosts. But if ye do not this, may Allah the Compassionate have mercy upon thee—as well as the Lord Jesus and his mother—for by my troth, when—as ye must—you fall into my hands, each man jack of ye shall beg me 'fore I'm done, the boon of death!"

He read it aloud. When he'd finished he looked up, met his wife's eyes. What was in them now was a strangely disquieting thing. Ice-cold abysmal hate for one thing. And—a kind of speculation, as if some dim, barely formed idea was struggling to be born behind those eyes. An idea so monstrous that he saw them reject it, saw them clear. But it would be born again. 'Twas that he did not know.

145

Leovigild's great catapult was, of course, powerless to carry their walls. But what it could and did do was to make life utterly miserable. Every day it killed or maimed a man. A scullion. A stableboy. A groom. A splinter from one of the stones laid open poor Florinda from naval to crotch, as she bore water to the men who manned the walls. And among the various things that spilled out of her was a man-child, still tiny, but fully formed. She named Julio as its sire before she died.

To make it worse, they had no means of replying to that rain of death showering down upon them from the sky. Because Wifredo had got Alaric's engine wrong. It had to be torn down and rebuilt again from the beginning. Alaric got out the great military work of art *Epitome Rei Militaris*, and explained in detail to Wifredo what was required. During the week that passed before Wifredo finished the ballista—mounting the great steel bow, the winches used to draw it, the trigger lock—Alaric did what he could, which was to send extralong flight arrows whistling down upon the men who worked Leovigild's trebuchet. Even at that distance, he managed to kill one or two.

But he was weakening fast. Nothing would stay on his stomach. Whatever he ate came spewing up, mixed with thick, ropy blood. Now he could scarce drive his arrows out to the range where the great gyn sat, endlessly hurling huge stones down upon them. To make matters worse, he underwent a nightly torment which threatened to cost him what reason he had left.

For, when he proposed to sleep in the little cloister room off the hall, Clothilde smiled, and said to him: "Nay, good my lord. Why should we trouble your poor father with what he need not know? You will share my bed, as a husband should. Do not fear—I'll see that you have naught but rest!"

So nightlong throughout that week, she lay there at his side, naked as a naiad new risen from the foam. Sat nude before him, combing out her long silken hair. Bathed and perfumed herself in his full sight. But when he reached out to take her in his arms she brought that dagger out from the coverlet, and plunged it into his ribs so that its point sank in an inch or more.

He sat up, his hand pressed to his side, the blood escaping between his fingers.

"Now you have killed me, I think!" he groaned.

She smiled.

"Nay, but rest assured I will, my husband—should you try to make use of me. Now lie you down, and let me cure that scratch. For, by my troth, I do not want you dead. Do you know why, good my lord?"

"No, why?" Alaric whispered.

"The dead don't suffer," Clothilde said.

Yet he suffered less from that cause than she might have hoped. His strange illness deprived him of even that little strength needed to feel too keenly, not to mention accomplish the consummation of his desire. He was steadily wasting away, which she attributed to her treatment of him. But no pity showed in her pale blue eyes. Only now and again that oddly speculative look.

Then Wifredo and Khinsvilda appeared before him wreathed in two enormous grins.

" 'Tis finished, my lord!" they said. "And by St. Bartholomew's Holy Fire—certain is it works!"

Alaric stood there staring at the huge crossbow. They very sight of it made him feel strangely better.

"Wind up the elevation screw," he said to the smith. "No, no, you ass! That one there! That's it! Higher. Higher. Now—a trifle more. An inch, say. That's it. Now you, Wifredo, crank it up!"

Wifredo put his huge paws to the windlass of the winch. But the immense steel bow was beyond even his great strength. Khinsvilda had to help him. Inch by stubborn inch they dragged that stout cord of twisted and oiled cowhide back, back, until the great bow was bent into its full arc. Alaric dropped a dart as big as a horseman's spear into the slot, fitted its notch snugly to the cord. Put his hand on the lever. Took it away.

"Go call Father," he said.

The Count came and stared. He said "God's eyes!" twenty times.

"I offer you the honor of the first shot, my lord Father! Alaric said. "You need but pull this lever. . . ."

The Count put his hairy paw on the lever. Yanked it.

The great bow twanged like the lute string of the demon. That great spear whistled skyward, scribed an arc against the blue, grew tiny in the distance. When it passed over the gyn it was meant to strike, it was still two hundred feet in the air. Its range at the full exceeded one thousand yards.

"God's eyes!" the Count roared. "What a shot! Wind it up again, lads, and I'll spit the Emir in his palace in Córdoba!"

"No need of that, Father," Alaric said. "Look you, Wifredo, crank it down again. To almost level. It has more range than I thought. That's it. Now wind it up again. Father—there you are!"

Grinning mightily, Count Teudis shot again. This time the dart buried itself to its feathers in the earth, fifty yards short of Leovigild's catapult.

"One and a half turns of elevation," Alaric said, and waited until the bow was cocked. This time when the Count let fly, they heard the cries from the crew working Leovigild's gyn. The great spear stood and quivered in the crossbeam of the catapult.

"That's it," Alaric said. "We have the range. Now, Khinsvilda, get you below and prepare the fire arrows. . . ."

"You mean to burn this one, too?" Count Teudis said.

"Yes, Father," Alaric said. "If God wills, with any luck, we'll take no more stones of theirs. . . ."

The Count stood there. He was remembering, doubtless, the fearsome holocaust Alaric had prepared to wreck the ram. Much he misliked this style of warfare. Yet, what could a man do? Leovigild was making the courtyard and the walls all but untenable with his gyn.

"So be it, son!" he growled. "Aim you right well!"

Before Khinsvilda came back with the special darts, Alaric saw Clothilde walking atop the wall with Julio. She often did that now, stones or no stones; even upon the not too rare occasions when the Berbers dashed in close enough to send a rain of arrows whistling in. When Alaric had spoken to her about it, she shrugged.

"What boots it if I die or no, my lord?" she said. "I'll give you no sons, that I've sworn my solemn oath. So, wed to you, my life is over. Unless you feel magnanimous enough to get yourself killed and free me. . . ."

"For whom?" Alaric said. "For Julio? It seemeth me that—"

She put back her head and laughed right merrily.

"Now have you put a thought in my head, my lord husband!" she said. "I had no idea you could be jealous of a baseborn churlish knave. And I don't mislike Juli for a fact! He's a most amusing villain. I have need to laugh betimes, God wot. . . ."

Out of pride he'd reproached her no more about that. Yet, well did it seem that Julio wore a most complacent air. The whoreson! He'd always been sadly wanting in respect for his betters. And with Clo treating him like a familiar . . .

"Here you are, my lord!" Khinsvilda said.

The darts that the smith held out were of two kinds. A dozen had their shafts rammed into the necks of earthen jars—of some considerable size, the Count saw. When Khinsvilda held them out, he could feel the heat from them.

"Pitch?" he said.

"Aye, my lord," Khinsvilda said.

The rest were tipped with tarred rags like the ones Alaric had used to burn the ram.

Now Alaric heard Clothilde's voice behind him.

148

"Come, Juli," she said. "Let us see how sorcerers and magi fight—without danger to themselves, doubt it not!"

"My lady," Julio said with a grin, "a man who risks his skin when he doesn't have to is a fool!"

It wasn't easy. The earthen jars changed the flight characteristics of the darts. The first two fell far short. The third went over. Then Alaric found the range. He lobbed jar after jar of pitch into the catapult. They could see the Berbers flying out from under it. They'd well learned their lesson from his destruction of the ram.

But when he switched to the fire darts, which looked like huge meteors flaming down the sky, again he overshot. The fire darts were much lighter than the ones which bore the jars. They were lighter even than the normal darts with their heavy iron heads. They had to lower the elevation to a quarter turn above point blank before the fire darts stopped arching over. Now when they hit among the pools of pitch laid down by the bursting jars, they made a fearsome blaze. The catapult burned all day. The Berbers dared not approach it to put it out.

"And now, my lord magician?" Clothilde said.

"And now—we wait," Alaric said.

"For what, my sorcerer husband?" she mocked him.

"To see if they tire before we starve," Alaric said.

In none of the many books that young Lord Alaric had read was the truest maxim of military life set down: that when war is not terrible, it is a terrible bore; and it is often both at the same time.

So was it now. Their rations had been cut, then cut again. In the courtyard now, no single goat was left to bleat. Quite early after they had begun to feel the pinch, good Sisberto's son, Theodor, disobeying Alaric's explicit orders, put himself at the head of five other hardy youths, and climbed down the walls of a night to raid their foe's supplies. The Berbers caught them all, quite easily and at once. And Leovigild had them crucified at all four points of the compass, so that for a whole month the defenders, no matter which way they turned their gaze, saw them there: caught, from whatever quarter the wind came, their putrid stench; could not so much as lift their gaze without having to watch the ravens beaking those poor gaping mouths to tear out rotting tongues, or probing in sockets that once had held young eyes.

Small wonder that poor Sisberto went mad, and had to be put in irons, where he died, screaming out his rage and grief. And not until they had been reduced to skeletons and had fallen into a whitening heap about the bases of their crosses did it occur to Alaric to do what he should have done at once, to burn those crosses down with pitch and fire arrows. With those same terrible weapons he harrassed his foes, igniting their tents and stores until they moved them out of range of even his great ballista. After which he could do no more, but wait, and starve.

And study. He read everything he had on war, strategy, tactics. But it was history itself which gave him his next idea. In his day, men fought on horseback with lance, shield, and sword, and sometimes, rarely, with the mace. But the arm with which he was most skilled, the bow, was purely a foot soldier's arm among Christians and Moors alike. Yet now he learned that the Mongolian hordes, specifically the Huns under Attila in their sack of Rome, had used the bow as their principal weapon from the saddle. He studied that, reached two conclusions: the great Moorish bow was too long for a horseman's use, the puny Christian weapon far too weak. Was needed then a special horseman's bow, both short and strong, with a terrible pull to make up for its lack of length. With Wifredo, he experimented and finally hit upon a combination of blackthorn, horn, and sinew, glued together in layers to make a bow twice as thick as his long Moorish bow, but short and double curving. At first he could scarce draw it at all; but then mounted on his captured Berber horse, he galloped around the courtyard shooting at a dummy clad in stout chain mail. At close range his arrows pierced the mail twice, entering, transfixing the dummy, and protruding from its back. But he had no occasion to use it against his foes. Pitched battles were now a thing of the past.

The siege went on. Alaric's internal wound seemed to have cured itself, or had been cured by the diet to which he limited himself, in order to give his rations to his father and his wife, a little watery goat's milk from the one she-goat they had saved. And even that poor beast was drying up for lack of freshening or fodder. Soon they'd have to butcher her as well.

And, at widely separated intervals, a series of strange happenings.

The First: He came through the dark hall toward the little bedchamber where now he slept, because Clothilde had grown so thin that she doubted her skeletal figure could torment him anymore. Or so she had said, when she bade him leave their tower chamber, adding in bitter contempt: "A man would have taken me by force, ere now! But you're no man, are you, Alaric? At least not unless one of your spells or holy visitations is upon you! So leave me now, for by God's eyes, you sicken me!" But, before he had reached his chamber on that day, he heard the sound of a mighty slap; and Julio burst through the door, holding his hand to his jaw, and fled as though he were pursued by all the fiends from hell. Alaric entered his room and found Clothilde there, sitting on his bed.

"Might I know," he said, "for what offense you deigned to slap that Churl?"

"For no offense, truly." Clothilde shrugged. "The fool was trying to cheer me; and I, somehow, am in no mood for japes. He told some comic tale of a nature no more lewd than those I've listened to a thousand times, and even told myself, God wot. I suppose 'tis because I am with this monthly affliction of women that I took it ill. Alaric, tell me—what chance have we?"

Alaric looked at her. He decided only truth would serve.

"Barring a miracle—none," he said.

"And when the castle finally falls?" she whispered.

He studied her another while before answering.

Don't worry, Clo; I'll see that you do not fall into their hands—alive," he said.

She got up from his bed, went to the door. In the doorway, she turned. "Oh, don't be a fool, Alaric! I don't mislike the idea of being slave to some lusty Moor," she said.

The Second: He went upon a day to the chapel to seek out Father Juan, at his father's request. The Count was ill abed, and felt the need of prayer. But he found Clothilde kneeling before the image of the Holy Virgin. And of all fair sights his eyes had yet beheld, there had been none one tenth so fair as this. She might have posed as model for an image of a Virgin or a saint, so had hunger reduced her face to perfect, aching purity. Her eyes were enormous, filled with light. So moved was Alaric at this vision that he closed the door very quietly and left her there.

The Third: Turtura came to bring him his usual now hard crust, and a bowl of wine to dip it in. Like everyone in the castle, she was painfully thin. But her thinness hadn't affected her little round belly; in fact, as the rest of her had shrunk, her belly seemed to have grown. He stared at her with increasing conviction, said at last the single necessary word: "Who?"

"Julio!" she sobbed. "Oh the knave, the whoreson, the churl! Oh, how I hate him, good my lord! He hath not left a maid—nor for that matter, a goodwife—in all the castle!"

"Your hatred, methinks, is but of recent date, Turtura," Alaric said wearily. "For some little time agone you could not have found him ill if your belly's any indication—"

"My lord—he—he tempted me! With food, ye ken! Me and all the rest! Have you not noted how fat and fine he is, when all men else—even you, my poor lord, are down to skin and bones?"

"God's eyes!" Alaric said. "I knew that there was something right

151

rare about Julio these days! That's it! The knave has not lost an ounce. And—"

"And here of late, your lady wife hath put on flesh!" Turtura said bitterly. "Look to her, good my lord! For hunger hath a way of reducing all conditions to but one, and that one base! Look to her, good—"

But that was as far as she got, for Alaric's hand brought hard against her mouth, broke her lips against her teeth. She fled from his chamber, blubbering.

After she had gone, he considered her accusations, measured them against what now he knew of female jealousy, malice, spite. He decided surely that she lied. For even disregarding all the motives impelling the wench to mislay sober truth, her story could not withstand one major flaw: where in a castle where even the dogs had now disappeared, would Julio have been able to find food enough to tempt one woman, let alone them all? For surely that cowardly, clownish miscreant would not risk his precious hide by climbing down the walls—not after having seen what had happened to brave Theodoro and his band—or even before having seen it. Julio, God wot, was nobody's hero. Nothing would cause him to take a risk like that, not even his gluttony or his lust.

The Fourth, the last, the greatest of them all: Alaric took council with Count Teudis, trying to persuade his father to allow him what seemed to him now their final hope.

"The Moors, God wot, accept our custom of letting a single combat between champions decide the fray," he said, "but whether the Berbers can be trusted to hold to it, I do not know. Still, Father, 'tis our only chance. I can beat Leovigild, of that I am sure. Whatever his strength, I am faster far than he, and—"

"Ha!" the Count said. "Such as you are now, boy, the carrion crows would scorn you! Much do I doubt you could even lift a lance. That's one thing. The other is, what under heaven and above hell makes you think that merciless swine would keep his word? That fiend who hung six brave lads on cross all about us? What's to prevent him, should he see himself bested in the fight, from raising his hand and calling a cloud of savage horsemen down upon you? His word? God's death! He hath no word! A renegade against the True Faith; a man who leads those Berber dogs against his own people, against, as it were, his own flesh and blood. And in such a case, whelp of my loins, we could not save you. For though we sallied forth, still would they outnumber us twenty to one, and that twenty—Satan take them—full well fed!"

"All that I know," Alaric said, "but I mean to see that he doesn't live long enough to raise his hand. For this, Father, is the weapon I mean to use against him—"

152

Count Teudis stared at that short and powerful bow.

"From the saddle?" he said.

"Yes, Father," Alaric said.

"They'll complain that 'tis not fair—" the Count began.

"What's fair about *me* having to ride with a lance against a man who outweighs me by eight stone?" Alaric said. "The object is to kill that swine, Father, not to dance a pretty measure! He tops me by a head, his reach is double mine. And all our horses which remain uneaten are so weak that I doubt one of them could keep their feet against that monster of a Flemish steed he rides! This bow can send an arrow through chain mail, I've already proven that and—"

The Count shook his head.

"Nay, lad, better that *I* meet him, with the usual weapons," he said. "For if you down him this way, they'll have excuse to break their words. I, at least, have both his height and reach; and though I am sadly reduced in flesh, yet can I overmatch him blow for blow!"

"Against which," Alaric pointed out, "all your own arguments as to his treachery hold good, Father. That's one thing. The other is that he'll but refuse you. 'Tis *my* head he wants. By now he knows 'twas I who cut Eigebert down. Another is, we'll make a cunning defense against treachery. I'll have Wilfredo set up again that pivot beam we used to shower pitch upon the Berber's ram, but this time with a ladder of rope attached to it. Should they ride out to take me, my lord Father, I'll dash for the place we have the beam. Whereupon you swing it around to me, I seize the ladder and climb up, leaving them as booty one rack of bones of a horse, which I took from them in the first place! Oh, Father, let me try!"

The Count frowned.

"Say—that your trickery wins," he said slowly. "God wot, I've seen you perform miracles enough—or black arts enough, I know not which to call it—to believe you can do this, too. But say you kill Leovigild, climb back up that ladder, gain the walls, where are we, my son? What have we gained? We're still starving within these walls, still besieged—"

Alaric smiled.

"Father, how long do you think those Berber horsemen will hold, once that swine is dead? How long will they keep to their bootless business of besieging this rude heap of stones, with a whole mark to raid, maids to rape, cattle to run off? Were it not for Leovigild, they'd have gone long since! They fear him; but they love him not. Methinks they'll reward me for ridding them of him!"

But still Count Teudis held his way, out of love and fear for the safety of this his one remaining son. In the end they decided upon a sort of truce. The great dart from the ballista which would bear their challenge into Leovigild's camp would offer both of them as champions for their cause; but leave the election of whom he'd choose to fight to Leovigild; both sides to abide by fate's—or God's—decision.

An hour after Khinsvilda had wound the ballista up and Alaric's trembling hand had sent the great dart whistling across the sky, a rider rode out from the Berber host. He had a white pennant affixed to his lance. He pulled up his barb within bow-shot of the castle, and lobbed a headless arrow into the courtyard. Julio picked it up, came running to his liege lords, to drop on his knees in a great and clownish show of reverence.

Alaric took the arrow, unrolled the parchment from around it, scanned the message in Leovigild's own crabbed and villainous hand. He could feel his father's eyes upon him.

"I," he whispered.

The Count bowed his head.

"So be it," he said, "though God knows if one can trust this dog. When?"

"Tomorrow at dawn," Alaric said.

At dusk, itself, he retired to rest, hoping thus to regain some slight measure of his strength. What he needed most of all was food; that, he knew, was the one thing he couldn't have. He sat there staring at that stone-hard crust of bread and the bowl of wine. The wine was good enough—a trifle sour; but even if he soaked that bread all night, it was still like to break his teeth when he bit into it and it was useless to try to cut it. He was sitting there like that when he heard the knocking on the door. He got up, went to the door, opened it.

Clothilde stood in it; she was smiling at him. But that wonderful odor that came from behind her almost made him swoon.

"God's blood, Clo!" he said. "What in heaven's name—"

She stood aside. Then he saw Julio standing there behind, holding a tray, on which there lay—a whole roast suckling pig!

Alaric's brows crashed together above his eyes. Turtura had said that this lewd and villainous wretch had used food to—

He took a backward step. Julio marched into the room, set the tray down on the table. On it, too, Alaric saw now, was a richly ornamented silver flagon. Julio made a sweeping bow.

"Compliments of y'lady, good my lord! And, if you'll permit me—of y'humble servant!" he said.

"One minute, rogue!" Alaric said. "Before you fly, I must know—"

"Oh, Alaric, sit you down and eat!" Clothilde said. " 'Tis all for you, for tomorrow we must all depend upon your strength!"

"Still, Clo," Alaric said, "we've suffered hunger these several months, and now with a wave of your hand, you provide me with a feast. Methinks I have some right to know how you obtained this bounty. . . ."

"Full easily, good my lord," Julio said, laughing. "I fished the piglet on a line. And not just this one. I've taken others, that I will avow. Well do I know what that silly trull Turtura accuses me of! But how can she know the brat is mine? She who sheaths a different weapon every night—"

"Julio!" Clothilde said severely.

"Y'pardon, m'lady." Julio grinned.

"I'm still waiting," Alaric said, "for an explanation that hath a head or tail, or that a simple Christian can believe. Look you now, Julio, no tricks! How came you by this pig?"

"First, Julio said, "I'd have my lord observe it *is* a pig. That's the important part. . . ."

"Why?" Alaric said.

"Because those Mahound fiends don't eat 'em," Julio said. " 'Gainst their superstition, I'm told. Am I right, my lord?"

"You are," Alaric said grimly. "Go on, Julio."

"Oh, Alaric!" Clothilde said. " 'Twill grow cold."

"No matter! Get on with your tale, Julio!"

"Very well, my lord. The Moors don't eat them, so, unlike sheep and cows and goats, they run loose. And since, whatever be my faults and sins, a fool no man can call me, it came to me that my dry crusts made better bait than food. So I dangle them from the walls o' nights, on a stout line, with a great fishhook hidden in them. Comes friend porker, takes the bait, and starts to squeal, and I let fly with my bow and arrow. You know I've some skill as an archer, do you not, my lord?"

"Like all cowardly knaves—even I—" Alaric said bleakly. "Go on, Julio—"

"With another stouter cord affixed to the arrow. Betwixt the two I manage to haul him up. Except once when the pig turned out to be a full-grown hog, upon which occasion I went down the walls on a rope, and risked my hide for my belly's sake. The sentries, please my lord forgive them, are in on my tricks because I share with them. Now does my lord see?"

"Right enough, you no-good churl!" Alaric laughed. "Still this time I cannot fault thee, for your trickery has served me well. Clo, I beg you that you partake—"

"No, my lord husband," Clothilde said. "Julio hath a cold ham below for your august father and your humble wife to dine upon. We'll leave you now. Fall to with a will, good my lord, so that you may face that renegade swine with some strength—"

"Stay, Clo—" Alaric said. "I—"

"Nay, Alaric," she whispered throatily, "for I—"

"For you what?" Alaric said.

"I—I find myself in—far too complaisant a mood—" she laughed "—which would contribute to neither your rest nor your strength!"

Very lightly, for the first time since her parents' bloody heads had crashed down at her feet, she turned and kissed his mouth. Then, laughing gaily, she scampered out of there. With another clownish, mocking bow, Julio followed her.

Alaric sat there, staring at the pig and the wine. It smelt most wondrous fine; and yet—

And yet there was something that would be scanned. This sudden change in Clo; Julio's exaggerated buffoonery. Still—the simplest explanation for it all was that they wanted him to win; since their very lives depended on it.

He put out his hand to pick up the dagger lying on the tray, in order to cut himself a slice of pig; when once again, that knocking sounded at the door.

"Yes, Clo?" he said. "Come in—the door's not locked—"

But then the door swung open, and not Clothilde, but Turtura was standing there.

"Come in, child," Alaric said, not unkindly.

She fell on her knees before him.

"The wine, my lord!" she wept. "Beat me if you will, but by the love I bear you, do not touch that wine!"

Alaric stared at her.

"Why not, wench?" he said.

" 'Tis poisoned, good my Lord!" Turtura said. "I heard them plot it! I wanted to warn you afore now, but I didn't dare. Julio's been watching me all day. And when he wasn't *she* was. Your Lady; I mean. I think they suspect I know something. Mayhap they recognized my voice. I couldn't help but cry out a bit, when I heard them say that. I had my ear pressed to the keyhole of the tower room's door and they—"

"The tower door!" Alaric grated.

"Aye, good my lord, where these many nights foul Julio hath shared your lady's bed!" Turtura said.

Alaric got up from the table. From the wall he took down a small riding whip. Still on her knees, Turtura moved crabwise till she'd turned her back to him.

"Beat me, if you will!" she sobbed. "Shred all the skin from my bones; but I'll say it still: Your lady hath dishonored my lord's bed with that—"

The whip came whistling down. It cut through Turtura's dress like a knife. Brought blood. She moaned. Then she said very quietly: "My life is my lord's. Beat me to death if you will, but I speak the truth: Your lady hath—"

This time she could not hold back a little choked-off scream. But as he raised the whip again, she whispered: "Please, my lord—"

"Speak, wench!" he raged.

"May I not have a cloth—or something—to—put in my mouth—so that my cries will not—attract *their* notice? Whipping's a cruel way to die— and I—I have scant strength—now that I'm with child—"

"God's death!" Alaric swore. "I'd forgotten that! Get you up from there, wench, and get you gone from me afore I forget it for the second time! For by God's Holy Blood, your filthy lies—"

"I do not lie, my lord," Turtura said.

"Turtura, by heaven and hell, I'll—"

"And now I know how to prove it to you! That and the other thing you've never believed, my lord Alaric—that I love you more than life! Now, watch this!"

In one great bound, she came up from her knees, and seized the flagon. She raised it to her lips, drank it down. Alaric made no move to snatch it away, so sure was he she would but disprove her own malicious idle fancies.

"Now," she whispered, "now I'm going to die. And the dying speak the truth. They have betrayed you, good my lord! They'd sell you to the Moor in exchange for lifting the siege, as ibn al Djilliki promised in that note he stuck in her dead father's mouth. They lied about everything— even the pig—"

"Is it poisoned, too?" Alaric mocked her.

"Nay, my lord, the pig you can eat. But I was fool enough to tell Julio about—about—"

"About what, wench?"

"How I w-w-walk—how I w-w-walk—through—throoough w-w-walls—"

Then she loosened all over, went down like a stone.

"God's death!" Alaric whispered. He bent over her. She was not dead. Nor, he saw at once, was she like to die. From her full lips there came a healthy snore.

He pushed her, none too gently, beneath the high canopied bed, pulled one side of the coverlet down to hide her form. Then he sat down and devoured that pig. For come what may, now he needed strength.

The wine—drugged. That much was sure. And proof beyond his heart's denying of the truth of Turtura's words. He fought back the black nausea that flooded him. He could not afford to lose that life-giving meal on the eve of his trial by combat. Slowly he sank back down into his chair. The rage that tore him was a dreadful thing.

Craft for craft, ye villains! he raged. Trick for trick, lie for lie! And yet have you o'ermatched me, for I have no way of equaling your swinish adulteries!

He laid his head down on the table, with his right hand extended so that it rested on the handle of the knife he'd used to cut up the pig. It was very sharp, as sharp almost as the razor-edged dagger he wore at his belt. Well might it serve to dismember still another swine.

He lay there a long time, so long in fact, that his very bones had begun to ache, before Clothilde came through that door.

She bent over him, peering into his face. Unsure still, she moved around him cautiously, while he lay there, fighting his screaming nerves with all his strength, holding himself motionless, closing his throat against the explosive rush of nausea foaming at the back of it, while this woman whom he'd loved longer and more deeply than any other proceeded to kill his insanely stubborn, slow-dying hope, smothering it terribly out of life with her every gesture.

Now she grew bolder. Leaning her elbows on the table, she lifted one of his eyelids with her finger. He did not move. She shook him, slapped him with considerable force, dug her nails cruelly into his cheeks.

"He sleeps like dead! she laughed. "Come, Juli, mine, and bring the ropes!"

Julio came through the door, assaulting Alaric's nostrils with his usual stench compounded of sweat, garlic, and sour wine. He was, Alaric could tell from the thickness of his tongue when he spoke, more than a little drunk.

"With that potion, we have no need of ropes." He chuckled. "Besides, we have all night. That great bed seemeth me inviting. 'Twould add a fillip to our sport, if, while he lies here asleep—"

"Julio, don't be a fool!" Clothilde said.

"Aye, God, but I have such envy to stretch again this dainty sheath with my huge weapon!" Julio said. " 'Tis so soft, so silken, so—"

Alaric heard the sharp intake of her breath.

"Take your filthy paw off me!" she hissed. "Or else!"

"Else what, my dove?" Julio said, and pushed his other, unoccupied hand inside her bodice.

She slapped him then, hard.

"You whoreson churl!" she said. "Do you not know by now that Alaric's no ordinary man? I've seen him do things that—no matter. The fact is, you randy billy goat, I cannot enjoy even your great lust, unless I know he's bound—"

" 'Twould be wiser, for a fact," Julio said, and turned her loose. He bent, picked up the coil of rope from the floor, laid it on the table. He put both his hands, palms down beside it, and leaned forward, peering clownishly into Alaric's face.

"Sleep well, my young and noble lord," he said grinning, "while I put your cuckhold's rope of hemp about ye!"

Abruptly his voice died.

"What ails you, Julio?" Clothilde said; then terribly, she heard him scream.

Alaric rose with one slow, easy motion. But Julio didn't. He couldn't. He hung there staring at his right hand, where the knife stood and quivered, pinning it to the table.

Clothilde stood there. She did not move. She saw Alaric's hand go to his belt, come out with his dagger. Even her lips were white. But when he was close to her, she put her hands to her own bodice, stretching it apart. He could see the soft rise of her breasts, see the pulse beating at the base of her throat. It seemed to have an independent life of its own. He raised his gaze to her face, saw her eyes. They were very wide and soft; but there were no tears in them.

"Strike true, my lord! For well I have deserved this death," she said.

Alaric looked at her, and the sick rage in him was absolutely bottomless. But now it was directed at himself. Because he could not. He lacked absolutely what was necessary to strike her down like that. He saw her lips curl into a slow, inviting smile.

"What do you wait, good my lord?" she mocked him. "I am an adultress and a whore. I have defiled my fair body with that filthy lump of dung. So now, my lord must kill me, must he not? Or—"

"Or what, strumpet?" Alaric said.

"Or perhaps my lord is wise. Perhaps he realizes that a woman's hardly spoiled, by loaning herself to a hardy, virile churl—particularly when her lord husband has been guilty of—neglect. If—if—" and now right artfully she began to weep "—you'd dare take that blade away from me, any time during that week, I should have devoured you with kisses, my lord Alaric! If, at the beginning you had not spurned me, left me, slept alone, surely by now I should be great with thy son! But even so, even now—"

"Even now, what?" Alaric said.

"Come to that bed, and I will show you what you propose to waste upon grave rot and worms! What can be yours lifelong, in utter servitude, in total fidelity. True, you had not the dubious privilege of the taking of my maidenhead; but, believe me, my lord, the honor's slight; and the pleasure's nonexistent! After all, 'tis a paltry thing: a little blood, pain enough to spoil a night—while now such ripened fruit as you'll enjoy will make you forget this silly ritual so falsely prized of men. Oh, Alaric, I—"

She came very close to him. Her mouth was slack, parted, a little wet, inches from his own. But, in a sudden elongation of his vision's scope, he saw Julio's face, saw the greedy leap of hope in those little pig's eyes, the expression of mocking triumph about those slack lips, twisted though they were now with pain. A tidal wave of rage came surging back —ice cold now, a black, polar, glacial, completely controlled flow. He remembered her own mocking phrase: "The dead don't suffer!" It rang inside his head like a doomsday drum, hollow, booming.

"And he?" Alaric said, nodding toward Julio.

Clothilde shrugged.

"Kill him, or leave him there—it matters not! No, let him live—and watch. 'Twill be the greater punishment!"

Then she took Alaric's hand, led him toward the bed, sank down upon it, put out her arms to him.

But, instead of stretching out beside her, he raised up, put one knee against her breasts, knelt upon her with all his weight, pinning her there. Her eyes leaped open in her face.

"You—you mean to—to slay me still!" she said.

"Nay, good my lady, nay, gentle Clo," Alaric whispered then. "I mean only to reward you for your fidelity—your love. Much have I treasured them—"

"You're mad!" she wept. "Mad!" Then, for the first time, she screamed. "You've cut me!" she moaned. "You've cut my face!"

"Such a little cut, dear Clo—a mere nothing; now, let me see—"

She screamed, and screamed again, and went on screaming now. Her head thrashed about on the slim column of her neck. He caught her chin between the fingers of his left hand, held it still. Her hands came up, clawing at his wrists. He brought the point of the dagger down. Moved it now this way, now that. Her screams were awful to hear.

Count Teudis came pounding into the room.

"God's blood, Alaric: What—" Then he saw Julio. Saw what held him there. "God's death," he said, so low, the words were scarcely sound.

"This churl, good my lord Father," Alaric said, "hath been making the beast with two backs, in mine own bed, with this highborn strumpet you forced me to take as wife. By our laws, my lord, the punishment for adultery is death. But I, as you have often said, am too tender of heart to be your son; so now I pardon them. God grant them joy of each other. And now, my lord Father—"

"The Count stood there staring at that moaning, writhing figure on the bed. His face was as gray as his hair.

"Have the goodness to give me that hand mirror over there," Alaric said. "Methinks my lady hath need of it. Her hair is in some disarray. Please, good my lord—"

The Count picked up the mirror and handed it to Alaric. His great hand shook.

"You have the right," he said, "to mete out what punishment you will in such a case. But this—this is the work—of a madman—or a fiend. I don't know you anymore, my son. What manner of man are you, Alaric?"

"A rogue. A knave. A jackanapes. A buffoon full of sunning jests, of sports, of gambols, of japes of most infinite variety! Who knows?" Alaric whispered. "Or, mayhap—a poor, afflicted dreamer fool, who now hath proved that not even he can escape his age's, or his own, barbarity. Or is acquainted with even one quarter of the devils that dwell within his heart. Still less with the angels who dwell there, too; for I, good my father, have heard their voices very clear, betimes. Or, mayhap, cruelty's the very stuff of life, for certain 'tis the only lust we have that grows and grows in the very heat of play and doth not fail nor satiate even upon an excess of consummation. My lady, gentle Clo, your mirror! Look you into it—long and lovingly and well; thus making a rite, both sacred and profane; for as oft as you lift this burnished silver to your gaze you must remember me. Here, fair Clo, take the cunning device, which hath the power to repeat a face—to call up beauty's self, or the foul image of adultery. What one sees in it, I'm told, is what one hath within his heart. I beg you, good my lady, take it up!"

She took the mirror from his hand, lifted it, peered into it. Then she threw it from her, so that it clanged against the wall; for, being silver, it could not break. She got up from the bed, and knelt before Alaric.

"My lord," she said, "kill me. I beg of you. Slay me for my fault. For, if God's thy judge, and thou hast aught of mercy in thy heart, thou canst not let me live—like this!"

"I can—and do," Alaric said. "Now get ye all apart from me! I have some need of rest!"

VIII

First in the morning after he had armed himself, Alaric started toward the chapel to say a prayer. But when he had reached the door, he stopped. How many times had he prayed to God now, to no avail? And always before, he'd knelt in a state of relative purity of heart and spirit. Not sinless, God wot; but guilty only of such sins that his Savior and his Lord in His days on earth had always gently pardoned. Unhallowed carnal knowledge of a maid; a troubled doubt or two about the basic tenets of his faith: these were the furtherest limits of his guilt. But now—could a man kneel before an altar, could he, dared he pray with such a black and ugly burden on his soul as now he bore?

I should have killed or forgiven her, he thought. Either of those could I have in honor done, while what I did hath neither honor, excuse, nor pardon, on earth nor under it! Oh, Blessed Savior, I—

Then he raised his eyes and saw her standing a little way off. She was heavily veiled, after the Moorish fashion; but he could see her eyes. What was in them now was not easy to decipher or divine; for it was none of the things he would have expected to encounter there; no slighttest response to all the motives compelling her to vengeance which now in all good truth she had: neither blood lust, nor rage, nor hate. But what it was, he could not then decide, because he had never seen her look at him precisely this way before.

"Nor could I enter it," she said. "That door, methinks, Alaric is forever barred to us both. . . ."

"Yes," he sighed, "I fear me that it is, Clo. And now—"

"And now," she said, "dare I ask of you a boon, my lord?"

He looked at her. When he spoke, his voice was very low.

"Aye," he said, "ask what you will, Clo; and if it lies within my power, I'll grant it; for much do I repent me of this thing I've done."

"Do you, Alaric?" she said; and her eyes, gazing on his face, were very wide and soft. "If I retained the power of feeling joy for aught, I should be glad of that. But no matter. Take this—if you will, my lord— and wear it on your helmet or your sleeve as you ride forth to meet the man who killed your brother, and thus first distilled venom in my heart.

And, afterward, my father and my mother both fell surely at his orders or his hand. Yet 'tis not revenge I crave. . . ."

"Then what is it, Clo?" Alaric said.

"I—I don't know. Mayhap—justice. A lessening of the evil that bestrides the world. To forestall future sufferings to the innocence he preys upon. And, good my lord, before you strike—"

"Yes, Clo?" Alaric said.

"Forgive him. And commend his soul to God."

He stood there, staring at her.

"Clo—" he said.

"Yes, my lord?"

"Julio. So clownish and so foul. The very definition of a knave, a churl. Could I but understand that—"

"You'd pardon me? Nay, Alaric, pardon does not exist for me now, neither at your hands nor God's. And could you grant me it upon my mouthing some excuse, still am I lost, for I have none. Oh, he made me drunken on a day, with wine that where and how he'd got, I know not even yet. But to impute my fall to drunkenness would be to lie; and I have done with falsity, my lord Alaric! Not even to save my life would I employ it, more. Say that all the terror and the pain new heaped upon my heart awoke in me my till then well-hid perversity. Say that to assuage hate too deep for any balm, I needs must punish the sinful inclinations which called down heaven's stern recompense upon my head, by greater sin; degrade this fair and shapely form that caused Ataul's death, and nigh caused thine; by wallowing with that nauseous filth in seamy lechery. Say that, and what have I said? Where stands—or lies prostrate—what men call truth? And where is God to witness it? Both forever absent from this world, Alaric! So let me humble myself still more, exceed even my newborn want and need of pain; let me confess I enjoyed that baseborn villain, churl, peasant, knave, lout, oaf, swine— these are not epithets enough, my lord!—to the very full. Enjoyed him, garlic, sour wine, rotted teeth, greasy hide unwashed of water since the baptismal font, if then, stable stench and all. Tell you that I screamed with delight while impaled upon his huge and hurtful weapon. Still, despite all this—ugliness, yet dare I ask you, because I must: Will you wear my gage, my lord?"

"Methinks," he sighed, "I've forfeited the right to deny you aught, Clothilde. So wear it I will, though it be a pair of horns to affix to my helmet in the sight of men. For now, by my troth, am I as insensible to ridicule as to pain. And you might have asked me more. 'Tis but a little thing. . . ." He looked at the cloth she held still in her hands. It was a silken

163

kerchief, snowy white save for its center where she'd traced a single word "If" in what was surely her own blood.

"If?" he said.

"Yes, my lord. The saddest word in any language. If I had known my heart from the very first. If I had not been capricious, filled with pride. If I had not hated you for being what you are—most utterly unattainable! Oh, I should have surely had the loan of your body upon a day—you have your lusts like any other man—but *you*, or what there is in you of the eternal, deep hidden within this fair and pleasing fleshly temple, from whence you allow to shine forth such sweet, wild, strange glimpses now and again as must madden all the female world; that awesome, awful be-ing, all compact of angel, devil, saint, lover, man—so wondrously, fear-somely combined, that *you*, that real you and not this pale abstracted mask you show to men, I could not have, Alaric! For with that quiet serenity that was a prick, a lash, a goad to mine intemperate blood, you —that special you—moved always just beyond my—or, methinks, any woman's reach; bidding me by inference to curb my instinct for greedy possession, be grateful for what small coins of favor you might let fall un-thinking from your pockets; what crusts and crumbs of affection—when her piteous, hungry whines brought the matter to your attention—you might throw your she-dog. But I desired more of you than that. Being me, I would not less than all! Not even with your mystic guiding voices, your ghostly holy visitors out of the tomb return'd to council you, the rays from the sky that shone about your head, protecting you from a host of murderous blades—not even with all these, I tell you now, was I pre-pared to share you. Nor could I accept—because, no less than heaven's favor, it, too, freed you of whatever carnal enthrallment I might have used to bind you—the dark and terrible powers of magic in you, enabling you to slay your enemies from leagues away, hurl fire through empty air, erase the night with flame, burn up the world. So if, my lord! If I had been content with some infrequent use of your fair flesh; if I had not been born with the sluttish appetite of a common trull; if I had had more of tenderness, less of lust, or even the imagination to see past my acts to their consequences—in short, if I had not been I, but such a one worthy of your love, I should not now have to live out my days con-demned to death in life; and you—"

"—would not have hurled this unpardonable affront to mercy into the teeth of Him who died to teach us it," Alaric said.

"Unpardonable?" Clothilde whispered. "Nay, good my lord—for I forgive you freely—if my forgiveness has aught of worth to you. And God will, as well, knowing your repentance sincere, and how gross the provocation offered you. So now there remains the hardest part of all; the lesson that the arrogant pride, girt round about by the beauty you robbed me of—thus ending pride and beauty both!—would not let me see; the cruel teaching that all of this one last sleepless night, I've tried to get by rote—"

"Which is?" Alaric said. "Of what consists this lesson, Clo?"

"Of knowing what you are; and being thereby hourly appalled; of living on, though sore stricken by the wounds no man can see, hurts got in the war between the good and the evil in you; yet having in the end the courage and the magnanimity to forgive yourself. Because there's no one else to, Alaric. No one else can. Even the chapel's door is closed—if it were ever open to any effect that hath meaning to us here below. Can you, Alaric? Can you forgive yourself, and become once more whole of heart?"

He looked at her, and his eyes were very bleak.

"No," he said.

"Nor can I pardon me—ever," she said. "And that, not my scarred face, my lord, is the death in life of which I spoke. A veil can hide the A for adulteress you cut into my brow, the strumpet's S you carved into my cheeks; the whore's W on my chin; but what cloth exists that can swathe the fiery letters branded on my soul?"

"Clo—" he said again.

"Oh, ride you forth, good my lord! And bear you bravely! For—for lost honor's sake. In the name of unredeemable sin. For no reward. On behalf of cruel necessity. I—I am a little mad, I think. Or else, why else should I—"

"What, Clo?" he said.

"Have the gall to—to ask of you a kiss. In parting, my lord Alaric! Knowing what you are, and what I am, how grave the presumption; how close it approaches insult—yet do I ask it! One touch of tenderness, my lord! To heal me a little, to—"

"Now do you honor me, I think, for the first time in your life, and mine," Alaric said, and took her in his arms. But when she lifted that veil and he saw her ruined face, his eyes went blind behind a scald of tears.

"May God, in his infinite mercy, forgive me, Clo, for I—I never shall!" he said; and bending, kissed her tenderly.

He had got scarce two yards beyond the portcullis when he saw Leovigild ride out from amid his cloud of desert horsemen, no more than fifty long strides away, upon his moving mountain of a horse. The Goth renegade was heavily armored, and held in his high saddle by leathern straps which hooked into iron rings sewn into his belt, making it all but impossible to unhorse him. The lance he bore was made from the fair-sized bole of the white ash tree; and his shield was stout enough to stop a ballista dart, not to mention so light a thing as an arrow. He drew up the hugh Flemish charger, and stared at Alaric in obvious puzzlement. Because by then he had seen that his young opponent carried no lance at all, no shield beyond a simple leathern target; was armed only with a slender curving sword, a poniard, and a silly Christian bow, stuck in a saddle sheath that was wide enough to carry it already strung; and bore, slanting diagonally across his back, a quiver full of arrows.

"When you are ready, my lord of Tierraseca!" Alaric called out to him.

"Now, whoreson!" Leovigild roared back, and charged.

Alaric spurred his captured barb, and charged in his turn. At the last possible instant, when it seemed to the watching on the walls that mighty beam of a spear must lift him from the saddle, he pulled left rein; and went by and under it, slashing at it with his Moorish sword. That princely weapon of the very finest Toledo steel, cut through the tough ash shaft with one stroke, leaving Leovigild with a yard and a half of useless wood in his hands. His bellows of rage split the sky apart.

"Churl! Whoreson! Coward! Lackey! Knave!" he roared. "If it's swordplay you will, then I'll oblige you! For by my troth, I'll cleave you to your skinny arse or know the reason why!"

Alaric didn't answer him. He reined in his barb, and sat there, studying the situation. Not only Leovigild, but his elephantine horse, wore a shirt of mail. But unlike the rider, the steed had no shield, and the underpart of his huge corded neck as well as his red flaring nostrils were bare.

Small targets, Alaric thought. "Still, sir fiend, let's see how skilled you are at managing wild horses!"

He waited there unmoving, until Leovigild started his second charge. Then he leaned forward, brought forth his bow, reached backward over his shoulder and whipped one arrow from his quiver, fitted it to the string, drew that bow, held it drawn against its some fifty pounds of pull, until he was sure he would not miss. Nor did he. The arrow whistled, blurring sight, so swift it sped; it took the Flemish warhorse in the nose. The great beast went wild. He screamed in that awful way that wounded horses will, and went back on his broad haunches, pawing the sky.

Even strapped to the saddle as he was, Leovigild had all he could do to keep his seat. Like most of the Christian warriors, and be it said their enemies the Moors, he was but an indifferent horseman. Not even his long association with the finest riders in the world, the Berbers, who held both their Arab allies and their Christian foes in just contempt on this score, had taught him anything; for his native arrogance made him despise what he could not comprehend. When that great Flamond reared, Leovigild did precisely what Alaric had hoped he would: he dropped his mighty two-handed sword, and clung to the pommel of his saddle with both hands.

So it was that the people on the castle walls and the Berber hosts, both of which had thought to see a fight, witnessed an execution. Before Leovigild's charger had brought his forefeet down again, Alaric had sped three arrows to the feathers into the great beast's unprotected chest and belly. The Flemish war horse plunged in good earnest now. Leovigild had all he could do to hang on, having no hand even to manage the shield that might have saved him.

Coolly, Alaric rode circles around the plunging, dying horse, and sped arrow after arrow into Leovigild. What was terrible, even to him, was the number of shafts that evil giant took and yet remained wildly, roaringly alive. Perhaps the renegade's chain mail was extra stout, limiting the barbed shafts' penetration; but by the time the great charger sank finally to earth, drowning in the hemorrhage two of Alaric's arrows had caused in his lungs, Leovigild resembled nothing on earth so much as a huge porcupine. But still he lived. His hand came out, clawing at his dagger. Four quick slashes and he was free of the strap holding him to the saddle. He struggled to his feet, while wonderingly, Alaric stayed his hand.

Tottering like some great spiny prehistoric beast, Leovigild lumbered toward his fallen sword; picked it up, turned; and hung there, heaving, the blood trailing down out of his nostrils and his mouth into his mustache and his beard, dyeing them a thick and ropy red. Stricken though he was, he was still dangerous. Every instinct of prudence and of sense told Alaric to speed an arrow through his throat at point blank range. But something, the feel of a pair of wide, soft blue eyes he dared not turn his head to see, peering at him above a heavy veil; the white flicker at his elbow of a silken kerchief bearing a device dyed into it with blood, would not let him take the easy course. Instead, he sheathed his terrible bow, dismounted, drew his sword.

"Oh, Alaric, no!" he heard her cry; but then Leovigild's mighty blade flashed down, bit earth on the exact spot where half a heartbeat before he had stood; but now that slender, graceful figure was not there. So went the battle on—but now upon nearly equal terms; for though Leovigild had still twice Alaric's strength, Alaric had three times and more his giant foe's agility. He allowed no single blow to touch him, while his own blade constantly bit through the links of Leovigild's chain mail, drawing blood at every stroke. Grimly the butchery went on, until the Galician leaned there on his sword, heaving and vomiting blood.

"Own yourself vanquished!" Alaric cried. "Swear upon your son's grave to lift the siege—and I—I'll spare your life!"

"Strike and be damned, whoreson!" Leovigild got out. "I'll ask nor give you quarter!" Then he lifted that two yards of heavy steel as though it were a wand, and brought it down in a stroke that Alaric leaped away from almost too late. The whole of his left arm, from shoulder to elbow, chain mail and all, was opened by that blow. Though, as he ascertained at once by doubling his fist, raising the arm, moving even his fingers, the gash had too slight a depth to injure any muscle, it bled frightfully.

He heard Clo's almost voiceless wail from the wall, his father's despairing groan. Then, in his extremity he did what must be done: Lifting his leathern target with that bloody arm, he went under Leovigild's guard and drove the point of his own wonderfully tempered blade through the chain mail covering the Muladi's belly, until it protruded from his back.

Leovigild dropped his sword, clasped that blade that had found his life with both his hands. When Alaric yanked it free, it cut them to the bone. But still the former Count of Tierraseca hung there on his feet, while his life pumped out of him with every beat of his great, evil heart.

"What—art—thou—Teudisson?" he gasped. "In—heaven's name—or hell's—what manner of man—art—thou?"

Then, as a great tree goes when it is cut three quarters of its thickness through, Leovigild of Tierraseca, Leolchijad ibn al Djilliki, bowed to what he could not, would not now ever understand; and gathering speed as an axed oak does, crashed to earth at last, measuring his great length, his towering ambition, his black, thwarted rage, and his now, at long last, drained-of-anguish heart, at the feet of—intelligence, skill, complexity great enough to, in that moment, envy him.

Fighting the weakness that threatened to drag him down beside his fallen foe, Alaric bent and dragged off Leovigild's helmet. Then with one might stroke, he decapitated the dead brigand, picked up that gory grisly prize by its long hair, walked with it in his wounded left hand until he reached the place where his barb stood trembling. He mounted one-handed, and with some effort; then held he his awful trophy high, so that the Berber host might see it.

They stared at it with somber eyes. Then, to a man, they touched a doubled thumb to their hearts, and lips, and foreheads, and called out:

"*Qismah! Ya Allah!*" " 'Tis fate and Allah will it!"

And turning their swift barbs about, they rode quietly off and left him there, left Alaric, son of Teudis, in possession of the field, of their master's severed head, of his own bleak, weary, savorless, joyless future, his more than half unwanted life.

The knocking on his door awakened him. He opened his eyes, saw from the quality of the light that it was long past dawn.

"Come in," he said.

The door pushed open. Turtura stood there. She had a tray in her hands. There was a bowl on it. A big loaf of bread: another object covered with a napkin. Raising his gaze to her face, he saw that what leaped and sparkled in her dark eyes was joy.

"Look what I've brought you, good my lord!" she said; then she whipped the cloth away.

"God's eyes!" Alaric said, staring at that whole roast chicken lying on the tray, filling the whole chamber with its succulent aroma. "Turtura, how on earth—?" Then: "Don't tell me they have gone!"

"No, my lord, the Moors are still there, if that's what you mean," Turtura said. "But they're beginning to leave! From the walls you can see parties of them riding off. Your august father says that by tomorrow or the day after, he's sure they'll all be gone—"

Alaric lay there looking at the scullery wench, at that chicken.

"Turtura—" he said.

"Why should I let Julio have the best of all the tricks? I said to myself: 'If he can do it, so can I!' After all, 'twas me who taught him how! So last night I went out and scrounged around. Oh, 'twas most fearsome dark, I can tell you, good my lord! I was so afrighted that my hair stood on end and the cold sweat—"

"Who lifted the portcullis for you, Tura? By heaven and hell, I'll have his hide! To take a risk like that—"

"Nobody, good my lord! And hence no risk at all! How many times do I have to tell you I can walk through walls?"

"Turtura—" Alaric said again.

"One day I'll prove it to you! But now will it please my lord to eat?"

"Where'd you get this fowl, Tura? And are you sure it has no cunning potion in it? Or in the wine?"

"Of course I'm sure, my lord Alaric! I cooked it myself. Fact is, I caught it, too. There's a whole flock of them running loose on the farm poor old Sisberto held in fief from my lord the Count. The Moors missed them somehow. Mayhap the chickens were out afield when they passed through. Most likely that, 'cause they killed all the pigs and left 'em to rot, the devils! Ran off the sheep and goats. Anyhow, please eat it, my lord. You're so pale and sick looking and—"

"You went to Sisberto's place, which is more than two leagues and behind the Berbers' lines! You got out of the castle without anyone's lifting the portcullis for you. You caught a chicken, brought it back and roasted it for me. All this between last night and dawn. God's eyes, Turtura! Are you a witch, in truth, or am I mad?"

Turtura stood there grinning at him.

"A little of both, my lord!" she said. "I'll make a bargain with you: You eat that chicken all up, and tonight I'll demonstrate to you my mystic powers—take you for a little stroll right through the walls—through the Mahounds' camp, too. 'Cause I can do it in the daytime, but night's better. Agreed, my lord?"

Alaric looked at her—a long, slow time. Then he sighed. What matters it now? he thought. Even if this gravid trull can flap her arms and fly, what care I?

"Agreed," Alaric said; and sat up in bed. Turtura's black eyes became very round and soft.

"Ohhh!" she wailed.

"What ails you, wench?" Alaric said.

"Your—your body, good my lord; the Moors have ruined it now! And 'twas so very fair. Now it's—too thin, and all striped and scarred. It gives me pain to see you thus—"

"And me," Alaric said, "to see *you* bulging with unhallowed fruit! Now get you gone, and fetch my lady—"

Turtura stood there. Quite abruptly all the joy drained out of her face.

"Your—your—lady, good my lord?" she said.

"Aye, wench, my lady! For well I know you've not thought to bring her aught to break her fast—"

"But—good my lord, she—"

"You heard me, wench! Go fetch her!"

"My lord," Turtura said, "I cannot. For she—she's not here. She left last night—a little before I did—With—with Julio. I—I thought you knew! The Count, your father, said—"

Alaric stared at her.

"What said my father, Tura?" he whispered.

"That Julio was to be released—at your orders."

"That is so," he said impatiently. "And—?"

"So when I saw him start away, leading your poor lady by the hand, naturally I thought—"

"You thought! God's eyes, wench! I suppose you're going to tell me that Julio and my lady Clothilde also went blithely strolling through the walls!"

"To be sure, my lord! That's just what they did! I—I told you. I taught him how—"

"God's death! Alaric said. "Now surely am I mad!"

"I—I thought you'd sent her away, my lord! She—she was crying so! Almost I pitied her despite—"

"Despite what, Tura?" Alaric said tonelessly.

"The way she treated you, oh, good my lord! But now—"

"She—was crying, you say?" Alaric said. "Crying, Tura?"

"As though her poor heart would break. I doubt me not now that Julio worked some trickery upon her, some cunning deceit to make her think you'd put her by. Or else—"

"Else what, Tura?" Alaric said.

"Why would she consent to lower herself to the kind of life Julio can give her? And why else would she cry?"

With that mask of ugliness I left upon her, Alaric thought, what hope has she? Or what choice, either? Julio or the convent; for certain is no man of quality would have her now. Her choice, however reluctantly made, is made. And made, 'tis base! To no nunnery will my Clothilde hie, for in the cloister one needs must sleep alone. Between her orisons and Juli, Juli. Between the matinal bell, the silent prayers, the peaceful service of Our Lord; and its opposite, that opposite: the beast with two humped, furious backs, the seamy bed, panting lechery! Fie on her! Devil take her! For she—

—Was crying. As if her poor heart would break. Sinner forgive thyself! For this is the last and greatest of the commandments but one. And that one—forgive the offender. As I do. And would have her back again. Would take her unto me and heal and comfort her. What boots it, the mockery of men? What boots any consideration of this world except to arm ourselves against loneliness, to—

"My lord—" Turtura said.

"Oh, get you hence, Turtura!" Alaric said. "Begone!"

But when she had left him and he got out of bed, he staggered dizzily, so weak was he from hunger and loss of blood.

Out of grim necessity, he sat down and ate the chicken, drank the wine, though the bile of sorrow in him destroyed the wine's sweetness, the meal's savor. Still, they restored him greatly, which was what was needful.

It cost him great pain to dress himself, his left arm had stiffened so. But he managed it at last, to find that he'd got some advantage from the delay. For it had thrust upon him time for thinking; and what he'd thought was that some use might be made of Turtura's witchcraft, or her tricks. So he lifted up his voice and called her name.

Almost at once he heard her footsteps in the hall. She came into the room and stood before him. When she saw the clean bones on the trencher, her eyes lit up.

"You ate it!" she said. "I'm glad, my lord! Now—"

"Now," Alaric said, "you'll show me how to walk through walls."

"My lord, I—" Turtura said. " 'Tis far too perilous by day! The Moors would hear or see us, sure and—"

"Now!" Alaric said. "For by tonight even on foot they'll get beyond my overtaking—"

"But they're not afoot, my lord! Juli hath that mule of his cousin Urbano's. You know, the one that holds his lands in fief from a noble Moor. That's where they went. And there they'll bide. So there's no need for haste, my lord Alaric—tonight will do as well—"

"God's eyes, wench!" Alaric said. "Now mean you to tell me that Julio rode a mule through our walls?"

"Oh, no, my lord! A mule's too big by far! Only people can do it. And they have to know the magic word. I had it of old Jacobo. You know, he was in the service of the Black Duke, when this castle belonged to him. Was he ever the lucky one!"

"God's blood! Was ever *who* the lucky one, wench?"

"Jacobo. The Count sent him to take those two old nuns back to the convent, afore the Moors came. And he never came back. Stayed there, eating rich and fat, and performing some little services for the lady Abbess like—"

"Hell and death! God deliver me from idiocy! What care I about Jacobo, wench! Come and show me the business of walking through the walls, and now!"

She stood there looking at him; and then she began to cry.

"As my lord wills," she wept, "but I am sore afraid! Oh, gentle Lord Alaric, they'll take us and—"

Alaric picked up his short horseman's bow, a quiver full of arrows; buckled on his sword, his poniard, slipped his arms through his leathern shield.

"They'll not take us, Tura," he said. "Now come!"

They went up the stairs toward the tower room. At a certain place, a little before they'd reached the top, she halted, put her already lighted candle down, knelt upon the step, folded her hands in the attitude of prayer.

"My Lord Satan, Father of Night and Darkness!" she whispered,

"And ye, Old Lord Warlock, King of Sorcerers! And ye, Lady Melusine, Queen of all Witches! I invoke ye! I call upon ye all!"

Alaric stared at her. Her voice had changed; it had become hoarse, shuddery. That she believed implicitly in every word she said, was abundantly clear. God's death! Alaric thought; suppose 'tis true? Suppose she hath those powers? After all, there *are* witches in the world. All the learned fathers say—

"Give me strength!" Turtura crooned. "Grant me the powers! For now will I say the awful words!"

Alaric waited, holding his breath.

"Eko Eko Azarak!" Turtura cried: "Eko Eko Arada! Open, wall! I bid thee let us pass!"

"Now will I strike thee in they secret place! You hear me, wall? I bid thee let us pass!"

Alaric didn't move. Nothing happened. Nothing at all.

She put out her tough little fist and hammered at a stone. Before Alaric's startled eyes it turned smoothly, silently, as though it had been oiled. Turtura put her hand inside the cavity, caught an iron ring, pulled it. Just as smoothly, and as silently, a whole section of the tower wall turned inward, revealing another pair of narrow steps going down.

"It used to creak and groan like the very devil," Turtura said matter of factly, as she bent to pick up the candle, "but Julio oiled the hinges. Follow me, my lord—"

Alaric repressed his wild impulse to laugh, for it struck him now that this was no simple thing, but a confusion that lay at the very heart of this his world. That Turtura knew not where fact left off and fancy or folly began, was to be expected. But are her betters any wiser? he thought. We reject simplicity; we have a need of the wondrous. Duke Atanagild, of course. Being the black-hearted fiend he was, he'd provide himself with this cunningly worked means of escape against the day of reckoning, when all the gentlefolk and the base he'd wronged came to take him. But praying to the powers of darkness, mouthing nonsense, what connection hath all that with a simple mechanical device? Surely none. Yet both my father and Clo impute to me the powers of sorcery because I warred with engines known to our ancestors a thousand years and more agone; and which the Moors use right handily to reduce our strongholds. My poor lady mother called me saint because I'd dreamed or lied, or both, and this foolish strumpet had befouled my room with cheap perfume. And yet—I did know where to find Ataulf without taking thought, and in that fight I should have lost my life a hundred times. Clo swears the heavens opened and a light—hell and death! I am as bad as they! I—I want to believe! I have a hunger after marvels, a thirst for wondrous things! I have a desire to be a favored one of God, such a one as angels watch over, invisible shields protect. As they did! They must have or why else—

"My lord!" Turtura said. "Why do you tarry? Come!"

—do I live? Because— And now the sickness is in me like a host of cold and slimy crawling things—because that Moorish lord—that Sahib Ahmad—offered them so much for me—as object of his twisted loves, his perverted lusts, that they—

"Oh God, God!" he said aloud. "Is there aught but ugliness here below? Hath Thou taken away all wonder and all beauty from the world?"

"My lord?" Turtura said. "Are you unwell? If so, we'll wait—"

"No, trull! Lead on!" Alaric said, and started down that stair. But now, irremediably, all things had changed for Alaric Teudisson. For though he clanked in armor, bore terrible weapons in his hands of which he had the practice and the use, still went he naked and defenseless to meet his foes. Because what had departed from him now was faith. And that, not Turtura's nonsense, was the magic word.

The tunnel went on for a long, long way. But now he could dimly see daylight up ahead. They moved on until they came to that opening. It was thickly shrouded with blackberry vines. Alaric pushed them aside with his target, came out. When he saw where he was, he swore aloud.

"The treacherous dog!" he said. "And I—I let him go!"

"What ails you, good my lord?" Turtura said.

"We're beyond the Berbers' lines," Alaric said. "We could have revictualed the whole castle but for your fine Julio! Or for that matter, but for you! Why did you not show me this before, you worthless trollop?"

"I—I dared not, my lord! Juli would have beat me to death. 'Cause then he'd have lost all his advantages: the pigs he got off his cousin Urbano—'cause Urbano's master, being a Moor, let him raise them to his own profit; and the wine and fresh bread he sold to the men for all the money they had; and when that ran out, he buckled down to what he was really after: making them bring their wives and daughters to his bed!"

"God's eyes!" Alaric said. "They stood for that?"

"Hunger's an awful thing, my lord Alaric. And Juli said he wasn't asking 'em for the right of the first night like a lord. Said what with the used and shabby goods he took in recompense for all his risks and trouble, 'twas he who was getting cheated, not they. 'Sides, he said—oh, no! I'll not tell you that!"

"Out with it, wench! Or by heaven and hell, I'll—"

"He said—he said—please, my lord, forgive me, for 'twas his words,

174

AN ODOR OF SANCTITY

not mine—he said: Why should they be so stiff-necked when you weren't! That certainly your fair lady's sweet favor was worth more than anything their sluts and slatterns had to offer—oh, good my lord!"

"And I—I let the whoreson live!" Alaric whispered.

"Which you can remedy tonight," Turtura said. "Come, my lord—'tis a long walk, and afore long the heat will be upon the day. . . ."

"Walk!" Alaric said. "I mean not to walk, wench. Our Berber friends will provide me with a mount. Now wait you here, below the river bank amid the vines. I'll come back for you."

"My lord! My lord!" Turtura wailed. "Please don't leave me. I'm afrighted! I—"

"Oh, hold thy tongue, Tura!" Alaric said.

When he came out of the ravine, he could see the horses. They all had their forelegs bound together so they moved about in queer, stiff, plunging jumps. The Berbers hobbled them that way to keep them from straying too far afield. Only one man guarded them. He was mounted on a magnificent white Arabian mare.

Alaric made up his mind at once. Not only was the guard's mount a superb example of the world's finest breed of horses, but she was already saddled and bridled. He had scant time to consider his European prejudice against riding a mare; besides, he already knew the Berbers favored them over either stallions or geldings. From what he'd seen of those desert dogs' prowess in the saddle, he was by then perfectly willing to follow their example in anything pertaining to horseflesh. And he'd have to kill the guard in any event. No other course was open to him. He got down on his belly, crawled from clump of brush to bare rock, to dwarfed, gnarled tree. When he was sure the guard had his eyes turned in another direction, he ran a yard or two.

So came he close. Then he moved closer still. For a man possessing such a horse might have on a shirt of mail under his tunic. That he was guarding the horses meant nothing: the way the Berber's loved their mounts, they well might set one of their ka'ids to watching them. So closer yet, to make sure that his arrow would reach its target with force enough to pierce stout chain mail. He'd have no time for a second shot. The very first must kill.

He drew his bow, held it drawn until his wounded left arm jerked and trembled, let fly at the very last. The shaft was blinding in its speed. The Berber let out one great, terrible cry, and reeled from the saddle, the arrow in him up to the feathers. He was dead before he struck the ground.

Alaric was in his saddle almost as soon as he vacated it. The mare trembled, then answered to the bridle. Alaric started off at a slow trot; if some of them had roused themselves at the Berber's dying scream, they'd see a horseman moving about his rounds, not galloping madly away. Done in that cunning fashion, he might escape cleanly without having to engage in a fight he had neither heart nor stomach for, God wot, this day. So moved he off, unpursued, until he came to the river bend. There was no sign of Turtura, which was strange. She would have come rushing out to meet him; and yet—

"The silly wench!" he thought. "She's wandered off, just when—"

He dismounted, let the bridle trail, knowing that a trained barb would stand at no more than that. Then he scrambled down the bank; and stopped. A dozen curved Berber swords thrust for his throat. He leaped backward, clapping his hand to the hilt of his own; but their leader, a black-bearded, aquiline hawk of a man, said in *aljamía*: "Wouldst sacrifice thy wife and unborn son, O infidel dog? Or willst thou surrender quietly?"

Then they parted, right and left, and Alaric saw Turtura. Saw and realized in one giddy instant of bitter, silent laughter that the Berbers might well believe her his lady. For among them, such a stocky, broad-hipped wench as this, big-breasted, fecund, round, fit to drop a foal yearly, would be a pearl beyond price. They had neither the delicacy nor the taste of the Moors. And because they knew not that their utilitarian concepts of beauty differed from his own, they were sure they had him. One of them held a knife across Turtura's throat. Another held her arms twisted cruelly behind her. A third had the point of his curved poniard pressing into a spot high on her swollen belly. As Alaric watched, slowly he pushed it in until a swell of scarlet rose about the point.

"Nay, Berber!" Alaric said. "Withdraw your blade. Slay me if you will, but spare her life."

"Slay you?" the Berber chieftain laughed. "Why thou, Sahib Aizun, friend of princes, art worth thy weight in gold! We'd have thee alive, and guard thee right tenderly! For if ibn Ha'ad pays us one half what he promised those swine the banu Djilliki—may Allah reward thee for ridding us of them, for, verily, they were fiends from hell!—we'll be well repaid for all we've suffered at thy hands. Now throw down your weapons one by one—"

"And the maid?" Alaric whispered.

"She's not thy wife, then?" the Berber chieftain said.

"No," Alaric said, "nor is the life that swells within her of my making."

"Good!" The Berber laughed. "Then think I to take her unto me, if thou doth not force me to disembowel her before thy eyes! For, from her build, she is one of those who run to luscious fat. Is this not so, my lord Aizun?"

"It is," Alaric said. " 'Twas your siege that starved it off her."

The Berber looked at Turtura, and his teeth flashed in the blackness of his beard.

"And thou hath proved that thou canst foal, canst thou not, O Christian mare?" he mocked. "Speak to thy lord, that he force me not to make carrion of so sweet flesh as thine! For by the Prophet's beard, I'll have not only this issue of thee without so much as a night's labor, but a fat and winning wife, who'll serve me well! What say thee, O little she-goat rich in milk, whose udders bulge most cunningly?"

"Spare me!" Turtura wept. "Spare my lord!"

"As Allah the Compassionate bids us show mercy, I'll grant thee thy boon, O moon of my delight! That is, if thou, Lord Aizun, willst be so kind as to throw thy weapons down. Or wouldst force us to butcher this little ewe?"

Alaric stood there, looking at the Berber chieftain. I should chance it, he thought. I should hang my poor, miserable existence upon the toss of even such weighted dice as these, for what they'd sell me into is not only slavery but abomination. Against that, what's this poor strumpet's life to me? Or her bastard's, either?

But the weariness was in him like a weight, pressing intolerably upon his heart. What, in this world of ours, is not an abomination? he thought. I have myself of late been abominably cruel or abominably bewitched—or mad, which is the father and mother of all abominations. And life—even this poor witless whore's, and more, even this bastard churl's kicking now right lustily amid her coiling tripes—is none the less sacred even when, as now, 'tis sired by an abomination upon two legs who still walks the world in such happy pursuit, enjoyment, and use of abominable knavery as to insure the continued begetting of abominations in his image down to the end of time. And—

Clo. To entwine her long, sweet, pliant limbs with his scales and scabs and crusty dirt, open her thighs, her body, her life to his brute male probing thrust, impaling not only her own pledged honor thereupon, but mine as well—*but mine as well!*—what was that if not an—

He threw back his head and laughed aloud.

"Art mad, Aizun? Or wouldst thou play the fool?" the Berber chieftain said.

"No—" Alaric said wearily. "I've worn that habit lifelong, now; and by God's Holy Blood, I tire of the cap and bells! I've no more stomach for war, which is but another jape, a louder jest, a sillier gambol, is it not O Ka'id? My weapons you may have of me. My life, too, which is the emptiest buffoonery of them all. I leave unfinished business, but then, what man doth not? I am at your disposal, Sahib! Strike—or bind me—as you will—"

"Bind him!" the Berber chieftain said. "Veil her—for truly I mean to take this delicious roundness unto me—and 'tis not meet that her beauty inflame other eyes than mine! Thou, Hixim, go fetch the horses! For before those other desert dogs get wind of our luck, we must ride!"

"Where, good my lord?" the one called Hixim said.

"To Córdoba, O flea up a cur dog's arse! To Córdoba! For as sure as Allah's the one true God and Muhammad is his Prophet, there we'll have our fortunes made! Now get you gone about your task; and tarry not, or I—"

"Ya, Allah! I go, Sahib!" Hixim said, and whirling like a dervish, fled toward that herd of hobbled horses.

Book Two

AIZUN IBN AL QUTIYYA

IX

Alaric lay on a pallet spread out across a corner of the tiled floor and stared up at the window of ibn Ha'ad's slave jail. He ran his fingers through the heavy blond beard that had sprouted on his face during the months of the siege. He had scarcely noted its appearance then, so occupied had he been with great and terrible deeds. Yet here it was, grown fine and thick, as if to give visible confirmation to achieved manhood. He stared up at the bars in the window. They looked fragile, but they probably weren't. And even could he break them, he still would need some fifty good yards of stout rope to descend to the level of the street. Yet he owed it to his sister Gele, and to Goissuintha—Sor Fidela no more by now; of that he was sadly sure—to escape and try to succor them.

Escape? he mused. Escape where? And from what? Our bonds are forged upon us whilst we sleep still in our mothers' wombs; we bear our dungeons about with us as do the terrapin, the snail. And what Gele and Goissuintha suffer now is but the common destiny of female flesh. If—the mocking thought stole unbidden into his mind—indeed they suffer. Have I not learned what base appetites a slender, graceful form can house? God's death! I'll think no more on it, for I—

Then he heard the great key turn in the massive lock. The door opened, and three men came into the room. Two of them, Alaric saw at once, were merely the rude, muscular brigands who guarded the slave pens; but the third was ibn Ha'ad. He knew at once though he had never seen the trader before that moment; for although the Berber had delivered him into the hands of the trader's agent and ridden away with Turtura and their reward two days agone, ibn Ha'ad for reasons of his own had not deigned to come until now to inspect his new lot of slaves. Alaric studied him with curiosity and some care, for the renegade merchant was surely the strangest, most richly comic sight that ever Christian gaze feasted upon.

He was monstrously fat, poised upon slippered feet so tiny that he seemed to walk on tiptoe. And he was far enough below middle height to seem wider than he was tall. He had taken off his high Persian bonnet, and Alaric saw that his head was bald save alone for a fringe of bright red hair that bristled about his ears and oddly grew so copiously on the back of his neck and the underside of his skull that he'd—proudly, Alaric was sure—made a thick red plait of it, which he wore in a little bag of silken net, falling artfully across one shoulder. In the lobes of his ears he wore enormous golden earrings. In one nostril, a surgeon had made a slit, enabling him to set a huge and glittering diamond in that most unexpected place. All his pudgy fingers, including, be it said, his thumbs, flashed with precious stones. His globelike bulk was swathed in acres of yellow silk, gathered about his quite nonexistent waist by a sash of brocaded green velvet, from which hung a huge drawstring purse. Into the sash was stuck a curved Moorish dagger, sheathed and hilted in gold, encrusted with brilliant jewels.

He passed with a jiggling step among the slaves, tossing back over his shoulder remarks to the guards in Arabic. Alaric had no idea what these remarks were, but they convulsed the guards with laughter. As ibn Ha'ad moved about, pausing now and again to examine an especially likely boy or youth, the fat man never ceased to take sweetmeats from that bulging pouch he wore attached to his sash, and pop them into his mouth.

And now Alaric could see his face clearly. His round, pouting little mouth was ringed with a sparse hairline mustache that descended past the corners of his lips and joined the ridiculous little red spike beard that sat on the topmost of his various chins like a bit of fluff clinging accidentally to a new-laid egg. But when he was close enough to distinguish Alaric from the rest—no difficult task, since it was by his own written orders that his keepers had placed this prized piece of merchandise apart—he stopped and stared; and his little blue eyes held not one jot of good humor in them. Nor of pity, Alaric thought, nor of aught else that's good. You walk upright like a man; but truly you are a swine in soul as well as in flesh, are you not O ibn Ha'ad?

The trader bent down, peering into Alaric's face.

"Get up from there, my boy!" he said in a high-pitched womanish voice. His Romance was fluent and good.

Alaric got to his feet, towering far above him. Those little pig's eyes opened wide.

"God's eyes!" ibn Ha'ad shrieked. "A giant! Bearded like a lion! Shoulders outspanning a yoke of oxen! The look of a warrior! By the Prophet's beard, I've been cheated! By the Black Holy Stone, I am undone!"

"How have you been cheated, sir slave trader?" he said. "You find me disappointing, then!"

182

"Nay, lad—had I an offer for a warrior prince, I'd find you well enough—even superb. But—"

"For my lord Ahmad al Hussein's purposes, I won't do?" Alaric said.

Ibn Ha'ad's little blue eyes opened even wider in his round pink face.

"Who told you that?" he said.

"Dead men," Alaric said.

"Dead men?" ibn Ha'ad whispered.

"Aye, Eigebert of Tierraseca, Leovigild, his father. The banu Djilliki, to you. They boasted too loudly and too soon. So I found it meet to silence them."

Ibn Ha'ad went on staring at Alaric. Then his little pouting mouth spread into a grin.

"And yet—you're here," he said.

Alaric shrugged. "Trickery," he said, "the folly of a maid. But give me a target and a sword, and see how long you'd keep me here, Sahib ibn Ha'ad."

The trader went on smiling. "Think you I'm a fool, Aizun?" he said. "Let me see—let me see—hmmm—less bad, less bad. Methinks there's still a chance—"

"A chance for what?" Alaric said.

"To recover the monies I have invested in you. I see now what my informants meant. Truly you are most wondrous fair, yet—"

"Yet what?" Alaric said.

"I know not how to account for it," ibn Ha'ad said. "True enough, several moons have sped by since my lord Ahmad saw you; and though at your age the tide of life is swift, yet even so I'd hold the interval scarce long enough to accomplish so great a change. But the fact is plain: you left Córdoba a beardless, pretty boy, and have come back a man. What explication canst give for that, Aizun, son of the Goth?"

Alaric stared past ibn Ha'ad; stared through him. Then his gaze came back.

"Pain," he said.

"Pain?" the trader said. "Ah, so? 'Tis true that suffering can harden both soul and body. I've seen it before. No matter. That's not the problem, now."

"Then what is the problem now?" Alaric said.

"To return—or reduce—you to the aspect the Sahib Ahmad expects. For, if I judge well his tastes—and my fortune has been built upon my judgment—the way you are now will please him little—"

"Why?" Alaric said.

"Because my lord Ahmad is not a *cinaedus*, but a pederast," ibn Ha'ad said slowly. "Have you not noted that he is not womanish in his ways?"

"Yes," Alaric said, "though I fail to see what that has to do with me."

"This: You are too male, ibn al Qutiyya! Al Hussein's taste runs to pretty boys, soft and submissive, whom he can use as though they were women. He hath not, like many deviates, the desire to play the woman himself. So first the thick, new-sprouted beard. Off it comes. And if my lord al Hussein gives me time, I'll stuff you with sweetmeats, sherbets, creams, and the like, to restore in you some semblance of the baby fat he so enjoys taking to bed. . . ."

Alaric didn't answer that. When he spoke, he said:

"Six moons agone, or thereabouts, did you buy and sell two Gothic maids? One of them plain of face, but sweet withal? The other—a religious sister—a nun?"

Ibn Ha'ad seemed to be searching his memory.

"The plain maid," he mused, "it seemeth me—but no. Six months ago, I bought one hundred three blond maids. Goths, Vascas, Gallegas—how am I to know? 'Tis unlikely that my agents would accept a maid lacking in beauty, Aizun. Elementary rule of the trade—plain maids are hard to sell. But the other, I can give you my solemn oath: no. The tenets of the Moors' faith bids them respect ours. No agent of mine would be so big a fool as to touch a nun. The head judge would lay two hundred stripes upon his hide, and fine me a princely sum. So about that, you can set your mind at ease. . . ."

Alaric felt the iron enter his heart. But he realized with a curious sense of shame that he could and would endure this new hurt. After so many blows, he was arriving at an acceptance—nay more—a certain affinity for pain. He passed his tongue up over bone-dry lips, and got it out, his voice slow, quiet, grave; the phrase, itself, dead stopped, with no interrogatory lift of inflection at the end, carrying all the weight of certainty: "They were murdered, too," he said.

"Aye." The trader sighed. "They were. The trouble precisely was the fact of their religious sisterhood. As I told you, the Moors respect our faith, my boy. Even such renegade dogs as the banu Djilliki knew well that living, a pair of nuns—"

"My sister was not a nun," Alaric said.

"Ah, so? True—I'd forgot the details. No matter. She was an eyewitness to the fate of her friend. The point was that to try to sell a nun, even stripped of her cloister garb and guised in harlot's silks, was too great a risk. They knew of a certainty that I'd refuse to take her off their hands—his hands—for the son was dead by then, no? Ibn al Djilliki was aware of the fact that the matter inevitably would have come to the attention of the Metropolitan of Córdoba, who would have run screaming to the Emir. The punishment for offenses against our faith and that of the Jews could range from imprisonment and fine, even unto death, should the maid complain of carnal abuse—"

"So, thereupon, that Gallego swine ravished them both, and cut their throats," Alaric said.

"*He* did not," the trader said.

Alaric caught the emphasis, slight as it was, that ibn Ha'ad placed upon the word *he*. An iron fist clutched at his entrails, shutting off his breath.

"Look you, my boy," ibn Ha'ad said. "You had cut down his son upon the field but an hour before. He was in no mood for fleshy delights. So he—"

"—turned them over to his men," Alaric said.

"Aye," the trader said. Then: "God's eyes! Why don't you weep? 'Twill ease you and—"

"I," Alaric said, "have moved beyond the use of tears."

Ibn Ha'ad's own barber shaved Alaric, cut his hair into a long bob like that worn by youthful pages. Then the slaves stripped off his dust-stained, filthy clothing, and led him to his bath. The water was both warm and perfumed. Alaric lay in it, soaking the stiffness and tiredness out of his body. Then ibn Ha'ad came into the bathing room and stared at his fair young body.

"God's death!" he swore. He turned to his agent and burst into a crackling flood of Arabic. But Alaric could see his eyes were troubled.

"How now, sir trader?" he said.

"If thy master al Hussein asks thee aught of me, Aizun," ibn Ha'ad said, "tell him I have been called away to the East, and will not return these many moons! I pray thee tell him that—"

"I'll tell him," Alaric said, "but I'd know one thing of you, sir trader: when I say that, shall I speak lies or truth?"

"Truth," the trader groaned: "I dare not risk his wrath."

When Alaric came out of his bath, ibn Ha'ad's slave dressed him in robes of light blue silk embroidered with silver threads. The trader stood back examining the effect.

" 'Twill do," he said. "It goes wonderfully well with his fair complexion. Now, go call Djiha!"

Djiha, despite the sound of his name, was not a woman. That is, Alaric decided grimly, not quite. He tittered and cooed and minced in Arabic, Romance, and a mixture of the two.

"Oh, dear," he wailed to ibn Ha'ad. "Must you sell him, master? Couldn't we just—keep him here? Oh, dear, but he's the loveliest thing! Such eyes! Such milky skin! And—so strong! Couldn't we keep him, master?"

"Shut up, you airy fool," ibn Ha'ad said. "Employ your arts. See if you can make him look a little less like a young lion and more like a girl. At least enough to let me get an hundred leagues from here before al Hussein discovers the deception. Get busy now."

"Oh, dear!" Djiha sighed. "A pity! Well do I like that warlike look. Gives me the shivers! Now, Sahib Quityya, if you be so kind as to sit. . . ."

Alaric sat down on a low teak and ivory stool. At once Djiha set up a little folding table and placed it at his side. After that, he opened a richly ornamented casket, and began to take out flasks, jars, brushes, powders, paint.

Alaric stared at him. Delicately, Djiha dipped a brush in a dark liquid.

"Do me the honor of closing your eyes, O most noble Goth," Djiha said.

Alaric closed his eyes. He felt the brush tip caress his lids. It felt warm and sticky. He opened them.

"What manner of folly is this?" he said.

"Kohl," Djiha said. "Makes the eyes look bigger. And brighter. And that slant, master? Suggestive, isn't it?"

"Hmnn," ibn Ha'ad said. "I don't know—it seems to me—"

Djiha dipped another brush in a pot of red.

"Now a touch of this carmine to the lips," he purred. "Not only to relieve their paleness, but to give them more pleasing shape—a sort of rosebud, say? Or a cupid's bow?"

He extended his brush, touched it to Alaric's lips; but before he was halfway done, Alaric shoved his hand aside. Among Djiha's equipment, of course, there was a burnished silver mirror. Alaric snatched it up, stared at his face.

"God's death!" he swore. "Wouldst make of me a buffoon, sir trader? A clown?"

"You're right," ibn Ha'ad said sighing. "On your face cosmetics become a mockery. I'll have to trust to your native beauty, then. May God grant that it bemuse al Hussein long enough for me to get away; for, if not—"

"If not?" Alaric said.

"I run some risk of monetary loss—and, mayhap, even some danger. My lord pervert hath much influence in high places. I'd much prefer to incur not his displeasure—"

The trader's slaves bore Alaric in a covered litter to Ahmad al Hussein ibn Maliki's house. And, in a strange way, his reception there was like the first time he visited Córdoba on his tragically futile errand. Again he was ushered into a room empty of people, but so richly furnished as to be somewhat cloying—no, more than cloying, actually disquieting. He tried to study why this was, but he could not. It would be years before he learned that a man's taste reflects what that man is.

He was still puzzling his head over it, when a slave girl came into the room. She was clad in the conventional Moorish woman's harem dress, which departed from the norm by being considerably more modest than usual, making no use of transparent stuffs. But even if she had not been dressed in the graceful oriental mode, the fact that she was an Easterner was apparent at a glance. Her hair was so glossy black that it reflected light the way a polished ebony surface does, so straight it appeared to be lacquered, so long it fell below her waist. He could not decide whether she was pretty or not. He had the feeling she was either ugly or beautiful. About her body there was no doubt; her modest harem dress, swirling about her as she moved, only emphasized its near perfection; but the type of face she had lay outside the scope of his previous experience.

He was dimly aware that one's concept of beauty is a matter of habit; having always dealt with the dark-haired Celto-Iberians only in the capacity of inferiors, it had taken him some little time to see Zoë's subtle loveliness. Until he had met her, he had been almost unaware that a brunette maid could bring a man's breath to a sudden halt as effectively as any blonde. And now this maid moved as much beyond Zoë as Zoë had beyond Clothilde. Her skin was so dark that only the hawklike aquilinity of her features proclaimed her membership in one of the white races; and her lips were so full, so sensual, as to put even that in doubt. Her nose was high arched, bold, arrogantly Semitic; there was something imperious in the way it jutted from her face; but most startling of all were her eyes: in her totally unveiled face—he knew enough about Moorish customs now to realize how shocking that was, contradicting the curious modesty of her dress—they appeared like yellow coals, much lighter than he'd expected in a face so dark, and ablaze with what was so clearly murderous hate that his breath caught in his throat before it.

God's death! he thought. What on earth have I done that she—

But she dropped to her knees, bowed until her forehead touched the floor. Then she straightened up a little; but the fury in her eyes abated not one jot.

"Have you hunger, good my lord?" she said.

"Yes," Alaric said. Then: "Tell me, what are you called?"

"Afaf," she said. "Have I my lord's leave to go?"

187

Alaric started to detain her, but thought the better of it. He dismissed her with a wave of his hand; then he sat there, trying to remember where he'd heard that name before. Then it came to him: Zoë! Zoë had spoken of a slave girl hopelessly in love with her master, al Hussein. He remembered that Zoë had spoken—nay, more—had insisted upon, emphasized this maid's beauty and her virtue. From such a source, he was prepared to accept both. But what was beyond comprehension was why she should take so violent a dislike to him whom she'd never seen before. Before he came to any conclusion about that, Afaf returned.

This time she was not alone. With her were two night-black slave girls bearing urns of burnished copper that shone like gold. One of them had snowy towels looped over her ebon arms. Alaric looked at them with real pleasure: they belonged to one of the African tribes that grew to great height; both of them were as tall as he; slim, sylphlike. They were veiled, and literally clanked with gold coins and other ornaments. Alaric thought they were one of the most splendidly barbaric sights he had ever seen. One of them pointed to his hands. He held them out. One of the black girls held a basin below them, while the other poured perfumed rose water over them from one of the urns. Then they dried them with towels. Betimes Afaf placed the shining silver bowls on the table, and uncovered them.

Something in the way she did it caught Alaric's eye. Bowing, the two black slave girls went through the doorway. Afaf bowed too, started to follow them.

"Wait!" Alaric said.

Afaf stopped. She stared at him.

"Come here," Alaric said.

She came toward him sullenly.

Alaric smiled at her. "Of what land or race or nation art thou?" he said.

"Egypt," she said. "I was born in the desert, but I grew up in Alexandria. Now, may I go?"

"No," he said. "First you will have the goodness to taste a little of each dish, and to sip this wine. . . ."

She stood there a long moment. Then silently she bent and did as she was told.

Then she spoke. Her voice was gutteral, a little harsh. "My lord has enemies?" she said.

"That I know of, none," Alaric said. "But there was something in your look, Afaf, that—"

"I see," she said. "But my lord need not fear that I shall poison him. Though I am a woman, I scorn the coward's way."

He appealed directly to her then. "What have you against me, child?" he said.

She backed away from him until she stood in the doorway. She looked at him, and the great glaze in her eyes dimmed a little.

"What, Afaf?" Alaric said.

"Thy beauty, Lord Aizun!" she said, and was gone.

It was late before Ahmad al Hussein came into that room. Apparently he came from a banquet, for he swayed drunkenly. Alaric was not surprised at that, because he knew well by then how seldom was the Prophet's injunction against wine obeyed. In the months since he had seen the Moorish lordling last, it was painfully obvious to what extent al Hussein's looks had decayed. He seemed much older; he was markedly thinner, and there was a falsetto tremble in his voice that had not been there before.

"Ah, Aizun! Aizun!" he breathed, and clasped Alaric in his arms. He stood there staring into the young Goth's face with dilated, unfocused eyes, and his wine-laden breath stirred Alaric's hair. Then, leaning forward, he kissed the boy wildly, passionately upon the mouth.

Alaric was too startled at the first to move; then he tore his face away from al Hussein's and struck out with all his force. The Moorish lord measured his length upon the floor. He came up at once, shrieking in rage.

"Infidel dog! Thou art my slave, to make what use of thee I will! And if thou willst not be wooed, prepare to be forced!"

But since he shrieked all that in Arabic, having from childhood stubbornly refused to learn the speech of the mother who had given him his blue eyes and fair hair, Alaric understood not one word al Hussein said.

The Moorish lordling took a step toward him.

"Touch me again, and you die," Alaric said.

Al Hussein whirled, clapping his hands. In moment a swarm of eunuchs piled into the room.

"Seize him!" al Hussein said. "Strip him! Hold him down! For well do I mean to mount this wild Gothic donkey! And the feel of my goad will break his spirit, right enough!"

Alaric kicked one fat greasy castrate in the paunch, smashed another to earth with a mighty fist; but in the end they bore him down, but not before most of the furniture in the room had been reduced to splinters. They lay across him, panting.

"Strip him!" al Hussein howled, and powerful hands tore at his clothing. Then suddenly there was silence. It went on a long time. Alaric forced his head around as far as he could, and then he saw al Hussein's face.

The Moorish lord had both hands clapped to his own jaws. He was staring at Alaric's body with wide-open eyes. And what was in those eyes was horror. Alaric saw the greenish tinge get into his face; saw the first involuntary gulp of his nausea. Al Hussein whirled. In the doorway, he halted.

"Take him to the east bedchamber," he whispered. "Lock him in! Oh, when I get my hands upon that Mozarab swine, ibn Ha'ad! To cheat me this way! To cheat—"

Then he plunged through the door, running, going on.

The eunuchs got up slowly, turning Alaric loose as they did so.

He turned over, clawing the rags of his torn clothing up over his naked body. He stared at their thick, sullenly anguished faces.

"Is there one among you who speaks Romance?" he said.

The oldest of the eunuchs answered him. "All of us do, save alone Ivan, who was brought from Tartary; and the black, Joaquin," he said.

"All right," Alaric said: "I bear ye no ill will; your needs must obey your lord. But in God's name, what passes with him? Beyond his crooked lusts, which right well I know—what signifies this behavior?"

The oldest eunuch shrugged. "Thy body, my lord," he said. "To such tastes as his—Allah curse them!—'tis repugnant—"

"Repugnant?" Alaric said.

"Aye. Instead of being soft and fair, 'tis sinewy, muscular, and hard. Much too thin, mayhap, as well. All of which could be remedied, with time and the proper diet. But those warrior's scars with which thou art covered cannot be, my lord Aizun. The Sahib Ahmad is of those who sicken at the sight of blood, and thy scars call blood to mind to so finicky an imagination as his. You see, he'd thought to buy a fair youth with skin soft as velvet, round with fat, silken to the touch, girlish, complaisant. Strange—"

"What's strange?" Alaric said.

"These perverts affect to mislike women; and yet they seek as close a similarity to the female as possible. God's death! 'Tis little I can do now, but if by a miracle of Allah, I could be restored—"

"I pity you, friend," Alaric said.

"I want not your pity, young Goth!" the eunuch said. "Now come with me—"

"Where?" Alaric said.

"To your bedroom," the eunuch said, "where right peacefully you may sleep this night, for be assured he'll come not nigh thee—"

"And tomorrow?" Alaric said.

"Tomorrow he'll sell thee if he can—and to the cruelest taskmaster he can find. So enjoy your rest this night, it may be long ere you rest again. Now, come!"

Alaric made what repairs to his clothing that he could. Then he drew aside the curtains and examined the windows. As he might have expected, they were barred. Besides which, this richly feminine bedroom was high above the street.

He sat down on the edge of the canopied bed. Curiously, what moved through his mind was renascent hope. If escaping from the room seemed all but impossible, there remained the fact that the very circumstances involved in his being resold to a new master increased his chances. He'd have to be transported to another house, to a mine, a farm, a factory. And since the eunuch clearly had been sure that al Hussein's vengeance would take the form of selling him to the type of master who worked his slaves like animals, Alaric was prepared to take an animal's many opportunities for flight.

For certain is, he thought, that such a one who sees in a slave an alchemist's machine for converting sweat into gold, must by the very nature of things transport his human cattle hither and yon, making far less sure whatever vigilance he employs than is possible in this shut-in, perfumed, cloying world. I'll wait and see. For here in Córdoba there are refuges to which I can fly: the Prince; the Emir himself; the Jew; even— Zoë. . . .

He thought about her now, which was a thing he had not allowed himself to do these several months. But his mind was troubled. Fate and Turtura's folly hadn't permitted him to take any definite action that could extricate him from the hellishly complicated matter of his marriage to Clothilde. Though, he told himself, I can face Zoë with a clear conscience. I am innocent of Clo, though wed to her in the sight of—He halted there.

Is one ever innocent in this world? he mocked himself. Do we not come into it clothed and girt about with sin? Innocent, ha! The Berber screamed just as I was lifting Clo's skirt. Leovigild hurled his great stones—and her parents' heads—as I, with my arms about her, was mounting to our bower. Say I was checkmated at every turn. Say that curious law of life—that evil happens daily by coincidence, by chance; good, never—prevented me from husbanding my bride. Admit that my own reluctance was hugely false, that I have loved and lusted after Clo all my life, and where stand I? Left in possession of a virtue by hapstance cloistered, and hence no virtue at all. Submitting to poor Zoë a fidelity, woven warp of fate's base sporting, and woof of blind accidentality. I'll not do it! 'Tis too vile! I will not lie! I'll say to her: "Forgive me, dearest one, for I have sinned. You must accept concubinage, lifelong shame, for I—"

He stopped, for a sound had come over to him. The slow, ominously quiet turning of a key in the look of the room's one door. He sat there, staring at the door, and thinking: God's blood; not again! The door opened slowly, easily, and Afaf came through it.

Alaric sat there like one turned stone; even his breath was still. All his youth, his force, his life were concentrated in his eyes. And they moved slowly, gravely, as a cornered lion's will, from Afaf's face to that naked dagger in her hand.

When he spoke, his voice was tranquil, deep.

"Wouldst kill me, Afaf?" he said.

"Yes," she whispered. "No. . . ."

He went on watching her. She seemed confused. Most of the hate had gone out of her eyes.

"Which is it?" he said.

"I—I know not," she said. "I do not want to kill you. And yet, I fear to let you live. . . ."

"Why?" Alaric said.

"Because of thy beauty, my lord Aizun! Even I—am—moved by it. As long as thy fairness of the moon, the sun, those morning-star eyes of thine exist, my master will remain enthralled, living upon the hope of one day winning thee. And by that hope, mine own is slain. He will never turn to me, now! Those plump and pretty baby boys of his were never a threat—an amusement, merely. But thou—how can my lord Ahmad help but love thee truly; when his heart of mine which hath no room for aught else but him, beats and beats at the sight of thee?"

He sat there, smiling a little. He had learned a great deal about women by then. He put up his two hands and drew apart the rags of clothing, baring his breast.

"Strike true, Afaf," he said.

She stood there, and now her amber eyes went crystalline, light-filled, shifting, blind. Dumbly, she shook her head.

"Why not?" he said.

"Mayhap for—for Zoë's sake," she whispered, "for the sake of the lusty manchild, who kicks now beneath her heart—"

He was on his feet, staring at her.

"Good God!" he said.

"No!" she flared. "I'll not lie! 'Tis not for the little Greek, nor even for the unborn bastard she claims is thine: 'Tis only—"

192

"What, Afaf?" he said.

"That I—I cannot!" she wept. "Thou art too fair, Aizun! Thou art much too fair!"

"Afaf," he said.

"Yes, my lord?"

"Come here."

She took a step toward him. Another. Stopped.

"Closer," he said.

She came up to him.

He put his arms around her. Stood there looking down at her. Then he bent and kissed her mouth. Gently, with great tenderness; with an aching sense of loss, with sorrow for this splendor that could not now ever be a part of his life. He thought suddenly of Clo's gage, with the word "If" dyed into it with her own blood. "If," she had said. "The saddest word in any language—"

Afaf drew away her mouth, looked up into his eyes. A long time. A very long time. Then she sighed.

"Come," she said, "the time grows short. You must escape. I shall help you."

"How?" he said.

"I have the key. The head eunuch gave it to me."

"Afaf—" he said.

"Truly. At a price. See—here it is."

He went on looking at her. "What was that price, Afaf?" he said.

She shrugged.

"What was it!" Alaric said.

"I let him make use of me," she said calmly, "after his dirty fashion. Cheap enough payment to remove the threat of thy beauty from my life, Lord Aizun. For since he is totally altered, not partially, like some castrates, nothing he could do was any danger to my virginity. I endured his nauseous slobbering and pawing for one hour, in exchange for this key—to thy freedom. To Zoë's happiness. To—"

"To what?" he said.

"I know not. I was about to say: To mine as well. But I doubt that now. Aizun—"

"Yes, Afaf?"

"You—you'll not desert the little Zoë, will you? She—she is dying of love for thee. Were it not for the child, she'd be dead by now. She eats nothing at all. She doth not sleep. She babbles thy name, endlessly. I think she is a little mad. She hath suffered much, you know, and—"

"Afaf," he said again.

"Yes, my lord?" she said.

"Come with me! Do not waste your life this way! There'll be someone for you. Someone else! For—"

She shook her head. "No, my lord Aizun," she said, "I cannot."

"Do not be a fool, child! Men such as he—if they can be called men—never turn to maids. So says the learned Jew ben Ezra. For that sickness there is, he swears, no cure—"

"I'll cure him," Afaf said. "I'll make him turn to me! I'll—"

"You won't. You can't. I even think you know that. Don't you, child?"

"Aye," she wept, "but 'tis so hard a thing to live without hope—" Then suddenly, mischievously, she smiled. The tears danced on the upturned corners of her mouth. "Wouldst embrace Islam, Aizun?" she said.

He stared at her; said: "Why?"

"Because then thou couldst have four wives—"

He smiled. "You tempt me, Afaf," he said, "wouldst thou that I—"

But her face was serious again. "No," she whispered. "Zoë would never consent. Nor would I, were I in her place. As your first, it is her right to refuse. So sayeth the law."

"God's death!" he swore, "what says the law?"

"The first wife can demand that her husband take no other—not even a concubine—as a condition of the marriage itself. If she exercises this right and he is not willing, then he must refuse to marry her—or, if already wed, put her by with honorable divorce—for if he doth not either of those two things, he must take her as his sole wife, lifelong. If I were Zoë, I would demand that. I should never share thee. Tell me a thing, fair Aizun—"

"If I can," Alaric said.

"Is't certain that the child she carries in her womb—this too-great child that so terribly burdens her—is, or even could be, thy own?"

"It is mine, surely," Alaric said, "Zoë would never play me false."

"Aye. Thou art right. She is a noble creature, thy Zoë. Aizun—"

"Yes, Alaf?"

"Kiss me once more. In farewell. For luck. To celebrate—what might have been—if—"

"If!" he said. "God's death, I hate that word!"

Then he bent once more and found her mouth. He kissed her a long, slow time, cherishing her lips with his own. He would have gone on kissing her even longer, if Ahmad al Hussein's voice hadn't grated on his nerves like a rusty file.

"She-goat!" Ahmad screamed. "Lecherous lump of cow dung! Whore and daughter of whores, delivered in a ditch by that great grandmother

194

of all Lesbians who was thy mother and thy father both, having conceived thee by abusing herself with a tallow candle! Must I teach thee to touch not what is mine? Nor to besmear his clean limbs with thy fishy female smell? Filth, thy name is woman! Sack of entrails! Oozing blood and stench with each change of moon! Why—"

There was something strangely comic about his wrath. Alaric could not help but smile.

"What ails you, my lord pervert?" he said.

"And thou," Ahmad shrieked, "who might have had my love—to turn to this—this—" Even in Arabic's matchless vocabulary, he could find no word obscene enough; so he drew back and clapped Afaf stingingly across the face.

Then Alaric hit him with his doubled fist. In the belly. Hard. Ahmad sat down abruptly, his long legs spread out. His fluffy combed and frizzled yellow beard bobbed with his effort to catch his breath. But when he had caught it, he did not shriek again.

"Thou, O Aizun, art too much male," he said quietly, "so now I know what to do with thee. My friend, Harith ibn Abil'Shebl, head of the Mint, hath need of a young eunuch to squire his women about when they sally forth. For that, thou wilt serve right well. I shall have thee altered before the sun sets this day!"

He got very slowly to his feet. Alaric, of course, had understood not one word he said. But Afaf fell to her knees before her master. Alaric stood there amazed at her equally incomprehensible cries, her pleas, her entreaties. Though he knew it not, she offered herself to be whipped, to be slain, to be tortured to death, anything at all, if al Hussein would desist from his intent. All of which only spurred the Moorish lordling on. He smiled.

"I promise thee, fair Afaf, thy lover's severed weapon, preserved in a flask of clear wine, that thou mayest fondle it to thy heart's content! Consolation enough, is it not, O she-camel eternally in season? Now leave me, for I must be about the arrangements—"

Alaric saw her eyes; saw them flare with that mindless rage men only feel toward one who has been greatly beloved. He leaped toward her, impelled by something swifter than thought, than memory, thrusting her arm aside before he saw the dull blue lightning flash of that blade. In one way he was in time, in another too late. He turned Afaf's poniard far enough aside to miss the Moorish lordling's vitals, but not so far as to leave Ahmad unhurt. The edge of the dagger slid along al Hussein's rib, cutting a gash fully five inches long, which, while neither deep nor dangerous, bled frightfully.

Ahmad clapped a hand to his side, took it away, stared at it—at what it was covered with now, at what dripped spectacularly between his fingers. He took a backward step. His face went white to the lips.

"Compassionate Allah!" he whispered. "The wench hath killed me! I—I die!" Then quite abruptly, he measured his length upon the floor.

There was no time to examine al Hussein, no opportunity to determine the gravity of his wound. Nor, in sober truth, did it occur to Alaric to do so. The Moorish lordling's robes prevented their seeing how slight the gash actually was, while the spreading stains upon them magnified it out of all proportion to its relative insignificance. Besides, the months of warfare, of suffering he had undergone, had so hardened Alaric as to make him forget his own youthful sickness at the sight of blood. He put out his hand to Afaf, believing his own attempt to save Ahmad al Hussein's life had failed; not realizing that this malaise of the glands, nerves, blood, this induced emotional distortion strong enough to warp a man away from the basic male hungers into this futile, sterile denial of life's essential continuity, would naturally enough, by reason of its hysterical quasi femininity, extend to the ridiculous extreme of causing him to swoon at so small a hurt, to feel death itself in the sting of a little cut. Nor, upon the visible evidence, was it strange that Alaric believed Afaf's stroke mortal; for terror had lent Ahmad al Hussein's face a convincingly deathlike pallor, and shock had slowed his breathing into imperceptibility.

But Afaf hung there, resisting the pull of Alaric's hand about her wrists. Bending above her fallen master, her dark face was ravaged.

"Afaf—" Alaric began.

But she slapped the key into the palm of his hand, and dropped upon her knees beside al Hussein. Bending forward, she kissed the bearded mouth. But the Moorish lordling's head lolled lifelessly out from beneath hers. She knelt there, with both hands pressed against her own cheeks, staring at him.

"Afaf—" Alaric said again.

Then loudly, terribly, she began to scream.

Alaric heard the sound of running feet, converging upon that room. Bending, he swept a muscular arm about her waist, and lifted her bodily from the floor. It was like trying to carry off a lioness; her nails tore his face; her teeth sank into his throat; but he hung onto her grimly, pounding down flight after flight of stairs, until he had reached the street level. But there, to unlock that door, he had to put her down. The moment he did so, she whirled, blurring sight with the speed of her dash back up those stairs.

He started after her, but the elephantine herd of eunuchs were upon her by then; two of them bore her up the stairs, while the other three stretched out their hands to seize him. What saved him was the fact that they had already ascertained that their master lived; that, moreover, the Sahib Ahmad al Hussein ibn Maliki, was not even badly hurt. So, knowing how whimsical a fancy Lord Ahmad had, how often and capriciously it changed, how little enduring was his wrath, especially when directed against so fair a youth as this, they kept their daggers sheathed, depended upon their bulk and numbers to bring Aizun the Goth's son down.

Their miscalculation was very nearly total. Five mighty warriors would have had difficulty in holding Alaric Teudisson, now. Being what they were—things reduced to dropsidical grossness, their formerly hard male muscles softened into rolls of torpid grease—they had no slightest chance of retaining him. "How many jackals add up to one lion?" he thought, and won free of them with quite ridiculous ease.

He plunged into the protective darkness of the streets. Behind him, he could hear the eunuchs' lumbering footfalls halt; in a foot race their unnatural fat put them out of the running at the outset; and they knew it.

He ran on blindly until even his stout lungs could bear no more. Then he halted, leaned against an archway, panting.

"Afaf! Afaf!" he wept inside his heart. "I have not loved before this hour! I shall never love again. I swear it! Oh, Afaf, I—"

Then he moved on through the darkness toward Solomon ben Ezra's house.

X

The manservant who opened the door was clearly afraid. In Córdoba, at this hour, a visitor could only be the police or an armed robber. But what he saw, even by his lantern's feeble light, reassured him. The young visitor was unarmed, his clothes in sad disarray, and his blond fairness bespoke other blood than Moorish.

"May I ask the Sahib his name?" the manservant said.

"Alaric, son of Teudis, Lord of Tarabella the Greater," Alaric said; then, as the servant bowed, in preparation to withdraw, he added quickly: "Willst tell the maid Zoë I am here?"

The sound of her cry, echoing from an inner room, was a shattering of the very fabric of silence; it drove into his ears, sharp, penetrant; and to him, oddly, it had the feel of cold. He reflected tiredly upon how limited the means for expression of any real emotion are; beyond a certain point, tears must serve for the extremities of both joy and grief. He could hear her footsteps now coming on; they were heavy, faltering, slow; and it came to him that more than seven months had passed since last he had held her in his arms, had seen her small face twist into that tortured grimace of intolerable anguish that served to depict equally intolerable ecstasy—if he needed further proof of the frail human machinery's scant capacity for showing clearly what it sensed or felt, or thought, or dreamed; time enough to have left her gravid with his unhallowed fruit; time enough to destroy that lightness, that grace which had seemed to him always poised to skip or scamper; that needed only some such hint of a breeze far less weighty than a lover's sigh to dance airborne like a leaf, a cloud—

And now, hearing her coming, dragging toward him like some over-burdened beast—or like one mortally wounded, worked or driven unto death, the thought leaped unbidden into his mind—he had time to think on what 'twould be like to have a son; and he shuddered, as though seized of a palsy. He looked down at his hands and arms, crisscrossed and striped with the scars of multiple sword cuts; and before his eyes rose the pallid corpses of all the men he had cut down. A murderer's blood will course through your veins, son of mine, he thought, damning you forever; and on your forehead will be the mark of Cain—

He got to his feet, because she had come into the room—or half into it, for in the doorway she stopped and stared at him out of eyes that had almost totally eclipsed her face; her tiny head was skeletal on its wisp of a throat, her mouth an agony of tenderness, a hurt of longing, a wound of love, bleeding the life out of her; none of them—neither head nor eyes nor mouth nor throat—had any discernible relation to that grotesquely swollen monstrosity upon pipestem legs which had minded him once (in another life, another world, some seven eons ago) of a jungle orchid's slender stalk, blowing toward him sweetly, gaily, lightly, upon a summer's breath.

"Zoë," he whispered, pity and repulsion waging bitter war within his heart. "Oh, Zoë!" And he put out his arms to her.

But she did not move. She leaned there against the doorframe, her eyes blackening beyond night, as he came to her. She put out one arm that was a parchment of gray-white skin stretched taut over fragile bones, and let her fingers tremble, ghostly and remote, upon the furrows Afaf had clawed into his face, across the purpling, ugly, beginning-to-swell double semicircle of teeth marks on his throat. When she spoke, her voice was death itself, dust-dry and rattling, a scatter of dead leaves, wind-driven down a stony highroad on a bitter day.

"I am—thy slave, my lord Alaric!" she whispered. "And naught but what thou hast made of me. But what thou hast made of me is the mother of thy firstborn son—which is so high and proud a thing that surely even thou hast no right to dishonor it thus!"

Then she hid her face against the doorframe, and quietly, terribly, began to weep.

He made, in his inexperience, the classic mistake: he tried to explain. Life had not yet taught him how futile that approach is, with men and women alike. He did not know that the only respect-compelling attitude toward any accusation, true or false, is: "Take me or leave me as I am, and be damned!"—that explanations, however truthful, reduce a man to the knave's, the lackey's role, placing him upon a plane of humiliating inferiority from which there is no recovery possible without fatal injury to dignity and to pride. Worse, explanations are almost never believed. When they are accepted, it is for reasons of the acceptor's own, having naught on earth to do with our humbly proffered "whys." Zoë went on weeping, her back turned to him, while he stammered out his account of al Hussein's death, the reasons for Afaf's fury.

He was still trying to convince her when Solomon ben Ezra came into the room.

"Say that again!" he snapped. "You killed that sodomite?"

"No," Alaric whispered, "not I, good physician. Afaf struck the blow. I tried to thrust her hand aside, but—"

The physician looked at his face and throat.

"Because of—this?" he said dryly.

"Nay, learned leech!" Alaric said, anger hardening his voice so that now, accidentally, he took the proper tone. "I know not why she struck him—mayhap because of what he said to her—he was screaming at her like a fishwife in that barking of desert dogs that serves them as a tongue. Yet afterward she repented of her deed; determined to stay there and pay with her life for it. I tried to bear her away to save her from her own folly, and she—"

"A likely tale!" ben Ezra chuckled.

"Likely or not, 'tis true!" Alaric stormed. "What species of a goat or a swine think ye both I am? She had already told me that Zoë was with child, a fact I knew not till then—"

"Why not?" ben Ezra said. "The dropping of breeches, and the lifting of skirts have a fairly sure result when indulged in with sufficient frequency; and certain 'tis that you rode more leagues by night than by day upon your homeward voyage, young Goth—"

"I knew it not," Alaric said, and his voice was harsh, flat, calm. "Would you oaths, Jew? Upon my mother's grave—she whose throat was cut by the banu Djilliki's Berbers because she was past the age for carnal sport. I swear it! I further swear I have known no other maid but Zoë in all my life. What shall I swear that upon? Mayhap upon the honor that my sister was ravished of when she was sold into slavery here in Córdoba. Or would you rather that I swear upon the coif and veil that were ripped from the gentle nun who nursed my brother in his final agony? Or, methinks, I should take my oath upon the blood from these wounds with which I have bedewed so much dry and thirsty ground—"

Zoë had turned by then, and was looking at him, staring at the scars that showed through the rags al Hussein's eunuchs had ripped his robes into; at the rents and whorls and crescents silvery upon him, at that long gash Leovigild had slashed down his left arm; at the look of a warrior prince; at the set of a young lion bristling in his pride, and all unaware, her tears slowed, almost ceased to flow—

"And your father?" ben Ezra said. "God grant no ills have befallen him; for, by my troth, he is both a gentle man and just. I own I liked him well."

"No ills?" Alaric whispered. "Aye, good leech, no ills—if life itself is not an ill. He lives—though of the sickness of drawing breath time hath in its fullness a certain cure. No ills—if to be bereft of loving wife, both sons—one dead, as thou knowest well, of a bowman's cowardly shaft; the other sold to appease a pederast's lust—his daughter likewise taken, sold, for which gentle use and treatment my tongue refuses the vile utterance—his soldiers slain, some five of them crucified before his eyes—and before mine, good leech, and before mine! If these be not ills, why then my lord father hath indeed no ills; nor in sweet, kindly truth has any man!"

"Alaric—" Zoë whispered.

"Aye, Zoë?" Alaric said. "Aye, good my lady and my wife? Aye, Lady Countess of Tarabella the Greater, and of the Lesser, too, since of that princely house no single male survives? Aye, lady mother of a future lord to be—thought of what, I ask you, God? Of bleached and whitening bones? Of a ruined rude heap of stones? Of darkness and of death? But I stray. My mind wanders. Aye, gentle Zoë, who sees in me but a whoremonger, a fancier of trulls and trollops? What would you of this lewd and lecherous beast?"

"Oh, Alaric, please!" she wept.

"Ah, but I am not pleased! I should have been pleased had you met me with a loving kiss. I should have been pleased to sit and hold your hand and plan a kingdom, hacked, if need be, out of the hides of all my foes, that you might queen it over, and as a patrimony for our son. But doubts please me not, nor bootless accusations. So now, what would the lady Countess of the humblest of her servants, standing before her clad in the rags of his clothing and the tatters of his honor?"

"That you forgive me, good my lord," she whispered.

"Done!" He laughed, and kissed her. "How now, my Zoë? God's death! Except for that great tun of a belly, you are but skin and bones! Is it thus that you care for my lady and my son—by starving them equally and mutually to death?"

"Aye," ben Ezra said. "I pray God that now that you're here, I can get a sup or two into her. She runs great risks, my lord—as she is now, that great monster you left in her is like to cost her life—"

"Good God!" Alaric said.

"Amen," ben Ezra said. "Now speak to me of this of the pervert; for much do I fear that our Zoë must bear with your further absence for yet a while—"

"Oh, no!" Zoë wailed.

"Oh, yes," ben Ezra said. "For if he has been party to the killing of a man so highly placed as that practicer of the swinish abomination for which God destroyed Sodom and Gomorrah, his life will not be worth an obol or a fal here in Córdoba."

"Then mine will be worth even less," Zoë said simply, "for if he dies, I'll die."

"You're like to die as it is, of a too avid embracing of female folly," the doctor said. "But hold your tongue, daughter, if that be possible, while your warrior lord tells me of the pervert's death. . . ."

"Hmnnn—" ben Ezra said, once the tale was done. "Less bad. To me the essential thing is to get you out of Córdoba, young Goth—and for some years, till this thing is quite forgot. Fortunately, Ahmad al Hussein, old Prince Maliki's son, hath no kindred that I know—and he himself has removed from his life the possibility of heirs who would normally avenge him. So, but one problem remains—time. Already one can make out the minaret of the mosque against the sky. Dawn comes on apace, I fear. Yet, before noon, you must be well on your way. I shall send you to a friend of mine—the wealthiest merchant in Toledo. His name is Hasdai ben Sahl; mark that well. He will give you employ; your knowledge of the Greek tongue will be of great value to him; and from him you can learn much. He is a man of the highest probity: the direct opposite of his bitterest rival, that swine ibn Ha'ad. A scholar. A Talmudist, of course. His Hebrew is exquisite; his Latin classical. You'd better be prepared to crack your head on Aristotle, Plato, and Socrates, as well as upon his Byzantine accounts. One warning: he has a son, a youth of your age, one Saadyah. Stay clear of that ne'er-do-well. Saadyah's never earned an honest penny in his life—or, to be fair, a dishonest one, for that matter. Knocks about with poets, dancing girls, gamblers, pimps, public women, and other riffraff—all of which poor Hasdai could stand were it not for that young clown's complete dedication to rationalism. Denies all religions as nonsense—even ours. You'd have to know Hasdai ben Sahl to understand how all that sits upon his stomach. But no matter. First, while we procure you decent clothes to cover your too attractive nakedness, I'll write to Hasdai a letter—in Hebrew, which will slow matters somewhat—I'm out of practice—"

"Master—" Zoë whispered.

"Aye, child?" ben Ezra said.

"Will your friend receive me, too? For whither Alaric goeth, there also shall I go—you know the verse?"

"The Book of Ruth. To be sure, he'll allow our northern barbarian to bring along his wife. That's not the problem. The problem is that you're entirely unfit for travel. I forbid it. As your physician, I forbid it absolutely. You'd abort before you got to the Iron Gate, and die of a hemorrhage before I could be fetched to save you—"

"Oh, master!" Zoë said.

"Besides which, you'd slow this young heathen down so much they'd catch him two leagues beyond the walls. And since they'd likely crucify him for so serious a crime as this, I'd have you dead—or mad upon my hands in any event—"

"Dead," Zoë whispered. "I'd take mine own life before witnessing that—"

"Zoë—" Alaric said reproachfully.

"The matter's not all that desperate," ben Ezra said. "Two months from now—no, say four—after you've had your Goth bastard, and recuperated, I'll send you to Toledo with a reasonable chance of your getting there alive. Fits in well. Gives Alaric time to establish himself, which, if he stays out of Saadyah's clutches and applies himself, will not be difficult. The very contrast between him and that disgrace to all Jewry will help matters.

"Now, enough of talk. Zoë, child, think you that you can apply the arts I taught you? For 'tis nearly daylight now, and he must pass the gate. What say you to—a Byzantine priest, bearing letters to his patriarch signed by our local bishop over some matter in dispute between the Eastern and Western rites of your Nazarenes? A man well sunk in age so that the special guards will be inclined toward gentleness toward his years—and toward his sanctity? You know the Emir is most stern toward those who abuse the dissenting minority faiths within his realm, so they're sure to let him pass if they see not through his disguise. I'll attend to the holy forgery, while you, daughter, alter his looks. But subtly. Don't make his hair black—that would only call attention to the blueness of his eyes. Brown—mouse-brown well sprinkled with gray. A beard to match, reaching to his knees. Color his skin, too; but lightly. A cinnamon here—like a well-baked cake. Wrinkles, resinous gum to pucker his forehead into lines, then the dye over that; and you'd better apply the stain to his whole body; those guards can be a suspicious lot of louts at times. Feel up to it, child? Or shall I call Sarah?"

"No!" Zoë said. "Any other woman who touches him, dies!"

Alaric smiled. "You are ready, then, to make of me an ancient bearded monkey of a priest, my Zoë?"

"No," Zoë whispered, "or rather yes, because I must; though I should much prefer that 'tis time that makes you ancient and bearded, as time will. And reduce me, too, in its fullness to a palsied quavering crone—even that, Oh love of my life, will be a fulfillment, as long as we suffer it together. Now come, let me make thee old and ugly, and thus keep thee safe until I am once more at thy side—"

Riding away from ben Ezra's house in the full light of day, accompanied by the manservant the physician had wisely sent along as a living completion of his disguise—for in all good truth so venerable a priest would not normally ride alone, needing at least one retainer to care for him on the way, and ben Ezra had provided that retainer lest the guards at the gate find his absence odd—Alaric could feel the sadness in him like a weight, crushing his very bones. To an enormous extent, he had had his youth hacked and torn away from him in the tenderest bloom of his years, by cruelty, sorrow, deception, treachery, pain. But some of it persisted still; and the form that it took was confusion: a certain indecision of the heart. In all other things—force, purposefulness, reserve, soberness, seriousness of thought—Alaric Teudisson was a man long before his time; but his vagrant heart had beat not yet nineteen years, and was incapable of true election—if any man's heart ever is, at any age.

He knew full well that Zoë was worthy, that having passed her lying in and brought forth his son, she would surely regain her comeliness, nay, more—after the fashion of contented women, she would add to it, becoming softer, rounded, matronly. But he could not force Afaf's imperious, regal Egyptian beauty from his mind; the more so because she had rejected him, and for so unworthy a rival! Slowly, insidiously, the longing for the forbidden fruit gnawed like a subtle serpent at his heart. And, at the same time, to compound confusion, the thought of Clothilde, whose beauty, and thereby her life, he had so basely ruined.

At that thought, he pulled up his richly caparisoned mule—ben Ezra having decided that having him ride the humble sexless beast instead of a princely palfrey would lend more verisimilitude to his disguise—and his eyes went sick in his stained and bearded face. The shame that coiled within his belly now was a cold and slimy thing. It had the taste of utter vileness. He had stormed at Zoë, at the proud and prickly Jew, in defense of his own innocence; and now, within the appallingly short space of four months—the two which still remained before Zoë would be brought to bed of his sons, and the two more that would be needful for so small and slight a woman as she to recover from what promised to be uncommonly difficult delivery—he would be faced with the all but impossible task of convincing Zoë that his marriage to Clothilde had been both forced upon him and unconsummated. It was characteristic of Alaric's honesty when dealing with those he loved—for he had come reluctantly to accept the uses of trickery against his foes—that the simple fact that he needed only to keep his mouth shut and enter into a compassionate act of bigamy with Zoë, knowing the chances of this kindly deception being exposed were practically nonexistent, did not even enter his head.

The problem, as he conceived of it, was thorny: both Zoë and the physician had seen Clothilde, had gazed upon her blond and radiant loveliness. What remote possibility existed, then, that they would, or could, believe that he had touched her not? The thing was incredible even to him; the individual causes for his abstention seemed to him now explicable only in terms of witchcraft; surely both he and Clo had fallen prey to the mechanisms of some evil spirit. His boyish, innocent wish to keep his vows to Zoë, his anger at being forced into a marriage which, truth to tell, he had desired all his life and which had come to him, maddeningly enough, only after he had surrendered all hope of ever achieving it; Clo's rancor at his childish act of pique, that business of sleeping apart from her, that first night of what should have been their honeymoon—all these were within the bounds of human error, and believable as such. But could he, dared he say that the chastity he'd worn like a hair shirt thereafter had been an act of will on either his part, or on Clo's? No—there clearly to be seen was the intervention of fate, or malignant spirits, of the Devil—or of God.

And worse still was the near impossibility of bringing the matter before the ecclesiastical courts—all the proofs needful for an annulment had vanished amid the rubble of his former life. Such a churchly bill was entirely neeful now, for Zoë—poor, tired, heavy, tormented Zoë, suffering his love in her very flesh—had become a convert to the One True Church, Roman, Apostolic, Catholic, Eternal, having abandoned her subtle eastern creed for his sake. Therefore—

"Good my lord," the servant said fearfully, "why do you tarry? 'Tis hard upon nine hours, now! And 'twould be better that we passed the gate right soon, for—"

"Aye," Alaric sighed. "Thou hast much right, Yacob. Come—"

But his priestly mule had not taken two more strides before he pulled the beast up again.

"My lord!" Yacob shrilled. "I tell thee—"

"Be quiet, Yacob," Alaric said. "That fine canopied litter there, borne by those slaves, who by the sweat that covers them have been running long and hard—that lump of beardless fat that rides before it—it seemeth me—Stop them, Yacob! Bring them here!"

Yacob stared at the venerable bearded figure that hid the semblance of a young and princely lord.

"Stop them, I say!" Alaric said.

Yacob shrugged, kicked his own mule forward, turned it sidewise, blocking completely the narrow cobblestoned street that led to ben Ezra's house.

"Way!" the heavy figure on the white horse shrieked. "Make way, fool! I have a dying woman in that litter! I must see that she is attended by the Jew at once!"

"Silence, eunuch!" Yacob said. "My lord his Holy Eminence, would have a word with you. And surely his blessing is worth more to the dying than the black arts of a Jew dog!"

Alaric wondered momentarily why Yacob thus gratuitously scrupled not to insult his own religion and his race. Then it came to him: Yacob was probably of Christian origin, and one of those who, as ben Ezra had said this morning, convert to Judaism in order to obtain their freedom after seven years' service. That freedom gained, and hugging to his bosom the bounty which was incumbent upon his former master to add in such a case, good Yacob would promptly become a Christian once again; and spend the rest of his days amassing wealth upon the basis of that bounty, and the arts he'd learned in ben Ezra's house. All of which, Alaric thought wryly, will not prevent him from joyously reviling his former master at every second breath. Man, thy name is falsity!

Conscious of the eunuch's puzzled, uncertain stare, Alaric rode toward the little group.

"Good servant," he said, making his voice majestic and slow, "what have you in that litter?"

"A woman, your Eminence," the eunuch said, "who hath been whipped so cruelly that I fear for her existence. She made a foolish, unthinking attempt upon her master's life, for love of a pretty youth—and her lord ordered her flogged to death. A most inhuman sentence for a scratch that is already healed!"

"A scratch!" Alaric said. "Then al Hussein is not dead?"

The eunuch's eyes opened wide in his full moon of a face.

"Your Eminence—" he whispered. "It seemeth me that—" Then his little eyes narrowed. "Thou!" he said.

"Aye," Alaric said. "I—who have not the makings of a mummer. Nor a conspirator, either. Tell me, eunuch, wouldst betray me?"

The eunuch stared at him. Turned away his heavy face. Kept it averted a long, slow time. Turned back again.

"No, my lord," he said.

"Why not?" Alaric said. "Thou art no coward, that I know."

"For—Afaf's sake," the eunuch sighed, "who loves thee. As I love her. But butchered as I am, maimed, of my manhood deprived, my love is but a mockery. Take her, my lord! Bear her off with thee. For here in Córdoba her life is now worth a fal—"

"You said she is dying," Alaric said.

"She will die more cruelly if she stays here. Mayhap Allah will show her the favor she deserves, and let her live. For now there is no time. She must fly with thee—not even for the Jew's ministrations must we let this opportunity escape. Once beyond the walls, you can hide in that thick pine wood some twelve leagues from here till I bring the Jew to thee. If she be not dead by then, her life will be saved—"

"My lord," Yacob said, "do not entertain this folly. What care you for the life of a Moorish wench? I tell thee—"

Which was as far as he got. The eunuch's arms—which Alaric knew from having fought against him, retained a surprising amount of muscle still, concealed beneath the unnatural fat—shot out; his giant hand clamped around Yacob's throat; powerful fingers squeezed.

Alaric waited calmly until Yacob's face had turned a lovely shade of blue. Then he said, mildly enough: "Do not kill this dog, good eunuch, though well he deserves his death. We shall have need of him, you and I—or at least of his mount." Then, turning to the manservant, he said: "Get you down, Yacob, and regain your master's house afoot, for now your mule must serve to bear away her who saved mine honor and my life. Speak of this clearly to the learned Jew; but to the maid Zoë, no word, mind you! Or else my friend the al fata will squeeze harder the next time; will you not, "O head of al Hussein's household?"

"Aye, that I will," the eunuch said, "and with great pleasure. This scum hath occupied space and breathed air for too long, now!"

The manservant hurled himself from the mule. As he scurried away, it came to Alaric whom the Jew's slave reminded him of: Julio. There was no physical resemblance at all; but through their different flesh their common swinehood showed.

He got down from his own mule and pulled aside the curtains of the canopied litter, that luxurious couch mounted on long, springy shafts, piled high with silken cushions, and covered against covetous male eyes in which the noble, rich, and highborn Muslim dames were borne about upon the shoulders of stalwart slaves. A sweet and sickly odor of some healing balm smote him in the face; and through it, the heavy scent of blood. Afaf lay face down on the litter. She was entirely and understandably naked; for, from her neck to her heels, her whole back was one purpling, bloody, lacerated mass of striped and broken flesh. She was very still. He could not see whether she breathed or not.

"Afaf," he wept. "Oh, Afaf, my love, my own—"

The eunuch stared at him.

"Cease to weep, young lord," he said, "or you'll ruin your disguise past all repair. And 'tis needful that you retain it. Come, let us take council together. How can we arrange it that you may bear her beyond the gates?"

Alaric frowned, then his eyes cleared.

"Tell the slaves to lash the poles of the litter between my mule and the one that Yacob rode," he said. "In 'that fashion I can bear her away easily enough, even, doubt it not, with a certain comfort—"

"And the guards?" the eunuch said. "How will you explain so rare a sight as this to them, my lord?"

"We must turn her over, face up, and cover her. I'll tell the guards she is my wife whom I am bearing to a holy shrine in the East to cure her of the terrible sickness which is fallen upon her—"

"But, my lord!" the eunuch protested. "Remember that you are supposed to be a priest!"

"An eastern priest, good eunuch, who takes no vows of chastity, as all the world knows," Alaric said.

"True—I'd forgotten that," the eunuch muttered.

"Tell me thy name, friend," Alaric said.

" 'Tis Hagib, good my lord."

"Then, Hagib, I would know a thing: how came you to bear her so easily and publicly from al Hussein's house? It seemeth me that if he were so bent upon her death—"

"He thought her dead already," Hagib said grimly, "and that I bore forth a corpse. He knew that I loved her, having always held it the richest of all jests, so he granted me my plea to give her decent burial. . . ."

"He did not trouble himself, then, to make sure?" Alaric said.

"He troubled himself enough, the perverted dog!" Hagib said. 'Twas an awful thing, my lord! He could not watch it long, you see, because he hath this falling sickness at the sight of blood—which is why he fainted at the scratch poor Afaf gave him, and led you to think him killed. So he retired to the next room, and listened to her screams and the sound of the lash biting into her flesh. As soon as she had ceased to scream and had fallen into a swoon, I ordered the whipping stopped, but he rushed back into the room and mastered his weakness long enough to ascertain that she lived still. He commanded Joaquin to go on beating her—the poor black had tears in his eyes, for even Africans have feelings, good my Lord—but he dared not disobey. I died a thousand deaths, I tell you that! At last, when one needed to put a silver mirror to her mouth and determine only thus that she lived, I stopped it. I held the little mirror beneath my arm until it was so warm her breath no longer clouded it, thus convincing that degenerate swine she was dead."

"He shall pay for this!" Alaric said.

"Aye, good my lord," the eunuch said, "by the Prophet's very beard, pay he shall!"

Alaric looked toward where the slaves were tightening the last of the knots which bound the litter's poles to the mules' saddle girths.

"Why did you tarry so long, Hagib," he said, "before bringing her to the Jew?"

"I dared not, before. I feared that she might die. I bore her to my quarters, and nursed her till the dawn. My lord, will you tarry a while near her till the Jew can come?"

"Yes," Alaric said, "and in the pine forest you suggested. I remember it well, having camped there twice—on both my journeys to Córdoba. I'll halt hard by the road, openly, as an old man with a sick wife would—"

He put out his hand to Hagib.

"If ever I have need of a steward for my house—willst come to me, good Hagib?" he said.

"Aye, my lord. Allah willing—and if I live," the eunuch said.

There was one bad moment at the gates when a surly guard poked his head through the curtains of the canopy that covered the litter.

"The woman's sick, you say?" he growled. "It seemeth me ye bear off a comely maid for lewd purposes, dog of a Nazarene! Sick—hmmm—she doth have an air of malaise. Tell me, ancient billy goat, what sickness hath this maid?"

"The pest," Alaric said; and watched in grim satisfaction as the guard howled: "Pest! Get thee gone, graybeard!" and fled like a man pursued by djinn and demons back to his post.

Long before ben Ezra reached them, Afaf had regained consciousness. She did not moan, or move, or cry out, but lay there staring at him with grave and questioning eyes.

"Afaf—" he murmured; and her eyes opened wide at the sound of his voice. She put out her hand and touched the long false beard he wore. With one great jerk, he tore it from his face; which cost him some pain because his own had begun to sprout beneath it, and the gum which held it to his face yanked out his own fine blonde whiskers by the roots in several places, and here and there a strip of skin as well.

He could see her lips move, but her voice was below sound. He leaned close. Her breath was rank with the smell of blood. Inside her mouth, her tongue was a swollen, purplish mass, where she had sunk her teeth into it until they met in a vain attempt to lock in her cries. He thought that what she said was "Aizun"; but then, it could have been "My lord." He could not be sure. What he was sure of was that he could not bear her eyes, face the intolerable sadness in them now.

"Afaf," he wept, "my poor, poor Afaf—"

She put up her hand with great effort, let her fingers touch his cheek. His tears spilled over them. Somehow that seemed to comfort her. He sat there beside her, holding her hand in his, until toward evening, ben Ezra came.

The physician climbed down from his horse.

"How now, Aizun?" he said gruffly. "She lives still?"

"Aye," Alaric said, "but why do you call me 'Aizun,' good leech?"

"Because at heart thou art a Moor—at least as far as women are concerned—"

"Or, mayhap, a patriarch of ancient Jewry?" Alaric shot back at him.

"Well answered!" Ben Ezra laughed. "I see you know our history. At any event, 'tis not your fault you were born too fair for your own good. Now stand aside, my lord polygamist, and let me have a look at her—"

The physican's examination was brief. But when it was done, he went to work at once. He cleansed her stripes with a pale liquid from one of the many flasks he bore. She moaned deep in her throat at the bite of it. Then he applied a sort of thick salve, creamy and white, and having a most pleasant smell. At once Afaf relaxed and made soft murmuring sounds of relief and contentment. Alaric stared at her in pure wonderment.

"How goes she, learned sage?" he whispered.

"She'll live," ben Ezra said, "though she'll bear the scars of the whipping to her grave. I've applied a healing salve, the secret of which I got of a Persian magus's slave ibn Ha'ad brought back from the East. I'll leave a store of it in your hands, sufficient to last until you reach Toledo. But I'd better write out the formula for it, in case she is not entirely healed by the time your supply of the balm is gone—"

The physician turned to the pack mule he'd led behind his horse, and took down his folding table and collapsible stool. From one of the many leathern bags with which the mule was festooned, he took out pots of ink, goose quills, rolls of thick, fine silken paper. Then with grave calm he cut his quills and began to write in Arabic.

"God's death!" Alaric swore. "You act as though we were in your dispensary! At any moment now, they—"

"They," ben Ezra yawned, "haven't even left Córdoba. There's no pursuit as yet. Which is all to the good. You can rest here tonight, which is precisely what she needs—"

"No pursuit?" Alaric said. "Why—"

"The sodomite counts you already beyond his reach—and considering the illegal methods by which he obtained you, he dare not raise the hue and cry. As for this poor child, it seems he believes her dead. A night's rest will do wonders for her. That balm's very nearly miraculous in its powers of healing. I confess I don't understand how it works; but work

210

it does. In that basket there, if 'tis not beneath your dignity to take it down, are wine, fruits, cakes, and a cold boiled chicken. Give her to sup. She needs food to restore her. By morning, her pain will have lessened considerably, and much of her strength returned. Then ride with her to Toledo. Though, by my troth, this doth raise up a problem. But I forget; you give this receipt to the Syrian chemist, in the Street of Goldsmiths, and he'll prepare the balm for you; but I beg of you not to tell him what use it hath, or he'll attempt to manufacture it in bulk, which will spoil it quite—"

"I'll do that," Alaric said. "But tell me, learned Doctor, what problem does my riding with Afaf to Toledo call up?"

"A grave one. Hasdai ben Sahl is an upright man, and very strict. One wife he'll accept of you; but two, no. To remain in his employ, you'll have to choose between this rarely lovely child, and Zoë—"

"What choice have I?" Alaric said. "Zoë carries my child. But since al Hussein is not dead, nor even greatly hurt, what need is there for me to flee? I'd much prefer to remain in Córdoba with Zoë and—"

Solomon ben Ezra shook his head in wonder.

"Your alternations 'twixt manhood and childish lack of thought never cease to astonish me," he said. "For murder, and a failing attempt at it, the difference is slight when the victim of either is as highly placed as that practicer of abominations. You'd die in any event. His response will be exactly that of a thwarted woman: blind, unreasoning hate. Your scorning him sealed your fate—and the wound this eastern beauty gave him serves well enough for excuse. Soon he will rouse himself from his present stupor long enough to realize that while you live he runs some risk of being exposed for the crimes of abduction and conspiracy. When he does, he'll soon set himself the task—for which he is well fitted, doubt it not!—of elaborating a tissue of lies intricate enough to hide his own guilt in these matters, and to persuade al Rahman to issue a warrant for your arrest. This he *must* do if you remain in Córdoba where your presence will feed daily his anger, his lust, his jealousy, and his fears—"

"And if I flee to Toledo as planned?" Alaric said.

"He'll gradually forget, come to feel secure again, find, or buy himself, another pretty youth to love; then you'll be safe. Now tell me, Aizun ibn al Qutiyya—Alaric Teudisson—what propose you to do about this maid who hath suffered so cruelly for your sake?"

"I know not. Could not your friend take her likewise into his employ —as a servant, say? She has many skills, that I know—"

"I doubt not that you do," ben Ezra said dryly.

"That one skill I know not if she possesses at all," Alaric flared. "For that she is virgin still I'd be willing to stake my life!"

"A matter sometimes easy—sometimes impossible to ascertain," ben Ezra said, "since an awkward fall, too rough a gallop while riding astride, even a curious, exploring finger can destroy the apparent signs of virginity. However, I'll accept your word that you, at least, are innocent of her—"

"Again," Alaric said tartly, "for you'd already accepted it once before on this very issue. No matter. I'll tell the merchant that I brought her with me to save her life, in recompense for the fact that she hath saved mine—and at great cost. If you will lend me a sum of gold at what usury you will, I'll hire her lodging apart from me, and the services of a woman skilled in nursing to care for her until she is well. Thereafter I shall support her with my earnings like a sister till she is wed, and settle a dowry upon her, too, if I have gained wealth enough by then—"

"Spoken like a true and gentle man," ben Ezra said. "A most laudable intent. But I'd advise you to inform ben Sahl freely of all this. For, if he discover it later, you'll be hard put to convince him you are not as loose of morals as his own clownish lout of a son. You're not too young to realize that what a man has suffered becomes a sore and galling spot in his heart, causing him to judge others in that particular with unmitigated harshness. So it is with Hasdai; he hath become a zealot in matters of moral purity and religious faith—"

Afaf said something then. The words came out muffled, distorted by her swollen tongue. But from their sound, Alaric realized he could not have understood her in any event; for 'twas in Arabic she spoke and to the physician.

Ben Ezra stared at her.

"You wish it, child?" he said in Romance.

Afaf nodded weakly. The physician turned to Alaric.

"I beg of you to apart yourself from here," he said, "or at least to turn your back. She asks of me a certificate of virginity, granting me the right to examine her. 'Twill be of use, Alaric. With your high station so sadly reduced, what I offer you may be, God willing, the means of your finding a new road to wealth and power; but any doubt of your probity, your decency, your honor, would ruin you from the outset with Hasdai ben Sahl, embittered as he is by Saadyah's goatish folly. I pray thee, young lord, turn aside thy face—"

Slowly Alaric turned his back. After some moments he heard the physician give a curiously gentle sigh.

"Virgin and intact," ben Ezra said, "so entirely that your bridegroom will have his work before him on thy wedding night. God grant thee a patient, gentle man with naught of brutishness in him, my child, or—"

He stopped, following the light-locked pointing of her gaze; watched it soften.

"'O Lord, my Lord, how excellent is Thy Name in all the Earth!'" he quoted; then added, with a sound halfway between a chuckle and a groan: "But couldst Thou not have made life a little simpler, O Master of the World?"

Ben Ezra then wrote out for Afaf the certificate she sought, in Arabic, Romance, Latin, and Hebrew. Before departing, he handed Alaric a purse and said, "Repay me when you can—and without usury. And God be with you, ibn al Qutiyya!"

"I thank thee, good physician, both for thy blessing and thy help," Alaric said.

"The blessing counts far more. So here's another one: May God's wisdom shine upon thee, and enlighten thy heart."

"Amen," Alaric whispered. But watching the wise doctor riding away, it was not light that he felt. Rather it was a darkness without end, a night which bore no promise of a dawn.

XI

In the blue mist of dawn, from where he lay some yards apart from the litter, a sound awakened him. He looked up and saw Afaf. She had wrapped herself in the sheets, in order to cover her nakedness, and was clinging to the canopy, trying not to fall.

With two great leaping strides, he was at her side. Sadly she smiled at him.

"Nay, good my lord," she said, the words heavy and thick, but much clearer than they had been the night before, " 'Tis not meet that you aid me, now. If you will have the goodness to cut me a staff to hobble upon, it will suffice. Please, Lord Aizun?"

"Methinks my arm is staff enough," he began, but she shook her head.

"If I were your wife, or even promised unto you, 'twould be acceptable. But now, 'tis not. The body is an ugly beast, its natural functions unlovely. You'll permit me to attend to them alone? It seemeth me you've shown my modesty some respect. I pray thee, continue to. I am your ward, your slave, your—"

"My sister," Alaric said.

She laughed then; but her eyes were misty.

"Why do you laugh, sweet Afaf?" he said.

"Because that is the last thing on earth I should want to be to thee," she whispered. "But no matter. You'll cut me a staff, fair Aizun?"

"Yes. But if you should fall, or otherwise have need of me, you'll call?"

"Of course. Strange—"

"What's strange, sweet Afaf, little sister of my heart?"

"I was thinking—nay, wondering—that on some future day, when—if—I shall have need of thee, Aizun, can you—will you—come?"

There was no answer to that question, and he knew it; nevertheless, he answered it.

"God willing, yes," he said.

She laughed again—a curious little sobbing note breaking through her laughter, like a white-capped wave of pain.

"Zoë willing—yes," she corrected him. Then: "My staff, good my lord?" she said.

By the afternoon of the third day of their slow journey toward Toledo, she was well enough to leave the litter and ride behind him on the mule—Alaric, fearing for her safety, would not permit her to ride the other alone. As they rode, they talked, and he found himself, under her urging, divesting himself of the many burdens on his heart, sparing neither her nor himself of the anguish, the pain, the total truth of all that had transpired with him since his first journey to Córdoba. Long before he had done, she was weeping. "Afaf!" he groaned. "It is not meet that one so lost, so damned, should cause you tears. . . ."

That night, when they stopped to camp, she said: "After we have supped, my lord, I will commence to teach thee Arabic."

He stared at her and said: "Why, Afaf?"

"You must embrace Islam. Don't you see, fair Aizun, that it is the only solution to the troubles that beset your life? If you remain a Christian, you can never wed Zoë, and your son must be born a bastard. While if you enter upon the Prophet's Holy Way, your Christian wedding counts for naught. Besides which, if you will, you need only to pronounce the sentence of divorce against your faithless wife, and your son can grow up in honor—"

"True—all true, sweet sister," Alaric said, "except the central thing, the heart of the matter: Zoë changed her religion for my sake; I cannot ask of her that she change it again. And she changed it merely from one form of our faith having, mayhap, as much right to its claim as mine has, being separated from it only by the accidents of history and not by deliberate heresy. So your solution, I fear me, is no solution at all."

"Aye, but it is! As people of the book, the Nazarenes and the Jews have their faiths respected of us. A Mussulman can take a Christian maid to wife or a Jewess, without requiring of her that she change her faith. I know Zoë well; and I am a woman. Think you she'd hold thy apostasy against you, knowing it done for her sake, and the sake of the child?"

"I—" Alaric whispered. "—have never told her of this of Clothilde. I had not valor enough; and even now I fear—"

"Tell her and fear not! Oh, she'll weep and storm at thee, and try to get from thee the most salacious details of the infidelity. She will never, as I do, believe you innocent of the fair Gothic maid. For I, alas, believe it only because thou hast no need to lie to me; and because thou hast confessed it due far more to fate's malign trickery than to any virtue on thy part. But in the end she'll only love thee more. We women are curious little beasts! We want not what no other of our sex desires. Her fear, her jealousy will make her cherish thee more. So thy objection counts for naught. Besides, there are other potent reasons for your accepting Islam. I shall set them aside, for the nonce, the chief one: that it is the only true faith, for I do not wish to waste the whole night in arguments with thee. I give you instead, another most practical motive: If you become a Mussulman, you can return to Córdoba, because if my lord Ahmad attempts aught against thee, a trial must be held before the Supreme Cadi and I, myself, have more than once witnessed sentences handed down in favor of a beggar, against the injustices of the highest and the wealthiest in the land. Hagib will testify in your defense; as will I, and show those stripes to demonstrate my master's cruelty; besides, the cadi will order ibn Ha'ad, his servants, and even the Berbers, if they are to be found, into court, to confirm or deny your statements. That trial you would of a surety win; and thus be able to live in peace in the city best suited to your talents. Is this not a good enough reason for you, my lord?"

"Not quite. Methinks the finest one of all is the fact that as a Mussulman, I can have four loving wives—"

She bowed her head, looked up again; said, her voice grave and quiet: "As well as innumerable concubines if it pleases thee, my lord. But rest assured of one small thing—"

"Which is, sweet Afaf?"

"That none of them—shall be I."

He looked at her a long, slow time, studying her amber eyes, her burnt bronze face, the Horus-beaked jutting of her nose, the wine-dark fullness of her mouth.

"Why not?" he whispered.

"Because I love thee," she said very simply.

"And *that* is the reason?" he said.

"Aye, I would not share thee—not even with Zoë. And she has a sacred right to thee. Come, my lord, let us prepare the evening meal together. Thereafter, if you will, I shall commence your lessons—"

"I will," he said with a sigh. "But to change the faith one was born to is a hard thing. I do not know if I can—"

"You can," she said. "Against the Prophet's Way, no lesser faith can stand. But for now, the lessons will be enough. 'Twill be very hard; yet, within a year, I'll have you speaking our tongue like one born to it; and writing it like a scribe. The rest will be up to you—"

"Will it?" Alaric said morosely. "Is the rest ever up to any man?"

One other thing Afaf insisted upon, and Alaric saw at once the wisdom of her suggestion: that since ben Ezra had said—and time had proved him right, for so slowly had Afaf's cruel stripes forced him to travel they'd have been taken long since had the contrary proven true—

—they were not being pursued, it would be much wiser that they enter into Toledo dressed in more normal clothes than the ones they wore. For one thing, Alaric's disguise had long since gone to seed. Given to frequent bathing, he had washed the stain from his face and body in the first stream he came to; his own blond beard was downy and soft upon his young face; and his priestly robes, therefore, were an object of curiosity when contrasted with his youth and strength—though not, mayhap, with the premature frosty bleakness of his eyes.

"Nor, Lord Aizun," Afaf said, lapsing back into Romance, after vainly trying to force him to understand what she meant in Arabic, "can I ride into Toledo clad in a bedsheet! So, in the next great town, which is, I believe, either Abenojas or Malagon, you will buy me stuffs, needles, thread, and scissors, and I will make us simple and sober clothing."

So it was that when they came into Toledo—which though much smaller than Córdoba, was a proud and princely city in its own right—they were clad in simple, yet decidedly elegant Muslim clothing. Alaric had sworn a volley of great oaths at her insistence in turning him into a Moor even in his garb; but once he had donned the soft, creamy silk shirt, the long Persian coat of a dark forest green, the pearl-gray trousers, likewise of Persian cut, Afaf had made, and the pointed, turned-up-at-the-toe Moorish slippers she had bought for him in the market place, serenely ignoring the stares at her beggar's garb, he had to admit that he looked very fine. On his head he wore a scarlet bonnet—not so high crowned as to give offense to the Moorish nobles, for whom the high Persian bonnet was reserved, nor so low as to give the impression that he was plebian, a member of the 'amma, or mob—though his fairness and his bearing left little chance of an observer's falling into that particular error.

For herself Afaf chose several bolts of cloth, all cotton save for one of tawny silk, between beige and gold, whose beauty she could not resist —being after all a woman. Of her purchases she made herself simple knee-length dresses, under which she wore the shintiyan, baggy ankle-length trousers of the same cloths and colors, completing her garments with a simple headcovering and a chaste veil. All her robes were identical in cut, each but of a single color; yet the indefinable thing that men call taste made of each of them a garb of rare and subtle beauty.

On the morning that they got up, with the roofs and minarets of Toledo already visible upon the horizon, Afaf surrendered to an acutely feminine impulse, and donned for the first time that robe of tawny silk. As she stepped out of the curtains of the litter, Alaric's breath caught in his throat, and his heart made a hammering that drowned her voice. 'Twas not in answer to her, "Dost find me pleasing, my lord?" that he said:

"God's eyes, but you are fair!" and stepping forward, he took her in his arms.

"Aye—" she whispered. "Kiss me, Aizun—for the last time. The very last time. Here, where 'tis safe, for I—"

It proved less safe than either of them had thought. She tore her lips from his at the last, buried her face against his chest, and cried.

"Afaf—" he groaned.

She looked up at him. Made a brave attempt at smiling. It failed. The tears danced on the trembling corners of her mouth.

"I thank thee for thy favor, good my lord," she said, "but we must not risk so much again. Come, cut the litter free of the mules. We'll leave it here, having no further need of it. I'll follow you upon the second beast, some yards behind, with modest, downcast eyes—as a simple Moorish woman should. For this day begins a new life for us. May Compassionate Allah grant us peace!"

The first thing they saw when they entered the South Gate was the mob. They had surrounded a humble dwelling house, and were shrieking with that senseless fury which Alaric was already beginning to realize was characteristic of mobs everywhere. At first he could not see what mischief it was that engaged their brutish attention, so thick was the press of the bodies before the door; but the wind shifted, and the acrid sting of smoke made his eyes water. He turned his mule toward them.

At once Afaf cried out sharply: "Oh, no, my lord! The Toledo 'amma is perilous!"

But he pushed his mule forward all the same. And now, from the high vantage point of a mounted man, he could see what they were doing: they had formed a line from the opened—or rather smashed, for it hung crazily askew on its hinges—door of the house, and were passing books, hundreds of books, from hand to hand, and dumping them into a huge bonfire that smoldered in the street.

Alaric stared at that strange sight, and the rage that hit him in his middle was absolutely bottomless. By inclination, by natural instinct, by the all-pervading love he bore for learning for its own sake, Alaric Teudission was a scholar. The remarkable skill he had acquired at arms —violation though it was of every fiber of his contemplative being—had been due to his scholarship. Other men fought by exercise of the brute power with which nature had dowered them. But not he. Reluctant warrior, forced into the use of arms by the iron necessity of his age, Alaric had read, reread, studied the treatises upon the employ of weapons, the arts of warfare; then swallowing his inner repugnance at the shedding of blood—nay, even at the sight of it—he had applied to those arts

—obscene though he knew they were—all his basic scholar's qualities of intelligence and skill. He had thereby won, being less a warrior than a strategist, a tactician. So it was that the life he had led this last terrible year had done nothing to dull his worship of knowledge. Nay, more, it had made him long for his interrupted studies, for his monastic tower room, with an anguished yearning that conceivably could, in some future year when his ardent young blood had cooled, overmatch his love for womankind and make him renounce the flesh forever. So it was that the sight of men burning books had upon him the effect that vandals wrecking a cathedral might have had upon a priest.

He heard Afaf's "Please, Aizun! Oh, my lord, my love—please!" but her voice was but a meaningless murmur against the mob's cacophony.

"To burn books!" he raged inside his mind. "God's blood and death, there is nothing worse—nothing in the world! For, kill a man and you have but hastened what time in its fullness would, in all events, have done. And though 'tis true you murder with him what thought, what dreams, what noble unsung songs remain in him, who can tell what worth they might have had? But this! Oh, bitter, vengeful hell of artless, dull-witted clods! Here rob you generations yet unborn of a heritage worth more than all the gleaming gold on earth. Here kill you pity, compassion, solace in grief, comfort against the onrushing dark. Here assassinate ye, doubt it not, the only immortality man is certain of! O forever silent, all-permitting God, how canst even thou allow this thing?"

Still his rage had not overmatched his wits, his prudence, nor would it have, had it not been for another thing: A tall man came out of the house. He was clearly very old, but straight and thin as a young birch tree, despite the snowy hue of his beard. He wore an equally snowy turban, indicating that he was either a lawgiver or a theologian, since among the city dwellers—in direct opposition to the custom of the Berbers—only those two professions wore the puffed, many-folded head covering. Yet it was not his simple dress that held Alaric, but his face. It was—to say it truly—a beautiful face. No other word could describe it. But to use the word *beautiful*, Alaric realized at once, you had to divorce it from all fleshly connotations. The purity of the old man's face was awe-inspiring. Every line, every wrinkle incised into his flesh by his more than seventy years, only added to that pure, that awesome, saintly beauty. The serene sadness of his dark eyes—enduring even this destruction of what must have been his life's work—spoke louder than the mob's savage tongues, telling of how long since, how completely the lusts, fears, hatreds, ambitions, greeds that so debase the commonality of men had been in him vanquished, declaring to those who had eyes to see a spirit so lofty as to seem to the young Goth angelic.

But Alaric was not to be left in the quiet contemplation of the only kind of beauty he was by nature designed to truly love. For the mob surrounded the tall, yet curiously frail old man, screaming epithets at him, shaking their grimy fists under his nose, even spitting upon his garments and into his beard. Yet, Alaric saw, beyond that, they dared not go: not one of them had the kind of courage it took to do real violence to the serene old man. In a very real sense, they feared him, not the reverse. In the dim flickering of the dull maze that served them as intelligence lingered tribal memories of soothsayers and sages, of wise men and magicians on whom it was not prudent to lay hands, or even to kill, lest their restless, vengeful ghosts return to haunt their murderers. Among the curses they shrieked at the old man, Alaric's ear, sharpened by Afaf's lessons, could distinguish one word, repeated over and over again. He turned in the saddle.

"What is it that they say?" he asked her.

"They are calling him philosopher," Afaf answered. "They consider the word an insult. For, to them, all philosophers are heretics, when they are not worse—"

"Worse?" Alaric said. "There is something worse than heresy?"

"Aye, Sahib. There are the rationalists and—the atheists. Among us, many philosophers are both. Which is why, in all likelihood, they burn his books. To do that, they must have obtained a judgment against him from the religious judge. Please, Aizun, let us go from here. They will not harm him. I don't think they dare. While you, if you intervene, they'll tear you limb from limb, glad of a more human object to vent their rage upon. There is naught that you can do for him now; were you to try, you'd but risk your life needlessly—"

But Alaric lingered still, held by that wondrous old face. So it was that he was there when the youth—of his own age, or mayhap some years more—came running around a corner, and leaped into the middle of those surrounding the old man, hammering at them with no more potent weapons than his own two fists. Which, God wot, were potent enough. The youth—Alaric saw that he was European, perhaps even a Goth, because his hair and beard were fiery red, and he wore a more or less Frankish, or even German, style of clothing—laid four of the mob out in a row; and the rest fell back before his fury.

But only for an instant. Now they came roaring in, and Alaric saw the flash of knives in their hands. This rash youth was going to die, and quickly, unless—

He kicked his mule forward. Afaf's cry was the almost voiceless wail of pure despair. But he ignored it, and rode on. Not until he had forced the mule through the press to where the youth, already bleeding from a dozen cuts—none, Alaric judged, of real consequence—faced that howling pack, did he remember that due to his leaving Córdoba in the guise of a Byzantine priest, he bore no weapons at all. Even the little dagger with which he had carved Afaf a staff to hobble about upon in the first days until her hurts were cured, and which they had both used to cut their food, was packed away in the saddlebags of Afaf's mule along with the cooking utensils. He had and used what substitute lay to hand, his whip. With it, he beat the 'amma back, reached down one sinewy arm to the youth, and slung him, aided, of course, by the youth's own agility, up behind. Then he tugged the mule's head about, and got out of there, greatly helped by the fact that the crowd had blooded their daggers' points in the beast's flanks, which encouraged him to so great a speed that, even doubly burdened as he was now, he caught up with Afaf's mule, and would, in fact, have passed him, had not Alaric pulled him back. Better to let her ride ahead. With his whip he'd keep them off long enough for them all to escape; but if Afaf fell behind, what that mob would do to her was not to be contemplated even in thought.

He slashed off the last of the clutching hands, and the two mules galloped clumsily down the street, almost abreast. Behind them streamed the mob, keeping a respectful distance from that terrible whip, but pounding after them with determination, forgetting their original prey in the heat of this new chase.

"Turn here!" the youth shouted gleefully, "and I'll show you how to distance this pack of pariah dogs!"

Alaric waved his intent to Afaf, and jerked his mule's head about. She turned her mount at the same instant, and they pounded through one twisting cobblestone street after another until the last of the mob, winded by so much unaccustomed running, gave up the chase.

"I thank thee, noble Goth," the red-haired youth said, and now, for the first time, Alaric noticed the cloud of wine perfuming his breath, "but I must, I fear, ask a further boon of thee—"

"Ask what you will," Alaric said, "for by my troth, he who defends learning against brutishness hath a claim on whatever services lie in my power to give. . . ."

"Spoken like a true and gentle man." The red-haired youth laughed. I like thee well, Goth! For though thy people are barbarians and hath cruelly oppressed mine, yet thou hast a scholar's air—"

"My people have oppressed yours?" Alaric said. "Then you are—?"

"A Jew. Can't you tell? A rascally Jew. A Jewish rascal! Watch you, good Goth, or I'll have usury of you! Or rob thee of thy fortune by cunning tricks. Look you now: my nose. See how it hooks? 'Tis the curve of avarice—"

He turned his profile, and ran a long finger down a nose that was perfectly straight, in a merry, ruddy face, as handsome almost as Alaric's own.

"And my lips—they have the thickness of sensuality! Ho, good wife, good maid, good girl, good chick, good cluck, wouldst be ravished by me? I am a first-class ravisher! A knavish, clownish, villainous Jewish raper of Moorish maids, and Christians, too—though of Christians not oft, not oft—I tell you that!"

In spite of himself, Alaric had to laugh.

"Why not, sir Jew?" he said. "Why don't you often ravish Christian maids?"

"The smell, my lord!" the young Jew said. "You Nazarenes have scant respect for soap and water. And that cunning little treasure 'twixt a maid's thighs hath other uses whose perfume is best scrubbed away. Now, my boon. Wouldst bear me to my house in Jewry? I don't trust my legs, truth to tell. The first half of last night, they danced away; the second, they entwined themselves about those of the Head Rabbi's youngest daughter. She hath cross eyes, but her thighs are straight, Jehovah be praised! Or they were until I bowed them. So now, my knees lack strength. And wine, oh, bless thee, Bacchus!—hath addled what wits I have. Tra-la-la! A cup! A cup! And devil take the Jews! Besides which, I'm bleeding like a pig. Not Kashruth—Father would hardly approve. You know my father? Hasdai ben Sahl, the merchant prince! A Daniel come to judgment—and a most imposing man!"

Alaric stared at the youth. He looked at Afaf. She was smiling. Despite her veil, he could tell that from the bright twinkle in her eyes. He turned back to the youth.

"Saadyah ben Hasdai, I give you greetings!" he said.

"You know my name?" Saadyah said. "How now, young Goth? You have the advantage of me. I knew not that my good fame was so widespread throughout the land—"

"Rest assured it is," Alaric said. "I come from thy father's friend Solomon ben Ezra, the great physician—"

"The great butcher!" Saadyah said. "He butchered my good weapon. He cut a yard and a half of foreskin from it when I was but a helpless babe, thus forcing me to be a Jew. A cruel fate, is it not, noble Goth? Before he shortened me, I could begin from below right piously and reach high enough to tickle the back of a maid's tonsils. At two months of age, I did that to my nursemaid. She laughed so loudly that my father—"

"My lord," Afaf said gravely, though Alaric could hear the shake of laughter beneath her voice, "thy language offends my maidenhood. I pray thee speak of other things. . . ."

"Right willingly. Thine eyes, for example? Knowest thou that thou hast the eyes of a lioness? Like coals of fire, consuming my evil soul. O moon of my delight, how art thou called?"

"Not moon of your delight, in any event," Afaf said. "Rather of my lord Aizun, if Allah will it—"

"I'm sorry. I'm a churl, an oaf! A knave. God of Abraham, but thou art beautiful! Ho, Aizun—Aizun? That is a Moorish name; while you—"

"I am a Goth, as you have divined. The Moors call me that: Aizun ibn al Qutiyya. My name is Alaric Teudisson, heir to the County of Tarabella—"

"My lord Count!" Saadyah said. "From one who counts not, homage! How can I count? To ten, to twenty, yes. I have all my fingers and my toes. To twenty and one half, even. But not to twenty-one, because that butcher hath shortened me. So, my lord Count, count me not, for I—"

Then quite abruptly he reeled forward and crashed down from behind Alaric to the ground.

So it was that, having asked the way of passersby, Alaric came to Hasdai ben Sahl's house with the merchant's son dangling across his mule before him. A maidservant opened the door, and set up such an outcry that all the servants came running into the hall. From their unrestrained outpouring of fear and grief, Alaric saw one thing very clearly: if Hasdai ben Sahl loved not his son, he was alone in that opinion, for everyone else in his household did.

Alaric waited with Afaf in the hallway, staring at the austere, sober, yet costly furnishings, and wondering whether any of the servants was even going to remember he existed, until an inner door opened, and a maid came through it. Alaric saw at once she was not a servant; her dress was too quietly rich for that, and she wore a considerable amount of jewelry, more, in fact, than most western women would have within the confines of their homes. Nor, unlike the majority of the female servants who had come screaming and gabbling out at the news of Saadyah's injuries, was she veiled. To Alaric's eyes she appeared as western, or Nordic, as Saadyah had. Her hair was a darker red; but still red; her eyes a soft, greenish blue. As she came closer, any lingering doubt he may have had that she was Saadyah's sister vanished; two people so alike had to share a common parentage. There was, however, a subtle difference in her appearance from that of her brother; to Alaric this difference could be summed up in the observation that, despite her fair and rosy coloring, she

223

looked rather more like Afaf than like Clothilde, or even Zoë. He groped for the word, and found it: this maid, as fair as any Goth, looked oriental. And though he did not know it, he had hit upon a rare and wondrous thing: the retention of the heritage that Father Abraham had brought out of Ur of the Chaldees when he departed from that place, the look of Sarah, herself; this richness, this eastern opulence, this somnolent promise of fecundity, this vein of vitality, of sheer nerve which shone through the maid's pale Nordic coloring like a light. She was plump to the point where another pound or two would have been a disaster; but she had kept a ganerous shapeliness; and she walked with such grace, such lightness, that she made no sound at all.

"I give you greetings, my lord Aizun," she said; and her voice was dark-toned, rich; a true mezzo-soprano, so musical that Alaric guessed that when she sang, listening to her would be a glory. "That *is* your name, isn't it? I confess I find it strange, now that I've seen you. My drunken lout of a brother keeps muttering, 'My friend Aizun. Fine fellow, Aizun. Saved me. Saved my life. A prince. No, a count. Count Aizun of—' Then, having tantalized my imagination and my curiosity both, he goes back to sleep!"

Alaric smiled.

"Yes," he said, "my name is Aizun. Or rather that's how the Moors render it in their tongue. In Romance, 'tis Alaric. Alaric Teudisson at your service, my lady—"

"Oh," she said, "and you are a count?"

"That I know not," Alaric said. "When last I saw him, my father lived. 'Tis likely—and God grant that it be so—I shall have to wait some years before I can assume the title. That quite barren title, carrying with it the lordship over a burned out, ruined town—some barren fields, a drafty, ugly pile of stones, in which one freezes in winter, bakes in summer, and fights vermin all year long."

She laughed; but the sound of it was edgy, taut with nervousness.

"I like your candor, Lord Alaric," she said. "Still, it puts me in a quandary—"

"What quandary, my lady? My lady what? May I know your name?"

" 'Tis Ruth. My father is devoted to Talmudic studies, so naturally he had to give me a Biblical name. . . ."

"Well chosen, I'd say. The faithful Ruth. As you are. I'm sure of that. Aren't you?"

"I suppose I am." She sighed. "Please, Lord Alaric, I don't know how to say this—but—"

"That quandary again?"

" 'Tis hard. You see, I'd thought you were one of the riffraff Saad is

224

always bringing home. So I'd planned to give you a purse, and dismiss you as gracefully as I could—and as quickly—"

"Why?" Alaric said.

"My father. He's in there with Saad now, and he's getting angrier by the minute. Poor Father! He's so disappointed in Saad. 'Twould be better that you have gone before he comes out. The servants have already told him that a strange Christian with a Moorish wife brought Saad home like that—even more drunken than usual, and all cut up. That must have been quite a brawl!"

"It was," Alaric said. "Your brother, fair Ruth, faced a mob bare-handed in defense of one lonely old man. I find that admirable. I find him admirable; and I fear me that, in this one particular at least, your father is a fool!"

"You're right. 'Tis he who—hath—hath distorted my brother, by try-ing to force him into a mold for which he was not made. But, please, Lord Alaric, tell me where are your lodgings that I may come later with Saadyah to thank you properly. Then take your wife and go, for Fa-ther—"

Afaf spoke up then, her voice a little dry.

"I am *not* his wife, my lady," she said.

"Oh," Ruth said. "Then what are you?"

"His slave," Afaf said, "in *all* ways, my lady."

"Oh!" Ruth said again, helplessly. "No matter. You'd—"

But the door opened again, and Hasdai ben Sahl came through it. He was a big man in every dimension save height; though, in truth he was tall enough, being but an inch or two shorter than the even six feet that Alaric had finally reached. It was the merchant's immense breadth that made him appear shorter than he was. He was soberly dressed in dark green cloth; but Alaric, who was beginning to notice such things, was aware that the cloth itself had cost a fortune. A heavy gold chain hung about his neck, only partly hidden by his short, well-trimmed beard; on the end of the chain was a golden replica of a scroll. On one side of the scroll there was a six-pointed star; on the other, some words in a script that Alaric guessed to be Hebrew. He wore a jeweled dagger at his belt on the right; on the left a heavy purse hung. His face was heavy, stern, and mottled with anger. His hair was a rich brown, well streaked with white, indicating that his children must have got their red hair from their mother. It was a not unhandsome face; both Saadyah and Ruth had something of his look; but again it lacked the lightness, the delicacy that they possessed, clearly from the maternal side of the family.

"I take it," he said in a drum-deep bass, "that you are friends of Saadyah's—and that you've done him some service. Mayhap, as he claims, you've saved his life. For that, I would not seem ungrateful. Hence this purse. But I've sworn my solemn oath to receive no more of Saadyah's motley friends in my house. So take this and be off with you!"

"Father!" Ruth wailed. "You're wrong! They—"

"Be quiet, girl! In what way am I wrong? Look at them! A tall lout of a Goth, accompanied by a Negress—"

"Ya Allah!" Afaf gasped.

Hasdai ben Sahl looked at her more closely. Grunted.

"At least a Moor—and not uncomely, though swart enough, for all that, making a motley pair. So tell me, daughter, in what way am I wrong?"

"In a certain want of courtesy, sir merchant!" Alaric's lighter voice ripped through the echoes of ben Sahl's bass like a blade. "And most assuredly in the lack of a discriminating eye. If you judge your goods as ill as you judge men, ruin stares you in the face. Look upon me again, and with a trifle more attention. Then tell me, if you can or dare, that I am a lout!"

"You threaten me, young sir?" ben Sahl thundered.

"Nay," Alaric said, "for to threaten is the act of incertitude, of cowardice. When there is need to strike, I strike, and the matter ends at once. But now no such need presents itself. For what I see before me is but that sort of wrath which springs from bafflement, the want of grace born of inner hurt. Keep your purse, master of vast fortunes. I envy thee not who hath already found the worth of whatever treasures thy coffers hold. What coin, good merchant, can buy a man an hour's happiness, a day of peace? Or a son's obedience, respect—and love?"

And now, finally, the merchant was staring at him with real attention, studying that comely, intelligent young face.

"I withdraw the word 'lout,'" he said heavily, "but more from your speech, which hath a certain polished turn of phrase, than from your looks, though they, too, in all good truth are more than fair. If you want apologies, you have them. Not all Saadyah's friend are ne'er-do-wells, though, unfortunately, those who are not are usually more dangerous—"

"How so, good merchant?" Alaric said.

"Purveyors of false doctrines. Deniers of religion, and of God! Clever enough, but 'tis an evil cunning. I hope you are not of those—"

"Nay sir. I remain within the Faith of my fathers," Alaric said.

"Good. Though you Christians have used us ill, yet you retain a belief in the Torah. I prefer that to total nonbelief! And this girl?"

"Is a devout follower of the Prophet," Alaric said.

"Good, again. With Mussulmen, we have no quarrel. Now, young sir, since I remain in your debt, and you refuse my purse, what would you of me?"

"Father!" Ruth said. "He is a nobleman!"

Hasdai ben Sahl gave a quick snort of laughter.

"Have I not Christian nobles enough among my clients, daughter? When hath a title filled an empty belly? How many such have I saved from ruin with generous loans renewed time and time again, advancing my monies at rates set by the Emir himself—and plagued low at that, scarce worth the risk—only to have them damn me for a usurer, call me avaricious Jew, sneer at my holy religion and my chosen race! 'Tis that you would, young sir? A loan? Then take this purse, not as a loan, but as a gift, for I—"

"Father," Ruth wept, "*must* you be so boorish?"

"Aye, that I must!" ben Sahl said. "I know not how to cringe before the Christians, child. I am a man; I'd have my weight felt; my presence respected. Come, young Goth, what would you of me?"

"Little—or much," Alaric said. "That depends upon you, sir. At the moment, merely that you read this letter from your great and learned friend, the physician Solomon ben Ezra."

"What!" ben Sahl said. "You come from ben Ezra? A sage. A true and noble sage. But why did you not say that in the first place? I thought you Saadyah's friend, so naturally—"

"You thought well, Master ben Sahl. I *am* a friend of Saadyah's, though I first set eyes upon him an hour ago. I saw him stand off a mob barehanded in defense of an aged Moor, and came to his aid. His courage earned my respect; his gallantry, my admiration; his gaiety, my love. You have such a son as many a man might envy you, sir! And—mark me well, recall my words, and the hour that I said them—you will be proud of him yet, once he hath found his way. Which he will—especially if I am granted the chance to help him—"

And now, Alaric saw, he had won this big, gruff bear of a man utterly. In ben Sahl's gray-green eyes there shone such a wealth of anguished tenderness, so great, so terribly thwarted a love, that the very sight of it was moving.

"How?" he said, his big voice dropping to the echoes of far-off summer thunder. "How do you propose to do that, young sir?"

"By proffering him a brother's love," Alaric said gently. " 'Tis a poor substitute for thine which he craves with all his heart, I know—"

"Ha!" ben Sahl snorted. "He craves my love, say you? That would be scanned, young Goth. For surely even Saadyah is not so great a fool as to think to earn it by drunkenness, fornication, and impiety!"

227

"He craves it," Alaric said, "and his behavior is but evidence of his cruel hurt. He'd have you love him, sir; love the man he is, and not a limp and dangling puppet of your own making. But, methinks I can bring him to some measure of reason; and by the use of suasion instead of tyranny. I do not share his views; but I hope to win, rather than force, him to mine."

"And what are yours, young lord?" Ben Sahl's voice had a hint of respect in it now.

"That God lives. And though we cannot comprehend His ways, we must so order our little span beneath His sun that life shall have meaning, dignity, and grace, by fearing Him and keeping His commandments—"

"Father," Ruth said quickly, earnestly, a note of entreaty fluting through her tone, "you must keep him here! You must! At any cost, for—"

"Silence, girl!" ben Sahl said. Then his voice rang out harshly, but without, Alaric was sure, real anger; rather in acute need to ward off danger, and possible hurt from his house. "And doth your God command you to murder us, as your people hath always done?"

Alaric studied the merchant's face; thought well before he answered. When he replied his words smelled faintly of the scholar's, the dialectician's lamp; but, as they came measured and grave and slow from his lips, he found with faint surprise that he meant them—which lent them enormous force.

"My God is the same as yours, good merchant," he said, "my Law inscribed upon tablets of stone on Mount Sinai. And it commands me: 'Thou shalt not kill.' Without distinction. Neither Jew nor Gentile. Nor Moor. Nor black. Nor any man of any clime. I've kept it ill, God wot; there's a fearsome burden of blood upon my soul. But only because I was thereto forced, in defense of those I loved more than life. And—" he paused, with sure instinct for oratorical effect "—be you, good sir, assured of this: not one drop from the veins of that ancient race from which my own Lord Jesu came, has ever stained my hands. Nor ever will. You have my oath on that. Within the limits of our right to differ, we share one Faith, for my Lord said: 'I come not to overthrow the Law, but to fulfill it.'"

"So?" ben Sahl said. "He fulfilled it plagued ill, then! But no matter. Come into my study, young sir, while I read Solomon's letter. . . ."

"And Afaf?" Alaric said. "May she not come with us? For she, too, is concerned in it."

"Aye, bring her in, bring her in! But tell me, what is she to you? Your wife? But that cannot be, for one of you would have had to change your faith, and you said—"

"She is my sister," Alaric said, "though only by the love I bear her, and by my gratitude toward her for having saved me from the vilest kind of servitude—and this, sir, almost at the cost of her life. . . ."

"Ah, so? Then bring her in; but I warn you, I'll tolerate no irregularities in my house. Now come!"

"Father," Ruth said, "may I also—?"

"That, no! Go tend to your brother, child. Methinks he hath some need of it. . . ."

"So you know Greek?" ben Sahl said; then abruptly he continued in that ancient tongue, speaking it very clearly with none of the usual barbarous Levantine trader's accent. "A valuable accomplishment, if true—"

"Of that, be you the judge, good sir," Alaric replied, with the flawless and cultivated Byzantine accent he had got of old Paulus; "I claim some mastery of this noble tongue, though more in the reading and the writing of it than in the speech—"

"I'll have you write me out a sample letter," ben Sahl said, speaking once more in Romance, "though methinks you may consider yourself already in my employ. For my letters, drafts, bills of sale, receipts, demands for payment to and from the Byzantine Empire, and that great part of the East where Greek remains the lingua franca, are a sore burden upon me, since until now I could not delegate them to another because among my secretaries there is none who hath the use of Aristotle's tongue. Oh, there are several scholars among my friends who know it well, but they have no time for such mundane things, being busy about the translations of the great works with which I, too, would occupy myself had I the leisure for it. Mayhap you'll grant me that leisure, Teudisson! By Father Abraham, this is passing strange! You Goths are usually far from erudite, and yet—"

"I was fortunate," Alaric said, "in that I had both the inclinations and the opportunity."

"What other tongues know you, my boy?" ben Sahl said, a note of something close to affection creeping into his voice.

"Latin," Alaric said. "That is, pure Latin of the times of Virgil, of Cicero, rather than those debased mouthings we use now. I can write it well, too. Better than Greek."

"No Hebrew, of course? No Syriac, Persian, or Arabic?"

"No, sir," Alaric said sadly, "though Afaf is beginning to teach me the Prophet's tongue."

"Good. But I'll set learned linguists over you, for it seemeth me you have the gift for languages. Now about your wages—"

"No wages at all, good merchant," Alaric said quickly, "beyond my keep, until you've had some months to judge my worth. And even then I owe your learned friend a sum of gold, which I'd prefer you'd pay for me, and count my services for a term against it."

"Done," ben Sahl said. "Now—about this maid. Solomon's letter is on the cryptic side. In fact I find no mention of her in it. Canst tell me something of her?"

Alaric told him the story, omitting only the kisses they had exchanged, the tortured tenderness between them. When he had done, the merchant swore angrily.

"I wonder why God doth not destroy those practicers of abominations as he did in the days of Sodom and Gomorrah! The traffic in women is bad enough, but this! Very well—" He turned to Afaf, and began to question her in Arabic. Afaf answered him in a modest, even humble, tone of voice, her eyes downcast, until, Alaric guessed, the merchant ventured upon the precise nature of her relationship to Alaric himself, couching his words so as to place grave doubts upon her virtue. Then the color flared in her cheeks above her veil, and putting her hands into the folds of her tawny robe, she came out with ben Ezra's certificate.

When the merchant had read that, he smiled.

"God guard thee, daughter," he said gently, "and grant thee a worthy husband. You'll serve my own daughter. I've long needed such a one as you to attend her. The work will be light; 'tis companionship more than aught else she needs—"

He turned back to Alaric, changed once again into Romance.

"And your wife, the Greek maid ben Ezra mentions in his missive; when she hath brought forth your firstborn, you'll want them here?"

"If you permit it, sir," Alaric said.

"I more than permit. I approve. I don't think a young couple should be separated. Makes for trouble, while a wife and a child are a steadying influence. Would God that Saadyah—"

He stopped. "Tell me," he said, "have you eaten?"

"No, good sir," Alaric said.

"And you don't object to kashruth practices?"

"Nay, my patron. In thy house, thy ways are mine," Alaric said.

XII

And now time stood still for Alaric Teudisson. To him, it seemed not to move at all. Those two months he spent waiting for news from Córdoba—penning betimes missives full of loving cheer thrice weekly to his Zoë, filling them with words whose tenderness he no longer was sure he meant, for he wondered whether his vagrant, restless heart had not moved beyond this love—went by on leaden feet. The worst of it was that he had of his bride to be, the mother of his unborn child, no word at all, which added hugely to his misery. Yet, 'twas a quiet time, withal. After all the things he had lived through, suffered, and endured in that last three quarters of a year, to find himself once more at a writing desk industriously scribbling away at Latin and Greek was strange, indeed.

The letters he wrote for Hasdai ben Sahl had for him a curious fascination, for, embracing a trade that covered the whole known world of his time, they appealed to both his intelligence and his imagination. They were about such diverse matters as bills, warrants, prices, the cost of transport by pack mule, by camel caravan, by ship; the buying selling of goods upon which he would never set eye, the wages of men who were but names on paper to him—but whose manner of being, whose personalities he came very soon to know; the hiring out of monies in the form of loans against a man's due bill, warranty, signature and bond, for which good use a certain additional sum had to be paid, said sum having no name as yet beyond the Church's ugly and unjust term "usury"; the purchase of notes outstanding against a traveling trader like ibn Ha'ad, say, in far off Alexandria, paying, through an agent in that city, gold to the Greek or Egyptian dealers in peacocks, ivory, apes, and slaves to whom ibn Ha'ad owed a goodish sum, said payment being always less than the amount owed, varying according to the urgency of the dealer's need for ready coin; then dunning the wily Mozarab trader in everything from a maid's virginity to a man's life, for more, much more than the amount of the debt he had hoped to escape paying in the first place, knowing the Emir's stern judges would force him to honor his own signature and the risk charges on the transaction, thus turning ben Sahl a tidy profit—of such esoterica did Alaric treat daily, until they became his world.

Yet, truth to tell, he loved it. His keen mind soon absorbed all the complexities of that infant science which centuries later would come to be called banking; he delighted in working out and discussing with his employer intricate combinations which brought gold flowing into the coffers of the House of Sahl. Before the second month of his vigil had passed its first fortnight, he was able to say:

"Look you, good patron: if we buy of Ibrahim ben Xubruf his notes outstanding against Theophilus in Alexandria, we can suggest to the Greek scoundrel, to whom honor is a stranger, that he deliver to our warehouses near the Pharaos those rugs that ibn Ibasi is bringing from Damascus on speculation, though Crystemenes says in his missive 'tis on a promise from ibn Ha'ad to purchase them that ibn Ibasi courts the risk. Surely the Damascene will take Theophilus' coin with scant regret, that coin being a tenth part less than he owes ben Xubruf, which we can manage easily enough; and the cunning Greek will count himself the gainer to be so cheaply acquitted of his debt. While we—"

"—will squeeze that pork-eating swine ibn Ha'ad till he squeal like his brethren he hath devoured?" ben Sahl said. "Such is your intent, Alaric? Methinks you have small love for your coreligionist. Wicked of you, my boy. A man should defend the members of his own faith—"

"As he defended me when he sold me to the sodomite?" Alaric said.

"Vengeance is an unworthy motive, my boy," ben Sahl said. "You know, of course, that ibn Ha'ad hath promised that particular lot of rugs—which are uncommonly fine—to Qitab, the Emir's favorite, for the summer palace?"

Alaric hesitated; then decided, as usual, that truth was the wiser way.

"Aye, patron, that I did," he said. "I paid out three gold dinhars from my pocket for that information. . . ."

Hasdai ben Sahl put back his head and roared.

"Now here is a living marvel!" he boomed. "I have a son whose head is full of vapors, who knows not how to turn a profit of an obol or a fal. While now before me stands the pretty goy who—Look you, Alaric, we are an honorable house, with a reputation for just dealing that extends over many lands. Nay, even more than that: the House of Sahl is noted for going past justice into generosity. This thing you propose—"

"—is entirely lawful, patron!"

"Aye, that I know. But full many a man, my boy, has had to cut his throat because of pressures put upon him entirely within the law. I like this not. It hath a Levantine trader's smell. Already the goyim of Toledo

232

marvel that I have placed one of their faith on so high a footing in my house. Let this be noised abroad—as it will, doubt that not!—and they'll say I've corrupted you, made of you a cunning avaricious Jew—"

"Let them, sir!" Alaric said. "God knows *their* hands are far from clean!"

"Which hath nothing to do with the state of yours. Yet, when I consider that 'tis ibn Ha'ad whom—You want to do this thing?"

"Aye, patron, that I do!" Alaric said.

"Then yours be one half of all the profit gained; and all the shame," ben Sahl said gravely, but there was a gleam of approval in his eye. "Alaric—"

"Yes, patron?"

"How goes this of Saadyah?"

"Ill. He calls me your Sabbath Goy and would naught of me. He seems to think that I work with a certain zeal, and pass my evenings with the linguists, expressly to curry your favor and to make him look worse in your sight. I cannot convince him that I like my work, and that I love learning for its own sake—"

"Your teachers say you are remarkably apt. And already you converse in Arabic with the slaves. . . ."

"'Fetch me water. Take this away. Zubah, my breakfast!' These, good patron, are the limits of my domination of the Prophet's tongue. Methinks I'll never master it! For—"

"Al Qatan swears you've learned more in less time than any other foreigner pupil he's ever had. But as to Saadyah, keep trying to reach him. 'Tis far from ill that you set him so good an example. It seemeth me he hath sallied forth much less of late—"

Alaric's mouth tightened in his face; but he said nothing. What he knew of Saadyah's motives for tarrying at home would not add to Hasdai ben Sahl's happiness; nor—for no man loveth the bearer of evil tidings— add to his own credit with a patron clearly grown fond of him. But with so keen and shrewd an observer as his patron studying his face, he had no need to speak. Ben Sahl's fingers gripped the arms of his chair.

"So!" he whispered. "'Tis that! He'd tumble that sweet maid you brought here—and in my house! Adonai—Elohim! Why am I cursed with such a son?"

"Patron," Alaric said, "he is young and—"

"He hath three years more than you have, Alaric! And the little Afaf's a good and gentle creature. Ruth fairly dotes on her. Don't worry, boy. I'll put a stop to this!"

"Nay, patron," Alaric said. "I beg of you that this matter, too, be left

233

within my hands. For if you intervene, he'll think me a talebearer, though in God's Holy Truth I told thee not. And I must win his confidence, if I'm to do aught with him. If you please, sir—"

"Oh, all right!" ben Sahl said shortly. "Look you, my boy, what of your wife? She should be very near her time by now—"

Alaric looked down, looked up again. His young face was utterly bleak.

"I wait," he said with a sigh. "Each time your messengers ride to Córdoba, I send her a missive—a simple gift or two—fair words of love. And having, as your post riders do, changes of horses every twenty miles, you know what speed they make. Yet in all this time I've had no reply. I fear me that—"

"What fear you, my boy?"

"Oh, I know not! That she is ill. Or—"

"She's not dead," ben Sahl said. "That, you'd have learned at once. I'll write a letter to ben Ezra, myself, and put the question to him. And now, methinks, we've talked overmuch to work's detriment. Back to your desk, my boy!"

As he passed the window, he could see Saadyah, in the courtyard below, practicing at boxing with his groom. He stopped to watch a moment, and had the dubious reward of seeing Saadyah lay the groom out with a backhand blow. As he helped his fallen servant to his feet, all the courtyard was loud with Saadyah's laughter.

The groom fetched Saadyah a lusty clout on the side of his head. Which was a mistake. The merchant's son swarmed all over him, dealing out blows with such speed that he seemed to have as many arms and fists as a Hindu idol. The groom went down. But this time, when Saadyah put out his hand to help him up, the Mozarab did not move. The last Alaric saw of the two of them was Saadyah walking from the courtyard, carrying the groom's big and powerful form in his arms as though the Christian servant weighed nothing at all.

Saadyah, as usual, did not come to supper, which now, as a mark of the favor he had found in this patron's eyes, Alaric took with the family. To Alaric, these suppers were a strain. The food was plentiful and excellent; but one of Afaf's duties was to help the manservant serve the table. It was the only time during the day he ever got to see her, and her beauty and her grace took away not only his appetite but his breath. He was aware that Ruth was observing with ill-suppressed glee the way his gaze followed Afaf's every movement. To make it worse, he was almost sure that the Lady Sarah, Hasdai ben Sahl's wife and mother of Saadyah and Ruth, was aware of his emotion as well. But he could not help it. He was sure, with a bitter certainty, that neither Hasdai ben Sahl nor his wife had had anything to do with the fact that he encountered the Egyptian slave girl as rarely as possible, and never when she was alone. He knew from the glances that passed between Afaf and Ruth that they had arranged this avoidance of, and escape from, what he knew as well as they was an impossible situation. The arrangement was all to the good; it removed great temptation from his path; yet, none the less, it irked him; and for no simple reason. He took some pride in his continence, his mastery of self. 'Twas achingly true that since his brief sensuous beddings with his Zoë, he had had carnal knowledge of no other woman; nor, holding himself in God's own truth a man, did he descend to that childish vice for which God condemned Onan. His chastity was dearly won; dreams of naked odalisques plagued his sleep; whole passages from that masterwork of erotica the Emir had had him translate from the Greek came crashing and thundering back into his mind. Endless cold baths and a sparse diet helped what they could not cure. And 'twas his own lack of faith in his continued power to resist her now fully restored charm that made him resent Afaf's course in removing herself from his path all the more.

So it was, that having finished his meal and taken leave of his employers with grave courtesy, upon reaching his room he was out of patience and in no mood for sleep. Nor did Zubah, his manservant, a black from the Sudan, help matters. As soon as he saw his master, the Negro prostrated himself before Alaric, bumping his forehead against the floor.

"What ails you, Zubah?" Alaric said in his halting Arabic.

"Bless me, my lord Holy Man!" Zubah cried.

"Bless you?" Alaric said. "Art daft? How can I bless you?"

Zubah looked up at him in awe, and a flood of Arabic gutturals burst from his throat. Alaric got not one word in ten. He caught the expression for urine; the word for pot; then he heard the great gusty roar of Saadyah's laughter.

"What is he saying, Saadyah?" he asked.

"That you're holy. He's right. You're most holy, Teudisson—a saintly, holy pain in that part of my anatomy upon which I sit. Upon the basis of incontrovertible evidence, he holds you a saint; that evidence being traces of semen in your urine, when he empties your chamber pot of a morning. Which means you're chaste; among Muhammad's followers chastity is incomprehensible, unless a man be a saint. To me 'tis even further beyond comprehension, lest a man be a fool! Which is it, Teudisson: sanctity—or folly?"

"Mostly folly, I suppose," Alaric said evenly. "Wouldst enter, Saadyah? I'd have a word with you—"

"Nay, San Alarico," Saadyah mocked. "I'm off to rid myself of precisely such evidence of holiness. Some other time. Let fornication reign! Down with saintliness!"

So it came to pass that the first time Alaric Teudisson was called saint, his poor mother confused a whore's scent with the odor of sanctity; the second, a roisterer hurled the name into his teeth in mockery. The third? There'd be no third, he thought; not if I can help it! But even as he sank into sleep it was as though strong and gentle hands were tugging at his heart.

Some three hours later, well past midnight, he judged, he came awake and sat up in bed, trying to recapture the dream that dwelt within him still, lingering disturbingly just beyond the threshold of memory. So it was almost with relief that he heard, just beyond his door, the sounds of a scuffle, muted bass laughter; then clearly, insistently, filled with terror, Afaf's voice calling his name.

He leaped from his bed—his long nightdress flapping about him, because, since coming to work for ben Sahl, he had adopted the chaste and pious custom of the Jews of sleeping in a robe—and went to the door. He jerked it open. The voice he had heard was Afaf's, right enough; with most of her clothing ripped to shreds, her young breasts bare, she struggled like a trapped doe in Saadyah's great muscular arms.

Considerations of caution, of self-interest, might have caused another man to remember that the offender was his employer's son; that despite Hasdai ben Sahl's avowed disapproval of Saadyah's wildness, his love for his errant offspring was the ruling passion of his life; to Alaric's credit be it said no such consideration entered his head. He acted at once and without thought. His hand shot out, closed on Saadyah's shoulder; one powerful jerk sufficed to whirl the young Jew about; then Alaric's good right fist not only tore him free of Afaf, but sent him crashing against the wall.

Saadyah hung there, a trickle of blood coming out both corners of his mouth, for Alaric's blow had broken his lips against his teeth. Then, slowly, he smiled.

"You have struck me, Teudisson," he said, "so now I claim the forfeit! Let us descend to the courtyard now and settle this!"

"Aye!" Alaric said. "And as the offended party you have the right of choice. What weapons choose you, son of Hasdai?"

Saadyah laughed; held up his two great fists. "These!" he said.

"My lord Aizun!" Afaf wept. "Do not go! He hath much skill in this of fighting with the hands. Today he broke Antonio's jaw, and—"

"Silence, Afaf," Alaric said. "Wait you here in my chamber till I return—"

They went down into the courtyard, Saadyah whistling cheerfully through his swollen lips; but there they found it fearsomely dark.

"Attend me, Teudisson," Saadyah said, "while I go fetch Antonio to hold a torch. He will not speak of this—have no fear of that. He can't!"

He went away to return after a lengthy space of time with the groom Antonio, who bore a torch. By its light Alaric could see the groom's face was swathed in bandages; and a spasm of fear twisted somewhere deep in his middle. Saadyah was a big and powerful youth, and supremely confident of both his force and skill. But there was a layer of fat about his waist that betrayed his Epicurean style of living. Hope flared in Alaric's mind. If, he thought, I can escape him for the while, he'll tire. While I, who've lived the life of a monk and avoided all fat and honeyed foods lest they inflame my blood to fleshly desire, can endure longer than he, if his blows do not injure me overmuch at the outset. Mayhap, by watching, I can learn of him his tricks and—

"Ready, Teudisson?" Saadyah said.

"Aye!" Alaric said, and thunder and lightning exploded inside his head. He found himself upon the paving stones of the courtyard, blinking up at the stars. Antonio's torch flared above him; and through the dim, flickering dark he heard the gusty roar of Saadyah's laughter.

"Admit thyself vanquished, Teudisson!" Saadyah boomed. "Concede me Afaf as spoils of war, and I'll let thee off this lightly!"

Alaric didn't answer. He lay there, gathering his forces; came up on one knee.

"Wouldst more?" Saadyah said in a tone of mocking wonder.

"Aye—" Alaric whispered.

Two seconds later he was stretched out on the paving stones again. He got up again more warily. Now he managed to keep his feet for five full minutes, before Saadyah sent him down again. The next time it took even longer. He did not know, of course, that by then, having made what hasty repairs she could to her torn clothing, using for pins twigs from Zubah's broom, from the window above gentle Afaf watched; and wept for him; nor, even remotely, did he consider the almost unimaginable consequences of this boxing match. For, after the fifth knockdown, Saadyah did not manage to floor him again; and almost imperceptibly command of the combat passed into Alaric's hands. Because, by then, it had occurred to him that fisticuffs were oddly like swordsmanship. The trick was to dodge or parry your opponent's blows while doing as much damage to him as possible with your own. It was an idea that occurred naturally enough to a mind by then accustomed to innovation—that anathema of his religion, race, and age!—a mind which, lodged in a slender body and cursed with a temperament unfit for war, had always been forced to substitute strategy for power in order to survive; and it gained its surprising effectiveness against a man trained to fisticuffs from the fact that the brutal gladiatorial sport of fist fighting, as practiced by the Romans, of whom the Hispano-Roman Mozarabs, like the groom Antonio, had learned it, retaining it unchanged for nearly four hundred years, was a matter of standing toe to toe and battering at your opponent with both hands until he—or you—went down.

So now the puzzled Saadyah found himself suddenly expending his terrific force upon the empty air; his crushing blows, instead of shattering Alaric's nose or jaw, bounced harmlessly off his forearms. Worse, he found himself taking counterblows that, while much less powerful than his own, hurt him sorely enough, and tired him even more. He fell back, giving Alaric time to catch a second breath. Then he came roaring in. Alaric eluded him easily, taking his cue from another Spanish heritage of the Roman love for blood and pain, the bullfight, already well enough developed by then to have caused strictures upon it from the churchly lords. The combat went on, both of them tiring now, but the slim and graceful Goth far less than his heavier foe.

Then Alaric found Saadyah's Achilles' heel: his belly, well larded over with fat as the result of many a nightlong feast. It seemed to the young Goth that his arm sank to the elbow into it, the first time he reached it. Saadyah let out a great "Oooof!" and sat down on the stones. He came up at once, roaring. Alaric sent him down again with the same blow. Three times the same thing happened, until Saadyah clapped both hands to his sore middle. Seeing his opportunity, Alaric went to work with both hands on his foeman's head. Saadyah crashed to the ground, lay there; came up with painful slowness. When he stood up at last, Alaric saw that he was swaying on his feet. Exultingly forgetting caution, and the simple fact that a wounded lion is a lion still, Alaric rushed in.

Wildly he pounded Saadyah, saw his foeman's knees buckle, his greater bulk start down; dropping his own guard, Alaric danced gleefully in to finish the contest; but to his own vast surprise, Saadyah's big fist came whistling up from somewhere in the neighborhood of his still buckling, sagging, giving knees; and red fire and utter dark burst eerily inside Alaric's skull, while far away and faint he heard Afaf's despairing scream.

He opened his eyes at long last. Tried to get up. He couldn't. Inside his head a legion of tiny jinn and demons were at work with iron hammers and red-hot tongs. He fell back until the pain lessened. Raised his head again. Saw Saadyah, some distance away, stretched out unmoving, like one dead. Try as he would, Alaric could not discern whether or not he breathed. From far above, he heard Antonio's groan of pure terror, muffled though it was by the bandages which would not let the groom speak.

Alaric rolled over, a great and terrible fear moving through his heart.

"I've slain him!" he thought. "Oh, God in heaven, no!"

Painfully he crawled over to where Saadyah lay, and hung there, propped up on his elbows, staring into the young Jew's face. Saadyah's eyes came open, blinked, cleared. He grinned at Alaric with astonishingly good cheer. Then he swept one great arm up, and locked it around Alaric's neck. He tugged Alaric's head down, and planted a bloody, sweaty kiss upon his cheek.

"Thou art my brother, Aizun!" he chuckled. "And a man! Thou hast thrashed me fairly. To the victor, the spoils. I renounce her from this hour, and here's my hand on't!"

When Alaric came into his room he saw his lamp was lit, which puzzled him, for he had not left it so. He stood there blinking foolishly at it until Afaf came out of the shadows and locked both her arms around his neck. She leaned against him, sobbing.

"I thought thee dead!" she wept. "I thought thee dead, my lord! And, oh, I knew then I could not live! Not without thee, fair Aizun. For until thou camest, I knew not what love was!"

Alaric bent and kissed the top of her dark head.

"Methinks you know not even yet," he said gently. "Now get you hence, sweet child, for by God's Holy Blood, I'm wearied unto death—"

She looked up at him, saw the blood that trickled from his nose and mouth, from a cut above his left eye which was already purpling. Her fingers strayed over the mottled splotches on his chest and arms, which, before morning, would be a greenish blue.

"Aye, how he hath hurt thee!" she sobbed.

"I hurt him worse." Alaric grinned.

"Aye, that I saw. Ya Allah, but thou art a lion, my Aizun! Now lie thee down, and I will tend thy hurts—"

"Afaf—" Alaric said, and his voice edged, grating across her name.

"My lord?" she whispered, a little fearfully.

"How came you to be in Saadyah's arms? You sleep in the chamber of your lady Ruth, in a little alcove not two yards from her side. He'd not dare enter there, even shameless as he is. So—"

"So—" she said, and her eyes went blind behind a scald of tears. "So

239

you think me vile, my lord! I, who have resisted thee, whose very touch turns my bones water!"

He looked at her, in anger, and in doubt; but her tears unmanned him.

"Thy pardon, Afaf," he said, "I am sore hurt, and tired, and confused. Though, methinks, confusion is the plain upon which my whole life is spent—"

"It matters not," she said, "and thou hast right: it doth have an evil look, doth it not? My lady Ruth received this night a missive from her aunt, the Lady Rachel, wife of the great merchant Ibrahim—"

"Ben Xubruf?" Alaric said.

"The same. The Lady Rachel is the sister of the Lady Sarah, wife of our lord; and my lady Ruth loves her much. A servant of the merchant Ibrahim, whom my lady recognized at once, brought her a message saying that the Lady Rachel was ill and would have her beloved niece at her side—"

"For which good service, doubt it or not, our fine Saadyah tossed the churl a weighty purse," Alaric said.

Afaf's eyes widened, staring at him.

"Yes—" she whispered. "So it was! So it must have been! For why else would he have been hidden in my lady's room when I entered it? Oh, Aizun, my love, my lord! I fought him with my nails, my teeth; broke free and came to thee—only to have thee in the end accuse me of—oh, Compassionate Name of Allah!"

"Afaf," he said, and put out his arms to her.

She came to him at once, and stood in the circle of his arms, trembling. Then she drew back a little, wrinkling her beaked nose with tender mockery.

"Verily thou hast the smell of a randy goat—" She laughed, making a sound like lauds and flutes, reedy and tremulous "—who is the most wicked of all Allah's creatures. Lie you down, good my lord, while I bring cloths and warm water and healing balms to cure thy hurts and improve thy smell."

Watching her moving through the doorway, Alaric felt the devil in the flesh stir, rise up, his aching weariness sink abruptly out of consciousness or even memory. "How thou couldst heal me, thou wouldst not, child," he thought, and stretched himself out on his bed, deliberately breaching his own barricades against temptation, against swiftly rearing lust, welcoming it now, not for itself, but as a kind of defense against the Nameless, the Unspeakable. She would not, say I? I have but to kiss her twice when she returns; put my hand inside her bodice where Saadyah so usefully hath torn it and—

"Zoë," the thought cut like a blade through his self-induced fever, his devil-possessed downhill swinish rush, "what of her? What of that poor creature who loves thee and carries our child in her womb?" And now it seemed to him that his second thoughts had taken another voice, alien and apart from him, addressing him as *thee* and *thou* as though he were, himself, another person, a separate entity. He had heard that voice before, he was sure of that; but, for his very life, he could not remember where or when. And now it came again: "Wouldst do this thing, Alaric? Wouldst add adultery to thy sins? For in Mine eyes Zoë is thy wife, albeit thy vows remain unsaid. Knowest thyself not, Alarico, my son? For thou art—"

"Alarico?" Alaric erected his musings like a wall against the slow-forming terrible words "—anointed unto me, and consecrated to my—" Saadyah called me that. San Alarico, using the Hispano-Mozarab, *alajamía* form. Saadyah and—no one else. I am weary. Or mad. My mind works badly. Fatigue does that; pain—

"—service," the alien voice went on implacably, forming its grave, tender accents inside his skull. "Wouldst sin so terribly, Chosen of Me? Thinketh thou to escape Me thus?"

"Aye!" he cried aloud, feeling the chill of his anguished terror congealing his blood into splintered ice, edged and cutting as a Roman spear, as myriadly penetrant as any crown of thorns; tasting in his mouth, bitter on his tongue, the contents of that cup that would not be taken from him, however much he pushed it away, put it by. "Aye! Thus will I escape Thee! Thus will I damn my soul to hell, where even Thou canst not—"

But he heard then Afaf's footsteps in the hall, and lay back down, closing his eyes, feigning sleep. But he knew that despite himself the fear of that great unknown was in him still, freezing all his flesh, drowning the fires of lust within him in dark, arctic torrents that flowed through and over him calling out to him in tremulous, haunting, unheard voices which none the less were very clear. "I will not!" he cried within his heart. "I cannot! I am not fit! Not fit for aught but lust and shame!"

And, as if to confirm his unspoken cry, he felt her soft hands moving on his face. He lay there with his eyes closed as she rubbed the balm into the cut above his eye, cleansed away the dried clots of blood from his nostrils and his beard. Then she stopped, murmured something in Arabic. He caught the word Allah; and the sound of her phrase was that of an invocation or a prayer. Then deftly she stripped the torn, ragged, blood- and dust-caked nightdress from his body, and began to bathe him as tenderly as a mother bathes a child. The sensation was indescribably pleasant. He stole a glance at her. Her small face was concentrated, rapt, alight with inner tenderness.

"I'll not touch thee, Afaf," he thought. "I leave the matter up to thy Allah. Mayhap thy desert god will protect thee—being worthier of trust than He who hath showered me with evil, grief, torment, loss—and now would use me for his fearful ends! I'll not lift a hand—so that even if the damnation come to pass, even should we couple in the dark, the guilt will not be mine. . . ."

And now again her slim hands moved, washing away the sweat and dirt from his arms, his armpits, his broad chest; but once more she paused. Her fingers slid from the cloth she held, and twined themselves helplessly in the downy golden thatch covering the lean in-hollowing of his belly. He heard her moan, deep in her throat, a sound so dark, anguished, sweet, that knowing that he, Lord Satan, and carnal lust had won, Alaric brought his arms up and drew her down upon him, exulting: "Mine! Mine! Woman's flesh and love and life and joy! All mine! Hearest Thou me, who'd have of me my soul?"

"No, Aizun!" she wept. "We cannot! We must not! Oh, my love, my own—no. No, no, no, no—No."

He kissed her mouth. It was honeyed, sweet; her breath had the smell of cloves. "Noooho," she muttered, mouth against his mouth. "Nooo—" the sound dissolving, melting, as her lips slackened, parted, broke open like some incredibly soft, noon-ripened tropic fruit with the sun's heat in them, and their own tart sweet scalding juices making a potent adhesive to weld them to his own; feeling that "no" repeating itself with the blind anguish of her dying will even upon the molten, serpentine thrust and probe exploring the interior of his mouth, even in the tender, wild, searching, agonized and agonizing fingertips learning his body by rote, gone beyond her control, her will; and he—deliberately stifling honor, consciously betraying not only Zoë, but all his sacred pledges, intentionally smothering his own essential decency; using, in fact, his innate acute and painful sense of guilt, of sin, perversely as a goad, a whip to lash the greater fury the rising red tides of his lust; matching, blasphemously, his own mad defiance—"I will not! I'll not, I'll not, I'll not—" with the pounding rhythms of his blood, his heart—reached up and ripped away the clothes she wore, helped by the fact that Saadyah's great paws had already torn them beyond effective repair; but aided more by her own two hands which came down to grip his wrists, but, instead, themselves a prey to blind instinct, went on past his, and thrust her shintiyan in one long, soft, silken slither over slim flanks, thighs, knees, calves, until it bunched about her ankles, while all the time, her freed mouth—for he was occupied now by richer, more ripened fruit, swelling and puckering under his hands, his lips—continued to moan and babble those meaningless, demented "No's" until in the very lists of love, the grinding heat of passion, he tried to enter her and found he could not.

It was as ben Ezra had said: she was virgin and intact. He saw her wine-dark lips go white with pain, and arrested his brutal thrust. In the throbbing silence all the longing, love, lust, desire, anguish, tenderness, hurt in him, pooled molten in his chest, halting his breath, stilling his very heart. And now again it seemed to him he felt those strong and tender hands move out of the pillar of fire, the luminous cloud, and draw him back from the edge of the pit, the brink of hell; from sin so black as to admit of no pardoning.

He was aware that her amber eyes had flared wide, glowing like coals in her dark face. Gently, he smiled at her.

"Thou art armored against my sinful lust," he said.

"Aye," she whispered. "Aye, lord of my life, but not against my own!" Then she buried her face against his breast, her mouth soft, hot, wet, trembling, opened against one of the hard, diminutive, atrophied male nipples, and arching her slim body like a bow, slammed it against his till then impenetrant maleness with all her force, convulsively sinking her teeth into him at the same time, so that the pain was mutual, and for them both.

And, after one blinding, unbearable moment, by them both forgot.

The sound of her weeping was the most dreadful thing he had ever heard.

"Afaf—" he groaned. "My love, my life—"

"Nay!" she stormed. "Thy slave, thy concubine, thy whore! Who hath damned thee to the pit! Who sought thee out—thou who hast been fair and honorable with me! And Zoë—what of her? Sweet sister of my soul, always gentle and loving toward me? To whom I brought my sorrows and hurts and received of her always comforting? Who loves me still, that I know—though I began to turn from her the moment that I saw thee! She-goat that I am! Dung and offal of all lechery! 'Tis as my first lady Saidat said: I am as lascivious as a monkey and am damned!"

But the sense of sin had gone from him; he lay enwrapped in lassitude, in peace. More than his seed had spewed forth from his loins into the undulant thrash and broil and heat of her; months of anguish, terror, grief, pain, loss high-piled upon his heart, had, it seemed to him, by this good comfort been dissolved, and pouring out of him had left him free.

"Allah people the world with monkeys such as thou!" he said. "Afaf, sweet child, hear me. I shall embrace your Faith. Then we can all live in peace, you and Zoë, and I—"

243

She came up on one elbow, staring at him, the lamplight making golden crystal of her tears.

"In peace?" she whispered. "You mean in hell! Knowest not that I should go mad, lying awake the nights when thou sought her bed? And she, equally, when thou deigned to honor me? That I know. We talked it out many a time at the market, or in the cool shade by the fountain waiting to fill our jars. Methinks that the women of those lords who have many wives love not their lords overmuch, if they love them at all. For true love cannot be divorced from jealousy. I would own thee utterly, Aizun, and be owned by thee. This milky flesh filigreed here and there with gold is mine! Thine, this swart, sun-whipped she-camel's hide, with its black camel wool that must be shaved away daily from armpits and the place of love—'tis valueless, I know, and ugly, but thine!"

"Lord!" Alaric laughed. "How sorely hath thy Allah afflicted me!"

"Aye!" she wept. "Sorely indeed, for I—"

But then he stopped her sobs against her mouth, drew her into his arms once more, and delighted her, and himself, until the dawn.

Ben Sahl took one look at his bruised and battered face, and let out a roar like unto that of a wounded lion.

"Thou, too, Teudisson! Carousing and brawling in the streets—with, doubt it not, my oafish son! I had thought better of thee than this. Come, boy; what have you to say? Wouldst explain this lapse of thine? I warn thee thy words had better carry truth's full weight, for by all the fires that flame in Hinon, by dark Sheol, itself, I'll show thee the nearest door!"

Alaric stood there.

"Good patron," he said at last, "I have no explanation to offer you, nor any excuse. Say I am but a man, and that temptation o'ermatched my strength. I have much sorrow for my sins, and think not to repeat them. But if you bid me go, I have no more recourse than to incline me before your will and leave your house—"

"Then leave it!" Hasdai ben Sahl thundered. "Upon the hour! For one drunken, brawling lecher is enough! I'll have not two—"

He stopped short, because Saadyah had come through the door without so much as a by-your-leave, and stood there airily stifling an elaborately theatrical yawn with the back of his hand.

"Two of what, honored and respected Father?" he said.

"Lecherous swine!" ben Sahl roared. "Street brawlers! Whoremongers! Frequenters of—"

"The purveyors of false doctrine," Saadyah finished for him. "What limited command of invective thou hast, Father mine! Remind me to teach you to really swear, one day. Your vocabulary is as limited as your insight, or you'd realize that there stands before you a man whose greatness of heart, whose gallantry outweighs that of princes!"

Ben Sahl glared at his son. "You refer to Teudisson?" he said.

"I do. But why 'Teudisson,' today? Why not 'Alaric,' or 'dear boy,' or 'my boy,' as usual? Own that you love your Sabbath goy right well, Father! And with reason. He is worthy of thy love. Mine, he hath, for whatever it is worth. In proof of which you see me up and dressed at this ungodly hour! I, to whom no day breaks before high noon. You see, I suspected you'd question—nay, not question! You never question, do you, Father? You only bellow like a shophar blown by a flatulent rabbi with a cold. So let me amend my thought: I knew that you'd see the bruises and cuts he got of me, defending the chastity of that Bedu maid from my drunken lust. And knowing the dulcet sweetness of thy temper, I realized that, without questioning him, you'd assume he'd accompanied me on my nightly prowls, fallen into evil company, visited whores, and engaged in street brawls at my side. All that, I knew. What I suspected—and I was right—was that he'd conceal his innocence to defend me from thy wrath. Ah, no, Father! I sadly fear that he is as saintly as he looks, and as—incorruptible. The fault is mine; mine the sin—though by my troth, well have I been punished for it—for 'twas he, not I, who was afoot at the last of it. So, good my Father, cease to roar. My head aches too badly to endure it!"

Hasdai ben Sahl looked from one of them to the other. "You speak the truth, Saadyah?" he said.

"Aye, Father, by Abraham, Isaac, and Jacob, I swear it!"

"Don't blaspheme, lout! Alaric, my boy, you have my apology. But you should not defend this fool at so great a risk. Now go to your desk—for what I have to say to this oaf is unfit for decent ears!"

He could hear the roaring half the morning; but when Saadyah came into the scriptorium where he worked, the young Jew's face wore a cheerful grin. Alaric smiled at him with what cheer he could muster, but being sunk by then into his inborn faculty for self-torment and busily engaged in flaying himself with the unrelieved horror of his guilt, his smile was dismal indeed.

"Your father has forgiven you then, Saadyah?" he said.

"Ha!" Saadyah laughed. "I have been outfooting the old man since the age of two. The trouble is that he loves me, which unmans him. You're good for him, my saintly friend. For now he loves thee, too, which makes up to him somewhat for the blackness of my sins. Tell me, how goes Your Saintliness today?"

Alaric sighed. "In a most unsaintly fashion," he said. "Saadyah—one thing I would of thee: How can you do the things you do, and stay so cheerful? Art never burdened with the weight of guilt?"

Saadyah leaned close, peering into his face. He threw back his head and loosed a peal of delighted laughter.

"So," he guffawed, "she rewarded thee for thy valor! Come, Alaric, tell me; how was she? Aye, God! I'll wager she drained the very marrow of thy bones, wrung thee dry as desert dust, twisted those long sweet limbs about thine, and drew the iron from thy poniard till it hung limp as a priestly banner on a windless day!"

"I know not of what you speak, Saadyah!" Alaric flared.

"Liar!" Saadyah hooted. "You lie in your teeth, Aizun ibn al Qutiyya, eater of pork and other unkashruth filth! Therefore thy tongue is forked and knows not truth. Ha! Saint Aizun, High Priest and Holy Pope of Fornicators, doth not know lying is a deadly sin? Yet twice already this day thou hast been guilty of it. And for the same motive: thy gallantry. I thank thee, Aizun-Alaric. Or is it Alaric-Aizun? And do not bridle so! She's thine; take you much joy of her. Bump bellies with her nightly till you fill her with thy fruit. I care not. Besides, you have naught to conceal from me who am your brother. You won't speak? Hoard to yourself the lovely details—for I have some experience of them already, brother! I, too, right off, hath seen twin cherry buds stand up and pout, begging for my kiss; hath felt the high spiced pouch of love gape and quiver and go creamy at my prying fingers' touch, hath—"

"Saadyah!"

"Your Saintliness? Do my words offend the chaste purity of thy morning-after heart?"

"They do offend me," Alaric said slowly. "I like not the way you make mock of all things. The love of man and maid for each other is no smirking ugliness to be caught in a net of words, Saad. I understand you not, my friend. The evils I have done, the blood and pride and lust staining my soul, torment me fearsomely. Yet you go to the public women almost nightly, drink, and game, and gambol and brawl your life away. If I did such things, I could not face my own countenance in the mirror—"

"That's because you're an egoist, Alaric," Saadyah said. "You think what you do matters."

Alaric stared at him. "Doesn't it?" he said.

"Not in the slightest. While I, knowing I am a worm, or at least a future banquet for the slimy tribe, can take my greasy carcass' share of joy. What else is there? Philosophy? The spinning of intricate nets of meaningless, self-contradictory words. Religion? The talking to themselves of poor mad children, afraid of the onrushing dark. The gaining of wealth, like my father? What will that wealth buy me in my grave? Even the blind crawling things despise hard gold, preferring my succulent flesh. Power? As transitory as the rest. Aye, no, brother! I'll take life, while I have it! I'll refuse no maid while my weapon towers like the minaret of the mosque and the muezzin within me calls upon all pious goodwives and virgins to prostrate themselves before it in the sweet attitude of holy prayer. I'll look upon the wine while it is red, and sing youth's long, brave song until the grave mold choke my voice. And so should you, brother mine; so should you!"

"Then," Alaric whispered, " 'tis true! You do not believe in God!"

"No," Saadyah said, "I don't. Why should I? What usefulness hath that idea?"

"Why," Alaric said, " 'tis a great comfort to know you have His guidance, His protection. That even as He sees the tiny sparrow fall, He seeth all danger, all hurt, that may befall you and—"

Saadyah laughed. "I go before you convert me!" he said. "Have I not pains enough being a Jew? A member of God's Chosen Race, who, while He was, mayhap, these many centuries occupied with keeping tally of sparrows dropping from the sky, hath been enslaved by the Egyptians, captured by the Babylonians, slaughtered by the Persians, cut to pieces and scattered over the earth by the Romans, chopped into mincemeat by the Vandals, treated with tender loving care by you Goths? What would come to pass should I become a Christian—as I might, for I dearly love a fat slice of pork! A practicer of holy cannibalism? As credulous as Father Joseph? As chaste as thy priests and monks and nuns? Surely some Nero would arise to feed me to the lions, for, I fear me, brother Aizun, I've had too much experience of that guidance and that protection of which you speak!"

"Saadyah," Alaric said sternly, "these blasphemies are ill! I'll not listen to this wickedness!"

"Then don't, Alaric," Saadyah said gently, "for in good truth I envy thee thy faith. I would not rob thee of it, having nothing to give you in its place. My hedonism is as empty as any other philosophy; and surely one as perceptive as thou art must see the sadness beneath my pretense at joy."

"I do," Alaric said; then suddenly all the dark doubts that had grown and festered in him since the day he had sickened at the sight of Saint Fredegunda's incorruptible arm, came flooding unbidden to his mind. "Saadyah—why don't you believe? I ask not to engage you in debate, but out of simple curiosity, out of a certain need to know—"

Saadyah looked at him.

"*You* ask me that?" he said. "*You?*"

"Yes," Alaric said. "You find it odd?"

"No," Saadyah said tartly. "I find thou hast an armored hide and no sweet rebellion in your shriveled heart!"

Then he got up and marched to the door. There he turned.

"Forgive me, Alaric," he said. "Go on believing. 'Tis a precious gift. Especially in such as thou. Had I had a brother arrowed to death from behind, a mother whose gentle throat was cut before mine eyes, a sister ravished first, then murdered, a wife turned whore with a swinish churl, a father left old and defenseless, myself sold to feed a pederast's lust—I doubt that I could manage it. Or—if I could, I needs must cry out like thy gentle Lord upon his tree: 'Eli, Eli lama sabachthani!'"

Alaric was on his feet by then. Even his lips were white. "Who told you all that?" he said.

"Thy Afaf—or rather she told it with many tears to my sister, who repeated it to me. You know how women are. Do not hold it against her, Alaric—"

"I don't," Alaric said slowly. "Saadyah, what you have said I—I have refused to look upon. I am a sinful man. Who knows that 'tis in punishment for the terrible things I've done that I have been bereft of those I love?"

"Thou!" Saadyah hooted. "Thou monster of inhuman vanity! Thy sins! Thy mighty, matchless, black and terrible sins for which others must die to afford thee the luxury of sufficient suffering! Ah, God! 'Tis bootless to bandy words with one so dense! Methinks you are a devil-worshiper, Alaric. Nay, I'm sure of it. Now sit you down; for, to cure thee of this want of humility thou hast, I needs must teach thee the Devil's Catechism. Hark me well; get it by rote. In a week—nay, in a month, for 'twill take that long for its subtleties to penetrate your thick Gothic skull—I'll have you say it back to me, and give me your interpretation. Art ready?"

"Aye," Alaric said grimly.

"Dost believe in the omnipotence of God?"

"Aye," Alaric said.

"And in His omniscience as well?"

"Aye," Alaric said.

"Dost believe that His omniscience, His total knowledge, includes the future?"

"Of course," Alaric said.

"Dost believe that mankind hath—or hath been granted—freedom of will?"

"Of a certainty," Alaric said.

"And in punishment for sin? In, precisely, eternal damnation? The fires of hell?"

248

"Aye," Alaric said.

"And in God's loving kindness? His tender mercy?"

"Very surely," Alaric said.

Saadyah shook his head, wonderingly.

"Dost believe that I am Beelzebub, am black as night, have cloven hooves, and wear a tail?" he said. "Horns, I grant you; the rabbi's youngest daughter hath adorned my forehead these two nights gone, the little bitch! Come on, Alaric; do you?"

Alaric stared at him, started to laugh; but Saadyah stopped him with a lifted hand.

"Do not laugh, my brother! Mayhap I *am* the devil in disguise. How dost thou know? For today I have subjected thee to temptation toward the original sin for which our first parents were expelled from Paradise. To eat of the fruit. To learn that thou art naked. As thou art. Naked to the miserable, barren soul thou thinkest thou hast—"

He stopped, seeing the hurt confusion in Alaric's eyes.

"Forgive me, brother," he said. "I would not change your ways. Pray for me, San Alarico! I have much need of it!"

"Saadyah," Alaric said desperately, "our minds are limited; we cannot understand—"

"What's beyond comprehension is likewise beyond use," Saadyah said mockingly. "Fare thee well, my brother!"

Then he went out of the scriptorium, closing the door very quietly behind him.

Alaric lay upon his bed. It was very late, but he could not sleep. His head ached dully. Since retiring to his chamber for the night, he had been puzzling over Saadyah's subtle mockery of a catechism. The key to it lay, he was aware, in Saadyah's own motives. For the creed therein exposed was conventional enough; a part, in fact, of the very dogma of the Holy Church. And yet, Alaric thought, he seemed to think me mad that I could hold it. Why? We're taught from childhood that—

He went over the Devil's Catechism point by point. There was no single item of belief that the sternest curate in this world could censor a man for holding. No single item. No single item! He sat up in bed, staring wildly into utter darkness. Because, dimly the outlines of Saadyah's mocking intent were beginning to form themselves. No single item—but take in conjunction? The fires of hell coupled with God's tender loving mercy? Omnipotence with man's freedom of will?

He thought: I used vile weapons in my struggle to escape. I befouled my body, damned my soul with seamy lechery to throw off those hands

249

. . . . I chose hellfire, the pit, eternal torment in preference to this road too high, too blinding, too exalted for my poor spirit. But what if I have no choice? If my freedom—even to damn myself—is an illusion? Being all powerful, He can bind me to His will, being all wise, He—Ho, Saadyah! I've found it! The flaw in thy reasoning! Being all wise, He can and doth, of His own vast wisdom, refrain from employing His unending power, thus leaving me free to—"

It is likely, given time, that Alaric would have seen that he had almost completely missed Saadyah's point; and that that point itself was unanswerable. 'Twas not between God's omnipotence and man's freedom of will that the essential conflict lay, but on quite another, much more subtle level, involving the nature of God himself. Only, he was not to be given time. For even as he was coming to grips with the dark angel of doubt, and finding his sable beauty matched curiously point by point that of his brother and his twin, the bright seraph of faith, he heard that light, brushing, almost inaudible knocking at his door.

He got up at once, and opened it, without thinking to blow out the oil lamp by his bed. By its light he saw Afaf standing there, her mouth a blurred tremble, her eyes wells of loneliness, longing, desire, abject shame, and bitter tears.

"Afaf—" he said, and taking her by the hand, drew her into his room, closing the door behind her.

She fell to her knees before him.

"Beat me!" she wailed. "Drive me away! That a man seeks out a woman is a meet and fitting thing, ordained of Allah since the beginning of the world. But when thy she-goat, thy female baboon, of lechery all compact, comes whining and wheedling before thy door, what then, my lord?"

"Why, then I am blessed," Alaric said, trying to force conviction into his voice.

"Nay, damned!" she stormed. "I lay there, waiting for my lady Ruth to fall asleep—she sleeps like one dead, you know—and all my body was lapped about with flame. I put my face against the pillow to stifle my moans, my cries, and kept it there so long I almost smothered myself to death. Oh, Aizun! Oh, good my lord, I—"

He bent and kissed her mouth, feeling the sense of sin in his very bowels, cold and cutting like a blade; but her hands were frenzied upon his body; her mouth, a scald, a wound, anguish given flesh, so that it was pity rather than desire that led him to grant her comfort. He found—for he was, despite himself, an ascetic in his heart—that an excess of passion is an ugly thing; that 'tis only tenderness, that all-embracing love which,

250

seeing beyond the graceful contours of a well-made form, beyond the febrile tactile and olfactory stimulants that Nature, in her mindless will to preserve the race, hath provided with such prolific generosity to the beloved entity, person, being within that lends a measure of beauty to our matings.

But now 'twas a furious gallop into the sirocco's sand-whipped heart; two desert riders pounding into night and pain; now her harsh gutturals were a goad of breath, thrusting into his ears; and not even the glistening rivers of sweat pouring from them both were enough to ease the irritant of flesh upon and within flesh grinding in bestial heat; humanity abandoned, lost in the savage lashing of teeth and nails, in the blasphemously prayerful exhortations of that two-backed race to reach what he could not reach at all, so great was the revulsion in him. Yet, when her eerie, high-pitched toneless final cry, the slackening of entwining limbs from his chafed and tortured flesh, told him she had found what she sought—that mere relief from tormenting desire, which taken as the sole motive for the act of love debases it into coitus, he did not let her go; but began sweetly, slowly to design with her the arabesques of tenderness, the slow, stately rhythms of temple dancers worshiping each other and love and God who hath given them this sweet, reverent magic of the flesh to their own increase, and to His greater glory. This time her final cry was flutelike, musical, and filled with joy.

She lay propped up on one elbow, staring at him.

"Allah bless thee, oh my lord," she said.

Briefly they slept. When Alaric awakened, Afaf was again propped up on her elbow, gazing at him. "Thinkest thou that—that Zoë—might be persuaded to accept me as thy second wife?" she asked.

"Lord!" He laughed. "But you have said—"

"—that I'd go mad if I had to share thee. Mayhap I would. But I cannot give thee up."

"I think—she might," Alaric said slowly. " 'Twould depend upon many things—"

"Then thou wilt embrace the True Faith?" she said.

"If you mean Islam," he said, a little sadly, "methinks I must. But 'twill be a hard thing for me—"

"Nay. I will make it easy for thee, when I am thy wife. And Zoë will accept me, right enough! To keep and guard thee, she would share thee with a Negress. Knowest that Abd al Karim ibn al Hixim, uncle of the Emir, hath married a Negress?"

"No," Alaric said, wondering at the sudden turns and twists of her thought.

251

"Well, he hath. Because of her wisdom and her wit. I know her well. She used to read the Qur'an to the copy girls in the Street of the Copyist. They have gone to live on al Karim's estates near here."

"Mayhap I have seen her. A crow-black little creature, as thin as a lance shaft?"

"The same. Though now she hath filled out and is rather beautiful after the fashion of the blacks. That came about when her master the copyist Harith ibn al Jatib, got her with child. A daughter. The Prince Abd al Karim would not keep his wife's former lover's child, so the child was given to Harith's brother Husayn. Harith could not keep her, for he no longer wanted to stay at the copy house, but wanted adventure and travel. Husayn had just wed a blond maid he had bought of ibn Ha'ad. So Harith pushed upon his brother both his daughter and his copy house and entered ibn Ha'ad's service as a guard for his caravans. Husayn and his wife, who hath the look of thy race and whose name is of a total unpronouncability, love the child much, having as yet no other children. And the baby is very pretty, with curly hair, and is only a little black, being about the color that I am. You like my color, Aizun?"

"I adore it, Alaric said. " 'Tis what I love most in thee. I find thy swartness exciting."

"Oh!" Afaf said. "Then wouldst marry a Negress, lord of my life?"

He laughed. "Why not? I find them barbaric and splendid. I doubt not that they are even wilder abed than thou art—"

"Then no Negress shall ever cross my threshold, not even Sumayla, whom I love well. Besides, my wildness displeases thee. Thou'd have me gentle, so gentle I shall be." She moved close, fitted her slim body into the contours of his own. "See how gentle, my lord?"

During the whole of the next week she came nightly to his bed. And if, during the day, he wrestled mightily with his guilt, betimes torturing his mind with the implications of Saadyah's diabolical catechism, trying to get them clear, during those nights she made him forget guilt, sin, the hereafter, and even God. She was a matchless lover, having no coldness in her, and once the desert heat of her blood had been eased and cooled by their good sharing and warm use of each other, she revealed an inexhaustible store of tenderness. They were very happy. So happy that he doubted it could last. He was right. It could not. Human happiness never does.

He came into his little cell-like scriptorium to find Hasdai ben Sahl waiting for him there. The merchant's heavy countenance was troubled, sad, even—a look Alaric had never seen upon it before—confused.

"Alaric," he said, "I want truth of thee! Tell me: when was that certificate attesting to Afaf's virtue written by ben Ezra?"

Alaric felt the ice enter his heart. A tiny shaking got into his limbs. But he mastered himself almost at once.

"Some several days before our arrival here," he said.

"And, upon your arrival, its contents were still applicable? Mark me well, my boy! There are sins and sins; and in this thing the element of time is all-important."

"It was," Alaric said.

"Is it now?" ben Sahl thundered.

Alaric bowed his head, looked up again. "No, patron," he said quietly, "it is not applicable now."

He stood thus, waiting for the storm. It did not come. Hasdai ben Sahl's face was slack with sadness.

"God guide me," he muttered. "Saadyah is right—I am often wanting in charity, harsh in my judgments. Alaric, my son, thou hast sinned. But of such sins of the flesh I too was guilty in my youth; though, be it said, as the Talmud commands us, and unlike my son, I married as soon as I could and ceased to commit them. Thou art too valuable to me for me to discharge thee from my service for such as this. If thou wilt wed Afaf, I'll retain thee in my employ—"

Alaric felt relief flooding over him like a warm tide.

"I mean to, patron," he said. "I've meant to from the first. I have hesitated only because of Zoë—for it means I must become an apostate against my faith or else—"

"Convert Afaf to thine," said ben Sahl.

"Which would mean abandoning Zoë," Alaric said quickly. "I am not so lusty as to incline toward polygamy, good patron, though thou must admit the patriarchs of thy faith—"

"—practiced it. In another epoch, in the desert, under conditions where the survival of my people itself was at stake. Even incest was at times permitted there so that the Chosen Race might not die. A man may change his religion, my boy, only out of true conviction. Which thou hast not. Methinks thou art unsure of the validity of any religion, even thy own—"

"But, patron—"

"Hear me out, Teudisson! That point is bootless now! One question more: Is my daughter Ruth correct in her belief that no more than a week hath passed since thou and that swart and pretty child first engaged in carnal sin? That, in fact, this came to pass the selfsame night you fought Saadyah in defense of the virginity you thereupon took, or were awarded, profiting from Saadyah's own shameless scheme of luring Ruth from the house with a lying message supposedly from my sister-in-law?"

"Aye, patron, thy daughter has it right," Alaric said.

"Mitigating circumstances, but no excuse. Wed her, Alaric—under what faith thou wilt. As now thou canst. And thank whatever god or idol or graven image to which thou wilt in the future pray, that thou art guilty of no graver sin than fornication! Which is forgivable. Murder is not. Not even this subtle slaying by indirection hast thou some share in, the guilt of which thou hast escaped—by a hair!"

Alaric stared at him, hearing the beginning of a roaring in his ears, the blind red stab of anguish in his gut. For he knew. Without asking, he knew. The sickness in him rose up in nauseous waves. There was bile and blood at the back of his throat. He knew. But he had to ask, in the forlorn, pitiful hope that ben Sahl would deny his knowledge, take from him this one more cup, this sop of vinegar lance thrust into the mouth of one now truly crucified. He licked a tongue over his dry lips; forced the word out on a dry death rattle of a breath.

"Zoë—?"

"Is dead. By her own hand. Taking thy son with her. Ben Ezra tried to save the child by making use of that operation by which the first of the Caesars came into the world. He could not. She had thrust her blade through her swollen belly first, before seeking and finding her poor, mad heart—"

Alaric put his hand against his writing desk to steady himself. He felt something under it, something hard. Looking down, he saw what that something was, recognized it with one part of his mind while the other, on a different plane altogether, was trying to gather together the implications of this new horror, trying to force through the whitish blur that was his lips, to shape into sound, that awful "Why?" that already did not matter because the means for escape from absolutely unspeakably outrageous fortune lay already beneath his hand, his fingers closing about it now without conscious thought, or intent, or even will, as part of that inevitability that seemed always to bind him to evil whether he would or no. But he went on trying to ask that question, to which he knew the answer; relegating with blunt and total honesty the detail of whether Zoë had known or had merely anticipated his guilt to the level of utter irrelevance upon which it belonged: only he could not. His shock-paralyzed vocal cords would not form that "Why?"

Ben Sahl, who, despite Saadyah, was not without sensitivity, guessed what he was trying to say.

"Why? Because that would-be Jew, that apostate Mozarab swine Yacob—whom many a time and oft I've warned Solomon against!—told her, lyingly, that thou hadst fled with Afaf. Because my messenger, who reached Córdoba ten days ago, three days before thou hadst become guilty of the infidelity that the poor mad creature equated in value with her life, when she asked him whether you'd come alone to my house, replied, innocently enough: "Oh, no—he came with his wife—a Moorish woman whose beauty is like a starry night!" So take what comfort thou can, my boy; in this of her death, thou hast no real guilt—What ails thee, boy? God of Abraham! Alaric! Alaric! Ho, Benjamin! Ishaac! Yusuf! Come! To me! To me! Someone! Anyone! Art there no servants in this house? Dost no one hear me? In God's name, come! This young fool hath stabbed himself!"

XIII

"Hmmn—" Solomon ben Ezra said. "Who treated him?"

"A healer of the town," Hasdai ben Sahl said. "Procured by my son here, who numbers all manner of oddities among the wide circle of his acquaintances."

"Yayya ibn Xuaib," Saadyah said, "is no mere healer, but an excellent physician, Uncle Solly. He has worked many cures. . . ."

"Don't doubt it," ben Ezra said. "You know of what is composed this plasma, Saadyah?"

"Yes," Saadyah said, "he wrote out the formula for me, and I had a chemist in the Street of the Astrologers prepare it. Here it is. . . ."

Ben Ezra took the paper and studied the flowing Arabic script. "Hmmmn," he grunted; then read aloud: " 'Pomegranate, frankincense, myrrh, aloes, sarcocole, quicklime, dried hares' skin, mixed with the white of an egg and Armenium earth.' Hmmmmnn—to be applied to the wound, the patient to be given a quarter drachma of opium—Hmmmmn—"

"Enough to kill him, eh, Sol?" ben Sahl growled.

"The strange thing is that it hasn't, Hasdai," ben Ezra said. "Of course, the weather's cool now; but still—let me see, let me see—"

He took instruments from his bag and began to remove the thick gray-white mass covering the wound in Alaric's chest. When he had it off, they could see that the stab was ugly, inflamed. Solomon ben Ezra didn't say anything. He simply picked up a knife from among the instruments he had brought, and cut into the wound, crossing the original stab. An evil-smelling mass of clotted blood and pus oozed out of it.

Hasdai and Saadyah stood there watching him, their faces paling, sweat beading their foreheads now.

Ben Ezra wrapped a piece of clean white cotton cloth around a wand of olive wood, and probed into the wound, cleaning out all of the foul-smelling mass.

"Lung's touched," he growled. "Been spitting blood?"

"Yes," Hasdai ben Sahl whispered.

"Got any more of that pomade, boy?" the physician said to Saadyah.

"Aye, Uncle Sol," Saadyah said, "only it's not mixed. Ibn Xuaib said it keeps better if the ingredients are kept separate and only enough for one application prepared at a time. But it can be—"

"No! Don't mix it yet. Now we can remove the superstitious nonsense, while keeping what is good. Because your ibn Xuaib is not unskillful. If he had not contained the infection, this poor young fool would be dead by now. Apart from a slight mortification in the wound itself—born of one of the ingredients of the plasma itself, doubt it not!—there's no spread of gangrene. The pomegranate, all right. Throw out the aromatic gums, and substitute oil of tuya. Cut the quicklime with that. And reduce the proportion of quicklime to one fifth what it is now—which is enough to keep the wound clean. Throw out the powdered rabbit skin, too. Corrupts on contact with the wound and *causes* mortification. And no more opium! He must be allowed consciousness enough to fight. The rest of this stuff won't hurt—or help, likely—so keep it in. Who knows? Every time I see a case like this, I wonder why I didn't take up your gentle form of highway robbery, Hasdai!"

Father and son both stared at the physician.

"Will he live, Uncle Solly?" Saadyah said.

"Don't know. He ought to. Been able to get any food into him?"

"Soups," the merchant said. "Broths. A little wine—"

"Excellent. Keep it up. Who mixes the pomade? Your alchemist-astrologer?"

"No. My sister Ruth doth," Saadyah said. "As I told thee, it needs must be combined afresh each time—and 'tis too far to the chemist shop—"

"Go tell her to mix some now—with the changes I told thee, lad. Then bring it back. I'll bandage him up again. Then, to bed! I'm dead of weariness. Methinks this young ass of a Gothic lord by seven holy devils and more possessed hath cursed me to ride more leagues than any other patient I've ever had. First to Bilad al Zila, or Qashtalla, that high hot dry land of many strongholds to cure his brother—dead upon arrival; then some dozens of leagues from Córdoba to heal the stripes with which that pretty Bedu lass was covered for his sake—"

"Stripes?" Hasdai ben Sahl said. "Stripes?"

"Aye, Master of Banditry by the stroke of a pen, stripes. In my life I've seen no other whipped like that, and live. Didst no one tell thee of how she saved him from the sodomite?"

"Yes. He, himself. A matter of a key purloined from an eunuch, or some such romantic, childish rubbish; but stripes? No one told me—"

"Wert not such a churlish bear, mayhap, those about thee would confide in thee more, my friend. Now this mad ride. I'm sure I have saddle sores upon my arse. Ah, yes, this son of my peoples' enemies hath caused me weariness enough, and some pain, too, I will avow! I loved that poor mad Grecian child. A pity—she'd have made him the perfect wife—"

"If he had not chosen to dally with others!" the merchant said.

Solomon ben Ezra looked at his old friend. "Most men dally with others, Hasdai," he said tartly. "Do not presume of thy fidelity to Sarah. Had she been less fair, or cold, who knoweth what thou mightest have done? And this adultery—were it that; the word allowable in this case, methinks—was with a maid who had all the flesh of her back made bloody ribbons for his sake. By the way, how is that thicklipped Bedu child?"

"Like to die," Saadyah said harshly, "for no morsel of food hath passed those sweet lips since this monster of piety butchered himself!"

"Have her brought here. I am too weary to descend or climb more stairs. I'll talk some sense into her—or have her force-fed like a Christian goose for one of their heathen feasts. Now get thee gone, my boy, and bring me that healing balm!"

When Saadyah came back to the room with his sister, the two of them supporting Afaf between them, because by then the Egyptain slave girl could scarcely walk, he heard the physician, their uncle by courtesy and by the lifelong ties of love binding their father to his learned friend, say: "Does he rave much?"

"Aye, that he doth," Saadyah answered for his father, easing Afaf down into the nearest chair.

"About what?" ben Ezra said.

"God," Saadyah said. "The quality of evil. Why it exists. Why God permits it. About his own sins."

"Dost call that raving? I don't. Or if it is, I've indulged in it oft, myself. But that's the chief danger now—"

"What's the chief danger now, Uncle Solly?" Ruth said, as she came forward and kissed the physician.

"Bless thee, child!" ben Ezra said. "The chief danger now is that he may will himself to die. Men do. And against that will, no art availeth. I've seen it happen right oft. Ordinarily I'd say he'd recover from this wound. But will he—from the others?"

"The others?" Hasdai said.

"Aye, Hasdai, the others. The ones that leave no scars our eyes can see. The ones that caused him to do this. The wounds life deals us all, but in general measured out, belaboring us at intervals widely enough spaced to permit some recovery betwixt one blow and the next. A catalogue of what hath befallen this poor lad in the past year would amount to punishment for the blackest sins a man might do in a lifetime; and penance and forgiveness, too; by my troth. And those he hath committed—some little fleshly dalliance, I'd guess, and precious little of that, or he'd have lost that angelic look he hath by now—as nothing against all he hath suffered. You've brought the pomade?"

"Yes, Uncle Solly," Ruth whispered. "Here 'tis. . . ."

"Good. Now be ye all still while I attend him—" the physician said.

"There!" ben Ezra said. "That should do it. How long hath it been since blood issued from his mouth or nostrils?"

"Last night," Saadyah said.

"I think that danger's passed. The lung is scarcely touched. A long cut, but shallow. With what implement did he this butchery? An ax?"

"Nay," the merchant said. "With an ornamental blade that hath no use beyond breaking the seals of scrolls and letters. Of copper, methinks. Without edge, and with a blunt point. The wonder is it penetrated at all—"

"He struck with fearsome force. Of copper, Hasdai? It doubled then! Hit a rib and was deflected downward from the heart, thus making this huge but shallow rip. So now—"

Ben Ezra turned then, and stared at Afaf. She was all eyes. Her flesh had wasted away in that terrible week; but her eyes were so luminous, so hot with anguish, sorrow, pain, that ben Ezra was sure that one could warm one's hands at them.

"Come here, child," he said to her in Arabic.

She pushed up from the chair, stood there like a dark and trembling shade from hell itself. Took one step forward. Another. Crashed full length to the floor. Saadyah and the physician both bent to pick her up; but she shook off their hands. She lay there prostrate, her face against the floor, crying.

Ben Ezra knelt beside her.

"Thou must not, child," he said to her in the Prophet's tongue. "Thou art all he hath now. Only thou canst save him, make him whole—"

"Noooh!" Afaf wept, the word coming out of her mouth in a long shudder. "He hates me now, for the sin I made him do! Besides, 'twas *she* he loved, not me! What wouldst thou, noble sage? What thinketh I could or dare do for him who is dying for the love of another?"

"Women!" ben Ezra snorted. "Nay, child, 'tis not of love he is dying, but of a sense of guilt. I fear his gloomy Teutonic mind more than his wound—that Gothic mind which not even four centuries of Spanish sun hath been able to warm to simple, sensuous joy—"

He could see that Afaf was listening to him now, so he went on, urgently.

"Mark me, daughter! Harken unto my words. 'Twas not who Zoë was that counted, but his feeling that he baselessly and without reason deserted her, and thereby caused her death. With his race's morbid hunger after guilt, he needs must forget that his separations from Zoë were on both occasions by circumstances forced; by evil fate, if you will. When he reached my house the night you helped him flee the sodomite, it was very clear that he no longer loved the little Greek—if, indeed, he ever did, having this faculty for persuading himself to respond with kindness to any maid's warm favor. And, being most matchlessly fair, that favor comes his way oftener than is good for him. I saw that night that he loved her not; but that duty, and the unborn child he'd sired, held him. Oh, he'd have made the best of it! Poor Zoë! Had not a renewed onslaught of her madness—you knew her, hence must have known that the touch of Allah's finger lingered upon her—taken her out of life, slain by an excess of unmerited suffering, her groundless jealousy, and her own poor tormented hand—Zoë would not have known a moment's grief, a moment's sorrow at his side. Nor wilt thou, daughter! For he loves thee. Not totally, but as much as he is capable of loving any woman. Thou must be content to share him with the inner voices that guide and torture him; with his rarely awful God. If only there were some way to rid him of his sense of guilt—"

"There is!" Saadyah's voice cut in harshly. "Aye, Uncle Sol, there is!"

Solomon ben Ezra stopped, looked at the ruddy, handsome youth, seeing his face unexpectedly and unusually stern, serious, grave.

"And how would you do that, Saad?" he said.

Saadyah looked not at the physician but into his own father's face. "By ridding him of his monstrous God!" he said.

"Saadyah!" Hasdai ben Sahl thundered. "His God is ours! Beyond this criminal nonsense of their Mashiah, the faith of the Nazarenes stems from ours. They even made an idiotic attempt to make a Gaon of their Mashiah by tracing his descent from King David through his sawdust-and woodchips-bedizened father, then negated their own fabrications without even perceiving the contradictions by basing their blasphemous claims to their Mashiah's semidivinity upon the especially repugnant contention that this selfsame carpenter Joseph was cuckolded by the Holy Ghost. God of Abraham! Had not a carpenter a stick among his possessions? Nor the manhood nor the wit to use it upon his faithless wife? Their nonsense aside, Saadyah, the Christians are our fault and our burden. They represent a failure somewhere to implement and enforce our holy teachings and our sacred laws. True, they hath used us ill, but even this hath a certain logic: if the very people of their Lord deny him, what becomes of their pretension to universality? So this I'll not permit thee! Thou'd rob him of the God of Moses, my son! And this blasphemy threatens not only his soul, but thine!"

"There are many gods, Father," Saadyah roared back, "and if he needs must have one, let him choose Allah who hath given his people dominion and power! Or Roman Jupiter who sent the Caesars' legions screaming across the world and gave them force enough to scatter us like dust over all the face of it! Or Ormazd, who informed his magi that to cleave a Jewish skull was pleasing in his sight! Or Amon Ra who instructed his pharaohs that we served well to make bricks without straw! Or Ba'al Mammon by whose Babylonian waters our forefathers wept; or cruel Ishtar whose Assyrian cohorts wreaked destruction upon our lands! Or—"

"Where art all those ancient peoples now, Saadyah?" the physician cut him off. "And where are we? Besides, heaven save me from my wordy, metaphysical race! Look you about you, my friends, upon what you might see had you eyes, or hear, if your ears remain undeafened by your own bellowings. A lad all but dying on a bed, in whose behalf the most elementary prudence, if not courtesy, counsels quiet. A maid whose health, if not her life, stands in some danger from starvation and the abuse of grief. I beg of you, postpone your theological hairsplitting for another day, and allow me to attend to what is needful here!"

"Thou art right, Uncle Solly!" Ruth said angrily. "Father and Saadyah, will you please, please be quiet for the nonce?"

"Sorry, Uncle Sol," Saadyah muttered.

"And I," ben Sahl rumbled. "This whelp upsets me so that I forget the circumstances. . . ."

"Very well," ben Ezra said. "Afaf, daughter, look at me!"

Slowly Afaf raised her head. "Yes, my lord?" she whispered.

"Only thou canst save him," Solomon said, "and thou must! Thou must give him the desire to live again; make him know life's sweetness and its savor. To do that thou must both save thyself—and repair thy looks! Thou hast become as ugly as a she-camel! Wilst thou save him, child? Wilst thou at least try? For if he dies now—"

"If he dies now?" Afaf echoed.

"The guilt be on thy head!" Solomon ben Ezra thundered.

Afaf stared at the physician. Her eyes were appalled. Dumbly she nodded. "Aye, my lord. I'll save him if I can," she said.

Upon the stroke of midnight Alaric Teudisson awoke from sleep, or, mayhap, from a state closer akin to death itself. He was in great pain. But, because that pain was physical, he welcomed it. It served for something, this slow, deep, searing ache. By concentration upon it, he could shut out that other hurt which had no name and was beyond his strength to bear. He lay there very still, keeping his eyes closed, conserving the flickering flame of consciousness, of being, within him until it spread out over his body like a feeble, searching blaze, moving in tiny tendrils, extending that bite, that sear, reduced to a prickling hot itch, along his veins, his nerves, until he could no longer deny its reality and his own renewed existence. The sensation was distinctly unpleasant, even painful; but since that pain had to bear comparison with the self-inflicted stab wound in his chest, and that long, long tearing scream of utter anguish that echoed in his heart, it was as nothing. He allowed his eyes to flicker open upon a world he'd counted lost, had no desire to see. At first they were unfocused, glazed; then they cleared. Their gaze rested like a pale blue glow upon Afaf's dark face.

She came up out of her chair very slowly, the motion angular, awkward, as though it were not her own volition that moved her legs, her arms. She did not cry out, or even speak. Instead she bent and took his hand, bore it to her mouth, covering it back and palm with slow, worshipful kisses, blessing it with her tears.

"Afaf!" Saadyah protested. "Thou must not! He—"

"—lives," Alaric whispered, "and must, methinks, continue to. Therefore, good Saadyah, beloved brother of my heart—"

Saadyah, too, was beside him now, kneeling on the other side of the bed; his fine ruddy face wet with the good tears of joy.

"Aye, Aizun?" he prompted.

"I pray thee, tell me—how," Alaric said.

"I tell thee, Aizun," Saadyah roared at him, one week later to the day, as he sat alone with Alaric in the night, "thou must become a Mussulman! Since all religions are nonsense, at least embrace a useful one! See all the advantages it hath: Thou canst rid thyself of thy carved-up strumpet by merely pronouncing sentence of divorce against her—nay, not even that; for in the eyes of Allah, the One, the Only, the Compassionate, the Wise, thou art not even wed to her, for no imam, cadi, alfaqui of His heard thy meaningless Christian vows. Thou must marry Afaf, and three others as different from her as suits thy capricious fancy—adding to the lot betimes as many luscious concubines as thou feels capable of belaboring in the night. Thou canst return to Córdoba as head of the branch of the House of Sahl Father is planning to open there—Oh, don't worry about that practicer of fellatio, sodomy, pederasty and other assorted unnatural vices! I've a plan afoot that will richly reward him for his sins, and cause him to take ship for distant climes. Which is why I am playing the dutiful son for the nonce. Father, poor soul, hath already consented to send me to Córdoba to purchase the land, and begin the construction of his counting house combined, which is to be the grandest in all al Andalus. Never you fear, I'll discharge his commission faithfully, betimes laying a trap for Ahmad al Hussein into which, being what he is, he cannot help but fall."

"When do you leave, then, Saad?" Alaric asked.

"That depends upon thee, brother. Thou hast, I flatter myself, some need of me still. I'd have thee afoot and walking in the sun ere I—"

"No," Alaric said. "Thy father's business should not wait for me. Go thou tomorrow, if the day be fair."

"Done!" Saadyah laughed. "I'm looking forward to this journey! The same old buttocks, breasts, and thighs I make use of every night begin to pall on me. As would their faces too, if I ever looked upon a face, which since it hath little or no use I do not. Aye, Córdoba! City of delights! But I digress. Let us return to you. Look you, fair Aizun, what the future could well hold for you! Once established in Córdoba, you can quietly let the Emir know of your presence, through his brother, al Mugira, say; write the Leader of the Faithful a verse—he's mad over poetry, you know—and when thy Arabic is no longer the stammering of an idiot child, then—"

Alaric smiled. He lay propped upon his pillows; he was as pale as death, and fearfully thin; but a hundred subtle signs indicated clearly that life had won out over death; that he would live; though his pale abstracted eyes looked longingly still, Saadyah thought, upon the Valley of the Shadow, yet his strength had increased to the point that he could be roared at, bullied, after the young Jew's wont.

"And thou?" he said. "What of thee, Saad? 'Tis meet that thou, not I, head thy father's new countinghouse—"

"Oh, I shall manage!" Saadyah said airily. "I have neither the head nor the inclination for such things. But as soon as I return, I'll take thee to an imam I know. A prince of a knavish fellow! Most wonderfully corrupt—"

"Saad—" Alaric said.

"Yes, Aizun?"

"I would not be an apostate from my Faith. Like thee, I have right oft been beset with doubts. I fear I must struggle with them lifelong. But to give up my Lord Jesu for the Prophet, my Lord God for Allah, seemeth me—"

"—six of one hand, and half a dozen of another!" Saadyah mocked. "But since thou'rt not convinced, I must be harsh with thee! Aizun, my pupil in deviltry, recite me the Devil's Catechism."

Alaric smiled.

"God is all powerful," he said. "God is all knowing. His knowledge includes the future as well as the present and the past. Despite His omnipotence, His omniscience, He grants me freedom of will, that I may choose between the good and the evil in me. If I choose good, He'll lift me into Paradise, make the light of His Countenance to shine upon me, grant me eternal life. If I choose evil, He'll throw me into hell, where I'll pay in endless torments for my sins. There! Did I get it right?"

Saadyah made a leg; bowed and kissed the ring on Alaric's finger.

"Beautifully, your Holiness! Just beautifully! Now, San Alarico, of piety all compact, let us play a little charade, thou and I! Thou for the nonce—" Saadyah folded his hands in antic reverence "—art God. And I am Alaric Teudisson. Agreed?"

"Agreed," Alaric said, "though God forgive us both for blasphemy!"

"And for gluttony, sloth, lechery, drunkenness, incest, sodomy, thieving and sleeping i' the church throughout my lord Bishop's sermons, though they be fearsome dull, I trow! Look you, Almighty. Consider Thy servant Teudisson. Who is not yet born. What knowest Thou of him?"

"Well—" Alaric said.

"Not well! He'll be a fearsome sinner, will he not? Speak up, Almighty, answer me! Thou knowest the future as Thou knowest this present hour. So tell me, will not Thy servant Teudisson sin?"

"Yes," Alaric said, beginning to catch Saadyah's drift and liking it not at all; because it was not the simple contradiction he'd thought, but of an unanswerable and disturbing complexity. "He'll be a sinner most awful, black, and foul, for which I'll punish him!"

"Wilt thou, now, Almighty? Good, good, good! Oh, good and rare and randy! Some brimstone piping hot, shall we say? A touch o' the devil's fork? A little pitch? Some molten lead? Fire i' the belly? Tongs to squeeze his lustful balls? A serpent nine clothiers' yards long to gnaw him where he most sinned? Good, good, good! Oh, most merciful Almighty!"

"Saad—" Alaric said.

"Not Saad. I'm Teudisson, remember. A black and foul sinner. And thou, Almighty, art all-knowing. Thou knew, didst Thou not—some moons before Thou didst allow me to be born that I'd lie in sinful congress with a maid named Zoë. Thou knew I'd pump her belly big with unhallowed fruit; and that from that simple giving and taking of joy would come events most murky, bloody, terrible. All this Thou knew

264

before Thou caused me to come into this best of all possible of Thy worlds, did Thou not? Answer me, thou capricious, cruel Fiend—Oh, I forgot; forgive me, Omnipotence! And answer me, Almighty!"

"Aye," Alaric said grimly. "A million, million years before I allowed thee, Teudisson, to be born, I knew that thou'd fornicate, murder, take awful vengeance upon a woman's weakness, lie, cheat, steal, contrive cunning plots for further vengeance, fornicate again, drive a poor witless child to her death—all this and more—till sickening of thy guilt, thou'd break My fearsome canons 'gainst self-slaughter. All that I knew!"

"Then, Lord Satanas—I mean Almighty—why didst allow me to be born? Or, having given me my miserable life, why didst Thou not, as elementary mercy demanded, remove these pitfalls from my path?"

"I gave thee choice, Teudisson! Thou wert free to choose the good thou spurned instead of the evil thou embraced! Therefore well hast thou deserved thy torments!"

"Thou liest in Thy holy teeth, Almighty, when Thou sayest that I had of Thee, or of Satanas Thy brother, choice! Or, if choice, vain; and, being vain, illusion! Come now, Almighty, don't be an almighty bore. Would say Thou didst not *know*, up there in Thy Cloud—Cuckoo Land, an eon ago—which choice I'd make, which choice I could not help but make, having the nature which Thou in Thy total wisdom gave me? Art trying to absolve Thyself of Thine own guilt, which consists of playing ducks and drakes with human beings created in Thy image? Or Thou in theirs— for who knows which came first, chicken or egg, egg or chicken? Yes, I am mad; but Thou hast made me so! Thou gave me choice? I laugh, but my laughter hath the taste of tears! Art Thou first cause or no? If Thou art, doth not all choice ultimately reside in Thee? Put me in a madhouse, in hall of mirrors; but call not what I do 'choice'! If *a priori* Thou knew I needs must choose—nay, make the proposition less even than that!—that I merely would of my own volition choose evil, and let me be born to choose it, then piled Sinai on Olympus by not stretching forth Thy allegedly merciful hand to stay me from doing that evil I had chosen willy-nilly—or by Thy leave! or by Thy leave!—why then dost hurl me into the pit? By what right? Answer me, why? Art tongue-tied, Almighty? Then let me say it! Because Thou delightest in cruelty, in pain; and the piteous screams echoing unending down all time art music to Thine ears! That being so, I beg of Thee the boon of removing Thee from my private heaven, my little cosmos, my minuscule universe—a poor and shoddy thing to be sure, but all I own! And before I'd see it peopled, throned, and ruled by a monster, I'll see it empty! Thou'll permit me to disbelieve in Thee, Almighty?"

"Saad—" Alaric whispered.

"I—I am of Thy Chosen People, Almighty—whose blood hath run red through half the gutters of this world! Who have been reviled, shamed, tortured, slain—in recompense for their steadfastness and their piety! So Thou, O God, let me alone! Allow me my human sins, and my merely human virtues! Let me take back from my son the freedom that I grant him, when I see him like to die of it! Let me intervene time and time again to save him from his own folly, lust, greed, crime, remembering he partaketh of my nature; let me realize that freedom of will is revocable for his own good; let me forgive him over and over, and never deny him! Let me know that no sin of his, no several sins, however fiendish, black, ugly, foul, art worth a single hour in hell, let alone eternity! Allow me—disbelief, and mercy both! Tenderness and love, for I—"

"Saad, 'tis not so! It cannot be! Our feeble understanding cannot—"

"Aye, but it can, Almighty! It can see the poor widow spitting blood from lung fever and starvation while her ragged scarecrows of children dance for obols to the tambourines she hath scarce strength to lift! It can comprehend the anguish of a pious maid forced to sell her body to bring her parents bread. It can even understand Clothilde's grief—I have her name right, have I not, Almighty?—when her father's blood and brains splattered on her robes; or mine—Thy servant Teudisson's—when he lifted his good and gentle mother up, and saw that second mouth the Berbers had slashed across her throat! Our feeble intellect can recognize bootless cruelty, unmerited suffering, gratuitous pain, easily enough! In all ages it hath cried out: 'Why doth the wicked prosper?' And, 'My God, my God—why hast Thou forsaken me?'"

"Saad—" Alaric whispered. "Oh, Saad!"

Saadyah stopped short; stared at him.

"Forgive me, Aizun!" he said. "For if there be sin, and if a hell exists, this that I have done to thee now is that sin and condemns me to that hell! I have no right—no right at all to—"

Alaric put out his hand to him.

"I bid thee good night, brother," he said.

"Aizun! I—"

"I love thee, Saad," Alaric said, "but this burden thou hast laid upon my heart now is mine. I have assumed it, fully. To bear it up—or lie broken beneath it. In either case I needs must try my strength alone. Hence, good night, my brother! And Godspeed upon tomorrow's journey—"

"I'll not go!" Saadyah wept. "I'll not go! For thou—"

"For I have need of a solitary time with no one at my side. Not thee.

Not even Afaf. Who would plumb hell must walk alone. No rancor, Saadyah! The God thou deniest, and of whom I would be free, bless and guide thee on thy way."

"Good night," Saadyah whispered. "Aye, good night—if any day or night be good! And all the angels thou bearest in thy heart, sing thee to thy rest!"

Then he bent and kissed Alaric's cheeks, and went out from there into the dark of night—not half so utter, lightless, black as that he left behind him.

XIV

The night that Saadyah ben Hasdai returned from his mission to Córdoba was soft and slumberous with spring, for three good months and more had passed by since Hasdai ben Sahl had reluctantly allowed his curiously changed and sobered son—this only, Saadyah knew, because Alaric was still too weak for travel—to undertake the first steps toward extending the House of Sahl's operations to Córdoba. In so doing, the merchant ran a calculated risk, for in the capital he would enter upon direct competition with that wiliest of all traders, the Christian ibn Ha'ad. But Saadyah rode homeward with contentment in his heart; for he had, as he would with all he truly cared about, succeeded brilliantly. The land for his father's new establishment was bought—and its location was, from a commercial standpoint, admirable. For on one of the city's busiest and most central streets, Saadyah's not unshrewd eye had seen a thing that not even his father would have thought to buy: an ancient tenement house, in so advanced a stage of decay that it had to be propped up with timbers to keep it from collapsing of its own weight, and swarming with filthy Mozarabs of the very lowest type, who, the young Jew was instantly certain, would be years in arrears with the payments of their rents. Three days of watching near the door sufficed: the rental agent came, only to be greeted with shrieks of rage in Romance and Arabic both. The haggling, which Saadyah wisely did not interrupt, went on for hours; in the end the despairing agent departed with less than one quarter of his rents.

Departed, but not too far. For at the very next corner Saadyah overtook him. A cup or two in a tavern, a meal cheerfully paid for, an insignificant bribe, and Saadyah had the name and address of the owner. A courteous visit that same night paid upon the pretext of securing the name of a rent collector to handle dwellings owned by his father, whose name, of course, the owner recognized; two whole hours of listening to the owner's bemoaning of his cursed fate, complaining of the impossibility of collecting rents in Córdoba, so supported were the rabble by the overtender law, enabled Saadyah not only to set the price for house and lot laughably low, but largely to resist the owner's sudden discovery of how valuable the house was, after all, when he found out the young Jew wanted to buy it.

The rest of the operation was of a nature which might have forced Hasdai ben Sahl, had he known of it, to thank his stars for his accidental choice of his son as emissary. For Saadyah did what Alaric would have been much too tenderhearted to do—if indeed it would have occurred to the young Goth to buy the miserable tenement at all, which is more than doubtful—he simply ordered his newly acquired tenants off the place; and, as they profanely refused to leave, commanded his crew of workers to pull the ancient firetrap down about their ears. The tenants—as Saadyah had known they would, and hence had already taken appropriate countermeasures—sent a delegation flying to the Head Cadi, who as the custom was, held public audience daily. But the head judge was burdened under a backlog of hundreds of cases, as usual; by the time he could hear their plea and send an official to investigate, official and delegation alike were confronted with a *fait accompli:* the Mozarabs' worm-eaten furniture and vermin-infested bedding polluted the air of the street, while their former residence was no more than a mountain of rubble which already lines of muleteers were beginning to cart away. More, when the indignant official ordered Saadyah to appear before his lord, the young Jew cheerfully acquiesced, arriving promptly the next morning with the following documents ready and in hand: the list of the arrears of his tenants to the former owner now become legally arrears to him, which fact he proved by a signed, stamped, and certified bill of sale; a judgment handed down by the Emir's own chief civil engineer condemning the tenement as unfit for human habitation and ordering the former owner to tear it down at once, said document bearing a date fully three years agone, its execution having been held off by numerous stays obtained by the former owner by judicious use of bribery; and a list—itself procured by a fat purse slipped into the itchy palm of the secretary of the Special Judge for Criminal Matters—on which appeared the names of at least one member of every family from the tenement, for offenses ranging from drunkenness, street brawling, and petty thievery, to pimping, prostitution, and murder, together with the fines, whippings, imprisonments, and even an occasional execution, with which these crimes, high and low, felonies and misdemeanors, had been punished, bearing the dates of their application—in many cases signed by no less than the head judge himself.

The Cadi al Aljama al Córdoba indignantly ordered the ring leaders of the delegation whipped with twenty stripes each and their followers driven from his court by the stout staves of his bailiffs. Whereupon good Saadyah further proved his shrewdness. Boldly he intervened on behalf of the groveling wretches, getting the judge to let them off with a heavy fine instead of the beatings, which he himself thereupon paid, thus causing the dull-witted rabble to hail him as their savior instead of murdering him during one of the nights he needs must still remain in Córdoba, as they otherwise would have surely done.

The rabble scattered to the four winds, the muleteers carting away the debris, the finest architect in Córdoba busy about the plans for the second House of Sahl—all his business, in fact, terminated with neatness and dispatch—Saadyah thereupon turned his attention to removing the threat to Alaric's safety once the fair youth had returned to Córdoba, represented by Ahmad al Hussein's residence in the capital and the high favor the pervert enjoyed.

Since Saadyah meant to bait a trap for al Hussein—the one, only, and inevitable trap that would ensnare the pervert—he reluctantly decided that his sacrificial lamb would have to be a Jewish youth. For the Jewish attitude was uniquely stern toward deviation, and only among his own religionists could Saadyah expect to find a father whose outrage at having a son corrupted by a Moorish lord would be not only sincere but implacable enough to be proof against the blandishments of conciliatory bribes.

After a month of mingling with Jewry of influence in Córdoba— those high enough placed and close enough to Moorish officialdom to guarantee a scandal of the magnitude suitable to his purpose—Saadyah found his lamb: Ishaac ben Abravanil, only son of the head of the local Yeshiva, petted alike by his highly regarded father, his mother, and his several sisters; he was a boy of great beauty and had the necessary air of effeminacy to make him fit bait for the twitching nose of Ahmad al Hussein. Deviously, Saadyah brought the boy to the pervert's attention, parading him before al Hussein's house until the eunuch Hagib approached them with an invitation. Whereupon Saadyah made arrangements both for himself to be unexpectedly called away and for the chief of police to intrude upon the appointed meeting after his own departure. All this he arranged through the complicity—and avarice, for he offered a purse—of the eunuch Hagib himself, who had scant enough reason to love his master.

All went off with the precision of a military exercise; stuffed with sweetmeats, drowsy with wine, his uncertain blood warmed with many a cunning aphrodisiac, young Ishaac proved deliciously easy for Ahmad al Hussein to seduce—at which moment Hagib gave the signal to the police chief.

So it was that Ahmad al Hussein, to his own incredulous dismay, found himself locked in a cell. The Emir had little patience with perverts, and would have brought al Hussein to speedy trial but for the advice of his head eunuch Nasr, who pointed out the folly of such a course. The Emir's own brother, Prince al Wallid, was thought by some to have had some carnal association with al Hussein—a rumor which surely would be brought out in the defense. As an alternative to a public trial, Nasr suggested a double remedy: first, the Emir should make al Wallid a present of the Gothic slave girl who had been bought for the royal harem (though she had remained unused for more than a year because of the religious madness that was upon her); this action would tend to cure the Prince of his rumored or real tendencies toward effeminacy; and the Prince's own gentle ways would certainly have a calming effect on the young slave girl, for that matter. Second, the eunuch urged his master to do nothing whatever but to forget the existence of Ahmad al Hussein in his guarded cell, leaving the matter of the pervert's fate in Nasr's humble hands. The Leader of the Faithful sighed and agreed.

As for the eunuch Hagib, he entered the service of Saadyah ben Hasdai and traveled with him to Toledo, whereat he was assured of proximity to Afaf, she whom he had loved well since the days of her service in al Hussein's household.

Saadyah was well pleased with himself on all counts. His good cheer, however, lasted him exactly one quarter of an hour after his arrival at Toledo. For within that short space of time his roars of rage and anguish had already begun to rock the whole quarter of Toledo's Jewry.

"Gone!" he bellowed at his sister. "Gone where?"

"I know not," Ruth sobbed. "Father put him from the house. Methinks he's lost his wits. The poor boy! He seemed determined to outdo your feats of debauchery, Saad. One night, a city guard brought him home. We never got the straight of it, but it seemed he'd done something so outrageous to one of those filthy creatures who sell themselves—to goats and monkeys like *you*, my fair brother—that even she rebelled; and the gross, fat creature who ran the house of ill fame—"

"Berta Broadtail!" Saadyah roared.

"The same. Or Milewide, or some such dreadful name—had him thrown into the street. I've heard he goes there nightly still, but that the fat woman denies him entrance. He, in his madness, fancies himself in love with the trull who had him ejected from that house. And poor Afaf—"

"Aye," Saadyah croaked, "Afaf—what of her?"

"—hath left us, unable to bear longer the sight of his degradation and disgrace. She, at least, fares well. She hath entered the service of a noble lady—a Negress, black as night—who is married to the uncle of the Emir—"

"Al Karim?" Saadyah said.

"I know not his name. But he hath an estate only four leagues from here on the main road to Córdoba. It seems Afaf knew her before she was elevated from the lowly position of a copy house slave to a princess. Strange—how could a man find a black woman beautiful? With their thick lips and woolly hair and—"

"Of tastes there is nothing written," Saadyah said. "So Father let her go, too?"

"How could he stop her? She was a hired servant here, remember, not a slave. Oh, I had to listen to two hours' nonsensical gossip about the black Princess who is brokenhearted because she cannot give her lord a son—apparently not her fault, for none of his other wives or concubines have been able to either; besides which, she left a bastard daughter in the hands of her ex-master's brother and his wife—who is a Goth, who looks like our Alaric, who is very gentle and so forth and so on ad infinitum and ad nauseam. In any event, as I said, our Aizun hath taken to drink and lechery. I think Father's sorry to have discharged him, because he continued to do his work well, even though blind with the effects of a night's carousing. Saad—"

"Aye, sister?"

"What willst thou do? We cannot let him—"

"Nor shall we. Have someone look after my new man. For, as weary as I am, I must ride—"

Finding Alaric proved no trick at all, for that saintly young sinner was precisely where Ruth's story had inclined Saadyah first to look, comfortably ensconced before the door of fat Berta's famed establishment. Beside him lay a leathern flask of wine, from which at intervals he expertly shot a thin stream into his mouth; before him, on the stone steps, he'd placed a slab of wood with a sheaf of papers pinned to it, on which he was scribbling happily, having also thoughtfully provided himself with an inkpot in a leathern case that hung from his belt, so that each time he dipped one of his dozen quills into it, he added another inkspot to the two score with which his Persian-style trousers were festooned already.

Saadyah put out his hand and touched Alaric's shoulder. The young Goth turned, blinked owlishly at him. Then his eyes cleared and over his face stole a smile of pure, seraphic beatitude.

"Saad—" he said.

"Oh, Aizun! Aizun!" Saadyah whispered. "How I have injured thee!"

"Injured?" Alaric said, getting to his feet. "Injured? How could you injure me, Saadyah? Know you not I'm proof against injury? All madmen are. 'Whom Allah's finger hath touched—' You know. Wouldst not kiss me, brother?"

Saadyah kissed him on both his cheeks, stood back. Alaric was painfully thin; and, indeed, a fire very like unto madness burned in his pale eyes, giving them a gleeful, mocking cast. Which was, in him, the saddest of all things.

"Aizun," Saadyah said, "you fool! You must come home with me at once. Father will forgive you. Ruth said he misses you sorely—"

Alaric blinked at him again.

"Can't," he said.

"Why can't you?"

"Must go in there—" He pointed to fat Berta's door. "Ah, Saadyah! You see before you the only man in the history of Toledo who was thrown out of a whorehouse with money still in his pocket! Berta won't let me in. Says I'm a troublemaker. She's right. I am. Where I go, trouble accompanies me. You see that man?"

Saadyah looked about him. He saw nothing. He caught a hint of movement in the deeper shadow; but 'twas but a breath of wind, he was sure.

"What man?" he said.

"That one there. In the dark. He hath followed me everywhere for two weeks now. I think he's the devil. Hath he not a devilish look?"

"Oh, Aizun!" Saadyah said.

"Come. See if you cannot persuade Berta to let me in. I must beg pardon of the fair Sancha. You know Sancha, don't you, Saad?"

"God, yes!" Saadyah breathed. "Now that's a fiery piece if ever— Alaric! Ruth says—So, 'twas Sancha! Tell me, brother, what was this awful thing you did to her?"

"Awful?" Alaric said. "Awful?"

"Aye. And it must have been horror's very self, for if I know Sancha, were she paid enough, she'd receive your favor standing on her head."

"Now, Saad, you wrong her. She's a good and pious maid, who—"

"She's a good and pious hypocrite! Oh, I know she goes to church on Sundays, confesses her sins—apart from whoring, which, I'm told, your priests hold not a sin, but merely work, since by it she gains her daily bread—but she employs this ostentatious piety but to add a fillip to jaded tastes—"

"She has the look of an angel," Alaric said.

"So far. Remember she hath not been selling her hot and perfumed little flesh more than a twelvemonth. Give her another two years, then look at her. Come on, tell me: What did you to that trull?"

"I? Nothing. She took one look at me and fled, screaming at the top of her lungs. Whereupon Berta threw me out. *Now* do you see him—?"

"Art mad, Aizun. Come. Tired as I am, I'd get to the bottom of this, before taking you home." He pounded on Berta's door with his great fist. "Open up!" he roared. "In the Name of the Emir of all the Faithful and His Law!"

The moment he pronounced this dread phrase used by the city police when about a search, the door flew open, and a trembling eunuch bobbed his thick body halfway through a profound bow; then halted it.

"My lord Saadyah!" he wailed. " 'Tis not meet to frighten the very life out of a body, thus! How fare you? Come in! Come in! For we have missed you sorely. When dist return, my lord? Wait here, and I'll fetch Berta—"

Then, seeing whom Saadyah had firmly by the arm, he stopped. His heavy forehead creased into a frown.

"My lord," he said, "my lady Berta hath forbidden—"

"I know, I know," Saadyah said. "Go and fetch her, Taliq! Hop now, O slender and graceful gazelle that thou art!"

The eunuch Taliq, who was as fat almost as Berta herself, made an elephantine caricature of a scurry. In a few minutes, the sound of heavy tread redoubled, for Berta came back with her manservant. She was a sight to see: her hair dyed red, her tiny mouth carmined in her great round face, which was plastered thickly with rice powder, with here and there a false beauty spot applied; she wore whore's garb still, made of transparent stuffs, so that her monstrous breasts, their nipples richly carmined too, plainly showed above the various rolls and ripples of her belly. But her hips, encased in brocaded and spangled drawers under the gauze of her shintiyan, were a wonder of wonders—even in a woman of her bulk they were disproportionate, and the original source of both her fortune and her fame, for dearly did the lower classes among the Moors, and all classes among the Berbers, love luscious fat in a woman. More than fifty now, she had clients whom she accommodated still, because they scornfully rejected "Those racks of bones" that even the plumpest of her girls were, to their taste. Yet, since Christians and an occasional lonely Jew made up the bulk of her clientele, most of her girls were slender in accord with European ideas of beauty. Seeing Saadyah now, her tiny mouth spread into a smile.

"My lord Short Sword!" she greeted him raucously. "Doth thy poor little maimed weapon ache thee tonight? Come, and I will ease thee—if thou thinketh thou canst mount a *real* woman instead of one of these narrowtails with twin pimples upon their chests!"

Saadyah grinned at her. The joke was an old one between them.

"I fear me I am too weary for your volcanic ardor, Berta," he said, "nor have I half the night to waste searching amid your various creases and folds for the proper one—for which, once found, Allah the Compassionate be praised, that I grant you! Truth to tell, I came on behalf of my friend, Aizun here, who—"

Berta stopped still. So still that almost all of her ceased to jiggle—no mean feat.

"Him!" she shrieked. "That holy madman! Out! Throw him out! Take him away from here, my lord Saadyah!" Then she made the sign against the evil eye.

"Oh, come now, Berta," Saadyah said. "Don't you call your establishment 'The House of All Delights'? Nothing is forbidden here, and you know it. Both ends, the middle, fore and aft, upside down, quaint and cruel devices, and even whips for those who enjoy giving, as well as those who lust after receiving, pain; peepholes for those who merely watch, pretty boys, trained animals—You'd tell me that my gentle, pious friend hit upon a method so rare that it outraged both Sancha and thee? If so, I'd know it! For verily it must be the eighth wonder of the world!"

"You wrong me, Saadyah," Alaric said, "for I did nothing to either of them. Nothing at all."

Berta crossed herself right piously. "He speaks truth," she muttered. "He *did* nothing. Oh, all right—bring him in. You'll guarantee he'll cause no further scandal in my house?"

"By my cut-tipped weapon, I swear it!" Saadyah said.

"Very well," Berta said, "come ye to my quarters. I'd prefer that the girls do not see him. He's caused me trouble enough, the saintly one!"

"I don't understand him," Berta said, as she put her great cup, emptied at a single gulp, down upon the low table. "Clearly he is a holy man, a saint—yet he comes here seeking fleshly joy. Why? Answer me that, Lord Saadyah? Why?"

"I cannot," Saadyah said. "Direct the question to him, Berta."

"Verily I will! Thou—thou touched of God—with thy archangel's face, what wouldst thou in a whorehouse? Tell me—what?"

Alaric looked at her with a gentle smile. "Escape," he said. "To flee so far down the road to hell that even He must let me go. As He hath, now. I have not felt His fingers around my heart for weeks. Therefore—"

Berta pointed a finger toward her own hennaed head. Made a circle with it.

"Mad!" she said. "Addlepated, for a fact!"

"Aren't we all?" Saadyah said. "But tell me, Berta, why did you throw him out?"

"Because your saintly madman of a friend was ruining my business! He came here—and though I marked he had this face like unto the Archangel Michael, this beauty that is more than human, my lord Saadyah, I shrugged, thinking: 'Oh well, we get all kinds!' And then I saw that though he was poorly dressed and had not the look of a man burdened by a heavy purse, all the girls were vying for his favor. 'Oh well,' sez I, 'he's a pretty lad for a fact. And having, as they do, to submit to every randy billy goat who hath the price, let them take what pleasure they can from his beauty—which is great, I trow. He'll disappoint 'em quickly enough abed'—for you know well, Lord Saadyah, not one man in ten—"

"Not one man in a million," Saadyah said gravely. "But I divert you from your tale, Berta! Say on."

"He—your friend, the holy madman—came here, and made his choice. Indifferently, methinks. They were all the same to him. Ininza, I mind me it was; no prize for looks; nor for years neither, good my lord! They ascended the stairs—and I forgot them quite, till it came to me 'twas nearly morning, and they'd not come down again. Curiosity o'er-came me, forced me to hoist my bulk up from this chair. I tiptoed up the stairs, and before I reached the head of them—I heard her cry that cry which can never be counterfeited, my lord Saadyah! That wail of pure, naked, undisguised delight that is torn from one when bursting on the inside, heart stopped, lungs afire, one dies and comes alive and dies again, knowing at the same instant hell and paradise. Ininza—that old whore petrified in sin—cried out like that. Like a green maid on her first night in the arms of a lad beloved beyond life itself. . . . I moved to the door, put my ear close, heard her sobbing like a child, babbling endearments like a bride—"

" 'Now here,' quoth I, 'is a living wonder!' and went back down the stairs. The next night, he came here again—and chose another. Estefania, I mind me now. Whereupon Ininza, who'd been watching him with eyes like two stars brought down out of God's own sky, was upon Estefania like a lioness! They wrecked the waiting room in their wild fray; neither I nor Taliq could separate them, until he spoke. What said you, Holy Fool?"

"That I'd have neither of them," Alaric said quietly, "because, me-thinks, a woman should be gentle. . . ."

"Whereupon, you went upstairs with—Berenguela. Same thing, my lord Saadyah! The whole of the night; and in the morning Berenguela, who is young and pretty, the prettiest of my girls after Sancha, on her knees before me, begging to be allowed to buy her freedom that she might follow him to the ends of the earth!"

"God of Moses!" Saadyah roared. "What did you do to them, my saintly brother?"

"I?" Alaric said absently. "Nothing—made love to them. Is that not what one comes to a brothel for?"

"But how, Aizun! Speak, man! What techniques did you use? What subtle arts? I'd known them, for possessing them truly am I Lord of Life!"

"Techniques?" Alaric said. "Arts? I don't know what you're talking about, Saad. We made love, that's all. Though first I explained to them my requirements—"

"Which were?" Saadyah bellowed. "God of Isaac, those requirements, boy!"

"That we should lie together and talk the while. That they should forget I was a client, consider me a friend, a lover. That they should tell me all they had in their hearts—what they hated most, that I be able to avoid it; what best they loved, that I should practice it—"

"And those things were?" Saadyah whispered.

"They differed from maid to maid; but only, methinks, in the faculty of speech, the way of putting it. In truth they were the same, though each poor, lost creature said it variously: They hated being despised, held in contempt, bought like so much goods for an hour, a night. . . ."

"And thou?" Saadyah said.

"Told them—nay, made them see—I loved them. That what I bought was not them, themselves—for a human soul remains both unpurchasable and beyond all price—but their company. Some surcease from loneliness, a little warmth against eternal cold; some sharing—I know not how to put it—"

"You loved them!" Saadyah jeered; but then he stopped, seeing Alaric's eyes.

"Aye," Alaric said, "as I love all God's creatures, Saad."

"But none of this saintly magic worked with Sancha, eh?" Saadyah chuckled. "I could have told you that. But say on, brother! What happened with that simpering trollop?"

"I know not," Alaric said. "We went upstairs together. She kissed me lingeringly on the mouth. Ah, God, but she was fair! Then she sat down, with mischief in her eyes, bidding me to take off my clothes. Unlike the others—who strip at once, and make forlorn gestures with their naked forms, designed, methinks, to awake lust, and which in me bring tears to see God's creatures so debased—Sancha retained all her garments. And when I asked her why, she laughed and said: 'Nay, thou first, Holy Fool! I'd see without delay thy unholy weapon which hath made lovesick girls of jaded whores!' But I had no more than removed my shirt when she gazed upon me in horror, and fled screaming down the hall—"

"And out the door afore I could stop her!" Berta groaned. "And on through the night till she came to the cloister's walls. There begged she refuge; and there she bides, lost to me, and to life—the fairest, most profitable of my girls! Even the lord Bishop hath interested himself in her case. She fasts and prays without ceasing, scourges herself till the blood runs down, hath achieved such fame for repentant piety that 'tis said my lord Bishop himself, after hearing her confession, hath allowed her to take the veil. And certain 'tis he hath sent emissaries here seeking out this holy man—"

"But why, Berta? In God's name, tell me why?" Saadyah said.

Berta crossed herself.

"Ask him to—to loose his tunic, bare his breast," she whispered.

"I?" Alaric said. "Right gladly, Berta—for I, too, would know—"

He opened his tunic. There on his left breast Saadyah saw the long, livid scar of the wound he'd dealt himself in the mad attempt to take his life. And then the other scar, crossing the first at right angles, that ben Ezra had made to draw the blood and corruption from the wound. Together, they made a rarely perfect Holy Cross, branded into the flesh of a living man. In the dim light, even to Saadyah's skeptical eyes, it seemed to glow.

Berta crossed herself fervently, a dozen times.

"Seeth thou now, Lord Saadyah, why I cannot have him in my house? He hath God's mark upon him!" she said.

The talk went on, more slowly now, for comfortably settled, good wine warming his belly, Saadyah was in no haste to go. In fact, it might have gone nightlong, had not Taliq pushed his head through the curtain of the alcove.

"My lords," he said, "there is a Berber here, who'd speak with the holy man. He claims to have some business with him too urgent to be denied. . . ."

"Befoul him! Saadyah bellowed. "Take a stick to him and bid him be gone, Taliq, or by thy Prophet's beard, I'll—"

"No," Alaric said, standing up. "I'll talk to him, Saad. Mayhap I can do him some kindness, that—"

"I doubt it not," Saadyah groaned, "who art of kindness all compact! So get thee gone, O brother of my heart; but return to me right soon; because sleep oppresses me, and we must be off—"

The man who waited in the salon was tall, beaked like the desert hawk he was, and clad all in black. But not in such brilliant black as the great and wealthy use, but a poor stuff, lightless, dull, that served him very nearly as a sorcerer's cloak of invisibility. For which use, clearly, it had been designed. In the dark, or even in a poorly lighted street, 'twould require the keenest kind of eye to discern this man's presence at all, though he stood close at hand.

Alaric smiled.

"You are he," he said, "who hath dogged my footsteps for a fortnight or more—clad in that cloak which blends with the dark itself. Might I in all good fellowship ask you why?"

"That you may," the man said, in a Romance much deformed by a harsh Berber accent. "But come apart. I like not the way these Christian strumpets devour you with their eyes—for it bodes ill for the accomplishment of the mission my lady put upon me. Ho, good eunuch! Hath not an alcove where my lord and I may sit and talk?"

Taliq bowed.

"This way, my lords!" he said.

"You know—you must know—that you are fair," the Berber said, "but I doubt me much that you have knowledge of just how fair you are—"

"I have had reason enough to curse my looks," Alaric said. "There've been times when I've thought to spoil them. A vial of vitriol would rid me of this fairness of which I take neither pride nor vanity, but rather shame, would it not? Men say 'tis painful, but 'tis not pain I fear, but rather the risk of blindness, which is great—"

"Don't be a fool, young master!" the Berber said. "Your beauty is a treasure beyond all price! 'Tis precisely that which brings me here tonight —after having, by following you half a month, learned your customs and your ways—"

"Say on, good Berber," Alaric said.

"I am in the employ of a great lady, whose kindness matches her beauty—though of her beauty she forbade me to speak, for fear that you, unaccustomed to women of her clime, might find her ill favored. In brief, while traveling in her litter of a day—she remarked you—nay, rather had you pointed out to her—"

"By whom?" Alaric said.

"By a slave girl whose name I know not, for I never saw her. I was on my lord's estates at the time. My lady summoned me into town for this mission."

"But when you arrived in Toledo, surely—"

"—I must have seen the girl? Nay, good my lord! Though what significance it hath I know not, upon the very day the maid pointed you out to her, she put that maid from her, sending her to aid in the preparation of my lord's palace in Córdoba against the day—which Allah willing shall be soon—that we all return there—"

"And?" Alaric said.

"My lady was so stricken at the sight of you that she hath slept no night through these two months agone! She invents dozens of pretexts to be borne into town so that she may have the joy of seeing you pass by. And now, so inflamed is she with love for you, that—"

"—she'd use me to betray her lord," Alaric said sadly.

"My lord—is very old, and very kind," the Berber said. "Of all things on earth, he desireth a son. And mark you, young lord, he is of a noble family who hath dwelt here in al Andalús so long, and hath so plentifully mixed their blood with Djilliki and Bashkunish women that they now have your morning-star eyes and sunset hair. So it seemeth me that in this you could favor my lord and my lady both—"

"By this cruel deception?" Alaric said.

"*Bism Allah!*" the Berber swore. "Well was my lady advised of the scruples thou wouldst have! Hear me, young lord, who hath twice thy years. A deception, yes. There thou hast much right. But cruel, my lord? My lady swears that if she doth not taste thy lips, she'll go mad, and die. 'Speak to him tonight, Hasham!' wept she. 'For by Allah, the One, the Only, and the True, if I hold not that angel's beauty in my arms right soon, I'll speed my soul to hell by mine own hand!' While my lord consults astrologers, soothsayers, magis, and physicians without end for a cure for the thinness of his seed; for he hath the humility to realize the fault's his own. Where lies the cruelty, good my lord? Only in thy refusal to grant great happiness to them both. What have you to lose? A son of thy loins might one day come to rule in Córdoba! Think on that! And think you even more upon this phrase that my lady said I was to tell you in the end—"

"Which is?" Alaric whispered.

"Wouldst regain two who love thee more than life—or wouldst have still another self-murdered woman's blood upon thy head?"

Alaric sat there. Even his lips were white.

"Regain two?" he murmured. "Two—?"

"Ask me not!" the Berber said. "For I know naught of that. Nor even the meaning of my lady's phrase 'another self-slain woman's—'"

"No!" Alaric grated. "Say that not to me again! I—I'll come with you, good Berber. Wait you here while I take my leave of—"

"No," the Berber said, "that thou must not, young lord! If all goes well, you'll see your friend again—and upon a reversal of your status, for then you'll be richer, and more powerful far than he. I know—that tempts thee not, for you have the saintly look of one who cares not for the riches of this world. Still, for my lady's sake, come away at once, because I'd not be questioned of thy friend. Like all his race, he is too shrewd by far. And my noble lady's very honor is at stake. In consideration for which—will you come?"

Alaric sat there. He looked at the Berber, looked through the Berber. Then his pale gaze came back from vast distances. From the windless spaces between the stars. From heaven, mayhap. From—surely—hell.

"Aye—I'll come with thee now, good Berber," he said.

XV

What was notable about the house was its age and its plainness. It dated surely to long before the Moorish conquest of Toledo, and showed signs of Visigothic construction. Here and there a tapestry, a curtain, a scroll had been used to approximate the Moors' elaborate concepts of luxury; but in this they failed, though not wholly. The house was beautiful in a strangely different way from all others he had seen—a way that Alaric decided at once he liked. It seemed to him that it combined the best of two worlds, being far more chaste than the complex decorativeness so prodigiously employed wherever an Arab designer set his hand, yet far less austere, less heavy than an Hispano-Goth architect would have—or perhaps originally had—built it. For certain 'twas that the added Moorish touches tended to correct that austerity, that heaviness.

"You find it poor, do you not, my lord?" the Berber, Hasham, said. "That is because it is rented, and not my lady's own. Which is, of course, a part of the deception—the necessary deception—of which we spoke. My lord has been told that my lady has gone to visit a sage of mine own race, an ancient Berber magician more than an hundred years old, who lives high in the mountains. I have of her already, should I succeed in fetching you to her side, orders to return to my lord with a certain formula for thickening his seed, and the intelligence that my lady must remain in her mountain retreat some space of time, drinking of the medicinal waters which gush from the ground there, and bathing in a certain magic spring—"

"While all the time the lady stays here in Toledo?" Alaric said. "Is there not some risk in that?"

"Little. It is my lady's intent to keep day and night within this house, and never sally forth. Not even its owner has ever seen her. Her servants consist of an eunuch, also a mute, because his former master, ibn Ha'ad, had his tongue torn out by the roots to cure him of his habit of bearing evil tales—albeit the tales were true, Allah witness that! He is called Imr, and will serve both you and my lady as cook, guardian, and perform whatever other duties may be needful, while only an ancient, half-mad crone attends my lady. Imr can't talk; the crone makes no sense when she doth speak—and you are from this hour so deeply involved that babbling on your part would but earn your death. And my lady's. But of that, methinks, I need have no fear."

"None," Alaric said. "And now?"

"I go. My mission is accomplished. You will wait here until Imr comes—which won't be long, because I'll tell him you're here before I go out. *Salaam*, O most noble Sahib!"

"*Bism Allah*," Alaric said.

He waited, after the Berber had gone, for what he estimated must have been a quarter of an hour. Then a Negro came into the room. He was a bent and wizened little fellow, showing only in his round and protuberant potbelly any trace of the eunuch's characteristic unhealthy fat. All the rest of him was painfully thin. He was dressed in a style that, while not poor, was far from the richness befitting a princess's servant, and plainly designed to attract the attention of the curious as little as possible. The black's thick, blubbery lips moved; but no sound came out of them; no sound at all. He made a gesture with his two hands, and bowed, indicating that Alaric was to follow him.

"Lead on, good Imr," Alaric said.

The little eunuch smiled, and led Alaric from the room. They came out into another which had been converted into a bathing room, and quite recently, Alaric saw, for the plaster on the walls, with its rarely lovely leaf and vine arabesque alfresco designs had not yet dried out. In it stood a round tub of veined marble, already filled to the overflowing with hot and perfumed water. Fresh robes of the richest kinds of stuffs lay on a carved ivory stool nearby, while closer, on its twin, were mounds of towels. A little farther away, on a low table matching the stools, being made of the same creamy ivory and having the same intricate carvings, were bowls of fruit, plates of little cakes, bottles of silver, which, Alaric guessed, contained wine, as well as tall alabaster and jade flasks of the kind the Moors used to hold perfumes.

Gratefully, he allowed the wizened little black to undress him, stepped into the tub, sank down. Lying in the water, he allowed his eye to wander around this transformed room. For, from its small size, Alaric judged it had been an alcove before, or a pantry, or a part of the scullery. It was impossible to tell now. Of one thing he was wryly sure: In this Gothic house, it had not been a bath. A Goth, on those rare and festive occasions he felt the need of a bath, would have had a big wooden tub made of hooped staves hauled into the kitchen and filled for him there; but to set a room aside for bathing would not have entered his head—or, if, perchance, so odd a notion did to him occur, it would have seemed to his frugal mind a criminally extravagant waste of space to devote a special room to a practice indulged in so infrequently.

But now a curious thing caught Alaric's eye. One wall of the bathroom, and that one alone, departed from the norm of its freshly applied, lovely, chaste decor. Here the plaster was not merely painted, alfresco style, but sculptured, the design a sumptuously complex mingling of leaf and flower patterns with the flowing Arabic script of texts from the Qur'an standing out in such high relief that many of its details existed fully in the round. Here restraint had been thrown to the four winds, and the artist's imagination allowed to run exuberant riot. This wall, too, was beautiful; but its sensuous richness was somehow disquieting. More, in a room perfectly square, this one lone carved wall destroyed the harmony. All four walls, yes; or two sculptured, and two plain—neither of these concepts would have violated the Arabic passion for repeated motifs in design. One wall like this one alone was a shock, for unrelated to all else in the bathing room as it was, it seemed to Alaric to have absolutely no reason for being.

Except its actual one, which now his keen eyes saw: These fretworks, scrollworks, arabesques gone mad were designed to hide the perforations through which the occupant of the bathing room could be observed in all his nakedness, as he was being observed now.

He lay there unmoving, thinking on that, for it violated all he knew of womankind. A maid, asked to describe her lover, might speak of his face, his eyes, his lips—even vaguely of the sweep of his shoulders, his strength, his athletic form. But no woman he'd ever known, not even one of Berta's girls, was like to gaze upon a man's naked body, and be by that sight inflamed, in the way that even so little as the half spill of a rounded breast from out its draperies can inflame a man.

Sighing, he stepped from the tub, making no attempt to cover himself. His body was still matchlessly fair, though much reduced in flesh and marred by a host of scars. He dried himself without haste, dressed, nibbling betimes at a bunch of grapes, a pear. But when he took a sip of wine, he spat it out upon the floor, so high-spiced a taste did it have. He suspected at once that such a one as would bore peepholes through a wall, might well add to his wine some subtle potion to arouse his senses, heat his blood. He was both right and wrong: the wine was loaded with cantharides but the taste it had was due to the spices added to conceal that ancient aphrodisiac's tart flavor. Much refreshed, he sat down on one of the stools and waited, enwrapped in that curious serenity that was, mayhap, a part of the madness which had come upon him from too much suffering, a kind of withdrawal, a spiritual distancing of himself upon some shadowy dimension at least once removed from life. Which served him well, now, at this absolute nadir of his existence, enabling him to dismiss without consideration from his mind the ugly implications of his being spied upon, drugged, as well as all speculation about the nature of a woman who would use these methods so foreign to all he knew about her sex.

How long he sat there, he did not know. Time flowed over and around him unperceived. He was not thinking, and certainly not remembering, for that, above all things, he had trained himself not to do. In an odd way, he was communicating, linking the slow, deep, somnolent life force within him with life's ultimate sources, with the unknown, the unknowable, with whatever lay behind, or was creation, though now he no longer equipped it with legs, arms, a belly, a long white beard.

Then the dry, wizened hand was a black spider on his arm. He looked into the eunuch's face; smiled.

"Aye, Imr," he said, "I'll come with you. 'Twill be something to do, will it not? Something to halt the upper and the nether millstones which grind across my heart—"

He followed Imr down a long hall in which no lantern or lamp shone. That he was able to do so without stumbling was due only to the little slipper-shaped lamp that the little black bore, holding it high above his head. But when the eunuch stopped before that door, and made the gesture which indicated Alaric was to enter it, even as the young Goth stepped forward, the Negro blew the lamp out.

Alaric paused. Utterly blinded by the sudden absence of light, he put out a groping hand and touched the door. It swung inward noiselessly. Clearly its hinges had been oiled. He took a step forward, another, released the door. Just as noiselessly, it swung shut again. He heard, behind him, the grating of a key, the hard, metallic sound of a bolt slamming home.

He took a step forward, halted. The room was not only dark, it was lightless. Because, not even by holding his eyes closed for a count of ten, then of twenty, then one hundred, did any hint of vision return to him. The windows, if they existed, must have been hung with triple thicknesses of black drapes, so that not even starlight, or a moonless night's faint phosphorescent glow, could enter them.

Therefore, he mused, I must depend upon that sense that needs no light. . . . And, lifting up his nose, he sniffed the air. It was warm and thick, redolent with perfume. He moved quietly, carefully forward; that scent redoubled. He noticed that it was not flowerlike, but musky, compounded of civet, ambergris, musk itself, containing no drop of the floral oils perfumers always add to these base, and basic odoriferents, having surely the same purpose as whatever potion it had been with which she had adulterated his wine. And failed equally, because it armed his willful heart against her, awoke doubt: What poor specimen of a woman must this one be, who needs must employ such artful weapons to entrap a man!

Still he moved toward her; and now at last he stopped because he was close enough to hear the soft rustle of her breathing. It had a ragged beat, moving in quick pulsations like a millrace, then, for the trice, halting altogether upon a note curiously like a sob. Wordlessly, he moved toward her, until the perfume with which she must have literally anointed all her body, rubbing it into her every pore, was stifling about his head. He was so close to her that he caught a lingering hint of the fragrant soap with which she had bathed: a flowerlike aroma of violets, a hint of rose; but through even that a faint, sharp, acrid odor that he recognized at once, having smelt it so often on himself: that peculiar, irritating, and penetrant scent that accompanies, or is caused by, the ice-cold sweat of fear.

"My lady?" he said in Romance.

"Here," she murmured, then, "here, O my beloved! Here!"

Her voice had a quality he had never heard before, a curious thickening of the very texture of sound, of speech, so that her perfect Romance took on a foreign note: not in the pronunciation, God wot, but as if it were spoken by one whose lips, tongue, throat, were formed to another language, other vowels from far away, from a land remoter than the desert from which Arabic sprang; from a clime hotter, wetter, more slumberous, more sultry that had robbed them of the crisp, incisive bite of northern consonants, making them blur the outlines of her words into haunting dissonances that were, nonetheless, utterly beautiful.

He sank down beside her. Her arms swept up and locked about his neck; and her mouth was on his, wider and softer even than Afaf's—of which with a sudden stab of bitter pain it reminded him—having a tart sweetness unlike any other he'd ever kissed; yet being, withal, both cold and dry.

He brought his two hands down upon her shoulders, finding with no surprise that they were bare, and pushed her gently from him.

"Why does my lady fear me?" he said, his voice grave, slow, tender.

"I?" she whispered. "I do not—yes! You are right; I fear you to my soul, Aizun! You are too fair; but 'tis not that—or not entirely—"

"Then what is it, my lady?" he said.

"I know not! I—I cannot put it fairly—"

"Try," he murmured.

"You—you're fair. But many men are fair. My lord—my husband is—the fairest of men. Only you are fair in a way that—"

"Say on," he said gently.

"That is not of men. Oh! I do not mean that 'tis of women, either.

There is no softness in your looks. Rather, she who looks upon you hath seen—an angel. A warrior angel. A leader of the hosts of light. Methinks I've chosen ill, for such as you could never stoop to such as I. Nor combine your unearthly beauty with—ugliness but one pass above the ape's. At least not fruitfully. And that is the vital thing, for I—"

"For you have need of a son, to insure your preeminence in your lord's house. And hence hath chosen me so that the child might have, mayhap, something of the northern fairness likewise possessed by your lord. All this I know. What I would know is: Do you love me? Even a little? Even to the extent of having for me some small kindness, some tiny, vagrant inclination of the heart?"

"Allah witness it!" she said, and now the warmth was there, like tides of a tropic sea, moving through her voice. "That is what most I fear, and 'tis what seemeth me most hateful of all in this!"

He stared at her, seeing what was but a long, slow quiver of deeper darkness on the dark.

"What is most hateful to you of all, my lady?"

"That with you, mayhap, I do in truth betray my lord, rather than render him a subtle service, by granting him the son he desires more than life."

"I see," Alaric said. "The distinction's fine cut; but it does you honor. Yet, the absence of any inclination toward me on your part would in turn dishonor me. However you propose to reward me—"

She said quickly: "Not, in good truth by giving you gold, Aizun! The moment I saw your mystic's eyes, your young saint's face, I knew better than that! Oh, I'd not buy you, dear, fair one. I'd borrow you a little, say, then restore you to your own—to two who mourn you as dead, and yet continue to love you more than life. Oh, do not ask who they are, for that would spoil it. Let me keep for a while the secret of this reward of mine which will be so doubly sweet to you that even the stain of this base coupling will be washed upon that instant from your heart—"

"Good!" He laughed, "but may I not have of my lady one small boon?"

He heard the sharp intake of her breath; then she said: "What boon, fair Aizun?"

"A little light, that I might see your face."

"No!" she said, and her voice edged, shrilled, a note of terror beating through it. "That, no! In all the time that you are here, you must never see me! You'll come to me in the night; and in the dawn's darkest hour, will you depart; for should you look upon my ugliness, you—"

" 'Tis that I would see," he said gently. "In all my life I've never seen an ugly woman. Much do I doubt that such exists—"

"They told me you were mad," she said, "and now you have proved it! You have perhaps twenty years, and in all that time—"

"I've seen no ugly woman, nor any man totally without favor. Mayhap, as you have said, in this lies my madness. For, in all His creatures, I see God's image. And though of late I've come to doubt there is a God at all, yet somehow I seem to see that image still. What men call ugliness is but a defense, an armoring of the will, the nerve, against the world's rejection, its indifference, or its hate, which methinks sets the very flesh into unlovely lines. But since I, fond fool that I am, reject no one, and love even mine enemies, those with whom I treat, sensing this, let such a flood of loving kindness flow forth from their hearts that by its workings all their visages change, transformed into the comely semblance of humanity. So, since surely I should find thee fair; I'd see—"

"No!" Her voice was bitter now. "For mine ugliness is not of my own making, nor doth it spring from the blows I've had of life. Rather 'twas itself the cause of all the hurts I've had, the many tears I've shed, by turning all men in hot revulsion from me. 'Twas born upon me, you see, Aizun, God's curse upon my fathers. So I'd not have you gaze upon me. Enough of words! Come, let us make lovelessly the beast with two backs! You'll perform upon me a natural function, done in the dark, without passion, nor with pain. And neither of us must take pleasure from it, which would reduce it to sin's image, uglier even than I! Why do you linger still? Art not a man?"

"Aye," he sighed, "man—and sometimes less. Sometimes a beast. Yet never a cunning device of wheels and cogs set in motion by a lever's pull, releasing it to the wind's force, or that of a fast-running stream. I have never bedded with a woman I did not love; and you, who refuse me all but your body, end by denying me even that. For my inert male flesh responds only to love, and cringes within his sheath at its absence. You'd have me see you not, and yet your lord, who sees you daily, loves you, I am told, above all his household—"

"He loves my mind," she said angrily, "not my body! He'd have of me verses and fair words, and fine-spun arguments of philosophy! By such conjurer's tricks of verbal legerdemain I've kept him from truly looking upon me! But one day he'll tire of words; and 'tis against that day that I must arm me with a son. 'Tis for that I need you, Aizun ibn al Qutiyya, and naught else! You're fair; but what care I for your, or any man's, beauty? Allah, or Lord Saithan, give me strength! For I—"

Then she hurled herself upon him like some great wild creature of the night; fastening her mouth upon his until she stopped his breath, while her hands were frenzied upon his body, stroking his flesh beneath the robe, but not, like a more feral woman might have, clawing or tearing at him. Her caresses were overfervent, too forceful, mayhap, but caresses for all that. Moreover, they showed a certain sureness, a hint of practice, which led him to suspect that 'twas thus she aroused her aging lord.

He drew his face from hers, said: "Not thus, my lady, not even thus—"

"Then how?" she grated. "In Allah's name, how?"

"You must love me," he said, "if you have it in you to love."

"Love?" she said, and he heard her voice go humid, thick with tears. "Love? If you have aught of Allah's wisdom in you, or His compassion, tell me, what is that?"

"This!" he said; and bending, found her mouth, cherishing it with his own, the kiss itself lighter than a breath, so gentle soft that touching, it seemed not to touch, lingering there upon her mouth, moving, caressingly, clinging, moving once again as though to mold the wide, soft, heavy-fleshed contours of her lips into some other semblance than that of thwarted rage and pain.

And now the moist unbidden spill on her unseen face was a flood, charging the tart sweetness of her great, wide, generous lips with salt, her hands lay upon him like a sensed presence, clasping, yet half afraid to clasp, warm, yet trembling with what was not the mad, forced determination of before; but with a real tenderness, with the beginning of desire.

He began the light and gentle play, the slow, sweet tactile awakening of her senses into carnal love, which is a thing far removed from lust— and, he mused, chiefly in this, that fleshly love is an offering of delights to the beloved, a giving, a sharing; a seeking to melt the barriers between the thou and I, and fuse them into one, the same indivisible, inseparable; while lust is but an ugly hunger demanding prey, debasing its victim into an apparatus of flesh to be most basely used. He dallied at the arts his Zoë had taught him so long that a choked-off, broken cry told him he had accidentally perverted them, forcing his unknown mistress to reach alone what should always be attained together. Which was but a small thing and easily remedied.

Thereupon he entered not only her body but indeed her life, achieving not once but several times that night that blinding, explosive, matchless instant when, solely 'twixt the moments of birth and death, one and the other halves of humankind are not pitifully, terribly, achingly alone; when all reserves are broken through; and more than flesh is with flesh conjoined. She returned to him again and again, softly importuning, seemingly insatiate, until at last she had wearied him out; and herself, too; for she pillowed her face in the hollow of his throat and moaned: "No more, sweet Aizun; for I—"

And upon that word itself, she slept. Which took him some little time longer, but when it came was like a mace blow on his head. He sank fathoms down into deeper dark, into dreamlessness; surfaced, it seemed to him, upon the spur of that same moment into day, into brilliant, noonday sun.

Its rays were strong enough to make mockery of those triple curtains; stealing around their edges in that subtle way that sunglow will, they bathed her bedchamber with a subdued, warm, dull-golden luminescence. Enough to bring her still slumbering face and body clear. And, looking at her now, her secret revealed through no betrayal of his own, he saw that she was black as night.

He studied her with curiosity and some care, for except for the two slave girls who had washed his hands before he dined on his first night of captivity in al Hussein's house, he had never been close to a black woman before. He could not see all of her face which was buried still against his throat; but he was aware at once that her body was very fine, slender and soft curving, and utterly harmonious of line. And now, as she moved, half turning in her sleep, flinging one arm wide, he saw that her breasts were perfect, more conical, firmer even than Afaf's, standing high even in her recumbent position, like hillocks molded of the very stuff of night. Her hair was strange. He touched it with a tentative finger. It was rigid, with no softness to it, and now as her face moved slumberously from his throat, he saw why: heated irons had pulled it into that hard, sculptured straightness. About her ears and brow, where sweat had touched it, it had begun to kink again into that tight, beaded, woolly thatch he'd seen upon more than one African slave's or eunuch's head. Where else he might have seen it in its original form, it existed not, for according to the Moorish custom, all her body had been shaved.

Her face, relaxed in sleep, was not uncomely. He supposed that some Negro tribal king would have found her a black pearl beyond price. But concepts of beauty, he realized sadly, are things of habit, education, custom, both learned and taught; he could not see in her blunt features loveliness.

And then, quite suddenly, by an effort of the imagination, by a deliberate lifting of his generous heart, by a total unwillingness to close his spirit or his mind, by a reluctance to reject all but the known, accepted, safe, he did see it, saw what in all good truth was so: this soft, velvety nightshade girl, not yet having passed the second decade of her life, was lovely in her own way, and by her very perfect right to differ from all he had up till that moment known.

So thinking, a great wave of tenderness washed over him; and he bent and kissed her mouth.

Her eyes flickered open, flared, too close for recognition, leaped like a trapped doe-thing's, as she tried to draw her mouth from his. But she could not. He went on kissing her till they closed again; until the tension, ice, and pain went out of her lips, allowing them to part like some great fleshy night-blooming flower under his own, the soft, adhesive underflesh clinging, softly, sweet-sighing, then going tart, scalding, demanding; and her arms coming up to lock about his neck. With no transition, they made love, silently, sweetly, slowly, her great brown eyes, while twice as dark as Afaf's, making the same startling contrast as Afaf's did, against the satiny blackness of her face—opened wide all the time, searching for something in, or behind, his pale-blue-smoke-on-a-frosty-morning gaze.

And afterward, when all the unheard music, harp, lute, double pipe, lyre was stilled, she lay propped up on one elbow, staring at him.

He smiled at her, said: "What are you thinking, now?"

"That you are good," she said in that dark-toned voice of hers, "and compassionate beyond all other men on earth. And a little mad. But that I like thy madness, Aizun. Aizun, sweet Aizun; sweet, mad Aizun, tell me a thing—"

"Aye, my lady?"

"You do not despise me?"

"In Allah's name, for what?"

"For two things—nay, three: My blackness. My ugliness. And this sin I've made you do. Do you, Aizun?"

He lay there, smiling at her, thinking how to answer her. Laughed a little as that answer came.

"Oft have I walked abroad by day, and ridden far under the sun," he said. "I've plucked fair flowers, and drunk of pleasant streams; but when dusk steals across the land, and I am wearied out, I sit and wait until a star appears. Then do I think, O dark lady of my heart, how lovely is the night!"

"Oh!" she whispered, gazing at him.

"I told you I've never met a woman without favor. But you, God wot, of beauty have been plentifully blessed. What boots is that 'tis not the same as the pale fairness of my race, my tribe? 'Tis beauty, still. Take in your hand a violet, and a rose. The violet's swart, the rose is fair. Wouldst say then that only roses are pleasing to the sight and toss all violets out to wither on the ground?"

A grimace of pain tightened her mouth. "Men do," she said. "How oft hath my former master Harith called me blubber-lips, or she-ape, or inky-hide? He only praised me for what I did for love of him, to couple with him like a wild thing in the dark. And even then he'd laugh, and beat upon me with his clenched fist, shouting: 'Faster! Faster! Oh, thou sweet baboon! Oh, she-ape of all lasciviousness! For such a ride as this, gladly do I endure your inky hue, and even the blackness of your sweaty smell!' "

"And where is Harith now?" Alaric said. "Plodding over the broad earth to guard with his poor life treasures not his own—"

She stared at him; then her face relaxed. "So Afaf told you of me?" she said.

"Aye, my lady Sumayla," Alaric said. "She did. Does it matter?"

"No," she whispered. "Say on, sweet Aizun—"

"Harith, your former master, spends his life guarding camels and donkeys, for being a donkey himself he needs must watch over his own. While you are a princess, because of, 'tis justly said, your talent and your wit. Yet methinks you sin in this regard as much as Harith doth—"

"I sin?" she said. "How so, Aizun?"

"By placing Allah's greater gifts below His lesser ones. You're much concerned with beauty which is but an accident of birth since, God wot, of his parents no man hath the choice. Again you're troubled past despair by your color which hath, it seemeth me, of significance even less, for Nature—to give but one example—hath never concerned herself to make a black steed less noble, swift, and fine than a white horse is. For that matter, since 'tis whiteness that you prize, then must you be much enamored of billy goats or the bellies of fishes, which are among the whitest things there are in the natural world. . . ."

"Wouldst comfort me, Aizun," Sumayla said, "then you choose ill your way. For 'tis not what I think that matters in this, since what I—and mayhap you—would believe flies counter to the opinion of all the world!"

He smiled. "Now once again," he said, "you fall into grave error. First by placing things of the mind, the spirit, below the mere appurtenances of the flesh. And second, by imagining that the world hath ever in its history had aught of right or could prevail against that majority formed by one good man and God. They crucified my Lord upon a tree, and who was victor in the end? They drove your Prophet Muhammad forth; and now his followers rule the world. But there is in you, my lady, a thing that is in all good truth a sin—"

"Which is?" she whispered.

"That you join your enemies; accept their versions of life, good and evil, history, justice, and even God. To bow before evil when it rides in overwhelming force, as right oft evil does, is pardonable. To believe evil—even of one's self—because 'tis roared forth from many mouths, is not. If you bemoan your beauty of the night, you blaspheme against God, who created the spangled skies of eveningtide equally as the day—and you, as well as me, in His own image. Hath seen Him, Sumayla? Canst swear He is not black?"

292

She threw back her head and let her dark laughter beat against the ceiling.

"And you, my sweet madman of a lover, most saintly, and most solemn," she said, laughing, "have you? Canst swear that He is not, mayhap, a She?"

The three months that he remained within her house were, withal, a happy time. And happiest of all in this: that for the first time in all his life Alaric knew a woman whose mind matched his own in full equality. They filled the gaps in each other's learning: what he had of the churchly fathers she, of course, knew not. But her knowledge of Eastern lore was vast. 'Twas she who taught him chess, and the princely science—sport of algebra. In those three months, she pounded an amazing amount of Arabic into his head. Before she was done with him she had him speaking it was well as—say, a bright child of eight or nine. From then on, practice would improve his knowledge daily. And to even the exchange, he taught her Greek.

For days on end they both forgot the perhaps kindly sin they did, in the calm joy they took in each other's company, reading together, playing the musical instruments on which they both performed with no mean skill; making love. Only on those nights she put him by because of the moon-wakened fountain of her blood, were they both reminded, and she wept. But he—lost, bemused amid the hundreds of books in Latin, Greek, and Arabic she caused him to be brought; finding as was his wont a mystic significance in the simple Pythagorean equations which seemed to him a perfect demonstration of the essential order of the world, devising cunning instruments for marking the degrees of angles which enabled him to determine by triangulation the height of the minaret of the great Mosque; dabbling in alchemy to the ruin of his clothes and the hurt of his fingers; watching the birds with childlike wonder, making little drawings of their plan forms, and pondering gravely why the broad-winged birds—the duck, the hawk—flew low and fast; the longer-winged ones—the stork, the crane, the goose—slowly and at medium height, while the long-winged vultures, falcons, eagles soared, black pinpoints against the blue of heaven, adding to his sketches designs for a device by which he meant to achieve the age-old dream of man, human flight—a pair of broad, hinged wings, of bamboo and of silk to which goose quills were to be sewn in abundance, the whole completed with a widespread tail modeled after that of the pigeon, the bird he was able to observe most closely at hand—forgot to count the days as they slid over the rim of the world. Procuring the materials for his flying machine, summoning the Berber Hasham once more into town for one more feat of his specialty, that of moving like a ghost through crowded streets, this time to find the name and the lodging of the white-bearded sage on whose behalf Saadyah had risked his life the day they met, Alaric, wrapped in his erudite, recondite, holy madness, his withdrawal from the teeming world that had dealt him such hard blows, forgot almost completely the ultimate purpose of his tender thralldom, this illicit romance, which, lacking all the elements that most adulteries have—furtiveness, desperation, sense of impending doom, shame, passion by those very elements driven mad—had all the calm tenderness, the many-sided sweet sharing, flesh and spirit and minds made one, of a good marriage between a pair who have each chosen his partner well.

The Berber came with his report: The sage, Marwan al Farrach, lived and was precariously keeping body and soul together by illuminating manuscripts; the Qur'ans by his skilled hands made being especially prized, so much so indeed that he might have gained from them some wealth, but for two things: the unworldly old man set his prices ridiculously low; and the wealthiest, best-placed of the Moorish and Muladi families feared, because of the judgment of heresy handed down against the venerable doctor, to employ him.

Alaric went at once to Sumayla's apartment to ask her to summon al Farrach to the house, knowing that to sit at the feet of a teacher so wise would be to her, as to him, the highest joy. But she was not there. Neither she, nor the aged crone, nor the little black. The apartment was empty. Her clothes, her perfumes, her casks of jewels, the boxes of iron tongs and pomades with which the old crone pulled the kink out of her hair, her slippers, the books which he himself had recommended to her, and which she greatly prized, all were gone.

He stood there looking upon that desolation, that emptiness, and the pain that smote him then was very great. He turned slowly and crept back to his own rooms like a man bent down by age and grief. Pushing open the door to his bedroom, he found it filled, almost to the extent of making movement impossible, with boxes and casks. On his bed lay princely robes, a scattering of jewels of great price, a scroll.

Which was to him then the only object in that room that mattered. He picked it up, unrolled it, saw the limpid Arabic script which now he could read passing well. The words leaped up at him, sang like whiplashes through his mind:

My own—Farewell!
Allah guard and keep thee. For 'tis certain now: a son of thy loins will sit in the highest councils of Córdoba; mayhap, if Allah wills is, rule as Emir there, one day.

I have left thee some trifling gifts, from which act I pray thee take no hurt! They include this house, which I have bought in memory of our love, and which can be thy dwelling whenever thou needs must come to Toledo, and also the swift steed who waits below to bear thee to Córdoba! Whither thou canst go now, for thy persecutor, al Hussein, no longer lives; justice for his sins hath overtaken him—twenty arrows found his life as he was attempting to escape from the Emir's jail into which he had been thrown for a crime of whose nature, since well do you know him, it is needless to speak. And whither thou must go, my love, to the Street of the Copyists, to the house of Husayn, brother of my former master, there to claim thy true rewards—Oh, not for this!—but for what thou art, a man with Allah's favor on him. So tarry not, Aizun, my lord, my love, my life! For there, happiness awaits thee in the fair persons of two who—even as I do—love thee more than life; and in whose summoning, arrangement, and care, I can claim some little part.

Thy Slave,
Sumayla . . .

He sat there a long, long time, like a man dazed. Then he sighed, stood up, went in search of Hasham, the Berber, found him, said:

"I pray thee, lead me to the sage Marwan al Farrach, and at once!"

"As my lord wills it," the Berber said.

XVI

During the next two weeks, Alaric made preparations for the journeys he knew he had to make, though which of them to undertake first, and what he needs must do at journey's end, were beyond him still. Nightly he tormented deaf heaven—and himself—with questions:

What should I do to become good, do good, even recognize good a quarter ell beyond my twitching nose? Find Afaf, make her my bride? So speak both my reason and my heart—the poorest guides, to judge from performances past, that ever a villian churl drowned himself in the mire afollowing! Demand of her that she desert the faith she was born to and believes with all her heart, to become the concubine of a man who cannot take her unto him as lawful, honored wife, because by the teachings of the Holy Church he is already wed. Wifeless, but wed, good Fathers! Well wedded to one who occupies another's bed—or his heap of stable straw!

Oh, I have another choice—'tis a thought I've had oft of late; and by the iron chill it sends through my blood, doubtless the best choice of all: for was I not meant for suffering, consecrated ere my birth to pain?—forgive Clo. Take her back. Make her in truth my wife. Smile into that sickening ruin of a face, that fleshly monument to all my sins, over our meals lifelong: blow out the candles of night, and gather her to me tenderly, denying to my churning gut that *his* stable stench upon her lingers! Aye, this is good, is it not? Good is what hurts, what bleeds, what crucifies!

This, my choice! Between Afaf, zebra-backed with stripes borne uncomplaining for my sake, and Clo, whose comely countenance I butchered into a horror in defense of my manhood, my husbandly rights, the home I never had. Which of them have upon me the greater claim? Clo, my wife in the sight of nonexistent God, abandoned to the stable to sleep upon dung-smelling straw; to bring forth every twelfmonth another replica of churlishness, blackguardery, poltroonery, unlovely sin? Afaf, by me of virginity deprived, robbed of honor, future, hope? To which of them shall I be tender, loving, merciful?

Tomorrow at the very latest I must ride. But where? To Córdoba? Where, according to Sumayla, Afaf awaits me, and—

He stopped dead, his eyes widening. Sumayla had *not* said that. In her farewell missive, she had not so much as mentioned Afaf! He realized now how sick he'd been, how ill his mind functioned still. What the black princess had written was: "Two who love thee more than life." Two. Afaf, surely Afaf. But the other? He gave it up. What mattered it, as long as one of them was Afaf? Yet—Clo. Afaf? Or Clo? Córdoba? Or Castilla? He'd have to make that decision now. Upon it all his future hinged.

Stiffly he climbed to his feet. Bedazed with weariness, half in his trancelike state still, he dressed himself, put on his shirt of mail, took up his weapons, went out into the stable yard, saddled and bridled the snowy steed that black Sumayla had given him, tied the mount to the hitching rail before the stable door, and once more entered the house. There he put a heavy purse of gold into his belt, ample to cover his needs during the journey; then, last of all, he tiptoed into the room where Marwan al Farrach slept; bent and kissed the old sage's hand too gently to awake him. That done, he went down the stairs and mounted the white palfrey—to ride whither he knew not, either in his heart, or his head.

The white horse pranced forth right bravely until he and his rider emerged from the city gate. But, once outside the city, the decision could be postponed no more. To the north, the road stretched narrow and broken toward the high plateau of Old Castile; to the south, it ran broad and fair toward princely Córdoba. There, Alaric Teudisson, Aizun ibn al Qutiyya, pulled up his mount and gazed long and thoughtfully in both directions, until at last Afaf's queenly dark face rose from nowhere and filled up his aching mind. So, with a fierce warrior's oath, he yanked the palfrey's head southward toward Córdoba, toward Afaf, toward all for which his young heart cried out in pain. But the white Arab balked. And neither whip nor spur could win from him more than a stubborn sidewise dance. Time and time again, Alaric tried to force him down that road; but that well-trained, till then obedient and gentle gelding toward Córdoba would not go.

Alaric sat there. If God were not, then omens were not, and signs and portents equally meaningless. The veil of the temple split, the darkness o'er all the world, a lion whelping on Palatine Hill, a guiding star, sudden thunder on a clear blue day—what were all these? And what a balky Arab steed? He threw back his head and laughed aloud.

"Whither wouldst go, fleet companion?" he said. "To succor a carved-up strumpet? To once more pay filial homage to my sire's gray hairs? To Bilad al Qila, fair Castilla, land of my birth, where on a morning all the sky was loud with birds and nothing ever more was the same again? Should I beg forgiveness of Saint Fredegunda's incorruptible arm? Bend and kiss that carrion bone? Incline my head before superstition, retreat into the savage night out of which I was hurled, or bloodily torn? Art thou the arbiter of my fate, angel in beast's disguise, messenger from above? I'll leave it up to thee and gladly! Choose for me, O desert courser! Clothilde or Afaf? Córdoba or Tarabella? Glory, wealth, luxury, ease, and fame—or that heap of vermin-infested stones in which I'll sink yearly deeper into drink and stupor in the classic Gothic way? I bid thee, choose!

And, at his word, the white horse turned his head north, and his hooves struck fire from the stones, as he cantered briskly on his way— away from Córdoba, from Afaf, from every hope or dream of joy left to his master in this world.

XVII

He came home again over the high trail. There was no reason at all for his doing that for at no time during his journey had he been in actual danger. He had seen, to be sure, now and again hoof-torn fields, a rubble of broken arms, an overturned cart with the lance-butchered mules still between the shafts, even a few dead men, bloating and stinking in the sun—but such sights were normal in the frontier marks at the beginning of every new reign, when each recently bethroned Emir in his turn felt compelled to prove his piety by launching Holy War against his stubborn Christian adversaries. But always the signs of battles fought were already days old when he came to them, proving that he rode some hundreds of leagues behind the second Abd al Rahman's raiders, or mayhap that he enjoyed divine protection, for no journey he had ever made had been as peaceful, as smooth, as wanting in event, and even in discomfort as this journey to Qashtalla undertaken at the insistence of a horse!

Yet, when he came to the entrance of the high trail, to that fork in the roads so unprepossessing that it was difficult to see it unless one knew 'twas there, he took it at once. The first time he had come home from Córdoba bearing Solomon ben Ezra with him in the futile effort to save his brother's life, he had ridden the high trail. But that had been out of cruel necessity, to avoid falling into the hands of Leovigild and Eigebert of Tierraseca, those Gallego brigands turned renegades, become the banu Djilliki, whom afterward he had slain. Now there was no reason at all for him to ride over that steep, rocky, difficult, dangerous trail instead of following the main road except—

That the first time he had ridden it, he had been with Zoë, so that now, knowing what bitter memories it would wake in him, taking it again became a kind of penance for his sins against her, a pilgrimage in honor of lost love, a ritual to his grief.

But Sumayla's four-footed gift went up that trail as though he were winged. Long before Alaric would have thought it possible, he sat there on his mount staring at the little chapel dedicated to Our Lady of the Forsaken, that selfsame chapel where praying with Sor Fidela for his brother's life, Clothilde had overheard some tender exchange betwixt him and Zoë. . . .

Slowly, he dismounted, went into the chapel, knelt before the image of the Little Virgin, tried to say a prayer. But as always now, no words rose to his lips, and his mind, his heart remained blank, void. So he got up from there and moved outside of the chapel to the side of the trail which here ran along the edge of the precipice. From there he could see his father's castle, sitting like a pustule on its pimple of a hill. He'd been happy there, once; but now all his childhood memories of felicity were gone, drowned in the black horror of his final months in that cold, dreary heap of stone. Suddenly he felt a wild impulse to put Jinni's head about—for so he had come to call the white gelding, because there seemed to him something magical about the horse—and flee, away from there, from the tasks he had imposed upon himself, from the coming sorrow, anguish, pain, accepted dishonor, all of which were by something in his nature so voluptuously embraced, that instead of a simple bowing before duty, his choice became, in a sense he could not quite define but vaguely sensed, a sin.

But he mastered the impulse at once, and remounted. Jinni's hooves struck sparks from the stones of the trail, moving off, striding easily, freshly, as though he had not put those many leagues from Toledo behind him, in a gay and dancing canter, going down that trail.

Before the portcullis, Alaric's memories rained down upon him, mace blows to head, blades stabbing his gut, the sickness in him so great that he could feel a hot wave of vomit choking off his breath at the base of his throat. Here, he'd seen his father's green and gold banner hauled down and the raven-hued pennant announcing Ataulf's death run up in its stead. There he had fallen from the saddle, had lain beneath his horse's hooves, pounding the earth in his mad grief. There and there and there and there and there and there six crosses had stood, marking the place where the banu Djilliki—nay! where Leovigild alone, for Eigebert was already carrion by then—had had the six brave lads who'd raided his camp for food crucified before their eyes. There he, Alaric himself, had burned Leovigild's Berbers alive beneath the flaming ruin of their battering ram. On that hill, Leovigild's great gyn had stood, hurling stones—and Marquis Julian's and his lady's heads—mark that! Clothilde too hath some excuse, she too was tortured, tormented, damned—into the courtyard, until the ballista Alaric had built had rained fire down upon the mighty catapult, too, utterly destroying it.

And inside the courtyard? His mother's and his brother's graves. The spot where Clothilde had spat into Zoë's face. The place where Zoë had bade him farewell and wept and wept and wept as though she'd known she'd never see him more! In the grim gray castle, the room where he had lain—sinlessly, God wot!—with Zoë. The room where he, though wedded now to Clo, had slept alone; the place where they (that swine, that whore) had tried to drug him, capture him, sell him into vilest slavery! That other room, somewhere in the castle (her's? or a stable stall of Julio's) where she'd opened her long slim thighs to—

God! God! God! I cannot! he thought. This is wrong! Evil and wrong! I have come back only to wallow swinelike in a sty of ugliness, of grief—

"Young lord?" the man's voice said close at hand; then there was silence. Frowning, Alaric looked down. The man had knelt wordlessly beside the horse, and was kissing his booted foot. And, as now he raised his rugged scarred old face washed with tears, Alaric saw who he was: the soldier carpenter, who along with the castle's smith had made the mighty weapons that had all but broken Leovigild ibn al Djilliki's evil power.

"Get to your feet, Wifredo!" Alaric said, his own eyes blurring at the sight of how his father's retainers loved him still. "It is not meet that you greet me thus!"

"Then how should I greet you, good my lord?" Wifredo said, his big voice shaking with emotion. "How else should I honor him who saved us all, now from the very grave returned?"

"Thus!" Alaric said, and leaping down from the white horse, took the old warrior in his arms, and kissed his bewhiskered cheeks right tenderly. Wifredo backed away from him, touched his forelock, and bowed.

"You honor me too much, Lord Alaric!" he said; then whirling, he split the very skies apart with a roar that any lion—or any pride of them, for that matter—might have envied!"

"Open the gates!" he boomed. "Hear me not, ye knaves, ye churls? Open up, I say! 'Tis young Lord Alaric come back again! 'Tis he! 'Tis he! I bid you, my lord Count, behold your son!"

In the courtyard, the first thing Alaric noted was how poorly dressed his father's retainers were—and how dirty. This last, he suspected, caught his attention only because he was new come from the dominion of the Moors where religious custom, and the existence of public baths, forced even the poor to maintain a reasonable degree of cleanliness. They were, God wot, no dirtier than they'd always been; but the patched raggedness of their attire showed things went not overwell in Tarabella now. Many of the faces were new. In such troubled times the Count had had no difficulty calling new liegemen into his service to replace those bucelarios slain in the recent war with the banu Djilliki. In fact, with the Emir's forces ravaging the countryside, Alaric was quite sure that the newcomers had volunteered their services to Count Teudis in order to put the castle's stout walls between them and the Moors.

While he waited for the Count to appear, Alaric embraced all the old retainers, starting with Khinsvilda, the smith, which called for some resolution on his part when due consideration be given to their smell. Thereafter, right graciously did he give his fair hand to all the newcomers whom Khinsvilda and Wifredo presented to him one by one.

That done, they both of them made labored talk to cover what Alaric was certain was their own embarrassment at the fact that Count Teudis still had not come to greet his son.

"Your magic gyns, my lord," Khinsvilda said, "hath saved our hides again! For when the Emir's raiders came, we beat them off at such great distances by showering them with burning pitch that they gave up the attempt to take us and rode off, seeking, doubtless, easier foes."

"Good!" Alaric said. "And these new men: how did they bear themselves in the fray?"

"Well enough," Wifredo said. "But then, they're not untrained in siegework and defense—since they came, most of them, from Count Avila's fief with our new lady—"

Alaric didn't say anything. He stood there, looking at Wifredo.

"God's death, you fool!" Khinsvilda roared. "Your tongue waggles worse than any woman's. Hast not brains enough in that great noggin to realize that the Count's new wedding and his bride are things best told by him to his lord son?"

"I—I did not think," Wifredo groaned. "Forgive me, Lord Alaric"

"You've done nothing amiss, good Wifredo," Alaric said slowly. "So my father's grief for my lady mother was of such short duration? Scant passing a twelvemonth ere she died, he needs must find another for his bed? And young and comely, I doubt not!"

"My lord," the blacksmith Khinsvilda said slowly, "you wrong your lord father now, methinks."

"How so?" Alaric grated. "Tell me that, good smith!"

"He thought you dead, my lord," Khinsvilda said, "and feared him much that his line must end with him. So made he some haste to wed while, as he freely told us most in his confidence, he still retained his manly powers. For age sits on him now, and has snowed his head. But he hath not forgot his beloved dead, in proof of which I give you his instruction to the priest: the child our new lady carries now, if male, is to be called Ataulf Alaric after both his fallen sons—supposedly fallen, in your case—if a lass, Godsuinta after your lady mother—"

"My lady stepmother is then with child?" Alaric laughed. "God's blood, but my father is a diligent husbandman! He doth not neglect his

302

plowing or his harrowing, nor the sowing of his august seed. But let us see what fruit he will harvest. For at his age, I doubt not that he has had some assistance at his labors all unbeknownst to him, God wot!"

"Again you wrong your father, my lord," Khinsvilda said, "and even more your lady stepmother, who is a gentle lass. Methinks she loves our lord the Count truly—having been deprived of a father's love as a child, she is most tender with your august sire. It seemeth me she loves him all the better for his gray hairs, for not having had a father herself, once having learned how good and gentle a man—for all his roars—is Count Teudis, she fairly dotes on him. Oft have I heard her say: 'Young men are churlish louts! Give me a well-seasoned man like my sweet Lord Teudis, for whom I thank Almighty God!' "

There was something in this that was wrong, a thing that did not gibe, Alaric thought. And, after a moment, it came to him what that thing was.

"But," said he to Khinsvilda, "if she be one of Count Avila's many daughters, how say you she knew not her father? For Ataulf, the same week he was wounded unto death, spoke of taking me there to choose one of the maids of Avila as my bride. At that time—a year and some months agone—certain 'twas that Count Ramon of Avila lived!"

"Ha!" Wifredo roared triumphantly. "Who is it that hath a loose tongue now, Khinsvilda? By'r Lady, yours is free on both ends and hinged in the middle! Let's hear how canst escape this one, ironmonger? Go on! Thy tongue waggled enough before. Speak, shoemaker to asses and other four-footed kindred of thine! Tell our lord the straight of it!"

Khinsvilda stood there; and now his rugged, burned, and scarred face was pitiful.

"My lord," he said to Alaric, "forgive me! But I beg to be released from my fealty to you in this small measure: that you do not ask of me that I explain this thing. The Count of Avila lives still, but the Lady Ramona—for she is called after him—knew him not. For that, there are reasons in God's own plenty; but 'tis the privilege of thy noble father to speak of them if he will, not mine. I beg you not to press me about this matter; and more—I pray thee forget my words, consider them unspoken especially before my lord Count Teudis—or else I risk some grave damage to my poor hide—"

"Done," Alaric said, "never ye fear, Khinsvilda; I'll hold my tongue on this, and make no comment, nor any quips, even should my father care to enlighten this devilishly murky matter. Which, mayhap, he will—for lo! He comes!"

Alaric stood there between the two bucelarios until his father was close. Then he saw a strange thing. Count Teudis was arrayed in fine robes, both in their colors and their cut, ill befitting his years. More, he had shaved off his beard! For the first time in his life, Alaric saw his father's naked face.

What washed over him at the sight of it was a kind of suffocation, a halting of his breath, his heart. Shaven, bereft of that great brush of reddish gold that stood about his countenance like a lion's mane, Count Teudis' face was diminished, somehow robbed of its gusty force, reduced to a pale replica of the face of everyman, tired, weak, showing the lip quaver, the jaw sag of impending and mayhap final defeat. Worse, it had precisely the opposite effect upon an onlooker than that which he's surely shaved away mustache and beard to gain. Alaric, in a burst of acutely painful pity, divined at once what had happened here: Married again to a young wife, the Count's surety of self had wavered; hearing no doubt the ill-concealed snickers of baseborn and gently bred alike, he had seen himself as he was: a graybeard husbanding a slip of a girl; had, in consequence, whacked away the honorable badge of his manhood and his dignity both; and reduced himself—with his clean-shaven face, shocking in its utter nakedness to those who'd always seen it decently clad, with his great body crowded into new, tight, too gay, stridently colored clothes— into that perfect object of ridicule: an old man trying to hide his honestly, bravely passed years, to regain his fond and foolish youth.

The Count came on now with a shambling gait until he was a scant yard away from his son. And the last thing that Alaric saw before dropping to his knees, taking his father's great, gone-gray, trembling hand and raising it in an agony of compassion, hurt, anguish, love to his lips, were the traces of dye the Count had been frantically trying tó wash from his hair—the thing that had thus long delayed his greeting his lost and re-found son.

But now, there was no time for shame or recrimination. With one great pull Count Teudis drew Alaric to his feet, crushed him in his great embrace, kissing him as though he were a babe, washing all his young face with great unashamed tears.

Then he pushed Alaric away from him, stood there holding him at arm's length and devouring him with his eyes, trying to assimilate this miracle, this resurrection.

"Aye, Father!" Alaric laughed, though his voice shook and his eyes were wet. " 'Tis I—in the flesh. Thought you truly to be so easily quit of me?"

"I thought you—dead," the Count rumbled; then: "Oh, the knave, the churl, the utter swine! Oh, the villain! The bloody, bawdy soulless villain! I'll—"

"Of whom do you speak, Father?" Alaric said.

"Julio, who else? He told me he'd found your body! Given you burial with his own two hands. In proof of which he brought me back your sword, your dagger, that little horseman's bow like the one you bear now in that saddle sheath—so in all good truth I thought—"

"—that I was dead, and not that he had my weapons of his Berber friends by theft or bribe, I wot not which. Natural enough, Father—but what I see not was his motive in telling you his lies—"

"Methinks he wanted me to restore him to my service—though to what end I know not even now. And in my grief I was disposed to grant him pardon till he let slip he wanted to bring along the lass—as his wife: So right soundly did I kick his wormy arse off the place. But enough of him—Tell me, my boy, how came it that—?"

"A long story, Father. And, by'r Lady I am too wearied out to tell it here. Besides, 'tis time I met my lady stepmother, don't you think? All the world agrees that she is most gentle and most fair—"

Count Teudis looked at Alaric.

"Son—" he said, and his voice was nakedly a plea.

"Oh, I understand it full well, Father," Alaric said. "Your old bones rattled 'twixt the sheets on wintry nights, without a bundle of hot and lissome flesh to warm them. I, who've been forced to it so oft and so long, know how ill it is to have to sleep alone. So, come—"

"Alaric—" Count Teudis said.

"Aye, Father?"

"You think that I dishonor your mother's memory, do you not?"

Alaric stood there. Said: "Aye, Father. Since you put it to me fairly, that I do."

Count Teudis bowed his head. The gesture was so palpably defeat that Alaric, who had loved his father all his life, whose greatest triumph had been finally to gain the Count's love and respect in equal measure to that which Ataulf had always had it, found it impossible to bear.

He put his hand beneath his father's bare chin, lifted the tired old face, and said: "I have no right to judge thee, Father. Nor do I—for my sins are beyond all pardoning; and these hands ill fitted for casting either the first or the last stone."

It was not until high noon of the next day, that Alaric met his father's bride. He bowed and kissed her proffered hand with all due signs and showings of respect; despite the fact that he knew now what she was. His father had sorrowfully confessed that his bride was not Count Ramon of Avila's daughter at all—though the Count in his senile folly believed she was—but the bastard child of a Norman groom, got upon the Countess

Mathilda's Frankish governess. But her face, as she gazed upon him, was sullen still. From its aspect one might think I've done her an injury beyond all pardoning, he thought.

He stepped back and looked at her candidly; from the size of her belly it was evident that his father's spell of mourning had been short indeed; but there were other things about his stepmother that pleased him even less. She was pretty, that he had to admit. A more generous eye than his might have held her beautiful. Aye, the fair Ramona was pretty, almost beautiful; but not—lovely. And that fine-cut distinction held all that troubled him. She was not lovely. Her beauty was broad-grained, coarse. Before she was out of her twenties, it would be gone. There was a shrewish down-tug to her mouth; her blue eyes were on the smallish side, alight with a peasant's narrow cunning—a Frankish peasant's at that, than which there was no more churlish animal in all the world.

"I give you greeting, my lord Alaric," she said in a high-pitched, rather harsh voice. "May God forgive you the many tears your good and gentle father hath shed needlessly over you!"

"Not needlessly, Ramona," the Count said uneasily, "for all my boy hath suffered merited my tears—"

"Oh, that I doubt not, my loved and honored lord," Ramona said. "But yet do I hold it ill of him to let you think him dead—"

Count Teudis took the hand she'd offered him. While he spoke she drew his great paw down and rubbed it fondly against her cheek.

"How could he advise me of his fate when he was a prisoner of the Moors?" the Count said. "Oh, come now, Ramona, though in God's eyes you're his mother now, I bid you forget that fact and give him rather a sister's love—for ye are much of an age—"

"That is evident," Ramona said, "though of love I have little to spare, for all of mine, and my life itself are centered upon thee, my lord—"

Methinks the maiden doth protest too much—Alaric thought; but then, startlingly, he saw she meant it. This maid of some nineteen years loved his aged father, loved her old graybeard of a husband. Loved him very truly, and would by her very peasant's shrewdness be exempt from any real temptation to betray him. She'll never forget, Alaric mused, who it was who raised her from the stable to the lordly hall—she who doubtless hath suffered her mother's ill humor, and the absence of a father's protection and his love, who hath been trained far above her actual station, imbued with dreams of just the sort of life she hath so unexpectedly attained. Ah, me! 'Twill not be pleasant to live here now—

Nor need I! he thought, with a sudden upward leap of hope. I'll return to Córdoba, engage in the trader's arts with Saad. And even if I am once more joined to Clo, no man in that place will hold it ill of me if I keep my woman hid. For that, better Córdoba than here. Canst imagine two such as Clo and this one beneath a single roof? God's eyes! What better description could a man invent for hell?

"What are you thinking, my tall and handsome son?" Ramona said.

"That having met you, my lady Mother," Alaric said smoothly, "my heart is light with relief. I came back home to care for my father in his declining years. But now I see that he hath gentler hands than mine to attend his wants—"

"And other attributes," the Count said, chuckling, "to attend those you're ill equipped to ease!"

"Oh," the fair Ramona said mockingly, "be not oversure of that, my lordly lover! Seeing him now, it is apparent why the Moorish lord of the strange persuasion was willing to spend a fortune for his sake!"

"Ramona!" the Count roared. "I hold your words unmannerly, and an offense to my son's manhood!"

"But true," she said imperturbably. "Yet freely do I beg your pardon, Lord Alaric! 'Tis not in the thought, but in the unkindness of uttering it that the offense lies. Am I forgiven?"

"Of course," Alaric said.

"You were about to voice a most interesting suggestion," she purred, "one from the very way it commenced, seems most like to please me."

"Aye, that it will!" Alaric said. "Look you, Father; there is no need on earth now that I remain here. I'll bide here with you for a while, then take my leave—"

"For where?" Count Teudis said, and the note in his voice was that of relief. Father's no fool, Alaric thought; already he knows his dainty spouse full well! Still, it hurts that he should acquiesce so tamely. . . .

"Córdoba. Oh, I'll visit you every year, sometimes more oft. But there I have a chance to make of myself one of the richest men in Spain. There I enjoy the Emir's favor; and there—" he shot a glance at his stepmother's face "—as well as here can I get you grandsons to continue your line—"

He had been right. Ramona's face abruptly tightened; all her obvious and open resentment of him was due to his return from the grave to take back the succession and the title—God, what a store women set by such empty things!—she'd dreamed of for her son.

"Well—" Count Teudis said.

"And one thing more, Father," Alaric said. "If the child the fair Ramona bears is male, I should prefer to give up the succession to him. This life is not for me. I am, as you know, but an indifferent warrior and the poorest administrator in this world. I have no ambition at all to be a Count. I prefer to be a rich and respected merchant of the town—"

"Like a filthy Jew!" his father roared.

"Aye, Father, like a Jew—upon whom we still must call when we have need of intelligence and skill—"

"That ben Ezra was all right," the Count conceded. "An exception, of course, still—"

"Still come you with the fair Ramona, and your nine new sons, in ten years' time to visit me in Cordoba, Father, and see then how I'll live!"

"Well—" The Count hesitated, knowing that this way lay peace, and mayhap happiness as well; but realizing at the same time that to surrender thus to the growing dominance of his youthful bride was pure and arrant cowardice on his part. And more, because a dull leaden ache in his middle told him how much he loved and would miss—his son. "You'll promise me not to change your faith, become a renegade like so many Christians have already done in Córdoba?"

"Aye, that I promise, Father!" Alaric said.

"Well—" the Count said. "Well—"

"Well, what, my lord?" Ramona said. "If he doesn't want to succeed you, I don't see why he should be forced—"

"Silence, wench!" the Count roared. "Let me see—let me see—I have it! We'll make a gamble of it—a fair throw of the dice! You'll stay here till Ramona gives birth! If it is a boy, he becomes my heir. If a girl, you remain my heir, even should I later sire another son! Fair enough?"

Alaric smiled, inclined his head slightly toward his stepmother.

"My lady?" he said mockingly.

"Oh—fair enough!" Ramona said.

XVIII

On the morning of the first of those three days that were to change
his life utterly, Alaric was awakened by the sound of his father's footsteps
pounding up the stair. He sat upright in the narrow bed on which since
his earliest childhood he had slept, just as his father burst into the tower
room. Seeing his father's face, he smiled.

"You haven't shaved, Father?" he said. "Good. 'Tis as I told you;
you're better with a beard!"

"And you're not," the Count said. "Your saintly face should be kept
smooth—as now. But enough of this chatter. I have news for thee, my
boy; news of great import!"

"So, Father?" Alaric said. "Tell me: what is this news of yours?"

"The Metropolitan of Toledo hath called a council of all the churchmen of the land—including those of Galicia, Navarro, and the two
Astures. It seems he hath the assurance of the Emir that prelates journey-
ing to the meeting will not be molested in any way, and will be allowed
to come and go through the city gates as they will. More, at the frontier
they will be met by a detachment of Moorish horse who will provide
them with escort to make sure no overzealous followers of the Prophet
doth them harm—"

"And to make doubly sure that they're not raiders in disguise," Alaric
said.

"That, too, surely," Count Teudis said. "Methinks al Rahman, who is
no fool, hopes to cool the fires of rebellion ever flaming in that city by
allowing Christian folk to air their grievances. But that's not the point as
far as you're concerned—"

"Ah!" Alaric smiled. "I was hoping you would come to that! What,
honored sire and good my lord, is the point precisely?"

"That the good fathers of every district, who dearly do love to con-
gregate at any excuse or none, exercise their tonsils, fill up their priestly
bellies, swill many a cup—and, I doubt it not, pinch every fair bottom
within reach—"

"Methinks you love not the priesthood, Father!" Alaric laughed.

"Nor do I. But don't interrupt, you impudent whelp! The point is, as
far as you're concerned, that this parish having been scourged and

ravaged more than most, and having thus doubly its share of grievances to air, hath been most prompt in holding a first preliminary meeting, over which his Grace, Martin, Bishop of Avila, hath kindly consented to preside—"

"Hardly strange, seeing that he's from here in the first place," Alaric said. "I have many memories of Father Martin, Father. 'Twas he, remember, who, through the agency of our own Friar Juan, was always trying to persuade or pressure you into making of me a priest—"

"Mayhap he was right," Count Teudis said. "You might have been happier in the cloth, son—"

"And mayhap your newcomer will be a girl," Alaric shot back at him.

"Spare me the edge of your tongue, whelp!" Count Teudis howled. "Can't you see what I'm driving at? Here at Tarabella, six leagues away, is this very moment sitting enough priestly croakers to annul all the mismated marriages of this world! Get up from there, Alaric! Ride to Tarabella, present your case! I'll go with you, betimes letting slip that if they really want a new roof to keep the rains from dripping down their saints' saintly backbones, hearing your plea with some favor might well dispose me to loosen my purse strings for a fact! Once free of that highborn trull, you can wed again. I'll send you on a grand tour of Navarre, Asturias, Catalona, Languedoc, even France. You're pretty lad; I doubt not that many Christian maids of any rank short of royalty, and mayhap even a princess or two of some princely house oversupplied with daughters—"

"Father—" Alaric smiled "—you rave."

"Mayhap I do. But in this of the ecclesiastical court I hold it certain—"

Slowly Alaric shook his head. "No, Father," he said gently.

"Why not?" Count Teudis roared.

"I—have wronged Clo grievously. As much, mayhap, as she hath wronged me. It seemeth me that as a Christian I can no more than pardon her, and beg her pardon in my stead. Forgetting the past, we can, me thinks, revive our wedding, live together in peace and sobriety—"

Count Teudis lifted his great head toward the ceiling of the tower room.

"What have I done, O God," he bellowed, "that I have sired such a fool!"

"To obey one of Our Lord's basic commandments hardly seems folly, Father!"

"Nor would it be," Count Teudis said, "with another kind of maid. Hear me out, boy! Many a man before now has pardoned a fall from chastity on the part of his wife. Women are only human, the flesh is weak, and to shew mercy doth well become a man. But to take back such a one in whom chastity now is not even a memory is, God wot, the purest folly! I happen to know that your Clothilde hath turned whore—I mean that in the literal sense. She now doth sell her favors for gold!"

Alaric sat there, looking at his father. His eyes were very bleak.

"Good my father and my lord, with all my obedience and my love, it simply is not possible for you to *know* this ugly thing you say."

"That I grant you. I don't *know* it; but I have evidence enough to give it credence. Look you, my boy—Julio hath joined a band of brigands —Berbers—who operate from a hidden camp in the mountains, somewhere along the high trail beyond the shrine. Took Clo along with him. And what is most sadly comic in the tale of the bedraggled pair is that our Turtura—if you're inclined to believe her—is queen of the band! Claims her husband is head brigand. Swore that were you here—for she damned Julio to his teeth, consigning him to hell's hottest pit before she'd believe you were dead, or that he'd bestirred his worthless carcass to bury your remains—you'd confirm her words—"

"And now that I am, I do. She speaks truth, Father," Alaric said.

"I suspected she wasn't lying. Neither about that, nor about your Clo. But I didn't want to add to her already overweening vanity by crediting her talk. You should see her, boy! Fatter than a brood sow— every rotund inch the queen. Prouder than Lucifer! I suspect that she makes Clothilde's life a hell, now that their roles are reversed. The scullery wench is queen, while the highborn maid is—"

"What, Father?"

"Exactly what I said! I know that Turtura's ever-wagging tongue doth to the prayer book no faintest resemblance bear; but from what I know of Julio—"

"What of him, Father? What of that swine?"

"More of a hog than ever. He hath turned renegade, become a Muslim; though from what Turtura says, Clo won't let him profit from that fact by taking other concubines, or brides—"

Alaric stared at his father, and the pain in his eyes was real.

"She is that enamored of him, then, Father?" he said.

"Enamored?" Count Teudis snorted. "Far from it. 'Twould appear she hates his wormy tripes. They fight like drunken fishmongers, Turtura claims. But he, being stronger, beats her fearfully. 'Twas he who forced her into that life, and lives at ease upon her earnings—even hating her as she doth, Turtura admits that."

"I'll kill him!" Alaric said.

"Nay, son. Because there is a point beyond which no man nor any woman either can be forced into anything. Turtura scornfully declares that Clothilde's resistance to fine Juli's scheme was slight. 'Twould seem, if our scullery wench turned bandit queen doth not make mincemeat of the truth, that our Clo is of those who—"

"What, Father?" Alaric said.

"Who hath a veritable sickness of lechery. 'Tis rare. Most women are on the tepid side, neither too hot nor too cold. But that little Clo hath always had a certain look which inclines me to believe—"

"That Turtura again spake truly?"

"Aye. Another point of evidence is that I've bathed in the river with all my men, when riding off to war. So I can vouch for the fact that nature's been unusually generous with Julio. Besides which, being a lazy clod, slow of everything save trickery and wit, he can prolong a woman's pleasure overlong—"

"Turtura again?" Alaric said bitterly. "On that you can accept her word, Father! Her knowledge is at first hand. She was herself bulging with his bastard when we rode away from the castle—"

"Aye, that I know. 'Twas her excuse for visiting me here. To show me her firstborn—a fair and lusty manchild. Anyhow, 'Twould appear that Juli's nightly bouts with Clo are the scandal of the camp. Seems she can be heard screaming four leagues away—"

"Father—" Alaric said.

"Aye, boy?"

"I'll still take her back. 'Tis my duty."

"Dung! Asses' dung at that! Don't talk rot, boy! You get up from there, ride over to Tarabella, present your case before the churchly fathers there assembled, get shut of her, find yourself a sweet maid and a chaste, and—"

"Father, I cannot. 'Tis my destiny to suffer. I must not put her by, be she the filthiest trull on earth—"

"Which she is, or very nearly. She careth not of which end of her use is made, nor of which she maketh use! I tell you boy—"

"Father!"

"Sorry, son," Count Teudis rumbled. "I tell you what; the council of churchly lords will be sitting all of a month. Which well doth give you time to convince yourself. Ride up to their camp—Turtura will see that no harm comes to you, for she hath much ascendancy o'er her swart lord—and see if you can stomach Clothilde now. Go on, get her out of your system! Lie with her if you will; mayhap that will cure you!"

"Of love for her in the carnal sense I was cured long ago, my lord father!" Alaric said. "But not of my love for God's Holy Word, and my need for keeping His commandments. And He commandeth me that a wife, once taken, cannot be put aside for any reason! Therefore I must—"

"Aye," Count Teudis said, "but the heart of the matter is that 'once taken' and according to you—"

"—I knew her not. That's true enough, Father. Only—"

"Only there is no sickness on earth less curable than that of being a fool!" Count Teudis said.

Alaric went up the high trail again, alone. When he had passed the chapel he turned aside, following a goat path that wound ever higher. No steed less sure of foot than Jinni would have ever managed it. Even so, at the last, Alaric had to dismount and lead the white palfrey. He rounded a jumble of broken rocks and stopped, for a dozen blades leaped out, their points held scant inches from his throat. He smiled.

"*Bism Allah!*" he said. "In the name of the All Wise, the Compassionate, the One—and in honor to His Prophet, I bid you take me to your leader—"

"By the Beard!" one of them swore. "The foreign dog speaks our tongue!"

"Poorly," Alaric said. "Yet I come as a friend. I'd have a word with your chief, and he permitting, with his Umm Walad, the Lady Turtura."

"The swords came away. Teeth flashed in swarthy faces.

"Come, then, O Sahib Qutiyya," they said, "but know you that if you lie—'twill be your last!"

"Oh, that I doubt," Alaric quipped, "for I am of those who will tell lies to my favorite houris in Paradise—"

They set up a roar at that.

"A right rare dog of an infidel!" they laughed. "But for his skimmed milk hue, he could be one of us!"

They led him into the camp. Their leader came out and glared at Alaric. Then recognition flared in his dark eyes. He grinned.

"A cushion!" he roared. "A cushion for my lord the Goth! For if I know aught of the Prince Ahmad al Hussein ibn Maliki—the Qutiyya suffers from a tender tail!"

"Nay, Berber!" Alaric shot back at him. "my arse is as sound as thine; and remains unstretched. While my lord al Hussein—"

"Aye, Goth, what of him?" the Berber chieftain said.

"He crossed the path of a flight of arrows," Alaric said, "loosened by the Emir's own archers. Which caused his health to deteriorate suddenly. And seriously. In fact, he's cuddling baby boys in hell."

"Good!" The Berber laughed. "Allah willed it! 'Twas but the dung-stirrer's due! Now tell me to what fortunate circumstance do I owe the honor of thy visit? Not surely to take vengeance upon me for having sold you—for in that case you'd not have come alone—"

"Nay," Alaric said, "for that I freely pardon you and here's my hand on it!"

The Berber took his hand and gripped it hard. "As Allah lives, and Muhammad's His Prophet, I like thee, Goth!" he said.

"And I, you," Alaric said. "My name is Alaric Teudisson, but my Moorish friends call me Aizun ibn al Qutiyya—"

"Good! Aizun—I am called Abdul. No more. I had neither father nor mother nor family. I was born of a lightning bolt which ravished a stout oak tree. Hence I am immune to death by fire. Now sit you down—I'll have some of my buzzards butcher a young sheep for thee. Betimes, a few cakes and nuts and fruits will have to serve. Now tell me—what would you of me?"

"A word with thy lady—in thy presence of course—"

"Done!" The Berber laughed. "Since 'tis to you I owe the capture of that luscious honeyed fat! Turtura!" he roared, and from within the tent that familiar voice piped up: "Coming, good my lord!" And in Arabic far far better than Alaric's own. Like many stupid people, Turtura had gift for mimicry.

She came out of the tent. Or rather she waddled out of it. For by then she weighed all of fifteen stone. She was dressed in Moorish garb, her face was veiled. But at the sight of Alaric she let out a piercing shriek and fell on her knees before him, and tearing off her veil, wildly she kissed his hands. Abdul only grinned at her. He seemed immune to jealousy.

"How, now, Turtura?" Alaric said in Romance. " 'Tis said that of all the fat women on earth you've been made the Queen—"

"I should be!" she groaned. "For much do I fear that I'm the fattest female who walks this earth. But—" she dropped her voice a trifle— " 'tis not all fat, my lord Alaric. I am once more with child—"

"Well did I discern that she could calve, this luscious cow," Abdul said in his good and fluent Romance. "But then, I had proof of that when I took her. Show the Sahib Aizun the Frankish brat!"

Turtura dashed back into the tent and came out with a baby. He was a handsome enough child, but his face had a curiously unpleasing cast. Then, after a moment, Alaric knew why. He looked like Julio. Which reminded Alaric of two things: the first of them being the original purpose of his visit; and the second that this was certainly not the moment to broach it. Abdul was no fool; surely he must know who had sired this child; so to ask after Julio now would be both a breach of etiquette and a tactical mistake. Best to keep the conversation general.

"Well, it seemeth me," he said, looking about him, "that you don't suffer want even in these wild haunts. For not only is the fair Turtura resplendent in her fat, but all your riders look sleek and plentifully fed. How do you manage that, friend Abdul?"

Abdul laughed aloud. "In Berber fashion!" he said. "Which is to say we extract tribute of passersby. Some we relieve of their goods; and others we offer our hospitality until such time as friends of theirs can arrive with sums of gold sufficient to compensate us for the heartbreak of having to part with them. In which regard your religious sisters make the best guests. The poor dears! They depart with such woeful faces—"

He left the phrase hanging, so Alaric asked the required question. "Why?"

"Because they're so disappointed at leaving us as chaste as they came," Abdul hooted. "I am most strict about that—"

"You don't need to be," Turtura said with a sniff. "Who'd want 'em, the whey-faced bags of bones?"

"Still," Abdul went on, "pity 'tis not to accommodate them. Look you, Aizun, at the moral and philosophical aspects of the matter: we could give them great pleasure, relieve them of a state highly burdensome to a woman, and contribute one bright memory which they could savor all their lives. And this with no sin on their parts! That is the delicate part, don't you think? They don't have to confess, or do penance or any of the unpleasantnesses of which your religion is so full, because their wills wouldn't be involved—or at least they could pretend even to themselves that they weren't. 'I? But, good Father, I was a helpless victim, never a sinner!'"

Alaric laughed aloud.

"Abdul the Philosopher!" he said. "Still, from what I know of the movement over these roads, there must be times when the pickings must be mighty thin—"

Abdul nodded gravely. "There are, though less now, since I founded my network," he said.

"Your network?" Alaric said.

"Aye, Aizun. Of spies. Whenever a mule train or a party of voyagers start out from Toledo, I know it; because a fast rider has preceded them from that place. So not only do I know the hour of their departure, their destination, but the exact roads over which they will ride. I have an even better organization in Córdoba. There, Allah willing, their work may be the cause of my pulling off the greatest coup in history—"

315

"Tell him about it," Turtura said with complacent pride. "He can be trusted, good my lord."

"Aye, that I will!" Abdul exulted. " 'Tis far too good to keep. But since it is the nature of a man to yield unto temptation with but scant struggle, I will hold back the names involved, so that even should he return to Córdoba—"

"I shall return there," Alaric said, "but not for another three or four moons—"

"Still," the Berber said, "lest you be tempted to hasten your departure in hope of material rewards great enough to interest even Count Teudis' son, I shall withold them still. For some moons now there have been negotiations between a certain wealthy merchant of Córdoba and a princely house in Byzantium. A marriage has been arranged—reluctantly on the young prince's part, who hath little desire to mingle his princely blood with that of a young brood sow, daughter of a swine—but the young man is greatly in the merchant's debt. I have verified the matter personally. And now, for the first time, my agents in Córdoba are taking an active rather than a passive role. Daily they spread tales about the great increase of piracy at sea, about storms, shipwrecks, and the like—"

"Why?" Alaric said.

"The merchant is an arrant coward. By this means we hope to persuade him to ride overland, bearing his plump pigeon of a princess yet to be. If you have any knowledge of geography, O Son of the Goth, you must know that to reach Byzantium he must pass through the Land of the Franks first of all. Which means that from Córdoba he can do no other but come *this* way. 'Tis the shortest route overland to that part of the Frankish domains that lies closest to Italy, whence likewise they must cross to reach their goal—"

"But," Alaric said, "suppose, despite all your spies' efforts, he goes by sea after all? 'Tis much quicker and safer to reach the lands of the Greeks by ship—"

Abdul shrugged.

"*Inshallah!*" he said. "What is written is written. We shall have other prey. Besides, he will not undertake the journey for some moons yet, until the weather softens into spring. So, me thinks we will have time enough and to spare to persuade this fat dog of an infidel trader. Now come, the evening meal is ready; let us sit ourselves down and dine."

Wisely, Alaric made no mention of either Clothilde or Julio on that night. He was shown to a comfortable tent, where right well did he sleep the whole night through. On the morrow, he joined his host and ten or twelve other Berbers on a hunt. With his powerful horseman's bow, he outdid them all, accounting for no less than four of the swift mountain goats by the simple expedient of galloping up the trail behind the graceful, agile beasts, and shooting them from the saddle. All of them greatly admired his skill. His short horseman's bow was passed from hand to hand and examined carefully. But being Berbers, not Arabs, there was no danger that they'd try to copy it. Not even the clear and admitted advantages of a new way would make them give up their veneration for the old. "'Tis indeed a mighty weapon!" they said, but in their minds the answering thought rose up like a refrain: "Yet our ancestors killed game enough without it!"

When they came back to the camp Abdul turned the carcasses of the mountain goats over to the women, ordering them to prepare a great feast. And now, at last, Alaric saw her; and his heart sank to his boot tops. She was veiled and garbed in the shapeless Moslem women's clothing. He was able to distinguish her from the others only by the whiteness of her hands and arms.

But then, as he stood there watching the women busily flaying and gutting the goat carcasses, Turtura came out of Abdul's tent, and walked over to him. He supposed the freedom that his ex-scullery wench enjoyed—surprisingly great even among the nomad Berbers where women had much more liberty than their city-dwelling Arab cousins did—was due both to Abdul's easygoing temperament and his absolute faith in her. She came on until she stood beside Alaric. At once, she discerned the object of his gaze.

"You'd speak with her, my lord?" she said.

"Aye," Alaric said, "but first, tell me how she fares among you—"

"Ill," Turtura said grimly. "Here *I* am queen, and it took more than one whipping to make her acknowledge that fact. She is a dirty beast—a disgrace to her sex, her race, and her class. All the young unmarried men make use of her. She will lie down for anyone!"

"But Julio," Alaric said, "doth not he—?"

"—object?" Turtura snorted. "Hardly! He grows rich and fat off the money they pay him for the privilege. In short, my lord, you are well rid of her. For she hath become what she always was at heart—the village whore."

"Julio," Alaric said: "where is he?"

"Lying abed in their tent, drunken as usual, doubt it not!" Turtura said. "My good lord Abdul, whom Allah be forever praised for granting me, hath twice banished him from the camp. The first time for drunkenness, the second for cutting through the back wall of a tent in which we were holding three young nuns for ransom, and ravishing all three. A leader less good-hearted than my Abdul would have had him killed for that. Only—'tis odd—even as my lord your father did, Abdul dotes on him. He makes my lord laugh, you see. Oh, he is a buffoon of the finest—and a swine of the lowest. Shall I call her to thee, my lord Alaric?"

"Aye," Alaric said, but his voice was so low Turtura had to strain her ears to hear it.

She cupped her hand to one side of her mouth, lifted up her strong, coarse voice and cried: "Clothilde, you filthy trull, come here!"

Alaric watched her coming toward him out of a kind of haze. Which was strange, for that morning was clear and bright. But then he heard Turtura's voice close beside him. It was dark with pity.

"My lord! My lord!" Turtura said. "She is not worth your tears!"

He waited as Clo came toward him with a shambling gait; until she was very close. Then he said, his voice low and sad: "I give you greetings, Clo."

"And I return them, my lord husband!" she mocked. "Hath come to reclaim your bride?"

Alaric stood there looking at her, and his eyes were bleak.

"Aye, Clo, that I have," he said.

The silence that followed hard upon his words was a true destruction of the very stuff of sound. 'Twas Turtura who broke it, her voice high and wailing, filled with sincere grief: "Oh, no! Oh, good my sweet lord, no!"

Clothilde did not say anything. She put out her hand blindly and let her fingers stray over his face. They stank of goat flesh and of blood. She took them away; and now at last the tears were there, hot and bright and sudden in her eyes. Slowly she sank to her knees before him. Reached out and took his hand. Raised it to her hidden mouth. Kissed it with aching reverence through her veil.

"Get up from there, Clo," Alaric said tiredly. "Go call Julio, that he and I may discuss what terms of compensation he may desire—"

She got up, took his arm.

"No," she said. " 'Tis thou and I who must hold a discussion first, Alaric." She turned to Turtura with a show of humility that was pure mocking malice, deadly in its spite. "Have I your leave to walk apart with him, my lady Queen?" she said.

"Aye," Turtura said grimly. "But not to lie with him, or else I'll have you splayed, you bitch! And not out of jealousy which Allah knoweth I no longer feel for thee. But because I'd not have an honest guest's clean parts rotted by your filth; by the loathsome diseases that devour thy loins. You hear me, Clothilde?"

"Aye, that I do," Clothilde mocked. "Not being either deaf or five leagues away, how can I help it, my lady scullery-wench-turned-Queen?"

Whereupon Turtura slapped her so hard that her head jerked sidewise on her neck. She reeled, would have fallen if Alaric had not caught her arm. He turned a furious face toward his former servant.

"Turtura, contain your wrath!" he said. "Have you lost all respect for me?"

"Nay, good my lord—and 'tis precisely upon that she gambles!" Turtura said. "For well doth she know, had you not been here, for far less than that I'd have had her killed!"

They moved down and away from the camp, until they came to the waterfall. It was very cold and damp by the pool into which the cascade foamed. Above them all the peaks of the Sierra were white with snow.

"Clo," Alaric said. "Oh, Clo, Clo, Clo!"

She smiled at him. At least her eyes did. What her mouth did beneath that veil he could not be sure. She was much thinner than before. What he could see of her neck looked scrawny. There were inky lines of dirt in the creases of her skin.

"Have you come to take me back, truly, Alaric?" she said, and now her voice was its old self again, speaking Romance with the cultivated accents of a highborn maid.

"Aye," he said simply.

"Might I ask you—why?" Clothilde said.

" 'Tis hard to say, Clo. Since I put you by, nothing but evil hath befallen me. Both Gele and your sister—are dead. So, too, is my Zoë—"

"Ah, so?" Clothilde said. "How came she to die?"

"By her own hand, taking my son with her, on learning that I'd betrayed her with a Moorish maid. Which maid I've left, for it doth not seem to me meet to continue with my partner in a sin that cost Zoë her life. Thus it came to me that God's displeasure lay upon me since I broke the holiest of all vows and put you from me. I'd have you back, as my lady and my wife. To be loved, honored, and ne'er reproached, no matter what you've done—"

She stared at him. "Alaric—which art thou: saint—or fool?"

"Fool. Though, mayhap, the words are synonymous."

"Methinks they are," she said. "But now, God wot, I'd better put the matter to some test. Wouldst come with me, my lord?"

She took him by the hand, led him back up the trail toward the camp. Then, abruptly, she stopped, left the trail itself, came to a clump of bushes by a rock. She pushed them aside, and now Alaric could see the yawning entrance to a cave. She bent, entered it. Quietly he followed her.

"Have you your tinderbox, my lord?" she said. "If not, much do I fear we'll freeze!"

Alaric searched in his sack, came out with the little box. She took it, struck flint to the steel, caught the sparks on a charred bit of linen cloth, blew it expertly into flame, bent down and lit a heap of twigs already prepared. They blazed; by the light Alaric saw that the cave was piled high with cordwood already cut. As she added larger and larger branches to the fire until all the cave was alight, he looked at the huge stack of wood questioningly.

"Juli cuts it for me," she said. "This is our place of business. Wouldst tell me you've never visited a bordello before?"

"Clo—" Alaric said.

"Don't worry—for you there is no charge!" she mocked. "But before I return to dull domesticity I'd know whether you have either the force or the skill to husband me properly, my saintly husband! Juli, for all his faults, is a champion rider of naked female flesh. Which is why Turtura hates me so—compared to him, all these Berbers are disappointing—"

Her hands came down, caught at the tail of her dress, pulled it in one easy motion over her head. She stood there naked to her waist, clad only in her shintiyan, her headdress, and her veil. Her body was a rack of bones. Her once proud breasts hung down over her oddly protuberant belly like sacks. Her skin was mottled with bruises, lined with dirt. There were teeth marks about her shoulders.

"Clo, please!" Alaric said.

She put down her hands and pushed her shintiyan down around her ankles. Her legs were pipestems, covered with bruises. On the inside of both of them, above her knees, were livid scratches, and what he would have sworn were more teeth marks, the actual festering wounds of bites. He could see, in the fireglow, the silken little inverted triangle of blonde pelt between her thighs gleam like a small sunburst.

She lay down suddenly, sprawled legs and arms agape upon a filthy heap of sheepskins, making by her posture a sudden and total crucifixion of the dreams he'd somehow stubbornly retained.

"Come, good my lord!" she mocked. Then: "Don't tell me my so long desired flesh hath lost the power to awake lust in thee!"

" 'Tis not that, Clo," Alaric said, " 'tis only that I—"

"Wouldst see my face? Odd! I usually do this veiled. . . ."

She tore away her veil, and now he saw again her pitiful, butchered face, saw the marks he had cut into forehead and cheeks and chin. Oddly, it had not changed much; behind the hideous scars she was fair still, until she smiled at him.

He reeled where he stood. "God's eyes!" he swore. "Clo, your teeth!"

"Juli knocked them out," she said calmly, "in various of his drunken rages. 'Tis better so—now those who prefer the Frankish vice need have no fear that I might become aroused and maim them. Come, divest yourself of your garments, my lord! 'Tis time at last that we had our wedding night!"

"Clo—" he whispered "—I—I cannot. There is too much sorrow in my heart, too much pain—"

"What better cure for it exists than this? Oh, don't be a fool, Alaric! I have no disease. Turtura lied. Besides, I want you. Can't you see I'm afire?"

"No, Clo," he said. "Like this—no—"

"Then how?" she mocked him. "Believe me there is not a position or method which I know not. I'll give you pleasure of which you never dreamed, my lord!"

But he stood there unmoving. Slowly he shook his head. The motion was utterly final.

She came up off the sheepskins then, clawed her clothes to her, climbed sullenly back into them.

"I knew that when I put the matter to the test, all your nobility would take wing and fly like pigeons harried by a hawk," she said.

"You knew nothing of the kind, nor do you know it now," Alaric said. "Come, let us go find Julio, and arrange the matter—"

She crouched there like a whipped beast, but what was in her eyes was wonder.

"Alaric—" she said.

"Aye, Clo?"

"You—you'd have me still? Me—a scrawny, skinny trull? The filthiest of all the trollops in this world? The most unspeakably vile of whores? I do anything, remember! Anything that's asked of me! There is no act so nauseous, so unthinkably loathsome, so abominable that—"

He smiled at her gently. "It doth not matter," he said.

"I—I'm with child! I—I think, by *him*. 'Twill surely be his image. When 'tis born, I should have to keep it with me. You'd see it daily, be reminded as oft that this toothless hag—"

"Nor that," Alaric said.

She came up to him then, stood there looking at him; and the firelight made crystalline gold of her tears.

"Say it!" she said. "I want to hear the words! Say: 'Clo, I love thee. Willst come home again?'"

Very gently he said it. "Clo, I love you. Will you come home again?" Then he bent and touched her lips as lightly as a breath.

She clung to him, shuddering. Then he raised her eyes to his, and on

321

her cheeks her tears were scarlet now in the firelight, a crimson spill, a flood.

Wordlessly she shook her head. Found her voice. "No, Alaric," she said.

"Why not?" he whispered.

She smiled at him then, through her tears. "Being what you are, let me honor you with God's own truth, my lord! Men, most men, are sentimental fools, so that the oldest legend on this earth is that of the whore with the heart of gold. She doth not exist, my lord! The marks of our trade are that we be stupid, lazy, and vile. All of us—even the ones sold into it as slaves; because if a captive be not a trull at heart, she dies within a fortnight of self-loathing, of disgust. So rid your heart of any suspicion that I am returning your touching idiotic saintly nobility in kind. I go not with you, because, truth to tell, I couldn't stand it. I couldn't bear your saintliness, your goodness, your solemnity! Within a month of my return to you, I'd be rutting with your stableboys in the straw—Why? Because I am what I am. I'd tire of your gentle husbandly love, beg you to beat me, bite me, ride me till I scream and scream and scream. Or to perform with me mutually the twisted acts whose very ugliness I've come to love. I cannot give up Juli. I need him. Only he among all the men I've known is big enough to hurt me to the extent I crave, or slow enough to cause my heart, my lungs, my loins to burst within me time after time before he reaches his own bestial pleasure. So, no, my lord Alaric! Honored and touched, but no! Selfishly, no. Truthfully, no—finally no, no, no! I love my work m'lord! And you would only cheat me!"

He stood there, staring at her. Sighed.

"Don't be a fool, Alaric!" she said harshly. "I'm nothing to regret—"

"Still, I regret you," he said. "Or mayhap 'tis the state in which you leave me, I regret. I am only human after all, Clo—"

"What state is that?" she demanded.

"Wifeless, yet wed. So that my line must die with me. I've wronged you cruelly, that I confess; and beg your forgiveness and God's. But still it saddens me in my heart that—"

"That what, Alaric?" she whispered.

"That you should hate me so!"

She came up to him then, and stood close to him, staring into his face.

"Come," she said to him at last, "let us go back. What doth it matter how I feel toward you?"

"Nonetheless, it does," he said.

She smiled at him then, in bitter mockery.

"Mayhap on tomorrow you'll learn just how terrible is that hate," she said. "Now come!"

Toward sunset, standing before the tent with his guards, Alaric saw Abdul coming up the trail toward the camp. The bandit chieftain was mounted on a magnificent gray. Behind him, on a fine dun-colored palfrey, Turtura rode, and at her side Clothilde, mounted on an evil-looking mule. Turtura was talking to Clo. They seemed, remarkably enough, quite friendly.

Then, lifting up his eyes, Alaric saw with an astonishment that made him doubt them and his senses, what came behind them. On a princely chair borne on the shoulders of twelve serfs—six to a pole, three before and three aft, so that distributed among twelve brawny shoulders on its double shafts, even the great weight of the chair and the imposing figure that sat in it were as nothing—sat Father Martin, Bishop of Avila. Behind him on various palfreys, donkeys, mules, rode a small host of minor clergy, among whom Alaric recognized Friar Juan. The whole of this amazing collection of priestly fathers was surrounded by Berber horsemen with drawn swords, so that they seemed to move in a veritable forest of flashing blades.

They came on until they had reached the clearing in the middle of the circle of tents. Gaily, Abdul leaped from his mare.

"I give thee greetings, Aizun!" he roared. "Behold my gift! Your freedom from this trull of thine—for here have we before us the first ecclesiastical court in history convened by Berber swords!"

"I thank thee, Abdul," Alaric began, "but I cannot—this is a terrible thing you've done! To have abducted an entire council of churchly fathers! Don't you see that in their wrath they'll not be inclined to—"

He saw the Bishop glaring at him. His words died in his throat. He walked past the two guards, who made no move to stop him, knelt at the foot of my lord Bishop's chair, bent and kissed the prelate's ring.

"Alaric!" Father Martin roared. "Is this thy doing? Wast thou who sent these fiends of Mahound down upon us? If so, thou'st earned excommunication! On pain of which, and also on pain of banishment, I charge thee, do not lie!" He held up his massive silver crucifix. "Now swear on this, and speak!"

"I swear before God, and by Our Gracious Lady," Alaric said softly, "that I had nothing to do with this abduction, my lord Bishop. It would seem that my Berber friends, wishing to render me a service, were overzealous on my behalf."

The Bishop stared at him. Then his eyes softened. He had known

323

Count Teudis' youngest son since birth and loved him well. Right oft had he commented with his secretary Friar John that the Church had lost a shining light when Alaric had not elected the priesthood as all the world had expected of him. Besides, his knowledge of men was vast. It was very clear that Alaric was not lying now.

"What did these heathens expect or want us to do on thy behalf, my son?" he said.

"To dissolve my marriage to the Lady Clothilde, my lord Bishop," Alaric said.

"Is she also present?" the Bishop said.

"Aye, your Grace. That is she there."

"Dressed as a Muslim!" Father Martin roared. "Come here, my child!"

Clothilde approached him. She bent and kissed the Bishop's ring.

"Hast turned apostate to they faith, daughter?" the Bishop thundered.

"Nay, my lord Bishop," Clothilde said. "I am a Christian—and a sinner."

"Then why art thou dressed like that?" Father Martin demanded.

"Because my husband demands it of me," Clothilde said.

The Bishop turned to Alaric in pure wonder.

"Why, in God's Holy Name—" he began, but Clothilde cut him off.

"Not he, my lord, but rather another—my Muslim husband, or if you will, he who serves me as a husband now—"

Alaric was sure that the vein in the good Bishop's forehead was going to burst, causing that godly man to perish of an apoplexy. All around them the Berbers watched, blades and teeth gleaming, watching this most strange spectacle with childlike joy.

But with immense effort, the prelate mastered himself.

"Is this why you wish an annulment, my son?" he said sorrowfully.

Alaric looked into Clothilde's face. As he turned back to the Bishop, he saw Julio on the fringes of the crowd, edging cautiously away.

"Nay, your Grace," he said quietly, "I do not desire an annulment. I only ask that my erring spouse accept my pardon—and grant me hers— for right grievously have I sinned against her. That she return to my house, to live with me honorably as my wife in the sight of God, his Holy Church, and man, for is it not written: 'Whom God hath joined together, let no man put asunder'—?"

The good Bishop looked at Alaric, and now his fine ruddy face was troubled. But, at that moment, Friar Juan came through the press of churchmen, bowed and kissed his lord Bishop's ring right reverently. He straightened up, and whispered in the Bishop's ear, so loud his voice carried to where Alaric stood.

"This is the case of which I told you, good my lord!"

Two spots of red showed in his Grace's cheeks. Mightily did he frown then.

"Then say I," he snorted, "that these children of Satan hath done well to bring us here! Convene the court, Brother!"

In a flurry of scurrying about 'twas done. The prelates sat themselves down on folding stools the Berbers provided them at Abdul's command. Writing materials were brought: paper, pens—a table.

Father Martin, Bishop of Avila, lifted up his eyes and prayed: "Our Father, inspire our minds and instruct our hearts. Lend us Thy Wisdom and Thy Justice. Amen!"

He turned to Alaric then.

"I take it then, my young lord Teudisson," he said, "that there are no grounds existent by which an annulment could be granted thee—"

Alaric thought about that. Above all, he must not lie; yet—

"I did not say that, good my lord," he said. "I only said I do not wish my marriage bonds dissolved! It seemeth me my duty to pardon my wife her sins and to take her unto me—"

"Thou sayest well," the Bishop said, but his voice curiously lacked all conviction. "Spoken like a Christian!" Then he turned to Clothilde. "What say you to this, daughter?"

Speaking, Clothilde's voice was utterly serene. "That I'll see him in hell first, the whey-faced, canting little priest!" she said.

And now, to Alaric's amazement, instead of being angered by her words, Father Martin seemed to find them pleasing. It came to him suddenly that the Lord Bishop *wanted* to dissolve this marriage; and the reasons why rang through his mind like the knell of doom: Who was it who was forever urging my poor mother to consign me to the seminary, if not this selfsame Father Martin, before he was elevated to the Bishop's chair? Who was it who pressed upon Father Juan the idea—not that the fisher of souls needed pressing overmuch? How oft did Friar Juan repeat: "Father Martin says the boy hath the look of an angel. Father Martin says 'God's Grace rest upon Alaric, my lord Count. You have one warrior son. Surely you could spare the Holy Church—' "

He could feel himself strangling. He felt trapped, the noose tightening about his neck. In desperation he shouted out: "I do not desire this thing, my lords!"

"But *I* do," Clothilde said. "And as a Christian dame of high degree, do I not have a right to present my case, good Fathers, Churchly Lords?"

"You have, daughter," the Bishop said. "But first I must appoint a Father learned in canon law to represent you, and another to undertake to argue in behalf of my lord Teudisson."

"I have no need of such!" Clothilde snapped. " 'Tis true I know little of canon law, but this I do know: if a husband refuses to consummate his marriage to the increase of Christian souls and in honor to his vows, that marriage hath no validity at all. Am I not right, my lords?"

There was a general murmur of mingled astonishment and assent, and, on the part of those fathers who had dreamed of drawing this fair youth with his disquieting look of sanctity into their number, of satisfaction.

"That is quite true, daughter," Bishop Martin said. "You say that my lord Teudisson hath not—"

"—lain with me in husbandly congress as is his duty! No later than this morning he refused me my wifely privileges once again. I say unto you, Churchly Lords; nay, I swear it upon the True Cross, that to Alaric Teudisson I have never been wife more than in name!"

The eyes of all present were upon Alaric now—some mocking, some pitying, some with respect, with awe. For in that day when chastity was held the highest good, men found the proof that one bound to no clerkly oath had maintained it outside the cloister's walls, evidence enough of sainthood.

"Ask him to swear upon thy miter and thy robes, my lord," Clothilde went on, "that he hath ever been husband to me. See, your Grace and Clerkly Fathers, if he dares take such an oath!"

Martin, Bishop of Avila by God's Own Grace, was looking at Alaric now.

"Nay, my ghostly lords," Alaric whispered. "Right freely do I confess that for a host of reasons, some good, some bad, some even, mayhap, mad, I have never possessed myself of my wife. But I say unto you that I repent me of my negligence, that from this hour I undertake—"

"I have no wish to be a priestling's wife!" Clothilde cut him off. "For that is in itself a sin. I prefer to cleave unto the husband I have now— who, for all his faults, is at least all man, not having undergone that subtle castration that a priestly vocation, accepted or not, imposes upon true maleness. I say unto you, my lords, that Teudisson's incapable! Let him if he will, if very truly he hath repented of his negligence, consummate his marriage now before you all! Let him prove that he—"

"Daughter!" the Bishop said. "Thy words are unseemly!"

"And she herself," Turtura piped up, "a filthy slut!"

"Who art thou, that clad in Satan's robes yet speak so perfectly our tongue?" Bishop Martin said.

326

"A Christian," Turtura said. "The Prophet's Law doth not require that we abjure our faith when we take one of His followers unto us for husband. If my lord Bishop will allow me to speak—"

"In the state of fornication in which you live, daughter," the Bishop said, "for marriage to one of them is in the eyes of the Church no marriage at all, your words are unacceptable as evidence—"

"Then neither are hers!" Turtura shot back. "For she is in the state of adultery, not only with him she calls husband but with half the men in the camp to whom she sells herself, my lord! I pray thee, let me speak! For I—"

Father Juan again leaned close to his Bishop's ear. His Grace smiled.

"We will hear you, daughter; but without your taking oath. Then we will have of Teudisson here, whose oath alone is at this juncture valid, his sworn statement whether, according to his knowledge, you speak the truth or lie. Now stand forward—"

"My lords," Turtura said, "he knows little—and that little hearsay. But there is in that big tent over there a Christian captive, who hath been with us these three moons awaiting a ransom. *He* knows first hand of what I speak, for he hath seen it with his eyes!"

"Then let him be brought!" the Bishop said.

After that it was already over—though Alaric had to endure another hour of horror. The captive, a merchant of Zaragosta, gave his evidence with zest. The things he'd seen Clothilde do in the open, in the center of the square, were enough to turn the stomach of a goat.

"They'd line up there, my lords," he said, "their robes tucked up, their breeches about their ankles and—"

God! Alaric wept inside his heart: God! God! God!

A half hour later he was a free man. The Bishop's great seal gleamed on a lettered parchment, granting him the annulment he had not asked for, did not want. Clothilde rested under excommunication until such time as she should confess her sins, repent of them, and give up her evil way of life—a penalty that seemingly troubled her not at all.

Before taking his leave and being escorted by the Berbers, along with the host of priests and friars accompanying him, back down the trail, the good Bishop spoke long and gravely to Alaric Teudisson.

"It seemeth me, my son," he said, "that thou art among those chosen of God. Another less chaste man than thou would have consummated his marriage despite his doubts. But since the hour of thy birth I've known that thou'rt an anointed of the Lord! When I came to christen thee voices spoke in my ear, telling me: 'Martin, Martin, Servant of God, behold one destined to become greater than thee in His service!' And light shone upon thy forehead, my boy; lauds and flutes and lutes and pipes made music, though God wot there were no musicians there! So seek not to escape your destiny! Pray upon this thing and meditate upon it all thou wilt. Then, son of mine, Chosen of God, come unto me!"

Alaric bowed his head. "I am a sinful man, your Grace!" he said.

"God's Mercy will wash you clean," the Bishop said. "Will you come?"

"If I cannot escape it," Alaric said.

XIX

The day after the christening of his half-brother Hermangildo, the third of Count Teudis' sons, and the fourth of the children that lusty old warrior had sired, Alaric departed from his father's house, forever—though in good truth such was not his intent. And though on the day of his going forth, all Castilla's beauty beckoned to him he rode away with sadness in his heart. One of the reasons for his mood was, he admitted, a paltry thing: the fair Ramona had flatly refused to have her son called Ataulf, as was Count Teudis' dearest wish, on the score that the name itself was clearly a harbinger of evil fortune. And such a tantrum did she throw, with such fishwifely screams, and so great a flow of tears, that Count Teudis for the sake of sweet peace within his halls had weakened and allowed her to call the newborn male infant what she willed. Whereupon Ramona had demanded of her venerable lord a list of all his forebears. That list supplied, she studied it most carefully, then elected a name that nowise upon it appeared—choosing Hermangildo for that very reason, hoping, thereby, Alaric was sure, to emphasize the commencement of a new dynasty. A pretty piece of female malice, petty spite—no more; but still it saddened him.

But now, as he cantered over the trail with the wind at his back, his heart began to lift. For well did it begin to seem to him that the path of duty lay along a more pleasant plane. Since Clothilde of her own volition had rejected him, his forgiveness, and his love; since, moreover, by the action of the highest authority to which in such matters recourse could be had, he was free, a bachelor again, it was not too much to believe that now the fair possibility existed of combining duty with joy, by righting the wrongs he had done Afaf, taking her unto him as his lawful wife—though between them still the differences in faith stood like a wall. Had the matter been reversed, had she been Christian and he Muslim, there would have been no problem; for the Prophet's followers were permitted to marry Christian and Jewish maids without their brides having to renounce their faiths. But unless he were prepared to become an apostate, or persuade Afaf from her beliefs, no marriage was possible between them. The Church sternly forbade, lest the bride become a convert first.

Whereupon, under Islamic law, for the crime of apostasy against her own, she died.

I am mad, he thought; I who have no faith at all—but a mere longing toward belief. And yet, and yet—

Then, looking up, he saw the Shrine of Our Lady of the Forsaken, tiny and forlorn, nestling on its high precipice. At once he reined Jinni in. 'Tis a waste of time and a folly, he thought; but after all, lean Abdul and fat Turtura served me well. And Clo—who, despite her harsh words, acted with a certain wry and bitter generosity. Mayhap what she said was true; but truer still, methinks, the tears she shed for my poor sake. Who knows that I cannot her some comfort bring. Aye, I'll ride that way. 'Twill cost me a day or two, no more. Methinks having been parted from sweet Afaf this long, another day, or even another week, will make scant difference.

In which conjecture he was absolutely right, though not for the reasons that he thought. His education in the ways of women, in the workings of the feminine heart, the female mind, was abysmally short of complete. But that he did not, could not know, as he tugged Jinni's head about, and started up that trail.

He reached Abdul's camp without incident. The sentinels posted invisibly amid the heaped-up rock recognized him at once; stood up, saluted with their swords, and waved him on.

But once within the camp, the first person he saw was Clothilde. She was more bedraggled, more slatternly than ever, and now monstrously great with child. She dragged herself toward him like a wounded beast, each step costing her an effort that was pitiful to see.

"Oh, Clo!" he wailed, and leaped down from his horse.

She looked rapidly around her in every direction. At the moment, there was no one in the clearing but the two of them, which Alaric should have realized even then, was strange.

"Get back up on that pretty nag, Alaric," she said harshly, "and fly from here. Should you remain, your life won't be worth a copper. For if you bide, you'll either have to join these thieving swine in a monstrous thing, or be held prisoner till they've done it. Thereafter it will occur to Abdul, or my Juli will point it out to him, that, living, you're the sole witness who can put their necks into the strangler's noose, or beneath the headsman's ax—"

"Surely, Clo—" he began.

"Surely, dung! Listen, you holy fool! Within two hours, for the lookouts have already sighted them, that fat filth ibn Ha'ad will ride by below here, bearing his plump pigeon of a daughter—"

The wealthy merchant from Córdoba *was* ibn Ha'ad, as Alaric had suspected. "So Abdul's spies persuaded him to go by land!" he said.

"Aye, the idiot! He rides well guarded, though. But since not even his mercenaries love that greasy swindler, methinks there'll be some slight slaughter, and then his men at arms will fly, leaving the Mozarab—fine Christian he is!—and his daughter to be taken—"

"Thus providing two other witnesses against Abdul," Alaric said, "since to obtain ransom, he must deliver them up alive—"

"Nay, Alaric! For God's love, don't waste time! Ibn Ha'ad hath not the courage nor the manhood to bear witness against his abductors! Nor will he allow his daughter to. The only one they'll have to fear is you; and doubt it not, they'll silence you forever—"

He smiled at her then, a little sadly. "That matters to you, Clo?" he said.

"God give me strength!" she moaned. "Nay! It matters not! Here, draw your dagger, cut your throat—see if I care! Oh, Alaric, Alaric, holy fool! Get on that beast and fly!"

"Come with me, Clo," he said.

"Fool!" she wept. "Tender fool! Holy idiot! Saintly ass! Go! You hear me! What do I have to say to make you get thee hence?"

"The truth," Alaric said. "Why are you doing this?"

She stared at him as though she were recreating him anew within the darkness of her mind.

"Because I love thee, Alaric, since you must know," she said flatly, calmly, slowly, her voice a little hoarse, a trifle strained; but making of her words a ritual, a litany, got by rote for this special occasion, whose pressing need for haste seemed to have flown from her reckoning. "I always have; I always will. I love thee before I was betrothed to Ataulf, and after. I love thee with all my heart, my half-mad mind, my lost soul, my by-seven-lustful-devils-possessed body. I love thee enough to give thee up, knowing that being what I am I would destroy thee. So now, having stripped to ugly nakedness my very spirit, having had of me this ultimate defeat, this final humbling of what pride in regards to thee I'd kept, will you by the love I bear thee, and my troth, get up on that dainty lady's palfrey—and fly?"

"Aye." Alaric sighed; and bending, kissed her cheek above the veil. Which small, gentle, courtesy forged of itself the last link in the iron chain that bound him to his destiny, for Julio came out of the tent at that moment, and saw Clothilde in his arms. Alaric felt the little shudder that she gave; bade her adieu, and mounting once more, rode down that goat track toward the trail.

331

One half hour later he heard a storm of hoofbeats behind him, the brazen clangor of arms, and looking back he saw a cloud of Berbers riding down upon him with Julio at their head.

He stretched out his hand and patted Jinni's sleek neck.

"Fleet companion," he said in Arabic, "if thou hast aught of magic in thee, aught of speed, prepare to employ them now!"

Jinni stretched his neck forth and melted into a creamy blur, pouring down that trail. Alaric had no need to use either whip or spur. With every stride the white palfrey opened the distance between him and his foes, until a pair of Berbers cut around Julio at a widening of the trail, and began to truly make a chase of it, their barbs as swift as Jinni or mayhap a trifle swifter, for well did it seem to Alaric that they were gaining upon him now.

Grimly he galloped on, down that trail where the slightest misstep would send both horse and rider crashing to their deaths; and just as doggedly the Berbers followed him. And now he could see the main road below, but it provided no refuge. He reached it, turned into it with the pair of Berbers hard on his heels. He heard something whistle by him, saw a Berber lance bite earth, stand and quiver some yards ahead.

"May God forgive me!" he muttered, and jerked his horseman's bow from its saddle sheath, reached over his shoulder and flipped an arrow from the quiver, fitted it to the bow, drew, and riding like that, the reins loose about Jinni's neck, at a hard gallop, he turned in the saddle, with the bowstring and the feathered butt of the arrow held as far back as his right ear against the terrible pull of that composite bow, against the ache in his left arm, until he saw the second Berber poise his lance to throw, and in that wafer-thin slicing of time let fly. The arrow sang its twanging, eerie whine. The Berber dropped his lance, clutched at that shaft protruding from his middle, reeled from the saddle, fell woodenly to earth. His mount, riderless now, galloped on. The second Berber drew his sword and died with an arrow through his throat long before he was near enough to chance a stroke.

The immediate dangers down and done for, Alaric turned his attention to his mount, in time to pull Jinni up and thus avoid crashing at full tilt into a milling crowd of heavily armed mercenaries, upon great war horses mounted, come from the direction toward which he fled now. And now he could distinguish their voices above the neighing and whinnying of their steeds, above the crazed clatter of their shields.

"'Tis a young lord, pursued by Moors!" they cried. "Hundreds of them! Flee for your lives! Turn and fly!"

The roar that burst from Alaric's throat then was Count Teudis' own. It soared above the clatter of their arms, the dancing, uncontrolled hoofbeats, the neighing of the horses, above their edging, shrilling, fear-shaken voices.

"Art dogs," he thundered, "or men? Ball-less wonders, castrates all! Hear me! Form ranks!"

There is a certain magic about authority at such a juncture. The milling ceased. They gazed at him in wonder. He sat there, a young war god now, his face terrible in its beauty, so that somehow looking upon him they knew to the man he could not fail. He was watching the Berbers, who had pulled up, one hundred yards away. He studied the situation coldly, the mystic in him, the saint, gone, pushed down into one tiny niche in his heart, while the blood of forty generations of warriors coursed through his veins; but controlled, mastered, seeing with quiet, awful joy a thing that only eyes like his would have seen, only an intelligence beyond the commonality could have grasped. Ibn Ha'ad had relied on Mozarab mercenaries, who being Christians, were armed in Christian fashion, with long lances, heavy shields, broadswords, and mounted upon great chargers. Now every time the Berbers had met such a combination in the field they had cut it to pieces, due to the superior swiftness of their barbs, their light armor or none at all, their matchless dash and skill of maneuver.

But now, God wot, they were not in the field, but massed upon a highway with towering mountains soaring up on both sides of it, leaving them no space for maneuvering at all. He wondered if they had seen in what grave danger they lay; but only for an instant. He lifted his sword skyward, roared out: "Lances at rest! Charge!"

It was a brave show there under the sun on that bright spring day. The mercenaries, under the spell of his grave beauty, under the magic of his voice, forgot what cowardly dogs they were and thundered forward in an unbroken line, filling the road from edge to edge. They hit the Berbers front and center. The crash when they struck was audible four leagues away. The slaughter, fearful. The light-boned, small, swift desert barbs could not keep their feet under the impact of mountainous horseflesh weighing twice as much as they, or more. Lances lifted the entire front line of Berbers from the saddle, spitted on the spear points. The mighty broadswords hacked the life out of the rest, as the big horses rode them down, and all the world became a cloud of dust out of which rose the roars of conquering lions who had tasted blood, the screams of dying men, the glitter of sunlight upon that forest of blades, half their blued steel lengths now dripping red.

It lasted the sum total of four minutes before the surviving Berbers broke and fled the fray. So fast did they ride that they almost caught up with Julio, who as usual, had decamped the moment he'd seen Alaric take command, before that fair youth had even had time to sound the charge.

And now seeing the mercenaries, turned warriors for the nonce, disposed in the battle heat of their blood to pursue the Berbers, Alaric ripped out: "Hold! Ye cannot win a horse race and the battle's already gained!"

They pulled up their big chargers and came back to him, saluting him with their swords.

"Who are you, young lord?" they said, their voices thick with pride, with awe, with wonder.

"Alaric, son of Teudis, Count of Tarabella," he said quietly, and before they could say more a rider dashed out from the mule train and galloped up to where they sat upon their foam-flecked, heaving horses.

"Our master, the merchant ibn Ha'ad, asks that the young lord be brought to him!" he cried.

Alaric shrugged. "Lead on, good lad," he said.

Ibn Ha'ad was afoot, having got down from the traveling litter borne on shafts between two mules. He was hopping up and down in his excitement, so that all his great bulk jiggled; the diamond set in the slit a surgeon had made in one nostril made scintillating ever-moving white fire, the huge hoops in his earlobes danced, and his pudgy fingers, covered, thumbs and all, with rings, made a multicolored blaze.

"A lion!" he cried. "A princely lion! A lion of a prince! Come closer, my boy! That I may thank thee properly!"

Then before Alaric could prevent him, the rotund little merchant had seized him in his arms, and soundly kissed both cheeks. Be it said that despite his fat, ibn Ha'ad was as clean as a Moorish lord, and much perfumed, so his kisses were not unpleasant. But now as he stood back, a startled light leaped in his little blue eyes.

"Thou!" he whispered.

"Aye, slave trader!" Alaric said evenly. "Behold him of whom you would have made a catamite for your noble pederast, al Hussein. Had I known 'twas you whom those desert dogs were after, I should not have lifted a hand!"

"Look you now, fair Aizun!" the trader said slowly. "Surely art not going to hold *that* against me? I knew not who thou wert, nor how highly favored among princes. Which now hath been abundantly proved the way thy friends arranged the pervert's death—"

"My friends?" Alaric said.

"Aye. That young Jew, Saadyah—son of my rival Hasdai ben Sahl. He had a principal role in it, I'm told; but the Emir himself took a hand, though ibn al Maliki's death cannot be traced to the Leader of the Faithful, since he left it all up to that son of Saithan and master of all intrigues, Nasr. I know not truly how 'twas done; but 'twas a veritable marvel. The sodomite caught abed with the son of a rich Jew—the one people on earth who violently object to a little deviate play from time to time—and lest al Rahman take the matter too lightly, accusations connecting the pervert with no less than Prince al Wallid, his own younger brother brought—whereupon we find Ahmad al Hussein imprisoned, then within a month escaping from that jail which hath held some of the stoutest brigands in this world, and no man in memory known to flee it—but slight, slender al Hussein free of those bars, those gates, those walls, and in a public street, where discovered by his guards, he's arrowed down. A marvel! A veritable marvel! I couldn't have done better myself!"

"I see," Alaric said. "Well, merchant, since now you've seen the error of your ways as far as I'm concerned, I bid you Godspeed, and take my leave of you. Nor need you fear any vengeance of mine. The past is dead. Let it rest in peace—"

"Nay, wait!" ibn Ha'ad shrilled. "You've saved my life—and the honor of my daughter! Name what reward you will, and it is thine! Ten thousand dinars? Twenty thousand? Fifty—"

"Not an obol or a fal," Alaric said. "To be quit of the sight of you, merchant, is reward enough. Again I bid you Godspeed! On your way!"

"Wait—if thou wouldst not have rewards, I beseech thee, Aizun, enter my service! Take command of my men at arms. I have never before seen them so inspired to valor as they were beneath thy orders! With such as thou to lead them—"

Alaric shook his head. As he did so, he caught sight of the look on a burly mercenary's face. The man was frowning, his countenance black with anger. 'Tis thou who captains this somewhat less than heroic band, and hence by my elevation would be deposed, Alaric thought. Ye need not fear me, friend! But ibn Ha'ad was pleading still.

"I implore thee, young lord!" he said. "The way to Byzantium is long, the dangers many. With thee in command surely we should arrive safely—"

"What matters it to me if the next band of brigands slit your gullet, merchant?" Alaric said. "Surely you hold not that I should entertain any sorrow over what might pass with you?"

"Nor over what might pass with me, good my lord?" that soft voice said.

"Jimena!" ibn Ha'ad grated. "I've told you and told you—"

"—to keep to my litter," Jimena said, "lest my beauty inflame your men. But beauty hath its uses, Father. Perhaps now 'twill serve to inspire this fair youth to change his mind—"

With that she coolly removed the veil which, Christian though she was, she at her father's jealous insistence wore.

Alaric smiled. He stood there feasting his eyes upon that face. It was round and plump and reminded him of Ruth's. It had the same slumberous, semioriental cast, though Jimena's hair was berry red above eyes of palest jade. Her figure, too, was plump, generously shapely, after the fashion that most men of his times found exciting. But Alaric was the exception. All his life he had loved slenderness in a maid. This plump pigeon was not at all his kind of bird. He admitted she was decidedly pretty; but it was that lazy, pampered, overfed prettiness that bred a certain languor, indistinguishable from torpor, which displeased him.

"The argument's powerful, my lady," he said, "and were my heart free it would have no force to gainsay it; but since it is not free—"

"Oh!" Jimena pouted. "Art wed then, fair Aizun?"

"Nay," Alaric said. "But I mean to be as soon as I reach Córdoba."

"Might I," Jimena cooed, "ask the name of the fortunate maid?"

"You'd scarcely know her, though your father doth, for 'twas he who brought her from Egypt, and sold her to al Hussein. Doth remember her, merchant? The Bedu slave girl, Afaf?"

Now truly the merchant was hopping about with pure delight; for now he saw victory in his grasp.

"Then come with us, ibn al Qutiyya!" he cried. "For naught awaits thee in Córdoba. Thou'rt free to travel—and, mayhap, so long a journey may serve to ease thy pain—"

"My pain?" Alaric got out. "What species of mockery is this, ibn Ha'ad?"

"My boy,"—the merchant's round face assumed a theatrical exaggeration of a sorrow nowise felt—"thou'rt a child in this of women, 'tis plain to see. Thou'st remained away too long. I tell thee, and my Jimena here can confirm it, that the night before we left Córdoba we were, my daughter and I, by special invitation of the fair Afaf herself, guests at her wedding to thy friend the Jew!"

Alaric hung there. He opened his mouth to say, to scream it out: "You lie in your teeth, you dog!" But nothing came out, no word at all. For looking at Jimena's face, he could see the truth of her father's words in the pity written there. He took a backward step, death in his heart, his face gone white; his lips parted to speak, to say—but what he would have said then not even he was ever to know; for at that pain-halted moment, Abdul and his brigands, totally unaware of Julio's abortive raid at the head of the men the bandit chieftain had left to guard the camp, struck the tail end of ibn Ha'ad's baggage train. They heard the thunderous crash, the metallic clatter, the mingled roars of Romance and Arabic oaths, the screams of bitter pain, the wild dance of hoofbeats, the battle cries.

"Aizun, I beseech thee!" ibn Ha'ad wept.

Alaric stood there. He thought: To die in battle is an honorable death—and no sin!

"I'm your man, merchant," he said. "Now have me brought a fresh mount. My barb's winded, and too light for this work in any event—"

"A horse!" ibn Ha'ad shrilled. "A steed for the young lord! In God's name, a horse!"

"Let him take mine," the black-browed captain of the mercenaries said. "Since I've been deposed, I leave your service, merchant! He can return it to me once the battle's over."

"I thank you, good Captain," Alaric said, and took the proffered bridle. It was at that moment he became aware of Jimena's face. It was very white. There was a hint of moisture about her eyes. She came to him then, stood very close so that her rich Moorish perfumes rose about his head like a cloud.

"Fair Aizun, no!" she said. "Thou must not!"

"I must not what, my lady?" he said.

"What you are thinking," she whispered. "That swart and fickle slave wench is not worth it! No woman is—not even I. Promise?"

He managed a reasonable approximation of a smile. "Gentle sorceress, reader of minds—" he began.

"Promise!" she said. She was, despite her somewhat excessive plumpness, in that moment very fair, standing there with her green eyes alight with tender concern for him at the very least, mayhap even more. A subtle thought invaded his mind: if, having promised this upon my honor, I in battle fall, surely I die free of sin, quit of any deliberate intent on my part to— He smiled.

"I promise, sweet Jimena," he said.

"Then wear my gage!" she said, and handed him the veil she had removed.

Ibn Ha'ad opened his mouth to say something, to protest; but he never got it out; for by then the first of his rear guard came hurtling past in wild flight, screaming: "Fly for your lives! Fly! All the Moors on earth are—"

Alaric mounted then, and turned to the mercenaries who had already served him well.

"Lads," he said, "Who have proved yourselves men, I bid you follow me and bear you bravely. Know you that you ride under a special blessing. Now, for God and Saint Fredegunda—charge!"

But now it was not the lesser men whom habitually Abdul left behind to guard his camp that they met, but his finest, most seasoned warriors: Berbers born, men swore, with a blade between their teeth and a horse betwixt their knees. Still the mercenaries' weight and height and reach told as before in that narrow stretch of roadway which left no room for Berber horsemanship. Hard pressed, Alaric fought in the thick of it; but his years of constant practice at arms, added to the analytical quality of a mind that had studied swordplay as though it were a game of chess, had made him very nearly invincible. Alone of all those on that field, he did not use a sword as though it were an ax, nor was his first blow aimed to kill; rather it was something analogous to a Black Queen's Rook's pawn, advanced to throw his opponent's defenses wide, sacrificed to leave an opening through which his own fatal thrust, sooner or later, like blued lightning came.

Seven or eight hundred years later, when the rapier would have replaced the broadsword, the dazzling array of thrusts, feints, paries that the Goth's son displayed upon that day would have become common-places of every fencing school; but in his times not even the the words "to fence" existed; men hammered each other to earth with the edge, or even the flat of the blade, and bull-like strength was all that counted. But wounded men withdrawing from the field, or those sound ones for the nonce unengaged with a foe, saw what he did and crossed themselves.

"Surely," they muttered, "he fights under Divine protection! Surely invisible shields turn aside those strokes that never reach him! Fair as he is—he calls down the heavenly hosts to aid him. God's eyes! Methinks I see them now! There! And there! And what is that light which about his bright head shows?

But 'twas not as easy as it looked; for unlike the Christian warriors, the Berbers, with their lighter, curving sabers, did have some notions of the art of swordplay. What gave Alaric domination over even them was the fact that he was by nature an innovator, while their swordsmanship, superior to that of the Mozarab mercenaries as it indisputably was, still went no further than a limited number of offensive and defensive strokes got by rote in boyhood.

But having cut down still another foe, Alaric found himself confronted with an opponent whose skill was on an order scarcely inferior to his own. For the mind that could conceive of the use of judiciously implanted propaganda to influence events in his own favor, the imagination that had leaped at once to the feat of abducting an entire council of priestly lords to serve the ends of a new-won friend, was scarcely the type to limit itself to boyish exercises with the sword. Like Alaric, Abdul had studied his weapon thoroughly; only a certain tendency toward sloth had prevented his equaling the Goth's total mastery of it.

Yet now, face to face with the fair youth for whom he'd done so great a service, Abdul's dark countenance showed no trace of the rage he might well have been expected to feel to find a guest so greatly honored, helped, riding at the head of his foes. Instead his teeth flashed white in the blackness of his beard. He locked swords with Alaric, leaned swiftly close.

"Make a good show of it, Aizun!" He grinned. "For I cannot slay thee. Turtura'd leave my bed forever, were it I who cut thee down."

"Agreed!" Alaric laughed. "And thy life is safe from me—not for Turtura's sake but because I love thee well, Abdul!"

The duel between the two leaders was the highlight of the day. All who witnessed it swore lifelong they had never seen such swordplay, nor two antagonists more evenly matched. Before 'twas over, each of them was wounded a dozen times, covering all the dark oiled chain with his blood. Then, with a mighty stroke Alaric smashed through the Berber's guard, leaving him with only the hilt of his weapon in his head; the blade snapped off, and by that same stroke, his sword arm so grievously wounded that Abdul could not lift it more.

"Kill him!" one of the mercenaries roared.

"Nay!" Alaric said, lifting his voice above the din of battle. "So brave a foeman deserves a Christians mercy. I give thee thy life, Berber! Let no man of mine touch him! Let him retire honorably from the fray."

So it was done, and by the doing the battle gained. Seeing their leader disabled, the Berbers lost heart, turned their mounts about, and fled.

Sitting there, watching them go, Alaric became aware at last how tired he was, how faint from loss of blood. He reeled a little in the saddle, then manfully bore himself upright.

"God hath granted us the victory," he said to the mercenaries. " 'Tis meet we thank Him for it! Doff helmets! Bow your heads!"

Afterward no man of them could agree with another upon his exact words; fierce arguments would arise as to exactly what it was the saintly young warrior said; but until the grave mold clogged each ear that listened to him on that day, all vouchsafed 'twas the most moving prayer they'd ever heard.

They rode back to where they'd left the merchant and his daughter. And now once more and terribly Alaric Teudisson was led to question his slowly returning faith, the existence, or at the least the benevolence, of God. For ibn Ha'ad lay on the ground, shrieking in impotent rage and pounding the earth with his fist beside the fair Jimena's traveling litter which lay overturned and empty beside him.

"Three men!" the trader howled. "Two Moors and their leader, a

339

Christian by his looks! Knocked me down! Threw Jimena across a riderless mount! And—"

"Julio," Alaric muttered. "Surely Julio—" Then, turning to his men, he
croaked wearily: "Come!"

He rode into the Berber camp with but two men at his side, under
the white flag of truce, for well did they know that to attack Abdul's
stronghold would be but to sign Jimena's death warrant. He found Abdul
sitting before his tent, stripped to the waist, while Turtura heated the iron
to cauterize the great wound in his arm.

"The maid?" Abdul said, speaking in Romance so that Alaric's guards
might understand. "The merchant's daughter? No man of mine took her!
By the Qur'an, I swear it! I give thee leave to search the camp, if thou
believeth not my word!"

"Nay, good Abdul," Alaric said, "thy word is enough. 'Twas Julio,
who now means to cheat you by keeping the entire ransom for himself. I
bid thee farewell, honorable foe, faithful friend. For now I must ride in
search of him . . ."

"And when thou findest him, slay him in my name, Aizun!" Abdul
roared. "Were I fit, I should accompany thee—"

"My lord Alaric," Turtura piped up, "you get down from there and
let me dress your wounds! You're white as death, and bleeding like a pig!
You hear me, Lord Alaric, get you down from there!"

"Nay, good Turtura," Alaric said, "there is no time. I must find that
churl before wine inflames his senses. The maid's most fair and—"

"—Juli more lecherous than a billy goat," Turtura snapped. "But if
you faint, you'll never find him! Get you down, I say!"

"Nay, Turtura," Alaric whispered, "I'll not swoon. Come, lads, let us
ride—"

Nightlong they beat through the pathless crags, dog-weary, sick,
most of them stiffening from their wounds, till in the dawning Alaric
pulled his charger up, murmured: "God's eyes! What a dullard ass I've
been! There! Surely there!" Then, lifting up his voice, he roared: "After
me! Ride!"

They left their mounts some distance from the cave, crept toward it
afoot, holding their scabbards away from their mailed thighs, wearing
their shields behind them lest they clatter. But all their precautions
proved needless; no one would have heard them had they ridden at full
charge.

340

For long before they reached the cave, they could hear her screaming.

Alaric was first into the cave. The fire was lit, enabling him to see clearly that which he'd have given his very life not to have seen. There were not three men there, but four. Julio who held one fair leg apart; a swart Berber who held the other; the second Berber who pinioned her soft arms; and the deposed mercenary captain, who humped his bare buttocks slowly, powerfully, between her white thighs, working into her with such lack of haste that Alaric knew that he and all the rest had repeated the brutal act of rape many times that night. The captain was of them all the most fortunate, for Alaric killed him then and there, dispatching him with a single poniard stroke through the back of his neck. The Berbers drew their daggers but Alaric's curved sword maimed one of them at once, dropping his hand still holding the dagger to the ground, while the Berber clutched the bleeding stump, sat down on the earth, and moaned. At which his companion in crime threw down his blade, and knelt before Alaric, his head bowed to receive the stroke that never came. Julio, seeing his chance, burst by Alaric through the cave's mouth, and ran straight into the arms of the waiting men.

Alaric tried to lift the mercenary captain's dead body from the moaning, weeping girl. He could not. His strength was too far gone by then. He had to call for help. Afterward he wrapped Jimena in the dead captain's cloak, and stumbled toward his charger with her in his arms. She put her bare arms about his neck and wept. The sound of it was absolutely unbearable.

He was unable to mount with her in his arms, so again a pair of the mercenaries had to aid him. They boosted him up on the taller charger, then handed Jimena up to him. Then the procession started off with Julio and one of the Berbers, their hands bound behind them, in the lead. The other Berber they left unbound, merely tying a tourniquet around his arm so that he would not bleed to death before they arrived. Even so, he kept falling off his horse, until they bound him to the saddle. In such fashion they gained the highroad where ibn Ha'ad's mule train waited.

Julio knelt before Alaric and wept: "My lord! My lord! Think of poor Clo! She is with child—and without me she will surely die! Who will provide for her when I'm gone? I ask thee, who?"

Slowly Alaric turned to the merchant, who was hopping up and down in his rage, shrieking aloud the thought closest to his avaricious heart: "Ruined! Who will marry her now? Even in my debt as he is Cyril

Indicopleustes will use this as excuse to escape me! Dogs! Ravening hounds! Kill them! But slowly! Flay them alive! I want to hear them scream!"

"Merchant," Alaric said then, his voice, despite the weight of weariness in him, crisp, "you're in my debt; you asked me before what reward I'd have of you. So now I claim of thee forfeiture of thy promise!"

Ibn Ha'ad stopped dancing about like an enraged dervish. He peered at Alaric in pure astonishment. Then he sighed.

"Aye, lad. Thou hast saved my life, and my daughter's not once but twice. And though thou couldst not save her virginity, 'twas no fault of thine. Ask what thou wilt, and if it lies in my power I'll grant it. What wouldst thou have?"

"Their lives," Alaric said softly, "that you spare them." At once the merchant began to dance about once more and scream his rage; but Alaric cut him off.

"You promised, merchant!" he said.

"No!" ibn Ha'ad shrilled. "That, no! They must die! These ravenous hounds must die!"

"Then I leave your service," Alaric said.

Ibn Ha'ad stood still. Owlishly he peered at the fair youth who swayed there before him barely able to stand. What the trader thought then could almost be read in his eyes: 'Tis far to Constantinople. Upon the way many dangers lurk. And that young princely fool Indicopleustos can be deluded. The Byzantine surgeons are most skilled—a stitch or two most cunningly placed will restore the semblance of what my poor Jimena's lost. Without this lordly young lion, with his face of a warrior-saint to lead them, these dogs of mine will revert to type. Keep him I must, so—

He smiled.

"You insist upon their lives being saved, Aizun?" he said. "That and nothing more?"

Alaric was too weary, too sick at heart to even speculate upon the meaning of the trader's question.

"Their lives, nothing more," he said.

Whereupon ibn Ha'ad turned to the mercenaries who guarded the captives.

"Cut them!" he said.

"No!" Alaric croaked, his voice a husk, a reedy scrape, struggling to break through into sound. "No! I pray thee, merchant—" But a cold strangling in his lungs rose up and choked his voice. There was sickness in him now like unto very death. He reeled back against one of the mule carts, hung there, staring at the mercenaries, at what they were doing now. He wanted to close his eyes but he could not. Gone beyond his will, they gazed upon that sight, so wide stretched that they throbbed achingly in their sockets.

It was quickly done. Brutally, the mercenaries tore the clothing from their captives, pinned them spread-eagled to the ground, holding them there like that, crying and struggling and begging the mercy they had not themselves shown. Julio was the closest to Alaric so that the young Goth saw what another, lesser man might have savored as his vengeance: rough hands seized the enormous male parts of which Julio had been so proud, dragged them up, held them.

"All!" Ibn Ha'ad said. "Seed sacks and goad! Leave him no means for pleasure!"

Alaric saw the knife flash. It must have been dull. Julio screamed and screamed as the mercenary sawed at him. His blood spurted, splattering over the hand that was gripping him, pulling at him, maintaining the necessary tautness.

There was a roar in Alaric's ears now. Vile, slimy things crawled about in his middle. A flood of nausea rose like a thick green tide, hit the back of his throat in a scalding rush. He bent his head to spew it forth, but all the morning roared and the ground leaped up and smote him in the face. From somewhere leagues away he could hear Julio and the Berbers screaming still.

Then even that was gone, or he had departed from it—from thick, hot blood stench, blade scrape, hoarse male voices edging, grating, shrilling into horror, from the ropy slime, the vile smell of the pool of his own utter revulsion in which, face down, the awesomely complex apparatus of flesh that normally he inhabited lay. He himself, person, entity, mind, had fled, had burrowed into the lightless womb of time; into what was much less loss of consciousness, perception, awareness, than the instinctive and total, if temporary, rejection of these means for maintaining contact with his rarely awful world.

Which was for Alaric Teudisson then, for his continued functioning as a rational being, a salvation of sorts. And for his remorse-torn, pity-ravaged heart, both a mercy—and a blessing.

XX

When he came back again he was in a traveling litter. He was stark naked now, and covered with a fine linen coverlet. When he tried to move he tore away the crusts of clotted blood gluing him to both coverlet and sheet, causing his wounds to bleed again, sullenly. The litter jolted and swayed. He thrust his head through the opening in the canopy and vomited once more. That made him feel a little better. He lay there like that, with his head hanging through the canopy with the cool air blowing down from the Sierras washing over his face. It revived him greatly; it brought him back fully into consciousness, into pain. Only the forward mule, who ran now like a deer between the front shafts of the jolting, jerking, swaying litter lashed on by his rider, as though fleeing all the fiends from hell, chose that moment to defecate, so Alaric was forced to draw his head inside once again.

He lay there, in the litter, bathed all over with the slow, sticky seep of his own blood. He was fully awake now; he could feel the searing bite of every sword slash that crisscrossed his shoulders, arms, upper trunk, even his left thigh. He could sense the weakness in him unto death; and yet he knew, with real regret, he was not like to die. He twisted upon his blood-stained sheets, all his mind blanched with recreated horrors.

The jolting of the litter was a dreadful thing. At the risk of killing his mules ibn Ha'ad was putting as many leagues between him and the Berber camp before nightfall as he possibly could. Alaric held his eyes tight shut; until finally his weakness, his fatigue, his pain, pooled above his heart and he swooned, or slept, or both.

When he woke again, it was night, and the canopy of the litter had been extended outward upon two poles to make a tent. Soft hands were washing and dressing his wounds.

Then suddenly they halted upon his flesh, went away, and a woman's voice, rising, edging, shrill, cried out: "In God's name, Berganza, look!"

He was aware through his half-closed eyes of another leaning swiftly forward. Fingers reached out and touched the crossed scars on his breast.

"Self-inflicted," the woman said, "in penance for some sin, surely. Get on with it, Teresa!"

344

Which reminded him once more of things far better forgot. A great tear made its way down his face.

"See—" another voice whispered. "He, too, weeps. The poor, brave lad! Mayhap because he came too late to save her—"

The language was Romance as he should have expected. After all, the merchant was a Mozarab; it was natural that his servants be Christians, too.

"Aye," he said in that tongue, "I weep for that, and for more. But tell me: How doth my Lady Jimena fare?"

"Ill," the eldest of them replied. "She hath not yet ceased to weep although she hath no tears left and both her eyes are swollen shut. Much do I fear she will die, or go mad of this. Men! What foul beasts ye are!"

"Berganza!" one of the younger ones said then hotly. "You dare say such a thing to this fair and godly youth covered all over with sword cuts got in her defense?"

"Hummph!" Berganza snorted. "Likely because he wanted her himself, and was by his own jealousy inspired to valor and to rage. I have not lived fifty years in this world for nothing! Now, get out of here, you silly trulls! For I mean to wash him and dress the rest of his wounds. 'Tis not meet for maids so young to look upon a man's nakedness."

When with disappointment in their eyes, they'd scurried away, she set herself to the task of bathing and dressing the wounds about his thighs. He suffered it, because her matronly air neither gave nor took offense.

"Now," she said, "I'll bring you to sup, because you must be faint of hunger."

"I am," he said, realizing suddenly that he was. "But first tell me, Berganza, those poor devils—did they—?"

"Die? Two of them, yes. The Berber whose hand you cut off, at once. He was already too weak to endure it. The other Berber an hour later. But that fat renegade swine lived. The mercenaries cauterized his wounds with hot pitch, and put a little hollow tube of reed in the front of him so that he won't heal shut and die of being unable to piss. Poor fat swine! He'll look like a woman now with everything cut away—"

Alaric shuddered at the remembered sight of the mercenary sawing at Julio, the still echoing memory of his screams.

"But—" he whispered, "what did they do with him afterward? Surely they did not just leave him there?"

"They bore him on a litter halfway up to the Berber camp. He begged of them. And methinks afterward they were ashamed of such a brutal, foul thing. The Berbers came down to meet them and took him in. Oh, he'll live, right enough. But 'tis said he hath a woman in the camp—"

345

"Aye," Alaric said, "he hath."

"Then God in His Mercy pity her!"

"Amen to that," Alaric said.

Three weeks went by before he saw the fair Jimena again, and then 'twas ibn Ha'ad himself who led him to her litter.

"She is dying," the merchant said with great dignity, and the tears stood and glittered in his little blue eyes. "She was too tenderly nurtured, you know, Aizun; therefore this outrage was more than her gentle heart could bear. So now am I left with nothing but useless wealth. 'Vanity of vanities,' sayeth the preacher. And, God wot, he sayeth true. Come, my boy; she is asking for you. She wants to thank you for your gallantry on her behalf, before she departs this life. . . ."

Alaric bowed. "Lead on, sir merchant," he said.

When he saw her, his breath caught in his throat, and he was hard put to restrain a cry. She was pitiful. In those three weeks no morsel had passed her lips. All that opulent, comely flesh had melted away, leaving her skeletal. He knelt there beside her looking at her. He had hoped that the fat little trader, much given to hyperbole, had been exaggerating her danger; but now he saw that her father, if anything, had understated the case. Jimena was clearly dying, largely because she willed it so. And suddenly this was too much, this final tragedy piled atop of the skyward-reaching mountain of his many hurts. He went on kneeling there beside her, but he could not see her anymore, so blind scalded were his eyes.

He was aware of movement, slow, uncertain. Something light and dry as parchment touched his cheek. He shook his head to clear his eyes and saw that something was her hand, thin, almost transparent, her fingers lingering on his cheek so that the great uncontrolled and uncontrollable wash of his tears bejeweled them, clinging to her fingers like diamonds in the morning light. And now he could see the pale flutter of her by then quite colorless mouth. He leaned close.

"For me?" she whispered. "You weep for—me, Aizun?"

Dumbly he nodded. His hurt, his grief, were beyond the possibility of speech. Nor would it be a kindness to tell her he wept for a succession of ghosts: for poor, mad, self-slaughtered Zoë, for Clothilde worse than dead; for Afaf lost to him; for Saadyah who'd betrayed him; for Gelesvinta, sister of his heart; for Goissuintha, of his soul; and last of all, for her—for Jimena whom he did not love, yet loved as he loved all of humanity. For this further waste of beauty, youth; for that maniac principle in life devoted to the blighting of all that's fair.

Her lips moved again; shaped the words: "Oh, Aizun, don't! I—" He leaned closer still. "I am not fit. A thing—dirtied—used—broken—tossed aside—"

He understood then, of what she was dying. Of hatred of self. Of self-loathing. Of that ancient hurt that has always disarmed the persecuted, the victims of this world: "If God lets me suffer so—if He permits this abomination to be done to me—why then have I not, all unbeknowing, somehow sinned? Am I not being punished for my unworthiness, my worthlessness, my sins of omission at the least, for the unhallowed desire I've felt at times for this one, for that; for my angers, my jealousy, my spite, for all the host of repressed, hidden, cowardly little sins I had not will nor strength to do?"

And because he, too, had almost died of that hurt against which we are forever without defense, her babbled, feverish words entered him like knives. He found them hateful. He had to halt them at any cost. So, bending forward, he stopped her mouth with the tender pressure of his own.

Her eyes flared wide, made emeralds, caught the light, splintered it into slivers along each mobile jeweled facet of her tears; then softly, sweetly they closed, while her mouth clung to his, allowing him to draw from her the hurt, the debasement, the loathing of self, the shame.

"Aizun!" the trader thundered. " 'Fore God, I—"

And halted, seeing his daughter's face, seeing what gleamed and glowed and fluttered there.

"Thou—thou'st saved her," he muttered, "and by a kiss. Methinks I must pardon thee—God's eyes, what a world it is in which we live! Come, lad—leave her now. I'll have Berganza bring her some food to break her fast. For methinks that now she'll take nourishment at last—"

"Father—" Jimena's voice came clear suddenly. "I—" Then it died. Ibn Ha'ad leaned close.

"God's death!" he swore. "She says—she says—"

"What, good merchant?" Alaric said.

"That she'll take food only from thy hands. Jinn and demons, ibn al Qutiyya! What manner of man or magician art thou?"

Within a week she was up and about again. Within two, she insisted upon riding at his side. She questioned him endlessly about his life, pried from him all his sorrows, all his griefs. Then, quite simply, she said: "We're both flawed, Aizun. Our lives have been damaged. And since you insist that you see in me no fault, while I, by the love I've come to bear thee, could pardon thee sins far worse than any of those paltry ones of which you accuse yourself, it is meet that we comfort each other. I am yours. If you wish it, when we reach Constantinople, I will wed thee."

"But the Greek?" Alaric said.

"That is Father's idea, not mine. Do not worry, Aizun, I'll make an end of that!"

He sat there on the white palfrey, looking at her.

"Methinks you love me not!" she said darkly.

"With all my heart," he said, wondering to what extent he lied; how much or little of his words were true.

"Then why don't you kiss me?" Jimena said.

But in another week, during which he was much beset with doubts, quite suddenly she withdrew from him, took to her litter, rode no more at his side. And, as always, once deprived of her company, which he in truth had valued little, he missed her sorely. Something very like unto love began belatedly to flame in his heart. He tried to see her, but Berganza barred the way. He got finally a note to her; she replied to it not one word. He could not let it go at that. He rode up to her litter, pushed Berganza gently but firmly aside, demanded of Jimena the reasons, asked if the trader had forbidden her to accompany him more.

She faced him and her lovely countenance was sullen.

"Nay," she said. "Have you not seen that my father is a puppet in my hands, Aizun?"

"Then why, Jimena?" he said. "In God's name, tell me why."

She turned her face from him, stared off into space.

"I have repented my folly," she said. "I hate all men, and thou'rt man, Aizun! Now get thee hence and leave me in peace!"

Nor, as he half hoped, half feared—for the idea of marriage had begun sharply to diminish in attractiveness in his mind—she would, did she change her mind. During the four months that the journey lasted, he caught glimpses of her, now and again. She seemed to have recovered fully—if anything she was a little plumper than before. Each time he saw her, he sighed and tried to valiantly put her from his mind.

During that four months they crossed the fair lands of Provence and Languedoc, past walled cities frowning with battlements, Narbonne, Nimes, Avignon, Sisteron; then wound over the mountainous north of Italy, Torino, Milan, Verona, Padua, Venice. Alaric, enchanted by that fairest land of earth, would have lingered long in each of her glorious cities, but the trader was a man possessed: in none of those fair towns by man's genius and his most subtle art made immortal did they linger longer than a single night. Now they moved past fair Trieste into a ruder, colder land, called by the Moors Jwarizini, by Christians, Cazimasium; more than once as they filed by the grim gray towns: Zagreb, Pokrac,

348

Belgrade, Sofiya, Plodiv, Ederne, Alaric had to unsheath his sword, and once or twice even to lead a charge. But then they came at last to the greatest city in the East, glorious Constantinople, repository of all true wisdom in the world.

Alaric succumbed at once to the heady intoxication of the Queen of Cities; during the two weeks when the official betrothal banquet celebrating the pledging of their troths by Prince Cyril Indicopluestes and the merchant's daughter was being prepared, he attended daily the lectures at the University, thus removing much rust from the surface of his Greek. He visited the glorious churches: St. Sergius, St. Bacchus, and the matchless St. Sophia, greatest, finest, richest cathedral under heaven. He had scant time for reading, but collected a library at no little cost; for ibn Ha'ad, being no fool, recognized the young warrior's value and his valor—the words being synonymous for once!—and paid him well. He piled up parchment scrolls with a lavish hand, until he had the words of Priscian, Musaeus, Eunapius of Sordis, and Socrates—not the great philosopher, but his orthodox Christian and vastly inferior namesake, and greatest of them all, Procopius, including the scandalous and unjust "Anecdota" so injurious to the great Theodora's fame.

Betimes he saw Jimena not at all, and her father seldom. The trader was beside himself with anxiety, lest some servant or guard let slip the story of his daughter's misfortune. He consulted with physicians, seeking some means to restore the semblance of the virginity which through no sin of her own poor Jimena had lost. Of which, in that corrupt age, in that wicked city, there were methods enough, God wot; more than one harlot, it was said, was enabled by the liberal use of gold, which, passing through the surgeon's hands, was transmuted into renewed virginity, to dye her nuptial sheets with the incontrovertible evidence of chaste blood. But Jimena refused to be examined, or otherwise arranged; she professed a perfect horror at being touched by male hands. Sick with apprehension, ibn Ha'ad did what he could; he quartered his muleteers, mercenaries, and slaves outside the city, sending them across the Bosporus itself to the teeming town on the Asiatic side, much to their disgust. The women he made absolute prisoners within his house. Only Alaric was allowed to wander freely about Constantinople at the slight cost of having to renew his sacred oath to speak of the ravishment to no living soul each time he and the merchant met.

He lost his temper at last and shouted at his employer: "What manner of villainous churl do you hold me, merchant? I risked my life in her defense; I'd risk it again and gladly to save her honor! I've told you I'd never betray this ugly secret; and I have not. So cease to plague me with your inquiries!"

349

" 'Tis that I am so worried, son Aizun," the trader almost wept. "If this proud marriage I've arranged for her fails through some babbling tongue, I'll never be able to find her a husband, never!"

He stopped short, and stared at Alaric. A little light of speculative cunning showed in his blue eyes. But he did not say his thought. What he said was: "Now come with me, for I must buy you silken robes, and some jewelry."

Alaric looked at him. "Might I know why this sudden favor, good patron?" he said.

"Oh, you're invited to the banquet, Aizun. She insists upon that. Says—and, methinks, rightly—we owe you that much and more. And since you have no suitable clothing—"

Alaric stood there. The pain in him was not paltry thing. Not only was he going to once more lose a maid not unpleasing in his sight, but must now witness the very ceremony of her betrothal to another. He shrugged. What doth it matter? he thought. I always lose—to human rivals or—to death. In this case am I fortunate—I had not time for my love to grow overstrong.

Slowly he inclined his head. "Very well, let us be about it, patron," he said.

The banquet given by the merchant ibn Ha'ad to celebrate the betrothal of his daughter to the young and noble lord, Prince Cyril Indicopleustes, was a marvel of opulence even in a city where luxury was a commonplace. Having neither rank nor fame beyond a certain notoriety, the Mozarab had to depend upon his wealth to sufficiently impress the supercilious and disdainful Greek aristocracy. Rumor had it he spent six hundred thousand sesterces of silver on that single banquet; rumor underestimated him; actually he spent seventeen thousand soldi, or "bezants" as the vulgar called the gold coin, a far greater sum. There were musicians and acrobats and dancers and performing beasts for entertainment; every delicacy the Near East had ever dreamed of graced his vast table; wines stood cooling in buckets of snow brought by relays of riders from the mountain peaks of the dark land above the Black Sea. Garlands of live flowers covered columns and walls. In a hundred cages, rare birds sang. The house had been renovated from top to bottom—every stick of furniture in it was both murderously, expensively vulgar and shriekingly new.

As the time for the banquet to begin drew nigh the merchant danced about like a madman from pure nerves. He had invited the city's lofty and its great; and now he was in a perfect agony of terror for fear they would not come.

He need not have worried: curiosity is one of the most potent lode-stones in this world. The deliciously gamy whiff of scandal, another. "My dear, just why is our Cyril marrying some trader's slut of a daughter?" the matrons whispered to each other. "I know he's up to his eyes in debt, still—"

So now the sedan chairs, the pole litters, gorged the street outside the merchant's house. The city guards had to be called out to restrain the imprudent riffraff, the swarm of beggars drawn like flies by the presence of so many of the rich and notable. And as they came tripping up his stairs, these godlike Greeks clad in robes of multicolored silks, heavy with jewels, redolent with perfumes, displaying all the tailor's, the dress-maker's, the furrier's art—for nothing was so beloved of the citizens of Constantinople than extravagance of dress—the little merchant was be-side himself with joy.

And, Alaric realized, the first part of the evening had gone amazingly well, as if that night the gods had smiled on ibn Ha'ad. He was able to observe everything in precise detail, because, having taken no wine as a precaution against the unwitting loosening of his tongue, the young Goth had the immense advantage of sobriety. He was able to study Prince Cyril most carefully: white of skin, black of hair, clad in a robe that bore the life of St. Sergius from birth to martyrdom hand-painted on tunic and skirt, Cyril was indeed a stunning sight. And he in his turn stared at the handsome young Goth. Of a race notoriously careless of the gender of its loves, despite the Emperor Justinian's code which punished pederasty by death, it was for a time unclear to whom Cyril planned to plight his troth that night, the fair Jimena or Alaric Teudisson.

Then, at long last, Jimena came into the hall. She was richly yet demurely dressed, and walked with her clear green eyes downcast. Alaric was prepared to swear he'd never seen another maid so lovely as Jimena was on that night; but as she passed close to where he stood, he was struck by how much heavier she had become. If she continued thus, in a year or two she'd be gross. As gross as Turtura, likely.

She saw his look, and a mocking smile lit her eyes. She said, without turning her face toward him, so that no one guessed that she spoke at all, much less to whom: "I took them off—all the lacings and the stays. For what care I now—if it shows?"

Which made no sense. No sense at all. Alaric studied her all through the banquet. Her hands and arms were thinner than before. Her throat swanlike. There was a hint of a hollow about her cheeks; but her green eyes were—feverish. They were—excessively bright. Seated, she looked as slender as Zoë had been, as Afaf. Then he saw Cyril was staring with undisguised horror at her waist. He followed the young princeling's eyes, and then, with an ice-cold, abysmal cessation of his breath, his heart, he knew. There was no disguising it. He knew.

He did not hear Cyril put the question to her; but those about the young Prince did, and a little silence spread out from the presumably happy pair and grew and grew until there was no sound within the banquet hall; neither the clink of goblets, the rasp of knives nor the patter of talk, of laughter.

Her voice rang out clearly, gaily, in most perfect Greek: "What care you, my lord? 'Twill spare you some labor on our nuptial night—a labor which, to judge from your looks, you fancy not at all, Cyril, dear—"

Cyril said something too low for Alaric to hear. But again Jimena lifted her voice. It rang like crystal.

"The father? How should I know? Any of three—nay, four it could have been. Ah, but you Byzantines are less civilized than I'd thought! Don't tell me you take seriously so small a thing?"

Cyril was on his feet, shaking, white. He used the Greek equivalents for strumpet, trull, trollop, whore.

Jimena looked him straight in the eye; said but one word; but that one deadly: "Pederast!"

Whereupon Prince Cyril slapped her face. The next instant he found himself lifted bodily from the floor to come to rest a little below the hanging lamps. The whole assembled company gasped at that matchless sight: Prince Cyril resting horizontally across the arc formed by the young Goth's rigidly upstretched arms, reposing there among the flickering candles, his mouth gaping open soundlessly, high above that bright blond head; above that calm, purposeful, perhaps too handsome face, which turned slowly from right to left, to right again, clearly looking for a window through which to throw Prince Cyril, thus adding mayhap fatal injury to what was already deadly insult, until some of the Byzantine ladies broke the general stupor by the small appoggiatura of their whimpers, which quickly gave way to the rising, swelling, shattering dissonance of their screams.

Jimena laughed right gaily.

"Oh, for God's sake put him down, Aizun!" she said. "Scant honor's to be gained in such a fray. You've proved your valor already in my defense against men. And *that*—whatever it is—most surely is not a man. So put it down. Let it scurry away to wherever boy-lovers go. . . ."

On his feet once more, Cyril recovered his dignity. "One of the four!" he sneered. "Or was it four dozen?"

"Oh, I don't recall, m'lord," Jimena said airily. "I didn't really keep count—"

And 'twas then that young Prince Cyril Indicopleustes fled.

Ibn Ha'ad was a one-man dancing troupe. He leaped, he pivoted, he whirled. He pounded the columns with his fists—to his knuckles' detriment, since the columns were of marble made. At intervals, he tore what was left of his hair.

"Ruined!" he shrieked. "Ruined! Canst explain this behavior of thine, Jimena? For what reason under heaven didst endeavor to convince all Constantinople that thou'rt a harlot? To prove to all the world my daughter played the whore?"

Jimena lifted her pale green eyes. She wasn't even crying. She stared at her father as though she were seeing him for the first time, Alaric thought. And as though the sight were loathsome.

"I am four months with child, Father," she said. "In my womb quickens a bastard of whose sire I know not even the name. Why, then, to continue this folly? Why wed that effeminate, perfumed little fop, only to have him put me by?"

"He wouldn't have dared!" ibn Ha'ad shireked. "This is Constantinople, not Córdoba! He is too greatly in my debt. Had you kept silent and not made your shame public—and worse, putting upon it a guilt it doth not have!—he would have accepted it in good part, and—"

"—gone back to that actress Thespis, whom he keeps in a house near the quay; to the strumpet Lysistrata; to Helene; and—to Adonais, Basil, Justin, et al; for our Cyril is completely ambidextrous in his loves," Jimena said, "while I sat at home and nursed my bastard child; or, after the fashion of this sickeningly corrupt place took lovers in my turn, or cooled my neglected ardor upon the bodies of my maids. Alexandria, where you hid me as a child, thus enabling me to learn the Grecian tongue—for which I thank thee now!—was bad enough, but this—this is worse! Wouldst make a proper Byzantine dame of me, Father?"

Ibn Ha'ad stopped whirling for the nonce. He peered at his daughter.

"Who told thee all this? By heaven, I'll have her flayed alive!" he said.

"No—her. A spy. A paid spy whose wages came out of mine own pocket. Am I not *thy* daughter, Father? Or—because until now I have been honest—do you doubt it still?"

The merchant, Alaric saw, was at that moment in grave danger of death by apoplexy. His mouth, his eyes, resembled nothing more in this world than those of a huge fish tossed upon the shore by a wave and dying for the lack of his natural element.

"Aye, Father, I know that, too. I've known it since the night Alaric

353

brought me to my litter, bleeding like a pig from the gentle attentions of four men, from whom *thou* didst not lift a hand to save me. I could tell thee how many strokes of that bull's hide whip, its thongs leaded to make them bite, it took to flay the flesh from my mother's back until her bones showed through. I could tell thee how many hours it took fair Diego to die, hanging there nailed to that cross in our garden, strangling upon those parts of him which, because they'd done the immediate offense, thou hadst him bereft and crammed into his mouth. Thou'rt long in vengeance, as thou'rt short in valor, not so, my father? Hence this comedy. Hence this ugly, obscene farce I played—for vengeance. For have I not your ugly need of it, as well? Which should be some comfort to you, Father—by the evils I have this night done, I prove my heritage of thy blood!"

"Berganza!" the trader howled. " 'Twas she who told thee! By heaven and hell, I'll—"

"Do nothing," Jimena said, "nothing at all, my father, if you wish to see my face again!" She turned then, suddenly, to Alaric; and now at long last her eyes were awash.

"Yet now do I repent of this thing, my lord," she whispered, "for your sweet sake. I saw—I saw your eyes, the hurt in them; and I wanted to cry out to thee: forgive me, Aizun! As now I do cry it out: Forgive me, my lord, my love, my life! Were it not for this—this monster growing in me, you'd have in me such a slave as would cut her throat before your eyes the first time she did aught that earned thy lightest frown!"

" 'Twas for this you put me by?" Alaric said. "For this paltry thing you made me suffer so?"

"Paltry? Dost know what it cost me to break off with thee, four days after I'd pledged thee my lifelong love, my sacred troth? Think you, Aizun, that I am of those who could lay such a burden upon the man I love? 'Tis a marvel I am not mad by now! I even toyed with the idea of coming to your tent at night, of lying with you—as Berganza urged me to do, so that in your fond folly you might come to think—But no. I could not play you so villainously false; besides—" a grimace of pure horror twisted her mouth "—it may be black as Satan, for the chances are double its father was a Moor; so I could not in any event have deceived thee long—"

Alaric smiled at her then. "Since now I am not deceived," he said, "and indeed the whole truth I know, I have a thing to say to you, fair Jimena—"

"Which is?" she whispered.

He came to her then, knelt at her feet; put out his long, slender hands, took her small plump ones.

"Will you, Jimena, by and for the love I bear you," he said, "do me the high honor of becoming my lady and my wife?"

She stared at him. Her tears were a rain, a downpour, a flood.

"Nay, Alaric!" she sobbed. "Oh, sweet, dear, noble fool! I'll love thee till I die; but no! I cannot. This is too much to ask of any man, let alone so gentle a soul as thou—"

Ibn Ha'ad was dancing again, hopping from foot to foot, wildly.

"Daughter!" he shrieked. "Don't be an idiot! He's no ordinary mercenary! That learned muleteer of mine, Harith—you know him! Ibn al Jatib—remember how he proved to me that he could read, write, and cipher, and is no mean calligraphist?"

"Aye," she said indifferently, "the ex-copyist. The one whose brother is married to a Vasca, or Gallega or some other fair-haired race. What care I for him, now, Father?"

"He swears that Aizun is a Gothic noble!"

She shrugged. "How could *he* know that, Father?" she said.

"Because his brother's wife—" ibn Ha'ad began, and stopped, seeing Alaric's eyes upon him.

"Go on, merchant!" Alaric said with deadly quiet. "What of the Moor's brother's wife?"

"It would appear that—that she is from your mark, Aizun," ibn Na'ad said hastily. "A maid of the town of Tarabella, captured by the Moors and—"

His voice died under Alaric's gaze.

"It would appear," Alaric said, "that she is either the fair nun, Sor Fidela, or my sister, the maid Gelesvinta; about whose deaths, as in all else, you lied. Which is it, slave trader?"

Dumbly ibn Ha'ad met his gaze. He knew, at that awful moment, it made no sense to lie. It is probable he took some courage from the thought that men ordinarily do not kill their prospective fathers-in-law; and much less so when the father-in-law question can measure out a hundred times and more his weight in gold.

"Which?" Alaric said.

"Thy—thy sister," the trader murmured.

Alaric went on looking at him. "And the other?" he said. "The nun, Sor Fidela? Formerly the maid Goissuintha, daughter of the departed Julian the Frank, Marquis of Tarabella the Lesser, may God rest his soul?"

Jimena was staring at him, her green eyes wide. "Then 'tis true!" she whispered. "Thou'rt—"

"Alaric, son of Teudis, Count of Tarabella the Greater. Nay, of all Tarabella Greater and Lesser both, since the banu Djilliki murdered

Julian the Frank, who left no male heir. Which matters not a fig! Go on, dealer in outraged innocence! What of sweet Goissuintha, fairest, purest maid under God's blue heaven?"

"The Emir—bought her of me. 'Tis said he touched her not, because she'd gone mad of grief. But lately—"

"But lately—" Alaric prompted.

"She hath recovered. And because of this of the death of Ahmad al Hussein, the Leader of the Faithful gave her to his youngest brother, al Wallid, in hopes that her beauty would cure the Prince of his tendency toward effeminacy. With some success, for I hear she is now with child. No mean fate, Aizun! A son of hers may one day sit upon the throne! So, my boy, if—"

"Don't call him 'Aizun,' nor 'my boy'!" Jimena snapped. "Bow when you speak to him, and say 'my lord'!

Alaric looked at her. His eyes were both amused and sad. "This matters to you, Jimena?" he said. "This business of titles and of rank?"

"No," she whispered. "Now I hate them, because they stand in my way. You see, my noble, princely lord—how could I have ever gazed upon you without knowing you were that, and more?—being a woman, I should soon have repented of my scruples in this matter. My heart would have dominated my repugnance at the thought of imposing upon you another's child; I'd have told myself that since you knew and had accepted it, I could with a clear conscience accept thee in my turn—as I so long to do! But now—"

"But now?" Alaric said.

"You are a count's son, perhaps his heir, and I but the daughter of a trader of most unsavory reputation, at the best. At the worst, I am a used and broken thing whom no man of rank and honor—"

"Now you anger me, I think!" Alaric said. "My rank's of scant import; my right to the succession I have renounced in favor of my infant brother. I like not that life, and mean not to live it. But honor's another thing. I lay some claim to possessing it, Jimena; and I think it not so feeble nor so delicate as to be harmed by taking you to wife. In this, methinks, my honor reinforces my love, bidding it do not only what it would, but what is just and honest and pleasing in God's sight. So now I ask thee once again: Will you have me as husband, child?"

She sat there, her soft green eyes searching his face.

"Aizun!" ibn Ha'ad cried. "I mean, my lord Count—you won't regret this generosity, this honor you pay us! I'll set the dowry so high that—"

Alaric turned on him. "Nay, 'tis I who'll set it, merchant!" he said. "One millions dinars in gold—" He heard Jimena gasp, saw her eyes. He smiled, and went on: "—to be paid to the Metropolitan of Córdoba on the day that Jimena and I are wed, for the construction of a fitting cathedral where the faithful of the capital may worship God in a decent and pious way. And do not advance the prohibition against the building of new chapels for our faith. At my word the Emir will waive that unjust law. Besides which, in the contract it be stated you are not to make gifts, monetary or otherwise, to the daughter you have lost, the bride I have gained. She will live upon whatever little I may be able to honestly and honorably earn. Further, when I return to Córdoba, I leave your service, that no man may say I married into whatever wealth and eminence I may one day win—"

He turned back to Jimena, and his face was stern.

"I warn you, sweet Jimena, you will never the title of Countess bear. What's more, the possibilities, nay the probabilities, are that you may know hunger at my side. Far from ascending in life, you will be coming down—my skills are few; and the house where I might employ them, closed to me for reasons which at some future date I shall explain. I have naught to offer thee but my love; nor will I accept of thee aught but thine. We start, God and you being willing, from nadir, from that new symbol brought from India, which the Moorish mathematicians call zero, signifying an infinitude of nothing. That said, I ask you for the third time, and the last, will you, Jimena, be my bride?"

She sat there gazing at him, and what was in her eyes was wonder.

"Methinks," she whispered, "no woman hath been more honored in all of time. Many have there been, my fair and noble lord, who have sought my hand, their eyes blinded by the gleam of my father's gold. But you reject that and take only me, dishonored, gravid with another's child, shamed. I wonder if your pity does not o'ertop your love; but no matter, I'll not question more. Yes, Aizun. Yes—strange that so small and short a word can sound so sweet! So I say it again, babble it like an idiot child, like a mooncalf, lovesick girl: Yes, oh, my lord, my love, my life! Yes, yes, yes!"

"Aizun, my son,' ibn Ha'ad said, "the phrase is feeble, but for this relief, nay, this salvation, accept my thanks. We'll speak of the conditions when you're both of a more tranquil mind; for surely you'll not insist upon this childish and romantic folly—"

"Of marrying solely for love?" Jimena said. "Ah, but we will, Father! Hath not your own experience taught you that all other reasons for being wed are more foolish still? Alaric will never have to beat me to death for dallying with another! For if these eyes ever stray to another face, with mine own hands shall I upon the spur of that same instant blind them, clawing them bloodily from my head!"

"Jimena!" Alaric said.

"Nay, more! I pray thee, good my husband and my lord, that never you look upon me with doubt; never wonder what this combination of thief's and strumpet's blood I bear may drive me to. Should you ever doubt my love's power to vanquish my shameful heritage, I shall open my veins and let the strain that caused you one instant's trouble flow forth until I die. Yes, I am mad; but 'tis for love of you, my lord! Much do I like this madness—"

She laughed then, the sound of it tremulous, breaking, with tears still laden.

"Sweet Aizun," she whispered, "Alaric of the angel's face. My lord— of habits most ascetic; of aspect most pure—dare I ask you now one further boon?"

"Of a certainty," Alaric said. "Ask what you will, my lady. What wouldst thou?"

Jimena laughed again, the sound of it flutelike, silvery, soaring. "That you cease to stand there like the statue of a saint, and kiss me ere I die!" she said.

XXI

The next six months, while he awaited the birth of Jimena's bastard child, were for Alaric a time of healing and of peace. They had no difficulty at all in having the marriage ceremony performed; for the Catholic priesthood of Alexandria, whence they had come after their flight from Byzantium, had absorbed by the osmosis of daily contact some of the civilized urbanity and tolerance of the Conquerors. Nor, in the face of the consistent and coherent testimony of the witnesses—her women, Alaric, those of the mercenaries who had sailed with them as defense against pirates—could the Church hold that the fair Jimena was in a state of sin. Confessed and shriven, the pair were wed, and retired to ibn Ha'ad's lovely town house hard by one of the several branches of the Nile, where date palms moved in the evening breeze, tame gazelles played about the garden, peacocks preened, apes and parrots chattered in their cages.

Alaric, out of tender concern for her state, did not know his bride. By now he found his continued chastity a light burden; but Jimena suffered fearfully from jealousy. Only after Zobeida had been replaced by Habila, and Habila by Abbasa, and Abbasa by Buran, who remained only because she resembled homemade sin created by unskilled labor, did Alaric discover that each of these serving maids in turn had been dismissed by his bride because each of them had given vent to some remark about their young master's great beauty. When he reproached her gently enough for her jealousy, she wept, and gave vent to all the pregnant woman's secret terrors.

"How can you love me? Look at me! Great like a cow about to calve! Bloated, swollen, hideous—and the child not even your own! If you made use of one of my maids, who could blame you? I'd die, of course; but then you'd be free to do what you will! Mayhap I'll die in any case—or bring forth a monster with two heads! Oh, Aizun, Aizun! I—"

He kissed her tears away; held her till she slept. Between dreams she murmured: "Thou'rt good—good—too good for any woman born—"

"Would that I had aught of good in me at all," he thought.

Betimes, he worked dilligently in ibn Ha'ad's countinghouse, and in

359

his warehouses as well. In his free hours he wandered about the city, searching for manuscripts, the tattered remnants of what once had been the greatest library in all the world. He found only fragments, a page or two of Sophocles, Euripides, Aristophanes; enough to make his heart bleed with anguish for these lost glories he would never know. And the pagan writers awoke a chord in him: How much more sense did their warring, capricious, idle, mischievous, ribald, and cruel gods make than Christian or Muslim belief! They gibed perfectly with the senseless world he knew and suffered, in a way that Jehovah, gentle Jesu, or Compassionate Allah never did.

Still, in the cool of the evening, it was a moving thing to hear the muezzin's cry ring out, from a thousand minarets, liquid and sweet upon the crisp, dry Egyptian air:

" La Iha—il—Allah, Muhammad um Rasulu—llah!" Allahu Akbar! God is great! Allahu Akbar! Allahu Akbar! I bear witness that there is no God but Allah. I bear witness that Muhammad is His Prophet! Come to prayer! Come to prayer! Come to happiness! Allahu Akbar! God is great! La—laha—l—Allah! There is no other God!"

He would stand there, trembling a little, and let that cry enter him, finding it immensely moving. He would wait for the rest of it.

Occasionally he went to the Place of Reverent Prostration, took off his shoes along with the Faithful, faced the qibla, listened to the discourse of the imam; joined the Mussulmen in their prayers. But soon he gave this up, fearing the powerful hold this new faith in its natural desert setting had made upon his spirit. He went with his father-in-law on business up the Nile to al Qahira. He gazed upon the pyramids with awe in wonder, pondered over the immense temples, the glorious statues erected to dead kings, forgotten gods. And it came to him that mayhap, on some future date, Christ and Muhammad would be included in the mythologies by a people bowing to newer gods or none at all, along with Horus, Ra, Isis, Mammon, Ba'al, Astarte, Zeus, Hera, Aphrodite, Azor, Adonais, Mithradates, and the rest. Earth received not only her children's bones, but their beliefs; earthquake and storm threw down their temples; and they themselves slaughtered each other over such cosmic idiocies as whether God was One, or Three; in the end nothing abided; all was vanity.

He returned to Alexandria by camel caravan, saddened and chastened by what he had seen, arriving at ibn Ha'ad's town house in time to still fair Jimena's screams by the simple expedient of holding her hand all through the long agony of giving birth.

The child was a girl. She was as swart as Afaf, and her tiny head was covered all over with silken, inky hair. Though at the moment she resembled nothing on earth more than an ancient wizened monkey, Alaric saw at once she would be beautiful.

But when she was placed in Jimena's arms, the trader's daughter gave voice to the most piercing shriek of all.

"Take it away!" she shrilled. "For by God's Holy Mother, 'tis nothing human. An ape—or a blackamoor! Take it away!"

Ibn Ha'ad had already thoughtfully provided a wet nurse for the child; for then as now in defense of their figures, many highborn dames did not suckle their young. The fatherless—and Alaric thought sadly, motherless—infant was placed in that stout matron's arms. When it had been fed the wet nurse brought the infant back into the bedroom. By then, worn out by her ordeal and her grief, Jimena slept.

The nurse started to lay the child beside her; but Alaric said softly: "Nay, bring my daughter to me. . . ."

He took the dark little she-creature in his arms. It gurgled contentedly, woke with a little cry. He gave it the knuckle of one clean finger, upon which it sucked peacefully until it slept again. But his journey had been wearisome, his nightlong vigil hard; his bright head nodded, jerked upright again, nodded again; and he slept.

So it was that Jimena awoke to see her husband sleeping in his chair, the tiny babe clasped right tenderly in his arms. She lay there staring at him, and all her face was washed with the hot tears of remorse and shame.

"Aizun!" she called. "Aizun, my love, my lord—"

His head came up; his blue eyes blinked, cleared.

"Aye, sweet Jimena?" he said.

"Bring me—our daughter, good my lord," she whispered, "for thou hast made her so."

Alaric smiled, got up, went to his wife's bed, put the child in her arms; sank down beside her with the infant between them. The child woke up, began to cry; he gave her his forefinger; she took it greedily. Whereupon Jimena loosed the bindings about her breasts.

"Nay, little monster," she whispered fondly, "I'll not deny thee! For if my lord can love thee, so can I! Oh, Alaric, how swart she is!"

"Like Afaf," said Alaric without thinking, "and will be as lovely."

He did not hear Jimena's halted breath; but he felt after a moment the fearsome weight of her silence. Raising his eyes from the baby to Jimena's face, he saw the brimming lash flicker and fall of her immense and terrible hurt.

"Jimena, forgive me," he began. "Fool that I am, I—" But she smiled at him.

"Wouldst—wouldst like to call this fatherless little monster after her?" she said. "I'll consent to it, if you will, for already you have consented to so much with tenderness and love. . . ."

Alaric shook his head. "Nay," he said, "the name's unchristian; for my daughter I like it not."

"Then what shall we call her?" Jimena said.

"Theodora," Alaric murmured. "For is she not very truly a gift from God?"

"From God?" Jimena said, her voice a little tart, ever so slightly edged.

"Aye, who from a crucifixion brought us all salvation; and who, out of the great evil which hath befallen thee hath fetched forth this dark and tiny angel to be our joy—"

"Alaric—" Jimena whispered.

"Aye, my love?"

"You—you love this swart little monster, don't you? You love her! You can forget—nay, you have forgot, how she was sired? Oh, Aizun-Alaric, thou'rt mad—or—"

"Or what, Jimena?"

"Not of this world, which is what most I fear. To no other woman will I lose you; your goodness will keep you faithful to me—even, I believe it!—should dark Afaf once more cross thy path. But against my true rival, have I no defenses; and must pray for His forbearance and His mercy—"

"His?" Alaric said. "His?"

"Aye," Jimena whispered. "God."

When they reached Córdoba at last, little Theodora was six months old and as lovely as a tiny night-blooming rose. Children of Berber strain are often handsome, and that she was of that desert race was abundantly clear. Better that a thousand times, Alaric thought, than that she should inherit Julio's foulness, or wear his evil face.

Their arrival at the capital did not pass unnoticed—in part, blame for the small sensation it caused upon the head of ibn Ha'ad himself. His passion for secrecy, born of the fears engendered in him by his own marital misadventures, had caused him to bear Jimena away to Alexandria at the age of four; and after circumstances compelled him to bring her once more to Córdoba at sixteen years of age, to hide her so thoroughly that the overwhelming majority of the populace of his native city—in which, be it said, he was known even to the blind beggars on the street corners, to whom, oddly enough, he was often generous—became aware he had a daughter only some days before his departure with her for the courts of Byzantine. And now, to have him return—who had loudly proclaimed he'd come back no more—with daughter, son-in-law and grandchild, loosened the hinges of every curious and malicious tongue in that fair and princely city.

There was, God wot, material enough for speculation, if not for scandal. Was not the husband not only no prince, but not even a Greek? Those who had seen him upon the party's entry into Córdoba described him as being fair-haired, tall—of Gallego, Vasco, or Gothic stock. Speculation buzzed merrily about his identity, until the mystery took another turn: the young bridegroom himself made some inquiries about the whereabouts of the eunuch Hagib, stating he wished to employ the castrate as steward of his house. Now truly did gossip take wing: Was not said Hagib formerly head of the household of the late, unlamented Ahmad al Hussein ibn Maliki? Was not Hagib now employed in the home of the Jewish merchant-prince Saadyah ben Hasdai, whose wife—Allah witness it!—was none other than the former Bedu slave girl, Afaf, of the murdered Ahmad's household as well? Then who else could the blond young giant be but a former captive, sold to al Hussein by none other than ibn Ha'ad himself! The pervert's scattered retainers, his widows, as they had been wives, in name only, could witness that by the One, the Only, the Compassionate, the Wise, so much was true! A host of predatory demi-males, deprived by Ahmad's death of their chief source of income, slanged crossly the young Goth's beauty and his fame; stories about how he had procured his freedom from the sodomite's perfumed clutches by remedying the pederast's neglect of his women one by one, until he found one fond and foolish enough to aid him—which tales did Alaric's reputation among Córdoba's distaff population no harm at all— were spread abroad, chiefly by the members of the city police guard.

A woman seller of laces and broideries managed to penetrate into the trader's house; Jimena made no attempt to hide the child, and all to Córdoba's satisfaction was explained: The child was Moorish, much too big. Ibn Ha'ad, then, had been at some pains to buy his daughter a husband to hide her shame. If he had chosen a youth much too fair to have sired a daughter much too swart, why, then, he'd had to content himself with what was available; besides, the female peddler swore, the husband was of a beauty seldom seen in man, so mayhap the fair and erring Jimena had concurred in the choice.

So with the matter fully explained to its wry, realistic, even cynical tastes, Córdoba settled down; would promptly have forgot the whole thing, for nothing is duller than an old scandal, had not the Mozarab community been rocked immediately thereafter to its foundations by the news that the merchant ibn Ha'ad, whose generosity did not extend beyond an ostentatious gift to a beggar in a public place where well that generosity might be marked of men, was donating a whole new cathedral to his coreligionists, and this with the Emir's gracious permission, since the building of new churches was forbidden by Islamic law. The Metropolitan himself announced it, along with the tart addition—which Córdoba's Christian head, knowing ibn Ha'ad only too well, had forced the trader to disclose upon pain of refusing him communion—that the gift represented the dowry waived by the young and noble Lord Alaric, son of Teudis, Count of Tarabella in Castilla, who was to the fair Jimena wed. When to this disclosure—which the gossip mongers took right ill, since it violated all they knew of human nature—was added the new fact that the young couple had left the trader's palatial dwelling and were living in a small and modest house in a poor quarter, speculation reached heights bordering upon insanity.

People in all walks of life came to pay their respects to the newcomers, and came away with divided opinions, which yet had aspects of unity. Aizun ibn al Qutiyya, the Muslimn said, clearly had been touched by Allah's finger, and was quite mad; but with a holy madness. The Mozarabs, especially those who most immediately benefited from his generosity, declared him to be a saint, or at least a man with God's special favor on him. Others, of both religions, less kindly disposed, declared him a faker, a fraud, a charlatan. But these last soon found themselves constrained to silence, by an event to which they lent more importance than, mayhap, it had: At the height of all the speculation an elegant pole litter, borne on the shoulders of stalwart liveried slaves, stopped before the young couple's door; from it descended a personage whose robes were of a beauty beyond description. Quickly a small mob of the curious gathered; and, as always, there was among the idlers one who could identify so imposing a visitor.

"The Raven!" it was whispered; and that nickname flew from mouth to mouth: "Ziryab! The Raven! Ziryab! Ziryab! The Emir's favorite!"

A hardy soul dared question the slaves, and was rewarded with a confirmation: the gorgeously dressed courtier was indeed the Sahib Abu'l-Hasan Ali ibn Nafi, the celebrated Iraqian singer and musician, become for all fashionable Córdoba, from the Emir himself to the least cultivated of the wealthy merchants, the arbiter of elegance in music, speech, dress, household decoration, all things, in fact, in which questions of taste were involved.

Before Ziryab—which nickname the vulgar had fastened upon the

364

courtier because of the unusual darkness of his skin, though in sober fact most of them were darker still than he—had emerged from Alaric's house, all adverse criticism of the young Goth had either silenced or reversed itself; for a visit from Ziryab meant but one thing: those who therein dwelt enjoyed the Emir's favor.

Nor were the speculations on this precise point far from the mark: Ziryab in his courtly way had delicately dropped a hint that the Amir al Muminin, "Leader of the Faithful," would not be displeased by a visit from the Goth's son. To which Alaric courteously replied that he hoped Allah's Favored would excuse him for the some little time he needed to set his affairs in order; whereupon, on the very next day the matchless and witty esthete reappeared with the message that God's Representative in the Land of Andalús was disposed to be patient, and the sun-haired offspring of the Goth could come when he felt so inclined.

On the day after Ziryab's second visit, one month to the day after their arrival in Cordóba, Alaric went to pay a very necessary call, which truth to tell, he could easily have made before, save for the fact that he had been, curiously enough, dreading it. But make it he must, so he set out afoot, despite Jimena's plea that he maintain his dignity by hiring a litter or a chair, toward the Street of the Copyists, to the house of Husayn ibn al Jatib, become, now his discreet inquiries had already informed him, one of the leading publishers of Córdoba. Which did not mean that Alaric's brother-in-law had become rich—the copying of books of religion, history, science, and poetry was not a business in which one could hope to become an Hasdai ben Sahl or an ibn Ha'ad—but that he had gained both public respect and a modest income which sufficed to allow him to live in some comfort, the more so because Husayn, whose uxorious fondness for his blonde wife was notorious, had never taken another, not even so much as a concubine.

Walking down that street before the open houses, or rather sheds, in which an army of copyists, many of them women, plied their pens, taking down with feverish haste the words that a reader droned out from the manuscript affixed to his—or her, for again this profession was one of the few open to both sexes—lectern, Alaric moved with no little hesitation, uncertainty, and even some fear. For among the things which had come to his ear, in that city where all things were known, was the much commented upon fact that between Husayn's Christian wife and the spouse of the young Jewish merchant-prince Saadyah ben Hasdai, the relationship was closer than between most sisters.

"In God's name, what have they not confided to one another by now!" he thought, "and how ill hath my defenseless name been used! Nor can I defend it. Say I was mad, and then I must say why. So one ill to the next doth lead until I stand damned beyond the end of time!"

He moved on, trying to dismiss that from his mind; but another thought still uglier took its place:

"What a piece of work am I!" he groaned inside his heart. "I was prepared fully before God and man to take swart Afaf to wife. The idea that she may be there now at Gele's house, paying a cordial visit, is enough to stop by breath with longing and with pain. Yet I—say it—tell the truth, like not at all that a swart and bearded Moor should be husband to my sister! What boots it his hue if she fares well—and yet—"

A veiled slave girl admitted him to a latticed, pleasant and comfortable home. He sank down upon cushions of yellow silk, thinking with more favor of the idea that had brought him, which was—God, Husayn, and Gele being willing—to put the considerable sums he had saved from his wages in ibn Ha'ad's service into his brother-in-law's business, becoming thereby a partner to the extent to which his capital was proportionate to the whole. The slave girl brought him a cool sherbet; he sipped it while her master was sent for from his copy house. Husayn came, recognized at once his brother-in-law from his resemblance to Gele; kissed Alaric tenderly. Alaric's heart lifted with quite ignoble relief: for Husayn was slender, tall, and handsome as any prince. His skin was pale golden, his hair and eyes were black; his whole aspect that of an aristocratic and cultivated Arab gentleman, with none of the crudity of Berber, Yemenite, or Bedu.

"Long have we awaited this visit, my lord," he said. "Thy sister is exceedingly wroth with thee, much do I fear! When the news of thy arrival reached us, she was beside herself with joy; but a moon hath gone by and until now—"

"I feared to come too soon," Alaric said. "Tell me, good brother—art happy with thy bride? My sister hath a temper, that I know, and—"

"Allah witness it!" Husayn laughed. "First she made me swear I'd take no other—which hath proved the lightest burden in this world. Praises eternal to Him who granted me such a wife!"

"*Allahu Akbar!*" Alaric said piously. "God is great!"

"*Ameen!*" Husayn said. "Now she scolds me if I am late from work, or careless in my dress, or pay not enough attention to the children—we have two: a daughter, adopted; but that you know; and a son of our own, named—guess it?"

"Ataulf?" Alaric said, fearing that election because he had reserved the name for his own first manchild.

"Nay, Aizun, after thee. Indeed, I count it a privilege to sit in the presence of such a paragon! To thy sister, thou'rt a monument of all the virtues; a holy man with Allah's grace upon thee—"

"And yet, say you, she is wroth with me—" Alaric said.

Husayn smiled, and clapped his hands. The slave girl appeared like a djinni summoned up from the earth itself; or, more likely, Alaric thought, like one who crouches by the keyhole to hear all that's said within. She bowed deeply.

"Summon thy mistress," Husayn said.

Gelesvinta came sailing through the door, and threw herself into Alaric's arms. She hadn't changed much, except that now she was beautiful. Her features, plain, pale, and placid before, were in the first two regards exactly the same; but now the placidity was gone forever, and all of her was lighted from within, with spirit, verve, fire. Here was, God wot, not the Gele that he knew but a woman reborn of love, fulfilled by happiness, till almost literally she glowed; and 'twas that which made her beautiful.

"Gele—" he husked. "Little sister mine, I—"

She kissed him once again, pushed him away, stood there looking at him, her blue eyes jeweled with tears, alight with that pure, sweet, leaping, dancing fire: then wildly, madly, and with tremendous force, her right hand blurred sight moving, until it exploded open-palmed across his face. The sound of that slap was deafening; he reeled under the unexpected blow.

"Gazella!" Husayn cried—for such had been the transformation of her rude Germanic name upon an Arab's tongue; and in truth she had much of a gazelle's grace, and all that lovely beast's slenderness still, despite wife and motherhood. "Art mad, woman! You dishonor me and my house! By all the laws of hospitality, I—"

"Laws of rubbish!" Gele laughed. "This is my brother—the wicked, sinful, faithless lout! To him, good my husband and my lord, no laws apply, for none doth he keep! Oh, but I've been saving that slap for him these several moons. And though I love him well, I needs must keep my word. Now come, oh my saintly brother turned foul lecher, and let me kiss your swollen cheek, to take away the sting."

"God's death, Gele!" Alaric said. "You've deafened me, for fair—and broke my jaw, I doubt not. Why, in the name of everything, did you—"

"—slap you? For Afaf's sake. Now tell me, if you dare, you did not deserve it!" Gelesvinta said.

"Hmnn," Gele said. "No mean sum, brother! Might I know from what poor innocent you fleeced it? Or is it a gift from your wife? Ugh! What a choice! Ibn Ha'ad's daughter! Now all your children will be thieves and swindlers for fair!"

"How, good Husayn," Alaric groaned, "can you endure a woman with such a tongue? Were I you I'd divorce her, since your faith allows it!"

"Oh, but he doesn't want to divorce me," Gelesvinta said, laughing. "I have—well, other accomplishments—eh, Husayn, my poor wearied-out husband?"

"Allah witness it, and for it be praised!" Husayn laughed.

"You mean my sister, who all her life hath been frozen to the marrow of her bones, hath been able to manage a trace of warmth?" Alaric said, the words jesting, the question serious.

"Aye, but what a thaw set in upon our wedding night!" Gele said shamelessly. "Then did I disgrace myself and all the gentle teaching of our pious mother. By the way, Alaric, how do she and Father fare?"

Alaric kept his face quite still; his smile did not waver.

"Later," he said. "Business first. Well, good brother?"

"The money tempts me," Husayn said. "Well could I make use of it. But you must not think that this is a business which brings quick returns. I know through Afaf you've worked with ben Sahl—to say the truth you'd be wiser to throw your lot in with his son, who, I'm told, is a friend of yours—"

"Was," Alaric said grimly, "till he robbed me of Afaf."

"Alaric, art unjust!" Gele snapped. "You who returned to Córdoba with a bride!"

"Whom I married only after knowing Afaf was lost to me. No matter. The truth is, Husayn, I cannot join Saadyah. 'Twould be too painful for us both. And of this business of books I have some knowledge. I have brought with me from the East manuscripts which well might make your fame. Besides, I have in my house in Toledo—"

"So you have a house in Toledo?" Gele said. "Ha! Shall I tell you Afaf's theory of how you came by it?"

"Silence, woman!" Husayn thundered.

"Yes, my lord!" Gele said demurely; but her eyes were bright with laughter still.

"In my house in Toledo—however I came by it—lives an ancient sage, who has to perfection the art of illuminating manuscripts. I propose we bring him here, to instruct your most skilled calligraphists. Then we can place upon the market editions of a luxury unheard of in this land. Why—"

"Done!" Husayn said suddenly. "And here's my hand on it, brother!"

"Good!" Gelesvinta said. "I'm glad the business part of your visit is settled, Alaric, for you do not depart from here until you have told me all that has passed with you since I was captured; with particularly acute attention paid to explaining your abysmally foul behavior toward Afaf!"

"Nay, sister—" Alaric sighed "—it grows late, and my tale is overlong. 'Twould take all night—"

"No matter," Gelesvinta said; then turning to her husband: "My love, tell Fadl to bring me another cushion—and my too-handsome devil of a brother, with that lying deceit of an angel's visage that he hath, more sherbet to wet his throat! For this tale of a thousand nights and one well do I mean to enjoy!"

Before he had done her eyes were swollen shut with weeping; but she would not let him stop until she knew all—or thought she did, for right judiciously did Alaric edit his tale as he went along. Beside her, gentle Husayn shed more than one tear in his turn, affected by the story and Gele's grief.

" 'Tis no wonder you were mad," Gelesvinta whispered, "even as fair Goissuintha lost the rational use of her senses for a time. Poor Clo! She is possessed of devils, surely, even as you said. Poor, foolish Father! A shrew, you say? And baseborn at that! Afaf will hear a few choice words from me! Heaping all the blame on you—she did not tell me that she helped cause that skinny little Greek child's—whatever did you see in her, Alaric?—death. Poor, poor Jimena! So that explains all the scandal about the child! You'll bring her to visit me? Never you fear, I'll not let slip that you told me of her sorrows. But, Alaric—"

"Yes, sister mine?"

"Methinks there are gaps in your tale! That house in Toledo wherein dwells now your sage—how came you by it? Afaf hints that there is something evil in its origin, but states it might cost her life to say precisely what that evil is! And Julio—you say he was terribly punished. But how? What was the nature of his punishment? And—"

"And you have shed tears enough, Gele," Alaric said, "and I have suffered once again my memories. There are—I confess it—things I did not tell you. Nor will I, because they are not good for you to know. More sins of mine—further disasters—what boots which and why they were? What matters now is to forget, and let time work what healing that it will. But before I go, one question in my turn: Goissuintha—is she happy? Doth she fare well?"

"Aye," Gele said. "I have word of her right oft, and in her own fair hand. Her husband the Prince is, says she, the gentlest soul on earth—and she confesses now that she could not have had a true religious vocation or else she could not be so divinely happy as a wife. But now I'll tell you what I think, Alaric, though it please you not. I think that we, as a people, are ruder than they—or at least our nobility is. Less gentle. Certainly less refined. Mother—God rest her soul! To be butchered like that! I heard her scream, but I thought 'twas only fear—would have been enchanted with a land where people bathe every day. How much honor do poets have among us? What Gothic prince would give thirty thousand dinars to a singer because a single song enchanted him so, as the Emir did to Ziryab? Look at the high place enjoyed by the poet Yahya al Ghaza! What alchemist would be given the post in Asturias or Castilla of Royal Astronomer, as the Emir has bestowed such a rank upon Abbas ibn Firnas, though he spends less time observing the stars to guide the Emir's destiny and protect him from all harm than he doth about his nonsensical inventions. In all events, brother, I live with more comfort here—and a thousand times more cleanness!—as a copyist's wife than I did in Castilla as a count's daughter! If that be disloyalty to our noble Gothic race, make the best of it!"

"Nay," Alaric said. "I sadly fear that you are right, sister. But now truly I must take my leave; for dawn comes on apace. . . ."

So was it done. Marwan al Farrach was fetched from Toledo to instruct Husayn's calligraphists in the art of illuminating manuscripts. Some few of them failed miserably at it; the vast majority of the penmen gained an acceptable, if moderate, skill; and one youth, Mugaddasi by name, bade fair to excel his teacher.

'Twas to him that Alaric entrusted the task of illuminating a copy of the Qur'an he meant to present to Abd al Rahman. But seeing the task would take far too long, and having learned from Gelesvinta, who had a note from Goissuintha to that effect, that the Emir was beginning to take his continued absence ill, Alaric set his wits to the composition of a short poem in Arabic, the writing of which, at least, he had mastered almost totally by now.

He wrote dozens of graceful, courtly verses—and tore them up. Their emptiness, their near sycophancy sickened him. The Emir was indeed a just and noble ruler; but what could one say in his praise that had not already been said by a hundred fawning poets? Then it came to him: a man who'd earn the favor of a ruler as wise as Abd al Rahman II was, would do well to neither praise nor fawn. A Prince surrounded by wealth, luxury, lovely complaisant women, witty courtiers, every pleasure that money could buy needed—the stern voice of prophecy; needed reminding of the brevity of existence, the total democracy of the grave.

I, Alaric thought, who have lived more sorrows than he hath ever known, can supply that lack. And if, enraged, he call for the executioner

and separate my head from my shoulders on the spot? So be it! What
have I ever gained from being wise? Do I possess one obol, one fal
gained through prudence? I own a princely house in Toledo—a woman's
recompense to me for consummate adultery! I have a lovely, charming
wife—gained by my pity, not my love. All I have in this world of sin has
been won by the sword, or the base prostitution of my body, or by aiding
and abetting my swinish father-in-law in his most diligent thievery! So
now to throw another pair of dice—weighted in my favor by the fact that
the Emir has no stomach for slaughter. Let me see—let me see—

Two days later he had it done, and in Mugaddasi's hands to be
copied out, and illuminated. And like many another doting husband, he
blandly lied to Jimena about its contents, showing her one of his earlier
efforts, which she, as brides will, pronounced a veritable marvel, and had
him say it to her aloud. Alaric did so, besides and betimes kissing, fondling, and playing with the dark and pretty child, which provoked a pout
from fair Jimena.

"Wouldst love her if she were fair, Aizun?" his wife said, "and looked
like me instead of—Afaf?"

Whereupon Alaric laughed, and kissed her in her turn, and reflected
upon his own great happiness. In God's own truth, it was a rare thing,
and based upon the curious circumstance that he liked his wife, he was
immensely fond of her, he admired her looks, her charm, her gentle ways,
but he did not love her. Hence he was spared the cruel intensity of that
devouring emotion; with Jimena, he suffered much less than most men do
with their wives. Her feminine quirks, her occasional want of logic
amused him; he endured the spasmodic and tepid nature of her ardor—
easily getting over his surprise at the fact that she, like nearly all women
under heaven, was capable of wild carnal passion, but only on very, very
rare occasions. Her love was as placid as her figure and her face; never
cold, but seldom more than warm. He could, he knew, at the cost of time
and effort, arouse her to a desire matching his own; but he troubled
himself rarely in this regard; mayhap because the vein of asceticism in
him ran deeper than he knew; or mayhap because that other contradictory identity, that alter ego, distorted mirror image of himself, that
madman, mystic, saintly fool he kept chained at the exact center of his
being lest it break forth and upend his world, was his essential quality.
He was capable of desire, but he was not a sensual man. What manner of
man he truly was, he himself scarcely knew.

So on a day, all unannounced, he presented himself at the Alcázar. A
guard took his name, returning after the briefest possible wait to say that
the Leader of the Faithful was pleased to receive the son of the Goth at

once. Whereupon one of his fellows led Jinni the second—for Jinni the first had had to be sold in Constantinople once they had decided to return to al Andalús by sea—around to the stables. The chief eunuch, Nasr himself, received Alaric in one of the Bab al Sudda's vast halls, and led him at once into the Emir's presence.

Alaric, having made the customary prostration before al Rahman, raised up to find that the Emir was not alone. For now five others emerged from a curtained alcove where they had been dining. Ziryab he recognized; to the others he was by that matchless courtier courteously presented—though to one of them, the Emir's second brother, Prince al Mugira, the introduction was superfluous, as Alaric already knew him from his first visit to the capital. They were the poet Yahya, called in his youth the Gazelle; now in his fiftieth year, only the name bore witness to his former beauty; the Berber, Abbas ibn Firnas, Royal Astronomer to the Emir, who had been interrupted in the demonstration of a most intricate water clock of his own invention by Alaric's entrance, and who seemed to take that interruption ill; and last of all the Prince al Wallid, the Emir's youngest brother. This last Alaric studied with some care, for rumor had it he had been cured of marked tendency toward effeminacy by his marriage to Goissuintha. Alaric decided that rumor, as usual, lied: for true deviates there is no cure; and the spiteful are ever ready to accuse of perversion a youth of delicate, gentle ways. Al Wallid was such a one; and by that very token the perfect husband for such a maid as the former nun had been.

These courtesies done, the Emir engaged Alaric in conversation, keeping upon him that ever-blinking gaze. As convention demanded, the Leader of the Faithful made no mention of the carved ivory casket Alaric bore in his hands until after an hour or two of talk, during which he drew from the young Goth the story of his adventures since last they'd met. Wisely, Alaric told the ruler the truth, with, even more wisely, many omissions, whereupon the Abdal Rahman sighed and said, "Thou hast suffered much, Aizun. May Allah grant thee consolation. Now, tell me, what hast thou in that casket?"

"An humble gift for thee, my lord Emir," Alaric said.

Blinking his eyes faster than ever, al Rahman nodded to Ziryab, who took the casket from the young Goth and gave it to the Emir. Abd al Rahman opened it and took out the gorgeously illuminated scroll. He glanced at it, too briefly to have read more than a word or two, then gave it back to Alaric with his own regal hand. This, all present took to be a gracious mark of royal favor, but Alaric alone realized that it was less than that, or more; for the verses were in Arabic, while until that moment the conversation had been conducted in Romance. The Emir smiled in a

way more than a little ironic, so that Alaric wondered if he had not read it
after all, even in that half glance.

"I'd have thee recite it, Aizun!" he said.

Bowing a little, Alaric extended the scoll, and began to read, his
Arabic a little halting still, somewhat slow, not altogether free from fault;
but gaining in verve as he went on. Each of them stared at him after his
wont: Ziryab with cool, amused wonder, not unmingled with contempt
for this folly, Yahya al Ghazal with a frown of professional judgment, too
lofty for envy, Abbas ibn Firnas, himself the outstanding student of methods of scansion and the technical side of verse making, which failed to
make of him more than but an indifferent poet, most coldly, scientifically,
critically, as if to say: "Speak up young man! My judgment, I warn you,
will be harsh, but just!"

Al Mugira looked upon Alaric with sleepy content; he, after his own
lazy, good-natured way, appeared not even to listen to the words. But the
young Prince al Wallid caught their import at once, and held his breath,
his tender face gone white, with astonishment at this madman's rashness,
with fear at what he might be compelled to witness next, with concern for
this fair youth's life, of whom his own wife, Goissuintha, had spoken with
rare kindness.

The Emir listened gravely, his ever-blinking eyes fixed on Alaric's
face while that wise young fool read:

"Much have I wandered in lands grown old
 Where sands whip hard across the broken stones
 Of ruined palaces; drift above the bones,
 Of those who strode in purple, gleamed in gold . . .

"Slow crumbling altars dot the empty land
 Whence men appeased their gods with bullocks slain;
 And the wolf who howls above them on the plain
 From sleeping dust calls not the hero's band—

"Accept, my Lord, this tribute that I pay
 To thee, in truth's mayhap unlovely word
 But harken to thy fool, and having heard
 A fool's mad wisdom, unfearing face the day

 When thou must follow where thy fathers trod
 O Servant of the Servants of Thy God!"

The harsh Arabic gutturals of that final phrase broke like a whipcrack
against the silence. No one spoke. No one even breathed. They all stood
or sat like men turned stone, their eyes upon the Emir's face.

Slowly Abd al Rahman got up from his chair, moved wordlessly to where Alaric stood. Then before any of them could divine his intent, he, ruler of all al Andalus, bowed and kissed the young Goth's hands.

The silence lasted a moment longer. Then it broke into shouts and laughter, bravos! and cries of "Well done!" The poem was passed from hand to hand. Ziryab and Abbas ibn Firnas disputed wittily over the meter and the form. Yahya al Ghazal, despite his occasional coarseness, nobler than they, said simply: "Thou'rt a true poet, O Goth's son!"

Al Mugira laughed, his big voice booming. "Scared you out of an ell or two of kingly pride, eh, brother? By the Beard, but the Goth hath his brass! Come, Aizun, tell us if 'tis true that you lowered every shintiyan in al Hussein's house? If so, 'twould explain your gloomy verse! Nothing so inclines a man to piety and prayer than the fatigue after a merry two-backed ride throughout the night!"

"Brother!" Al Wallid's light voice was tight with anger. "Canst think of nothing else but dalliance? It seemeth me that ibn al Quityya is inspired—he hath both the look and the tone of prophecy. I pray thee, fair Aizun, that you will partake of the hospitality of my house—that we may speak of high and holy things while we break bread and take salt. I have some scrolls of ancient Greek, of which my royal brother tells me you're fully master. If you would be so kind as to sup with me on Wednesday next, I should be honored—"

"The honor's mine, my lord Prince," Alaric said.

But the Emir silenced them all with a wave of his hand. Indicating a cushion at the foot of his chair, he said: "Sit you down, fair Aizun, and discourse upon your verse. In this room I've heard much frivolity, many mundane things; but now I'd hear from your lips your own concepts of creation, the cosmos, God. Silence, all! Let ibn al Qutiyya speak!"

Slowly, in his halting Arabic, because neither Ziryab nor ibn Firnas possessed a command of Romance, Alaric began. He conceded from the outset his doubts. Humbly he proclaimed himself a freethinker—whom well he knew it was the Defender of the Faith's duty to separate from his head; which well might be a boon, for thought, vain thought, had ached it so.

"And yet, my lords, sahibs and rulers of the land, it seemeth me that I am possessed of God—that my life hath been naught else but headlong flight to escape His presence and the awful demands that He upon me makes, and hath made since to me He spoke out of matchless light when I was but a child."

"Which are?" the Emir said.

"I wot not, my lord. Mayhap that I die for them in some great and terrible way, to the edification of unbelievers, the repentance of sinners. I have hurled myself oft and terribly into sin; and yet, as oft as not from that sin some good hath come: happiness where none existed before; a return to virtue—For instance, at the sight of the Cross of Jesus on my chest, a harlot fled her haunts and was with God reconciled—"

"The Cross of Jesus?" Ziryab said. "Oh, come now, Aizun! Surely you exaggerate! You mean you wear it around your neck—"

"Nay," Alaric said, "I mean I wear it in my flesh." He opened his tunic, bared his breast.

"By the very Beard! 'Tis true!" dark Ziryab cried.

The others crowded around, staring at the double scar.

"Pity 'tis not a crescent, or I'd make thee head theologian of the realm," the Emir said.

"I think that God cares not for symbols or under what name men worship of Him," Alaric said. "Methinks that when the world grows arid, bitter, and dried souls are heaped up like cordwood, He speaks—or reaches out His hand to touch His chosen; a carpenter's son, a merchant trader, and through His sons, His prophets, those souls take fire, and all of evil in them is consumed while their shining good rises like a smoke to heaven—"

"Methinks He hath touched thee, Aizun," al Wallid said.

"No," Alaric said sadly, "for those touched by God must come to Him with willing hearts, and I am a coward, sore afraid. I'll plod my way through life, attached to mundane things: a wife, children, some trickery of trade, the base coinage of this world which can buy naught that matters. Aye! 'Tis a poor discourse I offer ye, my lords! I now, thus lamely, make an end to it!

"Me, Thou hast sought through all the nights I fled
Thee down all the twisted paths that led
To hell, which is Thy absence, oh my God!
And when Thy fingers left my heart, it bled.

"Yet Thou willst be my healing, this I know,
Who art forever with me where I go
To save me through anguish, cure me with pain
Until I render Thee the death I owe!"

"My lords!" he said, and bowing, walked from the hall without so much as a by-your-leave.

The next day, a train of six mules stood before his door, laden with costly gifts. Alaric accepted but the tenth part, bidding that the rest be sold to the benefit of the city's poor. To the Emir's command that he come to the palace as Secretary for Byzantine Affairs, the young Goth was bold enough, candid enough to point out what he had learned in Constantinople: There were no such affairs; intercourse between Muslim Spain and theocratic Greek Orthodox Christian Byzantium on the official, governmental level was nonexistent; their only contact being the ebb and flow of trade.

"I would not live upon your charity, my lord," Alaric told the Emir, "pretending to work at letters never sent. Let me return to my little business, which, because it hath to do with the increase of knowledge in this world, hath its value. Some patronage from Allah's Favored there I will accept—a command of holy books well penned for the new mosques that you and your favorites have caused to be built—but nothing more. To do otherwise would ill become me as a man."

"As God wills!" The Emir sighed. "Thou'rt a prickly soul, Aizun! And yet I love thee better for it."

"I thank my lord for his wisdom and his understanding," Alaric said, and once more took his leave. And it seemed to the Leader of the Faithful that this strange infidel he'd come to love was at that moment, as he bowed and turned away, wrapped in a quite visible glow, surrounded by a pearly luminescence. It moved with him, mistlike and soft, until he passed through the door, which closing, shut it out, leaving that brilliant palace, at high noon though it was, strangely dark.

The lordly Emir lifted up his voice.

"Lights!" he cried. "In Allah's name, bring lights!"

XXII

"I tell you, Aizun," Husayn said, "you should make greater use of the Emir's favor. Not that we haven't done well—those illuminated manuscripts have brought us many new clients among the rich and great. But, save alone for Mugaddasi, none of our copyists truly have the skill that the saintly al Farrach had—Allah grant him much surcease in Paradise—"

"And books instead of houris, which would please him more," Alaric said. "When my hour comes, I only hope I can die with such majestic tranquillity. In short, what you're delicately hinting, brother, is that the business goes not overwell?"

"Not exactly," Husayn said. "We have more clients now and greater sale of books than ever in my life I can remember. Only costs—"

"—have increased greatly, that I know," Alaric said. "But the heart of the matter, good brother, is the fact that 'twas folly on both our parts to ever have dreamed a copy house could produce enough revenues to support two constantly increasing families. Thy four sons, and thy delightful little Negress—what a joy she is!—my little Berber, and my own two rosy sprites add up to eight hungry mouths to feed. Methinks we had both make the pilgrimage to Mecca, or otherwise absent ourselves from our wives, or else—"

Husayn looked at his Christian brother-in-law.

"Aizun," he said, "could not you reconcile yourself with your wife's father?"

Slowly Alaric shook his head.

"His methods are too foul," he said. "I would not increase my wealth at grave peril to my soul. And not even the decline of his health suffices to change him. He'll die as swinishly as he lived. But I'll put my mind to some other solution to our mutual problem; at the worst, I can always beg of the Emir some minor post in the government; or create a new one for him that I could head: Custodian of the Royal Library, say . . ."

"Which would expose thee to the jealousy of my coreligionists." Husayn sighed. "Nay, brother, thy policy of keeping out of official life has been most wise. But solution we must find, and soon, for much do I fear—"

A great gale of feminine laughter coming from the interior of the house cut him off.

"Ya Allah!" Alaric said. " 'Tis strange that our wives between them can make such a noise!"

"Today they have reinforcements," Husayn said with a smile. "One of whom hath played some little part in your life, Aizun, though the other, methinks, you know not. So naturally their gooselike gabbling hath redoubled, since today are four, not two—"

"Who are the others?" Alaric said.

"The Princess Sumayla, the Negress who was my brother's slave, and who is to the old Prince al Karim wed. Yet wonder of wonders, she hath given him an heir, whom not even the malicious can deny is his, for though the princeling's skin is swart, his eyes are as blue as al Karim's. You know how it is with the royal family—they keep getting sons upon Bashkunish and Qutiyya concubines until they are more of your race than ours. Besides, the child hath other attributes much like the Emir's uncle—a certain comeliness of face, and—"

He broke off, staring at Alaric. "What ails thee, Aizun?" he said.

"I? Nothing," Alaric said. "Surprise, I suppose, that so great a lady condescends to visit your humble house. Methinks she'd want to forget her past—"

"Nay, 'tis that very past she seeks. Oh, not Harith! The child al Karim would not let her take to his house, but he graciously consents to her visiting whenever she will; especially since he knows my poor brother no longer lives—"

"*Bism Allah!*" Alaric said. "That I did not know."

"Nor did I until a month or two agone. His comings and goings were most irregular, you know. And his death—unheroic. The randy fool let a merchant of Toledo surprise him in the merchant's own bed, busily entertaining the merchant's youngish wife. A dagger stroke cut short poor Harith's sport, and his days. The curious part about it is that I had news of the tragedy not from your father-in-law in whose employ, you doubtless know, my brother was, but from Sumayla herself. Her aging lord, it seems, had an oppressive, morbid jealousy of my brother—to the extent of accusing Sumayla of having again got herself with child by him, until the child himself gave the lie to the accusation with his bright blue eyes—and spent considerable sums having poor Harith watched, whenever my lusty lout of a brother was within the borders of al Andalus. Thereby, methinks, giving Sumayla priceless opportunities to adorn his wrinkled forehead with horns from other sources, a thought which seems never to have occured to the senile fool!"

"But the other guest?" Alaric said. "You said there were two—"

Husayn smiled. "Thy lost love—Afaf," he said.

Alaric sat there.

"I see," he sighed; then: "I don't suppose there's any danger of Gele's bringing her in here? After all, she's married to a Jew, so the usual rules don't apply—"

"The rules by which you've dined almost weekly those many years at Prince al Wallid's house and never caught so much as a glimpse of his wife, though she is a friend of thine from infancy," Husayn said with a little laugh. "What a poor opinion you Nazarenes must hold we have of women! Nay, brother—'tis human nature we do not trust. Gazella is thy sister, or you'd never have seen her either. But this is a good Muslim house; women guests, whatever their faith, must leave by a private door—after having slanged and blackguarded us right royally after the manner of good wives everywhere! Come with me! This will amuse you."

Alaric got up and followed his brother-in-law. They went down a passage, and came into a little niche, much decorated with verses from the Qur'an. Alaric started to say something, but Husayn put a finger to his lips. In the abrupt silence Gelesvinta's voice came over to them clearly.

"So there I was," she was saying gaily, "standing up there on the slave block—all but naked. By the Holy Mother, I thought I'd die of shame! Poor Goissuintha was in worse state than I, being by nature more modest, having been a nun—"

"Then your lord Husayn appeared?" Afaf's dark voice came through and stopped Alaric's heart.

"Oh, no, dear!" Gele laughed. "Whenever has my poor gentle husband been first at anything?"

Husayn hugged himself, and doubled over with silent mirth.

This is unworthy, Alaric thought; but intriguing! Oft have I wondered what women say of us when we're not there; so now—

"Then who did come, Gele?" Jimena said.

"Nasr. The head eunuch at the palace. I thought I'd swoon from pure terror. But, good wives and gentle friends, I need not have worried! He looked me over, gave a contemptuous grunt; and said to thy august father, Jimena, in Romance—the sexless dog!—to make sure I should understand it: 'If you continue to bring in scrawny cows like this one, merchant, you'll lose all your clients!'"

Husayn's silent laughter redoubled. He made the gesture of pretending to slap his knees.

"So then?" Sumayla's throaty voice cut through; her tone was amused, a trifle bored; Alaric knew at once she was indulging Gele in the telling of a tale told many times by now.

"Jimena's sweet, lovable sire then exhibited poor Goissuintha to that lump of useless fat. And I mean that, exhibit, literally. Tore off every stitch—"

"That's the part Father enjoys most," Jimena said.

"Well, that poor, modest, sweet creature was something to enjoy! I'm a woman, but even I could see 'twas a criminal waste to let a form like Goissuintha's rot in a cloister!"

"Oh, innocent chaste sister of my heart!" Alaric murmured.

"And then?" Afaf said. If she hath heard this tale before, Alaric thought, it retains its power to enthrall her, for she sheweth no sign that 'tis not dewy fresh upon her ear—

"Nasr bought Goissuintha at once, for a fabulous sum. He didn't ever haggle. The day wore on. All the other girls were sold. Even the pretty boys were picked up by the wealthy perverts. Only I was left. I'd thought I'd known what shame was; but until that last hour I hadn't any idea—"

"What do you mean, Gele?" Jimena's gentle voice was genuinely puzzled.

"Look, dear—I know you're married to my saintly brother—"

"Saintly!" Afaf hooted. "If Aizun's a saint, then I'm a virgin!"

"You should know, dearest!" Sumayla said.

"I *do* know," Afaf's dark voice edged. "God and Jimena forgive me! But what stirs my none too gentle soul to wrath, my lady Princess of the Blubber Lips, is—"

"Afaf!" Gele's voice was like a blade.

Husayn put an arm about Alaric, squeezed him fondly, the tears of repressed mirth starting from his eyes.

"Sorry," Afaf whispered. "I humbly beg pardon of you all. Including you, Sumayla—'Tis not your fault Allah made you black—"

"When He got around to thee, my sweet," Sumayla purred, "He had run short of celestial ink so that He had to cut your hue a bit—with milk. She-goat's milk, I'd say from your behavior. 'Tis sad poor Saadyah needs a prop beneath his chin to help him support the weight of all his horns—"

"That's a lie!" Afaf flared. "You lie in your teeth, black strumpet! Just because you betrayed your lord with Ai—"

"Stop it, both of you!" Gele's voice was cold. " 'Tis bootless folly to hate each other over a man neither of you can have, and a want of courtesy of the most abysmal sort to slang each other thus in the presence of his wife. Jimena, I'm sorry. I thought this day, in your presence, they'd behave themselves. I should have known better."

"It—it doesn't matter," Jimena said. Her voice was odd; she sounded as if she were strangling.

"Oh!" Afaf's voice came over to Alaric. "I—we—we've made her cry!

Jimena, dearest, forgive me! I wouldn't have hurt *thee*—not for anything under Allah's heaven! Oh, I am so sorry!"

"And I," Sumayla said. "Allah witness it! We had no right at all to make this poor child suffer so. Afaf, I beg thee join me in this oath: By the Compassionate, the Wise, the One, I swear never to fight with thee over this again!"

"*Ameen*," Afaf whispered. "*Bism Allah!* In God's name, I swear it!"

"Good!" Gele laughed. "*Now* can I finish my tale?"

"Yes, Jimena whispered; but her voice was humid still. "I needs must know what this new shame of thine was, sister—"

"The worst that any woman who is a woman can know," Gelesvinta said, and now her voice was grim, remembering it. "To stand naked in a marketplace, and not only not have lewd men assault your modesty with lecherous eyes, but to have them turn away indifferently! Put it this way, dear: suppose that with the wonder-workings, the black arts of an evil magician, you found yourself in a public square stark naked: How would you feel?"

"Terrified!" Jimena said. "And like to die of shame!"

"But suppose that after you'd crouched there with arms and legs all contorted to conceal those parts of our bodies we keep hid from all but our lords, nobody looked, or looking, yawned? What would be the response of thy woman's heart when it came to you that nobody at all was even moved to ravish you?"

"Gratitude," Jimena whispered.

"Ha!" Gelesvinta snorted; then: "In thee—mayhap—yes. In thee, that I can understand. But I was furious! And ashamed. I suppose that up until then, my father's and my brothers' fondness for me, and the absence of a pretendant to my hand of suitable rank, had kept me from finding out what a miserable example of femininity I was—"

"Oh, come now, Gele!" Jimena said.

"Yes, miserable! Poor skinny me—whom nobody wanted, not even as a slave! Whom nobody desired in that evil way at whose mention we publicly blush but which occupies our thoughts—in fascinated terror—or terrified fascination—much of our girlhood until that day it happens to us and we chant hozannahs to Him who put such evil in the world—"

"Gele!" Jimena said.

"Don't be silly, child!" Gelesvinta laughed. "I tell you all *that* is shame! So when poor dear Husayn appeared—with his downcast eye and timid look; and being not exactly ugly, I—"

"What?" Afaf breathed.

"I caught his eye. I was too furious by then to think of the usual simpler kinds of shame. So I smiled at him. Flirted with him outrageously.

Poor, timid boy! I thought he'd faint. And when at last I saw him approach that monster ibn Ha'ad—Oh, forgive me, Jimena!"

"You're right, Gele," Jimena said sadly. "My father *is* a monster—"

"Oh, I doubt that!" Sumayla said. "I think that to really be monstrous—to embrace true evil—one must be female. The male animal's too simple—too preoccupied by his idiotically simple lusts that beg only to be appeased, and involve no more consequences to him than some slight fatigue."

"Sumayla," Afaf said suddenly, "hast thou—ever loved?"

There was a silence. A curious kind of silence. It came over to Alaric like a felt presence. Like the prickling in the air before a storm.

Sumayla's voice was very harsh. When she spoke, 'twas very clear she had forgot Jimena's presence, mayhap her very existence.

"You ask me that?" she said; "You who have known him, too?"

"Aye!" Afaf said. "Hast ever said with wonder: 'I am alive and he is not here, God and Jesu how can this be? How can I bear his absence and still live?' "

"I have loved," Gele said. "But like that—no—"

"But I, yes!" Sumayla's voice was a brazen cymbal struck. "Like that. Or worse. Because I have added, Afaf, sister of my sorrows, he is *there*, not far off—and I dare not call him to my side. For if he came, he would be slain; and if he refused my summons, as well he might, I'd curse Almighty God, and die! Canst match that, sister?"

"God in heaven!" Gele whispered suddenly. "What manner of man is my brother?"

Jimena's voice came over to Alaric then, soft and slow.

"An angel. And a saint. But not quite human, Gele. Something less— and something more. I—I am surrounded by women who love him. There is not a serving wench in my house who'd not die—nay, more!—who'd not be torn to pieces by wild beasts for his sake! And men too, only slightly less. 'Tis a quality he hath that he knoweth not himself he possesseth—a power to inspire love so great as to be a terrifying force. Sometimes you can see it—believe me, I do not lie!—surrounding him like a sort of glow, a misty, pale luminescence. Ziryab told me once that upon Alaric's quitting the Emir's presence, the Leader of the Faithful called for lights—at full noontide—because after my sweet lord had gone a weight of darkness fell upon his heart and oppressed his sight. And there is more—you'll swear each of you by your several Gods never to mention this to a living soul when you have gone from here?"

Alaric's hand came down hard on Husayn's shoulder.

"In God's name!" he hissed. "Let me out of here!"

But Husayn shook his head. Clearly Jimena's voice, its utter sincerity, had caught him too. He waited as the women did within for what came next.

"*Bism Allah!*" Afaf and Sumayla said. "In God's name!"

"By sweet Jesu, crucified," Gele whispered.

"You all remember Omar, the blind poet who had a post hard by the mosque? He who sat there and improvised verses for the coins the pious gave him?"

"Ha!" Afaf said. "That impostor? He's no more blind than I am!"

"I thought that, too," Jimena said, "until the day he came bursting into our house—God be thanked Aizun was not there—tears pouring down his face, and babbling so that no one could catch a word he said. At once I dismissed the maids and talked to him alone. When one lives one's whole life in terror as I do, forever mounting stratagems in defense of what slight hold I have upon Aizun, it sharpens one's wits. It pleases you, does it not, Afaf, to hear me say that? It needn't. You'd not have more. No woman would. But I digress. What that fool Omar, of the excruciatingly bad verses, was babbling in that Yemenite dialect of his was: 'I can see! I can see! Thy fair lord touched me, and the darkness lifted from mine eyes! His face shone upon me, and its beauteous light pierced the veil of darkness! I see, my lady, I see!' "

"Good God!" Gele said.

"*Ameen,*" Jimena said. "I knew then that I had to do something at once, or a horde of filthy beggars, men deformed, sightless, maimed, leprous, would descend like locusts upon my house. So I told Omar that Alaric had cured the lame, the halt, the blind, hundreds of times before; but that the permanency of the cure depended upon his silence. I warned him that if he spoke a single word to anyone, darkness would again fall upon him. He promised me that, in real and abject terror. But I could not let it go at that—I knew I'd never sleep a single night through with my happiness at the mercy of a half mad fool. That night I talked to Aizun— but carefully: 'My Lord,' said I, 'didst chance to pass the mosque today?' 'Aye,' said he. 'Why, Jimena?' 'No reason,' I said carelessly. 'Didst talk with blind Omar who sits before the door?' 'Aye, that I did,' he said. 'Why, Jimena?' 'Oh, an argument I had with Gele. She says he s not blind; I say he is. What think you, Aizun?' My lord replied: 'He can see. His sight is dim, but he can see.' 'How knowest that?' I said. My lord answered me thus: 'Today I stopped and chatted with him. He was bemoaning his lot, as usual. So I put my hand in my purse and came out with a silver dirhem—'twas all I had. In fact, 'twas to buy me my noon-time meal—which as a result I went without, so we are no worse off. Then I rested my hand on his head and said: "God have mercy upon thy affliction, Omar." I gave him the coin then and strode away. 'Twas strange—all the strength had gone out of me suddenly so that my knees trembled as I walked. But—' and here my sweet lord laughed '—before I'd got five ells away, what an outcry burst from that impostor's mouth! He'd discovered 'twas a dirhem I'd given him and not an obol or a fal. I heard him cry out: "My lord! My lord!" but I hurried on. I was not eager for his effusive gratitude, because of this sudden—sadness—that had fallen upon me. As though all virtue had gone from me, leaving me—empty. And very tired—' "

"So?" Sumayla said.

"I realized that Aizun knew naught of the mad fool's claims. So I sent a servant to my father's without telling my lord what Omar had said, or what I meant to do. Within a week Omar was seized, transported to Alexandria, put up for public sale, and bought—on prior agreement—by a debtor of Father's whose bills were pardoned by one half in return for his buying Omar and putting him only to light and pleasant tasks. And I could breathe again—until the next time that my-lord-by-sanctity-possessed wittingly or unwittingly works another miracle—"

"Oh, come now, Jimena!" Gele laughed, but her laughter was shaky. "Don't you see Omar had to protect himself against the fact he'd given himself away by crying out at the sight of the silver coin?"

"Why would he have cried out at that?" Jimena said quietly. "He's not that big a fool. I'll warrant that had it been but that, he'd have buried it under the coppers in his bag and said no word. Besides, when he was taken by my father's thugs, I had his purse brought home to me. I wanted to retrieve that coin lest somehow—I was half crazed by then with fear—it turn up again in evidence against my lord. But, mark ye, there were several silver dirhems in his purse! Gifts from penitents who'd taken a vow, I doubt not. So why should he cry out at the sight of one more? And why should he of his own free will abandon an imposture that brought him in an amazing amount of money without his having to stir his stumps to earn it? Besides, after that, I began to watch my lord more closely. I have already mentioned the light that sometimes surrounds and accompanies him. But you, Gele, must have noticed how silently he comes and goes. One day I caught him at his wonder-working! He came drifting across the room, his feet a hand's breadth or more above the carpet. But when I screamed at him aloud in wonder, know what he did?"

"No—" Gele breathed.

"He forbade my taking wine at my meals for a whole month!"

In the great gale of laughter Gele's voice was silvery above the others. "Dearest," she hooted, "tell him to work a wonder about the business—before we all starve to death!"

Alaric caught Husayn's arm, pushed him with no little force toward

384

the door. As they went out, the last thing he heard was Afaf saying with real concern: "Things go not well with thy affairs, sweet Gele?"

That night, he whom his dear wife had accused of sainthood, of working holy miracles, had with her a most unsaintly quarrel. To the servants listening beyond the door they sounded as husbands and wives have since the very beginning of time.

"Why?" Alaric stormed. "In God's name, Jimena, why did you have to tell such outrageous lies? Me healing blind men! You abducting them! Shipping them overseas! What monstrous folly is this?"

"No folly, good my lord, but truth!" Jimena said. "It occurred just as I said. . . ."

Alaric hung there, staring at her.

"And you—and you," he whispered, "had that poor mad beggar sold into slavery because he claimed—Ay, God! You are the trader's daughter, after all! And like him—vile!"

"And thou?" Jimena wept. "Art not vile, too, Aizun? I go to visit thy sister and find myself surrounded by thy women! A Negress—blacker than a baboon! Thy Afaf, only a shade less swart! God's eyes, what taste thou hast!"

"I married thee!" Alaric said.

"I know And oft I've been sorry for that particular instance of thy want of taste, my lord! Tonight I looked upon our children and thought— that she-ape hath a child of his—of thine, my lord!—a son! She's happier than I who can breed only daughters! And your little blackamoor may sit upon a throne and hold thy daughters' lives and fortunes in the hollow of his apish hand. Sometimes I wish God would let me die before—"

And 'twas at that inopportune, or most opportune, moment—God alone could say which it was—that the knocking on the door drowned out her voice.

Alaric strode to the door, tore it open wrathfully. Stopped there like a man turned stone.

For in the doorway, his eyes alight with mocking mischief, and something else, something more—tenderness, Jimena decided—Saadyah ben Hasdai stood.

"Thy maids, dear Aizun," he said, "feared to interrupt your slanging match. But since I indulge in them daily with my honored, loved, and respected spouse, they bore me. The subject's always the same: Which slut it is now upon whom we have bestowed our manly favors? By Father Abraham, had I the time, the energy, or even the inclination to—but no matter! Well, Aizun, beloved brother of my heart, behold the Mountain to Muhammad come!"

"Saadyah—" Alaric said. "I—"

"Thou'rt a fool. As usual. And I, also. Likewise as usual. Only more so! Alaric, brother, I've missed thee—"

"And I, thee," Alaric said.

Whereupon Saadyah gave a bound, and seized Alaric in his great arms, lifting him bodily from the floor and whirling him around like a child.

"Fool!" he roared. "Tender fool! Saintly idiot of folly all compact! I married thy Afaf—but only after thou'd cast her out—"

"I?" Alaric said. "God's eyes, Saadyah! Put me down!"

Saadyah lowered him gently to the floor, stood there grinning at him; said: "Well, not cast her out exactly. Only thy holy stupidity extended to the celestial lengths of believing a woman can keep a secret! Since thy Jimena already knows—a fact which I gathered from your dulcet whispers passing through that stout oaken door—I can do no further harm. Sumayla *told* Afaf, Aizun. They had one of those sweet, tigerish little discussions to which the dark of skin and hot of blood are so prone; and the only way Sumayla could win that particular match was to bring out her cherished secret and belabor poor Afaf with it. So—"

"So?" Alaric said.

"Thy wronged, deserted, and abused love arrived at my house, bathed in tears, on vengeance bent. 'If Aizun, High Priest and Holy Pope of all Fornicators, can betray me with my friend, then I with his—' You know how female reasoning goes! Only I was not in an obliging mood at that moment. You know me, Aizun, know full well that had the contrary been true, I'd tell thee to thy teeth; but I did not. Not then, not ever till we were wed. Behold one Saadyah taken in chastity! Chaste Saadyah, pure Saadyah, refusing the favors of a maid!"

"My lord," Jimena whispered, "I think it best that I retire—"

"Nonsense!" Saadyah roared. "Stay with us, O rose of all delights, and learn a little of the ways of man! Item: I was tired. I still am. The business is a hellish chore—of which we'll speak later when I've melted thy hostility with the crystalline purity of the truth! 'Tis a fatigue of—of the mind—the nerve, I wot not—but oft it leaves me wih scant desire for aught but sleep. Item: despite my bellowing I am a—a most curiously subtle beast—"

"And a tender one," Alaric said.

"Mayhap. I love *thee* well, that I admit. Now if a maid throws herself at my handsome head for love of me, intrigued by my port, my shoulders' span, and what brute male force may in me reside—ah, well! Good! Happy to be of service, m'lady! But by that randy adulterer David, by Esau, and by Jacob, I like not being used. Which I told her in none too gentle terms, bade her be off, find another sacrificial goat—"

386

"But," Jimena said gently, "having left the Lady Sumayla's service, she had nowhere to go. . . ."

"Exactly. So I dispatched her to my sister's house. Ruth took her in. Thereafter, I saw her oft—too oft. She is a splendid swart she-animal, Aizun—as well thou knowest! And she had begun to have some respect for me, since I refused to play stallion at stud and service her vengeance. Finally it came to me there was no female about I disliked less—that I was living like a monk, for the business left me no time for roistering, and that I owed my upright and worthy father grandsons. So I married her; without a by-your-leave, m'lord! We've been more or less happy, more less than more, being human, lacking sainthood. And knowing how over-delicate thou art, hear this: you enjoyed the woman I'm married to— before we were wed. Which damaged her not at all, and taught her, mayhap, a trick or two. I should have joyously served thee equally had not that porcine animal, who hath the gall to imagine he could sire a rose like this, not kept thy Jimena so well hid. I knew not she existed until now. So I do not curdle the milk of human kindness in me, thinking on the past. I have forgot it quite; and so must thou. Agreed?"

"Agreed!" Alaric laughed. "Jimena, love, fetch wine, and some cold meats and—"

"—all thy children, whom I would see!" Saadyah said. "We've none so far. Poor Father! He's so disappointed. He dotes on Afaf, especially since she embraced our—his—faith of her own free will. I went to see Uncle Solly and slanged him well! 'Look you, Uncle!' said I. 'You cut me too short! Another inch and I should be Nasr!' "

Jimena doubled over with laughter and fled.

" 'Tis not charity I offer thee," Saadyah said. "I need thy aid, Alaric, more than you need mine. You're a good linguist—you've traveled in the East. You have this heavenly choir of little angels already got—so you can get away. And, if in your absence fair Jimena supplies thee with a son not too unlike thee, why wink at it, and say: 'Eleven months of gestation! I thank Thee for this miracle, Lord!' "

"Saadyah!" Jimena laughed. "Art a wicked, wicked churl!"

"Aye, so I am," Saadyah said complacently. "The point is, boy, that betwixt us we can a fortune amass that will make even your father-in-law ill with envy! A copy house. Bah! Listen to me, Aizun—you know what wealth the East affords! silks, spices, pearls, furs, carpets, gems, slaves—"

He stopped short, peering at Alaric.

"Ah, there I have touched a nerve!" he said. "Fret not! I won't make a slaver of thee, Alaric! I have rude brigands enough for that dirty trade."

"Since you know it dirty, why do you engage in it?" Alaric said.

"I am a trader," Saadyah said, "like thy lovely father-in-law. I'd deal in lost souls with Lord Satan, if the price were right! Since I entered into the filthy world of buying and selling and putting out money to usury, I've learned why it hath so great a hold over those who practice it. 'Tis fascinating in itself, Aizun! The rewards? Bah! What care I for wealth?"

"Then why are you here making me your wild proposals?" Alaric said.

"Because the game itself enthralls me! I swore that when *you*, dog of a Nazarene, with your three-headed God, fornicating Holy Ghost, and sacred cannibalism—"

"Lord Saadyah!" Jimena said.

"Forgive me, my sweet." Saadyah grinned. "I forget thou'rt not accustomed to my blasphemous banter. I mean not a word of it. To please my father—and mayhap something in myself—I've returned to kashruth practices, than which God wot there is no greater nonsense in this world. I seek thee out, Aizun-Alaric, Holy Sinner—because I'd have vengeance upon thee for thy greatest sin—"

"Which was?" Alaric said.

"The day thou butchered thyself over thy skinny Greek, and thus tricked me into finding out I was my father's son! That I could love this whole mad world of chicanery, trickery, deceit, fraud, slander, assassination, and—"

"Slavery," Alaric said grimly.

"And slavery, that we call trade. Win or lose, I love it! I care not, I repeat, not a fig for wealth; yet upon entering it, I swore to die richer than my father, if for no better reason than to prove to him I could. Yet, methinks, you owe me some service for entrapping me this way. You'll not deal in slaves for the excellent reason that your tenderheartedness would ruin my business; but in such materials only where your good eye and exquisite taste—again proved by your choice in women!—would be an asset. What say you, lad?"

"I like not even associating with a house which deals in human flesh," Alaric said.

"Dung!" Saadyah roared. "Asses' dung at that! Setting apart the making of eunuchs for which there is no defense possible, and which I'll never touch, I tell thee, saintly idiot, that nine out of every ten captives brought into al Andalus *better* their condition over what they enjoyed in their native haunts! Free? Who is free in this world, Aizun? Thou? I laugh. Enslaved by both thy fair Jimena's fecundity and by God. I? In thrall to my counting house, my ever-sinking ships, my caravans by Bedu brigands robbed! Tell me truly, thou who hast seen the lands of the Bulgars and the Slavs: Who among them there, including their savage

388

kings, live in such comfort, cleanliness, and health as those of them who've had the great good fortune to be brought here as slaves? I'll press the matter closer home. Sumayla—leave a mind like that in the jungle to be cowed by superstitious mumbo jumbo into savage negroid idiocy? Goissuintha—leave a beauty like hers to rot in a cloister in the service of an ice-cold eunuch's God who demands at least spiritual castration of his followers? Thy sister—leave her to go to waste in one of your grim, freezing Gothic stone heaps where the true lords are the lice, the flies, the stench; marry her off to one of your classic drunken, brutal Gothic louts, instead of gentle Husayn? Asses' dung, say I!"

"There you have a point," Alaric said with a sigh. "Gele said much of the same thing the other day. And, greatly do I fear me that since of my own volition I chose to live in the world of men, I cannot afford to refuse your offer, especially since you do this thing out of love of me. 'Twas Afaf, was it not, who told thee of our pecarious situation?"

"Aye. Which matters not. Look you, Alaric—I'd have you spend some months in Alexandria—"

"In Alexandria?" Alaric said. And what came suddenly into his mind then was the face of blind Omar, who, through his unwitting fault, so grievously had been wronged.

"Aye, Alexandria. Methinks my agent there is robbing me blind and—"

"Say no more, Saad," Alaric said. "I have a thing to do there myself. I am your man."

XXIII

Three weeks almost to the hour from that day, Aizun ibn al Qutiyya sat at a teak and ivory table in the House of Sahl's establishment in Alexandria. And though he had come ashore only that morning from the great bireme which, propelled by favorable winds and the brawny arms of the slave oarsmen, had made a record crossing from al Andalus, he was already hard at work. Four secretaries, all of them Greeks, came and went, bringing him mountains of papers. At his feet, an Arab youth sat, his nimble fingers playing upon the beads of an abacus as lovingly as though they were lute strings.

Finally, the Gothic lord, whose presence there, armed with letters from Hasdai ben Sahl and his son, had caused some wonder among the employees of the house—that a Jew should send a Goth to mind his business was, all things considered, an innovation!—pushed back his chair. His face was utterly calm, but as stern as the Angel of Judgment.

"My lord?" the eldest of the secretaries said.

"Thy master, Oribasius," Alaric said. "Summon him!"

The four secretaries stared at one another, their eyebrows arching.

"My lord," Priscian, the senior secretary whispered, "that would not be wise. At this hour, he—"

"Summon him!" Alaric said.

And now the four faces were one face, a quadruplicate mirrored comic mask of terror.

"My lord, we dare not," Eunapius, the second secretary, lisped. " 'Tis his hour to recline, and should we intrude, his wrath would be terrible!"

Alaric stood up. He was clad in cool and pleasant robes of white, against the heat; and moving, he seemed enwrapped in light.

"Then lead me to his house," he said, "and I will intrude. . . ."

The secretaries bowed. Then, among themselves, they began a rapid debate in Greek over how to evade or escape his orders, until Alaric cut them short with a phrase which to their consternation revealed his perfect mastery of that ancient tongue.

"Enough!" he said. "Know ye all this, Valens Oribasius is no longer master here, so ye need fear naught of him. What ye must fear, Priscian,

390

Eunapius, Aetius, Anthemius, is your degree of complicity in his thefts. Now I order you: lead on!"

He silenced the frightened babble of their claims of innocence with a lifted hand.

"Ye'll find me lenient," he said, "if you do not further try my patience—"

Valens Oribasius' house was only a street away from the ben Sahls' establishment. It was white and lovely beneath the date palms. In fact its very luxury proclaimed how much Oribasius had stolen from his employers.

A giant Negro barred their way, grew surly at Alaric's insistence, rose to wrath in his master's defense. He lunged forward as though to seize Alaric. A moment later he lay on his back at the foot of the stairs, blinking his dull, bloodshot eyes into the glow of the setting sun.

The four Greeks stared at the slender Goth, not yet in his thirtieth year, who had done this thing. For their very lives they could not tell how it had been done; all they knew was that the huge black had rushed at the tall, fair stranger, ready to rend him limb from limb; and the next thing they knew the Negro was hurtling through the air toward the ground below, his bull bellow gone woman-shrill with fear. So far as they could perceive, the young man had scarcely moved; and yet—

They faced Alaric with gaping jaws; but he ignored them. Now he strode easily through the door, moved up the broad marble stairs.

Valens Oribasius was at home, indeed. He lay abed with a lissome slave girl on his right, and an equally lissome youth on his left. A huge silver flask of wine stood on a night table; and Saadyah's factor in Alexandria was making full and very nearly simultaneous use of all three.

Alaric stood there, looking at Oribasius. The factor was not a pretty sight. He was gross with the fat of gluttony, slack-lipped and puffy from depravity. Naked and dripping with sweat, stinking from his labors, he, nevertheless, as small men will, drew on the robe of wrathful dignity.

"What folly is this?" he roared. "Who art thou who invades my house—accompanied by all four of my dingy scribblers? By the waters of Zeuxippus—"

"Get up from there," Alaric said, "and depart this house, of which I hereby take possession in partial recompense for all the monies thou hast stolen from my partner and my friend, Saadyah ben Hasdai."

"Stolen!" Oribasius roared. "Why, you idiotic barbarian of the North, I—"

Then his voice died. It had, the secretaries recounted afterward, been strangled in his throat by that unwavering morning-star gaze.

"At least give me leave to dress—" he muttered. "Then we'll discuss—"

"—nothing!" Alaric said. "I have full proof of thy embezzlements, Oribasius. Wouldst thou that I lay them before the head judge? Or dost prefer to leave this house and my employ with no further punishment than disgorging what thou hast left of thy thefts?"

It was Eunapius who saw his former master's small black eyes change. To his own astonishment, not knowing why—what was it, this strange, this compelling thing the fair-haired stranger had?—he ripped out a warning: "My lord Aizun, take care! He—"

Then Valens Oribasius was out of the bed with a speed incredible in a man of his bulk. He reached the wall, tore down a sheathed Moorish poniard hanging there; the blade flashed free; in one long, bull-like rush he was upon the slender Goth. Aizun ibn al Qutiyya gave a little sigh; moved back and away from his assailant.

On the bed the naked girl started to scream. The dainty youth joined her, making a duet of soprano voices. The four secretaries hung there staring at their new master. He had, they saw, his left arm crossed above his heart. He drew it away, and there on his silken robes bloomed the dark, exotic flower of his blood.

But he stood there like a rock, with all his left side dyed red, maintaining his posture despite the flooding of a clearly fatal wound. Oribasius stared at his dripping blade in wonder.

"Thy heart!" he muttered. "I pierced thy heart, and yet—"

Alaric's voice was like a strain of music, drifting through the dead-stopped air. It came from far away. It was infinitely sad. But it had great and terrible echoes in it.

"Depart from here," he said. "Take up thy robes and go. For this madness thou hast my forgiveness, Valens! But thou must ask God's as well!"

Oribasius hung there, all his sweaty bulk aquiver. He looked for all the world like a frog but a moment ago emerged from a stagnant pool, with the ooze and slime glistening upon him still.

"Die—" he croaked. "Why dost thou not die? I have slain a score of men and never needed a second stroke. But thou standest there with thy heart pierced through and—"

Then without warning he hurled forward once again.

Alaric scarcely seemed to move at all. The quality of his motion was that of smoke. He flowed off to the left of Oribasius' blade. The factor had no time to halt his thrust. The blade bit wood; yet curiously, the sound they heard was the ghostly echo of a cry.

Oribasius crouched there, making a statuelike pantomime of arrested motion, congealed, as it were, into the attitude his body had assumed as he had driven home his blade. But now his little black eyes widened in pure horror. His hand came away from the hilt of the poniard, he sank to his knees, making in his gross nakedness, his hairy, sweaty bulk, an obscene caricature of piety, as he knelt before that hand-carved wooden icon of the Holy Mother, into whose very breast he had plunged his blade.

Then, for the first time, he seemed to become aware of what dripped redly from the poniard. His little eyes rolled in his head till only the whites of them showed.

"I've slain Her!" he shrieked. "Dear little Mother, I—see how she bleeds! She bleeds!"

Then, in one wild tearing rush that combined both his hurling bulk and his despairing wail, he was across the room in a splintering of furniture, a crashing of screens, a shattering, even, of masonry, of iron, and had burst massively through that high window, leaving the long, long trailing of his final scream lingering on the empty air like a banner.

The secretaries peered through the gaping window from which Oribasius' great weight had torn the iron gratings.

They turned back to Alaric, their faces gray, working.

But Alaric was not looking at them. He put out his hand and drew the poniard from the icon.

"Thou hast forgiven him, hast Thou not, Little Mother?" he whispered. "What is one more wound to Thee—or me?"

The lissome slave girl came up from the bed.

"My lord," she whispered, "lie you down! I'll do what I can to—"

"Thou'll do naught, child," Alaric said, "but cover thy nakedness and get hence from here. And take this pretty confusion of genders with thee—"

"But," the girl wailed, "thy wound—"

Alaric smiled. " 'Tis already healed," he said, and drew apart his tunic.

On his chest glowed the ancient crossed scars. But no newer wound. No wound at all.

All of them—even the pretty effeminate—crossed themselves at the sight of that. The four secretaries sank to their knees.

"Oh, get up from there!" Alaric said. "I'd not have ye kneel to me. Go attend your former master. And, Priscian—"

"More?" Priscian got out.

"Yes, my lord?" the oldest secretary whispered.

"His burial is at my cost. That, and one thing more—"

"Aye. The twenty masses I charge thee to have said, for the salvation of his repentant soul—"

Eunapius came into the countinghouse and bowed low before his new master. His hands came out of his robes, with a small sack in them.

"My lord," he wept, "this represents the half of all that I, too, stole. But if you will give me time, I promise to restore from my wages the full amount—"

Alaric stared at him. "And the others?" he said.

"They wait without. And beg your clemency. No more than that swine Oribasius did we expect the Jew to send a wonder-worker down upon us! On their behalf, as well as mine own, I beseech your mercy! Thou whose wounds heal upon the instant they are dealt thee—"

Alaric felt the slow ache in the fleshy underside of his left arm, bandaged now, and thought with sad irony, what pity was that miracles have always such simple explanations. Oribasius' blade had severed a vein, which accounted for all the blood that had dyed his robe when he instinctively pressed his wounded arm to his chest. Fools, he thought, could not ye see that the garment itself bore no rent? But Eunapius was babbling still.

"Art great enough of soul to spare our lives, and not slay us with thine awful eye as thou didst Oribasius!"

"Who slew himself," Alaric thought, "by a hellish combination of fear, drunkenness, and outraged piety. What a piece of work is man! That icon was—furniture to him. A decoration. Nightly he has fornicated and indulged in deviate vice under its poor sightless wooden eyes. But when he struck it with his blade it came alive to him. Bled with the blood I lent it! Ah, well, I have lent my blood to lesser women than Thee, Holy Mother!

"They need have no fear," he said. "Tell them to set about their tasks, as usual. Today I have other things to do."

"My lord," Eunapius whispered, "about Thetis—"

"Thetis?" Alaric said.

"The girl. She hath no other home. She too begs that you—"

"—retain her in the house? Very well. Set her to what tasks in which she may have skills, apart from the major one of harlotry. Warn her she cannot expect to share my bed. I have no need for such as she—"

"Oh, that she knows!" Eunapius said. "She swears you are no mere magician, but a saint!"

The task of finding an honest man to act as agent, factor, manager, retained him in Alexandria far longer than he had meant to stay. He was beginning to believe his Diogenean quest impossible, for right well did it seem to him that Alexandria's upper classes—who alone had the learning and the languages necessary to manage the ben Sahls' great establishment, into which, borne both by the camel caravans of the desert and the broad-beamed, great-oared galleys of the sea, flowed the treasures of half the world—were hopelessly corrupt. Betimes he ran the Egyptian countinghouse, warehouse, trading post, exchanges, himself. But now, unlike his earlier beginnings in the House of Sahl, he no longer found fascination in the work, though he was often greatly moved by the beauty of the goods he handled—the luminous mist of a string of pearls very nearly beyond price; the scintillating green fire of emeralds; diamonds' blinding glitter, the sheen of silks; the iridescent glow of peacock plumes, the downy softness of ostrich feathers, the creamy luster of carved ivory, the intricate, elaborate patterns of Iranian rugs.

But the routine of bookkeeping, letter-writing, labeling, cataloguing, making inventories, bowed his spirit beneath a weight of boredom. In the great house he had of the unfortunate Oribasius, it seemed to him that the slave girl Thetis crossed his path daily with ever growing frequency. That she treated him with marked respect, even with veneration, was truer; but truer still the fact that three full months had gone by since he quitted the comforts of Jimena's bed. To escape both ennui and temptation, he rode more and more out into that wild, clear, sweeping wilderness where half of humanity's beliefs, and more than half its gods, were born. Which, for such a one as he, was surely an error. For sitting there upon his mount under the high blue Egyptian sky, in the shimmering desert light, with the wind-driven sand lashing stingingly across his face, Alaric could feel the words far off and faint, forming themselves deep within his mind:

"Aizun, My son, My son—"

And hearing them, he whirled his steed about and fled.

But inescapably, driven by a compulsion beyond his resistance or his will, he came again and again to that desert place, feeling that here he was very close to the deep, slow beating heart of time, to the answer to all mysteries, until the words were terrible thunder in his heart:

"Aizun, Aizun, my son, my son, why dost thou flee Me still?"

"I am not fit!" he wailed aloud; "I am unchaste! My hands are stained with blood! I doubt Thee! I am without faith! I—"

His absences lengthened, till on one occasion it was night before he returned to the house in Alexandria.

Thetis greeted him in alarm. "My lord, I thought thee dead!" she cried. "Without thee I would not live!"

For a moment Alaric debated with himself over the question of taking this pretty, corrupt child to bed, to escape the compulsion, the thunderous words, that sat on his spirit like the weight of his weariness.

"I thank thee for thy kindness, child," he said. "But leave me. Get thee to thy bed. For I am sick of heart, and of weariness very faint. I pray thee, sweet Thetis, go—"

"My lord," she said quickly, allow me to bring thee a cup—and some warmed and perfumed cloths to ease thy head and—"

"—your own soft flesh to ease the rest of me?" he said.

Her teeth were a flash of pearl between warm, moist lips of scarlet.

"Aye, Sahib Aizun," she whispered. "That most of all. . . ."

He went on looking at her. "Why?" he said.

"With my lord Valens—I—was forced. I hated him. He was fat and gross and given to vile practices—even with me, who am a woman, hence making unnecessary such rarities as men do with boys. But thou'rt fair, my lord! Methinks I've seen no other half so fair in all my life. And thou art also very gentle, very good. Who else would have paid out princely sums to have masses said for the soul of him who tried to slay thee?"

"In recompense for which, wouldst make with me the beast with two backs?" Alaric said.

"You put it harshly. Nay, good my lord! In recompense for nothing! Because I love thee—and am afire!"

He went on looking at her; and smiling at her in a way that was a negation in itself.

"Nay, sweet Thetis," he said with a sigh. "For should I grant you this, you'll remember me—if at all—as one more man among all thy men. I'd leave a gentler memory in thee—of him who refused thy love, for his soul's sake, and thine. Cold comfort! But one day, when you're old, you'll mind you of my words and know I spoke truly: 'Tis only the loves we lose that in God's good truth we keep—undiminished by sweat and dishevelment and carnal odors and the erosion of the years. Till I die, thou'lt remain in my heart and mind as thou'rt now: as lovely as an angel, slightly soiled; and I—"

"For me thou shalt always be the morning star, without blemish, for want of whom I die!"

She put her arms to him; but he shook his head.

"Nay, child," he said, and went into his chamber, closing the door behind him. Thus to his growing personal hagiology was another element added. For by then all Alexandria knew how he had pointed a slim finger at a monstrous black, and invisible spirits had hurled the huge Negro down a stair; how, receiving a knife thrust through his heart, he had made the sign of the cross above it, and the wound had healed at once, leaving only a glowing white image of the holy sign he'd made branded into his very flesh; how his assailant, trying once again to slay him, had plunged his knife instead into an image of the Mother of God, whereupon the image had cried out, commenced to bleed; how the holy man had turned upon the wretch the holy blue fire of his eye, and the miscreant had been with such remorse smitten as to throw himself from a window and thus depart this life. . . . Now upon all this sacred nonsense was piled this one last, final proof. Now Lord Aizun's wonder-working was crowned by chastity, by his kindly refusal to make use of that utterly delectable morsel Thetis. That, to Alexandrian eyes, was the greatest wonder of them all, the more so since all the world already knew the fair Goth never frequented boys.

In a day or two more, Thetis herself would begin to speak of it with pride.

Before his departure from Córdoba, Alaric had had of his wife the name of the man whom ibn Ha'ad had pressured into buying blind Omar. But Jimena knew not where Muhammad Ali—for thus was he called— lived. When she had asked her father, the trader had snorted, "Oh, hard by the quay!" which now was all Alaric had to go upon.

But it proved less difficult than he would have thought. The name Muhammad Ali was, of course, a common one. But Muhammad Ali, by profession a merchant of the town, reduced the matter to more manageable proportions. By name clearly a Muslim—which eliminated the bulk of Alexandria's population in that year of Our Lord 833, still in the majority Greek. By the same token it eliminated both Jews and Persians, both of whom could still be distinguished by their patronyms.

All that being taken into account, there were still a surprising number of merchants named Muhammad Ali. And some twenty of their number owned slaves named Omar. But bought of ibn Ha'ad? The purchaser pardoned by that wily schemer of half his debts thereby? Aye, that rang a bell!

"You mean, my lord, the *honest* Muhammad Ali! That solemn young fool who rode all the way to al Qahira to return an hundred dinars he'd overcharged a client by mistake! The faithful Ali!—faithful unto starvation—for since he will not adulterate his goods nor alter his balances and weights, he can no profit make!"

"Why?" Alaric questioned. "Cannot an honest man profit here? The ben Sahls do, and they, I know, are honest. . . ."

"But also great. They have a far-flung empire of trade more vast than that of ibn Ha'ad. What they lose on the one hand, they gain on the other. But what small merchant can afford the luxury of total honesty? Muhammad tries it, but in the end you'll find that he—Where doth he live? In the Street of the Fishmongers, near the Avenue of the Pharo, down by the quay—"

"Take him!" Muhammad Ali said with a laugh. "Take my Omar! With my luck I can scarce feed myself, not to mention him! Besides, he costs me some trouble. I have to conceal from the authorities that our fine Omar hath become an apostate to his faith—for which, as you know, the penalty is death. But since he swears a Christian holy man gave him back his sight, he needs must become a Nazarene!"

Alaric looked at the young Egyptian. He liked what he saw. Honest though he was, Muhammad was gay, not solemn.

"This of your luck," he said. "Things go not well with you?"

Muhammad Ali frowned. "I am an honest man, ibn al Qutiyya!" he said. "Ask whom you will, and they will tell you that! Honest Muhammad! Faithful Ali! So naturally in this den of thieves I starve. I am a merchant—formerly I traded with ibn Ha'ad; but he comes here no more. The last time he was in Alexandria was when his daughter had to be quickly married to the Goth—*Bism Allah!* What a fool I am! Forgive me, Sahib! I did not recognize who it was that so honors my humble house!"

"You honor me," Alaric said, "by your hospitality. But say on: With whom trade you now?"

"The House of Sahl. When they ran the local establishment themselves, I prospered, for the ben Sahls are honest men; but once they left it in the hands of that unspeakable swine Oribasius, trading became impossible. Valens Oribasius is dead now—may Saithan roast him well in hell!—but this new factor they have now is a stranger. So having very little to offer, I have not dared—"

"I bid thee dare, Muhammad, my friend. Present thyself at the countinghouse tomorrow—"

"To meet the new factor?" Muhammad said.

"Nay, for him you have known all your life," Alaric said.

"Known all my life?" the young Egyptian said. "Then it must be—Basil Belisarius? Cyril Dionysius? Justin Boethius?"

"No Greek," Alaric said.

"A Jew, then, surely. Yacob ben Israel? Sholem ben David? Ibrahim ben Yahvli?"

"Not a Jew," Alaric said.

"Then one of us? I give up! I have known thousands of Egyptians all my life—"

"But none as well as this one," Alaric said.

398

"Ya Allah! By the very Beard you tantalize me, son-in-law of ibn Ha'ad! Who can the new man be?"

Alaric smiled.

"Thou," he said.

And now, at long last, he could sail for home. For after a few days of watching how the young Egyptian took hold of affairs, Alaric was content. Part of that contentment was due to Omar's refusal to return with him to al Andalus; for there the former blind man would prove a fearsome burden. But in Egypt Omar had found a wife, had sired a son; and his former master Muhammad Ali would provide him with work as a freedman, a state Omar complained of as being more burdensome than that of being a slave.

"No one to look out for you, master!" he said to Alaric. "But if you'll give me your blessing I'll have naught to fear!"

Alaric smiled. "My blessing you have, Omar," he said, "so long as you do not go about spreading this nonsense of my having restored your sight."

Omar stared at him. " 'Tis no nonsense, good my lord!" he said. "You cured me! You put your hands upon my head and prayed to God for me. When your hands touched me, I could feel your power flowing into me—like—like heated wine! Then you moved away, and I turned my head in the direction of thy footsteps and lo! I saw thee! You were the first human being I'd ever seen. I thought you an angel you were so fair! If you wish me not to speak of it, I won't, but don't tell me thou didst not restore my sight!"

"All right, all right." Alaric sighed. "Speak no more on it! My head aches so. I sail tomorrow, good Omar. Can I do aught else for thee before I go?"

Omar bowed his head, looked up again. "One thing my lord Aizun—I know I shouldn't ask it, but—"

"Ask what you will, Omar! I owe you some recompense for your sufferings," Alaric said.

"My wife's sister, Hypatia. She—she is possessed of devils, good my lord."

"You mean she's mad?" Alaric said.

"No. For most days she is as sane as you or I. Then her demons seize her and she runs through the town, tears off her clothes, dances naked in a public place. Twice now wicked men have tried to ravish her, but her devils aid her in fighting them off, for they make her wondrous strong."

"You want me to lay hands on her head?" Alaric said. "Look you,

Omar, I have no such powers as these you think I have. Much do I doubt such powers exist; so ask me some other boon than this—"

Stubbornly Omar shook his head. "No other boon than this, Saint Aizun, Holy Man of God! Who else could work the wonders that you do? I beg you, I beseech, come to my humble home. If in truth you cannot cure her, what harm will have been done? You'll have wasted an hour, had a pleasant walk, given my wife Eulalia the greatest joy of her life— she is Christian by birth, you know, and it delights her good soul to hear me speak of thee! When I told her that the holy man of whom all Alexdria is speaking—the great Saint Aizun—"

"Omar," Alaric said sternly, "saints have to be cononized by His Holiness in Rome—"

"Or by the Patriarch in Constantinople!" Omar said. "My wife's Greek, so speak not of the Roman persuasion to her, I beg you, good my lord! Anyhow, when I told her that the miracle worker of whom all men speak with wonder is none other than he who cured me of my blindness— she was beside herself! So—"

"Omar," Alaric said, "you could see before! Admit it! Do not lie. I charge upon pain of blindness in all truth—"

"Well," Omar whispered, "a little—outlines—forms. But without clarity, my lord—until you came and—"

"Rubbish! Your sight has been growing better of itself. Admit that, too—"

"But so slowly, Sahib! I had of this quack in the Street of the Alchemists, this water of silver and—mayhap it helped somewhat; but 'twas thy touch which cured me, Lord Aizun! Before Jesu Crucified, I swear it!"

"There is nothing more invincible in this world," Alaric said, sighing, "than the will to believe. And the more idiotic the belief, the stronger it is held. Very well, Omar, I'll come with thee. Mayhap the air will clear my aching head—"

But fortune was not kind to Alaric on that day, for long before they reached Omar's house in one of the poor sections of Alexandria, they heard the shrieks, accompanied by the delighted bull bellows of male laughter. And rounding the corner they saw her, dancing in wild fury, rending the very air with her screams, her thickset body entirely nude, a moving whitish blur.

"God help me!" Alaric thought, or prayed, or both; and moved toward the plump, not uncomely peasant girl who was delighting the horde of loiterers with her mad gymnastics.

Someone in the crowd—a woman surely—saw his face, marked its brooding beauty, its tender sorrow. " 'Tis he!" she hissed. " 'Tis he!"

" 'Tis he! 'Tis he!" the whispers ran from one woman to another until even the brute male bellows died. " 'Tis he! The holy man! The wonder-worker! Allah witness he is fair. By Lord Jesu, 'tis an angel come down to earth. Mark ye how he moves in light. I tell thee there s a glow about his head!"

"Nonsense, woman!" a burly laborer said with a guffaw. " 'Tis a pretty youth—no more. One of Oribasius' lovers, surely—jinn and demons! One so fair could tempt me to turn from women, myself."

Alaric's eyes rested on the profane one. "Thy tongue is foul," he said quietly. "Take care what use you make of it, brother, or silence may fall upon thee like a leaden weight—"

"Ha!" the laborer scoffed. "I'll go on roaring till Lord Saithan crisps my soul black in hell! As for thee, pretty catamite, take care I do not here and now make use of—"

Those blue eyes rested upon him like the mists above a northern fjord.

The laborer's great voice died in his throat. He opened his mouth wider. His tongue moved up and down between his broken, filthy fangs. Beads of sweat stood and sparkled on his forehead. The muscles of his thick neck corded, jerked; but no sound came out of his mouth, no sound at all.

Nor from any of those who witnessed it. They had one and all of them ceased to breathe. Even the whirling naked girl was silent now. She danced on, her eyes rapt, withdrawn; but no longer did the demons within her scream.

And now the big man fell to his knees. His great grimy paws tore at the neckband of his shirt; ripped it to shreds; while his brute animal's face turned purple before their eyes. Then, at long last, he acknowledged defeat: he raised his two hands, palm pressed to palm, fingers upward to the gesture of prayer; and two great tears penciled the dirt upon his face.

Alaric sighed. "Thy sins are forgiven thee," he said quietly. "Go thou and sin no more. . . ."

Then he put out his slim, long-fingered hand, and touched the man's head.

A roar of joy burst from the laborer's throat. "Master forgive me!" he wept. "From this hour, I swear—"

"Do not take oaths lest you should break them," Alaric said. "Go thou and—"

"Master, I beg thee," the laborer said, "let me stay and see thou heal her, too!"

Alaric sighed. The pain oppressing his heart was very great. I have no powers! he thought. But they believe I do—and their belief dominates even the workings of their flesh. And being largely sane, I can reach them. But what is more hopeless than this? How can I strike through to this darkened mind?

He came up to her. Hypatia ignored him, went on whirling. The way she danced was in itself an act of ritual devotion to her unknown terrible demon gods.

"Give me thy cloak," he said to an old woman. The woman passed it over.

"Hypatia," Alaric said. He did not raise his voice; but it made music of her name; made silver bells and a twanging lute, and Grecian Panpipes orchestrating a triad, rising, falling, and endlessly sweet. "Hypatia, my child—"

She went on dancing, but her wild black eyes fixed themselves upon his face. Again and again, as her whirling brought them around to him once more, to leave, to whirl out upon that blank sea of dark faces, to return.

"Hypatia!" he cried out now. "Be still!"

She went on whirling: but suddenly now, she spoke, her words thrust out upon the ragged, spurting, panting staccato of her breath.

"'Tis not I, master! 'Tis not I—who dance! 'Tis they—'tis they—who—who buffet me about—who whirl me so! Oh, sweet master—cast them out! Cast them—out—of—me—that I—that I—may rest—"

Alaric lifted his eyes.

"Thou who pursued me lifelong down all the roads I fled thee —who torment me worse than even suffers this poor child—who claim me for Thine own—Where art Thou now? Where is Thy voice which twists my heart? Now that I need Thee! Speak—"

But no voice spoke to him then. No tender, infinite whisper echoed through his heart. In all that crowd, many of them kneeling now—Omar crouching at his side, making frantic crosses on his own breast—Alaric was alone. He could feel the ebbing of his strength, leaving in him a weakness like unto death; so, because he knew not what else to do, he lifted up his voice, made brazen thunder, crashing like cymbals, reverberating like a temple gong.

"Leave her! By sweet Lord Jesu, I cast thee out!"

Hypatia ceased to whirl. Her dark eyes glowed like embers. She hung there, plump, naked, short, bedewed with sweat, her black hair sticking to her face, her neck, her throat; her hands coming down now in the instinctive gesture of modesty to cover that dark-furred inverted triangle. Then with a little moan she slumped unconscious to the ground.

402

He bent and covered her with the woman's cloak. He turned to Omar.

"Pick her up," he said. "Bear her to thy—"

But at that moment a woman standing by the swooning girl began to scream. Wildly, her hands tore at her garments. She whirled. Then another took it up, and another, until every woman in that crowd was shrieking like all the fiends from hell and tearing at her clothing.

"God in Heaven!" Alaric said. Then he raised his two hands high.

"Be gone from here!" he thundered. "By God's Gentle Mother, leave this place, and trouble no woman of this land more!"

"Nor no man, either! Say that, my lord!" Omar wept. "Or else—"

"Nor any man!" Alaric cried, and silence fell upon them, like a prayer.

The women ceased to whirl. They stared at their torn garments, their bared breasts. Hastily they made what repairs to their clothes they could.

And now, truly, Alaric stood alone. For all that multitude knelt at his feet. He smiled at them tenderly, sadly.

"Bless thee, my children," he said; then, turning to Omar: "I charge thee, good servant, bear her to thy house. . . ."

'Twas only the next morning, when he was preparing to leave the house, with his baggage—which consisted mostly of gifts for Jimena and his daughters, for Gelesvinta's children—to go aboard the great galley that waited by the quay, that he discovered the magnitude of the error into which compassion had driven him. Muhammad Ali, come to bid him farewell, arrived with his clothes in rags.

"*Bism Allah!*" he gasped. "There's a mob of madmen before thy house, patron! By the very Beard, they've all but murdered me!"

Alaric stared at the comely young Egyptian.

"Why?" he said.

"That I should intercede for them! That I should beseech thy blessing upon each and every verminous head! That I should pray thee to cure them of bloody fluxes, running sores, boils, swellings, leprosy! And demons! An hundred dervishes howl and whirl before the door! Come to the window! Look, they've ripped my clothes to shreds. Ya Allah! Before my God and thine, good patron, now they bring their cripples and—O Merciful, Wise, and Only—their dead!"

Alaric stood by the window, staring at the sight. In the center of the crowd knelt Omar, his wife, and the plump Hypatia. The girl was decently clad now, freshly scrubbed. Her dark eyes were filled with adoration.

Alaric turned back to Muhammad; but a curious little whimpering sound caught his ear. Looking down, he saw Thetis kneeling at his feet. Before he could divine her intent, she drew forth a vial of costly perfume from her robes, and poured it all over his feet; then, slipping the loose Moorish sandal off one of them, she began to dry it with her long black hair.

"Thetis!" he said. "What manner of blasphemy is this?"

She looked up at him now, and he recoiled from her in horror, seeing the raw furrows she had clawed into her cheeks with her own frenzied nails, catching full in his nostrils the hot stench of blood; then, as she collapsed against the floor, her full, warm, opened mouth pressed against his bare foot, covering it with fevered kisses, he saw that the back of her dress was in ribbons and glued to her flesh by the slow-drying ooze of the terrible stripes with which, from shoulder to waist, she was covered.

"Mother of God!" he wept. "Who hath done this, child! Tell me: Who hath beaten thee so?"

"I—" she whispered. "I—I ordered it done, master. By—by the eunuchs and women of my departed lord—who dared not disobey me. 'Tis—'tis my penance for—for trying to tempt—a saint. . . . I followed thee on yesterday . . . I saw thy miracles—Oh, master, my saintly lord, forgive me! Forgive my sins which are as scarlet—Bless me and—"

"And what, child?" Alaric said, though now he could scarcely see her for his tears.

"Make me good, my lord! Make me chaste! Throw out the demons of lust from within me! Please, San Alarico, I beseech thee!"

He brought down his hand, let it rest upon her head. What matters one more lie, one more act of this mad comedy, now? he thought.

"Thy sins are forgiven thee, Thetis," he murmured. "From now on thou shalt be as pure as snow."

He turned, then, seeing Muhammad's dark eyes upon him.

"Care for her, Muhammad, when I am gone," he said.

"I hear and obey," Muhammad said. "But, master—how mean you to escape them? They are all around the house, and in their mad devotion they'll tear you limb from limb!"

How right Jimena was! Alaric thought. But I can scarcely transport this mob of poor hopeless fools to Sind or far Cathay— He stood there at the window, staring at them. Then suddenly he threw back the curtains and leaned out. The sunlight struck his bright blond head and gleamed.

The roar that went up from that crowd at the sight of him wracked sound out of existence, and was, in itself a compendium of all human

404

anguish, all man's longing for relief, his stubborn, slow-dying hope, his agonizing need to believe.

"My children!" Alaric cried. The silence in the square before his house now was death itself. "Return to your homes! I grant you all my blessing! And those of you whose faith is strong, and upon whom God's mercy rests, will from this hour of your ills be cured. Peace be with you! God's peace I grant unto you! Go ye all and sin no more!"

Five minutes later, no single person lingered in the square.

Muhammad stared at Alaric with awe.

"I, too, crave thy blessing, good my lord," he said.

Alaric stared at him. Muhammad saw the tears in his blue eyes.

"And I, thine," he whispered, "and thy pardon, too—"

"*My* blessing? *My* pardon?" Muhammad said. "Art daft, Sahib Aizun?"

"Nay. I crave the blessing and the pardon of an honest man; for I can no longer ask for God's—"

"For what?" Muhammad whispered. "For what wouldst be pardoned, master?"

"For blasphemy. For fraud. For unbelief. Though what I have done—this monstrous charade—was torn from me by pity. Lord God, they suffer so!"

"All men suffer," the young Egyptian said.

"Aye," Alaric sighed, "and most of all in one particular, good namesake of the Prophet—"

"Which is?" Muhammad said.

"That we, of all creation, are born knowing we must die, and thus are continually condemned to reinvent God. A meaningful God for a meaningless universe. Too great a task, my friend! And now—"

"And now?" Muhammad whispered.

"I go," Alaric said.

XXIV

"*He* does not go on journeys!" Jimena wept. "Oh, no! Not the great Saadyah ben Hasdai, merchant prince! *He* does not absent him for years from his wife and daughters of marriageable age. Nay, he sends thee."

"Hardly years—" Alaric said, sighing.

"Years! That voyage to Sind and Cathay; how long did it take you, Aizun? Tell me that!"

"Well," Alaric conceded, "that one, yes—"

"Three years!" Jimena shrieked. "Three long years without my husband! And with Theodora growing daily more unmanageable! Of course, in God's own truth, you cannot be blamed for that. 'Tis that savage blood she got from her blackamoor of a father—"

"Hardly a blackamoor, Jimena," Alaric said mildly. "A Berber, yes, and swart. But no matter. I too, my too plump pigeon, have been thinking that this business of constant voyages 'twixt here and Alexandria has to come to an end—"

"Ha!" Jimena said. "I know why you don't like going there!"

"Do you?" Alaric said.

"Aye! Because there they *know* you for what you are! A holy man. A saint. Every time you come ashore from the galley the sick are already waiting for you to cure them! Which you do—hundreds of them—by the use of your miraculous powers—"

"Who told you that?" Alaric said.

"Aizun, I spent most of my childhood in the East. Father took me there after—after that of Mother and Diego. I have many friends, who write me letters. For these several years all my friends in Alexandria, and their husbands, have been plaguing me to tell them what 'tis like to be married to a saint. I know all about it—even to the story of the Greek prostitute who is now Mother Superior of the convent because you refused her favors. Tell me, was it true that she mutilated her face and scourged herself almost to death in repentance for the sin of trying to tempt thee?"

"Yes," Alaric said.

"And didst kill a man by looking at him? Turn another mute, then restore his voice? Cast out devils? Cure lepers? Raise the dead?"

406

"Jimena, what you ask cannot be answered by a simple yes or no," Alaric said. "I did not kill Oribasius. He killed himself—out of fear because of a blasphemy he had unwittingly done. The man who lost his voice did so because *he* believed I had power to bereave him of the speech he used most foully. The women possessed—also a matter of faith. Their faith in me. The dead child was not dead, but in a deep trance, from which I called him because my voice hath a quality to it which, methinks, eases fear. The lepers, no. I have never been able to cure a true bodily illness. I can ease the terrified, the deranged, the sick of soul, because I have so much pity for them, so much love. But not even pity, not even love availeth when the flesh hath become corrupt and death lingers in the blood. But in this thou hast much right. I do wish to stop my voyaging to the East because of these things. I come home sick with pity, half dead of anguish because I cannot truly do what they believe I can. As God's my judge, I'd perform miracles gladly to rid the world of suffering, cruelty, horror, sickness, pain. But I cannot, Jimena. You call me saint—as have others before you; but now I confess to thee a great and terrible thing: I have no faith. I do not believe."

She stared at him, her face gone white.

"You—you do not—"

"—believe. Nay, sweet Jimena, good wife of my body and, mayhap, of the soul I doubt I have. I should give anything, including my life, to achieve belief. I have been close to it at times—the times when I am close to madness. Then I hear voices, dream dreams, and am myself possessed. But that passeth, and I return to this my world. This very pleasant world which my voices say I must leave—"

"Leave," Jimena said. "Leave how, oh, my sweet lord? Enter the cloister? Become a monk?"

"Nay, love. My voices say that in some great and terrible way—I must die."

"Die! Oh, no! Oh, Aizun, no! You cannot! I'll not have it! No, I don't care who tells you that! You must not leave me! Without thee, I should die!"

"Do not fear, Jimena. 'Tis some trick of the sense—that comes upon me when I am overwrought, or tired, or sick. It afflicted me in the desert, when first I journeyed to Alexandria for Saadyah. And another time when I was for some months mad of guilt and grief for having caused poor Zoë's death. And yet, upon other occasions, when I have equal or greater reason to be deranged, as when I knelt at my poor father's grave by the gracious leave of the young Count of Tarabella, my half brother Hermingildo—the fat, porcine little animal!—no voices speak to me at all. I mind me to survive long enough to dandle my grandsons on my knee, and plague their grandmother about her fondness for sweetmeats and rich pastries! Now, enough of this holy nonsense. Attend me well, for I have a plan to end the voyages. Art willing that I risk our savings on a venture?"

Jimena hesitated. "What sort of a venture, good my lord?" she said.

"Dost recall the cup I brought thee a month agone—the one Abbas ibn Firnas made?"

"Of course! What a treasure. 'Tis as clear as spring water—one can see one's fingers through it when one lifts it up. I know you gave up trying to explain to me how 'twas made, but I wish you'd try again. I never saw such a wonder before!"

"Nor did anyone else, since ibn Firnas invented the process himself. 'Tis made of melted sand, potash, and burnt lead. We call it glass, or crystal. Ziryab swears that the wealthy and exquisite will pay fortunes to possess such goblets and other objects made of glass. What think you of this, Jimena?"

He held out a small flat square of glass to her. She took it, looked into it, gave a cry.

"By'r Lady, never have I seen a mirror half so clear as this! Silver ones, no matter how one polishes them, aren't ever as bright as this. Another of that wizard's inventions?"

"Nay," Alaric said. "This one is mine. An accident, I confess. I was visiting Abbas' laboratory, and I dropped a piece of crystal he had made—the beggar hadn't warned me 'twas still hot, his idea of a jest, I suppose—and as luck would have it, it fell into a sticky mass of paint. You've no idea what a swine pen that laboratory of ibn Firnas' is! The heat of the glass dried the paint; the paint cooled the glass. This is the accidental result. Now tell me, sweet Jimena, would not most ladies pay well to have mirrors as good as this?"

"And dearly! Aizun—you mean you want to invest our savings—"

"In a manufactory of glass. Mirrors, goblets, cups, even dishes. Who knows what cannot be made of the wondrous stuff?"

"Aizun—it—it would not fail, would it? I shouldn't like our being poor in our old age—"

"Of that you need have no fear, my sweet. I said *our* savings; by which I meant the monies we have accumulated since we were wed. The fortune thy late lamented father left thee I have not touched; nor mean I to, ever. So poverty is not a thing you need to fear, Jimena. Besides, methinks my glassworks cannot fail. Abbas is most clever at inventing things; but he himself knows and admits he hath no head for business. While I do. I will have the papers so drawn that I control all negotiations, while he invents and develops his alchemist's wizardry to its furtherest limits. Art agreed, then, that we go into this thing, since of a surety 'twill keep me at thy side?"

"For that I'd agree even if I had to beg alms in the street!" Jimena said.

"Good! I told Abbas I'd not venture upon it without your consent because the matter involved some risk to monies in part thine. Ziryab is planning to invest in it, too; and Prince al Wallid. Ziryab will not be able to invest a great deal, for his extravagances hath limited the growth of his fortune. But he will be the more valuable partner for all that; for his influence over the notables will insure that objects of crystal become the rage of fashion. In the end I shall be able to buy him out, and the Prince as well. For though al Wallid possesses considerable wealth, he will not dare venture much, because he is timid by nature. Poor gentle soul. I know not whom he loves most, Goissuintha or Natalia—"

"Natalia?" Jimena said.

"Their third child. A daughter. 'Tis said she is as beautiful as an angel. The name is Slavic—curious they should have named the child that. And now, my love, I'd best go draw up and sign those papers before Abbas ibn Firnas blows himself up, or departs this life by poison, or self-mutilation. I'll demand of him the formulae for glassmaking in writing, because considering the idiotic risks he takes with his experiments—"

"Aizun, you stay out of that laboratory! Mayhap what thy voices meant was—"

"Nothing, fair Jimena! Voices never do," Alaric said.

The day he presented his resignation to Saadyah was not a remarkably happy occasion.

"Friendship, be damned!" Saadyah bellowed. "I brought you into the business only because Afaf would give me no peace with her harrowing tales of your poverty! And—"

"And now, having obeyed the Talmudic instruction toward charity, 'twill trouble you little to let me go," Alaric said.

"Shoel and Gheminna! You're a prickly beast, Aizun! I was about to say that my wife's lingering dreams of thee—which, had she married thee, she'd be well quit of by now!—forced me into the best investment I ever made! You're worth your weight in gold, Aizun! No one else ever managed to straighten out those thieves in Alexandria; and thy long voyage to Sind and Cathay brought in treasures enough to make me consider any reasonable demand. Look you—I'll augment your share! *Half* the profits! Will that suit you, Aizun, plagued son of the plagued Goth?"

Alaric smiled at him. "Nay, Saadyah, I want not gold," he said.

"Aye, I forgot. Since Satan dragged that fat swine of a father-in-law of yours down to his just deserts in hell, you could probably buy *me* out. By Cain, the originator of fratricide, is *that* what you want? To go it on your own? To set yourself up in rivalry to me, take the late, unlamented ibn Ha'ad's place? Aye! And I can tell you the reason! Our wives! Our precious little she-keepers! For the dubious privilege of bumping bellies with them, methinks we give up too much! Afaf would have me abduct thy Theodora, since she cannot obtain that lovely child by legal means. And why? To mirror her vanity—to be able to walk abroad with a daughter who's her image. Odd they look so much alike, isn't it?"

He stopped short, aware at last that Alaric was laughing at him.

"Then what is it?" he said.

"A simple desire to stay at home," Alaric said. "The time comes on apace when I must find husbands for my daughters. Jimena's sickly—a want of exercise and an inherited tendency toward gluttony hath made her much too stout, from which, and from fear, her heart hath weakened. And I tire of voyaging. Lastly, for thy information, good Saad, I propose to become a manufacturer of crystal—"

"Like those bowls you brought back from far Cathay? You know how to make them, boy? That puts another face on matters. The prices people were willing to pay for those bowls astounded even me—and I'm not easy to amaze, you know. Make me such an article of luxury and I guarantee the sale of your entire production. All right, I accept your resignation, Aizun, but only on one condition: that you cut me a fat slice of this! Half shares—and you name your price!"

"Done!" Alaric laughed. "But not halves. I cannot. Ibn Firnas owns half, since he invented the process. Ziryab hath taken ten percent of the shares, al Wallid five; and the rest are mine. But I'll divide with thee—seventeen and one half, each—"

"Good!" Saadyah said. "How much?"

"Don't know. How do you determine the value of an unborn baby, Saad? We must find a building, set up furnaces, train workers. It may be years before your shares have any value at all, my friend. The problems are not insurmountable, but they are plaguedly difficult—"

"Less than you think. Building, you've got. My old warehouses out in the Munyat Adjab section. Workers? How about foundrymen? It's similar, isn't it? I'll detach twenty good lads from my gold and silver foundries—slack season at the moment and—"

"Saad, the miracle worker!" Alaric said.

So it was done. The glassworks prospered from the start. Ziryab convinced all Córdoba that only barbarians ate upon silver plates, waxed lyrical about the beauty of wine glowing like liquid ruby or pale amber in

410

crystal goblets. Abbas ibn Firnas invented new methods every year, until his fertile brain discovered how to make great sheets of transparent plate, and no lesser personage than the Emir himself had a glassed-in veranda built into his newest palace.

During the next several years Alaric accomplished many things. One of al Rahman's elder sons, the Prince al Mundhir, saw Theodora passing through a busy street accompanied by her half-sisters. So smitten was he that the Emir was forced to take a hand. Once more Alaric was summoned to the Alcázar; when he left, a marriage had been arranged, save for the delicate business of obtaining Theodora's own consent, for well did Alaric know that his stepdaughter had a will of her own.

"Tell him to come in person, Father!" that saucy minx said, laughing. "Well as I should like becoming a princess, I'd like better having a husband as handsome as my father. 'Tis a pity I cannot marry thee who art the only man I'll every truly love. Tell me—doth he blink his eyes like his royal idiot of a father?"

"No," Alaric said. "The only sign of idiocy he hath displayed to date is his taste as far as maids are concerned. But in the fullness of our youth, in the heyday of the blood, few there be of us from whom sweet reason doth not depart, at least upon occasion."

"Father, tell me something," Theodora cooed.

"If I can, and if 'tis suitable for your tender ears—"

"Why'd you marry Mama and not Aunt Afaf?"

"Mayhap because I was mad, and like all madmen, very wise," Alaric said. "Enough of questions, Theo! I'll suggest to the Emir—whose blinking eyes are a sign of humanity rather than folly; his father, al Hakam, forced him to witness a terrible deed in his youth and the shock of it caused that strange habit which lingers with him still—that Prince al Mundhir be allowed to call as though he were a noble Christian youth. Speaking of which, I've already stipulated that in the event of this marriage's taking place, you are to retain, and freely practice, your own faith—"

"And I," Theodora said, "am going to stipulate—in the event I like his highness—that I be not shut up in anybody's smelly old harem; that I be allowed to go and come as I please, and that for every extra wife or concubine *he* takes, *I* be permitted to even the score with a new lover—"

"Theo!" Alaric said.

"Oh, don't look so shocked, good my Father! When you were my age one poor lovelorn fool had already cut her throat over thee; you'd been married to a highborn lady, from whom you procured an annulment because her morals were many degrees below her station; one creature of gay nocturnal habits entered the cloister for thy sake; and that ugly, red-

haired mulatto son of old Prince Karim's just might be my half brother—
or to put it more justly—could possibly have been my half brother, if I
had been yours, which I should have loved—even if it meant a simpering
idiot like Aurea or Munia—"

"Methinks," Alaric said with a sigh, "that even if this of young al
Mundhir doth fail, I had better find you a husband, if only for the
purpose of keeping you away from dear Afaf's loose and malicious
tongue—"

"I note thou dost not say 'lying tongue,' my lord Father!" Theo
laughed. "How good you are! Even to the extent of refusing to misues the
truth in self-defense. . . ." She stopped laughing suddenly; skipped over to
where Alaric sat; leaned forward swiftly and kissed his cheek.

"Might I ask why this sudden courtesy, daughter?" he said.

"For that," she whispered; "because I *am* thy daughter, though I bear
not thy blood. Mama has always hated me, remembering the terrible way
I came to be born. But you—who, being a man, should have loathed the
sight of me as a reminder that other men have shared the body of thy
bride—have always loved me; always treated me with every kindness.
Even with special favor. You are a saint, Father. Who else but a saint
would have not only endured, but actually loved, a brigand Berber's
swart bastard child?"

"There are no bastard children, Theo," Alaric said, "but only bas-
tardly fathers. But enough of this. Go prepare thyself; for from what the
Emir tells me of his son's impatience, when I grant him permission to call
upon thee, he will appear within the hour—"

"Father—" Theo whispered. "I—"

"What, child?"

"Oh, I would not leave thee!" Theo wept. "Not for any prince! I'd
stay with thee lifelong and—"

"Nonsense, child. To marry and live in the same city is not to leave
me. We'll see each other as often as we like. Young Mundhir seems a
reasonable lad—"

"I hope so." Theo sighed; then a flash of her old mischief lighted her
eyes. "Tell me, Father, is he—handsome?"

"Very," Alaric said.

A year and six months from that date, Alaric was already a grandfather—if only by courtesy, by the love he bore his dark stepdaughter—
and Theodora had carried her perversity, her contrariness to the point of
confounding all speculation by becoming a sweet and dutiful wife.
Within that same year Aurea had gone starry-eyed to the altar with young
Garcia Sanchez, the son of Alaric's most important Christian client. But

'twas gentle little Muna who caused them all the most concern. At Saadyah's house she met his tall and handsome nephew, fair Ruth's eldest son. Young Hasdai, named of course, for his grandsire, took one look at Munia, and, with an impetuosity matching his uncle's own, proposed. Munia came home in tears.

"I love him, Father!" she wailed. "At least methinks I do! Oh, but he is good to look upon. So tall! And his voice—like thunder a long way off. Grave and tender! But, Father, he is a Jew. Which means he doth not believe in Our Lord at all! Even the Muslimn do, though they reduce Him to a mere prophet. What will Mama say? She grumbled enough over Theo's marrying Prince al Mundhir, though Theo could do that and keep her faith. Father, must I give him up? I have never met a youth like him before and—"

"Let me think on it, and see what can be done," Alaric said.

What could be done was a special dispensation by which little Munia was allowed to keep her Christian faith, worked out between the Metropolitan of the Church and the Head Rabbi of Córdoba's Jewish community. For in those days there was peace still between all the faiths living under the benign Muslim rule. And pity 'twas that this enlightened toleration of a different belief was not to last. Four years almost to the day of Munia's wedding to young Hasdai it was destroyed—and, as usual, by Christian arrogance and bigotry.

But this exercise in religious statesmanship did not entirely solve the problem presented by a Jewish-Christian mixed marriage—in a way that a Muslim-Christian marriage never did, since the Moors accepted Christ—for fair Jimena, as her years increased and her health declined, took, as the fearful will, increasing interest in matters of religion. Despite her warm and continuing friendship with Saadyah, himself, her opposition to her daughter's marriage to his nephew was total. When her shrieks and tears availed her not against Alaric's firm contention that Munia had the right to marry whom she pleased—a contention based, his wife was shrewdly aware, upon his secret conviction that all faiths are at bottom nonsense, and hence hardly matters to disrupt two young people's lives over—Jimena took to her bed with the stated intent to die of her grief and shame.

Poor distraught Munia at once offered to forgo her own happiness; but Alaric, angered by one of the few things in life that truly offended him, the imposition of one person's will upon another by force, was firm.

"When 'tis done, thy mother will get up from her bed, and reconcile herself," he said. "Thy Hasdai is a noble lad, with all his uncle's force, and

413

with far better manners! I like him well. When you bring thy mother home a fair and lusty grandson, you'll see how entirely she'll forget this folly."

"Oh, I hope so, Father!" poor Munia sighed.

But to Alaric's surprise, Jimena did not rise from her bed once the wedding was celebrated. Instead she seemed very like to carry out her threat. In some fear, then, Alaric had the aged physician Solomon ben Ezra brought to his house, though that wise old man had long since retired from active practice.

Within a few days ben Ezra had Jimena much improved, largely by talking to her about religion. Subtly he insisted upon the fact that her Lord Jesu was a Jew, and what's more a good Jew who wished only to reform His ancient faith, not to overthrow it; he showed her Latin translations of the Gospel—which, of course, due to the Church's not at all unwise conviction that the Bible was too dangerous a book to be placed in the hands of laymen, she had never seen—let her read for herself her Lord's words undistorted by the priestly fathers' dogmas. In fact, the wise and good physician came close to anticipating history, by making of Jimena a creature which would not occur to history itself to create for some six hundred more years—a Protestant; but for the fact history chose that moment to intervene.

'Twas Saadyah who brought the news. He descended upon the glass factory with a countenance unusually grave, and a voice that spoke without a single roar.

"Look you, Aizun, I bring terrible news: the Norsemen, Normands, Madjus, call them what you will, have sacked Sevilla. And no mere raid, either. They've come in force. Fifty-four Viking galleys, a host of tow-headed savages—the country is in some danger, methinks—"

Alaric waited.

"I have called a meeting of the leading Jews. So, methinks, should you of Christian notables. No man hath more standing in the community than thou—"

"And having called them, lead them forth to war?" Alaric whispered.

"Aye! We owe al Rahman that much! Where else on earth may Christians and Jews live in peace? Where else is friendship possible between us? We have a stake in this reign, boy! A debt of simple gratitude! The Moors bought half of your churches did not turn you out, neither slaughtered you nor violated your women—except for a few eager Christian goodwives who volunteered their services; but there are always women in every community who rape with astonishing facility! And we

414

Jews were freed from centuries of persecution by their coming. That you, a Goth, and I, a Jew, could break bread together; that my nephew could marry your daughter not only with no opposition on your part but with your active support, and good miracles, Alaric! I want them to continue. I want the Moors to go on ruling in Spain; I want not the land I love—our land, boy, yours and mine!—to revert to its native arrogance, intolerance, savagery. We Jews have not the numbers to rule Spain, Aizun; you Christians, with all due respect to thee, would turn it into a charnel house, reeking with the stench of charred human corpses from end to end in the name of gentle Jesu! So this is a good fight, boy, waged in defense of civilization against barbarity. We must show the Emir that the minority faiths within his reign are worthy of his trust and capable of simple gratitude. What say you, lad?"

"That you're right, Saad. I—I'd hoped to never more lift a sword in anger. But what must be, must be. Much do I fear the effect of this upon Jimena. Her heart is truly weak, Uncle Solly says—"

"Then don't tell her! I'll do your lying for you. You have to absent yourself to inspect a new lead mine near Cadiz, say. You cannot afford to shirk this, Alaric. The Emir holds thee in too high esteem. And under the circumstances, the precarious condition of Jimena's health, your passion for the truth becomes too great a luxury. So leave the lying to me, will you?"

"Aye." Alaric sighed. "Now let us be off—"

On the twenty-fifth day of Safar in the 230th year since the Hegira, as the Muslims reckon time, or Tuesday, November 11th, 844, by later Christian reckoning, three of Abd al Rahman's generals took the field. Abd Allah ibn Kulaib, Abd al Wahid al Iskandari, and Muhammad ibn Rustum held their mixed corps atop the heights of Ajardafe which dominated Sevilla to the east; while on the Plain of Tablada below the volunteers under the command of the chief eunuch Nasr—many of them Christians and Jews, who, though exempt from military service in consideration of a tax, which to that effect they paid, had none the less chosen this means to demonstrate to the Emir their gratitude for the peace and prosperity they enjoyed under the benign and tolerant Moorish rule—charged headlong against the Viking hordes. And in their van rode Saadyah ben Hasdai, who commanded a company of his coreligionists, raised by his efforts and armed and equipped at his expense; and Aizun ibn al Qutiyya, who had combined his own similarly raised and outfitted company of Mozarabs with Saadyah's Jewish volunteers.

Both of them bore themselves with great valor, handling their largely untrained men with intelligence and skill. That their combined company

415

of storekeepers, clerks, copyists, foundrymen, glassworkers, and even students, did not flee the field at the first sight of the gigantic Scandinavians was a tribute to the quality of their leadership. But not even their skill or their valor sufficed to gain the victory. For now Alaric was forty years of age, Saadyah forty-three. They found to their dismay how much the years had robbed them of. Within half an hour, they were both spent, panting, bleeding from the usual sword gashes of battle, holding on only because of stubborn pride. Slowly they and their men gave ground, falling back before the two-handed swords and the battle-axes of the Norsemen. By now their company was sadly reduced, by wounded men sent to the rear, by those who had no stomach for the fight, and had wisely fled; by those who in their country's defense had offered up their lives.

But then, abruptly, the tide of battle turned. From the height on the edge of the plain, ibn Kulaib sent his horsemen plunging down upon the Vikings. The great blond savages fell back under the shattering impact of the Muslim cavalry. The air itself was torn by the neighing of steeds, the shrieks of the dying, the berserk roars of the Vikings. Alaric and Saadyah prudently got their bleeding, reeling, half dead infantry out of there, sent them to the rear, in the correct, but somewhat premature belief the day was won.

"By Esau's hairy hide, I'm spent!" Saadyah growled, as they watched the battle from a little rise. "But methinks we have them now, and our fat-bellied townsmen have done all they could. Not half bad, were they? They'll have a lifetime of glorious lies out of this day. God's eyes, Alaric! Look at that!"

Alaric turned his head in time to see a tall Negro, whose horse had outdistanced his fellows, like him mostly blacks, crash into the Viking ranks. A battle-ax all but decapitated his mount; the Negro crashed to earth, rose up groggily, his helmet gone; and now Alaric saw his tightly curling hair was red. Nor, seen now clearly, was his skin entirely black, but rather a rich mahogany hue. But whatever his color or the marked oddity of his looks, 'twas clear the mulatto warrior was doomed. The Norsemen had him surrounded now, cut off from any possible aid.

"Don't look!" Saadyah said harshly. "Turn away thine eyes!"

"Don't look?" Alaric whispered. "Turn away—?"

"Aye!" Saadyah grated. "I know thee, Aizun! Thou'rt not fit to see a son of thine die, bastard though he be, and half an apish black—"

Alaric was staring at the young mulatto now. As the youth turned his head desperately in search of aid, Alaric saw the flash of eyes like a summer sky set by some malicious mockery of nature in that teak and caoba head.

"Sumayla's?" he croaked.

"And thine!" Saadyah said. "She admitted as much to Afaf—Alaric! Thou fool! Thou tender fool! Thou canst not! God of Isaac, pity me! For now I, too, must die!"

The three of them made a difference even against that press of foes. They held the Norsemen off, cut them down; fought on, even after their mounts too were axed to earth. Alaric leaped before his son, shielded young Prince al Kamil ibn Karim with his target, with his good sword, with his own body. He took within an instant half a score of wounds; but 'twas an ax blade through his helmet that brought him crashing to earth, a flood of frothing red gushing from his nose and mouth.

And then it was that the young prince's own company arrived. They slaughtered the Norsemen, drove them back to the Guadalquivir, set fire to their ships. And behind them like a dark cloud of flesh from which their lance points and their swords made lightnings, the three corps of Muslim horse thundered into the breach. The Vikings broke, fled, re-embarked in what long ships they had left, some twenty-odd out of the original fleet of fifty-four, leaving one thousand dead upon the field, four hundred captives in Moorish hands, whose gory heads would adorn every butcher shop in Sevilla on the morrow.

Which meant nothing to Saadyah ben Hasdai as he knelt there with Alaric's head upon his knees, sobbing aloud great, terrible, hoarse-voiced cries of rage and grief, the tears streaking the blood and dirt on his face with sudden white, as he roared and raged and bellowed.

"For this! For this blubber-lipped swart bastard got with a she-ape! Of all the idiotic ways to die! God! Thou Cruel Monster in whom I don't believe, why? Why not this kinky-haired lump of dung instead of him? This offal of that black whore, Sumayla?"

"Look you, Sahib!" Kamil growled. "Thou'rt my savior in a way, and hence safe from my hand! But take my mother's name out of thy foul mouth, or else—"

"Or else give myself excuse to slaughter thee—black whelp! Look you upon him! Look upon this my friend! Know you who he is that for *thee* is dying?"

Kamil stared at Alaric, at that pure, quiet, singularly peaceful face; at the bright blond hair, dyed crimson now, at the flood of scarlet pouring still from nostrils and from mouth.

"Nay," he whispered, "I know him not. Who is he, my lord?"

"Thy father, fool! Thy father in the flesh, and not that behorned old goat whose name you bear! I tell thee—"

Saadyah stopped, seeing young Kamil's strange blue eyes, seeing them scald, glaze over, melt, disappear. The young Prince dropped, nay crumpled to the ground; then he leaned forward, and kissed that awful bloody face.

"Lord Aizun," he wept, "my lord Father. By the Compassionate, the Wise, the One, now must I die—for never can I face my mother more, having caused *thy* death—"

Saadyah looked at him, pity drowning his rage.

"You knew?" he said.

"Aye," young Kamil said. "I knew."

They watched beside Alaric for upward of an hour. Then the mulatto princeling raised his eyes to Saadyah's face.

"He lives still," he whispered, "and the bleeding hath all but stopped. Mayhap—"

Saadyah leaned forward, pressed his ear to Alaric's chest. The heartbeat was faint, irregular. Still it was a beat. Wild hope tore at him.

"Come," he said gruffly, "help me bear him up, your Highness. But gently, pray! Methinks that if we can bear him without too much jolting into town—"

"Aye, my lord," Kamil said. "Allah will spare him! That I know. The Compassionate will not require of so just a man his life. . . ."

They moved with him carefully over the war-torn field. As they passed a little heap of dead and dying men, one among them stretched out his hand to them.

"My lords!" he gasped in Arabic. "Take me, too! Do not leave me here to die!"

But they moved on, until a sudden tug halted them. Looking down, Saadyah saw the Moor's swart fingers were entwined with Alaric's, a curious interlocking of dark flesh and fair, unlike the usual handclasp.

"Release him, dog!" Saadyah roared. "He is dying and thou—"

"My lords! my Lords!" the soldier groaned. "I clasp him not! 'Tis he who holds me! Who gives me—who gives me—"

"What, soldier?" Prince al Kamil said.

"I—I know not," the soldier whispered. "But something flows between his hand and mine. A—warmth—a tingling—methinks 'tis—"

"What, archer?" Saadyah said, noting his broken bow, his empty quiver.

"Life!" the fallen soldier said.

Then Alaric's fingers opened slowly, let the Moorish archer's hand fall. The man lay there, staring up at him.

"May Allah the Compassionate have mercy upon thee, holy man," he prayed. "For now methinks I can endure till help comes—"

"Which will be soon, soldier!" Prince Kamil said. "I'll send after thee—"

So moved they with Alaric, son of the Goth, from the field. Men who had known him, Christians, Jews, and Muslimn alike, sprang to their aid. A litter was made of lance shafts and long shields as the custom was, and the archers, swordsmen, pike bearers of the infantry took turns in bearing him on their shoulders. And openly and all unashamed, they wept.

Others seeing the weeping volunteers with their still burden passing by, asked who the dying warrior was.

"Aizun ibn al Qutiyya," they were told. "Alaric, the Goth's son; a mighty champion—and a wise and holy man withal. A pity. The world hath need of such as he—"

Thus it was that, when the post rider reached the Alcázar at Córdoba with the news of the great victory at Tablada, though Alaric lingered on betwixt this world and the next, by rumor's facile distortion of the truth his name was included among the notable dead, for scant need there is to say that of common soldiers fallen, no such list was kept. Al Rahman, reading it there, rent his regal garments, and wept. In great alarm the courtiers sent for the Royal Physician; but the Emir waved him off, and cried: "Send for my son al Mundhir! At once!"

Prince al Mundhir came, heard the news, returned with doleful face to his Theodora's side. 'Twas said that the darkly lovely Umm Walad, the Princess Mother, quite literally took leave of her senses. So wild was her grief that her young husband ordered the servants to bind her to her bed lest she do herself fatal harm. But on the morrow she opened, as far as their puffed state would permit, her eyes, looked upon al Mundhir's terror-stricken face, forced through the blood-caked swollen lips she'd bitten through a whisper too faint for the Prince to hear. He leaned close, heard her say again: "Mother—hath—hath she been told?"

"No, O my beloved," al Mundhir said. "We thought it best—considering—"

"Release me!" Theodora said.

"Please, Theo—Please, O Starry Night, I—"

"I'll be good, Mund," Theodora whispered. "I promise. But who else can tell Mama but me? Willst send a note to my sisters, asking them to meet me here?"

"Aye, that I will," al Mundhir said, "and I'll go with thee to thy mother's house—"

"Thou'rt good, Mund. Now thou'st all my love since—since he no—no longer lives! Oh, Mund! Not my father! Not he who—I—I'll stop it now. Call my maids. I must repair my face. If Mama sees me like this, she'll—"

But in the end she was forced to wear a veil, and a Muslim woman's head covering to hide the raw red patches of bald scalp where she'd torn great hanks of her lovely black hair out by the roots. But being the strongest of them all, she took command, scolding and bullying her sisters till at last they ceased to cry. Then all three of them—with their husbands riding somberly beside the covered litters—were borne to Alaric's stately house.

Leaving their husbands in the salon, they tiptoed into the sickroom and stood, stricken mute, beside their mother's bed.

Jimena's green eyes opened, stared from face to face. Finally her pale verdant gaze rested on Theo's veiled countenance and lighted wrathfully.

"Take off that badge of Mahound's shame," she stormed, "and let me see thy face, Theo! Something's wrong! I know there is! Why else would all three of you come at once, who have neglected your poor mother most shamefully? Take it off! You hear me, Theo!"

"Mama—" Theodora whispered. Which was as far as she got. Before Theo could prevent it, her mother put out a trembling hand and clawed away her veil.

"Theo," Jimena said, "he—thy father—by the love he gave thee—yes. Thou'd weep for him like this. Thou loved him more than these witless chits I gave him! Tell me—is he—is he?" But she could not force her lips to shape that word.

Numbly Theodora nodded.

Jimena came up from the bed. Took one blind tottering step before she fell.

"Mother!" Aurea and Munia screamed.

Theo bent above her mother's prostrate form, sprawled across the floor.

"Mother," she whispered; "thou must not. I love thee. Thou'rt ill and—" Then her voice died into a sort of choked-off breath gone strangling, to rise again shrill, penetrant, terrible, knifing through the walls separating them from their three young husbands. Garcia, al Mundhir, and Hasdai burst almost abreast into that room.

They found Theo lying across her mother's body, and weeping awful, dry-eyed sobs that ripped from her throat like the tearing of the very tissues of her flesh. Aurea lay curled up, half swooning in a chair. But little Munia stood erect, and what was in her streaming eyes was pride.

Hasdai put his arms around her.

"My love—my orphaned love," he rumbled in his drum-deep bass, "I am more sorry than I can say or thou'lt believe, knowing how she opposed me. 'Tis a terrible thing! I—"

"Nay, Hasdai!" Munia said. "Not terrible. Wondrous, rather. Behold a woman! Look upon her well! There are not many such. And, sweet husband, good my lord—"

"Aye, Munia?" Hasdai murmured.

Munia's voice lifted, soaring, clear, and proud, so that at the sound of it even Theo's sobs were stilled.

"God grant that should you be the first to go, I, too, so honor thee and love," she said.

Book Three

SAN ALARICO

XXV

Let it be said at once that Aizun ibn al Qutiyya did not die; that due to the titanic efforts of the Royal Physician, Ishaq ibn al Abbas, sent by the Emir himself upon relays of his fastest horses as soon as the news reached Córdoba that the Goth's son lived still, lingering betwixt this world and the next—due mayhap also to the fervent prayers of Ayyub al Rumât, Job the Archer, who appeared at the sickroom, his abdominal wounds which should have surely killed him, healed, he swore, by the dying saint's mere touch on the battlefield—Alaric survived, began perceptibly to recover.

Or did he? Strange that so evident a thing could be so equivocal. For right oft thereafter, all who knew him wondered if the man who rose from that bed of pain, bearing the scars of the holes ibn al Abbas had drilled through his skull to insert the instruments to relieve that terrible fracture, was the same man who'd been placed upon it on that all but fatal day. For Alaric Teudisson had changed. In a hauntingly subtle way, he was not the same man at all.

Despite the physician's boasts—and the archer's—his recovery was painfully slow. All three of his daughters came down to Sevilla to care for him in the rented house Saad had procured for him, though Aurea and Munia were both with child by then. Saadyah returned reluctantly to Córdoba, bowing to painful fact that neither his own business nor Alaric's glassworks would admit of further neglect. With him he bore, almost by force, young Prince Kamil, for so greatly had the mulatto princeling come to love his father that he was prepared to give up his high place in the world, proclaim his own bastardy, renounce the fortune which his late, reputed sire, old Prince Karim, had left him. None of Saadyah's pragmatic arguments could move him, bemused as he was by the apparent saintliness of the wounded man, exalted by the first flush of youth's high idealism, touched by the revelation that the man who'd got him 'twixt unlawful sheets had loved him enough to lay down his own life for his sake. Not until Alaric fixed him with those great sorrowing eyes of his and

425

said: "Thou canst not shame thy mother thus, my son," was the boy persuaded to leave.

The girls had many a whispered conference among themselves, and nightly pillow consultations with their husbands.

"He—he is not *here!*" Theodora wailed. "He sits and smiles at one, but he—his heart, his mind, are a thousand leagues away!"

"And his speech!" Aurea wept. "So—groping. So slow. As though the words come not to him clearly—"

"He's grieving for Mother," Munia said. "Mayhap he blames himself for her death—"

"When I saw Mund and Hasdai, between them, trying to teach him how to walk again, I had to stuff a kerchief in my mouth not to cry out aloud," Theo moaned.

"That goes better now," Munia said. "Hasdai is sure that within a month he'll be able to put away his canes. We've received a long, long letter from Uncle Solly, how to deal with a case like this. He's too old to come himself. He writes that function not totally lost returns with use, that we must force Father, if need be, to exercise all his limbs increasingly every day, though excessive fatigue is to be avoided. 'Twas that which worried me so much at first—this—this apathy of Father's. But now—"

"He *is* trying!" Aurea said. "He does little gymnastics with his hands and feet, even in bed. I've seen him. He *is* trying."

As spring came on, Alaric's efforts to recover his faculties increased apace. He wore himself out with exercises, until by the end of April 845, it was clear he had won. For by that date, five months after he'd been brought to the door of death by the blow of a Norseman's battle-ax, he was able to mount a horse again and ride forth in company of his sons-in-law. His speech, too, became firm, precise, and clear, though it did not regain its former speed. Strangely his voice had deepened; always before it had been a pleasant tenor, sinking at times to a light baritone; but now it darkened, gravened into a bass but little less heavy than Saadyah's. Yet it retained a matchless musicality, to which a certain authority was added, so that a single word of his had the power to halt the rapid give and take of conversation between his daughters and their husbands.

Which increasingly became a necessity—for a new thing was abroad in the Emirate: a growing, sharpening, edging controversy between the different faiths. Among Mundhir, Garcia, and Hasdai, dispute at times became heated.

When Garcia, with that monumental arrogance that was to characterize the holders of his faith throughout all history—especially when they were of his nation and his race—proudly proclaimed that he was of "The One True Faith" Prince al Mundhir exploded.

"True? How preposterous a claim! By Allah, Garcia, I do not comprehend you Christians. Well do I know that you have wise men, sagacious princess, illustrious philosophers among you. Nevertheless you believe that one is three and that three are one; that one of the three is the Father, the other the Son, and the third the Spirit; and that the Father is the Son and is not the Son; that man is God and is not God; that your Messiah has existed from all eternity, and yet was created! What's more, you believe your Creator was scourged, buffeted, crucified, and that for three days the universe was without a ruler! More arrant nonsense than this have I yet to hear!"

"And you, worshiper of Mahound the Adulterer!" Garcia shot back at him. "That camel driver, smelling of animal dung, who gained his fortune by marrying a rich widow old enough to be his mother! Why—"

"Garcia," Hasdai said, "this fashion of disputing is unworthy. You may not agree with the ideas of a philosophy or a faith, but to attack the personality of its founder is unworthy. Whatever might be said of the Prophet Muhammad, be it admitted that he was an enlightened and tolerant man, willing to accept your Lord Jesu, and our patriarchs, as authentic. It seemeth me you might well respect that tolerance which permits you not only to exercise your faith, but even to grow wealthy in the benign clime imposed by our rulers—"

"Who," Garcia spat, "would never have come here if you Christ-killers had not invited them in to save your avaricious hides!"

Hasdai smiled. He had little of his uncle's turbulence of temper.

"Christ-killer?" he said. "But that is impossible, Garcia. How could we have killed a man who never existed? Ye have no proof of him beyond your Gospels, which your Church forbids you to read for fear that you might discover other uncomfortable facts, as that they don't even agree among themselves; while no impartial historian, not even that treacherous swine Flavius Josephus even mentions your Jesu, and Josephus was born in Palestine during the lifetime you assign to your Yeshu'a or shortly thereafter. I think you Christians invented him as a means to an end—say to cover your general incompetence in business, your wrongheadedness in philosophy, and your lack of civilization—"

"Jew dog!" Garcia spat. "Why, I'll—"

"Hold thy tongue, my son," Alaric said quietly. "Harken unto me, all of you. I like not to forbid a subject, for methinks that only through discussion can enlightenment come. But this ugly way of disputing I cannot permit. Men, my sons, slang each other only when their arguments are weak. And since, by the very nature of the subject, all arguments are suspect, this business of religion is best not discussed at all."

They all stared at him.

"Father Alaric," Hasdai said, "men call you holy, say you're a saint, and yet—"

"And yet I sometimes think that theology is the tribute that nonsense pays to sense." Alaric sighed. "Look you, my sons—of all Creation man bears the heaviest burden: the knowledge of his own approaching death. And since he finds—in his mad vanity—the destruction of so perfect a masterpiece as Garcia Sanchez, say, or Mundhir ibn al Rahman, or Hasdai ben Yahvli intolerable, he hath been compelled throughout history to invent gods—"

"Invent!" Garcia roared. "Why, Father Alaric, this—even from you—is a monstrous blasphemy!"

"Aye, that it is," Alaric said, "and I am heartily sorry for it, son Garcia. I envy thee thy stormy faith. I would, if I were able, gladly return to it; become simple as a little child, as He commanded us. But I cannot. I cannot condemn millions of souls to hell because they were so unfortunate as to have been born during all the uncounted ages before He appeared, eight hundred short years ago; nor those who in mountain and jungle and far-off isle hath no opportunity to hear His word. Nor even those who reject it. I know well the dogma: 'Before truth, error hath no rights'; but it seemeth me that arrogance so great is in itself a sin. I know not what truth is, nor, I submit, doth any man. I believe, humbly and from afar, that God—if He exists—might well reveal Himself to various races, nations, men, in various different guises, at widely different times. I have doubted His existence—"

"And yet," Garcia said, "you work wonders!"

"No, son. I work no wonders. Everything in this world hath explanations. In my case I have been able to reach the deranged, the mind-sick, the victims of fancied illnesses—and they suffer as cruelly as doth those whose pangs are real—because I was born with an excess of pity, a surfeit of love. I never have been able to hate for long, not even those who had injured me. I cannot work miracles. Could I do that, the first one I'd perform would be to restore my own lost faith. Betimes I worship Him— or It, the life force behind the universe, the great and icy mind that disregards us totally, holding us, justly, to be unworthy of either heaven or hell, save these paltry ones we create in our own hearts—from afar off, knowing it doth not matter whether I believe or not, except to me. That I am nothing, dust, and that so are all men. Neither their lusts, follies, crimes, obscene cruelties, nor their justice, honor, pity, love, piety, sanc-

428

tity matter a jot in the scale of things. I bear humility in my breast like a wound, a brand, and so I ask ye all three, each according to his several faith: What art thou, that thou holdest thyself worthy of the attentions of a god?"

They looked at him, their young faces troubled now.

"I am going away," he said. "I mean to make a pilgrimage to the Holy Land, to see if I cannot hear once more the voices that spoke to me in my youth, to try to win my way back to the comfort of a faith. On that journey I mean to visit all the holy shrines that lie athwart my path, and pray in each of them, though it be mosque, synagogue, or church; for I hold God not so small as to take into account the puerile and meaningless differences of belief over which men murder one another. What cares He, Mundhir, if I drink wine, which you Muslimn are forbidden; or eat kid seethed in its mother's milk, Hasdai; or enjoy a fine fat roast of a Friday, Garcia?"

"You eat nothing," Garcia muttered. "Hence in this you avoid all sin—"

"I have graver sins upon my soul, my son, than these childish and futile subjects for dispute. Gravest of all, mayhap, is having the skeptic's mind which makes me wonder if, when Muhammad, Moses, and Jesu are brought before God on Judgment Day, He may not turn to the Recording Angel and inquire: 'But just who are they?' "

"Father!" his three sons-in-law chorused.

"Aye. I shock you. Mayhap you need a shock or two. But I'd have of you your solemn oaths that, for my daughters' sakes, for the children who'll bear my blood, and for your own, you'll refrain from such disputes in the future, and split not asunder what hath been united by love. Do you promise this?"

"Aye, Father Alaric, that we do," they said.

With fair May smiling across the land, Alaric rode forth upon his pilgrimage. Before he departed he shocked all Córdoba into speechlessness by dividing the vast fortune his departed Jimena had passed on to him intact from the late ibn Ha'ad, equally among the Metropolitan, the Head Rabbi, and the Grand Vizier for distribution to the poor, the sick, the maimed, the blind, of the three faiths, thereby causing the representatives of each of the three to forget what nominal gratitude they might have felt in their enormous rage at seeing so much go to their hated rivals.

That done, Alaric took his leave of Córdoba. He rode without attendants, without arms; he wore rough and simple pilgrim's garb. Yet to his weeping daughters, as to all else who witnessed his departure, no prince of any realm had ever seemed one half so fair. At forty-one years of age Alaric's face remained unlined, though his blond hair was silvering rapidly. Yet no one would have mistaken him for a youth. Asked to guess his age, most people gave him a year or two more than he actually had. Why this was 'tis hard to say; mayhap the look of brooding sorrow in his eyes, or the subtle circumstance that his beauty had both heightened and deepened, having gained that ageless patina of the spirit—with nearly all sensuality burned out of him—that is beauty's purest manifestation, its very self.

His pilgrimage began just outside the gates, at the Mozarab cemetery, where he knelt before the earliest of his shrines: Zoë's grave, wherein lay his first love, and their unborn son. From thence he moved to Jimena's tomb, where slept the fair companion, mother of his daughters, good and gentle wife, who likewise for his sake had died. Thereafter, his road ran straight to High Castilla, where he stopped to pray at Ataulf's grave, his mother's, his father's—reflecting sadly that a man of forty hath behind him already a host of beloved dead. He found the spot where they lay with some difficulty, for of his father's castle not one stone was left standing; the last Holy War had tumbled it to the ground. In the end, he had to engage his good friend and sometime foe, Abdul, brigand chieftain and fat Turtura's husband, to lead him to their burial place. 'Twas Abdul, upon whom the weight of years was heavy now, who pointed out to him that the fair Ramona slept also beside Count Teudis, thus making matters a trifle awkward when all three awoke in a Christian's paradise. But fat, porcine Hermangildo had by his wits escaped, and had these two years enjoyed the favor of Ramiro I, King of Asturias, now that Alfonso the Chaste had been gathered to his fathers. 'Twas said that Count Teudis' youngest bade fair to become a power in that northern kingdom. So, sorrowfully, Alaric included his father's second wife in his prayers. But one further grave not even Abdul nor fat Turtura—white of hair and benign, surrounded by a swarm of grandchildren—could help him find, for they knew not where it lay: that of poor, lost, damned, pitiful Clothilde.

"I doubt me that she was buried at all," Turtura said. "She died of a hemorrhage, my lord. Julio kicked her in the belly in a drunken rage because she was once more with child by one of the many men who mounted her for coppers—or for naught at all, if she felt so inclined. Losing his balls did nothing to improve that fat swine's temper. So he killed her—without meaning to. Oh, not from jealousy, but because until she should be brought to bed of this one more bastard brat, fine Juli could not longer live upon her earnings as a whore. She had many children by as many fathers, no one of whom she could with any certainty name—

mayhap because she loved children, and scorned to make use of the arts by which harlots protect themselves—"

"And Julio," Alario whispered, "what of him?"

"His sons rose up and slew him for what he'd done," Turtura said, "led by the eldest, who almost surely was his very own. You see, they loved her. Strange—the longer I knew Clothilde, the more I liked her. She was by jinns and demons possessed; but mostly she had bad luck. Could she have remained with *thee*, my lord—"

"Aye, mayhap." Alaric sighed. "But if her sons killed Julio, surely someone must know—"

"Where she is buried? Nay, good my lord—and precisely for that. They were children still, so they became frightened at their own crime. They hid both bodies, Allah the Wise alone knows where, and fled. And since, as I have said, most of them were snot-noses, still wetting their beds of nights, I'd wager that they merely tumbled them into a ravine, or covered them over with brushwood. At best, in their haste, they must have buried the bodies too shallowly, which accounts for the fact that though Abdul's men searched most diligently all they could find was a scattered bone or two—and hereabouts there are many bones. Surely the dogs devoured them. My lord! Thy pardon! I did not mean to make thee weep!"

"No matter," Alaric murmured. "And the sons—where are they now?"

"In Asturias, we've heard, where they've taken service with the king. You'll bide with us a while, my lord? 'Twould be a great honor. It hath been long since you—"

"Nay, good Turtura, I must be on my way," Alaric said.

The first of the great shrines was near at hand. He needed only to make his way northwestward to the province of Galicia, in those days part of the kingdom of Asturias. There he stood in the small and rather mean church Alfonso the Chaste had built as a repository for the bones of St. James the Greater, Son of Zebedee, one of the Twelve Apostles, a man who had seen Our Lord in the very flesh. He listened gravely to the young priest whom he had accosted in the street and who had voluntarily forgone other, perhaps more pressing errands to bring him to the shrine, as that handsome young curate told the story; but all the time his relentlessly logical mind compared it with what he knew of James and John, the Boanerges, "sons of thunder." And, unhappily for him, he knew a great deal; he had read in Greek, Latin, or Arabic, works considered too dangerous for the ear of the faithful, except in selected cullings misquoted and badly interpreted from the pulpit.

"It happened thus, noble pilgrim," the young priest said, his eyes alight with enthusiastic faith "For six years the great Apostle preached in Spain—"

Alaric nodded. Possible. Just barely, but still possible. The Apostles had traveled widely, though not one jot of proof existed that any of them had ever reached lands lying to the westward of Rome.

"Then he returned to Jerusalem, where Herod had him beheaded."

Alaric locked his teeth together before his instinctive protest could escape him. Herod the Great, the last king of that name to rule in Jerusalem, died in 4 B.C. His son Herod Antipas was Tetrarch of Galilee; while his other son, Archelaus, who *was* ruler of Jerusalem, had been disposed of in A.D. 6, when Augustus made Judea a Roman province, under a procurator. Whoever had ordered the execution of St. James, it was most certainly not King Herod. But he did not say that. To expect a priest to know history was asking too much. History was such an untidy affair, affording man scant comfort, nor any support at all to the beautiful fables he desired so ardently to believe.

"How, then, good young Father," he said quietly, "did his bones come hence to Spain?"

"Ah, that is the wondrous part!" the young priest cried. "His followers embalmed his body with loving care, took it aboard ship, and sailed with it to our noble land. They landed at the Roman port of Tria Flavia on the coast of Galicia—"

Alaric thought about that with profound sadness. Was it the *sine qua non* of faith that a man had to be a fool? He enumerated silently in his mind all the damning why's with which one could demolish the really splendid idiocy of this story that had brought millions of pilgrims trooping like the muttonheads they were into Spain. Why should anyone embalm a dead body and row thousands of leagues with it with all the teeming expanse of the Holy Land there before them into which to excavate a simple grave? Why should the Roman procurator surrender the Apostle's body instead of leaving it upon the cross to rot, to be beaked by crows and vultures as a warning to other fanatics as the custom was? He realized suddenly with a pang of apprehension that the same objection applied to the crucifixion of Our Lord; but once entered upon the testing of a thing by the harsh light of truth, one must proceed with it however little one liked the results of that testing. And granted that which he was little prepared to grant—that a band of madmen had brought the saint's body to Spain—why not Greece, Turkey, Egypt, Syria?—why had they selected Galicia as the place to disembark? Nothing in the tradition confined St. James' preaching to Galicia. Nothing—no word declared he had *ever* preached there. All the venerable tradition said was "Spain."

He could hear the young priest's voice like a buzzing in his ears as he recalled the many times he had made quite similar voyages. How vast the sea was! What absolutely murderous labor it cost to win a league or two across the wine-dark depths. And yet this pious young fool—oh, splendid piety, oh, enviable folly!—was capable of believing that men who had toiled by Cyprus, circled Sicily, won past Sardinia, crawled by Corsica, driven on by the Beleares, straining nerve and sinew and human endurance to their limits and beyond, would, having sighted their landfall, their ultimate destination Hispania (again, why Spain?), despite the fact that they'd be almost dead by then of weariness, circumnavigate the whole of the huge land mass of the peninsula to land at an obscure Roman port on the farther, the Atlantic side.

This did not strain credulity; this broke it. Yet Alaric stood there, growing increasingly cold and numb of heart as the curate went on with his tale of how a hermit had seen a star, had heard celestial music, and thus had found the tomb whose location had for these many centuries been by men forgot—not knowing in his piety, his enthusiasm, his faith, that he had lost his audience long since. Alaric had lived too close to the seats of power, knew how well great men employ the fear and superstitions of the lowly. Alfonso el Casto had needed something to counter the Moors' fierce conviction that he who died in battle for the Prophet's sake was issued upon that very instant's span into Paradise; hence this too-fortunate discovery of an improbable tomb in an impossible location; hence this elevation of the mingled bones of executed thieves, or fallen soldiers, or the victims of assassins—who could tell the origins of the skeletons of at least three men, mayhap four, jumbled together in that urn?—into those of Zebedee's son, a man who in all likelihood had never heard of Spain. And Alfonso's successor, young Ramiro, giving to his men the cry, "St. James! Close ranks, Spain!" had proved but his understanding of human nature, by making use of one fanaticism to counter another, and winning thereby the great battle of Clavijo.

So it was that Alaric departed upon his quest, knowing from the outset that it was going to be futile; that the stern integrity of his intellect would not bow, not even to the yearning of his mystic's heart. But stubbornly he continued his journey, made his way across France to Italy, tarrying long in that fair land where there were shrines and saints' bones in God's own plenty; but upon his leaden heart, his head that injury, surgery, life itself had left with the slow torture of an almost constant ache, they had no impact. So he crossed the calf of the boot, took ship, and sailed to Egypt, coming ashore as always at Alexandria.

And also as always, within hours the news of his arrival spread through the town. He was forced to lay hands upon and pray above the heads of hundreds of sufferers. It quickly became intolerable. For, if he was torn by pity for the dying, fly-infested, rotting-while-still-alive human wreckage for whom he could do nothing, he was even more shaken by the cures he was able to perform. His powers had deepened: his grave, sweet voice reached in an instant into troubled minds and hearts. Always he succeeded in casting out devils—he who doubted the existence of devils, other than in human form; and, increasingly, he was able to restore the sight to a certain type of blind man—those who had no visible cataracts or other impediments in their eyes. Were they malingerers? Now, not even he could be sure. And the people in deep, comatose trances—that last woman now, who had at his command got up and walked—even to his own eyes she had seemed truly dead.

So, enwrapped in night, he fled the city, made his way at last to the Holy Land. He dwelt there two long years, wandering from shrine to shrine, teaching himself Hebrew in order to read the ancient manuscripts that shepherds brought him, swearing they had been found in caves. And there, in the end, peace came to him; he realized that he must accept and live with his unbelief. For if here he was shown where the angel had announced to Mary that she would bear God's Son, there he had seen where equally Virgin Het had given birth to the Sun God Ra; if on this spot gentle Jesu had ascended into heaven, upon that one Muhammad had risen into Paradise upon a steed with a woman's face and a dragon's tail. A linguist and a scholar, he knew that everything the Christians of the West believed unique to their faith were Eastern commonplaces; that both Osiris and Horus had risen from the dead; that Osiris, Attis, Dionysius had all died to redeem mankind, and were called Savior, Deliverer, and, in the case of Dionysius, even "Lord"—that every claim made for gentle Jesu by His followers had been made in these God-drunken mystic lands by followers of other Saviors, other Lords whose names were legion.

So when he gazed upon the stable where the Savior of the world had been worshiped by the Wise Men, he wondered unhappily if he were in the right stable, in the correct town, since he was well aware that there had been Bethlehems in both Judea and Galilee; and references to the Magi awoke in him the painful suspicion that some inspired copyist had added it to the ancient manuscripts from the quite historical visit of Tiridates of Parthia come with three magi laden with gifts to worship the Emperor Nero at Rome, proclaiming him the Lord God Mithras.

In the end, he sailed home again, convinced that to discriminate between the nonsense of one or another faith was an impossibility; that all were false, and all were true.

For almost a year after his return to Córdoba, he led a quiet, peaceful, if somewhat lonely life. He attended to his glassworks, giving away all his earnings save alone the little he needed to sustain life in him. He read unceasingly, attended mass, fasted, prayed. And because his doubts, the quiet anguish of his unbelief, were a secret between him and his father-confessor, he rose by his natural piety, his almsgivings, and his blameless life to the position of the leading Catholic layman of the city. The Emir wanted to make him Comes, or Count, of the Christian Community, in which desire he was supported by the overwhelming majority of the Mozarabs themselves, but Alaric begged to be excused from so demanding a position, and convinced al Rahman by showing him the huge white scar that all but bisected his cranium, that mark of an honorable wound got in the Emirate's own defense.

"There are times, my lord," said he, "when this poor head functions plagued ill; and others when I must keep to my bed, it aches me so. Moreover, it hath two holes in it—here and here—each the size of a dirhem, which should I, by misfortune, there be struck the slightest blow, my departure from this life would follow upon that same instant. Methinks, therefore, that the interests of thy Mozarab subjects would be better served by the appointment of a sounder man than I."

"Aye; in this thou hast much right," the Emir sighed, "for well hast thou earned a reposeful life, Aizun. But 'tis a pity. For what with these mad new priests who have come among ye Nazarenes, thy wisdom, tranquillity of spirit, and diplomacy could have served me well. But, *Inshallah*—so be it! I shall have to look about for another."

So it was that Alaric was allowed, so far as he was able, to retire from public life. Which, be it said, was not so very far. Alaric Teudisson, Aizun ibn al Qutiyya, as he was known to one and another of the rapidly dividing communities of Córdoba—as exalted fanatics among the Christians awoke an answering fanaticism in the breast of the Muslimn with whom they'd lived so long in perfect peace—was not such a man as to pass unperceived through life. For one thing, there was his notable piety, which few knew was based on hope rather than faith; for another, his rare, seemingly more than human beauty, his face of angel, saint, unlined even at forty-five, and betraying his maturity only by the brooding sorrow of his luminous blue eyes; for a third, the persistent rumors, brought back by travelers from the East, that he was none other than the San Alarico venerated by all classes in Egypt, in whose name at Alexandria a veritable cult had been formed, complete with disciples professing the power to work wonders by the mere invocation of his name. That these rumors gained no firm credence in Córdoba was due to the fact that too many people had known him as husband and father, knew him now as grandfather. To the religious-minded of his day, sanctity and perfect chastity were inseparable concepts. Goodness they granted him, sanctity no, who had with women in sexual congress lain. And he, all unwittingly, preserved his privacy, his peace, by refraining from wonder-working in Córdoba, out of the wry knowledge that a prophet is forever without honor among his own.

In this semiretirement of his Alaric's sole diversions were an occasional visit to the houses of his daughters—he was far too wise a man to wear his welcome out—receiving their much more frequent visits to his own (especially those of the Umm Walad, the Princess Theodora, who literally worshiped her adoptive father), playing with his ever-increasing swarm of grandchildren, and debating philosophical and religious questions with Saadyah, whose wit had lost none of its corrosive bite.

Now and again, of course, he was summoned to the Emir's court, where he read Abd al Rahman a somber poem or two. But this was all. This, then was the even tenor of his way, resigned, as he was, at forty-five to premature old age, believing all things behind him now—even grief.

But of this last, before spring came whispering through the land, he was to feel one more bitter pang. The Umm Walad Goissuintha, the former Sister Faith, sleeping in her garden on a deceptively benign day, was by an unexpected downpour soaked to the skin; a careless servant, not knowing her mistress there, had bolted the one door leading from al Wallid's palace to the tiny walled private garden that was her mistress's pride. Some time passed before poor Goissuintha's cries were heard; by then capricious March had reverted to winter. When she entered the harem at last, the Princess' very lips were blue. That night she fell into chills and fever; al Wallid, alarmed, summoned the Royal Physician. Ishaq ibn al Abbas, taking into account how greatly al Wallid loved her, and the consequent danger to the continued association of his head and shoulders should one of his own bold and simple remedies fail, applied to her all the Galenic ancient nonsense in the medical books. Poor Goissuintha was cupped and bled until the likelihood is 'twas of the Royal Physician's remedies rather than of her illness that she died.

When the news of her death reached him, Alaric wept and prayed for the repose of the soul he rather hoped she had. Nor was his grief diminished by the fact that he had not seen her since that awful day when fate, his evil star, Satan, or mayhap God, had constrained him to choose Clothilde instead of her or even his own sister to save from their Berber abductors. In Moorish Córdoba, this circumstance, which would have been unbelievable in the capitals of Christendom, was not even strange. The moment that Goissuintha became the wife of a Moorish prince the possibility of any meeting, even by chance, between her and Alaric ceased to exist. And this despite the fact that al Wallid was one of the best friends Alaric had in this world. For Alaric to have suggested it would have ended at once a friendship that he prized; coming from Goissuintha herself the suggestion would have been worse than inconceivable: to a Moor, there was only one reason for a woman to display interest in a man other than a brother or a father—that she was upon adultery bent. So, loving her husband, doting upon her children, the former nun had lived with a circumspection beyond that attributed to Caesar's wife—extending it, in Alaric's case, to never even visiting Gelesvinta, though Alaric's spritely sister was a frequent and welcome visitor to the palace, which mayhap was an indication of something, if no more than a fond memory of what-might-have-been that died aborning. . . .

So with Goissuintha dead, one more link to his past was severed. He felt very lonely now; the more so because his lean and vigorous body, kept unintentionally slim by the frugality of his appetite, well-muscled and erect by the exercises he had fallen into the habit of performing daily lest the torpor due to his head injury return, occasionally reminded him that he was not truly old. His health—save alone for those headaches whose murderous intensity made him at times lies for days on end abed— was surprisingly good; and, as a healthy man, even in his middle years, will, he felt the slow, stubborn stirrings of desire. Which, be it said, he repressed sternly, would have, in fact, gone on repressing forever, had not upon an April day less than a month after the Umm Walad Goissuintha's death, the Prince al Wallid appeared unannounced at his house.

The Prince came without attendants and afoot, clad in mourning garb, his every lineament showing how bitter was his grief for her whose sake he had forgone without a qualm a Muslim prince's perfect right to fill a harem with beauties brought from the four corners of the earth. He hath come doubtless to seek of me comfort, Alaric thought sadly. I who am myself of all comfort bereft.

But he smiled and said: "My house is honored by thy presence, my royal friend—"

"Honored?" al Wallid said. "Nay. Look you, Aizun, you'll pardon me if I dispense with the usual hyperbole of courtesy? I must come immediately to the point. "There is need for both haste and secrecy in this affair—"

Alaric indicated a divan. The Prince sat. He began at once, his voice harsh, strained:

"I speak, of course, of my daughter Natalia," he went on. "I know better than to speak to thee of dowry. To a man who gives away the fortunes you do and is in all quarters proclaimed a saint, 'twould be an insult. But I should like to settle upon her an independent fortune to relieve you from having to give too much thought to her care. Further, if you will, I will designate to what charitable purpose you may name the sums that normally would come to you, even though it be Nazarene—and that, my friend, to a brother of the Commander of the Faithful, involves some risk."

"But—but—" Alaric said, "surely, my lord, you—your words cannot mean what my poor ears seem to hear!"

Al Wallid smiled sadly. "Aye, but they do," he said. "Let me say it then, quickly and baldly. Will you, my friend, do me the honor and favor of taking my daughter, the Princess Natalia, as thy wife?"

Alaric stared at him speechlessly.

"The trouble is, she hath been reared as a Christian. Having given me and Islam two tall sons, Goissuintha insisted that I allow our daughter to follow her way. What is worse, or rather more difficult, is the fact that when my poor angel knew that from her illness she would never arise, she begged me as her dying wish to marry the girl to thee."

Alaric found his voice.

"But—but," he protested, "she is a child! 'Twould be unseemingly for a man my age—"

"Nay, Aizun, Natalia is all of twenty—and many a man of forty-five hath married, quite unashamed, girls younger still. Nor will Córdovian society censure what it sees every day, what is a commonplace here. My daughter is of great piety, which means that thou, whom even the Bishop calls an ornament to the Christian faith, will be most suitable for her. I confess I hesitated at first; but thou art still slim, still fair—fairer, in fact, than any man I know, so I am sure you'll not be unpleasing to her—"

"But she herself," Alaric whispered. "What says she to all this?"

Prince al Wallid smiled. "She objects with a certain violence, which only proves how much she is intrigued," he said. "That is no problem. You know how women are. 'Twas months before my poor Goissuintha would let me touch her hand; but I was patient, and had of her a love that would make all the bright hosts of God chant hosannas in the end. There are difficulties much more serious: the scandal that will break about my poor head once this marriage hath been announced; my brother's wrath— for though he loves thee well, Aizun, as Leader of the Faithful he, too, will be the target of much criticism when the fanatical and vulgar learn that his own niece hath married an infidel."

How arrogant art men about their beliefs! Alaric thought sadly; but aloud he seized upon the point as a perfect means by whose judicious use he might escape this intolerable situation into which Goissuintha's understandable longing to safeguard her daughter's person, and her faith, and

Prince al Wallid's uxorious desire to comply with his beloved wife's dying wish, bade fair to thrust him.

"Aye, there you have much right, my Prince!" he said. "Lesser events hath sent armed rebellion flaming through our streets ere now. 'Twould be both more prudent and the better part of valor to—"

He stopped short before the look of deep hurt in al Wallid's eyes.

"Aizun, old friend," the Prince said, "if thy departed Jimena had prayed thee marry thy daughter to this one or that, wouldst not comply, the risks being what they may?"

Slowly Alaric nodded. "There you have me," he said softly. Then he smiled. "Truth to tell, my Prince—and this I can say, for since I have never seen your daughter, you cannot interpret my words as a reflection upon her person or her charms—I am afraid. I'd resigned myself to the thought of growing old alone. And at our age, old friend, one doth not burn with such ardent heat of blood as not to weigh carefully all that might be said against the institution of marriage, as well as its undeniable delights.

" 'Tis a grave thing you ask of me—on the other hand. On the other, I am both touched and honored by your trust. I know not what to say—"

"Then say nothing, Aizun," al Wallid said. "By asking thee this I have already complied with my poor Goissuintha's dying wish. That she had equal faith in thee doth not change the fact that thou hast made her no promises. I cannot, nor will not, force thee to wed Natalia. But what I do ask of thee is to keep an open mind on the subject."

He stopped short, seemed to be meditating. Then he smiled sadly.

"*Inshallah!*" he said, "so be it! Now both of you and this headstrong child of mine, who, being her mother's image, dearly do I love, hath forced me to a concession inconceivable to any man to Islam born: Ye must meet, unwedded though ye be. 'Tis contrary to all our ways, but then ye are both Nazarenes, which gives me some excuse to waive for the nonce my custody of my daughter, and permit what we have held a grave affront against the modesty of a highborn Moorish maid. Ye must look upon one another—shameful as that seems to me—and then, if this reluctance on both your parts persists, Allah and my dear departed forgive me, for I can do no more. I put it in this wise, Aizun, old friend: if, having gazed upon my daughter's beauty—and Allah witness that 'tis great!—she find favor in thine eyes, thou hast my leave to follow the dangerous and immoral Christian way, in short to woo my daughter, win her consent—"

Alaric grasped at that final straw.

"And if I cannot?" he said.

"Then I will command her to wed you, pointing out 'twas her mother's final wish. But that will not be necessary. I have never known a woman who, meeting thee, did not become at once slightly deranged, my friend. My dear aunt Sumayla, for one—that was a secret kept plagued ill—though while he lived no one dared tell that doting old fool my uncle Karim that. Thy friend Saadyah's wife Afaf—Allah preserve me from such a shrew! And from what my poor spouse told me of thy youth—she had the story of thy sister, though it would seem she witnessed part of it herself—there have been many such. Thou hast a way with women, Aizun. And not because of thy beauty; many women prefer ugly men. Nay, 'tis a quality thou hast—this frightening power of thine to inspire love. That coarse, lecherous ruffian of a brother of mine, Mugira, swears 'tis the root of thy sainthood; that most women wear their faith betwixt their thighs; and that religion and desire in them are one and the same. He may be right. There must be some way of accounting for the success of thy lewd priests who seduce thy women even in the confessional—"

"We do have a few good and devoted priests who keep their vows, your Highness," Alaric said, a little tartly. He was growing tired of all the bickering and slandering of one another that had grown up among the three faiths of late.

"Mayhap, but one never sees them!" al Wallid said. "But no matter. Will you at the least match my sacrifices in this regard, by riding forth into the country south of town? I'll bring along Natalia that you may meet. What say you, my old and gentle friend?"

Alaric hesitated. His life, he was forced to admit, had been dreadfully lonely since Jimena died. And a vision of Goissuintha on the day he'd seen her first, weeping beside Ataulf's wounded, bloody hulk, rose up and filled his mind. Natalia was her mother's image, the Prince had said.

"Aye—God forgive me, but I will," he said with a sigh.

XXVI

For a man of middle years, bent upon avoiding an entanglement with a maid young enough to be his daughter, Alaric dressed himself on that morrow become today with quite contradictory care. Emerging from his bath, he applied clean and subtle scents, then donned the garments of Persian mode designed for him by no less than the *arbiter elegantiae* of al Rahman's court, Ziryab. His baggy trousers were the color of new honey, his long frock coat of green slashed brocade underlaid with gold which showed through the slashes. His tunic, or shirt, was of a watered silk so tawny rich that it took on the hue of cream; the broad sash about his waist of cloth of gold. From a casket he brought forth his jewels, which he had not given away to feed the poor only because he'd wanted to leave his daughters some souvenir of him upon his death; but in the end he put most of them back again, wearing only a pair of golden earrings, and a heavy matching chain upon which a cross was hung. For a headdress, he decided upon a turban of snowy silk—for was he not a theologian of sorts? Then, at the last, he debated with himself upon one final detail: whether to shave off his short, new-sprouted beard, which dated to less than a month agone, or keep it?

Most of his life he had been clean-shaven; but as age came upon him, and his place among those who fancied him their coreligionist grew, he had decided to let his beard grow, as most Mozarabs who resisted being Arabicized did. For, as a general rule, Moors were clean-shaven—with the notable exceptions of judges, theologians, lawyers, and some dignitaries such as the Emir, himself, while the Christian Mozarabs generally wore beards, as did all Jews past their middle years. On both sides—in fact, among the followers of all three faiths—there were those who did not follow the rule, so he was quite free to do as he pleased about the matter. But now, in a curiously indirect way, he took council of his daughters. Remembering their outcries of pure dismay when he'd begun to let his silver and golden whiskers sprout, Alaric shaved off his beard.

Verily on that spring day in 849, as he strode from the house, he was a princely sight, and the very portrait of a man who would acourting go; but his appearance in no wise reflected the state of his feelings. Rather

441

'twas a tribute to the subtlety of his mind. For, if he came to meet the fair Natalia carelessly dressed, al Wallid, who was not a fool, would be quick to read a motive behind that fact and take offense. Nay, far better to ride forth in splendor like a prince, and to use his considerable knowledge of feminine ways to see that Natalia had no change of heart.

True to his decision to outwardy play the role into which he had been thrust, he stopped at a jeweler's on the way, and bought an emerald on a chain, likewise a princely bauble that cost him no mean sum. He reflected sadly that he was tossing away on the gem monies that could have fed twenty poor Cordovian families for a year—to which use, ordinarily, come Christmastide, he would have put the heavy purse the jeweler had of him for this evilly beautiful lump of frozen green fire. The jeweler fitted the necklace into a tooled leather case, remarking at the time that 'twas said this very emerald was the one Lord Nero watched the gladiatorial contests through. And the lions which upon poor Christians fed, Alaric thought, but aloud he said: " 'Twill grace a fairer throat than that mad swine's, jeweler! I bid thee make haste!"

The jeweler finished wrapping the package in silken papers soft as swansdown, bowed twenty times, called Alaric "my lord sage" fifty, all the time staring at his client with a combination of astonishment and curiosity. To which, of course, Alaric paid no attention, so preoccupied was he with his oddly intriguing plight. But he should have. For long before he had returned from his first meeting with Natalia, the story of his purchase, his cryptic remark concerning his intent, and the unusual richness of his dress—he who was noted for the chaste simplicity of his attire—had flown from whispering mouth to receptive ear, in endless series, until by nightfall not only his three daughters, his sister Gelesvinta, and Princess Sumayla, widow of al Karim, had all heard it, but worse still, bored, fretful Afaf, in whose rebellious heart Jimena's death had waked all sorts of enticingly illicit dreams, had too—which involved a chain of consequences like unto a train of Greek fire laid down to burn a city.

But of all this Alaric had no inkling yet, as he rode forth on the latest of the long line of snow-white horses he had owned, called like them all, Jinni, though by now he had difficulty recalling if this were the seventh or the eighth of the strain. He had been advised by a trusted slave of the Prince's what route to follow, so right briskly did he canter along under a sky washed with April's pearly light, until in an olive grove where all the leaves blew silver, he saw two palfreys tied—a lordly barb of purest midnight sheen, and a dainty dappled gray, fit mount for a highborn maid.

At once he drew Jinni up, and sat there, deep in thought. Then quickly he dismounted, let Jinni's bridle trail, to which that intelligent beast had been trained to stand, then proceeded afoot. Mayhap, he thought, 'tis less than honorable of me to come upon them unaware, but in self-defense some little dubious tactics art permitted to a man, or they ought to be. . . . So thinking, he moved as quiet as a ghost until he came abreast of the two horses. And now for the first time he saw her—or rather her doubled-over slender back, shaking with wild sobs.

"No! No!" she wept. "I'll not, Father! Thou canst not wed me to a graybeard! Nor for that matter to a youth! I'd much prefer the cloister's walls to the lecherous brutal animals that most men are!"

"Now child," al Wallid groaned, "my friend Aizun is most fair, and—"

"I care not!" Natalia stormed. "Even if he has the beauty of angels I'll not have him!"

"Then," Alaric said in his grave, musical voice, "it remains but for me to pay my respects to the Lady Natalia and offer her a small token of my esteem, in hopes that it will for the discomfort and sorrow to which I, all unwittingly, have put her, in some small measure make amends."

"Oh!" Natalia gasped, and whirled to face him.

His voice died in his throat. For she was not her mother's image, but Clothilde come back to life. All that vital spark, that leaping fire, that splendid young Norse goddess' beauty was there, except—or mayhap his willful heart read what it would instead of what was—it seemed to him her eyes were kinder. Her hair, he saw now, was a trifle darker than either her mother's or her aunt's had been; in her, the Moorish blood she of al Wallid had, though much diluted by the royal family's constant miscegenation with blond barbarians, had deepened its gold to a tawnier shade; but her rose-on-snow complexion showed no hint of Afric strain.

She stared at him with wide, astonished eyes; and so clearly could he see her astonishment had not the quality of disappointment but rather the reverse, that he ventured to smile at her.

"Willst forgive the graybeard for his presumption, child?" he said.

"Presumption?" she whispered. "Nay, good my lord. For my mother had much right. Lifelong she sang thy praises, until—"

"Until she sickened thee quite of me?" Alaric said.

"Aye!" Natalia said, and a tremulous little laugh broke through her voice. " 'Ah, but he is fair!' she'd say. 'No man is fairer, none more good, more gentle!' To such effect that I once told her if she went on so, Father would have to cut thy throat—"

"Instead methinks I shall have to wed thee to my daughter," al Wallid said. "Come, Aizun, sit you down and partake of our little repast. For thee I have brought wine, since 'tis not against thy faith—"

"Nor against mine, Father!" Natalia said. "And now, I confess, I feel the need of a sip to—to steady this trembling that hath got into my hands. See!" She held them up; quite visibly they shook.

"I note thou hast ceased to weep, daughter mine," al Wallid said a little tartly. "Art thou, then, so easily won?"

That glorious little heart-shaped face went scarlet. Her head came up proudly.

"Methinks I shall never be won by any man, Father," she said, "since the sole representative of thy sex I love is thee! I think that Lord Aizun, being very wise, will not mistake my courtesy for more."

"Nor must you, vain chit," al Wallid snapped, "mistake his for aught else either! I had to drag him forth to this meeting almost by force!"

"Ohhh!" Natalia whispered, and the scarlet left her cheeks, leaving them deadly pale.

Alaric, who knew women all too well, realized how matchlessly skillful was al Wallid's stroke. Face them with indifference when all their barriers against ardor erected art, and watch how swift those barriers tumble down! he thought. He went on smiling at her with gentle sadness.

"And now—and now that you have seen me, my lord Aizun," she said, "art of the same opinion still?"

"Since I'd never looked upon my lady before this hour," Alaric said smoothly, "I scarce could have formed an opinion. My reluctance to come had another cause—"

"Which was?" Natalia whispered.

"The difference in our ages. I have daughters older than you are. And, I confess it, a certain slothful disinclination to change the peaceful tenor of my way—"

Her blue eyes took fire. In anger she became again Clo's very self.

"You need have no fear, my lord!" she said. "But satisfy a woman's curiosity upon one delicate point, the same one which with so much art you evaded before: Now that you have seen me, do you feel the same?"

He went on smiling, said, his voice grave, tender, sad: "Nay. Now I like the idea even less than I did before."

It took her half a minute to force that "why" through her throat's appalled constriction into sound.

"Thou art a child, my lady," Alaric said, "a glorious child—but still, a child. At my age, the blood flows humbled through the tired veins, and the possession of all the quintessence of female charms that thou art means less to me than companionship against my loneliness. What would we talk about, thou who hath never lived, and I who have lived too much? Would not to take the lily stalk of thy form betwixt these hands befouled of myriad sins be not itself a profanation? What could I teach

444

thee that would not sadden thee?—" He halted suddenly, began again in swift Arabic verse, of which he had now all the Moorish fluency and gift for improvisation:

> "The wisdom that I have, if such it be,
> Is ill designed to grace one dear to me;
> For age's sagacity of dust is spun
> Blighting to beauty, humbling to the free—

> "So sadly would I, if I could, from this
> To great honor fly, escape this bliss
> And ask that thou grant thy senile fool
> From youth's renewing lips a parting kiss—"

She stood there staring at him, until her eyes were hidden behind a scald of tears from pure exasperation sprung.

"Then take it!" she said, and despite her father's presence, leaned swiftly forward and kissed his mouth.

'Twas al Wallid's outraged strangled cry that waked her at last to how great her miscalculation was. For instead of the light brushing mockery of a kiss she had intended, her lips on his had gone soft, grown adhesive, melting, sweet, sighing, parting tender; her reason told her she should draw them away, but she could not; gone beyond her will they clung and clung, moving on his, confessing wild wondrous things she did not know she knew, until his hands came up and capped her small face between them like a grail, a chalice, and the great blue brooding sorrow of his eyes was luminous as gently he forced her lips from his, some little space.

She stood there like that, gazing into his eyes.

"Natalia!" her father cried.

"I—I—forgive me, Father," she whispered. "And thou, too, good my lord. I—I meant not to kiss thee thus—"

"Your Highness, for this breech of the proprieties, I humbly crave your pardon," Alaric said.

"You did nothing, Aizun! But this brazen wanton of mine shall this night feel my rod!"

"Good Prince, old friend," Alaric said, "I beg thee constrain thy wrath. Let us partake of thy good wine, break bread together. I'll make so bold as to offer thee a cup, for hath not the Prophet said of the occasional good use of forbidden things: 'Mention the Name of Allah o'er it'?"

Al Wallid laughed shortly.

"Always the perfect courtier, eh, Aizun! Very well. Let us eat—and talk. For now methinks we have only the details to work out. The problem's thorny. In these troubled times my brother's wrath will be surely great—"

"Father!" Natalia said. "That kiss was what he asked of me—a token in farewell! Thou must not think—"

"Oh, be quiet, child!" al Wallid said.

They rode back into Córdoba together, entering the suburb of Munyat al-Agab; thence they crossed the old Roman bridge. Once across the bridge, at the very gates almost of the palace, where they needs must part, they found their way blocked by a dense crowd. The motley rabble were staring at something on the ground. From their high vantage point on horseback, they could see what it was: a poor devil of a starveling boy, some twelve years of age, moaned and foamed at the mouth and bit his own tongue through in the paroxysms of some demonic seizure on the ground.

Pity washed over Alaric in a wave. The boy was so young, so terribly thin. His wild twitching spasms were horrible to see. Now and again he thrashed his arms and legs about, kicked with his feet like a dying ass.

Alaric sat there, trying to contain that pity, his lips moving in silent prayer. Then he felt Natalia's eyes upon him. Turning, he saw the tears in them.

"Poor boy!" she whispered. "Poor lost, starved, mad little thing."

At that, Alaric climbed down from his horse; he laid his two hands on the backs of the stalwart churls who blocked his way; they turned snarling, met those wondrous eyes, touched breast and lip and forehead in sign of respect, fell back and let him through.

In all his princely finery he knelt beside the possessed child on the ground; stretched out his hand and laid it on that grimy, louse-infested head.

Instantly the boy was still. Alaric knelt there beside him, his own face strained and white as that terrible ebbing of strength out of him into the boy's still form took place. He prayed silently for a moment more; then rose up. He stood there looking at the unconscious boy. Then suddenly, terribly, his voice was brazen thunder, as he cried out: "In Lord Jesu's Name I bid thee leave him, Saithan!"

The crowd fell back in terror. The boy opened his eyes.

Alaric smiled at him. "Come, my son," he said in that grave musical marvel of a voice. "Get up from there. Let us go and sup, and after that a bath. What say you, good lad?"

"That God bless thee, Holy Man!" the boy whispered, and climbed to his feet.

The crowd stood there stricken dumb. Then a woman fell to her knees. "Thy blessing, San Alarico!" she said.

"Call me not that, woman," he rebuked her, "for I am not—"

"Who casts out devils is not a saint?" she said. "Then no saint hath ever been! Thy blessing, I pray thee, please!"

"Thou hast it," Alaric whispered. "So have ye all. Now cease to bar my way. This poor child must be—"

"Alaric—" Natalia whispered. "I mean—my lord—I—"

"Aye, sweet Natalia?" he said.

"I, too, would have thy blessing," Natalia said.

The whole of that next day she wrestled with her love, her doubt. That she loved this strange and wondrous man she already knew; but she had been brought up by the most Christian of mothers, and was herself by her very nature devout. She prayed to the Holy Virgin, to Jesu, to the saints for counsel. But when that counsel came her woman's heart rejected it. So she prayed again for humility, for the strength to do what she needs must do.

"Who am I to deprive the world of a saint?" she wept. "Married to me he will be but chained to the flesh, to common carnality, and this— this sacred gift he hath dissipated, lost—" She knelt there, thinking: Mayhap we can together in full chastity dwell. He could. Aye—he could do aught God wills. But I? I who stood there before mine own father's eyes, clinging to Lord Aizun, mouth to mouth, bewildered by my blood? God help me!

She bowed her head, let her tears rain down. "I must give him up! I must!" she moaned.

She got to her feet with sudden desperate strength; took up the case containing the emerald. Right fervently she kissed it. Then she closed it again, veiled herself, snatched up a cloak.

I'll return it to him in person, tell him why! she vowed, and scampered down the hall like the girl child she was still. She need not fear encountering her father; she knew precisely where he was at that moment 'twixt dusk and dark. Prince al Wallid was in the servants' quarters with the boy. Having found by questioning that the mysteriously restored child was to Islam born, the Prince had insisted upon bringing him home, vowing to take him into his household as a page. For the Prince was greatly troubled: What to do with a child of Allah by Christian wonder-working restored?

'Twas easy enough for Natalia to leave her father's house. There were no eunuchs in his household, no guards. And by this hour the Princess' own women were busy about the preparation of the evening meal. Only when 'twould be served some hours from now, would she be missed and the alarum given. Silently Natalia tiptoed forth into the night, making use of a bunch of keys she had purloined from her father's study. Crossing the gardens of the Alcázar, within whose confines, like those of all the Emir's brothers, al Wallid's minor palace lay, was more dangerous. But she had oft, upon a sleepless night, watched the palace guards about their rounds. By timing her swift rushes from shadow to shadow between their receding and approaching footfalls, she gained the gate and freedom. She ran breathlessly through the silent streets. She had no idea where Alaric's house was; but at that early hour of the night there were still passersby about the streets. She went on through the maze of crooked streets, getting lost, asking again, leaving behind her a trail of witnesses who would make the task of her uncle's police laughably easy, she knew, until she found the house. To her disgust, it was but a street or two away from the palace grounds, and she'd wasted an hour finding it. Worse still, by then she was too late.

Afaf was there before her.

Natalia hung there by the door, her hand upraised to knock, but frozen in that very gesture, listening to those terrible words.

"You had of me my virginity, Aizun! And with it, all my heart—forever. And how served you me? Tell me that! By deserting me, that's how. By consorting endlessly with those filthy Toledo whores, at Broad Berta's place, hard by the gate. And, after that, when I'd have forgiven you, taken you back again, you turned to that black she-baboon of a Sumayla! Gave her thy child that she might therewith deceive her lord—"

Alaric murmured something so low that Natalia could not hear what it was.

"Tell her she lies!" she wept within her heart. "Deny these horrible things, my lord! Deny them, I beseech thee, please!"

"I thought you mad—or dead!" Afaf raged. " 'Twas only out of excess of loneliness did I turn to Saadyah! Poor gentle soul, for all his roaring. I've made his life a hell—and that's thy fault, too!"

And now, Natalia had to see her. She did not want to, but she had to. She tried the door. It swung open noiselessly, and at once she saw Afaf standing there facing Alaric. She herself was in plain sight of both of them but neither knew. She hung there, studying that dark, thin, tense and tigerish woman in her fortieth year, or mayhap beyond it: lath-lean, fallen of breast, sinewy of throat, the silver glittering in the blackness of her hair, her eyes deep-ringed, aflame.

"What would you of me, Afaf?" she heard Alaric say, with infinite sadness.

"You ask me that?" the woman laughed. "I'd have you—your immortal soul, Aizun! The occasional loan and sweet use of thy fair body, too. But most of all that you desist from this folly of marrying a mere chit of a girl—who thinks its only use is to make water from it!"

"Oh!" Natalia whispered. "Oh, vile! Thou shalt never have him! Thou shalt not, for I—"

Afaf was raging on. "If you have need of a woman, you have me, Aizun! You've always had. At any time during all these terrible years had you but crooked your little finger, I'd—"

It was too dangerous to remain where she was, Natalia realized now. Aizun had but to lift his eyes to see her standing there. She backed swiftly from that door, went down the stairs, circled the garden path until she came to a window she judged would give upon that room. She was right; it did. Uneasily she turned her head. Yes, she could still see the gate from here, would have time to fly if the Emir's police started to enter in pursuit of her. But Afaf's desert gutturals dragged her gaze back through that window.

"Allah witness that I'd have come to you! But no matter! 'Tis the future we must consider. Whenever you feel the heat and languor of your blood, you have but to send me word, and I'll come to thee, as I've come now!"

"And Saadyah?" Alaric said.

"Will know nothing. He cannot lift his eyes above his ledger books! I could have by now deceived him a thousand times—"

"And thou hast," Alaric said sternly.

"Nay, twice—thrice. No more. You see, my love, there was but one of you; and 'twas that which safeguarded my fidelity. Possessed by another—by ibn Ha'ad's fat, stupid daughter! Oh, I was patient; but I'll wait no more. Enough of this! Come, take me to bed, that I may cool the desire that leads thee to this madness. You'll find no green lovesick girl can match my arts—"

Natalia's fingers on the trellis ached. Her breath had stopped. So had her heart.

"No, Afaf," Alaric said.

"Why not?" the dark woman screamed at him.

"Saadyah is my friend, faithful and just to me. Nor would I make of thee an adulteress."

"Then take me to wife!" Afaf wept. "Within a little month I'll be a widow, say you but the word!"

Again Natalia's breath caught in her throat until he spoke.

"How?" he said.

"No matter! I'll tell thee naught! For you'd only—"

"How, Afaf?" he said. His voice was quiet.

"A—a poison. I had it of the Umm Walad Tarub. The—the Emir's favorite. She wants me to try it first—"

"Why?" Alaric said.

"She'd insure that 'tis her son Abd Allah who succeeds her lord upon the throne, and not that motherless brat Muhammad. She—she had the poison of the new physician al Harrani. She gave me some—to make certain 'tis swift and effective because young Muhammad and the Emir must both die within a single hour for her son to reign. She knows how unhappy I am. And now that your wife is dead, she thought—Aizun! Look not upon me thus! I have not—not yet—"

"Murderess," Alaric whispered. "Harlot and murderess. And to think how many nights I wept for thee! Art vile, Afaf. Damned and vile. Depart my house! For I—"

And 'twas then, at that precise moment, that Natalia heard the heavy footfalls coming on. She turned a face gone white toward the gate. But the big man running toward it was no soldier. He wore the type of clothes that rich merchants usually affected; his big lion-like head, haloed by a wild brush of fiery hair and beard, was bare; and, as he came on, Natalia saw by the street lamps' glow, the blue blaze of the naked sword he had in his hands.

Natalia leaped backward from the window and ran down the garden path toward the rear of the house.

"There must be another door!" she wept. "There must! Lord Jesu help me find it! Holy Mother, help me! For if he dies—for if he dies—no longer can I live!"

There was another door. The servants' entrance. Natalia entered it, and scurried through passages, opening doors, closing them, until she found the chamber that she sought. His bedchamber. From just beyond it she could hear the man's voice thundering in the hall.

"Thus doth thou serve me, Aizun, my friend? This is thy idea of vengeance? Saintly Aizun! With all the town echoing to the news of thy miracle, thou'd cap and crown it with adultery! And thou—my Afaf, sweet Afaf—wife of my bosom! 'Fore God, I'll—"

Natalia heard the explosive sound of a slap, heard the woman moan.

Then Alaric's voice came over, grave and slow: "Nay, Saadyah; this is unworthy of thee. To strike a woman is beneath all the many things thou art—"

"I'll strike thee, villain! Oh, thou saintly churl! I'll have payment for this in thy blood! Thou, who doubt it not, these many years hath horned me!"

"Saad," Alaric said tiredly, "thou art a fool."

"Aye. There thou hast much right, Aizun! I was. For by my troth, I loved thee! Eloheim and Yahveh witnessed how I loved thee! I made of thee a God—an idol of flesh, fount and head of all my idolatry!"

His big voice broke, and Natalia realized with sudden pity that he was crying.

" 'Tis for that sin I pay now, Aizun—brother of my soul! And this night will I end it! For this thing thou must die. Take up thy sword! For by King David, the holy adulterer, I—"

Natalia tore away her veil. Dug fingers in her hair, dragged it loose so that it fell over her shoulders in a shimmering spill of tawny gold. Reached up and ripped her bodice until her two proud breasts were almost bare. Kicked off her sandals. Whirled and tugged the coverlet from the bed, the sheet; wrapped herself in that.

As she pushed open the door she heard Alaric say: "Nay, Saad. Slay me if thou will; but never in life shall I lift a sword against thee, brother. . . ."

"Brother!" Saadyah howled. "Fine brother who—"

His big voice died. He stood there blinking at the vision who knelt before him.

Natalia drew apart the sheet in which she was wrapped, baring her sweet bosom like a sacrificial lamb.

"Me first, my lord," she said gently, "since without him I'd not live—"

"Good God!" Saadyah whispered. "Who art thou, child?"

"Natalia," she said.

"And thou"—thou wast in there—all the time—"

"When this swart madwoman came? Aye, my lord. I told him to send her away; but he is too gentle, and too kind. So I—" she turned, still on her knees, until she was facing Alaric "—had to hear from her lips her version of thy life, sweet my lord! Tell me 'twas not so, I beg of thee! Tell me even if you die, lest my heart burst of too much grief! Oh, Aizun, Aizun, my lord, my life, I am like to die of too great hurt—"

He came to her then, lifted her to her feet, held her weeping in his arms.

"Tell me that she lied!" Natalia wailed.

"Nay, child," Alaric said sadly. "She did not lie. I have done all the things she said, and more—"

Wildly, desperately, Natalia tore free of him.

"God in glory!" Saadyah howled. "Afaf, you randy bitch, recant! Take back every lying word, or by heaven I'll—"

Afaf's cruel eyes faced him. "I spoke the truth, O prince's daughter; and though this gross lout slay me, I'll not recant," she said. "Thou canst not preserve thy innocence of mind forever—and this night, 'tis clear, that of thy body thou hast already lost. Aye, he is a glorious lover, is he not? Come, Saadyah, let us leave the lovers to their bliss; since on this night we both upon a fool's errand hath come—"

"Nay," Saadyah growled, and took Natalia's weeping face between his hands. "Look upon me, child," he said.

She stared up at him, her blue eyes both wide and wet.

"I would have died for him," Saadyah rumbled. "I'd do so still. And so would all who ever hath enjoyed his lightest favor. Toss not away what thou hast because of the idle rantings of a jealous—and aging—female fool. To be close to Aizun is a privilege—for by that very token thou'rt closer to the host of light, to God Himself, than mortals ever are. I'll not deny he hath his sinful side; but even that is derived from his great goodness. Aye, Natalia, they have much right who call him saint! For saints right oft are sinful men who do but bear God's grace in their hearts—"

"And yet," Natalia whispered, "you would have slain him!"

"And followed him in death upon the hour when I had to my senses come. Say I then this. His life before you entered it was his own, to use as well or ill as he saw fit. Mostly he used it well. God witness he hath relieved much misery in this world. But now 'tis thine. And from him, as poor sweet Jimena thy predecessor did, will thou have unswerving fidelity. He hath need of thee, I think—"

"No! No!" Natalia wept. "I but deter him for his way, turn him from his saintly mission with my love. 'Twould be a sin, Lord Saadyah; 'twould be a terrible sin were I with him to wed—"

"Then thou hast not—? Aizun! Saintly sinner! High Priest and Holy Pope of all Fornicators, this thou canst not do! Not this sweetness, this innocence! Nay, brother, this night I'll play the heavy father, if she hath not one—"

"Of a certainty she hath, great churl!" Afaf spat. "She is al Wallid's daughter. The Emir is her uncle!"

"Good God!" Saadyah roared. "Look you, saintly fool, if thou wouldst thy head and shoulders in close association keep, hie thee to the mosque and at once!"

"The church." Alaric smiled. "Natalia, too, is Christian. Wouldst find me a pair of witnesses of our faith, Saadyah? Surely you have enough

Nazarenes so deeply in thy debt that you can even at this hour rouse them out. . . ."

But coming from the church, which Alaric's own waived dowry had built, Natalia was troubled still.

"What if I do but turn you from your holy way, sweet my lord?" she said; "All saints of whom I've ever read were celibate. Aizun, my dear sweet lord, if thou willst, I will with thee as a sister live, so that the uses of flesh impair not thy sanctity. Wouldst have it so?"

He threw back his head and let his laughter beat against the dome of heaven.

"And thou?" he said. "Wouldst also have it so?"

Gravely she shook her head. "Nay, good my lord," she whispered. "Mother hath oft complained that I had of Aunt Clothilde her ardent blood. I fear me 'tis true. Thou'rt my husband now, so I can say it without shame, can I not?"

"Of course, child. Say what thou will—"

She hid her face against his breast. "If—if you do not take me in thy arms when we get home, methinks that I this very night will die!"

But when, in fact, they reached his house they found the whole street a howling uproar. A detachment of the al Khurs, the Emir's special guards, had the house surrounded. All three of Alaric's daughters were there, white and speechless with fear and rage. Their husbands stormed and thundered at the captain of the guards, who shrugged.

"I do but follow orders," he said.

Within half an hour Alaric stood before the Emir. Abd al Rahman's face was lined and angry.

"This of abducting my niece, Aizun," he said, "is a crime equal to treason, and punishable by death. Before I turn thee over to the Kadi I'djama'a I'd have of thee some defense of thy conduct. You have served me well, been wounded nigh unto death in defense of my realm. How, then, wouldst thou explain this madness?"

"My lord," Alaric said, "I cannot. I have no defense—beyond to say that when thy guards arrested us, the lady was already my wife."

The Emir stared at him, blinking his black eyes furiously.

"Wouldst mock me, Aizun?" he thundered. "Wouldst tell me that this night for the sake of my niece thou hast abjured thy Yeshua in whose name I'm told thou hast done miracles?"

"Nay, good my lord, I have not become an apostate to my faith," Alaric said.

"Then thou hast done a fouler thing!" the Emir said. "For if a child of my blood has denied the Prophet for thy sake, thou must witness her execution; for the penalty for such is death. Princess or no, she shall die!"

"My lord!" al Wallid's thin, piping tenor rang out. "Allow me to explain—"

Abd al Rahman listened, his face growing ever darker, his eyes blinking ever faster.

"So," he said at last, "there is no crime! Thy daughter, thou weak and spineless fool, stole thy keys, escaped thy house. Hence she was not abducted. And thou, fond idiot, in defiance of thy sacred duty, not only allowed thy sole wife to remain a Nazarene, but also to rear thy daughter as one! So neither do we have apostasy! In Allah's name, what do we have?"

Natalia's clear, childish soprano rang out, from where she stood between two huge eunuchs set over her as guards.

"My wedding night, which thou'rt spoiling, Uncle," she said.

The Emir opened his mouth; but gone beyond his will, a great gale of laughter burst from it.

"Come here, child," he said.

Natalia came to him.

"Sit on my knees as thou used to when thou wert small," the Emir said.

Natalia sat on her royal uncle's knee; put a slim arm about his neck; reached up and kissed his bearded cheek.

"Please, Uncle, do not be wroth at me," she said.

"Allah deliver us from women!" the Emir said. Then he smiled at her right fondly. "What wouldst have as a dowry, child?" he said.

"A necklace of pearls like the one you gave Shifa," Natalia said, "and a bale of silk, saffron-colored like you bought for Ihtizaz; and golden plates to eat on like those of Mu-ammara; and jewels like Tarub's—"

At mention of Tarub's name, Alaric stiffened; for Afaf's words came back to him.

"And a duplicate of everything you've given to Fakr, and the three Medinese, Fadl, 'Alam, and Kalm. And thou must make my husband Grand Vizier, or at least Comes of the Christians, and—"

"Natalia!" Alaric cried.

"Oh, I am but teasing, sweet my lord! Uncle's used to it. Aren't you, Uncle?"

"Aye," the Emir sighed. "Art as bad as mine own daughters. I am too indulgent, which is why you young gazelles use me ill. I must begin to

454

impose respect among my own. For instance, niece, thou shouldst call me 'my lord Emir,' at least in public!"

"Nay!" Natalia laughed gaily. "I won't! Thou'rt everybody's Emir, but only *my* uncle, Uncle dearest! So give me a kiss and let me go—" she leaned close to his ear; but so clear was her voice that her whisper carried from one end of the salon to the other "—for I mean this night to leave my ancient creaky bones of a husband so worn out that he'll never look upon another!" she said.

When the general laughter died, the Emir turned to Alaric.

"Aizun, thou hast joined my family now," he said. "I bid thee welcome. The 'amma will take it ill that I sanction this marriage; but, under the Prophet's teachings, which bade us respect you Nazarenes as a 'People of the Book,' I cannot forbid it. 'Tis within the law, and entirely legal. Now, before I let thee go, what boon wouldst thou have of me?"

"A word with thee in private, good my lord, nothing more," Alaric said.

"I thank thee for thy warning, Aizun," al Rahman said, "though methinks 'tis but idle vaporing on Tarub's part. She hath not so evil a heart as this. Nonetheless, I'll take thy advice and appoint a royal taster for my dishes. Mayhap I'll have her taste a few herself, the silly trull! Now, Allah go with thee and grant thee many sons!"

"*Ameen* to that, my lord," Alaric said.

XXVII

First in the morning, Alaric came awake to the great blaze of the sun reddening his eyelids. It was late, very late for him to lie abed, he who always arose at dawn's first faint glimmering. He guessed that it must be all of nine o'clock; but he didn't care; he stretched out his long legs in luxurious slothfulness, feeling all his blood moving soft and languid through his veins. He was very tired, and very peaceful. He was also, he was surprised to realize, happy.

So thinking, he turned to his bride. She was sitting up in bed, with her back turned to him. The morning glow came through the garden window and sculptured that back exquisitely; lingering over her lithe, firm young nakedness, the light itself seemed half a caress.

He put out his hand to touch her, to take her in his arms, but halted the gesture in mid-air. For now he saw how her shoulders shook, heard the stifled strangling of her crying.

"Natalia!" he said.

She doubled over until her head was pressed against her knees, and her long hair spilled over the edge of the bed. The sunlight caught in it, and blazed.

He stretched forth his hand again, and let it rest upon her shoulder.

"No!" she shrilled. "Do not touch me! Do not touch me, sweet my lord! Do not thus dishonor thy sainted hand!"

"Child," he said gently, "how have I offended thee?"

She straightened up then, whirled to face him.

"Thou?" she sobbed. "Thou offend me? Never! Even if thou wert to order my death, I should hear thy sentence as a blessing! Nay, Aizun! Nay, good my lord! 'Tis with me the offense lies! I—I never dreamed that I could be so wanton!"

He smiled at her. . . . "Sweet child," he murmured. "Little angel given into my keeping, thou couldst not be wanton if thou tried—"

"Oh!" she whispered, staring at him.

"Didst expect to find love unpleasant?" Alaric said.

"Nay—I—I expected it to hurt. My serving women all said that—that the first time it hurts, terribly. They were—half right. It did hurt at the beginning. But not terribly. . . ."

"I'm sorry, child," Alaric said.

"You mustn't be. I forgot that soon enough! How could one remember a little pain when one is dying and going to heaven, and drowning out all the lauds and flutes and trumpets of the angels with one's demented cries, and coming back again and melting on the inside and bursting and being destroyed and loving one's own destruction so much, so much! Ohhhh! The things I said! I was so happy, Aizun! So very, very happy, until —"

"Until what, child?"

"Until I hadn't the heart to plague you anymore, and let you go to sleep. And even after that I was happy, lying there and staring at your outline in the dark. Only—"

"Only?" Alaric said.

"It came to me that I—that I—Ohhh, Aizun!"

He waited.

"That I'd behaved exactly as that dreadful swart woman said I would! So then I started remembering her and all your other—mistresses—and I was so miserable I wanted to die! 'He'll think I'm no better than the rest,' I thought, 'as lecherous as a she-monkey!' So I decided that in the morning I'd beg your pardon and promise to be more chaste—"

"Heaven forbid!" Alaric said.

"And then it was light, and thou wert still sleeping and I—I bent over thee to wake thee with a kiss and I—I saw—this!"

She put her hand out and let her fingers quiver over that terrible cross cut into his very flesh.

" 'Tis nothing, child," he said. "An accident—which hath no meaning now—"

"No meaning? To bear Our Lord's Cross branded upon thy body, my sainted husband? No wonder thou canst work miracles! When I saw this, thy holy stigma, I knew how great the sin I'd done, how basely I had profaned thee! How far I was beyond God's pardon! Oh, Aizun, sweet my lord, put me from thee! I have not the strength or the will to go myself, but thou must put me by. Thou must!"

"Must I?" he said solemnly, trying to keep the tender amusement from his voice. "What will you do then?"

She looked at him, and her small, heart-shaped face was filled with such utter woe, such complete conviction, that he was suddenly afraid.

"Die," she whispered.

"Natalia—" he said reproachfully.

"Not even in that could I gain merit with thee," she said, "for I should only be number three. The Greek who—who cut her throat, having lost thee. Thy Jimena—my mother told me about that; she had the story of thy sister—who when she was told by error you were dead, simply died in that instant of her grief. Know what I said when I heard that, Aizun?"

"Nay, odd sweet child—"

"I said, 'Oh, nonsense, Mother! People don't die of love, not in these modern times!' You see, I didn't know you then, couldn't understand what Mother was talking about when she kept saying what a wondrous man you were. But they do die of it, Alaric. Methinks I am dying a little now, just to think that I must leave thee—"

He took her small face between his hands. "But you mustn't," he said gently. "In fact, you cannot. Methinks you listened ill when your mother was instructing you in our faith. We are Muslimn, child. And though I respect that faith, and find much in it of good, yet do I fear it takes the institution of marriage much too lightly—as thou'rt doing now—"

"No, sweet my lord, I—"

"Hear me, Natalia!" His voice was suddenly commanding, stern. "You speak of sin; yet now you sin against one of God's own sacraments! And you'd have me join you in that sin. Our Lord said: 'Whom God hath joined together, let no man put asunder.' Last night before the Bishop, you joined me in swearing, ''Till death us do part.' Death, Natalia, not the Head Cadi! Not an idle phrase pronounced three times before the door of the mosque—"

"Ohhh!" she wailed, and hid her eyes behind her hands. But soon she was peeking through her fingers like the child she was. "Art—art wroth with me, Aizun?" she said.

"Very," Alaric said.

At once she started to cry. "I am bad for thee, I am!" she sobbed. "Shall I fetch thee a rod that thou mayest beat me?"

"No," he said gently, "but thou must learn to be a woman—and a wife."

She knelt there looking at him. Then she whispered: "I will do all that my lord commands. What would my lord of me?"

Then he said it, voiced the greatest, most enduring longing of his heart.

"A son, sweet Natalia," he said.

But even as their wedding night had been disturbed, so was their first day of married life. The Emir had seen fit, due to the bitter feeling between the two faiths that of late had risen up, to forbid all news of Alaric's wedding to his niece to be noised abroad, even going so far as to send a politely worded warning to that effect to the bishop, who had married the erring pair. That the royal efforts in this regard were futile need hardly be said; but they did serve to delay confirmation of the wild and fantastic rumors flying like a conflagration through the town.

The Muslimn had it that the Nazarene Holy Man had been jailed for rape, and would be shortly crucified upside down, adding to the story a perfect wealth of brilliantly obscene detail; the Christians that he was being martyred lest the superiority of their faith be demonstrated by his miracles—by then the demon-possessed boy had become a dead virgin whom Alaric had resurrected by dropping a single chaste tear on her forehead; while the Jews cannily kept their mouths shut, lest they get all the worst of a dispute not their own, as usual.

So it was that before midmorning, the Lady Sumayla appeared at Alaric's house, forcing them to arise from bed in haste—for the fair Natalia, after due consideration, had found wifely obedience to her sweet lord much more congenial than the idea of saintly chastity—and dress themselves to receive her.

The Black Princess, now a widow and a woman of respectable age, could go and come as she pleased. Moved by genuine concern for Alaric's safety, she was greatly relieved to find the wild rumors had no foundation. And, unlike Afaf, having entertained no fond and foolish dreams of recapturing the Goth's son for her very own, she was both sweet and kind to Natalia. Too much so. Betimes she managed to stud her conversation with so many references to "My son Kamil," adding the one detail that Natalia did not know—the fact that in an attempt to save Prince al Kamil's life Alaric had received his almost fatal head wound—that the bride was moved to ask: "You have no other children, my lady?"

"Nay, sweet infant!" Sumayla purred. "Just that one. You see, my late husband, Prince al Karim, was very old when he married me, so I was most fortunate to be able to present him with even one. Becoming an Umm Walad cost me some trouble, I can tell you, dear—"

So it was that when she left, sweet Natalia threw a temper tantrum most wondrous to behold.

"You'd have of me a son, my lord?" she screamed. "For what? Do you not have one of my black she-ape of an aunt? And I was eating my heart out because I'd drawn thee back into the world—Oh, Saadyah had it right, thou High Priest and Holy Pope of Fornicators!"

Alaric sat staring at her in purest amazement. Then he said, in an unsmiling pretense of anger: "Go fetch me my rod!"

Natalia subsided at once. "Ohhhh!" she wailed. "Now thou'd beat me, too! Already thou'st ceased to love me!"

"Thee I love," Alaric said. "But not this changeling shrew who hath

459

taken thy place. Had I wanted a termagent in my house, I'd have chosen Afaf. Come here, child—"

She came to him, her face downcast.

He put a finger under her chin, lifted it, kissed her long and tenderly.

"Aizun—" she breathed.

"Yes, sweet Natalia?"

"No one else will visit us today, think you? Oh, I hope not! For—"

"For what, infant?"

"How can I give thee a son, if I have to spend all day in the salon, talking to people?"

But that was precisely what she had to do; and the next time it was even worse: for at high noon all three of Alaric's daughters, accompanied by their husbands, appeared—with Theodora at their head, the banners of a great and terrible wrath flying visibly in her eyes.

Which Prince al Mundhir helped not at all by giving vent to a low and soulful *"Bism Allah!"* when Natalia appeared. At the sound of his voice Aurea and Munia glanced quickly at their husbands, and what they saw in Garcia's and Hasdai's all too appreciative male eyes caused them to close ranks with their dark half-sister.

"Father!" Theodora grated, her voice an exact duplicate of Afaf's own. "What's come over you? For days the wildest rumors have been flying about: You buying jewels of great price; you riding forth attired in robes richer than the Emir's; you being seen with a mere slip of a girl; you—"

"True," Alaric said, "all true. She is but a slip of a girl; but I have pardoned her her youth, and so must you, daughter mine—"

"Ohhh!" Theodora wept. "'Tis as I feared! He's mad! Mund—ride and ask thy august sire, the Emir, to send the Royal Physician! For surely, Father, at your age the blood is humbled and—"

"I am happy you know so much about it, daughter," Alaric said.

"He—he's laughing at me!" Theodora shrilled. "He sits there with his trull—"

Alaric glanced quickly at Natalia, seeing the color drain abruptly from her face until even her lips were white.

"Theo—" he said, and his voice was very deep and quiet.

"Yes, yes, Father: thy trull! For what decent maid would marry a graybeard? Surely she hath been told that your wealth is great and—"

"Silence, woman!" al Mundhir cried. "For by the very Beard, you shame me! Hath never seen innocence? Hath never gazed upon it? Art lucky *I* did not see this little angel first, or by Allah and Lord Saithan both, I'd—"

"But you *did* see me first, Cousin Mundhir," Natalia said. "In fact, we played together as children—though you never could have married me even if you'd wanted to. Our degree of consanguinity is too great, considering that thy father and mine are brothers—"

"Natalia!" al Mundhir shouted. "God is great! The little Natalia! I did not recognize thee—so greatly hast thou changed! And for the better, methinks! Why—"

"So, good wives and ladies all," Hasdai rumbled in his drum-deep bass, "it would appear that the designing creature ye've been slanging all the way over here is a Princess of the Blood! Didst not any of you know your own father well enough to realize he'd be too wise to stoop beneath him?"

Munia and Aurea looked frightened now, but Theodora did not know what fear was.

"I withdraw my hard words and crave your Highness' pardon," she said directly to Natalia. "But you must admit this winter-spring mating is most passing strange. And there is still much about it that wants clarifying. If this *is* a marriage, what was all the uproar about last night? I assure you, I wept nightlong thinking my father in a dungeon, or dead! For surely mine eyes did not deceive me! Those *were* the Emir's own al Khurs who came and dragged you both away last night?"

Natalia stared at her in pure incredulity. Clearly she had never had such liberties taken with her before in all her life. But when she answered she displayed the advantage of an education at the Emir's court.

"My uncle, the Emir, looks upon me almost as a daughter," she said smoothly. "And when my father—who, as you doubtless know by now, is the Prince al Wallid, his youngest brother—found out that I had fled his house, they both leaped to the conclusion that my sweet lord husband had abducted me—"

"And hadn't he?" Garcia said. "*I* would have without a second thought!"

"And I!" Hasdai boomed.

"Men!" Aurea and Munia said.

"No," Natalia said shamelessly. "Quite the reverse: *I* abducted *him!*"

"Now, child," Alaric said.

"Well, I did—almost. Please, husband, sweet my lord—oh, I do love thee, so—give me leave to speak. Thy daughters have some right to an explanation and 'tis meet that I, thy handmaiden and thy slave, should offer it."

"Gracious of you, Natalia," Alaric, "but methinks that by their monumental display of bad manners, they have forfeited whatever rights they may have had to ask of thee anything!"

"Nay, sweet my lord," Natalia said gravely, "for well do I understand it. Had *my* father brought home a new wife as young as I, I fear me I should have clawed out her eyes! Or an old one, for that matter. 'Tis always thus with maids who love their fathers, truly. Even when we marry, methinks we do but seek our sire's dear image—"

"Is *that* why you married me, child?" Alaric said.

"Nay. For thou'rt nothing like my father. My father's short, and thou'rt tall; he's timorous, and thou'rt bold; he's good: but thou'rt a wonder-worker and a saint; he's fair—but thou'rt beautiful!"

"*Bism Allah!*" al Mundhir said.

" 'Twould seem you—you love him truly," Munia said in a startled voice.

"Love him? I worship and adore him!" Natalia said. "I have bitten him all over to see whether 'tis possible to devour him entire; but he's tougher than he looks I can tell you—"

"Natalia!" Alaric said.

"Oh, do allow me to plague them a little longer, dearest!" Natalia laughed. "I do so enjoy it!"

"Very well," Theodora said. "Now that you've had your vengeance, Princess, would you mind telling us just *how* you came to marry my father?"

Natalia looked at Alaric, with a merry and mocking little smile, and began to speak. Before she was half done, Alaric realized he was listening to a masterpiece of the storyteller's art. No single word that his gay and mischievous little sprite said was untrue, but, oh! how she heightened the suspense, achieved all sorts of weird and wonderful effects in the telling!

" . . . So," said she in her soft, sweet voice, "when I reached home I became frightened. It seemed to me that to marry so saintly a man was a mortal sin—which could I do but turn him aside from his holy mission? So while Father was talking to the boy my lord Aizun had cast the devils out of, I slipped from the house and came over here to tell him I couldn't marry him after all—only it did not turn out that way. There—there were some people here. And I'd come in the back door, so when I came out of his bedroom with my hair all loose, they thought—"

"Father Alaric!" Hasdai roared.

"Now don't be wicked, young man!" Natalia said primly. "One of the people was a woman, and she was throwing herself at his head so brazenly that I took my hair loose on purpose to make her think that! So after that, my poor old graybeard, my darling ancient creaky-bones, decided he'd better marry me at once before I caused him more trouble. So he did. So you see, dear Theodora, in a way 'twas I who abducted him, because I compromised him so fearfully that he had to marry me, although he didn't want to. It wasn't my intention to do that, but my poor dear mother always said I was a silly goose; and, oh, I'm so glad I am, for how else could I have caught me a husband so sweet and saintly good and beautiful? Anyhow, when we came back from the church the police were here, because my uncle the Emir was foolish enough to think that my Aizun is one of those dirty old men who go around abducting girls—"

"Instead of," Theodora said with mocking malice, "your being—"

"—a dirty little girl who goes around compromising old men?" Natalia said. "But I don't—not usually, Theo. Just him. Did I tell you how I kissed him in front of Father's very eyes? Poor Father! How outraged he was—"

"But you *were* arrested," Aurea said. "I *saw* the Silent Ones take you and Father away. When Garcia came and told me you'd been released, I was so relieved! I kept him watching in front of the palace half the night, the poor boy! But tell me, your Highness, how did you manage to be freed the same night? Usually when the Silent Ones take a person, 'tis months before he's *seen* again, if he ever is! How on earth—"

"Oh, that was easy!" Natalia said. "I simply talked Uncle out of his wrath. Uncle loves me. I can talk him out of anything. So he turned us loose, and we came back here—"

"And—?" Hasdai, Garcia, and al Mundhir chorused.

Natalia made a face. "By then we were so tired we fell asleep at once," she said. "In fact, we just got up this instant—"

"That, I'll wager!" Garcia said.

But none of them seemed disposed to go; the young men because they had fallen completely under Natalia's vivacious spell; the girls because her artfully artless tale had but heightened their curiosity. Over the noontide meal it occurred to Theo that the religious controversy was the fatal flaw in Natalia's story; for while a Muslim could marry a Christian woman without either contracting party's having to change his faith, a Christian, in order to marry a Moorish maid, had absolutely to convert to Islam. The problem was thorny, and was one of the principal questions that was worsening the relations between the two faiths. Both sides were at fault: the Church would not permit such a marriage unless the maid became a Christian, whereupon the Muslim promptly beheaded her, for in the Emirate the punishment for apostasy against Islam was death. Therefore, a Christian in love with a lissome Moorish lass had either to give her up or renounce his Church, which, having no real power under Moorish domination, could only excommunicate him.

463

"And that, Father would never do!" Theo thought triumphantly. "Now I have her. Let's see this clever little vixen escape from this!" She put the question with dry malice.

Thereupon Natalia smiled at her most sweetly, and replied: "But I am a Christian, dear. I always have been. Didn't you know that?"

"A Christian!" Theo said.

"Aye. My mother won that concession from my father, that I be brought up in her faith. She was one of thy father's oldest, dearest friends, a neighbor of his since his infancy. She was the daughter of a Frankish nobleman long settled in Spain. But due to a great misfortune, she was brought here to Córdoba as a captive. Surely my sweet lord must have told you of the demoiselle Goissuintha?"

"Goissuintha?" Theo said, searching her memory. "The name's familiar but—"

"She was a nun before," Natalia said. "She was called Sor Fidela in her cloister. Only—"

"Say no more!" Theodora exulted. "I remember now! My Aunt Afaf told me—and also about her sister, thy Aunt Clothilde, whom doubtless *you* resemble, dear!"

"My mother always said I did," Natalia said sadly, "especially when she was wroth with me. But I hope I don't, because she was a very wicked woman. Do I, good my lord?"

Alaric smiled at her with tender mockery. "Thou'rt her image, child," he said.

"Oh!" Natalia whispered; and stared at him. At once her eyes filled up, brimmed, began to spill.

"Father Aizun!" all three of his sons-in-law said wrathfully.

"Only physically," Alaric said. "So dry your eyes, my little goose! Besides thy Aunt Clothilde had much in her that was good and more that was generous—"

"That I've heard," Theo said tartly. "She was generous with everybody—"

"Thy Aunt Afaf's word bares scant resemblance to the prayer book," Alaric said. "I think that poor Clothilde was an authentic example of demonic possession. No one I've known could be sweeter, gayer, finer one day, and more—"

"Vile?" Theo suggested.

"I would say—demented," Alaric whispered, "the next. Would God I could have helped her!"

"Why didn't you, Father Aizun?" Garcia said. "Why did you not just bid her demons leave her?"

Alaric smiled at the earnest youth. "Because a prophet is forever without honor in his own country," he said, "and no man is a hero to his wife. Besides, son Garcia, I have no power to cast out devils. I have no powers at all, save that in a way I do not understand, my voice has a quality that strikes through to the troubled, the demented, hidden-like-beast things in the thicket of their fears. I have failed as often as I have succeeded, and I am most loath to attempt it, because it drains all strength from me, and leaves me spent. Moreover, it causes people to come to me with illnesses for which there is no hope at all: leprosy, canker, blindness—"

"Be that as it may, Father Aizun," Garcia said, "since yesterday your fame as a healer hath spread abroad throughout the town. In which regard, two of my dearest friends have asked to meet you. Have I thy leave to present to you the young Father Eulogius? Never have I heard our Faith defended with such fire! And I should like also to bring along my good friend Alvaro—"

"That renegade!" Hasdai snapped.

"Oh, I know his family is Jewish, Hasdai," Garcia said, "but because he had the wisdom to choose the True Faith, you have no need to slang him! Why—"

"My sons," Natalia said, her voice crisp, commanding, all traces of its habitual childishness—which Alaric was already beginning to suspect pure theater—gone. That phrase on her lips halted them at once. "Well, you *are* my sons now," she said firmly, "and therefore you must obey me who am thy mother. Or at least thy mother-in-law, which is even more imposing and terrible. I have lived all my life in a house of mixed religion—my father and my brothers Muslimn, and my mother and I Nazarenes. Therefore I tell you all I am heartily sick of this endless debate. Since to prove the rightness or the wrongness of either side we all needs must die and go to heaven, and see whether the Christian and Jewish God, or the Muslim Allah sits upon the celestial throne, or if they are not all the same God, which is what I think, this quarrel is bootless. So stop it! I command you!"

The sight of that sweet, girlish face set in lines of stern command was so irresistibly comic that they all laughed, and good humor was restored. But Garcia persisted, politely, with his request.

"Oh, bring whom you will, Garcia!" Alaric said. "I am always happy to talk with religious men, whatever their beliefs—"

"Father," Munia said, "tell us about that boy Nat—the Princess—spoke of. Oh, we heard the most fantastic things! That you raised a virgin from the dead, and—"

"No, daughter," Natalia said. "That wasn't here. That was in Alexandria, wasn't it, my sweet saintly lord?"

Alaric stared at her. "Who on earth—?" he began.

"—told me about Alexandria? Mama, poor thing. She had it of thy sister Gelesvinta, who had if of thy—thy—Oh, Aizun, how it hurts to say that word of another!—but no matter—of thy wife, the Lady Jimena, who, I take it, was the mother of all these great strapping daughters I have inherited. Mama said you never spoke about it, but she said that big man who was here last night—the merchant?—could confirm it, because he hath business in Egypt. And—"

"I should greatly appreciate it if ye all would let this subject drop," Alaric said tiredly.

"Oh no, sweet husband! Since I have the responsibility and the fearful burden of being married to a saint, *I want* the world to know it. Thou canst and doth do miracles! Take the day I met thee. There I was, dead set against thee, crying and screaming at Father and swearing I'd die first before marrying a graybeard! Then you spoke to me—and 'twas finished. Before I even turned my head to see thy face 'twas finished. I could *feel* thy voice, my lord, inside me, spreading out along all my veins like grave, sweet music—melting me, making my heart leap up and float away like a leaf, a cloud—"

"That miracle's common enough, Natalia," Theodora said. "You merely fell in love—"

"No, no! Not merely! Not even merely. Nothing about him is *merely,* Theo. Can't you see that? Then I turned and saw him—not old, not young—but oh, so fair! So—so beautiful—not as men are beautiful but as angels are! He said some commonplace or courtesy, and I could not make out his words for the music of his voice. By then the miracle was done. From hating the idea of marrying a man my father's age, I had turned in a thrice to being terrified at the thought he mayhap did not want me. And it turned out I was right. He didn't. He'd only come along to please Father—"

"Natalia, please!" Alaric said.

"But 'tis true, my lord! Before three minutes were out I'd kissed him on the mouth like a wanton! I, who'd never kissed a man before save my father, my brothers, and my uncle the Emir. Not even you, Mundhir— though you tried to often enough! And never ever them on the mouth. Ah, God, but that kiss was sweet!"

"My love," Alaric said in his grave voice, filled with its freight of amused tenderness, "methinks you mistake the very nature of miracles—"

"Mayhap. Though that thou canst love me is the greatest miracle of all. But no matter. In Alexandria, thou looked upon a blasphemer and a thief, and from the terror of thy gaze he died. Thou struck a profane churl dumb, then out of pity restored his voice. Thou cast out devils from a girl named Hypatia. Thou forced a courtesan—a harlot, to say it out—to so repent of her sins that she is today Mother Superior of a convent under the Grecian rite. Thou raised a little girl from the dead. Thou cured hundreds of people there. And even before that, a woman called Sancha, likewise of ill repute saw—Ohhhh, Aizun! Now I know what it was!"

They were all staring at her now in utter fascination; at the bitter, hopeless way she cried.

"Child—" Alaric said tenderly.

She looked up at him, her blue eyes streaming. "Forgive me, my lord," she whispered brokenly. " 'Tis a weakness, I know; but whenever I think of another woman's having known thee, touched thee—something in me dies. Methinks it is—my heart—"

"Infant," he said, "I have never loved another as I love thee. The hour I saw thee something young and new and splendid came into the world. So cease to grieve for shadows, or to accept these misinterpreted, twisted tales as evidences that I am a saint—"

She sprang to her feet then, her motion unutterably graceful; came to him; put her small hand into the neckband of his tunic; stood there staring into his eyes.

"Thou'rt not a saint, my lord?" she whispered. "Then how doth thou account for—this!"

With one wild pull she ripped his tunic to the waist. They all saw it then: the great white double scar, making a rarely perfect cross carved into his living flesh. Against the pale suntanned hue of his skin, it glowed.

What broke the breath-halted silence was the heavy thump of Garcia's knees as they struck the floor. He knelt before his father-in-law, his dark eyes aflame with faith, with devotion.

"Thy blessing, good my lord!" he said.

In half a heartbeat all three of the girls were kneeling beside him, while Natalia beamed upon them with maternal pride. Then she, too, sank down beside them. Al Mundhir and Hasdai looked on uneasily, even their stoutly held faiths a little shaken by this sight.

Alaric looked upon them kneeling there, and wept. Because he knew. Now very perfectly he knew that his end was upon him, that the long flight from inevitable destiny that his life had been was over. It might extend a year or two longer, but upon a day not far off his own Golgotha, his private Calvary, would find him.

And now once more, at long last, he heard that soft, matchlessly tender, mayhap self-induced, autosuggested voice whispering: "Alaric, My son, My son—"

Then Gelesvinta's voice cut through irritably: "Alaric, where are you! 'Fore God, brother, you drive a person out of her mind! Working miracles and abducting baby girls and—"

Her voice died abruptly as she saw his face, saw what glowed upon it now, saw that perfect image of sanctity, of sainthood; saw the great droplets bejeweling his cheeks, which—mayhap because the sunlight passed through a crystal flask filled with wine before striking them—were red. Then her gaze drifted down to his ripped tunic to that white—horror? glory?—tortured into his very flesh.

"My God!" she whispered, and got clumsily and creakily to her age-stiffened knees.

"Bless me, too, brother—and take from me my sins!" she said.

XXVIII

There was no peace. There would never be peace again. Alaric was sure of that.

"Oh, no!" Natalia wept. "Oh, how can Uncle be so cruel?"

Alaric looked away from her to where the al Khurs, the Silent Ones, were beating the mob of cripples, blind men, spastics, people so ill they had been borne there on stretchers, from before his door. He did not know how the Emir had come to be advised of their presence; but certain 'twas that Abd al Rahman II had known of that strange and pitiful gathering even before he had; for when a servant had knocked on his bedroom door to tell him of the crowd of miserables before the house, howling and weeping and imploring his blessing, the al Khurs were already upon them.

He let his hand rest for a moment longer on Natalia's shoulder; then he gave that fair, soft roundness a little squeeze and started through the door.

"Aizun, no!" she screamed. "Thou must not! Oh, Gentle Jesu, he'll be killed!"

She came out of the door behind him; but he turned to her, smiling.

"Go back into the house, child," he said quietly. "No evil will befall me this day. You have my word."

Then he turned and walked out into the street, where the Silent Ones were beating that crowd of scarecrows who twitched and jerked and howled under the blows and wept great tears—some of them from glazed and sightless eyes—but stubbornly would not move from before the house.

"Little Sancho," Alaric said to the captain of the Silent Ones, who was the son of Sancho the Frank, head guard of the palace gate, and therefore was known throughout Córdoba as "Little Sancho" to distinguish him from his father, though in sober truth he was even bigger than his father was. "Must follow orders so explicitly?"

Sancho turned a hot red face to his questioner, and now Alaric saw that there were tears in his little blue eyes.

"I like this not at all, good my lord," he said. "Thou knowest I am a Christian like Big Sancho, my father. It sickens me to my tripes to beat these poor hopeless fools. But, good my lord Aizun, they refuse to budge! So what can I do? Disobey the Emir's orders? Thou seeth perfectly well that I have but one head, which is joined to my shoulders by but one neck, so—"

"So suppose you let me carry out your orders for you, Little Sancho," Alaric said. "If you will command your men to cease beating them, I will see that they disperse. They will obey me."

At once Sancho lifted his hands and made a gesture. This was necessary because the Emirs did all in their power to prevent the al Khurs from learning either Arabic or Romance, and become thus accessible to the public who might divide their loyalties. Many of the al Khurs were Negroes; the rest were Bulgars, Tartars, Slavs. Only their officers were Franks, because the Frankish variety of Romance was, with some difficulty, still comprehensible to the populace. But no al Khur whatsoever was ever an Arab, a Berber, a Muladi, or a Mozarab. Dependent totally upon the Emir, who paid them well, supplied them with not too bad slave girls for their beds, and all the good coarse food they could eat, these foreign mercenaries could be depended upon absolutely to put down the all too frequent popular revolts with murderous thoroughness. 'Twas this occasional use of sign language by their officers to overcome the difficulty of speech that had given rise to the popular belief that they were mutes.

At Sancho's sign, they all ceased to beat Alaric's suppliants, stood back and watched what happened next with grave, uncomprehending eyes.

"My children! Gather about me!" Alaric called. "Thus! But leave me some little space to breathe. I have not yet learned to live without air—"

The gibbering, jerking, tottering, groping, and unmoving hulks debased almost out of humanity by their sufferings, drew back, or were drawn, in the case of some of the paralytics, by their friends.

Slowly Alaric knelt before them in the street.

"Those of ye who can," he said, "kneel and pray with me. Those who cannot, follow the prayer, if only by moving your lips—"

Again, unquestioningly, they obeyed him.

"My Father God," he began; then he paused, for three young men came swiftly around the corner of the street. One of them was dressed in the cassock of a priest; but the other two wore rich clothes of the sort usually worn by Jews or Christians. When they were close enough he recognized one of them. His son-in-law Garcia Sanchez. With, he thought wryly, Alvaro, the ex-Jew; and the fiery priest—Eulogius.

They stopped short, their eyes opening wide in wonder. Garcia and young Alvaro, who was a handsome lad indeed, stopped where they were,

470

folded their hands together reverently, and knelt down. But young Father Eulogius came on, pushing his way without ceremony through that stinking mob of diseased and broken human wreckage until he reached Alaric's side. He stood there a moment, staring at Alaric with hot and fierce little black eyes which seemed to have coals of fire in their depths. Then, with an apparent humility that was but the sinful reverse of teeming pride, he knelt down beside Alaric.

"Please continue, good my lord!" he said.

This one hath—or is—a devil, Alaric thought. Then with furious concentration he dismissed him from his mind.

"My Father," he prayed, "behold Thy suffering children! Whether their pains are punishment for sin, I wot not, nor is it meet of me to say. Thou'rt just, well know I that, my Lord; but just this once for Thy Sweet Lady Mother's sake, willst temper justice with mercy? I ask not their deserts, nor mine, for what man is there who meriteth not death and hell?"

He heard Eulogius' fervent "Amen!" to that phrase, and it angered him.

"I ask thy mercy, Lord Jesu—thy infinite compassion. Thou who scorned not the Magdalene nor the woman at the well, nor she who dried thy sweet feet with her own sinful hair, nor Lazarus, the publican, nor even the Roman centurian who came in faith to ask of thee a boon. Thou who loved sinners above the whited sepulchers, the hypocrites, the vainly pious—"

"Amen!" Eulogious said again.

"—I beg Thee lift the darkness from the eyes of those who—"

And then, before he could finish that phrase, a voice screamed out terribly: "I see! I see! I see!"

Alaric knelt there shivering a little, feeling the weakness in him unto death. From all that crowd a wave, a current, a desperate need was clawing into him, dragging forth his life, draining the vitality out of him, as though it were blood instead of sweat that oozed from his every pore.

He did not lift his gaze to seek out the man who claimed to have recovered sight, for with sick conviction he knew what he would see: one of the sightless who have no visible damage or veiling to pupils or iris; and who—he knew, he knew!—refuse sight because of some horror too great by their—thenceforth insulted, outraged, denied—eyes, in defenseless childhood seen.

We have many ways to flee life, he thought bitterly; not all of them so obvious as self-murder. The cloister: to make a god of joy-hating chastity in the Name of Him who celebrated the marriage of Cana with divinely created wine. To close our eyes to it, as these self-willed blind men do. Or to blink it away as doth the Emir ever since the Day of the Pit, or to wallow in drunkenness and lechery as doth the majority of mankind. But dark and obscure are the roads down which have fled all those whom I have the power to cure! O God, may I not ever help a sufferer whose hurts are real? Must I deal forever with these poor fools by their own sick spirits maimed?

He heard Eulogious stir, rise up. Some moments later, he heard the young priest's voice say triumphantly: "Kneel here beside us, my son!"

Then Alaric caught full in his nostrils the beggar's stench. He turned his head from it, and his eyes fell upon the face of a young woman who lay on a stretcher just before him where her bearers—her brothers, surely, from their looks—had upon that instant swiftly placed her. She was a lovely, piteous child, about his Natalia's age. There was absolutely no resemblance, of course; the paralyzed girl was of Hispano-Roman stock with some Moorish, mayhap even Negro, strain. Her skin was very white, but her black hair curled too crisply and her features had a hint of Afric bluntness. But what held him were her soft doe-eyes, so enormous as to almost eclipse her face. They stared at him with what was less hope than—love, less faith than melting tenderness.

"Thy blessing, sweet my lord!" she said.

That phrase, which was Natalia's own:—"Sweet my lord!"—stung his eyes, tore his heart.

"Only my blessing?" he said harshly. "And not that I make thee walk?"

"Nay, sweet my lord," she whispered. "To have seen thee is enough. I shall go happy to my grave, having held converse with the Morning Star—with one of the hosts of light. Thy blessing will illuminate my days till God sees fit to end my misery. So, if thou wilt—"

"Thou hast it!" he said tiredly. And now he could feel that murderous ache begin inside his skull; the legion of fiends with crowbar and ax and pinchers go to work under the two gaping holes Ishaq ibn al Abbas had left in his head; a lake of fire flow out under the scar the Norse battle-ax had cleft in his cranium. He had had these headaches before, but never so murderously bad as this. Still he concentrated fiercely, gathering inward blood and breath and pity like unto a blade, and that ache that was killing him and all his will, against his doubt, against his knowledge that this thing was utterly impossible, and screamed at her, his voice rising, soaring, brazen and awful, breaking above the sea of bowed, terrified heads like a whip crack, like the crash of doom, like, finally, a piteous and pitiful sob: "I bid thee rise and walk!"

The frail girl stared at him. Then she put down her hands and pushed. Came up to her knees. To her feet. The silence before his house was very death. She took a tottering step, another. No one spoke. No one breathed. Silently, like a sleepwalker, like a temple dancer, she tottered and limped and stumbled and gathered certitude and speed and walked and paraded up and down before them, and still they watched her unbreathing, until Natalia's clear soprano lifted: "Forgive me, O God, for my unpardonable sin! He is not mine, but thine! He—"

And then the whole street erupted into sound, human voices gone beyond humanity into exultation, exaltation, madness. The sound was inside his skull and it was killing him. And Sancho, captain of the guards, was kneeling at his feet and kissing and slobbering at his hands, and crying like a giant child, and all the mob with one frenzied howl was upon him, tearing at his clothing, knocking Eulogius down in the process and trampling upon him, and Sancho, recovering his wits a little, trying to protect both Alaric and the fallen priest, and Garcia and Alvaro fighting their way to his side, and he, his knees loosening, giving, his face covered with the spittle of a thousand ferocious kisses, his fair body all but naked now, so naked that some one of them saw at last—among all the dull white marks of old sword wounds upon his shoulders and his arms, but away from them all, clear and centered above his heart—that white cross sculptured in ridged scar tissue like a bas relief in his very flesh, and screamed out: "Look! God's Holy Cross! Upon him! See it! Look!"

And those who had been fighting like savage dogs a moment before for a bit of his clothing, a hair torn from his head, were still. One by one they knelt down, while Alvaro and Garcia and Sancho and the battered, bleeding Eulogius lifted his unconscious form and bore him into the house.

When he came back again it was night and four tall candles flickered at his head and feet. The priest Eulogius knelt beside his bed and tormented deaf heaven with a continuous drone of Latin prayers. From the salon came a babble of mingled male and female voices, and the sound of terrible weeping. Alaric lifted his head. It still ached dully, but the pain was receding, was bearable now.

"Natalia?" he said.

Eulogius got up from his knees.

"How art thou, my saintly son?" he said, his hot little eyes boring into Alaric's face.

Alaric felt anger stir in him; but he contained it. He was utterly drained; totally spent.

"Thou," he whispered, "who have half my years—still call me son?"

"I am thy Father in the Spirit," the young priest said proudly, "and thou must heed my counsels. The opportunity we have now is priceless! And most humbly do I thank God for having given thee into my hands—"

Alaric stared at him. "Into—thy—hands?" he whispered.

"Aye, saintly son! Long have I prayed for this vindication of The One True Faith! Outnumbered, surrounded, corrupted, seduced by Mahound's subtle wiles, we children of God long hath had need of such proofs of our rightness as thou hast given! Thy miracles I can toss into that blinking fiend al Rahman's very teeth! With thee to inspire them, I can raise such a crop of martyrs as to drown all these Moorish dogs in blood. In never-ending files will we bow our necks before the ax, accept the beasts, the tortures, the cross itself—"

Alaric's gaze was a blue flame flickering over his face. "Thou—thou'rt mad!" he said.

Eulogius smiled.

"Mayhap," he said, "but 'tis a holy madness. And by its fires I shall burn up this false faith, destroy this evil world!"

Alaric turned away from him. For this I suffered, he thought, for this I nearly died! So that the monster of monstrously perverted piety can—

He turned back again. "Natalia," he said. "Send her to me!"

Again the young priest smiled. When he spoke it was in the patient tone of one who tries to explain a grown-up matter to a child.

"Nay," he said, "I have forbidden her thy presence—"

Alaric was strangling. The rage in him was death and hell. "Thou," he whispered, "thou hast forbidden—my wife—"

"Not thy wife," Eulogius corrected him kindly, "thy sister in Christ Jesu. I have the question of an annulment up before my lord Bishop now. 'Tis certain he will grant it—though the problem of upon what grounds is knotty. Our Sister in Jesu Natalia, hath already agreed to take the veil. For 'tis not meet for one of God's saints to live in carnal congress with a woman, however pious—"

"God's death!" Alaric's voice shook the windows with a roar like unto that of a wounded lion. "Get thee hence! Remove this holy madman from my sight, or by heaven and hell I'll rend him limb from limb!"

They came pouring into the room. Garcia, Alvaro, Theodora, Aurea, Munia, Gelesvinta. Alaric noted at once that neither Hasdai nor al Mundhir nor his brother-in-law Husayn was present. He wondered whether the mad priest had forbidden all non-Christians his house. That the fanatical young fool was capable of it, he was already sure.

Then Saadyah came through the door leading Natalia by the hand.

"I pray thee, Aizun," he boomed, "that thou grant me the pleasure! This raven from the caves of ignorance this very evening tried to bar thy door to me! So let me have him! First I'll whack off the balls he hath no

474

use for, and cram them down his gullet. Nay, better still—I'll lead him to Eulalia's house of joy and have the girls take turns at him. Ho, little priest! What sayeth thou to martyrdom through a fine excess of fornication?"

"Now, listen Jew!" Alvaro flared.

"Aye," Saadyah rumbled. "I am a Jew. My member hath been shortened piously. But thine, oh, pretty youth, what of thine? Let's have it out for inspection. Oh, have no fear, all the good wives here hath been deflowered with the holy consent of rabbis, bishops, imams, and other practices of abysmal irrationality. So the sight of thy tiny toad-sticker cannot offend them. Doth thou so love pig grease, lad? Or is it our prohibition against sodomy that offends thee?"

"Saadyah, please!" Natalia wept.

"Nay, good chit, I am not pleased! Especially am I wroth with thee who would sin against nature at the first mouthings of this fool. Wouldst hide these cunning little bulges, that delicious little jiggle thou hast when thou walkest, these long sweet thighs and that little treasure 'twixt them in a cloister with only graybeards in cassocks to fumble at it—and wrong end to, at that, I'm told?"

Eulogious lifted up his crucifix.

"Fly, Satanas!" he barked. "By the True Cross, I exorcise thee!"

Saadyah stared at him with pure incredulity. Then he threw back his great head and roared. His laughter beat about their heads like a gale, like a wild, deep hurricane blowing up from the south.

Bringing sweet reason with it, Alaric thought. For now he could see the twinkle in Gele's eye; Theodora openly and irreverently had started to grin; and though Aurea and Munia were pale and frightened still, even the corners of Natalia's sweet lips had begun to twitch.

Alvaro caught Eulogius by the arm. "Come with me, my Father!" he flared. "Let us leave this evil presence! Tomorrow we can return and—"

Tomorrow, Alaric vowed, 'twill be too late!

But still one more act in the tragicomedy—for at that date, in the spring of 849, the relationship between Christian and Muslim had not yet taken its ever steepening, sliding, accelerating swoop toward the edge of the precipice over which, before another year was out, it would plunge—had that selfsame night to be played out. Saddyah lingered, sitting by Alaric's bed, roaring at him, making his poor head ache.

"But how do you know the wench couldn't walk before, or that the ragged swine of a mendicant couldn't see? Three quarters of the lame, halt, and blind leeches that infest our streets are frauds! I tell you, boy—"

"Why do you doubt him, good Saadyah?" Natalia said reproachfully.

"I don't, little pastry pie, little bowl of honey and fresh cream—give me but a spoon and by heaven I'll eat thee—What I doubt is miracle working itself. I don't believe nature's laws can be violated, not even by so holy an idiot as our Aizun. Why—"

"And if God will it so?" Natalia said.

"Thou'rt young, my little currant pudding, my darling hot cross bun, and 'tis mayhap a cruelty in me to say it out; but the years, time, experience, and history's damning evidence leave us but two workable hypotheses for God: that He gives not what droppeth into the Bishop's pit privy for mankind and all his works, or He simply is not there. Which, methinks, is mayhap the kinder interpretation—"

Two spots of color showed in Natalia's cheeks.

"Oh, good Father Eulogius hath right!" she said. "Thou'rt wicked, Saadyah!"

"Nay, child, I am good; and that I have not thus far ravished thee proves it! Oh, what a rosebud! What delectable little tits! What a lovely, lovely behind! And that tiny waist which my gross paws could span! Were I you, Alaric-Aizun, High Priest of Belly-bumpers, I'd keep her hid and under lock and key!"

"Sometimes the way you look at her convinces me of the need," Alaric said, laughing.

Natalia pouted, tossed her head, made a face; but that she was not angered at Saadyah's playful grossness was abundantly clear. Natalia was all woman, and no woman is ever offended by sincere admiration, no matter how crudely it is put. Of that Alaric was entirely sure. I wish Saad would go home, he thought; for this night must I counteract that braying clerkly ass's influence, or see my autumnal season ruined.

"Sweet child," he began; but the thunderous knocking at the door drowned out his voice.

"I'll go," Saadyah said. "Methinks thy churls and wenches are abed by now—and with each other, likely! And I'll award the back of my hand to whatever oaf 'tis who makes such a racket at this hour—"

He left the room. They heard his footsteps cross the salon, the creak of hinges, the mingled rumble of bass voices. Then Saadyah came back again.

" 'Tis Little Sancho, captain of the Mutes," he growled, but there was a hint of worry in his tone. "Says he has orders to bring thee before the Emir—"

"Oh, no," Natalia wailed.

"Quiet, chit!" Saadyah said. "I asked him if this were an arrest, to which he replied: 'No, not exactly. I had of my lord the boon that I be allowed to come alone, so 'twould not appear thus to all the world.' He seems distressed, the poor fellow! Aizun, if thou dost not feel well enough, I'll go in thy place and present thy excuses. The Emir's usually reasonable; though with your exalted party of Nazarenes braying and kicking in their stalls he hath reason enough to be irritated—"

"Tell Sancho," Alaric said, "to go and hire me a litter or chair; give him a purse for that, Saad, and return. By then I'll be up and dressed. You may assure him he need not fear that I shall fly. The Emir and I are old friends—we can easily settle matters between us—"

"I'll come with thee, sweet my lord!" Natalia said.

"No, 'twould be unseemly, child. Just wait here till I return—"

"If you return!" Natalia wept. "Uncle can be most cruel at times!"

"Look you, Aizun," Abd al Rahman said, "I confess that I was wounded by the evidences laid before me of thy defection from thy loyalty to me—"

"Defection from loyalty!" Alaric said. "How so, good my lord?"

The Emir sighed. "Methinks 'twill be but a thing already known to thee, when I say I have informers everywhere. 'Tis an ugly necessity which—Allah witness it!—I dislike. I know that there hath grown up of late a band of fanatics among the Nazarenes who have as their avowed aim the overthrow of my rule. Nay, more! The overthrow of the reign of Allah and his Prophet throughout all al Andalus! The leaders of this band, I tell thee upon thy oath of secrecy—" He paused, waited.

"Thou hast it, O Commander of the Faithful!" Alaric said.

"—art one Alvaro, a renegade Jew turned Christian, and a priest called Eulogius. Up until now, not one word nor any shred of evidence hath linked thy name with theirs. But now, unhappily, I could throw thee in a dungeon, Aizun! Thou knoweth full well that for any subject of mine to blaspheme against Islam is a capital crime—"

"Who says that I have done so, lies," Alaric said calmly.

"No one hath accused thee of blasphemy by word, Aizun!" al Rahman said sternly. "But by deed? Scant days agone thou cast out the devils in a Mussulman boy, in the Name of Jesu. What is that but—"

"My lord, I thought him a Christian," Alaric said.

The Emir stopped, thought about that.

"Aye, that would be sufficient defense," he said, "and I am glad that thou hast offered it. But about this morning? Thou hast worked more wonders before thy house, in which thou wert joined by that selfsame pair of birds of evil omen, Alvaro and Eulogius! More, thy son-in-law Sanchez hath clearly been drawn into their circle—"

"And my other sons-in-law?" Alaric smiled.

"Were forbidden thy house by this croaking raven! Mine own son

477

Mundhir was told he was unwelcome in the dwelling of his wife's father! I tell thee, Aizun, tolerance hath its limits and—"

"My lord," Alaric cut him off boldly, "have I thy leave to speak?"

"Aye, Aizun, speak! For much do I mislike this thing!"

"And I, my Emir. My two sons by marriage, al Mundhir, thy noble offspring, Allah grant him and thee long life—"

"Do not make mock of Allah, Aizun!" al Rahman thundered.

"I do not, my lord. My sincere belief is that He and our God are one and the same; that in His Wisdom and Compassion, He hath revealed Himself to different races of mankind in different guises, according to their capacity to understand—"

"A happy thought! I like this line of reasoning. Developed, it could soothe the unrest in my realm. Say on, Aizun."

"My two sons-in-law, al Mundhir and Hasdai ben Yahvli, who are both much more congenial to my temperament since they are reasonable young men, than is Garcia, who is not, were forbidden my house while I lay unconscious, after that howling mob had ripped the clothing from my body, bruised and buffeted me, who am no longer strong since this of my wound—"

"Got in my defense! Art a courtier, Aizun! How smoothly thou hast reminded me!"

"I meant it not thus, my lord," Alaric said, "but no matter. 'Tis true that Garcia hath fallen under the spell of this mad priest—a truth I mean to remedy. 'Twas he who asked—and got, I will not deny it!—my permission to present Eulogius to me. But when I consented to that, my lord, I knew nothing of the character of the man. Methinks he is of devils himself possessed. So greatly hath he imposed his will upon Natalia that now she is threatening to leave me, to take the veil, on the score that a holy man, a wonder-worker, would be, needs must be, corrupted by the sweet uses of the flesh. Whereupon, my lord, I ordered Eulogius from my house—"

"Hath proof of that, Aizun?"

"Witnesses: my sister, wife of Husayn the copyist. My daughter Theodora, wife of thy noble son. My two younger daughters, Aurea and Munia. Saadyah ben Hasdai, the merchant—"

"Whose oath alone would be of value before the courts, since he is in no wise related to thee. Very well. Send Natalia to me, and I'll cure her of this folly! Wallid was a fool to let her be brought up as a Nazarene! But thou, Aizun, this of thy wonder-working is a troublesome thing. Canst do miracles, truly?"

"Nay, my lord." Alaric sighed. "I can reach through to darkened minds, troubled spirits, the fearful, no more. In no person I have cured is there evidence of any prior organic or bodily defect. To put it simply, they *believed* themselves crippled, devil-ridden, blind; I ridded them of that belief, nothing more. And I could do this thing for Mussulmen in the name of Allah, as easily as for Nazarenes in that of Jesu. The point is that they must have faith, believe. In what that faith consists, in whom they believe, is a total irrelevancy. Bring me a follower of Beelzebub, and I'll cast out devils in his name—"

"So you remain a freethinker still?" the Emir said sternly.

"Say, rather, my lord, that my heart knoweth God exists, but that my mind rejects him wholly. And upon that cross am I hourly crucified. The priests of my religion damn me for intellectual pride; but 'tis not pride— Allah witness I am humble!"

"Then what is it?" al Rahman said.

"I know not—lest it be the cohabitation in my breast of warring contradictions. A philosophy whose basic concepts negate each other, and leave but the bleeding wounds of uncertainty, of doubt. A difficult foundation upon which to live, my lord. Yet I am forced to endure it—for to deny reason is to return to beasthood; I cannot murder my intellect without thereby assassinating my integrity. Something in me hard and bright and pure resists with all its strength our current versions of the witch doctor's cave, or mumbo jumbo in Latin or whatever other language uttered. I cannot live upon my knees, bowed before the images of human fear and ignorance in the temples of unreason; I must walk upright like a man i' the sun! And yet. And yet—"

"And yet?" al Rahman said.

"And yet, another thing in me contradicts this bright hardness totally. And it—which for want of a better word I call my heart—shouts that my reason itself is God's highest gift, for which I needs must glorify and thank him—"

Abd al Rahman stared at the tall, wondrously fair, yet somehow now frail appearing Goth. His dark eyes almost ceased to blink.

"Tell me, Aizun," he said; and his voice was low and sad. "If I ordered thee to cease thy wonder-working, wouldst obey me?"

"And if I obeyed thee not, my lord?" Alaric said.

"Thou would fulfill Eulogius' fondest dreams—to make of me a Nero—by heading the list of martyrs for thy faith. Wouldst force me to that, Aizun, knowing how I love thee?"

"Alaric bowed his head. "Nay, my lord," he said. "I would not force thee to it; for me martyrdom would be a mockery and a travesty. I have scant fear of death, which seemeth me but a sweet sleep and a forgetting. But I have no right to die for that which I do not truly believe. I have refrained these many years from my so-called wonder-working within thy realm, for I doubt that it does any real or lasting good. I should have been content to forever from it abstain, if my pity had not upon that day unmanned me. In which regard, I crave of thee a boon—"

"Which is?" the Emir said.

"That thou have it noised abroad that I am under orders to cease from these practices on pain of death—"

Slowly al Rahman shook his head. "Nay, Aizun—that is our secret, yours and mine. Thou'rt not a fool, nor am I, my friend! Surely thou seeth that this notice would be but to give thee a cheap and comfortable martyrdom in which thou wouldst live in peace and enjoy the admiration, nay, the veneration of thy fellows without paying for it, as true martyrs must, with thine own life. Thou'rt not a coward, Aizun, nor, methinks, a trickster! All governments, even a benevolent despotism like my own, rest ultimately upon the consent of the governed. I cannot slay all the Mozarabs of Córdoba! Yet, if they rise up, to which mad act thou as a symbol of my cruel and unjust persecution of thy faith—Ha! of the faith thou dost not e'en believe!—might well inspire them, 'tis that I'll be forced to do. Nay, *thou* must publicly renounce thy wonder-working, giving for that renunciation what reasons thou wilt, save this one, that I ordered thee to it!"

"Thou'd have me lie, my lord?" Alaric whispered.

"Nay. I hereby withdraw the order. I merely ask thee, as a patriot and a friend, to refrain from putting weapons into the hands of angry fools. Without too much pride I ask thee this: where else—in what dominion where men pray not to Allah is peace among the different faiths possible? In Antioch we keep a special police in your churches to keep you from slaughtering one another over some weird metaphysical question or the other. Whether the Son was coexistent with the Father, is it not? No matter. Aizun, Aizun, few Nazarenes are as civilized as thou art. What sayeth thou, my friend?"

"That thou'rt right, my lord. I ask only that, as kindly as you can, you bar their access to me lest my pity too greatly tempt me. And now, good my lord, with thy leave, I bid thee farewell, for I left thy niece weeping and fearing for my life—"

"In God's name, what slaves we are to women!" the Emir laughed. "Methinks thy mad priest Eulogius hath more than half the right of it in this regard. Go to her, Aizun. And when thou hast filled her belly with thy fruit, so that she hath a manchild to occupy her and thus hast won a little freedom, return to me. For by the All Wise, I vow I value thee above a kingdom!"

"My lord, you honor me too much!" Alaric said.

"Nay, far too little. Now get you gone, Aizun," the Emir said.

When she heard the door open, and saw him there, Natalia came flying toward him. But a yard away from him she stopped; and her small face was pitiful.

"No," she whispered, "I must not kiss thee. I must never kiss thee again. Oh, Aizun! Oh, sweet my lord—how terrible!"

"Aye," Alaric said, "so it is, my Natalia. That for this mad perversion of our faith, I be denied the son I've longed for all my life—"

"Thou hast a son!" she said tartly.

"Aye. In secret, and in shame, who can never sit at my feet and thus rejoice my heart. Who, though good to look upon, is—alien, strange, wears not truly my image. Whom I did not see in his cradle, did not hear prattle, finally mouth the syllables for *Father*. Nor have I seen him creep, cling to things, stand up, take his first step, totter, fall—and howl until I picked him up and comforted him. Whom I watched not growing into boyhood, at his books, practicing his archery, riding, writing verse—ah, God! Who hath not had that, hath not lived! My daughters? Ah, yes; great joy I had of them; but a son, Natalia, a son! Methinks 'tis our sole chance at immortality. That I should have had of thee—seen thee made Madonna with thy Holy Infant in thy arms, for all children are God's, and all fair young mothers in the sweet semblance of Our Lady made—"

"Oh, Aizun!" she wailed.

"But at the first bray of the holy ass, thou'd deny me life, take from me the comfort of my declining years—"

"But thou'rt a saint, my lord, and saints—"

"God's death, child, what know ye of it? Were not the Holy Apostles saints? They, nearly all of them, had wives! So, too, did the very brothers of Our Lord! This denial of the very principles of life is evil! and I—"

He stopped short, and she saw the tears upon his face.

She came to him then; put up her fingers and let the droplets spill over them; stood there staring up at him with woeful eyes.

But in the end, she wailed: "My lord, my lord, I am afraid!" and fled.

He lay there upon his bed alone, and the bitterness in his heart was very great. For now he knew he had loved no other in all his life as he loved this tender, gay, and splendid child. He loved her totally, her gaiety, tenderness, spirit, fire; and the thought that that hot-eyed, black-robed little monster dared, even in the name of ghostly, improbable God, to tamper with these qualities of hers, sent pain screaming along his nerves, so great he groaned aloud.

Instantly his door opened, and the light axed half the dark. She stood in it, clad in a nightdress of silk, through which the lamp behind her silhouetted her form. His breath caught in his throat at the sight of all that loveliness denied him, making a strangling note, curiously like a sob.

At once she was beside the bed, leaning over him, whispering: "Art ill, my lord?"

"Nay," he said harshly. "For want of thee, I die!"

"Ohhhh!" she wailed. "But what if I damn thy sweet soul to hell? My lord, I cannot! We must not—'tis not meet—"

His hands came up and caught her, dragged her down, slowly and powerfully, yet with great tenderness. Her mouth on his was salt with tears, babbling still: "Art holy—a saint—not—not meet—not meet—"

He silenced it, feeling it blooming under his own, swelling, adhesive, soft, wet, parting, until he knew that he had won; though 'twas not till some time later, while employing all his unmatched skill, gentleness, restraint, in the worshipful, rhythmic cherishing of her body, that he realized how Pyrrhic his victory was. For the sweet breath spurting past his ear formed words, formed a litany, a prayer, that drove ice through his beating heart.

"A son. For him. A son. For thee, too. In Thy Holy Image Please. I know 'tis sin. This we do—ahhh—sweet!—is sin. 'Gainst chaste sanctity. But if Thou canst forgive—A son. I beg of Thee—a—for my saint—a son—"

'Twas not to be borne. Her selflessness destroyed him. Woke him in a terror that chilled his ardent blood, halted the motion, the rhythm, the tenderness.

Her blue eyes opened wide, fixed upon his face. Then without a word, she began to anew the motion, the rhythm, that sweet, slow, worshiping of life, of creation, that utter denial, defiance of negation, death; until she roused him from his pain, his stupor, brought him to, and joined him instantly in, that final bursting, small death, transfiguration, glory, different both in quality and in kind from any they had ever known before, going on so long, so long, that bemazed mind, overtaxed heart, tortured lungs all shuddered to a total halt, and darkness drifted across the world, musk-laden, redolent with the high spiced scents of achieved love. Then from somewhere afar off beyond black, lightless seas, he heard her throat gulp air, and her voice, rising upon the ragged tides of exaltation, exhaustion, triumph, cry: "Now truly do I thank Thee, God!"

On the morrow when Eulogius came once more to the house, one look at the glowing heaven in her eyes told the fiery young priest that he had lost. He took it ill; for hours he stormed and threatened; but Natalia sat there holding her husband's hand in her own and made no reply. And when at last the priest paused for breath, with grave reverence, as one might a Holy Grail, a Chalice, she raised Alaric's white hand palm upward to her lips and clung her mouth to it unbrokenly until Eulogius fled.

A month from that night she was happily vomiting up her breakfast every morning, and demanding for supper impossible dishes such as onions flooded with cream. Yet oft betimes, in those months of waiting that followed, he surprised a look of fear in her blue eyes. And finally, toward the end of her pregnancy, she astounded him by kneeling heavily and clumsily at his feet.

"My lord, I crave thy forgiveness for a thing I've done," she said.

"What thing, child?" he murmured gently.

"I—I have pledged—our son—to God. Since I have stolen thee from Him, I thought it meet and just to offer Him this recompense. Art—art wroth with me, sweet my lord? I—I'll give thee many sons! I swear it! But thy firstborn—mine—must be God's or—or else I fear—"

He gazed sadly at the utter terror in her eyes.

"If he hath a true vocation, I'll not object," he said.

XXIX

Saadyah ben Hasdai stood in the outer hall. Every time Natalia screamed, he beat his great fist against a marble column. All his knuckles were cut, and the blood ran down the back of his hands and splattered on the floor. But Saadyah did not notice that at all.

Now, abruptly, her screams ceased. Saadyah stopped breathing, crept to the door of the bedroom. He heard a rustle, a low moan, a hard slap, a loud and lusty wail.

"God of Abraham, I thank Thee!" he said.

The silence lengthened, crawling along his nerves with a thousand, thousand tiny, obscenely slimy feet. Then the door opened, and Alaric came through it.

"Aizun!" Saadyah bellowed happily. "Hath it a sword or merely a sheath? Must it stand or squat to pizzle 'gainst the church door?"

" 'Tis male," Alaric whispered. "A manchild. Perfect. Huge—like my brother Ataulf, after whom I'll name it. Or my father—a great lout of a Goth, goddam its soul!"

"Aizun! Dost not mean—Nathalie!" he rasped, giving the name, as he always did, the Frankish pronunciation. "Oh, no! She's not—she's not—?"

"Dead? Not yet. But if ibn Abbas doth not halt the bleeding soon there is no hope. The child was—too big. She—she is fearfully torn. If we cannot keep life in her till tomorrow or the next day, he says—he says—"

"Oh, no!" Saadyah roared. "Oh, no, Black Saithan and all thy host from Hell! Oh no, thou fiendish Monster who rules over men! Not Nathalie! Not my little angel! Not she!"

He turned upon Alaric, his eyes wild. "Thy miracles, Holy Man! Perform one now! By Beelzebub! By all the whores who dance in heaven! By all the saints in hell! Do something! Call up the Devil! Conjure up Old Wood Chips' Son!"

Alaric's blue eyes were very bleak.

"There are no such things as miracles, Saad," he said.

"Are there not? Just wait and see, Oh despoiler of chaste beauty! Oh belly-ripping assassin, wait thou and see!"

Then he was gone from there in a crash of splintered tables and chairs, knocked over in his haste. In his rage, his fear, his blindness, he

484

forgot he had a horse. He ran all the way to the palace gate a few short streets away. He pounded on it with both fists, roaring like a pride of lions, outbellowing a herd of bulls.

"The Emir! In Allah's Name, the Emir! Tell him his niece is dying!"

Fortunately for him, Little Sancho now guarded the gate, since the death of his father, Big Sancho, a month agone. And Little Sancho, the Frank, knew Saadyah well. He had made his acquaintance at Alaric's house where, since the day of Alaric's wonders before it, he had formed the habit of visiting almost daily, to listen to the holy man's words with doglike devotion. Moreover Sancho knew how much the Leader of the Faithful loved his spritely niece, preferring her even above his own myriad daughters.

Five minutes later Saadyah stood before the Emir, with his tears dripping into his great bushy beard. His emotion added force to his tale; listening, Abd al Rahman's knees buckled under him, he was forced to sit. He clapped his hands, shouted commands; in a trice the whole palace was in an uproar.

And not one quarter of an hour after he had crashed through the door of Alaric's house, Saadyah marched back into it with a perfect swarm of physicians, leeches, healers, astrologers, and imams at his heels.

Alaric stared at them in wonder. Saadyah pointed.

"This," he said, "is al Harrani, who before he died last year, my Uncle Solly told me is the finest physician he'd ever seen. The rest are quacks. I'll keep 'em out. And throw that old fool Ishaq ibn al Abbas out of there too! Let al Harrani attend to it!"

The new Royal Physician, who, though Alaric knew it not, had already superseded al Abbas in the Emir's favor, entered the bedroom. He examined Natalia briefly. Consulted politely with ibn al Abbas. Came out again.

"My lord Jew," he said, "you have, it seems, the Emir's ear. Tell him I need a troop of cavalry—the fastest and best riders in the land—"

"A troop of cavalry?" Alaric whispered.

"Aye, my lord Goth. To ride relays to the Sierras above the town. I have need of snow. Much snow. Fortunately 'tis January now, and all the peaks are white. Suggest to my lord that he arrange the posting of horses every five leagues. Until that can be done, they'll have to kill a few fine mounts, but no matter. I must control this hemorrhaging. Then we'll see, we'll see—"

Before dawn bloodied the peaks above the city, al Harrani had the bleeding stopped, by the simple expedient of packing her slender loins with snow. Then he resorted to drastic measures: he had a young calf brought, and cut it jugular in the salon outside the bedroom, caught cup after foaming cup of blood; poured then down Natalia's barely conscious throat. She gagged on them, vomited them up, but the physician kept on pouring hot animal blood into her, until some of it stayed down.

By noon there was a hint of color in her cheeks; a broth of young squabs heightened it, cups of wine. She slept, woke refreshed. Seeing Aizun sitting there beside the bed, she smiled at him, said something in a whisper so low he could not hear her. He bent close to her all but colorless mouth. Her breath was fever-laden, faint, but there was no death rattle in it now.

"Art—pleased—with me, sweet—my lord?" she said.

Alaric nodded, kissed her, not daring to trust his voice. Then he went outside, crushed Saadyah in his arms, and big as his wildly roaring friend was, lifted him high in the air, whirling him about before he set him down again.

"She's saved, Saad!" he shouted. "She's saved! Thanks to thee, she'll live!"

Saadyah stared at Alaric. Then he did a strange and wondrous thing. Sitting down at a table, he bowed his big head on his enormous arms, and wept.

"Now if you will, my lord," al Harrani said, "you may have some women of your family in to care for her. 'Twas wise of you not to call them before when tears and hysteria would have but increased thy lady's danger; but now that the peril's past, 'twould be wise. 'Tis my experience that serving wenches are not to be trusted, lest they have over them some dame they both respect and fear—"

"My sister Gele, then," Alaric said. "God wot she must apply a whetstone in her tongue to keep it honed to so fine an edge!"

" 'Twould not be amiss to send for her, my lord," the physician said, and bowing, took his leave.

"He must cost you a fortune," Saadyah said, looking after him.

"Until now, I have been unable to pay him a fal," Alaric said. "The Emir dotes upon Natalia, Saad. He hath taken all the charges of her treatment to his own private purse. He sends her fruits, sherbets, gifts, daily. When he received my word that she was out of danger, 'tis said he placed al Harrani on a balance and then equaled his weight in gold!"

"And yet," Saadyah said quietly, "thy Nathalie is a grave danger to his reign."

"I know," Alaric sighed; " 'tis for that we ceased attending mass at the Cathedral. At first we went to the little church of San Acisclo, but as she grew more gravid, I had good Father Perfectus come to say mass for us here. I mean to continue that practice—"

" 'Twould be wise. All the 'amma need to learn is that the Emir hath a Nazarene niece, and they'd run riot through the streets. What is most strange is the fact they have not found it out ere now!"

"Nay, Saad, 'tis not. Natalia was in a Mussulman household reared. The first time she sallied forth where the city mob could see her was when her father brought her to meet me. Returning from that meeting, she rode at my side, while al Wallid rode some distance behind us. Even when I, in my monumental folly, stopped to aid that boy, there was no reason for the crowd to connect her with the Prince, but rather with me. And who, looking upon Natalia, would dream she is the child of a Moor?"

"Nobody," Saadyah said, "but then who, looking at al Wallid, would dream he is a Moor? Of them all, only the Emir himself shows his Afric strain. The Royal Family's peculiar in that regard—when they yank down a shintiyan, if a maid's nether foliage is not golden, they send her to the executioner, I'm told!"

"Nonsense," Alaric said laughing. "In the first place, Moorish good-wives shave their bodies; in the second, my lord hath concubines who range from Negresses to Norse—"

"Aye, that he hath. Still, Aizun, I am much worried about this matter. There is no way they can touch Nathalie, is there?"

"None. She was born Christian, so the laws against apostasy do not apply. And certain 'tis she'd never dream of publicly, or privately for that matter, insulting the religion of her father, his brothers, and her beloved uncle, the Emir. True, there might be some disturbance if the mob learned that the Emir's own niece is married to a Christian, but methinks all danger of that no longer exists. Only one man knew it for a fact: jeweler of whom I bought the emerald, and who, methinks, did speak of it overmuch, and he is dead. His shop was broken into by thieves, who cut the throats of him and his good wife both, and departed leaving the shop swept bare—"

Saadyah's lips curled sardonically between his mustache and his beard. "Thieves, Aizun?" he said.

Alaric stared at him. Whispered: "Good God!"

"*Ameen*," Saadyah said. "What quicker or more effective cure for diarrhea of the jawbone than that? And that fat little eununchoid fool being a jeweler—"

"Saad," Alaric said, "God grant you are wrong!"

"*Ameen* again," Saadyah said, "but I don't think I am. The knowledge of Nathalie's parentage, and her religion, are dangers to the state—

especially since that braying holy ass Eulogius got started. The Emir's spies heard the fat fart breaking wind through the wrong opening in public, ergo—"

Alaric bowed his head.

"Don't take it to heart, Aizun! To have the Emir's special protection as thou doth is no mean boon! 'Tis that which will save thee when these mad fools finally exhaust the Emir's all but miraculous patience, and he with much justice sends them to bend their stiff necks beneath the headsman's ax. . . . By the way, have they ceased to attempt to draw you into that clandestine group of theirs, in which, though they know it not, every third man is one of the Emir's spies?"

"No," Alaric said. "They plague me still, though now, Got wot, their methods hath become less direct. What think you of this, Saadyah?"

He took down a roll of parchment from a shelf, and gave it to his friend.

Saadyah glanced at it, grunted; said: "I've read it before—'tis the work of that old fool Spera in Deo—a demonstration of the falsity of the teaching of the Prophet Muhammad. Lacks all interest, Alaric—what care I, or any rational man, what any one idiot says of another? All religions are but superstitious folly, and the time they waste attacking one another only proves it—"

"Oh!" Alaric said. " 'Tis not that scroll I meant to give you, Saad, but rather another—though I don't agree that the works of the Abbot Spera lack all interest, since they are the fountainhead of all our growing unrest. Didst know that Eulogius and Alvaro both attended his school in the parish of San Zoil? That 'twas there, in fact, that they met?"

"Ha!" Saadyah said. "Should have known neither of those fanatical asses had brains enough to dream up a doctrine for himself—By Satan, Alaric, what *are* you looking for?"

"This!" Alaric said in triumph, and handed him another scroll.

Saadyah unrolled it, read: "My fellow Christians delight in the poems and romances of the Arabs; they study the works of Muhammadan theologians and philosophers, not to refute them, but to acquire a correct and elegant Arabic style. Alas! the young Christians who are most conspicuous for their talent have no knowledge of any literature or language save the Arabic; they read and study with avidity Arabic books; they amass whole libraries of them at great cost; they everywhere sing the praises of Arabic lore."

He looked up; said: "Alvaro? And referring, of course, to thee?"

Alaric smiled. "I thank him for that 'young'; and for 'conspicuous' for talent," he said, "but still he uses me ill. The next time he comes here I shall give him a lesson in Greek. This was occasioned by his finding me at work upon an ancient fragment in Arabic. Methinks it is a page from Aristotle, which in my leisure I am putting back in Greek to see if I can recapture something of the original flavor. But now fine Alvaro says I have naught but Arabic—"

"You should give him a lesson in Latin, too. God knows *his* is plagued bad! This, then, is a part of the subtle approach you spoke of?"

"Aye. Were it but that, I should laugh at it—but failing to get me—the holy man, the miracle worker!—to commit suicide by voluntarily becoming a martyr to their cause, now they're trying to trick me into martyrdom! Methinks 'tis of Sancho they had information that the Emir forbade me to work more wonders upon pain of death—"

"Did he?" Saadyah said.

"Yes. And in another breath withdrew the command, asking me as a patriot and a friend to refrain from acts which needs must but stir the Exalteds up the more. So now, whenever I sally forth, there whines some blind man, some leper, some cripple in my path begging that I restore him. Of late they've refined the tactic even more: now nearly always 'tis some beauteous maid suffering from some largely hysterical disorder. In this I see Eulogius' fine hand—"

"Why Eulogius'?" Saadyah said.

"I have observed him closely. His fervor is but a perversion of his lust. I would take my oath that he keeps his vows of chastity; but 'twould be better for Córdoba and for him if he did not. His fervor, his fever of exaltation, his fire of religious devotion, would sink and calm into acceptable religiosity had he a 'housekeeper' or a 'niece' to cool the heat that rises to his brain upon occasion. . . ."

Saadyah glanced toward the closed door of the bedroom.

"The tactic's not intelligent," he said. "Surely having seen what you've got in there, he must realize he can't tempt you that way—"

"Aye, but he can!" Alaric said. "And knows it. Whenever I see a fair and suffering maid my pity all but unmans me precisely *because* I am reminded of Natalia or my daughters. The Satanic little beast is not unsubtle, Saad. Besides—"

"Besides what?" Saadyah said, eyeing Alaric closely now, for the deep sadness in the Goth's tone had not escaped him.

"Besides—upon your word, you'll breathe not a word to Afaf—for if this spreads abroad it only could have been known through thee, since to no other have I told it—nor shall I—"

"Mouth's sealed. Sewed up. Speak, brother!"

"Al Harrani says that the next time my Natalia is with child, I am not to send for him, for he will not come. Rather I am to turn myself over to the nearest cadi as a deliberate murderer—"

"Good God!" Saadyah whispered.

"*Ameen*," Alaric said softly. "So now, married to all that young splendor, I must like a monk live—"

"Hardly!" Saadyah said. "Don't be a fool, boy! Go down to Eulalia's once a month and draw the temper from your weapon—that's what I do. Easier than overcoming Afaf's constant evasions, or watching her close her eyes so she can pretend that I am you—"

"Poor Saad," Alaric said. "Poor me. Poor—us!"

"You have said it! Doth she know?"

"No, and I'll not tell her. I'll evade the issue. If forced to it, though I hate lies above all things, I'll swear that I dreamed an angel spoke to me commanding us to live like brother and sister—"

"I couldn't. I'd go mad," Saadyah growled.

"You think I shan't, brother?" Alaric said.

At the end of the fourth week of Natalia's convalescence, good Father Perfectus of the Church of San Acisclo sought Alaric out. He was fairly beaming.

"I have consulted with the physician al Harrani, my son," he said, "who, though an infidel, is yet a man of skill—"

Alaric smiled at him.

"Strange, he tells me that *you* are infidel, Father," he said.

Father Perfectus' face turned purple; then he saw Alaric's smile.

"I do wish you'd not jest about high and holy things, my son," he said. "But no matter. Al Harrani says that the Lady Natalia can now be borne upon a litter to the church with no danger to her health. I know thou hast delayed the christening so that she can attend it, as is meet and just. I have informed the Bishop who has graciously consented to officiate—"

"Father," Alaric said, "we cannot go to the Cathedral—"

"Aye, that I know, my son. 'Twould be dangerous if the vulgar herd of infidels found out thy sweet lady is the Emir's niece. I laid that problem before Bishop Saul. He, out of his admiration for your learning, and the respect inspired in his august breast by the saintly wonders thou hast done, is perfectly willing to come to my humble chapel. What say you to that divinely inspired youth Alvaro as godfather?"

"Never!" Alaric said.

Father Perfectus' face fell. "Why not?" he said.

"Say I prefer one who knows what is Caesar's and what is God's," Alaric said. "Alvaro, Eulogius, and their exalted followers are going to bring down the Emir's wrath upon the whole Mozarab population, Father. And, when they do, they will be guilty of murder—"

"And if they, themselves, are martyred, my son?" Father Perfectus said sternly.

"When a man embarks upon a course of action deliberately, with the full knowledge that his own death must inescapably result therefrom, he is committing suicide—which is also against our canons, Father."

"My son," Perfectus said, "I find this line of reasoning strange. Strictly applied, you could make the same accusation against the saintly martyrs of the early Church—"

"No, Father. For they suffered for *being* Christians. For refusing to renounce their faith. They resisted to the death the blasphemy of worshiping the Emperor's statue as a god. Here, nothing of the sort entails. Here, Eulogius seems bent upon provoking a slaughter of Christians in a land in which we dwell in perfect peace and in the full exercise of our faith. We are *not* forced to worship Allah; we do not have to hail the Emir as a god. We've been for the most part able to keep our churches open, hear mass, confess our sins, bring up our children in our way, without let or hindrance. What need have we for martyrs here? Martyrs which we can only produce by insulting a faith that hath treated us and ours most kindly?"

Two spots of color showed in Perfectus' face.

"Kindly?" he said. "We are forbidden to parade our sacred images in holy procession through the street! We may not sound a bell to call worshipers to prayer. Their cadis and theologians proffer insulting interpretations of our faith, and should we reply, we risk death! How oft have I been stoned by the children, spat upon, abused by the mob because of my clerkly garb? Hardly kindly, my son!"

"And yet that mob, those children, are, save for the rarest exceptions, children and grandchildren of Catholics, my Father. I say only, very mildly, that there must be something vital in a doctrine that can win from them so fierce a loyalty. Daily we lose converts to them—and not only from the lowly, but from our highest and best."

"Seduced by their luxury, their splendor, and their abominable vices! Which is why we *must* overthrow them!"

"To be overthrown in our turn when some new creed comes along." Alaric sighed. "Earth is filled with the graves of gods, Father. Every land hides an hundred forgotten faiths—"

"But not the One True Faith which is ours!" Perfectus thundered.

"Is it? I give thee Pilatus' question, Father: What is truth? And being humble, I confess I know not. Let us not quarrel, good my Father, in matters spiritual! Instead of overthrowals and massacres and self-immolations, let us rather follow the way of the Man whom methinks the Church hath quite forgot: He who despised processions, kept no fasts at all, associated with publicans and thieves and harlots, praised God in wood and plain, on hilltops, by the seashore, while walking in fields of corn; who entered a temple but twice in all his life—once to dispute with the learned Fathers as I dispute now with thee; once to drive forth those who were profaning it with questions of barter, sale, and taxes—which is Alvaros' and Eulogius' chief rallying point, is it not, Father Perfectus—the taxes which we pay?"

"Which are crushing, ruinous! They have right, my son! Not to mention daily abuse, and insult!"

" 'Render unto Caesar that which is Caesar's,' Father; 'and to God that which is God's.' 'If any man smite thee on thy right cheek, turn unto him also thy left.' 'If any man require of thee that thou go with him one mile, go with him two.' And above all, 'Father, forgive them, for they know not what they do.' Methinks we lose too much with our processions, and images, and liquefying blood, and unrotting arm bones of long-dead saints. In our religion of ritual, hatred, death worship, putrefaction, and decay—in our life-denying, self-torturing morbid faith, Father, we've managed to leave Him out, haven't we? Oh, we have Veronica's veil, wood from the True Cross, the sudarium, thorns from His crown: the chalice from which He drank—everything but Him—everything but love, forgiveness, tenderness—"

Perfectus stared at him, and frowned. For a long time he was silent. Then quietly he said: "Thou hast much of right, son Aizun—and now I see why men call thee saint. Still, if we do not resist them, they will destroy us—by wearing us away, by leaving our churches empty, while showing our young a heaven in which each man has six concubines. But it grows late. Whom then would you have as godfather for your son?"

"The Exceptor Gomez, of the Emir's staff, who is both a Christian and gentleman. The Lady Sara, widow of the merchant Sanchez, mother of my son-in-law Gracia, will stand as godmother. And my son is to be called Ataulf, after my brother, who died in the Faith. Will you tell the Bishop that, my Father?"

"Aye, that I will." Perfectus sighed. "Would God I had thy powers, my son!"

"I have no powers, Father—save alone the power to love. Methinks 'tis of that I shall one day die."

Perfectus stood there, staring at him. "Why doth thou think that, son Aizun?" he said.

Alaric smiled. "Those who love cannot help but give," he said. "First they give of their goods until all material things have gone. Then of their service, of their strength. And when strength and the ability to serve have

492

departed them, having nothing left to give—they offer up their lives. I bid thee good night, Father!"

The old priest stood there staring at him. And to him as to many another who had talked long with Alaric Teudisson, lingered in his presence, it seemed to him that the Goth's son moved in light, was cloaked in it, haloed. And though he did not see him go, of a sudden the old priest was alone. He made the sign of the cross above his heart.

"We shall never win him to our cause," he muttered. "Never! I wonder if 'tis good or ill, the thing we do. . . ." Then, taking up his staff, he moved through the door, out into the street, where the darkness lay drifted deep, and there was no light at all.

The christening having been accomplished, peace of a sort returned to Alaric's house. Alaric was pleased to note that Alvaro and Eulogius had apparently given up their attempts to trick or win him into martyrdom.

Nor have they had better fortune with any man, he thought wryly. To die for a cause to us all seemeth a noble thing. But when we look old bony death in his hollow eye, how fast doth nobility depart us! Besides, they hath fallen into that trap which doth unmake those who'd move and shake the world in every age and clime: when a death's required, one must lead—and not push another victim forward. If they do not encounter a volunteer martyr soon, methinks their movement will of its own weight collapse—

Such were his thoughts as he rode forth from his house one day—a thing he did now and again with increasing confidence that his sojourns would no longer be interrupted by cripples, blind men, hysterical young maids planted in his path. So occupied was he with his thoughts that he did not hear the hoofbeats coming after him till 'twas too late. Before he could turn, the rider was abreast of him.

"My lord!" he cried out in Arabic. "A word with you, if you please!"

Frowning, Alaric pulled up his mount. Then he let his face relax. The young man who had hailed him clearly was not one of Eulogius' followers. Of purest Arabic strain, by dress and bearing both he was of the highest aristocracy, mayhap even a prince.

"What would ye of me, my young and noble master?" Alaric said.

"A boon, Lord Aizun," the young man said. "That you accompany me to my house. A maid lies ill there—methinks dying. And you—"

The frown returned to Alaric's face. "Art Christian, then?" he said.

"Nay, good my lord. I am a faithful follower of the Prophet. But the maid of whom I speak is of thy faith and—"

493

"Thy name, young sir!" Alaric said sternly.

The young man smiled. " 'Tis Yahya ibn Zakariya' al Khashab, and since that name will mean little to you, I will add that my mother was sister to her who caused to be planted this orchard through which we ride—"

"And built the leprosarium yonder, which gains its sustenance from the fruits of the demi-paradise," Alaric said. "The Munyat Adjab named after that great and pious lady, favorite of the late Emir al Hakam. I am honored to salute her nephew, young lord. . . ."

"And I to bow before a Holy Man," the young lordling said. "But first, let me set your mind at ease upon the point I know is troubling you. My aunt is a frequent visitor to the court of my cousin, the Emir. I am well aware of the prohibition against wonder-working my royal cousin hath imposed upon you. Nor am I even secretly a Nazarene—though there doth to me seem much that is noble and pure in thy faith—and I have no connection with the priest Eulogius at all. That said, I humbly beg thee to come to my house and do what thou canst for the maid Baldegotona, for much do I fear that she will die—"

"You know, O nephew of Adjab," Alaric said, "that if I should do this thing and word of it reach the Emir, my head is unlikely to maintain even a nodding acquaintance with my neck?"

"Which is why no word of it shall reach him. He hath of thee thy promise to do naught that will lend fire to the fervor of Alvaro, Eulogius, and their zealots. Nor seemeth me that to undertake to cure, in the privacy of a Muslim home, a maid stricken dumb by cruelty and fear, and dying of starvation, can be construed as a rupture of thy promise—"

"Speak to me of her, good Yahya," Alaric said.

"Baldegotona is a maid most passing fair," Yahya said, "though not, methinks, so fair as her sister Flora, who, not she, is the root of all the trouble. . . ."

"How so, young master?" Alaric said.

"Because poor Baldegotona's not headstrong, while Flora is. The story, to put it briefly, is a commonplace: a follower of the Prophet, wed to a lovely Nazarene; two daughters, secretly by their mother brought up to worship the Son of Mary, your Messiah. One son, he the eldest, following his father and Islam with all his heart and mind. The father dies and the household splits apart. The lovely Flora, daring to a fault, defies her brother. In a rage he beats his sisters—and being, Allah pity him, a hard man—is overgenerous with his blows. I should not leave a mule in the state he's left poor Baldegotona now."

"I see. And Flora—?"

"I know not. She hath taken refuge in a Nazarene home, as she professes to despise the race one half at least of whose blood she bears, and the religion of her own sire, calling us infidel dogs. I know not where she is. But Baldegotona came to my aunt's house, her back in ribbons, unable to speak. That was five days agone, and since then no morsel hath passed her lips. As I said to thee before, my lord—if someone doth not win her from her present state, much do I fear she'll die. . . ."

Alaric sat there, thinking. Then he sighed. "I'll come with thee, good Yahya," he said. "For to let a person die whom one might possibly save is to be guilty, at least in part, of another's death."

Baldegotona was, as Yahya ibn Zakariya' had said, most fair. Despite her Gothic name and a hint of that blood in the whiteness of her skin, her hair and eyes were dark. She had been most cruelly caned; her back and arms were covered with bruises. But 'twas abundantly clear that her brother's blows were but a minor part of her distress. Something rested on her mind, her heart; some great and terrible burden that had caused her tongue to cleave to the roof of her mouth, allowing neither words to escape nor food to enter.

Yahya's mother and his Grand Dame of an aunt paid Alaric the tribute of veiling themselves; but they had no intention of leaving the room. Alaric sat there by the bed, and looked at this graceful, pretty child. He said no word; he simply sat there, looking at her.

At first her great brown eyes leaped with fear; but slowly, under the wondrous tenderness of his gaze, they softened. Now they were studying his face with awe, then with something else. Hope—Alaric thought.

"Now canst speak, can't you, child?" he said to her in Romance.

The nod she gave was barely perceptible. Then her eyes swept fearfully from the face of Yahya's mother to that of his aunt Adjab, coming to rest at last upon Alaric's own. If eyes can be said to speak, Baldegotona's spoke then.

Alaric turned to the two highborn Arabian ladies. He addressed them in the Prophet's tongue.

"Have the goodness to leave me alone with her," he said.

He could see the expression of outraged shock cross both their faces. To leave a man not yet bowed down with years alone with a comely maid to them was unthinkable.

"I'll not ravish her," he said dryly, "nor she, me, methinks. Have the kindness to leave us, gracious ladies—for she will not speak unless ye do. And 'tis from her words alone that I can judge the best method for curing her."

Still they hesitated until Yahya burst out: "Allah witness that women are witless fools! Hath it never occurred to thee, my mother and my aunt, that there *are* men who are not concerned with the gratification of their lust every instant of their lives?"

"I never met one who wasn't—unless he was asleep, too ill to lift a hand, or dead," Adjab snapped. "Still—"

"Still you insult my visitor who is a holy man," Yahya howled. "Now get out of here!"

When they had gone, muttering to themselves the way women in their middle years will, whatever be their faith, their race, their clime, Alaric turned to Baldegotona.

"Now you can speak, child," he said. "Tell me whom it is you fear— your brother?"

"Nay, good my lord," she whispered. "My brother is terrible when he is wroth; but only then. Generally he is most kind. Even—even—this—" she touched the welts and bruises that showed on her arms above the coverlet "—is but evidence that he loves me—"

"Then who is it that you fear, sweet Baldegotona?" Alaric said.

"Flora," Baldegotona whispered.

"Thy sister?" Alaric said.

"Aye," Baldegotona said.

Alaric sat there studying her face.

"Why?" he said. "Is thy sister evil?"

"Oh, no!" Baldegotona said. "Flora is wondrous good! She is very nearly a saint! Always about her prayers; her fasts, her mortification of her body—"

Alaric's eyes were very deep and sad. His voice came out measured, slow.

"Only," he said quietly, "she is not kind."

"Oh!" Baldegotona whispered.

"She is very straight, very pure," Alaric went on. "She hath no doubts at all. Father God sits up in Heaven with Lord Jesu on His right hand, with hell yawning at their feet into which they both will hurl all who believe not precisely as fair Flora doth. All Islam's lordly, knightly sons, all those who follow the Grecian rite, all the teeming millions who had the misfortune to be born before Our Lord came; all the swarming races of mankind now alive who have not even had the opportunity to hear Our Lord's Word. No matter if there be just and decent men among them; no matter if there be wise men, healers, saints. Art not a Christian—and of the Roman persuasion? Thy screams will sound unendingly in hell!"

Baldegotona did not move. She let her breath out in a long, long sigh.

"Thou knoweth her, my lord!" she said.

"Aye," Alaric said, "though I have never seen her face, I do. Her name is legion, child. And, methinks, I know thee, too. Hast thy doubts at times, do you not, sweet Baldegotona? You find life sweet, and would live it, not bow thy head beneath the headsman's ax. Art not convinced the Prophet's way is totally wrong; nor Lord Jesu's entirely right. Or—if thou art, thou hast not in thee such stuff as of which art martyrs made. Wouldst live and say a prayer to Allah and to Jesu both when thou'rt hard pressed, fearful, sore afraid. Have I not the right of it, my child?"

"Aye, good my lord! Methinks my brother's right! He tried reasoning with her first; but she was so stubborn that she enraged him, so he fell to beating her—and me, because as I kept silent, he was sure I shared her views. And I do! I do! I am a Christian, my lord! Only—"

"Flora is not. Nor is anyone who knoweth not that the essence of our faith is to forgive. You'd save your life, live in what peace you can find or win—even if it meant giving at least lip service to the Prophet's way? Then do it, child! For 'tis thou, not she, who hath the better part. Any faith that denies life becomes a perversion and a vice. Life is to be lived—as decently, kindly, chastely—in the sense that thou should cleave only to thy husband, the father of thy sons—as possible—"

"But Flora says that—"

"—to save your life, you damn your soul. Upon which she, of course, is the ultimate authority. I say unto you, Baldegotona, that God careth not a jot if ye call him Allah, Jehovah, Eloheim, Ra, Azor, or even Ba'al—as long as you love him with all your heart, and your neighbor as yourself. Return to your brother, child! Become a good Muslim. Face Mecca when you pray. Much good hath from that direction come: tolerance, peace, the veneration of learning, music, art, science—even cleanliness—"

"But," Baldegotona protested, "I fear hell, my lord!"

"And I," Alaric sighed, "which exists solely in the hearts of men full of hate, who invented it to have a place wherein to consign their foes. But more than hell do I fear those who walk in the arrogant surety of their rightness, child. Methinks we owe ourselves, our lovers, brethren, friends, all of humanity, and mayhap even God—the kindly humility of a little decent doubt—for no amiable skeptic in all of history hath ever slain a man over what can never be proven anyhow, while behold the hecatombs we've piled up in the name of the Prince of Peace. Do as I command thee, child; upon my soul, if this be sin, rest the burden of it!"

He turned then, clapped his hands. When Adjab came rushing into the room, followed by Yahya's mother, he smiled at them, said: "Bring food, and wine. Let us eat, drink, and be merry—to celebrate our daughter's return to life!"

He rode homeward again, accompanied by Yahya ibn Zakariya' al Khashab almost to his house, and his heart was filled with peace. But that peace ended the moment he opened his door. For Natalia came flying to his arms and clung to him and wept and wept, beyond all hope of speech.

"What ails thee child?" he said. "Hath aught passed with Ataulf?"

"Nay!" she sobbed. "For that at least God be praised! Oh, Aizun, Oh, sweet my lord, they—"

But once again a gale of weeping drowned her voice.

"They?" Alaric said.

"The al Khurs! The Silent Ones! At Uncle's orders they arrested poor Father Perfectus! They led him before the head judge! And—and—Oh, sweet my lord, go to my uncle! He loves thee much! Bow before him! Humble thyself if need be for—"

"For what, child?" Alaric said.

"For Father Perfectus, Aizun. For my poor confessor whom the Kadi l'djama's hath found guilty of public mockery of Islam and condemned to death!"

Alaric stood there. His eyes were, at that moment, very bleak. "So now it begins," he thought. "So now those monsters of piety have won. Poor Perfectus. Poor gentle old fool. I wonder how—"

He looked down at her bright head, at her quivering shoulders.

"Aye, child, I'll go there now," he said.

XXX

But for the first time in all the many years he had known the Emir, Alaric was unable to obtain an audience with the Commander of the Faithful. At the palace gate, Sancho the Frank begged him to go away, tears of rage showing in his little blue eyes.

"I beg thee, my saintly lord, to get thee hence from here!" he whispered hoarsely into Alaric's ear. "The Emir's wrath is fearful to behold! And who, I made bold to ask, would make these infidel dogs better prey than thou—the holiest of all men, whom these very eyes hath seen do miracles?"

"I am far from holy, Sancho," Alaric said with a sigh. "And methinks the Emir will not harm me. You know well I have enjoyed his favor these many years. Mayhap I can soften his heart toward poor Perfectus—who is not of the stuff of martyrs, by my troth! I have had many discussions with the good Father, who, though strong in his faith and devoutly orthodox, clinging to the letter of the law while the spirit escapes him betwixt the lines, is not unreasonable. Even he must know that the fleabites and pinpricks we suffer under Muslim rule are not worth dying for. I find it passing strange that he, and not some other more zealous one, should be the first to offer up his life for the cause—"

"He did not offer it, my saintly lord!" Sancho hissed. "He was tricked! A group of Mussulmen engaged him in debate upon the relative merits of their Prophet and Our Lord. He had of them their promise that the discussion was to be a private affair, in which each side would maintain a decent courtesy and each man's opinion be respected without making of it a matter for the police or the law. But you know how slippery *that* subject is! Soon they were shouting at each other—and the good father, losing his temper quite, slanged the Prophet as a blackguard and an adulterer. Whereupon a silence fell upon the group. Which of them betrayed him, I know not. Mayhap none of them. As loud as the good father was bellowing his insults, any passerby could have heard him and reported him to the cadi. All I know is that I was sent to arrest him, which after having of him both his forgiveness and his blessing, I did. So now—"

"So now," Alaric said, "thou wilt go and beg an audience of the Emir for me, Sancho."

"As thou wilt, my lord! I have told thee 'tis not wise; but 'tis not my

499

place to gainsay thee!" Whereupon the huge Frank turned and clanked away toward the interior of the Alcázar.

But when he came back again, 'twas not to the royal quarters that Alaric was led but rather to the smaller, less richly furnished offices of the administrative staff. And there, sternly frowning as though he were the Emir himself, the head eunuch Nasr received him.

"Look you, my lord Aizun," he began at once, "I warn you 'tis not wise to interest yourself too vividly in this affair. All too often now, your name has been linked with these fanatical fools. I know, I know—you do not share their views; but weigh you well the danger of defending them— even out of pity!"

"I don't defend them, my lord al Kabir; I merely say that poor Perfectus is not of their number; that he was tricked into a discussion which I, for one, right oft have warned him to avoid. Further, the crime of *Istikhfaf*, or blasphemy against Islam, involves the basic concept that it must be publicly, openly done. A discussion among friends over the differences between their faiths, even when it becomes heated, is a private matter. Well it seemeth to me that here the law against Istikhfaf doth not apply."

"Nor would it," Abu l'Fath Nasr said, "but for the fact, attested to by twenty witnesses, that the good father made his views public, by standing outside in the street and roaring his maledictions upon Allah, Muhammad, God's Prophet, and the occupants of the house. Oh, no, the charge is both clear and just. Nor would he recant before the head cadi—by which act alone he might have saved his life."

"I see," Alaric said; then: "May I not have a word with thy lord, the Commander of Allah's Faithful?"

Slowly Nasr shook his head. "Nay, good my lord," he murmured.

"Why not?" Alaric said, his voice a whip crack suddenly.

"Because he himself hath expressly forbidden it. 'For no reason at all is ibn al Qutiyya to be admitted unto me,' he said."

Alaric sat there looking at the eunuch. "Might I know the reason for his change of heart?" he said.

"His heart hath not changed. He loves thee much, Lord Aizun! 'Tis but to spare both himself and thee the pain of the refusal he must give that he will not see thee. Thou'rt not unsubtle, Goth though thou be. When thou hast thought this matter through, thou wilt see that Perfectus is the one man in all the Emirate that the Defender of the Faith can in no wise pardon."

"Why not?" Alaric said again.

Nasr's smile was the embodiment of evil. "Because of thee, my lord," he said. "Because of thee!"

Alaric sat there, feeling the hammers beginning under his skull, the mailed fingers closing around his heart.

"Because of—me?" he whispered.

"Aye, Holy Man, Worker of Wonders, because of thee! Were the Commander of the Faithful to pardon of his crime the father-confessor of thy house, all the world would ask why, would seek for reasons beyond the fact that thou'rt the Emir's friend whom well he loves. Upon thy head is Perfectus' blood, O Son of the Goth! Thou condemned him the day thou stole al Wallid's daughter from his house; thou murdered him when thou didst wed her in the Church; thou rammed his poor witless head down upon the block the hour thou chose him as thy wife's confessor. For should my regal lord set this bellowing idiot free, how long thinkest thou 'twould be before someone learned that the Emir's own niece is to a Nazarene wed, and though guilty of *Zandaka*—heresy in thy tongue, is it not?—yet lives?"

"And in thine, O Nasr—since thou, equally as I, wert to Romance born! And just as equally thou knowest that my lady cannot be charged with either heresy against, nor apostasy from, a faith which she hath never held!"

"True," the al fata said blandly. "But wouldst thou, ibn Qutiyya, like the task of explaining these fine points to the mob? I'll grant thee privilege gladly, having some respect for this ugly and useless hide I wear. Thou'rt a wonder-worker, truly, Aizun! And of all thy miracles, none is greater than this: that upon a long series of thy heedless acts the very state bids fair to stand or fall!"

Alaric bowed his aching head, looked up again. "I see," he said.

"So let the clerkly idiot die. What is one man's life against the good of all Andalús? And should hot rebellion flame through our streets, rest assured the very gutters would run red with blood—some of which might well be thy own. Nay. I'll not take that tack! For having seen thee in battle against the Norsemen, when thou wert briefly under my own command, I know how little fear of death impresses thee. Say, rather, some of it might well be thy gracious lady's. We'll give the old fool a merciful death—one stroke with a sharp ax and 'tis done. Besides, he hath some weeks left yet in which to recant—for the execution is scheduled for the Day of the Breaking of the Fast. If betimes thou canst from his fatal folly persuade him, the possibility exists, due consideration being given to the Emir's well-known and, methinks, excessive tendency toward mercy, that he might still be saved, my lord!"

But the first person Alaric saw when the jailer unlocked the door to Perfectus' cell was Eulogius; the second, Alvaro. And yet they wot not, he thought wryly, that the very fact that they can visit him, that they, the known leaders of the opposition, are permitted this, is *ipso facto* a refutation of their claims of cruel persecution.

He said: "Clerkly fathers, my lord Alvaro—I give ye greetings."

There was a silence; then Eulogius said grandly: "I bid thee welcome, son Aizun!"

Alaric looked past him to where Perfectus sat. "And you, my good Father in matters spiritual, do you also bid me welcome?" he said.

"Need you ask that, my son?" Perfectus said. "Sancho told us how you went to the Emir to intervene in my behalf. For which, my thanks—"

"Though you should have consulted him first—or me—to see whether such a step was desirable," Eulogius said.

Alaric's soft blue gaze met Eulogius', small dark eyes and held them. But 'twas the priest who broke that silent war of wills by gazing up at the dust and cobwebs of the ceiling.

"Why?" Alaric said.

"Because, God wot, martyrdom is a privilege," Eulogius thundered, "of which no godly man can be without his own consent robbed!"

Alaric stood there looking at the young priest. Then he murmured in Arabic the classic phrase: "Whom the finger of Allah hath touched—" and turned to Perfectus once more.

"What did you say?" Eulogius said angrily.

"That thou'rt mad, my Father," Alvaro said, supplying the translation for him. "By now thou knoweth what this devil-worshiper, this evil magician is like! I bid thee come away, good Father, and—"

"Nay!" Eulogius said sternly. " 'Tis my duty to stay, for the protection of the immortal soul of this our brother in God, Perfectus, lest this son of Satan tempt—"

"Eulogius, my friend," Perfectus said, "you talk rot. I have known this my son Aizun for these many moons, since in fact he returned from the Holy Land. I have never known a man purer, more free of evil, or of sin. You forget that the very cathedral in which our good Bishop Saul now sits was built entirely at his expense out of monies that should have come to him as a dowry upon his marriage to that good and pious lady Jimena, daughter of the late, unlamented ibn Ha'ad! You see before you a man who could, if he so willed it, rival even the great Jew Saadyah ben Hasdai in wealth, but who lives modestly, even meanly, because he gives not a tenth, but nearly all his earnings to feed the poor! The orphanage of my parish San Acisclo derives its total support from a tax he himself imposed upon the earnings of his glassworks, and will continue to do so by his express command, imposed upon his heirs, even after he is dead! And thou, thyself, hast seen his wonders; why—"

"Yet he himself admits he doubts the verity of our Faith," Eulogius said. "And when, after his wonder-working on that day, when he had the peerless opportunity to glorify the True Religion and God's Own Church before all men—he refused to submit to discipline; insisted upon remaining in the stew, the sty of carnality, of filthy lust! I tell thee, brother—"

"—that he speaks with much justice when he calls thee mad, Eulogius. 'Tis normal and good that Christian men cleave to their wives. Our Lord himself commanded that. And here is one further thing thou does not know: He married his sweet lady at her own father's request, because the Prince, infidel though he is, felt bound, as the gentleman he also is, to comply with the promise he made to his Christian goodwife on her deathbed—that the Lady Natalia, brought up in our Faith, be wedded to a pious Christian gentleman! And furthermore—"

"Father," Alaric said.

"Aye, son Aizun?"

"Could we not cease to discuss me and my doings as though I were not here? You make of me a demi-saint, while I, God wot, have a fearsome burden of sin upon my soul. Nor do we have time to waste upon these quarrels, which, methinks, lack all reason and all sense. What I have come here for is, if thou and God permit, to save thy life."

"To—to save my life?" Perfectus whispered.

"How?" Alvaro said.

Alaric ignored him. "You must recant, Father!" he said to Perfectus. "Let me go to the head cadi and tell him you are willing to withdraw your words—"

"—that Muhammad was a blackguard and an adulterer?" Alvaro sneered. "How can he, since those words are true?"

Alaric looked at him. "Were I to shrivel your evil tongue in your mouth," he whispered, "would you believe me then when I say you lie? The Prophet was the kindest, most generous, and the best of men—and of God truly favored. That he hath upended this our world, proves him so. You, young Alvaro, art a learned man; you know as well as I that the patriarchs of our mutual Jewish-Christian faith had many wives, had indeed to have many if the race itself were to survive—but no matter! I came here not to dispute with you but, if I can, to save the life of this good and just man whom ye have entrapped into doing for ye both what ye have not the valor to do for yourselves! If it is a life your cause requires, I bid ye—offer up your own!"

"Apostate," Eulogius thundered, "who thus defend Muhammad, Satan's own son!"

"God!" Alaric cried, putting his hands to his own aching head. "Good Father Perfectus, hear me! Withdraw thy words in the interest of thy parish, of all God's poor who need thee! Do not be led to the slaughter by these blind and fanatical fools!"

Perfectus looked up at him, and his old eyes filled up with tears. "I thank thee, Aizun, gentle son, in God's Name," he whispered, "but I cannot. I owe my sore oppressed people, and my God, this death. Aizun, Aizun, my son, my son—do not thus weep for me!"

But Alaric knelt there at his feet, took his gnarled old hands and kissed them, bathing them with his tears.

"I beg of thee thy pardon, good father," he said.

"In God's Name, son Aizun, for what?" Perfectus said.

"Thy blood is upon my head. For had I not chosen thee as father-confessor of my house, surely thy sentence would have been much lighter, or mayhap thy pardon granted; but as it is—"

"As it is, what?" Eulogius said, seizing upon these words with sure instinct."

"He means the fact that his wife's the Emir's niece hath been carefully concealed from the city mob," Perfectus said. "Were it noised abroad, the Emirate itself might be in danger—for then the Commander of the Mussulmen would perforce have to explain how he came to have a Christian niece; how she came to be married in the church by our good Bishop Saul, prove to all the world that she be no apostate against Islam, and furthermore—"

"Father, good Father," Alaric said, "put not this weapon in their hands!"

But by then it was too late; only by looking into Eulogius' eyes and by seeing the flame of triumph flaring there, that, any man could tell.

The days crawled by. Natalia did not eat at all, scarcely slept an hour through. She became so thin, so fragile, that her very flesh seemed transparent. And being himself comfortless, Alaric was powerless to comfort her. He began to fear quite seriously that she might go mad or die of grief. As it turned out, his fears proved groundless. For before Perfectus died, she had already begun to recover her health, her strength, her matchless beauty. And what saved her was a sadly mundane thing.

They were walking in the garden some weeks still before that April day on which poor Perfectus was doomed to die.

"Let's go back in, sweet my lord," Natalia said. "Methinks it's going to rain, and I—"

That sound cut through her voice; half a quaver, half a sob.

Natalia stopped still, her exquisite little head, its delicate bone structure showing clearly through her all but vanished flesh turned upon the reedlike thinness of her neck, poised there, a poem in arrested motion, as she stared toward the gate.

"Didst hear, my lord—" she began; but that sick, hurt, desperate wail rose up, gathering strength, clarity, form.

"San Alarico!" it cried.

Natalia's face came around to him, her eyes great star sapphires, her mouth rounding into a pale pink O; and then, as he started toward the gate, she found her voice.

"Don't go! Don't go, Aizun, sweet my lord! 'Tis a trick! I'm sure. Please, Aizun! I—"

But by then he had reached the gate; tore it open, looked down. A moment later Natalia was at his side, staring down at the woman, nay the maid, the girl who had flung both her arms about his ankles, and was kissing his slippered feet as though they were the sweetest objects in all the world. For the first time since little Ataulf's birth high color flared in Natalia's face.

"Who is this one, good my lord?" she said. "Another of thy various loves, about whom I've not been told?"

"Hardly," Alaric said. "Look at her arms, Natalia!"

Natalia bent close, reeled back, clutched at Alaric's arm until the giddy sickness that assailed her passed.

"Poor thing!" she whispered. "Poor, poor little thing! What monster could have beaten her like this?"

Alaric bent down then and pried loose the girl's arms from about his ankles; then he lifted her from the ground. As gentle as his touch was, she moaned.

"Send a servant for al Harrani, child," he said to Natalia, "for, methinks, this girl is like to die!"

"No!" the girl whispered. "Please call no physician, my sainted lord—for that—for that—"

"What, daughter?" Alaric said.

"would be—to seal—my death—" she whispered. Then she loosened all over in his arms, became boneless, her head dropping to one side.

"Aizun!" Natalia cried. "She—"

"Nay, she is not dead. Go ahead of me, Natalia—have the servants prepare a room for her. And bring thy scissors, child—"

"My—my scissors?" Natalia whispered.

"Aye," Alaric said grimly, "for much do I fear her clothing needs must be cut away from her back—"

He was right. Even after having been soaked with warm water, her dress stuck to her stripes; and however gently Natalia's women pulled it away, she bled. And when they began to rub the healing balm into her welts, at their fingers' lightest touch, she screamed.

"Stop it," Alaric said. "Give me the balm!"

The women passed him over the little clay pots, their faces showing wonder, resentment, shock. Since nearly all of the serving maids within his house were of the Prophet's faith, that a man should offer to do this humble service for an unknown maid appeared to them outrageous, or unthinkable, or both. As very nearly, be it said, did it so appear to his Natalia, who was to their ways and customs born, despite her Christian faith.

Alaric sat down on a low stool beside the bed. The girl was naked to the waist now; but lying there, face down, her striped and lacerated back was hardly an object to awake desire. What Alaric saw to his astonished pity was that she had been beaten many times. Some of the stripes were old, beginning to heal; some of the bruises were fading into greenish yellow; while above them, crisscrossing them, were the new and terrible marks of a whip expertly wielded.

He put out his hand, dripping with balm; touched her bleeding, purple welted back. She gave a little choked-off moan, then she was silent. Intensely silent. He went on rubbing in the healing balm under Natalia's ever-narrowing eyes. She moaned again; but 'twas a curiously ecstatic sound.

"What say you, girl?" Natalia said.

"Sweet—" she whispered. "My lord's hands—are—sweet—"

"Aizun!" Natalia got out. "Do not tell me—do not dare—that you knew not this creature before!"

"Nay, child," Alaric said. "Not even her name do I know. What is it, daughter?"

"Flora," the girl murmured. Her voice was stronger now. "And she lied! My sister Baldegotona lied when she said that you, my saintly lord—"

"Her sister!" Natalia said. "Aha, Aizun! This is the one who crouched at the keyhole while you—"

"Natalia, my lady and my wife," Alaric sighed, "wouldst do me the honor to elevate your thoughts the barest trifle? I have suffered thy neglect without complaint; nor have I attempted to remedy it elsewhere, neither with this poor child, her sister, nor any other—"

"Oh!" Natalia whispered. "'Tis true that I—but, oh, Aizun—I—suffered so with Ataulf! I was afraid! I am afraid!"

"Natalia," Alaric said. Her name, nothing more. Without any sharpness in his tone. No hint of reproach. But his voice went through her heart like a blade. She subsided at once into silence.

But Flora didn't.

"Oh, no, my lady!" she said. "You must not think that of thy saintly lord! He is good! Mayhap too good! He cured my lying wench of a sister when she'd been struck dumb of fear, when our brother had beaten her, too—"

"Your brother did *this?*" Alaric said.

"Nay, good my lord. The city executioner whipped me, at the head judge's command. My brother hath beaten me a dozen times; but never like this! He hath neither the strength—nor, methinks, the cruelty—"

"What did the head judge order you whipped for, girl?" Natalia said. "Prostitution?"

"Na—tal—ia!" Alaric said.

"Well, that's one of the things for which wenches are whipped. That and petty thievery. Mayhap she stole some bauble from a lady in whose house she worked—"

"I am not a servant, my lady!" Flora flared. "Nor a thief, nor a whore!"

"Then what are you, girl?" Natalia said.

"A Christian," Flora said. "For my faith I suffered this, my lady. And for my Lord Jesu, and his Lady Mother, I am prepared to die!"

At their morning meal Flora, much rested and much recovered, told her tale.

"I tarried long before coming here, my lady," she said. "For when my sister Baldegotona would not take back her story that he urged her to return to that Satanic infidel's faith, I began to doubt your lord. But then Dhabba told me what he'd done for her—"

"Dhabba!" Natalia said. She put down her knife, and glared at Alaric.

Wonderingly, Alaric shook his head. "I know no one of that name," he said.

"Aizun," Natalia began, "methinks—"

But Flora cut her off. "Methinks you merit not so good and sweet a lord, my lady," she said crisply, "and that your jealousy's unseemly. Thy lord hath never laid eyes upon poor Dhabba, any more than he'd ever seen me before I came crawling to his gate, seeking his mercy like a wounded dog! And much do I fear that they have much right who say—"

"What, daughter?" Alaric said, the clangor of iron getting into his voice now, beneath its solemn music.

But Flora was not subtle enough to note that. True believers seldom are.

"That she is the chief obstacle to thy beatification, my lord! And that the fact that thou liveth with her in—in the full uses of matrimony—is the reason that thou canst no longer do thy miracles—"

"Ha!" Natalia snorted. "Much they know about it! My lord hath not done more than touch my lips since our son was born! And he doth no wonders because I won't let him, knowing that my uncle the Emir will cut off his head if he performs them! And thou, fair Flora, art much too free with thy tongue, and quick to judge thy betters, to my liking!"

"I," Flora said angrily, "have no betters, my lady—save alone my Lord Jesu, and his Sainted Mother. I was born free and to some place in this world, and even should you be, as you claim, niece of that black-bearded devil who sits upon the throne, I—"

"Daughter," Alaric said. His voice was very quiet, but it halted her in mid-flight.

"My lord?" she whispered.

"My lady makes no claim to perfect piety, while you do. Hence, 'tis you who must display that humility, sobriety of speech, and quiet modesty which are attributes of a Christian maid. To exchange harsh words ill becomes any daughter of the Prince of Peace, and I'll have no more of this from either of you. Ye both sin, methinks, from excess of pride, so now I command ye: exchange the kiss of peace, and slang each other no more, either in my presence or out of it! Go on, kiss each other, and mutually beg pardon."

He was hard put to repress a smile at the sight of these two fair young faces then. But they did as he bade them, though the peck they gave each other's cheek was henlike in its quickness, and the "I pray thee forgive me," they exchanged came close to strangling them both.

"Now, Flora," he said, "this of the woman Dhabba wants explanation. You say I did her a service, though methinks I know not such a one at all—"

"Nor do you, good my lord!" Flora said quickly. "But you raised her baby from the dead all the same, without ever having seen her or it, thus duplicating one of the miracles of Our Savior!"

"Now, Flora—" Alaric said.

Flora got up from where she sat and fell to her knees before him. "I swear before God and his Holy Mother, that what I say is true, and that I myself witnessed it! Amen!" she said, and crossed herself.

Now Natalia pushed away her plate and sat there staring at her unbidden guest.

"Get up from there, daughter," Alaric said. "Good. Now speak. . . ."

508

"Dhabba," Flora said, "is a poor Christian woman who comes to lend service in our house—to cook and clean and do the heavier chores. I know her name sounds Moorish, but since she was orphaned in childhood, 'tis possible that the form of it hath been corrupted by Arabic usage. Methinks 'twas Deborah, or suchlike, but there is no way to tell now. Her husband Jorge is a porter, and likewise of our faith—"

"Go on, daughter," Alaric said.

"Well, though many years wed, they had no child until this year. Then God granted them a boy. Only the child was sickly. Some weeks ago, upon a certain day, its illness took a sudden, desperate turn for the worse—"

"And?" Natalia said.

"Poor Dhabba had heard my sister speak of thy saintly lord, my lady—for since the day he gave her back her speech Baldegotona hath done naught else but sing his praises endlessly—though less, methinks, from considerations of religion than from the fact thy lord is indeed most wondrous fair—"

"Which interests thee not at all, of course?" Natalia said tartly.

"Nay, my lady," Flora said quietly and with complete conviction. "I long ago pledged my life to Our Lord's service, taking privately on that day a vow of perpetual chastity. In any event, poor Dhabba started out to seek for thy lord San Alarico—having heard from many others besides my sister the story of the wonders he hath worked. But as she left the house, Jorge called her back. ' 'Tis bootless now, goodwife,' quoth he. 'Our son is dead. Look ye how still he lies.' Whereupon poor Dhabba let out such a shriek that I ran to see what ailed her—they live, my lord, in a house behind our house, on some land belonging to my brother. I entered their little hut, and lo, 'twas true: the child was dead. He neither breathed nor moved, nor did his poor tiny heart beat. I turned to them to offer them what comfort I could, but Dhabba broke free of Jorge's embrace and fled—"

"Where?" Natalia said.

"To seek thy saintly lord, my lady. She found him finally at the jail, where he was visiting that hero of our faith, Father Perfectus. Not daring to ask admission, she crouched by the door till he came out again. And, says she, his eyes were filled with such great and terrible sadness that she was stricken dumb. So because she could do no more, she reached out and touched his cloak. He did not notice this at all—but Dhabba swears that a—a glory flowed out of him so great that it was as though light itself stabbed into her heart. She came home reeling, half blind, a little mad, to find Jorge dancing and howling and weeping before their door with the child in his arms—alive! And I—"

"And thou?" Alaric said.

"Knelt there beside them in the mud and prayed. 'Twas this that made me to decide once more to defy my brother though I was black and blue all over from his daily beatings. But he was so wroth with me that he delivered me to the cadi, saying since I wished to die, he'd not deny me the privilege! Only the cadi ordered me whipped—and sent me home again. And the thrashing dealt one by a brother or a father is as nothing to what an expert torturer can do!"

"That we saw," said Natalia. "How you must have suffered, child—"

" 'Twas dreadful, but I was sustained by my faith in Our Redeemer. As soon as my brother left the house I fled—and came here. The rest ye know—"

"Flora, daughter," Alaric said in a troubled voice, "art sure the child was dead?"

"As I am that my Savior lives! What's more, my saintly lord, Jorge and I, by questioning Dhabba, established that 'twas the exact instant she touched thy cloak that the child awoke and began to cry—"

"Aizun," Natalia said dolefully, "I am afraid! Thou'rt—"

And 'twas then, of course, that the servant came into the dining hall with Eulogius behind him.

"Aizun, my son," Eulogius said, "I know and am saddened by the fact that we see not eye to eye in many things. But word hath reached my ears this morning of another of thy wonders—a child raised from the dead! Is this thing true?"

"Aye, good my Father, it is!" Flora cried. "I witnessed it myself!"

Eulogius turned and stared at her. His hot little black eyes locked with her wide brown ones, and held and held until the very air sang with tension, went smoky, blue, seemed to whine. What passed between them was a recognition so complete, that 'twas in itself a kind of consummation.

"Tell me about it, daughter," Eulogius said. His voice, speaking, was deep and quiet; but a tender tremor had got into it somehow.

Whereupon, Flora began once more to speak; and her young, somewhat strident voice, too, had changed. Now it was flutelike, dulcet, full of half hidden little runs and trills, soft tremolos, breathless little pauses.

"Why," Alaric thought, less in amazement than in outrage, " 'tis—'tis the voice of a woman in love! And he—"

"I thank thee, daughter," Eulogius said. That was all. Just those four words; but at the sound of them Natalia's soft blue eyes leaped light-filled and startled in her face, sought Alaric's searching them, putting to him their silent, likewise amazed, outraged question.

Slowly Alaric nodded. Natalia clapped hands to visibly flaming cheeks; but neither the priest nor the virgin noticed that. Eulogius tore with noticeable effort his gaze from Flora's fair young face, and turned to Alaric once more.

"Son Aizun," he said, and now, for the first time since they had known him, his voice was truly gentle, "is it thy intention to attend the execution?"

"Aye, Father," Alaric said.

"Aizun, no!" Natalia cried. " 'Tis much too dangerous! The mob will be inflamed and—"

"God will protect him, daughter," Eulogius said. "He doth protect His Own, you know. Thou hast the right decision made, my son. And now, I go—"

"Father!" Flora's voice was shrill, edgy. "Ere you depart, willst hear my confession? I am in a state of sin and—"

"Here?" Eulogius said.

"Why not, good Father?" Flora said. "My lord will provide us with a room apart where—"

Eulogius' dark little eyes had coals of fire in their depths. His face darkened, mottled. Beads of sweat showed on his forehead.

Poor devil! Alaric thought.

"Nay," Eulogius said quietly, " 'tis not meet. Come to the Church of San Zoil at the tenth hour tomorrow, and I will hear it there."

Flora went on staring at him a moment longer. Then she dropped her gaze.

"As thou will, my Father," she whispered.

"Nay, daughter! As God wills," Eulogius said.

XXXI

Alaric came away from the square reeling, deafened, blind, the roar of the mob still ringing in his ears. He could hear again Perfectus' terrible words:

"I cry anathema upon thy Prophet and all his works! May God punish him for all the many souls he hath seduced into hell! And as for thee, Nasr, apostate from the True Faith, castrate in spirit as well as in body, upon thy head rest my dying curse! Thou wilt not live to see the anniversary of this day. Before many moons have fled thou wilt be delivered unto Satan, thy true Lord. And now, executioner, strike well! Thy blade is but the key which for me unlocks the doors of paradise! My blessing upon all those who in Lord Jesu do believe! Upon those who follow Mahound, my curse!"

There were those in that crowd who reached out to touch Lord Aizun as he passed. A woman produced scissors, cut away a snippet of his robe. Others were moved to follow her; before he reached the exit from the square, his clothes were in rags. But he moved on, all his face bedewed with tears, his heart and mind appalled by that sickening sight: how the axes rose, glittering in the sun; held for an instant, whirled into an arc; smashed down; the sound it made striking drowned out by the mob's bestial bellow. Then the executioner lifted Perfectus' gory, severed head—by one ear, for the priest's tonsured, close-clipped hair afforded his blunt fingers no grip. Perfectus' eyes and mouth were both opened wide, seeming to scream his terrible curses still.

Alaric could feel the sickness in him unto death, that awful ache beginning to assail his poor wounded head. His footsteps tottered, stumbled; he was about to fall when gentle hands reached out and took his arm.

He raised his tear-glazed, half-blinded eyes and stared into Natalia's small, sweet face.

"Come, sweet my lord," she murmured, "and I will care for thee as is meet and good in God's sight. I—I've been a coward, Aizun. But women must suffer to bring children into this world—and, oh, our little Ataulf is worth the price. Wouldst have a daughter next? Or another son? Whichever you prefer, I—"

"Ah, God, the single-mindedness of women!" he wept. "Sweet child, you know not what you say!"

"Ah, but I do!" she said. "So cease to weep, my lord! I've heard poor Perfectus died well and bravely. Surely he hath gained God's favor by his valor, and his sacrifice, so—"

Alaric stared at her, and now the tears were gone from his eyes. The ache in his head was still murderous, but even it could not dominate his wonder at the invincible oversimplifications of the human heart. Perfectus, he thought, died cursing millions of people because they believe not as he'd have them do. A priest of Our Lord Jesu, he could not in that awful moment recall that the essence of our faith is to forgive. Hath any man since Our Lord himself managed that? Did not the last Christian die at Golgotha upon a Cross?

"Besides," Natalia said, trying to keep the cheerfulness out of her voice. "once more our house is our own. Dear Flora hath left us, for which God and Our Lady both be praised!"

Alaric stopped short, looked at his wife.

"Oh, no! I had nothing to do with it, sweet my lord! Since she started going to San Zoil, she met a young nun, called, she says, Maria. So now to the cloister she must hie—and good riddance! She'll be safe there from her brother, the head cadi, and all the rest. And that monster of piety, Eulogius, can cease to torment himself, take off his hair shirt, throw away the whip he uses nightly on himself to still his desire—"

"Natalia," Alaric whispered. "You cannot know this terrible thing you say!"

"I don't *know* it. But I guess it. Ugh! Those hot little eyes of his! He hath undressed me with them often enough. But with Flora he goes further than that. Not only doth he strip her naked with his beady little gaze, but lays her down, hitches up his cassock, and—"

"Natalia!"

"Oh, but I am a strumpet at heart, sweet my lord! And this night I mean to prove it to thee."

"Child," Alaric said gently, "after what I have seen and suffered this day, not even thou couldst to love arouse me. For verily what I have in my heart is a kind of death—"

"Oh!" she whispered. "I am sorry, sweet Aizun. I wish you had not witnessed that. Your poor head aches you, doth it not? Come, I'll put hot cloths on it, and—"

She stopped short, staring at the woman who had stepped out before them, completely blocking their path. Then her eyes softened with real pity, for not even she could imagine that this poor bedraggled creature was one of Alaric's former loves.

The beggar woman dropped to her knees before them.

"My lord!" she wailed. "He hath died again! And I could not find thee to touch thy cloak once more. See—how still he is? Touch him, San Alarico—restore him once more to life—"

Then she held out that little bundle of rags to Alaric. Gently Alaric pushed them away, and looked into that purplish mottled mass that once had been a face, caught full in his nostrils that awful stench.

"Dhabba," he said gently, "I cannot restore him. His life hath fled him much too far—"

"Jorge says I should bury him," Dhabba said, "but I won't! He's mine! He's my son! Jorgito, niño—hear me! Hear thy mother! Come back to me—Oh, San Alarico, touch him with thy sainted hand and give him back his life!"

"Dhabba," Alaric said, "take thy son to the priest, and give him Christian burial. Tell the good fathers that I will pay all charges, and for masses, too, to insure his innocent soul's repose. But thou canst not keep him above ground—for already his poor body rots."

"No!" Dhabba shrieked. "He lives! He lives still! He is only sleeping, and thou, San Alarico, canst recall him!"

"Woman," Natalia said then, "don't be a fool. Can you not smell how this poor little lump of carrion stinks? 'Tis an offense in God's nostrils, and you risk the pest! Do as my lord commands you. Take thy child's body and—"

But now Dhabba leaned forward until her mad face was inches from Natalia's own. Her wine and garlic scented breath made a miasmic cloud about Natalia's head; and when to that was added the various odors of her Christian—and hence unwashed—body, plus the sweet sickening stench of putrefaction arising from the bundle in her arms, the wonder was that Natalia did not swoon.

"Thou strumpet!" the madwoman hissed. "Harlot! Scarlet woman— who hath destroyed his powers! Before, I touched his cloak and my son was to life restored; but now thou wallowest with him nightly in thy filth, and drain the virtue from his sainted loins! God's curse be upon thee, trull! For but for thee, thou slut, my son would live!"

"Dhabba!" Alaric's voice rang like bronze.

"Aye, my lord?" Dhabba whispered. "Aye, San Alarico?"

"Get thee hence, and give Christian sepulchre to thy son. I command thee, go!"

"Aye," Dhabba whispered. "I'll obey thee, Blessed Saint. For as for her—may she rot in hell!"

"Oh, Aizun, Aizun!" Natalia wept. "I am afraid! She—"

"She's mad, poor thing. Ah, God, but thou hast put far too much grief into this thy world! Come, Natalia—there is naught to fear. Come, sweet child, come—"

One month from that day Natalia lay gripping her pillow till her knuckles whitened with the strain. But her eyes were tearless.

"Aizun," she said, "why won't you love me? Have you taken a vow to live in chastity from now on?"

"And if I have?" he said.

"I'll respect it. But methinks I'll go mad—or die. I—I have such a need of thee, my lord! Have you?"

"No, sweet child," Alaric said.

He saw joy flare in her eyes.

"Then?" she murmured.

"I cannot," he said, "and I beg of you that you do not ask me why."

"Oh!" she whispered. "Aizun, is it because of Afaf? Hast promised her to—to husband me no more?"

"Natalia, don't be a childish fool. What need have I to promise Afaf anything? What was between us died long ago. Love with Afaf, marriage to Afaf, became forever impossible for me the day that Zoë took her own life, because of what had passed between Afaf and me. And this before thou wert born, child!"

"Ohhh!" Natalia wailed. "Thou—thou'st never loved another save alone that little Greek! By dying for thee like that, she's kept thy love forever, and I—"

He took her small face between his hands, looked into her eyes.

"Methinks that I have never truly loved until God gave me thee, sweet child. And in heaven above He knows how I suffer from this burden which He hath put upon me—"

"What burden, Aizun? Tell me!"

"No, Natalia. I cannot. 'Tis—too terrible—"

"Tell me, my lord. I can stand it. What I cannot bear is not knowing. Whatever thy secret is, I forgive thee for it, beforehand. I'll not weep, or slang thee, or throw tantrums. I promise. I'll be good. Please, sweet my lord—"

He looked at her. Sighed. Then he said: "Mayhap 'twould be better if you knew—"

"Tell me!" she cried.

"Al Harrani says—that if you're ever—with child again—you'll die."

She lay there staring at him, her blue eyes very wide, and soft.

"For me," she whispered, "as always. Oh, Aizun, Aizun, how canst thou be so good? All these months, because, because—"

515

"Because Ataulf needs his mother; and I need thee, child," he said.

But when he waked on the morrow she was gone from his bed, even from his house. The servants told him that she had called for a litter and departed, saying she had some purchases to make. Because she had never done such a thing before, and because she had left even before the shops in Córdoba were open, he did not believe that explanation. So worried was he that he sent a servant to the glassworks to tell al Firnas he would not come to attend to business matters that day. But at eleven o'clock she came gaily in, her arms full of packages, followed by servitors of every notable emporium in town bearing still more.

"Willst be so kind as to pay them, sweet my lord?" she said. "I ran out of money hours ago! Oh, but I've spent fortunes!"

"Natalia," he said when they'd gone, trying to keep the amused tenderness from showing through his voice, "might I ask for what reason you've brought me to the brink of ruin?"

"Because," she said, " 'tis a day of joy! I must deck my body for my lord. I must give him rare sweets to eat, and rare wines to drink in the event that his blood prove sluggish. I have been dying of want—and now need want no more. And you, my saintly lord, have been dying, I think, in like fashion—and can now be reborn!" She wound her arms around his neck, pressed her body to his.

"Natalia!" he said. "Little fool! Let go of me!"

"Nay. Nay. Never. Please, my lord. Sweet my lord. San Alarico. High Priest and Holy Pope of—"

"Natalia!"

"Oh, all right. I'll have to tell thee, and tease no more. I went to see al Harrani. This morning. I told him I felt most wondrous fine—except that I was starving to death for want of my sweet lord's attentions and that I was never born to be a nun. No woman of my family ever was—not even poor mother. I insisted that he examine me. Poor man! He was so frightened. Said that a physician should never examine a woman without her husband's consent, and that the examination should be done in my lord's presence. So I loosed a few choice phrases that Saadyah taught me to the effect of how he was ruining my married life. So he examined me. Pronounced me a marvel, fit to bear thee twenty sons. It seems that Ataulf's huge Gothic head stretched all the places where I was too narrow, so now I could give birth to a camel or an elephant without pain. Now there's a thought. Wouldst prefer a camel or an elephant for a son, my lord?"

"Natalia," he said, "if thou'rt lying to me—"

"Go and ask him! Send a servant to bring him here! No, don't. Send for him tomorrow. Nay, the day after. Mayhap I'll consent by then to release thee from these chores that bore and fatigue thee so! But, at the moment—"

"At the moment?" he mocked gaily, his heart full of joy.

Leading him by the hand toward their bedchamber, she said, "Thou must commence thy riding lesson. Thy wrestling match. Thy—" She said that phrase in Arabic. Both her accent and her words were appallingly, clinically precise.

"Natalia!" he said.

"Well, what do *you* call it, sweet my lord?" Natalia said.

By mid-July she was round and rosy with the lineaments of a new pregnancy. But her health was so obviously good that the ice-cold fear sleeping in him had no cause to raise its head. She laughed, sang, scampered about, played with little Ataulf, and ate enough to feed a regiment. She experienced no morning sickness at all.

But slowly, as fall stiffened into winter, and the Sierras beyond Córdoba stabbed heaven with their whitened peaks, he began to note a change in her. She laughed less often now, and when she did her laughter had a hectic quality to it. Now and again, he surprised in her glance what could have been the leap of fear. And she once more to sacred things turned her thoughts. He needs must have Father John of God, in to hear her confessions, say mass for her.

To his vast relief, Father Juan was sternly opposed to Eulogius and his Exalted Ones. "The first duty of the Church is to survive, my son," he said. "If those madmen provoke the Emir into destroying us, he hath the power to do it! Have they never thought that the Christian faith may vanish from all al Andalus because of them?"

"Methinks they think not at all, Father," Alaric said.

"They think—but wrongly, son," Father Juan said. "I, too, suffer from the burdens upon us imposed: the taxes, the prohibition against the sweet sound of church bells, the forbidding of passing our holy images in solemn procession through the streets, the occasional insult offered to my cloth. But none of these things threaten the existence of the Church! Martyrdom is justified when the faith's in danger. But here 'tis protected by the highest power of the state—and endangered only by mad fools like Eulogius and Alvaro who would provoke a tolerant and kindly creed into forgetting that tolerance and slaughtering us—"

"You justify Perfectus' death, then, Father?" Alaric said.

"Would we not in their position, do the same?" Father Juan said sternly. "Nay! Have we not under our Gothic kings done far worse? Could a man in those days, of his own free will, remain a Jew, or follow the Grecian rite, or cling to Arianism? If he persisted in his error, did we grant him so merciful a death as the ax? Did we not rather burn him alive? And will we not do so again, when we have the power?"

"Thou," Alaric said, "art a strange Catholic, Father!"

"I am a true one. I render under Caesar, Caesar's things. And I know Our Redeemer commanded us to remove the beam from our own eyes before casting out the mote from our brother's. To go the second mile; turn the unslapped check. To never lift the stone with sinful hands—"

Alaric smiled at him sadly then. "Nay, Father, thou'rt not a Catholic," he said. "Thou art a Christian."

Father Juan stopped and stared at him. "You'd imply they're not the same thing, my son?" he said.

"Sometimes. Rarely. In the same fashion that Our Lord was a Jew."

"Thou'rt strange, my son. But no matter. Might I, touching upon mundane things, suggest a thing to thee, Alaric, saintly son?"

"Of course. What thing, Father?"

"Call upon the physician al Harrani," Father Juan said.

"She is with child?" al Harrani said. "In God's name, Sahib Aizun, I told thee she would die!"

Alaric stood there staring at the physician. He could feel his knees buckling under him; a cold, sick wave of weakness extending along his nerves, his veins.

"She—she did not come to thee?" he whispered. "Thou didst not tell her—"

"In the Name of the Compassionate, the Wise, the One, I have not seen thy wife since I gave her permission to get up after her lying in," al Harrani said angrily. Then his voice softened, filled with pity. "So she lied to thee—eh? Told thee she was fit for childbearing? What ferocious little beasts women are when their maternal instinct's aroused! Sit down, my lord. Here, smell this vial. 'Twill clear thy head. Better now?"

"Aye. Tell me, wise physician, what can we do?"

"If she's early in her term, I'll force her to abort. Her pelvic girdle is far too narrow, my lord. 'Twas a miracle I did not have to resort to that murderous operation by which the first of the Caesars was born, in order to deliver her of thy son. 'Tis a most wondrous feat of surgery, right enough; and I can boast I do it well. Only women always die of it! How far is she gone?"

Alaric stopped and calculated. 'Twas December now.

"Five months," he whispered.

Wordlessly al Harrani shook his head.

"Too—late?" Alaric got out.

"I fear me that it is," the physician said; "still, I'll get my instruments

518

and come with thee. Nature is strange—mayhap there may be more hope than—I believe."

"Hmmm!" al Harrani said. "Hmm! 'Tis strange, but—"

"What's strange, wise physician?" Alaric said.

"That tale of jinn and demons she told thee—is not entirely false. She doth have more space now. Mayhap not enough, but still—"

"I—I'll live?" Natalia said.

"Aye. That surely," al Harrani said.

"And—and my baby?" she whispered.

"Ah—there's the rub. Of that I cannot be sure. If it is somewhat smaller than normal, I think so, yes. 'Twould be better if 'twere female— since girls right oft are smaller—"

"Oh, my lord Harrani, save it! I don't care about me! Save my baby! I—"

"Quiet, child," Alaric said; "you must keep your strength. . . ."

"For what? He said I'd live! It's my baby that—Oh, sweet my lord, I have no need of strength—"

"Ah, but you do," Alaric said grimly, "to bear the caning I'm going to administer thee, once thou'rt up from there!"

They came close to losing al Harrani's services; for the new Royal Physician became involved in the Lady Tarub's plot against the Emir's life. Secretly summoned by the head eunuch Nasr, turned now—as his twisted kind so often did—against his master, al Harrani was forced to prepare the poison; but a man devoted lifelong to healing is not easily constrained to kill. Besides, al Harrani loved and respected the lofty figure of the Emir; in good truth al Rahman was the noblest figure his race and times produced. At the risk of his own life, then, the physician managed to send a warning to the Emir through the lovely concubine Fakhr—she who had been her lord's favorite until displaced by Tarub. Warned, al Rahman invited Nasr to drink first from the fatal cup. So it was that of his own perfidy the chief eunuch died.

It is not too much to say that gentle Natalia's life hung upon these sad events; for much did she need al Harrani's care. Fortunately for her, and thereby for Alaric, Fakhr told her lord the truth about how she came to be warned. Abd al Rahman rewarded the physician handsomely. But, to everyone's surprise, the would-be murderess Tarub remained soft and smiling at his side. Not even proof of her criminal intent could shake the Emir's love for her. Freely he pardoned her, considered the incident closed.

But it was not closed. The Exalted Ones took Nasr's death as a fulfillment of the martyred Perfectus' prophecies. Their meetings redoubled. Now and again, they began to show their hand.

First was the Christian merchant Juan, accused of blasphemy because he swore by the Prophet's beard. Wisely deciding the crime hardly worth a death, the head cadi had him soundly thrashed, and ridden through the streets upon an ass, his face turned toward the ugly beast's tail.

More meetings. More ratlike scurrying about, furtive and secret in the night. More whispers. An increase in tension until the very air seemed to whine, smoke-blue, spark-shot. But nothing more. There matters rested until my lady Natalia, wife of ibn al Qutiyya, was brought to bed of her second child.

It went well enough, at first. Al Harrani was advised, and took up residence in Alaric's house so that his vigilance could be constant. Now and again he emerged from the bedroom to advise Alaric, and the alarming number of people who had descended upon his house—his sister Gelesvinta; his three daughters, Theodora, Aurea, and Munia, occasionally the husbands of all four, though the men mercifully did not remain, but came and went as their occupations permitted them; the Lady Sumayla, with from time to time her son, Prince al Kamil; Afaf; and always huge, brooding, his bearded face filled with a terror greater than Alaric's own, Saadyah—of her progress. Which was good. Which was astonishingly good—even normal.

Alaric began to relax, a little. He murmured a little prayer of anticipatory thanksgiving. Which was mayhap an error. But not an excessively great one. For when that cry rose up, naked, blade-thin, edged, hanging on the night like the embodiment of terror, it came not from the bedroom where poor Natalia fought her desperate battle to win the fight for which she was poorly armed, but from the servants' quarters.

Alaric turned, stormed through the door white-lipped with rage that the wenches should cry out so at such a time, entered the quarters of Natalia's women, to find Kalim, whose work it was to guard and care for little Ataulf, moaning and writhing on the floor, while between her lips issued a bloody froth.

"What ails thee, wench?" he said. "Art ill?"

Then, bending close, he saw it: the hilt of a common kitchen knife protruding from Kalim's belly; and the sullen dark flow welling up around it, dyeing all the nursemaid's robe with red. He looked at once into Ataulf's crib, for they had moved the year-old child into Kalim's room lest he wake at night and disturb his mother with his lusty howls. The crib was empty. Even the sheet and the coverlet were gone.

He looked through the ice-cold death that had imprisoned him, shutting him off from all the world, to see the other servants pouring into the room. But when he spoke his voice was oddly cold and quiet.

"My lord Harrani, the physician; fetch him. And tell the Sahib ben Hasdai to join me here," he said.

Then once more, Aizun ibn al Qutiyya, San Alarico, did a wonder perform. He knelt on the floor beside the writhing, moaning girl, put out his hand, and touched her forehead.

"Thou'll not die, Kalim," he said, his voice grave and slow, with angelic music filled. "Thy wound will heal within a fortnight. Even now it hath ceased to hurt—hath it not?"

Kalim's eyes came open, filled with awe, held by the tender blue luminosity of his gaze.

"Yes, my lord," she whispered, "it hurts no more. Oh, good my lord— my baby! My poor little Ataulf—she—she stole him!"

"Who?" Alaric said.

"A madwoman. Dressed—in rags. Stinking most fearfully. She said— that since—that since—"

Al Harrani and Saadyah came through the door. Alaric halted them with a lifted hand.

"That since?" he murmured.

"That since—my lady—robbed her—of her son—she'd—"

Alaric stood up.

"Remain quiet, Kalim," he said gently. "By Lord Jesu's tender mercy, I promise thee it will not hurt, even when the Sahib Physician draws out that blade. Nor will it bleed over much. And in a fortnight thou shalt be well. This in recompense for thy bravery. . . ." Then he turned, and Saadyah saw the screaming hell deep in his eyes.

"Saad," he whispered, "we must ride thou and I—fast and far. God grant we come in time."

The trouble was that they could not go directly to Dhabba's hovel, for they had no idea in which quarter of Córdoba it lay. All Alaric knew was that it was situated behind Flora's and Baldegotona's house. But since the question of the location of that house had never before arisen, Alaric knew not where it was, either. What he did know was that it must be somewhere near the Munyat Adjab, because Baldegotona had taken refuge in the house of Yahya ibn Zakariya' al Khashab, the nephew of the distinguished lady for whom that quarter was named.

So first of all Saadyah and he rode to that distant quarter. And there that utterly insane quality with which all of life is hedged about intervened. Yahya was not at home. He was, the servant told them, attending a meeting; then seeing in the lamplight the style and cut of their dress, he leaned forward and whispered excitedly: "A Christian meeting, good my lords!"

"The Lady Adjab?" Alaric said.

"Is at the palace visiting her departed lord's son, the Emir," the servant said.

"And my lord Yahya's lady mother?"

"Is here; but 'tis very late, and she hath retired—"

"Wake her!" Saadyah roared.

"But gently," Alaric said, "and do but ask her this: the street in which lies the house of the brother of the maid Baldegotona, whom I had the occasion to meet here in her house. . . ."

The manservant was gone above a half an hour. Then he came back, spread wide his hands in a hlepless gesture.

"My lady says she hath no idea where Lord Yahya's mad friends live," he said.

"Now what?" Saadyah growled. "Go we from house to house and knock on every door?"

Alaric sat there on his white horse, his head bowed upon his breast. At that moment he looked curiously old and frail. One who did not know that his forty-seventh birthday was but lately passed, would have thought him above three score years of age.

"Nay," he whispered, "we ride back to the Church of San Acisclo, and awaken Father Juan—"

"God's blood, Alaric, why?"

"Because he knows the name of the cloister in which fair Flora hath taken refuge," Alaric said, sighing; "and surely not even the fever and the chills of her devotion have caused her to forget the location of her brother's house. . . ."

By the time all that had been done, by the time the various obstacles had been overcome—Father Juan was a sound sleeper; awake, his senses returned slowly; the Mother Superior of the convent saw Lord Satan's hand writ large in the fact that two well-dressed gentlemen should long after midnight knock on the cloister's door; Flora herself believed them at first her brother's agents, and would not speak until from a latticed window she had beheld their faces—the night was fading into dawn.

They rode back, retracing exactly all their futile steps to the Munyat Adjab; and there, a few short streets from the Lady Adjab's house, they found the modest home of Flora, her sister, and her brother; and behind it the filthy hovel in which Jorge and his mad wife Dhabba dwelt.

Jorge knelt before them, tears in his eyes; all his work-gnarled body shaking with terror.

"I tried to get from her where she had stolen it, my lords!" he wept. "But she is mad, God wot! She would not tell me. And when I tried to take it from her arms—she screamed and swore she'd throw it down the well!"

Alaric passed a tongue-tip over bone-dry lips. "Hath—hath she harmed—my son?" he said.

"Nay, good my lord!" Jorge cried. "She'd never harm a child—not ordinarily. She sits within, cradling it in her arms, and crooning lullabies to it. Methinks that if all three of us were to—to rush her from different angles—we might—"

Alaric shook his head. "Lead her forth, good Jorge," he said. "I would speak to her."

But Dhabba screamed and swore and refused to leave her hovel. Bowing his head, Alaric entered it.

They heard his voice, grave and sweet and slow, filled up with all the tenderness in the world.

"Willst come with me, good Dhabba?" he said.

Then quietly, normally, almost sane, her own: "Aye, that I will, my saintly lord—"

She came out into the refuse- and rubble-filled yard of the hut, and now the sun was up so they could see her clearly. She held a bundle of rags in her arms, out of which peeked one plump and naked foot. But that foot was blue.

"Dhabba—" Alaric said.

"Yes, my lord Saint?" Dhabba said.

"Kneel and pray with me—"

At once she sank to her knees, as did good Jorge, and even Saadyah to whom all faiths were a mockery.

"Mother of God," Alaric's voice soared up, "ye see before thee a woman whose only sin is to love children beyond idolatry. In Thy Name, who loved thy Son, and in His who bade us suffer little children and forbid them not, for of such is the kingdom of heaven, I beg thee to restore her darkened mind. Thou willst, willst thou not?" He paused as though listening; then his voice was the music of church bells: "I thank Thee, dear little Mother of God!"

He got up then; put out his hand to Dhabba. Wonderingly she got to her feet.

"Now thou'rt sane, Dhabba," he murmured. "From now on thou shalt be clean and industrious and obedient to thy husband. In the full-

523

ness of time, mayhap God will send thee another child. Now give me my son."

"Thy son, my lord?" Dhabba said; then she looked down at the rag-covered bundle in her arms. Her face twisted into horror. "I—I stole it, didn't I? And I—I killed a woman! With a knife! Oh, good my lord—oh, San Alarico—how could I do those things?"

"Thou wert mad, Dhabba," Alaric said, "but now thou'rt sane. Give me my son and let us depart in peace. The girl thou stabbed lives, and all thy sins are forgiven thee—"

She passed that rag-covered bundle over. Quickly Alaric unwrapped it, looked into the face of his son. Then he turned and gave the child to Saadyah.

"Hold him while I mount," he said, "then pass him up to me—"

"But, Aizun! He—he's—"

"Give him to me now, Saadyah," Alaric said, "and get thee up, for we have far to ride."

"Alaric—" Saadyah said. Then he closed his mouth, passed up the child, mounted his great black. But of a sudden in a nearby street he yanked his mount to a startled, dancing halt, threw his gray-streaked bearded head backward, and split the night apart with an anguished scream, high, grating, edged, woman-shrill. "Willst Thou never relent?" he howled. "Is there no end to Thy fiendishness?"

"Saad—" Alaric whispered; but Saadyah reined his mount in close, threw one gigantic arm about Alaric's shoulder, and almost crushed him in that great embrace; bending his lion-like head above the dead child and weeping for it, for his friend, for Natalia whom he loved, for the sons he'd never had.

"Why dost thou weep, Saadyah?" Alaric said.

Saadyah's big head came up. The tears stood and glittered in his eyes, on his face, clung like frozen white fire to his mustache and his beard.

"Because," he rumbled, "I am but mortal and hence I can. Because I bear not the fearsome burden of being a saint—"

"I am no saint, Saadyah!" Alaric said.

"Aye—thou'rt no saint. Thou whose loving kindness extends to this—that thou hid from that poor mad bitch who'd smothered it the fact that thy son is dead! If that be not sainthood, then I'm Lord Saithan. As mayhap I am. As mayhap I am—"

Alaric looked at him. The ghost of a smile hovered about lips whiter now than all his face.

"Nay, Saad. Satanus thou'rt not. And hear me, brother, mark me well: One day thou shalt be with me in Paradise," he said.

They came up to the house. Entered it. Alaric had the dead child wrapped in its coverlet, so that none of them might see its bluish mottled face and cry out. But all the salon was filled with the sound of weeping.

He turned his eyes from one tear-stained face to another, while his own grayed slowly out of life. Saadyah caught his arm, held him erect; Afaf leaped up and took the baby from his arms.

"Natalia—" he whispered. "Is she—is she—"

"Nay, Aizun," Afaf said. "In that, thy luck holds. 'Twas the child. The loveliest baby girl—only—only—"

"What, Afaf?"

"Nothing al Harrani could do would make her breathe."

Alaric bowed his head. " 'Tis as God wills," he said. "May I see her now?"

"Of course!" Afaf said contemptuously. "*She's* all right. Satan looks after his own!"

"Afaf!" Saadyah rumbled warningly, but at that moment Afaf looked down.

"Sweet boy," she cooed, "my Ataulf—yes, my own. Thou'st come back to me, little angel? Thou'st—"

She halted. Her amber eyes dilated in her dark face, stretched, widened, flaming, speaking fire.

Then she began to scream.

Alaric sat by Natalia's bed, holding her pale bloodless hand. She had her eyes closed, but the tears squeezed out from under her lashes and penciled silver across her cheeks.

"Sweet child," he whispered, "do not weep. Thou'rt here, and that's all that matters. . . ."

"But my baby, Aizun," she sobbed, "my baby—she was so tiny—and so sweet—Oh, dear God, what sin have I done that I—"

"No sin, sweet child," Alaric murmured, "no sin at all—"

She lay there crying. Then she said, suddenly, her voice bright, hopeful, strong: "Ataulf! Bring him to me—I—I've neglected him fearfully of late. And now that he's all I've got—"

The door crashed open, flooding that darkened room with light. Afaf stood in it, tall, lean, terrible. Yet beautiful, somehow. An Astarte-Ishtar—the fires in her brazen belly more hot than those of her lord Ba'al. Her voice rasped, awful in its triumph. "Thou hast—nothing, Natalia! No fruits of the love thou'st stolen canst thou keep! For thy son, too—is dead!"

Instantly, Saadyah was upon her. One mighty blow hammered her to the floor. He stood there looking down at her where she lay, moaning a little. He shook his big head tiredly, stepped over her, moved into the bedroom, stood there looking down at Natalia lying white, rigid, tearless on her bed.

Then he turned and walked out of there, stepping once more over his wife's prostrate body. Alaric heard the front door slam suddenly. But after that there was no sound at all. It was so still that, listening hard, a man might hear the angels weep.

If angels ever weep, he thought, if pity's an attribute of God.

XXXII

"How is she, Aizun?" Saadyah said.

Alaric shrugged

"She lives," he said, after a fashion. Or rather, she exists. She eats and drinks the absolute minimum necessary to keep life in her frail body; as for the rest, she spends every waking hour studying the catechism, reading the lives of the saints, or at prayer. . . ."

"Strange," Saadyah rumbled. "Nathalie's never impressed me as being one of those female fools who approach God with thick, yolky cries. Methinks a good lusty belly-thumper could cure them of their religiosity in a fortnight—for if a woman's blood be not frequently and sufficiently cooled below, it rises to her head, and gives her the vapors."

"Nor was she," Alaric said, "albeit she had of her mother a certain inclination toward piety, which the mischief, gaiety, and sunny warmth of her nature served well enough to keep in check; but now—"

"But now?" Saadyah said.

"She is obsessed with the sense of sin. She considers herself the most unpardonably guilty of women."

"Not Nathalie! In God's Name, Aizun, why?"

Alaric bowed his head. Looked up again into the troubled face of his friend.

"Because of me, Saad," he whispered. "Because of me—"

"Same question! In God's name, Aizun, why?"

"You know that there's a school of thought hereabouts which holds that I am a wonder-worker and a saint?"

"Of which school thy servant Saadyah is a most devoted adherent!" Saadyah said dryly.

"Turn about is fair play," Alaric said. "In God's name, Saadyah, why?"

"Later. Get on with your explication of my little angel's trouble. She interests me more than you do, Holy Fool!"

Alaric smiled. "All right. Eulogius, failing to be able to use me for his demented ends—which were, methinks to force me to perform a series of miracles before the scaffold on which poor Perfectus was executed—"

"And this new mad fool, Isaac? Hath he approached you about that?"

"No. By now he knows better. In any event, failing to bend me to his will, he spread abroad—or more likely, since he is not given to lying, did not rebuke those who spread abroad—the tale that my fall from monastic chastity by entering into marriage with Natalia had cost me my miraculous powers. You know that after that uproar before my house at which time I am alleged to have made a blind man see and a paralytic maiden walk—he came close to inducing Natalia to take the veil, and leave him in full possession of me, so that he might make of me a saint—"

"God of Abraham!" Saadyah said.

"Amen!" Alaric murmured. "Now that, according to my poor child bride, was the beginning of her life of sin. She, according to her new portrait of herself, is as lecherous as a she-monkey, utterly depraved; she, according to what she now doth believe, is being punished for her terrible lustfulness, her carnality, by the loss of her children; she, according to what she hath been told by Eulogius' life-hating Exalteds, is utterly damned—"

"By which they mean she's a normal, warm, and loving woman?" Saadyah said.

"Aye. And not overwarm at that. Even before, she could go weeks, even months, without remembering her husband was alive—"

"Unless you reminded her—like every normal woman. Love lies forever sleeping in the female form, boy, and seldom wakes of itself. Even when enhungered, most females experience but a vague and diffuse discomfort. God, but they're lucky! While we—But I interrupt you. Get on with it, boy."

"The trouble is that there is an active climate of hostility to my poor sweet childish love, of which she first learned from her encounter with Dhabba. All the female Exalteds seem to believe that they were indeed deprived of my wondrous services—"

"Ha!" Saadyah said.

"Not in *that* sense, billy goat!"

"Aye, precisely in that sense, albeit they know it not. But the problem's thorny—thornier, indeed, than you think, Aizun. The best minds have wrestled with it from the beginning of history: How doth one explain gratuitous evil in the world? We're forced from infancy into the acceptance of cause and effect: 'You be good, Saadyah; or by heaven I'll flog thee till the blood runs down.' There you have it, Aizun! I remain good—by which my august father—rest his soul!—meant that I indulge not myself in stolen sweetmeats, flasks of wine, or between the rabbi's youngest daughter's creamy thighs, what a brood sow she hath grown up to be, *sic transit gloria mundi*—and my arse remains unstriped! Only, slowly, some few rare ones of us, thou, I suspect, and I, surely, among them, begin slowly and dimly to realize that we live in a universe where beyond a few severely simple limits cause and effect do not hold good; that one is evil, and grows rich and great, that one is good, truly good, like thou, and thy arse is forever purpling, bloody, and crisscrossed with blows! Hath thou, my friend, ever seen one provable case where the good or evil a man doth—beyond, of course, the simpleminded enforcement of idiotic concepts by society's police, scaffolds, whips, and jails—matters what the mule drops behind him on the street?"

Alaric held him with the soft blue luminosity of his gaze.

"It doth—to me," he said quietly, "though I grant you the rewards and punishments are irrelevancies. What more can a man ask of life than to be able to dwell with himself—in peace?"

"Oh, thou'rt an exception, San Alarico! But see you not that 'tis the necessity for equating punishment with sin that is destroying our little angel? She suffers, ergo she must have sinned! What sin, then, lies to hand? She came virgin to thee—if not to thy nuptial bed—"

Alaric smiled.

"To both," he said. "That charade of the torn gown was to prevent thy killing me. . . ."

"Bless her for that! She hath never stolen, lied unnecessarily, murdered, committed adultery—though if she needs must have a sin for which to suffer there's one I'll happily supply her!—so now she is freely granted one by the sisterhood of hangdown tits and frozen tails, by the brotherhood of dried-up balls, those castrates of the mind! She hath corrupted a saint! She who gave thee life; who put the smile of true happiness upon thy face for the first time since I've known thee! Ya Allah! 'Tis enough to make a body puke!"

"True," Alaric sighed, "but there it is—"

"The trouble is that thou *art* a saint, or reasonable replica thereof," Saadyah growled. "So fornicating good, you gripe my hairy arse at times! You upset my whole existence, Aizun. I don't believe in miracles, and then I *see* thee do them!"

Alaric laughed then, quietly. "Utter rot!" he said.

"Is it? Oh, I've heard your explanation: that they're unconscious malingerers—that is, they're not lying or faking exactly—they really believe they can't walk, see, are possessed of devils or what have you. Whereupon you relieve their fears, et cetera, et cetera, et cetera—"

"Well?" Alaric said.

"Well, hell! What about the archer? Kamil and I bore you from the field with your thick Gothic skull smashed like an eggshell, and though thou wert in a swoon like death, thou reached out and took his hand. Whereupon I looked down and saw a man with belly wounds the like of which no man survives. God of Esau, Isaac, Jacob, his stinking tripes were showing! Yet within a fortnight there he was, healed up and walking, San Alarico! And Dhabba! Hast seen her lately, Holy Fool?"

"No," Alaric said.

"Clean as a whistle, smelling of good soap, a hint of perfume! Almost pretty. She hath taken to making lacework, and broideries—an art which the good sisters taught her in the orphanage, and which she swears she'd quite forgot. But you touched her, prayed over her, and back it came! She sells them in the marketplace, and with the money thereby gained she has transformed her hovel into a home. Clean, shining, flowers before the door. And she is once more with child, which, due to the improvement in her health, she'll keep. Only—"

"Only what?" Alaric said; then he saw the sudden rush of tears to Saddyah's eyes. "Why, Saad!"

"Hell and death!" Saadyah howled. "I can't stand goodness! It unmans me! She wants to know if she can give the child to you and Nathalie to replace the one she robbed you of! She who loves children above her life. Ahhh, God, why can't everybody be vixens and blackguards like they ought and leave me in peace?"

"Sweet of her," Alaric murmured: "but no—You were saying?"

"And your Kalim, whose wound al Harrani swears is fatal ten times out of ten. But, no, San Alarico told her it didn't hurt, so Allah and Moses and Jesu bless us all, no pain doth she feel! So he sews her up—including the big gut which is pierced, which is, as usual, dripping feces into the abdominal cavity—and goes home waiting for the inevitable moritfication to set in—for her to swell and stink and rot living till the stitches pull loose and green pus pours out and she dies raving. So what happens? Nothing! No mortification! She lies there smiling at him with a hole in her gut which even with a whole drachma of opium ought to have her screaming thy house down, and swears: "But it doth not hurt, my lord physician! My sweet lord said it wouldn't, and it doth not!" And the next time he comes she's up attending to Natalia! And you say that you're no saint!"

"Nay, Saad. I am a humble sinner. These things I do trouble me. I understand them not myself. But they—they're all things of the mind. Of faith. If a man believes enough, even the body is affected thereby. Much do I wish I could do miracles in the true sense—for as God lives I'd do one now! I'd blast open the doors now closed to me, and stand before the Emir once again—"

"To plead for the monk Isaac? But, Aizun, that fool blasphemed Muhammad in the very Blue Mosque during the evening prayers!"

"To plead for him. But more to save the Emir, who is my friend. Methinks that I can show him that terror never works—and especially not for him whose heart is too soft to apply it to its furthest limits. Al Rahman can quell his unrest in two ways: by magnanimity or by massacre. Between those two stools, being what he is, he falls. . . ."

"He refuses to see you?" Saadyah said.

"Aye. And thinks, moreover, that indirectly I inspire the Exalted. He hath decided upon a policy of sternness, God help him! No blasphemer shall go unpunished, he swears, though he be a Prince of the Blood!"

"Thou art right." Saadyah sighed. "God, in His mercy, help him indeed!"

But having belatedly turned to rigor, Abd al Rahman II, Emir of Allah's Faithful in the Land of al Andalus, made the classic mistake: he veered too abruptly from one extreme to another. For, having allowed the Mozarabs to celebrate a public funeral for Perfectus, passing in solemn procession through the streets of Córdoba, he now attributed the increase in the Exalted Ones' fervor to the inspiration they had drawn from that moving ceremony. So, resolving never again to give them like cause, the Emir put flame to tinder by having the monk Isaac's throat cut, his dead body crucified upside down and thereafter burned, cross and all, and his ashes scattered over the surface of the Guadalquivir.

At least one version of this awful event had it so. Another contradicted it in the minor detail that the cadaver was removed from the cross before being burned. Which proved not so minor after all; for thereafter, near the place of execution, a rude chapel of sun-dried brick was quickly thrown up, in which the cross upon which Isaac's body hung—or a replica thereof—was exhibited by the Exalteds for the veneration of the faithful.

"Surely a replica!" Saadyah cried. "Unless my eyes deceived me—though frankly I gave the matter scant importance at the time—I'd swear I saw them toss him cross and all into the fire!"

"And those bloodstained ropes on the cross?" Alaric said.

"Pig's blood. Or goat's. Would you put pious fraud past Eulogius?" Saadyah said.

There followed the days when Alaric felt sure he would go mad. "Little" Sancho of the palace guards, former captain of the Silent Ones, cursed Muhammad within the very palace, and died upon the scaffold with matchless serenity, declaring that he would straight to heaven go, because San Alarico had these many moons agone blessed him.

Whereupon Alaric was dragged before the head cadi, who, finding that Alaric's blessing of the soldier had antedated, and had absolutely no connection with, Sancho's mad act, but yet fearing the aroused mob dared not acquit Alaric outright, sentenced the Nazarene holy man to a public whipping, advising the executioner *sotto voce*, due to the victim's obvious emaciation and frailty, that the stripes be limited to twenty-four and that they be laid on lightly.

Even so, due to the extreme thinness and whiteness of his skin, the executioner's first blow broke it open like a ripened gourd. When 'twas done, and the weeping, raging Saadyah had borne him away from there, his whole back was dyed red with his blood—into which, be it duly said, the Exalted women dipped their handkerchiefs to be preserved as precious relics.

But upon reaching home, barely conscious, he was met with further horror: Natalia lay like one dead upon the floor, her fair young back more striped, more bloodied than his own.

Saadyah's scream of anguish actually shattered a vase of crystal on the mantel. For half an hour his lion-like roars shook the house. A man-servant was dispatched for al Harrani, who came into bedlam. Alaric and his wife lay like bloody slaughtered animals upon the bed, while Saadyah, roaring and crying, was rapidly reducing two maidservants, Kalim and Begonia, into an even more pitiful state.

"Stop it, my lord ben Hasdai!" al Harrani cried. "By Lord Saithan and all the djinn and demons, what passes here!"

"They beat her!" Saadyah bellowed. "She-asses! Lumps of female dung! Take that! And that! And that!"

Al Harrani got in one expert blow with his staff across Saadyah's wrist, causing him to drop that terrible whip.

"Animal!" Saadyah howled. "Ye've broken my arm!"

"I hope so," al Harrani said coolly. " 'Twill mayhap for some moons at least keep thee from employing it in the abuse of the innocent."

"Innocent!" Saadyah roared. "They've all but killed her!"

"Oh, be quiet, Sahib ben Hasdai," al Harrani said. Then to Kalim, "What passed here, my child?"

"They took my lord away—to—to whip him," Kalim sobbed, "my sweet lord, who saved my life! And for—for a thing—no wise his fault—"

"That I know, child," al Harrani said. "But thy lady—who was it who hath beaten her thus? So terribly that she may die of it?"

"We did!" Kalim wept. "Begonia and I! She ordered us to! She holds that all my lord's misfortunes are fruits of her sin in marrying him! She commanded us to lay on two stripes for every one my lord received; and every time we tried to stop she'd scream: 'Another! Harder! Harder! Harder, you hear me! Hath neither of you any strength at all?' "

"I see." Al Harrani sighed, looking at Saadyah and shaking his head ruefully.

"In a mad world, the asylum keeper's king," Saadyah growled. "Can I be of help to you, good physician?"

"*If* I have not broken your arm, you may," al Harrani said. "In any case I am right sorry for it, for I recognize the provocation was gross. If you can, help me draw Lord Aizun and his lady a little apart, that I may cleanse and dress their stripes—"

"Done!" Saadyah said and bent over them. But as he drew Natalia gently apart, his lips went white under his shaggy mustache.

"It is broken, isn't it?" the physician said.

"Aye!" Saadyah growled. "But 'tis only by pain that asses are taught. To work, good physician! Save her—save her in Allah's name!"

They were both a full two months abed. Of the two, Alaric, because of his age and his now ingrained asceticism, came closer by far to death; but in the end al Harrani saved them both. And, in a way, those months were a blessing, for they were shut off from the full horror of the Exalteds' sheeplike trooping to the scaffold in search of martyrdom. For after Sancho, Jeremiah, Isaac's uncle, led five more monks from the monastery at Tabanos to bend with him their freely offered necks to the headsman's ax; then the priest Sisnandus, the deacon Paul, the friar Theodermir of Carmona. In those two months eleven godly men cursed Muhammad in public, and for their curses died.

"But not, note it well," Alaric raged, "either Eulogius or Alvaro themselves, my sweet Natalia! Oh, they can push others forward to die for their mad cause, or, as in thy case, to leave a lovely back a mass of ridges and scars, marking it for life!"

Natalia looked at him.

"They had nothing to do with that my Lord," she whispered.

"Then you obtained the idea from the Hagiology?"

She smiled at him with solemn tenderness.

"Nay, sweet my Lord; I merely took a page out of the story of Thy life . . ."

My life he said. "Aye. That girl in Alexandria, she of the bad life, who, having tried to tempt thee, was by her remorse so sore smitten that she took a whip of rawhide and—"

"Thetis. Oh, God, how fat doth folly grow, feeding upon its own example! But now I must leave thee for the nonce, child. I pray thee

533

that you'll do not further idiocy in my absence. Promise me, Natalia?"

"I promise. But tell me: Where go you, sweet my lord?"

"To the palace—to demand an audience with the Emir upon good right. This time he cannot refuse me. This latest arrest, of a young cousin of his, a Muslim of the highest circles, might well cost me my life, for young Yahya can swear with some truth that I influenced him—"

She sat there gazing upon him a long slow time; and when she spoke her voice was odd. "Thou'rt brave, I know, Aizun, my lord; so why is it now that you fear to die?"

He answered her then upon the moment's very spur, without reflection, without thought, out of the purest longing of his heart: "I fear it not, Natalia! Were it not for thee, I should welcome it. . . ."

Of all the errors of a long and troubled life, those words were to prove the most grave. But he had no way of knowing that, as he turned and left her there.

The discussion with the palace guards was sharp. They clearly feared he might bewitch them into some such madness as had cost their former captain, poor Sancho, his head. But they were upon the last persuaded to pass him to the offices of the new al Fata al kabir, the eunuch Sa'dun.

Sa'dun, a grave and cautious man, heard him out in silence; then he said: "My lord is ill—the troubles in his realm have undermined his health; but if you can give him some reason to save the son of the sister of Adjab I am sure he would be most grateful to you. Besides, after Tarub, there is no one in this world he loves as he doth his niece, thy lady wife—and al Harrani hath kept him advised of her sorrows. I am sure he will receive you now, since 'tis none of these mad Nazarenes you come to save. Be you so kind as to wait. . . ."

Ten minutes later Alaric was ushered into the Emir's presence. And when after so long a time he saw the change in his master and his friend, the ruler to whom in so many ways his own life was bound, unbidden tears stood and smarted in his eyes. The Emir, in the fifty-ninth year of his age, appeared to have an added score of winters on his brow. Fever glittered in his eyes; what sat upon him now was very death.

He stared at Alaric, with an ironic smile, and said: "Thou'st weep for me, Aizun, whose judges caused the skin to be lifted from thy back—and without just cause?"

"Aye, my lord," Alaric said. "Forgive me—but I am shocked to see the change in thee."

"I am dying, Aizun!" al Rahman said. "Which is a matter of but scant import. All men die—and I am but man; there's no divinity in me, such as all men see in thee—"

"Nor in me, my lord," Alaric said.

"No? When men die smiling for thy sake as Sancho did? When Yahya ibn Zakariya' al Khashab, son of one of my father's viziers and nephew of his favorite Adjab, hath committed Zandaka and Istikhfaf both against Islam under thy influence? When that angel sprite, my niece, matched every stripe that overzealous fool of a cadi ordered laid on thee, with two upon her own fair back, desiring to suffer with, and for, thee? *Bism Allah!* Why hath no woman ever loved me thus?"

"My lord, many women hath loved thee thus—and more. Al Shifa, for one, who gave thy heir Muhammad to suck from her own sweet breasts when his mother Buhair died; Fakhr, who warned thee of the plot against thy life—"

The Emir stopped him with a lifted hand.

"After thou hadst warned me first, two years and more agone. And even in this new warning thou hadst a hand—thou and thy strange friend, that burly, bearded Jew. But tell me not how my women love me: that I know far better than thou canst. How much, and how little. Aizun, Aizun—though piled high with cushions of damask and silk, no seat's harder nor more lonely than a throne. But enough of that. I thank thee, old friend, for this latest of thy many loyal services to me. Now speak— why hast thou come?"

"To offer thee my life, my lord, since I am accused in this of young Yahya's heresy and blasphemy!"

"Allah the Compassionate deliver me from prickly Nazarenes!" the Emir cried. "Look you, Aizun, before the law there is no charge against thee that holds. Didst advise either Sancho or this young fool, son of Adjab's sister, to curse the Prophet? No, thou didst not; and neither of them accused thee of it! All they said was that thy goodness, thy piety, thy miracles inspired them to the stand they took—and not, Allah witness, thy words! More, there is on record the testimony of my agents who were present at each of thy frequent disputes with the fiery fool Eulogius, and they all quote thee as defending the Prophet as a just, holy, inspired, and tolerant man—"

"As he was. Who else would have forgiven the woman who poisoned him except—"

The Emir smiled sadly. "Except this weak and vain fool," he whispered, "who hath forgiven Tarub against whom long ago and justly you warned me. This asinine question of thy guilt being settled, what would you of me, Aizun?"

"His life," Alaric said, "young Yahya's life. Please, my lord! As Allah is compassionate, thou—"

Abd al Rahman's head sank upon his breast. But in that position he shook it slowly. "Nay, good Aizun," he said.

"Why not, O just and noble Emir?" Alaric said.

The Emir raised his head, and Alaric saw the tears that sparkled in his black eyes.

"Death and hell!" he roared. "Have I not enough with Adjab here in the palace all these weeks to plague me? Think you that I love the stench of blood? And of this fair youth who by his looks resembleth Muhammad, my son?"

Alaric bowed his head. "As my lord wills," he murmured. "But now my heart is heavy—"

"And mine hath upon it all the fiery stones from Saithan's hottest pit. Seeth thou not, O ibn all Qutiyya, that 'tis *because* he is Adjab's nephew I cannot save him? My justice is never broken; my impartiality unsullied— twelve Nazarenes have died for this crime; am I now to pardon a Muslim because he is the son of the sister of my father's favorite? I tell thee this Aizun: were it one of my sons—Abd Allah, or Muhammad, or al Mundhir, or al Mutarrif—equally would I condemn him! Therefore, I beg thee, keep that sweet child, thy wife, away from those mad fools! For no daughter of my loins have I loved as I love Natalia! And should I ever have to pass sentence upon her, methinks my heart would fail me. So look to her, Aizun, my friend!"

'Twas not until he had returned home that the true meaning of the Emir's word come to be revealed to him. He found Natalia in the little chapel, prostrated before the image of the Holy Mother, praying and weeping bitter tears.

"Dear Little Mother, save her!" she sobbed. "*Because* I was jealous of her, *because* I hated her, save her please! She is better than I; purer, braver! She maintained her virginity, even as Thou didst, preserved her chastity! While I seduced one of God's own saints into his fall from grace! Hear the words of a Magdalene, a strumpet, a whore! Even vile as I am, in Thy great compassion thou canst succor me in this—since I ask nothing for myself, not even to be saved from the hell that yawns before me! But please, dear sweet Mother of God, save poor Flora, please!"

Gently he bent down, raised her to her feet.

"What has happened, child?" he said.

"Oh, Aizun!" she wept. "Oh, sweet my lord! Flora! She—she and Maria!—On yesterday they left the cloister. And they—"

"Blasphemed against the Prophet?" Alaric said.

536

"Aye! They went before the head cadi and called the Prophet an adulterer! They're in jail! And nothing can save them, nothing at all—"

"Unless they recant," Alaric said.

She looked at him with deep astonishment, then with anger, whispered: "Aizun, Aizun—wouldst have them damn their souls?"

XXXIII

It was late November now, of that year of Our Lord 851, of that two hundred and thirty-sixth year after the Prophet's flight from Mecca to Yathrib, and all the sky dripped sullenly—or wept, Alaric thought. More than the year was dying now; and the slate-gray heavens had reason enough to weep—for illusions gone, for youth fecklessly spent, for the dust of hope to dust returned . . . for—memory.

Allah witness she had been a she-hawk, a lioness! Her mouth had been wine-tart, bittersweet, combining honey and gall. He could recall her eyes glowing amber in her dusk-rose and burnt-copper face, as she bent above him, her hair cascading down between him and their bedside lamp, heavy, musk-scented, to shut out sight like a night without stars. Her loins had cradled fire then; and into them his sturdy youth had melted; those now still loins which henceforth only the blind, crawling things would explore. No kiss of his would ever more awake her where she slept, self-surrendered in one last great orgiastic bursting—into silence.

His tear-glazed eyes could see only desolation: a curtain of rain marching aslant a new-dug grave. The soft, sucking sounds the wet earth made as they lowered her (lowered Afaf! To think her name was in itself a cry of astonished rage and grief—could all that vitality, love turned anguished bitterness, come to this? To this!) into a bleak hole half awash with the tears of time; with the slow, cold drizzle which at the last drowned all fires, congealed once ardent blood, leached away flesh from the fine-sculptured, uncompromising bone, until it too crumbled, and there was naught. Could all she had been and meant and suffered come to this? To this?

Aye. It could. It had. It would for him, too, one day. Soon now. Please God, soon!

He felt something touch his arm, and turning, looked into Saadyah's eyes. They were veiled, brooding, dark with pain.

"Come," Saadyah said, and they walked through the rain to the gate of the Jewish cemetery. There they stood, two men by this single extinguished dark flame bereaved, sharing her legacy of grief, as they had shared her wonder and her joy, while the attendant mourners—so few, so few!—Ruth and her husband, their son Hasdai with Munia; Theo, weeping for her beloved "Aunt" Afaf as no one else there had or could; Sumayla and her son (mine, mine too! Alaric thought) al Kamil; the chief rabbi of Córdoba's synagogue, a handful of Jewish friends of Saadyah's —filed past and offered with mumbled word, pressed hand, quick kiss, the condolences that no matter how deeply felt, remained—even they knew it!—meaningless.

And now they were alone. Alaric took his friend's, nay, his brother's arm; and they moved off through the gray landscape; through the whisper and the whimper of the rain.

"Poor Afaf!" Alaric said. "Life and I, and mayhap even God, hath used her ill. . . ."

"She's better off," Saadyah said harshly. "Now at last she hath ceased to grieve for thee, my friend. She died willingly enough. By her own hand. Or by mine. I wot not which."

"Saadyah!" Alaric said.

"Oh, don't look so shocked! Suicide's a noble death, as thou'rt stoic enough to know. When existence becomes intolerable, what's better than to depart it with dignity? Or meaner than to cling weeping and imploring to this brief misery we call life? She died well. More nobly than she lived. I pray nonexistent God that he receive her imaginary soul."

"Thou'rt a hard man, Saad—sometimes," Alaric said.

"Am I?" Saadyah whispered; and now Alaric saw his eyes were wet. "I loved her, Aizun! God of my Fathers witness that! More than I've loved anyone in this miserable, evil world, save alone thee. I loved her long past the time she'd no longer permit me the luxury of illusion. But gradually she killed that love with her shrewishness, her adulteries. You thought I didn't know? I may be a brute, but I have never been a fool. Worse luck! Since folly's the price of happiness. . . . Such cheap little cowardly adulteries! Why could she not have been faithful to the glorious one I permitted her to maintain lifelong in her mind with thee? And yet—I mind me that when ye two came that night onto thirty years agone to my father's house she was—almost—sweet. . . ."

"She *was* sweet," Alaric said. " 'Twas cruelty and disappointment that soured her—"

"Don't blame yourself, boy. Methinks the way a life takes is always inevitable. This cruelty, or that one, what boots it? That disappointment, or another—what creature of gut and dung and blood escapes them?"

"Saad—how came she to die? I have not seen her since that night—"

"—that she demonstrated how bottomless is female cruelty. The night that thy little angel having all but offered up her life to give thee another child, and having lost it, my sweet Afaf had to tell her that her firstborn had been murdered as well. Let us hope that our reason plays us not false when it tells us there is no hell beyond the one we bear within our breast, for if hell exists, by that one act alone hath Afaf earned it!"

"God will pardon her, Saad. As Natalia hath, and as I have, knowing how great her sufferings. For if she had had a son of her own—"

"If wishes were horses, all beggars might ride! And stones, bread, no hunger there'd be i' the world!"

Alaric stared at him. "Forgive me, Saad," he said.

"God's blood, boy! For what?"

"For touching thee upon an unhealed wound," Alaric said.

"Magician! Sorcerer! Reader of minds—saint! There're no secrets safe from thee, are there? I could never fondle thy little Ataulf, lest of pure envy I should die. Oh, devil take it! With me that unique creation, that masterpiece of all the ages, Saadyah ben Hasdai, fornicator, adulterer, roisterer, drunkard, vain, noisy fool—dies, leaving neither image nor replica. And good riddance to bad rubbish!"

"Nay, Saad, with thee dies nobility enough to supply the needs of nations, a heart so tender, that, breathe upon it, and it lo! it bleeds. A love so great that thou hast always to hide it with bellowings and bluster—one of God's truly great creations. Aye! A masterpiece of the ages, and more. Who hath sustained me when no one else could; who sustains me now when no one will—"

Saadyah glared at him balefully; dropped a bushy eyebrow over one green eye.

"And Nathalie?" he growled. "Doth she not—"

"Sustain me? Let us not speak of that. Tell me: of what, precisely, did Afaf die?"

"Of a running issue of the left breast that was devouring her. Caused, mayhap, by her striking her tit against the floor after the buffet I fetched her in thy house. So likely I am an assassin. Which doth not matter either! What's one more sin? More immediately she died of a potion she took when the pain got too bad. Methinks al Harrani gave it to her—if so, he's a partial assassin, too. And she, a suicide in her own very good and perfect right! May she rest in peace. Come, let us dwell no more upon it, lest it sour the angelic sweetness of my disposition even further! Though, God wot, all subjects for talk these days are sad. Tell me, art going to attend the executions? They're scheduled for tomorrow, I am told—"

"Nay, Saad. To tell the sober truth, I couldn't stand it. I've seen men die, sent all too many by this bloodstained hand screaming from this

540

world. But never a woman. Methinks that sight would sicken me past recovery. And Flora and Maria art both so fair!"

Saadyah cracked his knuckles together, and grinned at Alaric with that wild antic humor that came upon him when he would from himself and the world conceal he was sick at heart, buffeted about by life, half dead of grief. Alaric knew that now, and pitied him. With a quick, nervous gesture, Saadyah stuck his big fingers into his bushy, tangled, gray-streaked red beard, and raked it into some semblance of order.

"You did your holy fornicating best to save them," he said.

"Aye," Alaric sighed, "but I failed. Methinks I never had a chance to accomplish it. After all, the Emir refused to pardon ibn Zakariya'. And note well who *he* was, Saad! Adjab's nephew! That Adjab who was al Hakam's favorite—who hath given her name to an entire suburb of Córdoba. If al Rahman could resist the tearful pleas of his father's favorite, of the woman who had been as much a mother to him as his own in his boyhood, how could I have even expected to succeed?"

"Young Yahya ibn Zakariya al Khashab died well. I've heard he invoked *thy* blessing even upon the scaffold—which did thee no good at all in the Emir's eyes, Aizun! Though in bitter truth, his case had nothing to do with your failure to save those two muddled-headed little clucks— when will women learn that only one end of them is of use?—the fact is that ye came up against far too redoubtable an adversary this time, Aizun, my boy!"

"You mean Eulogius? That I grant you! He bested me with sickening ease in that contest, Saad!"

"Not Eulogius. Eros. The mischievous little god. The sower of confusion—no difficult feat among you Nazarenes, considering your native tendency to confuse the spicy aroma arising from 'twixt a maid's thighs with holy incense—"

"Saad—" Alaric said reproachfully.

"He is in love with her. Mayhap she with him as well. Nathalie thinks so, in any event. But instead of tumbling her to the increase of Christians, the salvation of his allegedly immortal, hypothetically existent soul, and the general good of the commonwealth, he must murder her—by convincing her of the nobility and the glory of separating her useless head from her useful tail in the interest of bell ringing, street processions, and the reduction of taxes! Now there's a holy cause for thee, San Alarico! Which I must say he hath done most effectively, in quite respectable Latin. Hath read his *Documentum Martyriale?*"

"Aye. 'Tis in many ways a masterpiece."

"Madmen are quite often brilliant. One must have a mind to lose or

541

distort it. And love—or at least lust—in one's loins to pervert it. As this monster hath done—"

"Saadyah, your way of thought is sometimes distressing—"

"Isn't it, though?" Saadyah rumbled. "But then, truth nearly always is. Untidy *and* distressing. And farcical. And undignified. And sad. Look thou, Aizun, my friend—he loves her. This hot-eyed little monster loves our Flora. So naturally he hates her. Hate's always the reverse of the coin of love. She comes up to him and thrusts her proud and pouting little delectabilities up under his nose and coos: 'Hear my confession, Father!' So what can he do? He's a man of the cloth, so he can't take a good-sized bite out of 'em the way I'd do, flip up her dress, yank down her shintiyan or whatever 'tis your 'No, not evers!' wear under their robes, and get to work. Oh, no! He has to stand there and suffer her wiggling this at him, and jiggling that, until he's wild with lust, and even when he gets home to his monkish cell he cannot so much as invoke good Saint Onan to relieve his anguish. Poor devil! So by now he *wants* to kill her. If I had a pious goodwife or daughter—which Ba'al and Beelzebub be thanked I haven't!—I'd keep her well away from Father Eulogius. He's dangerous."

"That he is perilous, thou'rt right," Alaric said, "though mayhap for causes less farfetched than thy chaste and delicate exposition of the theory of thwarted love. Certainly he hath a murderous faculty for persuading others to die for his mad causes while risking his own saintly neck not at all. But now"—and Alaric's voice was grim suddenly—"God willing, I have a means to stop him permanently, from doing further harm."

"A hired assassin?" Saadyah growled, his green eyes glittering with a light that showed Alaric how close to madness he had been brought by grief and pain. "Save thy dinars, Aizun! I'll gladly do this pleasant chore for thee for nothing, well rewarded by the pleasure 'twould give me to shut forever that venom-spewing pesthole of a mouth! Since I have one death on my conscience now, what boots another? Name but the time and place, and I—"

"Nay, Saad," Alaric said gently. "A subtler plan; though one mayhap as twisted, as devious as he is. 'Tis my intent to persuade Father Juan de Dios to indicate to His Grace Saul, Bishop of Córdoba, the pressing necessity of calling a church council. I am already dropping a pearl or two of wisdom into the ear of Gomez, son of Antonius, the Emir's appointed Count of the Christians, to have the Emir indicate to His Grace that such would also be his royal pleasure—"

"Father Juan, eh? How're ye going to persuade that sweet old croaker of that? Damn me for a sinner, there's one shaved pate I like! And say you call it, what good can it do?"

"One thing at a time, Saad! I can with total justice point out to

Father Juan that hundreds of Christians have become apostates, and converted to Islam since these noisy fools started bending their necks to the ax—out of pure fear. And that if this madness of martyrdom without just cause continues, there'll be no Christians left, because if what my son-in-law al Mundhir tells me about his elder brother is true, when Muhammad comes to the throne he'll massacre those few hardy souls who have by then still resisted the overwhelming temptation to become Muslimn and live in peace, to the man. 'Tis Muhammad who is stiffening poor dying al Rahman's hand now. Our next Emir's hatred of Nazarenes hath come to be undiluted, unmixed, and pure—and with good reasons, I'll admit. A council of the churchly fathers can and must be called on the score that Eulogius and Alvaro are endangering the very existence of the Church."

"And once it's called?" Saadyah said.

"I'll beg leave to speak. And with all due solemnity and respect for form, I'll point out to the holy mitered heads therein assembled what all men seem to have forgot—"

"Which is?"

"That suicide is forbidden Christians under canon law. And that to voluntarily seek one's death—even by indirect means, such as to blaspheme the Prophet in the mosque—is precisely that. And lastly, such gentle souls as urge the faithful to so heinous a step can and must be excommunicated for their sins, or cease and desist forever from them!"

Saadyah stared at Alaric. Then he clapped him on his back so hard he made his ribs rattle. He threw back his own fiery red head—now well silvered—and roared: "A Daniel! A Daniel come to Judgment! Hear ye, O Israel! Aizun, my boy, you should have been born a Jew!"

"Art sure that there are *that* many apostates, Aizun, my son?" Father Juan said.

"Aye, Father! That I am. And there'll be more if Eulogius and Alvaro are not halted. 'Tis asking too much of ordinary folk, that they risk dying in the massacres that those mad fools are surely bringing down upon all our heads. Good Father Perfectus told me once he feared that all our faithful would be seduced by the lechery and luxury of their way. I tell thee now that they will be forced into it by terror! I tell thee—"

Father Juan smiled sadly. "Spare thy vehemence, son Alaric, to convince those not already on your side, as thou knoweth well I am. But let me acquaint thee with the facts of clerkly life, since thou, being as thou art, a saint, hath too little cognizance of the frailties of those mere men who go about with long and solemn faces clad in priestly robes they are for the most part plagued ill fitted to wear—"

"Oh, I know the common gossips: Ye all have 'nieces,' 'housekeepers,' even pretty orphaned 'boys'—Calumny, Father; pure calumny, nine times out of ten!"

"I thank thee for thy good opinion, son. 'Tis mostly calumny; but I fear me more are chaste from fear than from faith. But 'twas not to that I referred. See how it rains? And 'tis plagued cold. Out of sweet Christian charity, Aizun, remember that by the time a man's a bishop he's bent with years, and the rheumatism in his ancient bones is a fearsome thing. The Bishop would not call a council now, knowing as he doth full well the state the roads are in this time of year, and how many of his rank would not, or even could not, attend."

"So now many another fervent fool must die—for mark ye, my Father, there will be more than one silly maid to follow the fatal example that Flora and Maria will set on tomorrow—because of a little rain! Oh, no! Don't tell me that!"

"Art a poor observer of humanity, my son. Between Perfectus' martyrdom and Isaac's, how much time elapsed?"

"A year. Nay, thirteen months," Alaric said.

"Exactly. From spring to spring. Hast never noted that revolts, massacres, religious revivals, and the like always occur in midsummer? That when 'tis freezing cold nothing ever happens, God be praised? We'll have no more martyrs this year, my son, now that winter's come. Look you, even Flora and Maria committed their mad folly long ago when the heat lay on the land, awaking all the devils in the blood. They have been in jail these many months because that poor devil of a head cadi—who is a noble soul; he did his blessed best to convince al Rahman that Isaac was mad, that in fact all Nazarenes are, and hence not to be held responsible for their actions—"

"An opinion that, unhappily, I sometimes share," Alaric said with a sigh.

"And I," Father Juan said good-humoredly. "In any event, the head cadi hath spent all his time trying to get them to recant; but neither cajolery nor threats have served him. The poor man's actually fallen ill, so great is his repugnance at this slaughter. To return to my original point: Faith grows feeble when it must crouch before a fire to warm its shanks, Alaric, my son! Let us try then to induce His Grace to call the council for the balmy days of next spring."

"Methinks, sometimes, Father," Alaric said tartly, "that thou'rt as skeptical as I am, and even more of a cynic!"

"Neither one, Alaric," Father Juan said gently. "I merely believe that the Good God is indulgent of human frailty, and so must we be as well. Now, here's what I suggest: that thou and I devote the winter to gather-

544

ing evidence to lay before the Bishop—a sort of census of those who have left God's Church because of this mad and murderous folly. With that to convince him, I'm sure he will call it, for he hath the Church's interests truly at heart. Betimes, you pressure the Exceptor Gomez into obtaining the Emir's permission for such a council to be held. Then you and I will call down anathema upon these murderers by indirection, my son! And what joy I'll take of that sweet day!"

"And I, Father!" Alaric said, and bowing, took his leave of the wise and gentle priest.

When he reached his house it was very nearly night, for Afaf's funeral had been delayed somewhat by the heavy rain, had, indeed, gone forward only when the downpour of the early afternoon had slackened finally into that sullen drizzle so disheartening to behold. And thereafter, his conference with Father Juan had forced him to tarry for yet another while. Still, when he came into the house, Natalia faced him with that smile she wore almost always now—so otherworldly as to appear angelic.

I, he thought bitterly, prefer the way she was before—when she would have come running to greet me, to half devour me with kisses, or to weep and storm at me and throw perfectly hellish tantrums on the score that I was betraying her with another.

"Thou'rt soaked, my lord," she said. "Come sit here beside the fire, while I fetch thee dry robes into which to change—"

"The servants can do that perfectly well," he said irritably.

"But I am thy servant, good my lord," she said, "thy bondswoman, and thy slave. And I owe thee what services I can give in some small recompense for the heavy burdens I have put upon thee."

He stood there, dripping water from his robes, and considering how strange her words were, how utterly foreign to her habitual mode of speech. There was in them a formality of phrasing, a stately, liturgical quality that she seemed to have got by rote from—

Not from Father Juan! That good man's mode of speech was decidedly unpriestly. He delighted in a racy turn of phrase, a cleaned-up street argot he'd learned of the whores and thieves whom more than any other priest in Córdoba he was successful in reforming. Still, Father Juan was her confessor now. All summer long she had gone to San Acisclo, instead of having him come to their house, because, as she with some justice had said, the walk was good for her.

"Do as you like, child," he said, sighing, and sank down by the fire. Gently she turned and went to get his robes. No longer, he thought sadly, doth she skip and scamper now. It seemeth me that her feet beat time to slow and funereal music. She walketh like a matron sunk in fat and years, though she is more wraithlike than ever. Aye, God! A spring breeze could carry her away.

They never made love now, though al Harrani assured him that they could, that the danger of her becoming pregnant was remote, and the issue thereof as likely to be successful as not. For one thing, Alaric was conscious of a serious diminution of his vital forces; for another, though she did not refuse him, 'tis impossible for a man of even normal sensibility to embrace with desire a waxen doll, motionless, and but faintly warm. And Alaric was sensitive to a fault.

She came back with his dry clothes and fragrant towels. He stripped and dried himself vigorously. She glanced at his still remarkably fine body with complete disinterest, save alone to say: "How thin you have become, my lord."

Then once again she got up, and with that priestly, ritual stride went into the pantry to return with cold meats, cheeses, wine, cakes, fruit.

He nibbled at this, at that, leaving, as always, most of his supper intact. Nor did she reproach him for it, as she would have a year agone. In those days she had often wept in exasperation at his lack of appetite. But now—

They sat there in silence before the fire. Those silences, it seemed to him, had come to make up nearly the whole of their life together. And tonight, God wot, there were subjects enough for talk: Afaf's sudden (was it sudden? Had it been? Nay—'twas only that Saadyah had concealed from them his wife's illness lest one more bad memory, aching sorrow, be piled on hearts which already bore too much) death; the bloody termination upon tomorrow of two young lives which so desperately he'd tried to save; the whole sweeping question of martyrdom and the use of misuse thereof—

He stopped short, one instant before they heard that thunderous knocking on the door, and what leaped into his mind was not thought, but prayer: "I thank thee, Lord, for silence!"

Broken now by hideous banging; by—even before he reached the door he heard and recognized—those bull-like roars. He opened it, and Saadyah lurched into the room, the cloud of wine upon his breath making the candles flicker.

"By Lucifer!" he bellowed. "By Beelzebub! by Ba'al, I—"

Then he stopped, and swayed there like an axed oak, trembling at the last instant before its fall; but somehow, miraculously keeping his feet. His voice sank, murmuring like a far-off surf upon a golden isle; like the memory of storm.

"An angel," he rumbled. "I've never known an angel. Thou'rt lucky, Aizun! Still—'tis just. An angel—and a saint. While I—while I—"

His knees buckled under him then, but slowly. He measured his great length upon the floor. Natalia flew to him, dropped down beside him, cradled his great head in her slender arms.

"—am but a foul and lecherous lump of dung!" he wept, his tears in the firelight rubies, blood. "Don't touch me, li'l angel, lest—lest—"

"Lest what, Saad?" Alaric said.

"Lest she soil herself forever. I went—from Afaf's grave—from the burial of—my wife—a shrew—a termagent—she was—and unchaste to boot and—"

"Now, Saad!" Natalia said.

"Queen of the art—of applying—horns—"

"Saadyah!" Natalia said.

" 'S God's truth. But I loved her. Know what I did?"

"No, Saad, dear," Natalia said.

"Went to a house—a house of—a house of—what, Aizun?"

"Blessed if I know," Alaric said solemnly.

"Blessed if you don't, O Holy Pope of Fornicators! Spent half your youth in one—chasing the trollops and the trulls—into cloisters!" He began to sing suddenly; his big bass surprisingly musical.

"Drop down your skirt and take the veil, tra-la, tra-la,

Drop down your skirt and take the veil, my lovely!

For those dimpled knees no more you'll spread

Nay you'll fast and pray until you're dead, tra la, tra la, my lovely!

San Alarico came in the door, ta boom! ta boom! ta boomlay!

San Alarico came in the door, ta boomlay!

From whence no whore will ere walk more

But only restitched virgins, eyes on the floor, ta boom! a boom! ta boomlay!"

"Saad, you stop it!" Natalia said.

"Aye, li'l angel from heaven. Know what I did? Went to a house of ill fame. Why ill fame? Why not good fame? Or no fame? A brothel. But I—I couldn't, Aizun! Her face—her face—"

"Now, Saad," Alaric said gently.

"—kept getting in betwixt me—and that trull's. Couldn't. Then I looked and they—and they—"

"Poor Saad," Natalia murmured.

"They all had Afaf's face! Fifty harlots wearing my poor vixen's face—and she dead—dead. Dead! Ahhhh God, how could You?"

"Poor, poor Saad!" Natalia wept.

"Aizun! You did that! Another miracle! Put her poor dead face upon their necks so that I couldn't, couldn't, I couldn't—"

His head dropped suddenly. From his lips there came a curiously gentle snore.

Natalia looked up at Alaric; but a little smile bisected the track of her tears.

"How good he is!" she said. "All noise—and all heart. Aizun, sweet my lord, what will we do with him now?"

Alaric felt a little stab of pain somewhere in the region of his heart. 'Twas the first time she'd called him 'sweet my lord' since both their babies died.

"Put a pillow beneath his pate, and cover him with quilts. He's much too big to move," he said.

And on that morrow, one more thing: He walked with Saadyah halfway to his house, far enough to make sure his pale and tottering friend could get there safely. And when he returned, Natalia was not at home.

"Now where on God's green earth—" he began—then fear came out of the shadows and took him by the throat. "The executions! Flora's and Maria's! God's blood and death! Don't tell me that she—!"

He whirled, already running; but as he passed the sundial in the garden its shadow stood at an hour beyond noon. He was too late. At precisely high noon the two fair and foolish maids had—

The memory of Perfectus' death washed over him in a nauseous wave. He halted, hung over the garden gate, waiting for the sick giddiness to leave him. When he looked up again, he saw Natalia coming up the street. He stood there, waiting.

Then she was close enough for him to see what it was she held, most reverently between her hands. A silk kerchief. Her own. It was soaked. So much so that the excess ran out between her fingers, splattered black-scarlet splotches down the front of her gown.

He heard a voice, so thin, edged, woman shrill, that a moment passed before he realized it was his own: "In God's name, Natalia, give me that!" he screamed.

She smiled; and of all the horrors high piled on his heart, the most horrid was that smile's macabre sweetness.

"'Tis Flora's," she lisped. "I—I hated her, knowest thou? But now I don't. A most precious holy relic, sweet my lord. 'Twill guard and protect us 'gainst all harm—"

Wordlessly he reached out and snatched that blood-soaked kerchief from her, whirled, ran into the house, and threw it into the fire. It almost

548

put out the flames. A thick black smoke rose up, rasping his nostrils, searing his eyes.

He turned, choking, coughing, half blind, to find Natalia there. She was smiling still.

"See how her soul goes up to heaven, sweet my lord," she said.

XXXIV

The night before the council was to meet, Father Juan de Dios came to visit Alaric at his house. It was midsummer now, the first week of July, 852, and the night was very warm, so they sat before an opened window and talked. That the council was so late in opening was due to a circumstance upon which neither of them had counted: by eloquence, by fire, by the force of an indomitable will, Eulogius had won Saul, Bishop of Córdoba, wholly to his cause. Had the matter rested with His Grace alone, the council would never have been called; but by then Alaric and Father Juan were disinclined to tamely accept defeat. Armed with a list of the names, occupations, and rank of the hundreds of Mozarabs who had gone before the Muslim authorities and renounced Lord Jesu in favor of the Prophet since Perfectus had initiated the new martyrdom, said list supplied them by no less than the head cadi himself, sickened to his soul by all the poor innocents he was forced to condemn to death, reluctantly Father Juan followed Alaric's advice, and went over the Bishop's head, laying the matter before the man who was at that moment, by virtue of the accident of history, the highest ecclesiastical authority in all al Andalus, Recafred, Metropolitan of Sevilla. For now, already, the Exalteds' half-religious, half-political revolt was spreading to other cities. Ever-rebellious Toledo embraced Eulogius' cause with wild enthusiasm. But then, as Father Juan wryly put it, Toledo would embrace the devil, as long as His Satanic Majesty was against the Emir and Córdoba. And by so doing, it insured the cause's defeat; for every major city in the Emirate had long since learned that to follow where Toledo led was to plunge downhill to disaster. The news of rioting in that bellicose city tipped the scales in Father Juan's favor. After less than a week of consideration of the matter, the Metropolitan Recafred called a council of all the chief prelates of al Andalus to be held in Córdoba within a month—that is, the first week of July.

And in good time the riders sped from village to village bearing the Metropolitan's missive. All good Christian men felt relief—for outside of Córdoba the Mozarab communities could not for their very lives discern what all the shouting was about. Living in peace, in wealth, in ease—in a civilization unequaled in all of Europe—they found their taxes fleabites and well worth the payment, for compliance with this annoying obligation enabled them to escape service in the Emir's armies. Moreover, having no church bells to break their sleep at the crack of dawn on Sunday mornings, they genially went ever later to mass, or not at all. Surrounded by an Arab elite whose reaction to matters religious was an amused skepticism, the better class of Mozarabs gradually began to realize that fervor in unprovable matters was the hallmark of a narrow, unenlightened, if not downright vulgar mind, and that the passage or the nonpassage of the shinbone of a long dead saint in its silver casket through the street was a question worth at best a yawn; but certainly not a life.

But 'twas in Córdoba itself that Alaric and Father Juan found their most ardent support. Outside the monastery at Tabanos, that hotbed of martyrdom, no single churchman was in agreement with Eulogius' policies. In this they were joined by the overwhelming majority of Catholic laymen, anxious to stop this madness that threatened to destroy the whole Christian community because an infinitesimally tiny minority possessed lunacy's ever-unparalleled capacity for making noise. What precisely, they asked, was it that was troubling Father Eulogius? Had the Emir, or any Muslim whatsoever, forbade his father and his brother from amassing wealth until his family was among the comfortably situated elite of Córdoba? Was not his elder brother an honored official of the Emir's court, appointed to his quite respectable post by al Rahman himself? Were not his other two brothers such successful merchants that even Saadyah ben Hasdai himself had to reckon with them? Had any imam, cadi, fakir, or police forbidden Eulogius to become a priest? Had any Muslim whatsoever refused to allow his sister to take the veil? Where, in God's name, in his own family, in his own life, was the persecution of which so bitterly he complained?

"Saadyah," Alaric said to Father Juan now, glancing toward Natalia where she sat, busy at her broidering, halfway across the room, "hath a theory about that. He thinks that Eulogius is hungry for power—for, among other things, the power to persecute. Were we to allow him to burn a few heretics or Jews after the fashion of our gentle ancestors, he'd soon cease his clamor. What think you, Father?"

"That Eulogius is mad. And that Alvaro is a fool. Let us not speak of them, my son—for on tomorrow we have the power to defeat them utterly—"

"Have you, Father?" Natalia said suddenly from where she sat.

"Aye, daughter. I have sounded out the secretaries of every bishop who will attend, and save alone our own Bishop Saul, no one of them will support Eulogius. And after thy good husband hath expressed his views, certain 'tis that Eulogius and Alvaro will be forever silenced."

"Then," Natalia said, clearly, slowly, pronouncing the Romance words with icy precision, "thou, Father, as his spiritual adviser, must forbid my lord to speak. And thou, thyself, must keep silent!"

"Natalia!" Alaric said. "In God's name, what has come over you?"

"A concern for thy soul, sweet my lord, which I have endangered enough as it is, by intrapping thee into the filthy sty of carnal marriage! And for thine, my Father—whose cloth itself doth suffice to show you how terrible is thy error! Martyrdom is good and pleasing in God's sight; every drop of blood shed willingly for Our Redeemer's sake as precious as any jewel. So neither of you must commit this wickedness. I—I forbid you!"

And now, sickeningly, Alaric realized the source of Natalia's altered, new, strangely priestly phraseology. Eulogius! Who else? He turned bleak eyes upon Father Juan.

"Father," he said, "tell me a thing: Hath she attended mass almost daily at San Acisclo? Hast thou heard her confessions, or—"

Father Juan looked at Natalia with troubled eyes. To come between man and wife was a terrible thing, and yet—

"Tell him, Father. Nay, I will," Natalia said. "Sweet my husband and my lord, each time I told thee I heard mass, prayed, confessed my sins, 'twas the whole truth. And 'twas your own decision to separate yourself from the One, True, Holy Church that prevented you from learning that I went not to San Acisclo but to San Zoil!"

"To *his* church," Alaric whispered. "To the church of that madman!"

"Aye," Natalia said. "Why not, my lord? What surcease hath this lukewarm priest of thine to offer me? Only words of fire can cauterize the wounds I bear! My—my babies gone—in punishment—for—for the destruction of thy sainthood—with the foulness of my body. Madness, you say? Well, what explanation hath thou to offer?"

"None," Alaric said. "I pray thee go to bed, Natalia. For now truly am I sick at heart, and would speak alone with Father Juan."

"As my lord commands," Natalia said. " 'Tis a wife's whole duty to obey. Good night, my Father—"

Father Juan raised his head from where it had sunk upon his breast.

"Good night, my child," he said.

"So there you have it, Father!" Alaric raged. "My life! One long catalogue of horrors—God wot, 'twould be simpler to see it as Natalia

552

doth as God's punishment for my sins. But what when the punishment far
outweighs the sin? Outweighs all my acts in importance, outstrips them
far in number! Oh, I claim not blamelessness, my Father; but neither
have I the vanity to attribute to my sins more grandeur than they have.
I'll raise no defense of my conduct; but did my mother and she who was
to be my bride have to die to afford me the luxury of suffering? Did she,
whom lovelessly I called wife, have to damn her immortal soul to serve as
the implement by which Almighty God might chastise me? Or is not thy
God more than a torturer, an executioner? Hath he naught of tender,
loving kindness in him? Or shall we recite the devil's catechism together,
Father? Did God who in his prior knowledge of every act I'd do in all my
life, that knowledge which dwelt in him uncounted eons before he allowed or caused me to be born, then take into his divinely omniscient
cognizance the sins of lust, anger, murder, pride he knew I must commit,
sins he did not trouble to remove from my stars the day the midwife
smote breath into me, and equate with them as punishment the killing of
my babies? Punish me thus, with and through other lives, for acts he
knew *a priori* I'd do, nay needs must inescapably do, having the nature
that he gave me? Assent to this, and ye paint me the portrait of a fiend,
my Father—who'll leave me as mad as my poor Natalia is now! What
answer is there? What response canst thou give to the black and towering
evil that bestrides the world? Tell me that and I'll return to thy Church,
which surely Our Lord had no slightest intent to found, bend my poor
stiff neck, transform the wafer in my mouth into the savage's eagerly
devoured raw, red man meat, the wine to thick, ropy human blood!
I'll confess my sins, beat my breast, whine *mea culpa* to the end of
time! But for what, good Father, tell me that? In God's name, for
what?"

Father Juan bent his head. "I cannot answer thee thy terrible questions, Aizun, my son," he said, "being, unlike thee, truly humble. I do not
pretend, or even dare attempt, to comprehend the awful ways of God.
Instead I can but oppose your questions with another: Hast thou never in
all thy days heard and denied a call from God?"

Alaric stopped his tigerlike pacing, turned, stared at him.

"Aye," he whispered, "if God exists, and if I have not been right oft a
madman, I have, good Father!"

Father Juan smiled.

"Tell me about it, Aizun," he said.

"Before we proceed," the good priest said, when he had heard Alaric
out, had pondered over his dreams, visions, voices, visitations, "these

553

strange powers that thou hast—whether you call them miraculous or no—whênce think you they come? From Lord Satanas?"

Slowly Alaric shook his head. "Nay, Father," he said. "My powers, if I have powers, are of God."

"Good. Now one last question: Hast ever visited the armories at Toledo, seen there a Toledo blade being made?"

"Aye, Father, I have," Alaric said.

"How doth one make a sword, my son? Doth not one tear the ore from the ripped and bleeding bowels of the earth? Doth not one slaughter a thousand thousand trees to make the fire to smelt it down? Is it not, in its crucible, the very image of hell? Poured into a mold, it cools a while; but we do not leave it thus! Once more we heat it, beat it, pound it on the anvil into shape; then, bringing it to glowing red heat once again, we plunge it into a bath of oil. Then we grind it, polish it, buff it, incise it with veins of gold, fit a hilt to it, fit for the hands of a warrior!"

"So?" Alaric whispered.

"Thou'd have God try His saints less cruelly than this, my son? Temper them less through blood and pain? Serve His holy cause with inferior weapons, brittle under blows, blunt of edge, ignoble, base as lead? Methinks He loves thee much, Alaric, to have made thee suffer so! Now tell me, thou who wert to sainthood born, know ye what He'd have of thee? For it seemeth me that through works, charity, prayer, suffering, and the healing of His sick, already thou hast served Him well. If thou knowesth, tell me, what would God of thee?"

Alaric stood there a long, slow time, looking out of the open window at the blue velvet night, at the far, faint stars. Then, without turning his head, he said it, measuring it out upon a sigh: "The last thing I have to render Him," he said, "which is my life, Father. Which is my life."

When he retired at last to his bedchamber to rest, he found Natalia awake and awaiting him. She lay propped on one elbow looking at him and her eyes were as feverish bright as sparks.

"Aizun," she cooed; and her voice, miraculously, had leaped backward over two long, bitter years to the time before death and destruction and Eulogius' interpretation of the will of God had come between them, transforming her into something resembling one of ibn Firnas' clockwork artifices.

"Aye, Natalia?" he said tiredly.

"Kiss me, sweet my lord," she murmured, all the warm tides of spring fluting through her tone.

He stared at her. She had, upon occasion, taken the initiative in love before; but now he was no longer simple, no longer pure; his heart had been damaged, made complex by pain. Then he bent and touched her lips as lightly as a breath, straightened up, or tried to, for she clung to him.

"Oh, Aizun—wouldst—wouldst love me—this night?" she whispered.

A blade went through his vitals, twisted. He was sure now, very sure. But he kept his tone light, pleasant, dry.

"Tell me, good my lady, and my wife, what price must I pay for this so precious boon?" he said.

Before she would have been too quick, too subtle to fall into such a trap; but now she gazed up at him with a macabre counterfeit of love, an insane grimace meant to be a tender smile, and said: "That you do not speak before the council on tomorrow, sweet my lord!"

Gently his hands came up and disengaged her clasp.

"Good night, Natalia," he said.

On the morrow, Alaric Teudisson spoke before the council. He spoke last of all, only having seen the visible trouble in the eyes of the assembled prelates after Eulogius had spoken with great fire; after Saul, Bishop of Córdoba, had with stately eloquence defended the martyrs, defended, indeed, a Christian's right to choose martyrdom.

His, San Alarico's, precise words have not survived; the chroniclers speak of his voice, his tall, gaunt form, the glow of light that many witnesses of that day afterward swore they saw about his head, all evidences of mankind's incurable desire to rewrite history, reshape it—after brutal fact cannot any longer give the lie to his dreaming—closer to the heart's desire. The import of his words seem to have been that a Christian had no right to refuse martyrdom when that glorious fate was thrust upon him. Eulogius and Saul listened with delight to what seemed at first a defense of their position; but Alaric soon disabused them of that notion. Ordered to deny his faith, worship alien gods, he went on coolly, calmly, a Christian had no other choice but to die. But when in all the history of the Church, had her children been asked to die over a question of taxes? Over street processions and bell ringing? Did not Our Lord instruct us to render unto Caesar, Caesar's things; to go the second mile; to turn the other cheek? And if, as Father Eulogius insisted, the jails were full of priests, 'twas not for exercising their profession or their faith that they were there; but rather for brutally and stupidly insulting the professions and the faiths of others. Nor was it a question of whether that alien faith was sinful, or in error: it was that a Christian who returned evil for good, intolerance for tolerance, sinned before his own Lord Jesu, and his God. A man who was martyred in defense of his own faith, who died defending his right to worship God after the Christian way, earned undying glory and God's blessing; but he who sought his own death by provoking his execution was but a common suicide whose soul must plunge to hell.

How he said these things is not now known, the rolling, sonorous sentences of his remarkably perfect Latin have forever perished; but their effect was immediate. The council adopted a resolution signed by every bishop there save Saul, forbidding all Christians to seek in the future the voluntary sacrifice of their lives, which, said the resolution, was susceptible to interpretation as a kind of self-murder, forever forbidden by the Church.

'Twas at that moment that Eulogius rose, and wild with anger, went so far as to shake his fist in Alaric's face. Whereupon the Exceptor Gomez demanded the arrest of Father Eulogius and all the leaders of the Exalted party. While the council prepared to debate this measure Eulogius fled the Cathedral; but not before screaming at Alaric: "Thou'll not forget this day, vile magician! Never as long as thou shalt live!"

Not wishing to have any connection with the outcome of this debate, nor even so much as to influence it by his presence, Alaric asked, and got permission, to leave the meeting. But he had no sooner gained the street outside the Cathedral than Saadyah was upon him.

The big Jew stood there raging and raving and tearing his own clothing; scooping a handful of dirt from the gutter, he poured it over his own head. Terrible as they were, these ancient, symbolic, even racial expressions of his grief were also profoundly moving—the more so because the sounds that came out of his mouth were scarcely human, being less than that, and more.

Alaric lifted his hand and waved it slowly, steadily before Saadyah's eyes. Then he snapped his fingers with a sharp, explosive sound. The little knot of the curious who had gathered at the sight of Saadyah's wild behavior, thinking him surely demon-possessed, crowded closer now, avid for a miracle—and, be it said, to their own minds at least, obtained their desire.

"Thou wilt speak, Saadyah," Alaric murmured, his voice deep music. "Thou wilt speak clearly, and cease to weep. Now tell me, brother of my heart, what is it that passes with thee?"

Saadyah opened his mouth, but the voice that came out of it was not his own. 'Twas an ancient voice, gray, croaking, infinitely weary.

"Nathalie. And two young men. Georgius. Aurelius. In the great mosque this morning, offering injuries to the Prophet so gross that even I should have blushed to utter them. They're before the Kadi I'Djama'a now. Mayhap if you hurried, you—"

556

Alaric took Saadyah's arm. His expression had not changed at all. His eyes were infinitely calm and sad. They looked past Saadyah, through him, peering backward to the landscape of his dream. To a hill where three crosses stood, where impenetrable darkness drifted down a noonday sky. He bowed his head. Looked up again.

"Come, Saadyah," was all he said.

He knew it was hopeless from the first. But he did all the possible things. He visited the sick, gray, trembling figure of the Emir, who embraced him, kissed his cheeks, and wept.

"Knowest thou not that of this sentence I, too, shall die?" Abd al Rahman said. "Believest thou, Aizun, Holy Man, that I wouldst not remove it if I could? Pardon my niece? Allah the Compassionate remove from me this pain! Pardon her and have all Córdoba flaming with revolt within the hour, and those Nazarene fools ye've done so much for, my friend, being piled up in bloody heaps first of all! Nay, Aizun—save her I cannot—nor can I save myself. Aizun, Aizun, my friend, thou must force her to recant!"

How to do that? Alaric thought. How doth one influence a mind one cannot reach? I who so easily have struck through to other darkened minds am from this beloved one shut out as by a wall. 'Tis clear she doth not even hear me when I speak—nor is aware truly of my presence. She kneels there, prays, and turns deaf ears, blind eyes to a world methinks she hath already left. Still, what to do? One thing more—as useless as the rest—but do it I must, for 'tis my final hope. . . .

He went to visit Eulogius in his cell, for the prime mover of the revolts, as well as Alvaro and Bishop Saul, were all in jail by then.

"I came," he whispered, "to beg thee to send her word in thine own hand telling her to recant, for only thou canst, Father. She'll listen to thee—only thou canst save her!"

Whereupon Eulogius read him a sermon, stormily and at great length. Mostly it was a repetition of the words he had addressed to Flora and Maria when those two poor human creatures had weakened in their desire to obtain a martyr's crown. Halfway through it, Alaric turned and walked away from the barred door, unable to stand it more. Nothing would be gained by staying there, he knew. The obsessed are immune to reason; and Eulogius was obsessed—or mad.

The night before the executions, that night of July 26-27, 852, he spent on his knees in the corridor outside her cell. By morning he was speechless, all but blind, after pleading with her nightlong to recant. It was like addressing a statue, or the image of a saint. Not one word did she vouchsafe him; nor a glance, a tear, a sigh.

557

Some time after midnight he heard an uproar in the street outside her cell; the bull bellow of male voices, the sounds of blows, curses, the clangor of weapons. But 'twas not until morning that he learned its meaning.

A prison guard came up to him, as he was leaving the prison, said: "There is one who'd speak with thee San Alarico. If thou'll be good enough to follow me—"

Alaric bowed and followed him. The guard led him to that tier of cells in which male prisoners were kept, preceded him down the corridor, stopped before a door. Through the bars Alaric could see that gigantic, known, beloved figure. Saadyah was chained, feet and wrists alike, to manacles set in the wall. His face was gray below the bloody bandages swathing his big head.

"In God's Name, Saadyah!" Alaric said. "Don't tell me that you, too—"

"Hath blasphemed against the Prophet?" Saadyah groaned. "Nay, brother! I merely tried to tunnel through the walls of her cell, and drag Nathalie out of there. But the noisy fools I hired raised such a din that—"

"I see," Alaric whispered. "God bless thee, Saadyah! And now I go!"

There was one last hopeless recourse; but that one, too, he tried.

He bowed gravely before the Kadi I'Djama'a, and made his plea.

"She is mad," he said. "She hath not even wit enough left to recant. That being so, Your Worship, I beg of thee a boon—"

"Which is?" the head judge said.

"That I be allowed to suffer in her place," Alaric said. "Since the law requires a death for this crime, let me die for it. For is not a husband ultimately responsible for his wife's deeds? I did not observe her with sufficient attention to mark how serious was the deterioration of her wit, her mind; nor guard her well enough to keep her from this folly—"

"Nor didst thou inspire her to this action," the Kadi sighed. " 'Tis known of all men that thou'rt one Nazarene who respects truly, even venerates our Prophet. One day ye will come into the True Fold, Aizun! Of that I am very sure. But this thou asketh cannot be. Each must pay for his own, not another's crime. And, frankly, 'tis thy lady's identity, the august blood she bears, which makes it impossible to pardon her. The 'amma would be at our throats within the hour, screaming nepotism and baring their rusty blades, were that done. Ye have my profoundest pity, my friend; and surely God's, thou who hast walked uprightly all thy days. I pray thee bear this sorrow bravely. Thou'rt not too old yet who hath not reached thy fiftieth year. After this hath passed, in some little time, come unto me and I will instruct thee in our way; and thenceforth thou canst have many a sweet companion to take her place. . . ."

To take her place, he wept within his heart, she whom not even one of God's angels could equal in my sight! But he plunged on doggedly toward his house. 'Twas almost high noon, the hour set for the executions, when he reached it. He paused before it in the street, trying to dominate his thoughts, to hold in check the crippling pain that went screaming through all his body, heart, spirit, mind. He could not, dared not, let those images form, that despite him murderously were forming now: with an easy swing the executioner lifting his heavy ax, letting it hang almost perpendicular down his back, his coiling, bunching, obscenely thick arms making a backward-slanted, inverted, open V through which his bullfrog's head protruded. Then the tensing, the whirling blued-steel swing through three quarters of a circle's full circumference, flashing against the blue, catching the sun's rays, smashing down to make that sound you never heard because the crowd's anticipatory roar forever drowned it out; and the headsman bending now, pushing his thick fingers through that beloved, lovely mass of tawny gold, lifting by her hair that little goblet of flesh in which all Alaric's dreams had been distilled, that tiny, articulate, and magical globe that had contained, encompassed his world—Nay! Lifting by her gore-streaked tresses her severed head to stream great gouts and clots and ropes of blood as Perfectus' had! To stare out over that bestial, still bellowing mob, searching for his face with dead eyes, screaming his name with silent, gaping, likewise blood-filled mouth!

God God God God. His knees buckled; he bent half his length above the garden gate; raised his head at last to see through the opened windows of his house the figures of his daughters, his sons-in-law, even al Mundhir, which took courage on such a day, his sister Gelesvinta, his brother-in-law Husayn, Sumayla, his son al Kamil, others—come to be with him, tender him their love, help him, share with him—this horror.

It was not to be borne. He whirled, already running. Within mere minutes he approached the square. On the edge of it he stopped, raised up his eyes.

"Thou gavest me powers, O God!" he murmured. "Do not forbid me to use them now!"

He waved his hand in a slow, majestic circle above the crowd.

"Ye all hath been stricken blind!" he whispered. "None of ye can see! A cloud hath come down from heaven to veil my love and me from your sight! When it lifts again, and your sight is restored, we shall be far from here!"

He moved quickly, easily through the mob; and those who witnessed it, until their dying hour swore that no man marked his passage. Upon the scaffold, the executioner leaned upon his bloody ax—for Georgius and Aurelius were already dead by then; and in stupefied amazement rubbed his bloodshot eyes. No longer could he see Natalia where she lay, face-down, her wisp of a throat resting against the block. A half or a quarter stroke will do it, the headsman thought. 'Twill be cutting a reed, a wand, nothing more—poor child. But then the state of matters now got through even to his dull-witted, slow-working mind. "In Allah's name!" he roared. "I'm blind! By the very Beard, I cannot see!"

The mob stood there unmoving. Some rubbed their eyes. Others groped for kerchiefs or used their sleeves. The silence was absolute as San Alarico, wrapped in a mist, a cloud, existent only in the minds of those he had forced by his nerve-naked tortured will to believe it there, mounted the scaffold.

What was it then that failed? Did he in that last moment pause long enough to doubt the efficacy of his prayers, his powers? Or did his voices speak to him, moving like organ chords through his heart to blast him to a trembling halt by thundering: "Alaric Teudisson, Servant of God, thinkest thou thus to thwart Me?"

For certain it is that they who saw him not before, saw him now, bending above her to lift her from the block; and ten thousand animal voices burst from human throats in a roar that wracked sound out of existence. 'Twas then that the executioner smote him—lightly enough, 'twould seem—with the back of one huge, horny, bloodstained hand, but the blow sufficed to send him over the edge of the platform to pitch him headfirst to the ground.

He got up almost at once, with blood pouring from his nostrils, his ears, his mouth, even from his eyes. He moved out and away from there, stumbling, staggering, obviously blind, his hand put out to grope his way, and they not one of them making the slightest move to stop him until he had reached the edge of the square; and not even there, but instead some of them began to follow him, then more and more—until when the executioner finally lifted his broadax and brought it whistling down to end Natalia's life, the mob was already mobile, fluid, flowing out and away from there in the wake of a corpse that walked, a cadaver stumbling, shambling, tottering over ground.

He reached that place that Saadyah had shown him and entered it, the chapel Eulogius' followers had made to enshrine the cross—or a replica thereof; for almost all of Christianity's sacred relics are pious frauds; and what boots it, if men believe?—on which Isaac's dead body

560

had been hung upside down. 'Twas a rude affair, shaped like the letter X, a form more stable than the right-angled cross since two bars instead of one could be set into the earth. The ropes, stained with poor mad Isaac's blood—or a pig's, a goat's—were on it still; and he moved toward it unerringly, though 'twas clear he saw nothing at all. His hands touched it, explored its shape, found the ropes. He turned, slipped one arm through them, then the other, leaned back against that cross—and died.

The rest is legend, which would grow with the natural increment of human hoping, dreaming, vain, pitiful faith in arrant nonsense, refusal of fact, hungry embracing of surcease-granting illusion. Though there may have been more to it than that, hallucination, autosuggestion, the contagious hysteria to which mobs are so prone, some trick of light and shadow seen by eyes still dazed by too much sun, interpreted by childlike minds yet under the influence of a triple execution—who knows? Suffice it to say that the tales were wondrous: How light washed all that cross and the figure on it in a blinding glow, how a voice spoke from heaven saying: "Aizun, My son, My son, come unto Me!" And Lord Aizun's, San Alarico's, soul flying upward from his mouth in the form of a small white dove; and the blind among that crowd beginning at once to see, the deaf to hear, the lame to walk, and all who were dying at that hour being somehow miraculously restored, and even one or two dead a little time before it opening their eyes, beginning to speak, praising San Alarico and God—

But for legend, Reader, here have we no place; he who treats of more than totally verifiable fact, exists forever in a state of venial sin. Let us, therefore, turn once more to history, begging your indulgence for yet another while.

Six years from that date Saadyah ben Hasdai came, as his custom was, to sit and meditate beside Alaric's grave. He came also to toss angrily away the crutches left by some cripple claiming to have been by San Alarico's intervention cured; to tear up with a fierce oath the little scrolls attesting to lives saved in moments of great peril by the mere mention of the Saint's name, and others recounting the stories of those risen from their deathbeds because of prayers addressed to him—all the mindless paraphernalia of superstitious rubbish so tenderly held and believed in the face of all evidence to the contrary throughout the Mediterranean world; but, chiefly, Saadyah came to meditate, which, though he would not admit it to himself, was a kind of prayer.

And on that day, as he walked toward Alaric's and Natalia's graves, he saw two men in cowls and cassocks bending above a yawning pit, outlined against a mound of broken masonry and freshly dug, high-piled earth.

He rushed upon them, roaring: "Grave robbers! Brigands! Thieves! What do ye here?"

Whereupon they looked up at him with that bland and weighty expression of utter idiocy which hath been the hallmark of the pious since the beginning of time, and said to him, not in Arabic or Romance, but in horrendously bad priestly Latin:

"We have the Emir Muhammad's permission to bear these holy relics of the martyred saints away from the indifference and mockery of infidels to repose in Christian peace in our abbey, Saint Germain des Pres, in Paris, capital of the Land of the Franks, there to be forever venerated by the Faithful!"

For, Reader, Abd al Rahman the Second was dead now, too, having succumbed, said Eulogius and his Exalteds, to the vengeance of Heaven; nay, rather, said the cynics and the skeptics, to the Umm Walad Tarub's delicate attentions by eating of some dish, or partaking of some cup, prepared by her dainty hand; or—which is the humble opinion of him who pens these lines—to fatigue, weakness, grief, and, mayhap, a broken heart. The great and noble Emir of all Allah's Faithful in the Land of al Andalus was gathered to his fathers on the third day of the month of Rabi in the two hundred thirty-eighth year after the Hijrah, or, if you prefer Christian reckoning, the twenty-second of September of that year of Our Lord 852, exactly five days less than two months after the date that Natalia and Alaric died. May Allah the Compassionate guard and keep his soul in Paradise!

But to return to Saadyah and the Frankish monks, Usuard and Odilard, for such were their names. If the holy grave robbers expected this white-haired, snowy-bearded fierce old giant—all of the red having flown from Saadyah's hair and beard, 'tis said, the very moment he was of Alaric's death advised (how difficult it is to keep base legend out!)—to be awed by their cloth, they were of that notion soon disabused; for he lifted his heavy staff and roared: "Ye have *my* permission to depart from here with unbroken pates, O ravens from the caves of superstition and ignorance! For if ye heed me not, right gladly will I pleasure my heart by bedrubbing ye most soundly! Ye hear me, filthy croakers; be gone!"

It did not occur to him to inspect what the monks bore in their packs, which spared him the bitter fate of looking upon poor Natalia's fragile bones, jumbled together in true pious fashion with those of Aurelius and Georgius. Instead, he bent and looked into Alaric's grave, and—

AN ODOR OF SANCTITY

Thy forgiveness, Reader! The rest is myth and legend: How a heavenly aroma of sweet flowers and delicate perfumes arose from that broken grave, the true odor of sanctity; how Saadyah ben Hasdai, the pious Jew (for poor Saadyah would not escape life's insane irony; would pay for his sin of being a rational man in an irrational world, by being venerated in turn by that same irrationality) leaped into that grave and picked up San Alarico's sweet-smelling, totally uncorrupted corpse; how he kissed it tenderly with many a tear, and strode away, bearing it in his great arms straight into the light of the setting sun—into which he disappeared with his holy burden, neither he nor San Alarico's saintly body being any more seen of man.

What is fact is that to this day, no man knows where San Alarico's bones, nor those of his friend, whom the Cordovian peasants call *el Judio bueno*, the Good Jew, lie. But men and women of the Sierras and the plains round about Córdoba to this very day invoke them both in prayer with rare impartiality.

And who knows but they do not indeed hear the prayers of the humble and the poor, and intercede for them tenderly before the throne of God? That is, if men have souls which survive their deaths, and if there be a heaven to which humanity's desolate pleas can rise, or a just and merciful God to act upon them—

Which are things, Reader, that you, ere you come to the end of the chronicle of your days (less terrible, fearsome, strange than this, God grant!) must, according to your capacity for faith, or your lack of it, for yourself decide.

And may good San Alarico, patron of skeptics and doubters, be with you in that hour to grant you out of his hard-won store of it—his peace.